COPYRIGHT ACKNOWLEDGMENTS

Endpaper art by Darrell K. Sweet.
Frontispiece by Michael Whalen.

The Little Sisters of Eluria, copyright © 1998 by Stephen King; p. 19
  illustration courtesy of Erik Wilson
The Sea and Little Fishes, copyright © 1998 by Terry & Lyn
  Pratchett; p. 93 illustration courtesy of Paul Kidby
Debt of Bones, copyright © 1998 by Terry Goodkind; pp. 140–141
  illustration courtesy of Tor Books, publishers of *The Sword of
  Truth*
Grinning Man, copyright © 1998 by Orson Scott Card; pp. 216–217
  illustration courtesy of Tor Books, publishers of *Tales of Alvin
  Maker*
The Seventh Shrine, copyright © 1998 by Agberg, Ltd.; p. 257
  illustration courtesy of HarperPrism, publishers of the *Majipoor
  Cycle*
Dragonfly, copyright © 1998 by Ursula K. Le Guin; p. 335
  illustration courtesy of the author
The Burning Man, copyright © 1998 by Tad Williams; p. 399
  illustration courtesy of the author
The Hedge Knight, copyright © 1998 by George R. R. Martin;
  pp. 452–453 illustration courtesy of Bantam Spectra, publishers
  of *A Song of Ice and Fire*
Runner of Pern, copyright © 1998 by Anne McCaffrey; p. 537
  illustration courtesy of Michael Whelan
The Wood Boy, copyright © 1998 by Raymond E. Feist; pp. 596–597
  illustration courtesy of Avon Books, publishers of *The Riftwar
  Saga*
New Spring, copyright © 1998 by Robert Jordan; pp. 632–633
  illustration courtesy of Tor Books, publishers of *The Wheel of
  Time*

All other in-text illustrations copyright © 1998 by Michael Whalen,
  except for p. 146, which is illustrated by Keith Parkinson, copyright
  © 1998.

FOR MARTY AND RALPH
who certainly know why

CONTENTS

CONTENTS

INTRODUCTION

Here is a book of visions and miracles—eleven rich, robust new stories by the best-known and most accomplished modern creators of fantasy fiction, each one set in the special universe of the imagination that made that writer famous throughout the world.

Fantasy is the oldest branch of imaginative literature—as old as the human imagination itself. It is not difficult to believe that the same artistic impulse that produced the extraordinary cave paintings of Altamira and Chauvet, fifteen and twenty and even thirty thousand years ago, also probably produced astounding tales of gods and demons, of talismans and spells, of dragons and werewolves, of wondrous lands beyond the horizon—tales that fur-clad shamans recited to fascinated audiences around the campfires of Ice Age Europe. So, too, in torrid Africa, in the China of prehistory, in ancient India, in the Americas: everywhere, in fact, on and on back through time for thousands or even hundreds of thousands of years. I like to think that the storytelling impulse is universal—that there have been storytellers as long as there have been beings in this world that could be spoken of as "human"— and that those storytellers have in particular devoted their skills and energies and talents, throughout our long evolutionary path, to the creation of extraordinary marvels and wonders.

We will never know, of course, what tales the Cro-Magnon storytellers told their spellbound audiences on those frosty nights in ancient

France. But surely there were strong components of the fantastic in them. The evidence of the oldest stories that *have* survived argues in favor of that. If fantasy can be defined as literature that depicts the world beyond that of mundane reality, and mankind's struggle to assert dominance over that world, then the most ancient story that *has* come down to us—the Sumerian tale of the hero Gilgamesh, which dates from about 2500 B.C.—is fantasy, for its theme is Gilgamesh's quest for eternal life.

Homer's *Odyssey*, abounding as it does in shape-shifters and wizards and sorceresses, in Cyclopses and many-headed man-eating creatures, is rich with fantastic elements, too, as are any number of other Greek and Roman tales. As we come closer to our own times we meet the dread monster Grendel of the Anglo-Saxon *Beowulf*, the Midgard serpent and the dragon Fafnir and the apocalyptic Fenris-wolf of the Norse sagas, the hapless immortality-craving Dr. Faustus of German legend, the myriad enchanters of *The Thousand and One Nights,* the far-larger-than-life heroes of the Welsh *Mabinogion* and the Persian *Shah-Nameh*, and an infinity of other strange and wonderful creations.

Nor did the impulse toward the creation of the fantastic disappear as the modern era, the era of microscopes and telescopes, of steam engines and railway systems, of telegraphs and phonographs and electric light, came into being. Our fascination with the unseen and the unseeable did not end simply because so many things previously thought impossible now had become realities. What is more fantastic, after all, than having the sound of an entire symphony orchestra rise up out of a flat disk of plastic? Or to speak into a device that one holds in one's hand, and be heard and understood ten thousand miles away? But the same century that gave us the inventions of Thomas Alva Edison and Alexander Graham Bell gave us Lewis Carroll's two incomparable tales of Alice's adventures in other realities, H. Rider Haggard's innumerable novels of lost civilizations, and Mary Wollstonecraft Shelley's *Frankenstein*.

Nor did the twentieth century—the century of air travel and atomic energy, of television and computers, of open-heart surgery and sex-change operations—see us losing our taste for tales of the extraordinary. A host of machine-age fantasists—James Branch Cabell and A. Merritt and Lord Dunsany, E. R. Eddison and Mervyn Peake and L. Frank Baum, H. P. Lovecraft and Robert E. Howard and J. R. R.

Tolkien, to name a few of the best-known ones—kept the world well supplied with wondrous tales of the fantastic.

One change of tone did occur in the twentieth century, though, with the rise to popularity of science fiction—the branch of fantasy that applies immense ingenuity to the task of making the impossible, or at least the implausible, seem altogether probable. As science fiction— which was given its essential nature well over a hundred years ago by Jules Verne and H. G. Wells, and developed in modern times by such writers as Robert A. Heinlein, Isaac Asimov, and Aldous Huxley— came to exert its immense appeal on the atomic-age reading public, "pure" fantasy fiction (that is, fantasy that makes no attempt at empirical explanation of its wonders) came to be thought of as something largely reserved for children, like myths and fairy tales.

The older kind of fantasy never disappeared, of course. But in the United States, at least, it went into eclipse for nearly fifty years. Science fiction, meanwhile, manifested itself to the reading public in the form of magazines with names like *Amazing Stories* and *Astounding Science Fiction* and readerships composed largely of boys and earnest young men with an interest in gadgets and scientific disputation. The only American magazine dealing in the material we define as fantasy fiction was *Weird Tales*, founded in 1923, but that magazine published not only fantasy but a great many other kinds of genre fiction that might not be thought of as fantasy today—tales of pure terror, for example, with no speculative content.

The separation between fantasy and science fiction is not always easy to locate, but some distinctions are fairly clear-cut, if not entirely rigid. Stories that deal with androids and robots, spaceships, alien beings, time machines, viruses from outer space, galactic empires, and the like usually can be described as science fiction. These are all matters that are *conceptually possible* within the framework of scientific law as we currently understand it. (Although such things as time machines and faster-than-light vehicles certainly stretch that framework to its limits, and perhaps beyond them.) Fantasy, meanwhile, uses as its material that which is *generally believed to be impossible or nonexistent* in our culture: wizards and warlocks, elves and goblins, werewolves and vampires, unicorns and enchanted princesses, efficacious incantations and spells.

Fantasy fiction per se did not have a real magazine of its own until

1939, when John W. Campbell, Jr., the foremost science-fiction editor of his time, brought *Unknown* (later called *Unknown Worlds*) into being in order to allow his writers greater imaginative latitude than his definitions of science fiction would permit. Many of the same writers who had turned Campbell's *Astounding Science Fiction* into the most notable magazine of its type yet published—Robert A. Heinlein, L. Sprague de Camp, Theodore Sturgeon, Lester del Rey, Jack Williamson—also became mainstays of *Unknown*, and the general structural approach was similar: postulate a far-out idea and develop all its consequences to a logical conclusion. The stories about being nasty to water gnomes or selling your soul to the devil wound up in *Unknown*; those about traveling in time or voyaging to distant planets were published in *Astounding*.

But *Unknown*, though it was cherished with great fondness by its readers and writers, never attained much of a public following, and when wartime paper shortages forced Campbell to choose between his two magazines in 1943, *Unknown* was swiftly killed, never to reappear. Postwar attempts by nostalgic ex-contributors to *Unknown* to recapture its special flavor were largely unsuccessful; H. L. Gold's *Beyond* lasted ten issues, Lester del Rey's *Fantasy Fiction* managed only four. Only *The Magazine of Fantasy,* edited by Anthony Boucher and J. Francis McComas, succeeded in establishing itself as a permanent entity, and even that magazine found it wisest to change its name to *Fantasy and Science Fiction* with its second issue. When science fiction became a fixture of paperback publishing in the 1950s, fantasy once again lagged behind: few fantasy novels were paperbacked, and most of them—Jack Vance's *The Dying Earth* and the early reprints of H. P. Lovecraft and Robert E. Howard are good examples—quickly vanished from view and became collector's items.

It all began to change in the late 1960s, when the sudden availability of paperback editions of J. R. R. Tolkien's *Lord of the Rings* trilogy (previously kept from paperback by an unwilling hardcover publisher) aroused a hunger for fantasy fiction in millions of readers that has, so far, been insatiable. Tolkien's books were such an emphatic commercial success that publishers rushed to find writers who could produce imitative trilogies, and the world was flooded with huge Hobbitesque novels, many of which sold in extraordinary quantities themselves. Robert Howard's *Conan* novels, once admired only by a small band of ardent cultists, began to win vast new readers about the same time. And a few years later Ballantine Books, Tolkien's paperback publisher, brought out an extraordinary series of books in its Adult Fantasy series, edited by Lin Carter, which made all the elegant classic masterpieces of such fantasists as E. R. Eddison, James Branch Cabell, Lord Dunsany, and Mervyn Peake available to modern readers. And, ever since, fantasy has been a dominant factor in modern publishing. What was a neglected stepsibling of science fiction fifty years ago is, today, an immensely popular genre.

In the wake of the great success of the Tolkien trilogy, newer writers have come along with their own deeply imagined worlds of fantasy, and have captured large and enthusiastic audiences themselves. In the late 1960s, Ursula Le Guin began her searching and sensitive Earthsea series, and Anne McCaffrey co-opted the ancient fantastic theme of the dragon for her Pern novels, which live on the borderline between fantasy and science fiction. Stephen King, some years later, won a readership of astounding magnitude by plumbing the archetypical fears of humanity and transforming them into powerful novels that occupied fantasy's darker terrain. Terry Pratchett, on the other hand, has magnificently demonstrated the comic power of satiric fantasy. Such writers as Orson Scott Card and Raymond E. Feist have won huge followings for their Alvin Maker and Riftwar books. More recently, Robert Jordan's mammoth Wheel of Time series, George R. R. Martin's Song of Ice and Fire books, and Terry Goodkind's Sword of Truth tales have taken their place in the pantheon of modern fantasy, as has Tad Williams' Memory, Sorrow and Thorn series.

And here is the whole bunch of them, brought together in one huge anthology in which fantasy enthusiasts can revel for weeks. A new Earthsea story, a new tale of Pern, a new Dark Tower adventure, a new segment in Pratchett's playful Discworld series, and all the rest that you'll find herein—there has never been a book like this before. Gathering such an elite collection of first-magnitude stars into a single volume has not been an easy task. My gratitude herewith for the special assistance of Martin H. Greenberg, Ralph Vicinanza, Stephen King, John Helfers, and Virginia Kidd, who in one way or another made my editorial task immensely less difficult than it otherwise would have been. And, too, although it goes without saying that I'm grateful to my wife, Karen, for her inestimable help in every phase of this intricate project, I think I'll say it anyway—not just because she's a terrific person, but because she came up with what unquestionably was the smartest idea of the whole enterprise.

—Robert Silverberg
December, 1997

The Dark Tower

—

STEPHEN KING

stephen king

the little sisters of eluria

THE GUNSLINGER (1982)
THE DRAWING OF THE THREE (1987)
THE WASTE LANDS (1991)
WIZARD AND GLASS (1997)

These novels, using thematic elements from Robert Browning's poem "Childe Roland to the Dark Tower Came," tell the saga of Roland, last of the gunslingers, who embarks on a quest to find the Dark Tower for reasons that the author has yet to reveal. Along the way, Roland encounters the remains of what was once a thriving society, feudal in nature but technologically quite advanced, that now has fallen into decay and ruin. King combines elements of fantasy with science fiction into a surreal blend of past and future.

The first book, *The Gunslinger*, introduces Roland, who is chasing the Dark Man, an enigmatic sorcerer figure, across a vast desert. Through flashbacks, the reader learns that Roland was a member of a noble family in the Dark Tower world, and that that world may or may not have been destroyed with help from the Dark Man. Along the way, Roland encounters strange inhabitants of this unnamed world, including Jake, a young boy who, even though he is killed by the end of the first book, will figure prominently in later volumes. Roland does catch up with the Dark Man, and learns that he must seek out the Dark Tower to find the answers to the questions of why he must embark on this quest and what is contained in the Tower.

The next book, *The Drawing of the Three,* shows Roland recruiting three people from present-day Earth to join him on his way to the Dark Tower. They are Eddie, a junkie "mule" working for the Mafia; Suzannah, a paraplegic with multiple personalities; and Jake, whose arrival is startling to Roland, who sacrificed Jake in his own world during his pursuit of the Dark Man. Roland saves Jake's life on Earth, but the resulting schism nearly drives him insane. Roland must also help the other two battle their own demons, Eddie's being his heroin addiction and guilt over not being able to save his brother's life, and Suzannah's the war between her different personalities, one a kind and gentle woman, the other a racist psychopath. Each of the three deals with his problems with the help of the others, and together the quartet set out on the journey to the Tower.

The third book, *The Waste Lands*, chronicles the first leg of that journey, examining the background of the three Earth-born characters in detail. The book reaches its climax when Jake is kidnapped by a cult thriving in the ruins of a crumbling city, led by a man known only as Flagg (a character who has appeared in several of King's other novels as the embodiment of pure evil). Roland rescues him, and the group escapes the city on a monorail system whose artificial-intelligence program has achieved sentience at the cost of its sanity. The monorail challenges them to a riddle contest, with their lives as the prize if they can stump the machine, who claims to know every riddle ever created.

Wizard and Glass, the fourth volume in the series, finds Roland, Jake, Eddie, and Suzannah continuing their journey toward the Dark Tower, moving through a deserted part of Mid-World that is eerily reminiscent of twentieth-century Earth. During their travels they encounter a *thinny*, a dangerous weakening of the barrier between different times and places. Roland recognizes it and realizes that his world is breaking down faster than he had thought. The *thinny* prompts him to recall the first time he encountered it, many years before on a trip out West with his friends Cuthbert and Alain, when Roland had just earned his gunslinger status. It is this story—of the three boys uncovering a plot against the ruling government and of Roland's first love, a girl named Susan Delgado—that is the central focus of the book. While the three manage to destroy the conspirators, Susan is killed during the fight by the townspeople of Hambry. The story gives Jake, Eddie, and Suzannah new insight into Roland's background and why he may sacrifice them to attain his ultimate goal of saving his world. The book ends with the foursome moving onward once more toward the Tower.

The Little Sisters of Eluria

STEPHEN KING

[Author's Note: The Dark Tower books begin with Roland of Gilead, the last gunslinger in an exhausted world that has "moved on," pursuing a magician in a black robe. Roland has been chasing Walter for a very long time. In the first book of the cycle, he finally catches up. This story, however, takes place while Roland is still casting about for Walter's trail. A knowledge of the books is therefore not necessary for you to under-stand—and hopefully enjoy—the story which follows. S. K.]

I. Full Earth. The Empty Town. The Bells. The Dead Boy. The Overturned Wagon. The Green Folk.

On a day in Full Earth so hot that it seemed to suck the breath from his chest before his body could use it, Roland of Gilead came to the gates of a village in the Desatoya Mountains. He was traveling alone by then, and would soon be traveling afoot, as well. This whole last week he had been hoping for a horse doctor, but guessed such a fellow would do him no good now, even if this town had one. His mount, a two-year-old roan, was pretty well done for.

The town gates, still decorated with flowers from some festival or other, stood open and welcoming, but the silence beyond them was all wrong. The gunslinger heard no clip-clop of horses, no rumble of wagon wheels, no merchants' huckstering cries from the marketplace.

The only sounds were the low hum of crickets (some sort of bug, at any rate; they were a bit more tuneful than crickets, at that), a queer wooden knocking sound, and the faint, dreamy tinkle of small bells.

Also, the flowers twined through the wrought-iron staves of the ornamental gate were long dead.

Between his knees, Topsy gave two great, hollow sneezes—*K'chow! K'chow!*—and staggered sideways. Roland dismounted, partly out of respect for the horse, partly out of respect for himself—he didn't want to break a leg under Topsy if Topsy chose this moment to give up and canter into the clearing at the end of his path.

The gunslinger stood in his dusty boots and faded jeans under the beating sun, stroking the roan's matted neck, pausing every now and then to yank his fingers through the tangles of Topsy's mane, and stopping once to shoo off the tiny flies clustering at the corners of Topsy's eyes. Let them lay their eggs and hatch their maggots there after Topsy was dead, but not before.

Roland thus honored his horse as best he could, listening to those distant, dreamy bells and the strange wooden tocking sound as he did. After a while he ceased his absent grooming and looked thoughtfully at the open gate.

The cross above its center was a bit unusual, but otherwise the gate was a typical example of its type, a western commonplace which was not useful but traditional—all the little towns he had come to in the last tenmonth seemed to have one such where you came in (grand) and one more such where you went out (not so grand). None had been built to exclude visitors, certainly not this one. It stood between two walls of pink adobe that ran into the scree for a distance of about twenty feet on either side of the road and then simply stopped. Close the gate, lock it with many locks, and all that meant was a short walk around one bit of adobe wall or the other.

Beyond the gate, Roland could see what looked in most respects like a perfectly ordinary High Street—an inn, two saloons (one of which was called The Bustling Pig; the sign over the other was too faded to read), a mercantile, a smithy, a Gathering Hall. There was also a small but rather lovely wooden building with a modest bell tower on top, a sturdy fieldstone foundation on the bottom, and a gold-painted cross on its double doors. The cross, like the one over the gate, marked this as a worshipping place for those who held to the Jesus-man. This wasn't a common religion in Mid-World, but far from un-known; that same thing could have been said about most forms of worship in those days, including the worship of Baal, Asmodeus, and a hundred others. Faith, like everything else in the world these days, had moved on. As far as Roland was concerned, God o' the Cross was just another religion which taught that love and murder were inextri-cably bound together—that in the end, God always drank blood.

Meanwhile, there was the singing hum of insects that sounded *almost* like crickets. The dreamlike tinkle of the bells. And that queer wooden thumping, like a fist on a door. Or on a coffintop.

Something here's a long way from right, the gunslinger thought. *'Ware, Roland; this place has a reddish odor.*

He led Topsy through the gate with its adornments of dead flowers and down the High Street. On the porch of the mercantile, where the old men should have congregated to discuss crops, politics, and the follies of the younger generation, there stood only a line of empty rockers. Lying beneath one, as if dropped from a careless (and long-departed) hand, was a charred corncob pipe. The hitching rack in front of the Bustling Pig stood empty; the windows of the saloon itself were dark. One of the batwing doors had been yanked off and stood propped against the side of the building; the other hung ajar, its faded green slats splattered with maroon stuff that might have been paint but probably wasn't.

The shopfront of the livery stable stood intact, like the face of a ruined woman who has access to good cosmetics, but the double barn behind it was a charred skeleton. That fire must have happened on a rainy day, the gunslinger thought, or the whole damned town would have gone up in flames; a jolly spin and raree-show for anyone around to see it.

To his right now, halfway up to where the street opened into the town square, was the church. There were grassy borders on both sides, one separating the church from the town's Gathering Hall, the other from the little house set aside for the preacher and his family (if this was one of the Jesus-sects which allowed its shamans to have wives and families, that was; some of them, clearly administered by lunatics, demanded at least the appearance of celibacy). There were flowers in these grassy strips, and while they looked parched, most were still alive.

So whatever had happened here to empty the place out had not happened long ago. A week, perhaps. Two at the outside, given the heat.

Topsy sneezed again—*K'chow!*—and lowered his head wearily.

The gunslinger saw the source of the tinkling. Above the cross on the church doors, a cord had been strung in a long, shallow arc. Hung from it were perhaps two dozen tiny silver bells. There was hardly any breeze today, but enough so these smalls were never quite still . . . and if a real wind should rise, Roland thought, the sound made by the tintinnabulation of the bells would probably be a good deal less pleasant; more like the strident parlay of gossips' tongues.

"Hello!" Roland called, looking across the street at what a large false-fronted sign proclaimed to be the Good Beds Hotel. "Hello, the town!"

No answer but the bells, the tunesome insects, and that odd wooden clunking. No answer, no movement . . . but there were folk here. Folk or *something*. He was being watched. The tiny hairs on the nape of his neck had stiffened.

Roland stepped onward, leading Topsy toward the center of town, puffing up the unlaid High Street dust with each step. Forty paces farther along, he stopped in front of a low building marked with a single curt word: LAW. The Sheriff's office (if they had such this far from the Inners) looked remarkably similar to the church—wooden boards stained a rather forbidding shade of dark brown above a stone foundation.

The bells behind him rustled and whispered.

He left the roan standing in the middle of the street and mounted the steps to the LAW office. He was very aware of the bells, of the sun beating against his neck, and of the sweat trickling down his sides. The door was shut but unlocked. He opened it, then winced back, half-raising a hand as the heat trapped inside rushed out in a soundless gasp. If all the closed buildings were this hot inside, he mused, the livery barns would soon not be the only burned-out hulks. And with no rain to stop the flames (and certainly no volunteer fire department, not any more), the town would not be long for the face of the earth.

He stepped inside, trying to sip at the stifling air rather than taking deep breaths. He immediately heard the low drone of flies.

There was a single cell, commodious and empty, its barred door standing open. Filthy skin-shoes, one of the pair coming unsewn, lay beneath a bunk sodden with the same dried maroon stuff that had marked the Bustling Pig. Here was where the flies were, crawling over the stain, feeding from it.

On the desk was a ledger. Roland turned it toward him and read what was embossed upon its red cover:

REGISTRY OF MISDEEDS & REDRESS
IN THE YEARS OF OUR LORD
ELURIA

So now he knew the name of the town, at least—Eluria. Pretty, yet somehow ominous, as well. But any name would have seemed ominous, Roland supposed, given these circumstances. He turned to leave, and saw a closed door secured by a wooden bolt.

He went to it, stood before it for a moment, then drew one of the big revolvers he carried low on his hips. He stood a moment longer, head down, thinking (Cuthbert, his old friend, liked to say that the wheels inside Roland's head ground slow but exceedingly fine), and then retracted the bolt. He opened the door and immediately stood back, leveling his gun, expecting a body (Eluria's Sheriff, mayhap) to come tumbling into the room with his throat cut and his eyes gouged out, victim of a MISDEED in need of REDRESS—

Nothing.

Well, half a dozen stained jumpers which longer-term prisoners were probably required to wear, two bows, a quiver of arrows, an old, dusty motor, a rifle that had probably last been fired a hundred years ago, and a mop . . . but in the gunslinger's mind, all that came down to nothing. Just a storage closet.

He went back to the desk, opened the register, and leafed through it. Even the pages were warm, as if the book had been baked. In a way, he supposed it had been. If the High Street layout had been different, he might have expected a large number of religious offenses to be recorded, but he wasn't surprised to find none here—if the Jesus-man church had coexisted with a couple of saloons, the churchfolk must have been fairly reasonable.

What Roland found was the usual petty offenses, and a few not so petty—a murder, a horse-thieving, the Distressal of a Lady (which probably meant rape). The murderer had been removed to a place called Lexingworth to be hanged. Roland had never heard of it. One note toward the end read *Green folk sent hence*. It meant nothing to Roland. The most recent entry was this:

> *12/Fe/99. Chas. Freeborn, cattle-theef to be tryed.*

Roland wasn't familiar with the notation *12/Fe/99*, but as this was a long stretch from February, he supposed *Fe* might stand for Full Earth. In any case, the ink looked about as fresh as the blood on the bunk in the cell, and the gunslinger had a good idea that Chas. Freeborn, cattle-theef, had reached the clearing at the end of his path.

He went out into the heat and the lacy sound of bells. Topsy looked at Roland dully, then lowered his head again, as if there were something in the dust of the High Street which could be cropped. As if he would ever want to crop again, for that matter.

The gunslinger gathered up the reins, slapped the dust off them against the faded no-color of his jeans, and continued on up the street. The wooden knocking sound grew steadily louder as he walked (he had not holstered his gun when leaving LAW, nor cared to holster it now), and as he neared the town square, which must have housed the Eluria market in more normal times, Roland at last saw movement.

On the far side of the square was a long watering trough, made of ironwood from the look (what some called "seequoiah" out here), apparently fed in happier times from a rusty steel pipe which now jutted waterless above the trough's south end. Lolling over one side of this municipal oasis, about halfway down its length, was a leg clad in faded gray pants and terminating in a well-chewed cowboy boot.

The chewer was a large dog, perhaps two shades grayer than the corduroy pants. Under other circumstances, Roland supposed the mutt would have had the boot off long since, but perhaps the foot and lower calf inside it had swelled. In any case, the dog was well on its way to simply chewing the obstacle away. It would seize the boot and shake it back and forth. Every now and then the boot's heel would collide with the wooden side of the trough, producing another hollow knock. The gunslinger hadn't been so wrong to think of coffintops after all, it seemed.

Why doesn't it just back off a few steps, jump into the trough, and have at him? Roland wondered. *No water coming out of the pipe, so it can't be afraid of drowning.*

Topsy uttered another of his hollow, tired sneezes, and when the dog lurched around in response, Roland understood why it was doing things the hard way. One of its front legs had been badly broken and crookedly mended. Walking would be a chore for it, jumping out of the question. On its chest was a patch of dirty white fur. Growing out of this patch was black fur in a roughly cruciform shape. A Jesus-dog, mayhap, hoping for a spot of afternoon communion.

There was nothing very religious about the snarl which began to wind out of its chest, however, or the roll of its rheumy eyes. It lifted its upper lip in a trembling sneer, revealing a goodish set of teeth.

"Light out," Roland said. "While you can."

The dog backed up until its hindquarters were pressed against the chewed boot. It regarded the oncoming man fearfully, but clearly meant to stand its ground. The revolver in Roland's hand held no significance for it. The gunslinger wasn't surprised—he guessed the dog had never seen one, had no idea it was anything other than a club of some kind, which could only be thrown once.

"Hie on with you, now," Roland said, but still the dog wouldn't move.

He should have shot it—it was no good to itself, and a dog that had acquired a taste for human flesh could be no good to anyone else— but he somehow didn't like to. Killing the only thing still living in this town (other than the singing bugs, that was) seemed like an invitation to bad luck.

He fired into the dust near the dog's good forepaw, the sound crashing into the hot day and temporarily silencing the insects. The dog *could* run, it seemed, although at a lurching trot that hurt Roland's eyes . . . and his heart, a little, too. It stopped at the far side of the square, by an overturned flatbed wagon (there looked to be more dried blood splashed on the freighter's side), and glanced back. It uttered a forlorn howl that raised the hairs on the nape of Roland's neck even further. Then it turned, skirted the wrecked wagon, and limped down a lane which opened between two of the stalls. This way toward Eluria's back gate, Roland guessed.

Still leading his dying horse, the gunslinger crossed the square to the ironwood trough and looked in.

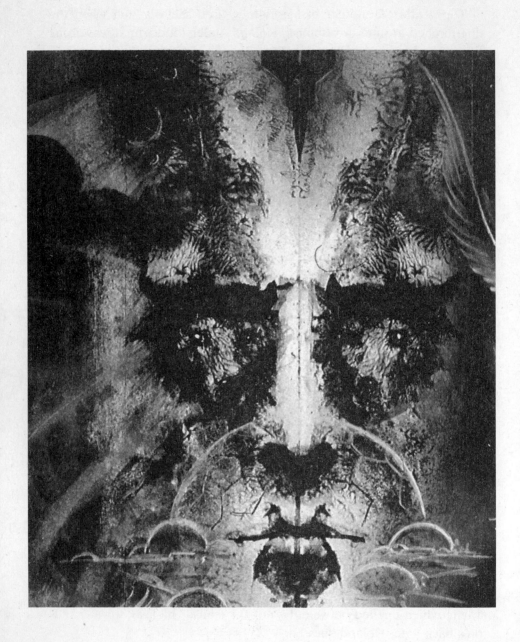

The owner of the chewed boot wasn't a man but a boy who had just been beginning to get his man's growth—and that would have been quite a large growth, indeed, Roland judged, even setting aside the bloating effects which had resulted from being immersed for some unknown length of time in nine inches of water simmering under a summer sun.

The boy's eyes, now just milky balls, stared blindly up at the gunslinger like the eyes of a statue. His hair appeared to be the white of old age, although that was the effect of the water; he had likely been a towhead. His clothes were those of a cowboy, although he couldn't have been much more than fourteen or sixteen. Around his neck, gleaming blearily in water that was slowly turning into a skin stew under the summer sun, was a gold medallion.

Roland reached into the water, not liking to but feeling a certain obligation. He wrapped his fingers around the medallion and pulled. The chain parted, and he lifted the thing, dripping, into the air.

He rather expected a Jesus-man *sigul*—what was called the crucifix or the rood—but a small rectangle hung from the chain, instead. The object looked like pure gold. Engraved into it was this legend:

James
Loved of family, Loved of GOD

Roland, who had been almost too revolted to reach into the polluted water (as a younger man, he could never have brought himself to that), was now glad he'd done it. He might never run into any of those who had loved this boy, but he knew enough of *ka* to think it might be so. In any case, it was the right thing. So was giving the kid a decent burial . . . assuming, that was, he could get the body out of the trough without having it break apart inside the clothes.

Roland was considering this, trying to balance what might be his duty in this circumstance against his growing desire to get out of this town, when Topsy finally fell dead.

The roan went over with a creak of gear and a last whuffling groan as it hit the ground. Roland turned and saw eight people in the street, walking toward him in a line, like beaters who hope to flush out birds or drive small game. Their skin was waxy green. Folk wearing such skin would likely glow in the dark like ghosts. It was hard to tell their

31

sex, and what could it matter—to them or anyone else? They were slow mutants, walking with the hunched deliberation of corpses reanimated by some arcane magic.

The dust had muffled their feet like carpet. With the dog banished, they might well have gotten within attacking distance if Topsy hadn't done Roland the favor of dying at such an opportune moment. No guns that Roland could see; they were armed with clubs. These were chair legs and table legs, for the most part, but Roland saw one that looked made rather than seized—it had a bristle of rusty nails sticking out of it, and he suspected it had once been the property of a saloon bouncer, possibly the one who kept school in the Bustling Pig.

Roland raised his pistol, aiming at the fellow in the center of the line. Now he could hear the shuffle of their feet, and the wet snuffle of their breathing. As if they all had bad chest colds.

Came out of the mines, most likely, Roland thought. *There are radium mines somewhere about. That would account for the skin. I wonder that the sun doesn't kill them.*

Then, as he watched, the one on the end—a creature with a face like melted candle wax—*did* die . . . or collapsed, at any rate. He (Roland was quite sure it was a male) went to his knees with a low, gobbling cry, groping for the hand of the thing walking next to it—something with a lumpy bald head and red sores sizzling on its neck. This creature took no notice of its fallen companion, but kept its dim eyes on Roland, lurching along in rough step with its remaining companions.

"Stop where you are!" Roland said. " 'Ware me, if you'd live to see day's end! 'Ware me very well!"

He spoke mostly to the one in the center, who wore ancient red suspenders over rags of shirt, and a filthy bowler hat. This gent had only one good eye, and it peered at the gunslinger with a greed as horrible as it was unmistakable. The one beside Bowler Hat (Roland believed this one might be a woman, with the dangling vestiges of breasts beneath the vest it wore) threw the chair leg it held. The arc was true, but the missile fell ten yards short.

Roland thumbed back the trigger of his revolver and fired again. This time the dirt displaced by the slug kicked up on the tattered remains of Bowler Hat's shoe instead of on a lame dog's paw.

The green folk didn't run as the dog had, but they stopped, staring at him with their dull greed. Had the missing folk of Eluria finished up in these creatures' stomachs? Roland couldn't believe it . . . although he knew perfectly well that such as these held no scruple against cannibalism. (And perhaps it wasn't cannibalism, not really; how could such things as these be considered human, whatever they might once have been?) They were too slow, too stupid. If they had dared come back into town after the Sheriff had run them out, they would have been burned or stoned to death.

Without thinking about what he was doing, wanting only to free his other hand to draw his second gun if the apparitions didn't see reason, Roland stuffed the medallion that he had taken from the dead boy into the pocket of his jeans, pushing the broken fine-link chain in after.

They stood staring at him, their strangely twisted shadows drawn out behind them. What next? Tell them to go back where they'd come from? Roland didn't know if they'd do it, and in any case had decided he liked them best where he could see them. And at least there was no question now about staying to bury the boy named James; that conundrum had been solved.

"Stand steady," he said in the low speech, beginning to retreat. "First fellow that moves—"

Before he could finish, one of them—a thick-chested troll with a pouty toad's mouth and what looked like gills on the sides of his wattled neck—lunged forward, gibbering in a high-pitched and peculiarly flabby voice. It might have been a species of laughter. He was waving what looked like a piano leg.

Roland fired. Mr. Toad's chest caved in like a bad piece of roofing. He ran backward several steps, trying to catch his balance and clawing at his chest with the hand not holding the piano leg. His feet, clad in dirty red velvet slippers with curled-up toes, tangled in each other and he fell over, making a queer and somehow lonely gargling sound. He let go of his club, rolled over on one side, tried to rise, and then fell back into the dust. The brutal sun glared into his open eyes, and as Roland watched, white tendrils of steam began to rise from his skin, which was rapidly losing its green undertint. There was also a hissing sound, like a gob of spit on top of a hot stove.

Saves explaining, at least, Roland thought, and swept his eyes over the others. "All right; he was the first one to move. Who wants to be the second?"

None did, it seemed. They only stood there, watching him, not coming at him . . . but not retreating, either. He thought (as he had about the crucifix-dog) that he should kill them as they stood there, just draw his other gun and mow them down. It would be the work of seconds only, and child's play to his gifted hands, even if some ran. But he couldn't. Not just cold, like that. He wasn't that kind of killer . . . at least, not yet.

Very slowly, he began to step backward, first bending his course around the watering trough, then putting it between him and them. When Bowler Hat took a step forward, Roland didn't give the others in the line a chance to copy him; he put a bullet into the dust of High Street an inch in advance of the Bowler Hat's foot.

"That's your last warning," he said, still using the low speech. He had no idea if they understood it, didn't really care. He guessed they caught this tune's music well enough. "Next bullet I fire eats up someone's heart. The way it works is, you stay and I go. You get this one chance. Follow me, and you all die. It's too hot to play games and I've lost my—"

"Booh!" cried a rough, liquidy voice from behind him. There was unmistakable glee in it. Roland saw a shadow grow from the shadow of the overturned freight wagon, which he had now almost reached, and had just time to understand that another of the green folk had been hiding beneath it.

As he began to turn, a club crashed down on Roland's shoulder, numbing his right arm all the way to the wrist. He held on to the gun and fired once, but the bullet went into one of the wagon wheels, smashing a wooden spoke and turning the wheel on its hub with a high screeing sound. Behind him, he heard the green folk in the street uttering hoarse, yapping cries as they charged forward.

The thing which had been hiding beneath the overturned wagon was a monster with two heads growing out of his neck, one with the vestigial, slack face of a corpse. The other, although just as green, was more lively. Broad lips spread in a cheerful grin as he raised his club to strike again.

Roland drew with his left hand—the one that wasn't numbed and distant. He had time to put one bullet through the bushwhacker's grin, flinging him backward in a spray of blood and teeth, the bludgeon flying out of his relaxing fingers. Then the others were on him, clubbing and drubbing.

The gunslinger was able to slip the first couple of blows, and there was one moment when he thought he might be able to spin around to the rear of the overturned wagon, spin and turn and go to work with his guns. Surely he would be able to do that. Surely his quest for the Dark Tower wasn't supposed to end on the sun-blasted street of a little far western town called Eluria, at the hands of half a dozen green-skinned slow mutants. Surely *ka* could not be so cruel.

But Bowler Hat caught him with a vicious sidehand blow, and Roland crashed into the wagon's slowly spinning rear wheel instead of skirting around it. As he went to his hands and knees, still scrambling and trying to turn, trying to evade the blows which rained down on him, he saw there were now many more than half a dozen. Coming up the street toward the town square were at least thirty green men and women. This wasn't a clan but a damned *tribe* of them. And in broad, hot daylight! Slow mutants were, in his experience, creatures that loved the dark, almost like toadstools with brains, and he had never seen any such as these before. They—

The one in the red vest was female. Her bare breasts swinging beneath the dirty red vest were the last things he saw clearly as they gathered around and above him, bashing away with their clubs. The one with the nails studded in it came down on his lower right calf, sinking its stupid rusty fangs in deep. He tried again to raise one of the big guns (his vision was fading, now, but that wouldn't help them if he got to shooting; he had always been the most hellishly talented of them, Jamie DeCurry had once proclaimed that Roland could shoot blindfolded, because he had eyes in his fingers), and it was kicked out of his hand and into the dust. Although he could still feel the smooth sandalwood grip of the other, he thought it was nevertheless already gone.

He could smell them—the rich, rotted smell of decaying meat. Or was that only his hands, as he raised them in a feeble and useless effort to protect his head? His hands, which had been in the polluted water where flecks and strips of the dead boy's skin floated?

The clubs slamming down on him, slamming down all over him, as if the green folk wanted not just to beat him to death but to tenderize him as they did so. And as he went down into the darkness of what he most certainly believed would be his death, he heard the bugs singing, the dog he had spared barking, and the bells hung on the church door ringing. These sounds merged together into strangely sweet music. Then that was gone, too; the darkness ate it all.

II. Rising. Hanging Suspended. White Beauty. Two Others. The Medallion.

The gunslinger's return to the world wasn't like coming back to consciousness after a blow, which he'd done several times before, and it wasn't like waking from sleep, either. It was like rising.

I'm dead, he thought at some point during this process . . . when the power to think had been at least partially restored to him. *Dead and rising into whatever afterlife there is. That's what it must be. The singing I hear is the singing of dead souls.*

Total blackness gave way to the dark gray of rainclouds, then to the lighter gray of fog. This brightened to the uniform clarity of a heavy mist moments before the sun breaks through. And through it all was that sense of *rising,* as if he had been caught in some mild but powerful updraft.

As the sense of rising began to diminish and the brightness behind his eyelids grew, Roland at last began to believe he was still alive. It was the singing that convinced him. Not dead souls, not the heavenly host of angels sometimes described by the Jesus-man preachers, but only those bugs. A little like crickets, but sweeter-voiced. The ones he had heard in Eluria.

On this thought, he opened his eyes.

His belief that he was still alive was severely tried, for Roland found himself hanging suspended in a world of white beauty—his first bewildered thought was that he was in the sky, floating within a fair-weather cloud. All around him was the reedy singing of the bugs. Now he could hear the tinkling of bells, too.

He tried to turn his head and swayed in some sort of harness. He could hear it creaking. The soft singing of the bugs, like crickets in the grass at the end of day back home in Gilead, hesitated and broke rhythm. When it did, what felt like a tree of pain grew up Roland's back. He had no idea what its burning branches might be, but the trunk was surely his spine. A far deadlier pain sank into one of his lower legs—in his confusion, the gunslinger could not tell which one. *That's where the club with the nails in it got me,* he thought. And more pain

in his head. His skull felt like a badly cracked egg. He cried out, and could hardly believe that the harsh crow's caw he heard came from his own throat. He thought he could also hear, very faintly, the barking of the cross-dog, but surely that was his imagination.

Am I dying? Have I awakened once more at the very end?

A hand stroked his brow. He could feel it but not see it—fingers trailing across his skin, pausing here and there to massage a knot or a line. Delicious, like a drink of cool water on a hot day. He began to close his eyes, and then a horrible idea came to him: suppose that hand were green, its owner wearing a tattered red vest over her hanging dugs?

What if it is? What could you do?

"Hush, man," a young woman's voice said . . . or perhaps it was the voice of a girl. Certainly the first person Roland thought of was Susan, the girl from Mejis, she who had spoken to him as *thee.*

"Where . . . where . . ."

"Hush, stir not. 'Tis far too soon."

The pain in his back was subsiding now, but the image of the pain as a tree remained, for his very skin seemed to be moving like leaves in a light breeze. How could that be?

He let the question go—let all questions go—and concentrated on the small, cool hand stroking his brow.

"Hush, pretty man, God's love be upon ye. Yet it's sore hurt ye are. Be still. Heal."

The dog had hushed its barking (if it had ever been there in the first place), and Roland became aware of that low creaking sound again. It reminded him of horse tethers, or something

(hangropes)

he didn't like to think of. Now he believed he could feel pressure beneath his thighs, his buttocks, and perhaps . . . yes . . . his shoulders.

I'm not in a bed at all. I think I'm above *a bed. Can that be?*

He supposed he could be in a sling. He seemed to remember once, as a boy, that some fellow had been suspended that way in the horse doctor's room behind the Great Hall. A stablehand who had been burned too badly by kerosene to be laid in a bed. The man had died, but not soon enough; for two nights, his shrieks had filled the sweet summer air of the Gathering Fields.

Am I burned, then, nothing but a cinder with legs, hanging in a sling?

The fingers touched the center of his brow, rubbing away the frown forming there. And it was as if the voice which went with the hand had read his thoughts, picking them up with the tips of her clever, soothing fingers.

"Ye'll be fine if God wills, sai," the voice which went with the hand said. "But time belongs to God, not to you."

No, he would have said, if he had been able. *Time belongs to the Tower.*

Then he slipped down again, descending as smoothly as he had risen, going away from the hand and the dreamlike sounds of the singing insects and chiming bells. There was an interval that might have been sleep, or perhaps unconsciousness, but he never went all the way back down.

At one point he thought he heard the girl's voice, although he couldn't be sure, because this time it was raised in fury, or fear, or both. "No!" she cried. "Ye can't have it off him and ye know it! Go your course and stop talking of it, do!"

When he rose back to consciousness the second time, he was no stronger in body, but a little more himself in mind. What he saw when he opened his eyes wasn't the inside of a cloud, but at first that same phrase—*white beauty*—recurred to him. It was in some ways the most beautiful place Roland had ever been in his life . . . partially because he still *had* a life, of course, but mostly because it was so fey and peaceful.

It was a huge room, high and long. When Roland at last turned his head—cautiously, so cautiously—to take its measure as well as he could, he thought it must run at least two hundred yards from end to end. It was built narrow, but its height gave the place a feeling of tremendous airiness.

There were no walls or ceilings such as those he was familiar with, although it was a little like being in a vast tent. Above him, the sun struck and diffused its light across billowy panels of thin white silk, turning them into the bright swags that he had first mistaken for clouds. Beneath this silk canopy, the room was as gray as twilight. The walls, also silk, rippled like sails in a faint breeze. Hanging from each wall panel was a curved rope bearing small bells. These lay against the fabric and rang in low and charming unison, like wind chimes, when the walls rippled.

An aisle ran down the center of the long room; on either side of it were scores of beds, each made up with clean white sheets and headed with crisp white pillows. There were perhaps forty on the far side of the aisle, all empty, and another forty on Roland's side. There were two other occupied beds here, one next to Roland on his right. This fellow—

It's the boy. The one who was in the trough.

The idea ran goose bumps up Roland's arms and gave him a nasty, superstitious start. He peered more closely at the sleeping boy.

Can't be. You're just dazed, that's all; it can't be.

Yet closer scrutiny refused to dispel the idea. It certainly *seemed* to be the boy from the trough, probably ill (why else would he be in a place like this?) but far from dead; Roland could see the slow rise and fall of his chest, and the occasional twitch of the fingers that dangled over the side of the bed.

You didn't get a good enough look at him to be sure of anything, and after a few days in that trough, his own mother couldn't have said for sure who it was.

But Roland, who'd had a mother, knew better than that. He also knew that he'd seen the gold medallion around the boy's neck. Just before the attack of the green folk, he had taken it from this lad's corpse and put it in his pocket. Now someone—the proprietors of this place, most likely, them who had sorcerously restored the lad named James to his interrupted life—had taken it back from Roland and put it around the boy's neck again.

Had the girl with the wonderfully cool hand done that? Did she in consequence think Roland a ghoul who would steal from the dead? He didn't like to think so. In fact, the notion made him more uncomfortable than the idea that the young cowboy's bloated body had been somehow returned to its normal size and then reanimated.

Farther down the aisle on this side, perhaps a dozen empty beds away from the boy and Roland Deschain, the gunslinger saw a third inmate of this queer infirmary. This fellow looked at least four times the age of the lad, twice the age of the gunslinger. He had a long beard, more gray than black, that hung to his upper chest in two straggly forks. The face above it was sun-darkened, heavily lined, and pouched beneath the eyes. Running from his left cheek and across the bridge of his nose was a thick dark mark which Roland took to be a scar. The bearded man was either asleep or unconscious—Roland could hear him snoring—and was suspended three feet above his bed, held up by a complex series of white belts that glimmered in the dim air. These crisscrossed each other, making a series of figure eights all the way around the man's body. He looked like a bug in some exotic spider's web. He wore a gauzy white bed-dress. One of the belts ran beneath his buttocks, elevating his crotch in a way that seemed to offer the bulge of his privates to the gray and dreaming air. Farther down his body, Roland could see the dark shadow-shapes of his legs. They appeared to be twisted like ancient dead trees. Roland didn't like to think in how many places they must have been broken to look like that. And yet they appeared to be *moving*. How could they be, if the bearded man was unconscious? It was a trick of the light, perhaps, or of the shadows . . . perhaps the gauzy singlet the man was wearing was stirring in a light breeze, or . . .

Roland looked away, up at the billowy silk panels high above, trying to control the accelerating beat of his heart. What he saw hadn't been caused by the wind, or a shadow, or anything else. The man's legs were somehow moving without moving . . . as Roland had seemed to feel his own back moving without moving. He didn't know what could cause such a phenomenon, and didn't want to know, at least not yet.

"I'm not ready," he whispered. His lips felt very dry. He closed his eyes again, wanting to sleep, wanting not to think about what the bearded man's twisted legs might indicate about his own condition. But—

But you'd better get ready.

That was the voice that always seemed to come when he tried to slack off, to scamp a job or take the easy way around an obstacle. It was the voice of Cort, his old teacher. The man whose stick they had all feared, as boys. They hadn't feared his stick as much as his mouth, however. His jeers when they were weak, his contempt when they complained or tried whining about their lot.

Are you a gunslinger, Roland? If you are, you better get ready.

Roland opened his eyes again and turned his head to the left again. As he did, he felt something shift against his chest.

Moving very slowly, he raised his right hand out of the sling that held it. The pain in his back stirred and muttered. He stopped moving until he decided the pain was going to get no worse (if he was careful, at least), then lifted the hand the rest of the way to his chest. It encountered finely woven cloth. Cotton. He lowered his chin to his breastbone and saw that he was wearing a bed-dress like the one draped on the body of the bearded man.

Roland reached beneath the neck of the gown and felt a fine chain. A little farther down, his fingers encountered a rectangular metal shape. He thought he knew what it was, but had to be sure. He pulled it out, still moving with great care, trying not to engage any of the muscles in his back. A gold medallion. He dared the pain, lifting it until he could read what was engraved upon it:

James
Loved of family, Loved of GOD

He tucked it into the top of the bed-dress again and looked back at the sleeping boy in the next bed—*in* it, not suspended over it. The sheet was only pulled up to the boy's rib cage, and the medallion lay on the pristine white breast of his bed-dress. The same medallion Roland now wore. Except . . .

Roland thought he understood, and understanding was a relief.

He looked back at the bearded man, and saw an exceedingly strange thing: the thick black line of scar across the bearded man's cheek and nose was gone. Where it had been was the pinkish red mark of a healing wound . . . a cut, or perhaps a slash.

I imagined it.

No, gunslinger, Cort's voice returned. *Such as you was not made to imagine. As you well know.*

The little bit of movement had tired him out again . . . or perhaps it was the thinking which had really tired him out. The singing bugs and chiming bells combined and made something too much like a lullaby to resist. This time when Roland closed his eyes, he slept.

III. Five Sisters. Jenna. The Doctors of Eluria. The Medallion. A Promise of Silence.

When Roland awoke again, he was at first sure that he was still sleeping. Dreaming. Having a nightmare.

Once, at the time he had met and fallen in love with Susan Delgado, he had known a witch named Rhea—the first real witch of Mid-World he had ever met. It was she who had caused Susan's death, although

Roland had played his own part. Now, opening his eyes and seeing Rhea not just once but five times over, he thought: *This is what comes of remembering those old times. By conjuring Susan, I've conjured Rhea of the Coos, as well. Rhea and her sisters.*

The five were dressed in billowing habits as white as the walls and the panels of the ceiling. Their antique crones' faces were framed in wimples just as white, their skin as gray and runneled as droughted earth by comparison. Hanging like phylacteries from the bands of silk imprisoning their hair (if they indeed had hair) were lines of tiny bells which chimed as they moved or spoke. Upon the snowy breasts of their habits was embroidered a blood red rose ... the *sigul* of the Dark Tower. Seeing this, Roland thought: *I am not dreaming. These harridans are real.*

"He wakes!" one of them cried in a gruesomely coquettish voice.

"Oooo!"

"Ooooh!"

"Ah!"

They fluttered like birds. The one in the center stepped forward, and as she did, their faces seemed to shimmer like the silk walls of the ward. They weren't old after all, he saw—middle-aged, perhaps, but not old.

Yes. They are old. They changed.

The one who now took charge was taller than the others, and with a broad, slightly bulging brow. She bent toward Roland, and the bells that fringed her forehead tinkled. The sound made him feel sick, somehow, and weaker than he had felt a moment before. Her hazel eyes were intent. Greedy, mayhap. She touched his cheek for a moment, and a numbness seemed to spread there. Then she glanced down, and a look which could have been disquiet cramped her face. She took her hand back.

"Ye wake, pretty man. So ye do. 'Tis well."

"Who are you? Where am I?"

"We are the Little Sisters of Eluria," she said. "I am Sister Mary. Here is Sister Louise, and Sister Michela, and Sister Coquina—"

"And Sister Tamra," said the last. "A lovely lass of one-and-twenty." She giggled. Her face shimmered, and for a moment she was again as old as the world. Hooked of nose, gray of skin. Roland thought once more of Rhea.

They moved closer, encircling the complication of harness in which he lay suspended, and when Roland shrank back, the pain roared up his back and injured leg again. He groaned. The straps holding him creaked.

"Ooooo!"

"It hurts!"

"Hurts him!"

"Hurts so fierce!"

They pressed even closer, as if his pain fascinated them. And now he could smell them, a dry and earthy smell. The one named Sister Michela reached out—

"Go away! Leave him! Have I not told ye before?"

They jumped back from this voice, startled. Sister Mary looked particularly annoyed. But she stepped back, with one final glare (Roland would have sworn it) at the medallion lying on his chest. He had tucked it back under the bed-dress at his last waking, but it was out again now.

A sixth sister appeared, pushing rudely in between Mary and Tamra. This one perhaps *was* only one-and-twenty, with flushed cheeks, smooth skin, and dark eyes. Her white habit billowed like a dream. The red rose over her breast stood out like a curse.

"Go! Leave him!"

"Oooo, my *dear*!" cried Sister Louise in a voice both laughing and angry. "Here's Jenna, the baby, and has she fallen in love with him?"

"She has!" laughed Tamra. "Baby's heart is his for the purchase!"

"Oh, so it *is*!" agreed Sister Coquina.

Mary turned to the newcomer, lips pursed into a tight line. "Ye have no business here, saucy girl."

"I do if I say I do," Sister Jenna replied. She seemed more in charge of herself now. A curl of black hair had escaped her wimple and lay across her forehead in a comma. "Now go. He's not up to your jokes and laughter."

"Order us not," Sister Mary said, "for we never joke. So you know, Sister Jenna."

The girl's face softened a little, and Roland saw she was afraid. It made him afraid for her. For himself, as well. "Go," she repeated. " 'Tis not the time. Are there not others to tend?"

Sister Mary seemed to consider. The others watched her. At last she nodded, and smiled down at Roland. Again her face seemed to shimmer, like something seen through a heat-haze. What he saw (or thought he saw) beneath was horrible and watchful. "Bide well, pretty man," she said to Roland. "Bide with us a bit, and we'll heal ye."

What choice have I? Roland thought.

The others laughed, birdlike titters which rose into the dimness like ribbons. Sister Michela actually blew him a kiss.

"Come, ladies!" Sister Mary cried. "We'll leave Jenna with him a bit in memory of her mother, who we loved well!" And with that, she lead the others away, five white birds flying off down the center aisle, their skirts nodding this way and that.

"Thank you," Roland said, looking up at the owner of the cool hand . . . for he knew it was she who had soothed him.

She took up his fingers as if to prove this, and caressed them. "They mean ye no harm," she said . . . yet Roland saw she believed not a word of it, nor did he. He was in trouble here, very bad trouble.

"What is this place?"

"Our place," she said simply. "The home of the Little Sisters of Eluria. Our convent, if'ee like."

"This is no convent," Roland said, looking past her at the empty beds. "It's an infirmary. Isn't it?"

"A hospital," she said, still stroking his fingers. "We serve the doctors . . . and they serve us." He was fascinated by the black curl lying on the cream of her brow—would have stroked it, if he had dared reach up. Just to tell its texture. He found it beautiful because it was the only dark thing in all this white. The white had lost its charm for him. "We are hospitalers . . . or were, before the world moved on."

"Are you for the Jesus-man?"

She looked surprised for a moment, almost shocked, and then laughed merrily. "No, not us!"

"If you are hospitalers . . . nurses . . . where are the doctors?"

She looked at him, biting at her lip, as if trying to decide something. Roland found her doubt utterly charming, and he realized that, sick or not, he was looking at a woman *as* a woman for the first time since Susan Delgado had died, and that had been long ago. The whole world had changed since then, and not for the better.

"Would you really know?"

"Yes, of course," he said, a little surprised. A little disquieted, too.

He kept waiting for her face to shimmer and change, as the faces of the others had done. It didn't. There was none of that unpleasant dead earth smell about her, either.

Wait, he cautioned himself. *Believe nothing here, least of all your senses. Not yet.*

"I suppose you must," she said with a sigh. It tinkled the bells at her forehead, which were darker in color than those the others wore— not black like her hair but charry, somehow, as if they had been hung in the smoke of a campfire. Their sound, however, was brightest silver. "Promise me you'll not scream and wake the pube in yonder bed."

"Pube?"

"The boy. Do ye promise?"

"Aye," he said, falling into the half-forgotten patois of the Outer Arc without even being aware of it. Susan's dialect. "It's been long since I screamed, pretty."

She colored more definitely at that, roses more natural and lively than the one on her breast mounting in her cheeks.

"Don't call pretty what ye can't properly see," she said.

"Then push back the wimple you wear."

Her face he could see perfectly well, but he badly wanted to see her hair—hungered for it, almost. A full flood of black in all this dreaming white. Of course it might be cropped, those of her order might wear it that way, but he somehow didn't think so.

"No, 'tis not allowed."

"By who?"

"Big Sister."

"She who calls herself Mary?"

"Aye, her." She started away, then paused and looked back over her shoulder. In another girl her age, one as pretty as this, that look back would have been flirtatious. This girl's was only grave.

"Remember your promise."

"Aye, no screams."

She went to the bearded man, skirt swinging. In the dimness, she cast only a blur of shadow on the empty beds she passed. When she reached the man (this one was unconscious, Roland thought, not just sleeping), she looked back at Roland once more. He nodded.

Sister Jenna stepped close to the suspended man's side on the far side of his bed, so that Roland saw her through the twists and loops of woven white silk. She placed her hands lightly on the left side of his chest, bent over him . . . and shook her head from side to side, like one expressing a brisk negative. The bells she wore on her forehead rang sharply, and Roland once more felt that weird stirring up his back, accompanied by a low ripple of pain. It was as if he had shuddered without actually shuddering, or shuddered in a dream.

What happened next almost *did* jerk a scream from him; he had to bite his lips against it. Once more the unconscious man's legs seemed to move without moving . . . because it was what was *on* them that moved. The man's hairy shins, ankles, and feet were exposed below the hem of his bed-dress. Now a black wave of bugs moved down them. They were singing fiercely, like an army column that sings as it marches.

Roland remembered the black scar across the man's cheek and nose—the scar that had disappeared. More such as these, of course. And they were on *him*, as well. That was how he could shiver without shivering. They were all over his back. *Battening* on him.

No, keeping back a scream wasn't as easy as he had expected it to be.

The bugs ran down to the tips of the suspended man's toes, then leaped off them in waves, like creatures leaping off an embankment and into a swimming hole. They organized themselves quickly and easily on the bright white sheet below, and began to march down to the floor in a battalion about a foot wide. Roland couldn't get a good look at them, the distance was too far and the light too dim, but he thought they were perhaps twice the size of ants, and a little smaller than the fat honeybees which had swarmed the flower beds back home.

They sang as they went.

The bearded man didn't sing. As the swarms of bugs that had coated his twisted legs began to diminish, he shuddered and groaned. The young woman put her hand on his brow and soothed him, making Roland a little jealous even in his revulsion at what he was seeing.

And was what he was seeing really so awful? In Gilead, leeches had been used for certain ailments—swellings of the brain, the armpits, and the groin, primarily. When it came to the brain, the leeches, ugly as they were, were certainly preferable to the next step, which was trepanning.

Yet there *was* something loathsome about them, perhaps only because he couldn't see them well, and something awful about trying to imagine them all over his back as he hung here, helpless. Not singing, though. Why? Because they were feeding? Sleeping? Both at once?

The bearded man's groans subsided. The bugs marched away across the floor, toward one of the mildly rippling silken walls. Roland lost sight of them in the shadows.

Jenna came back to him, her eyes anxious. "Ye did well. Yet I see how ye feel; it's on your face."

"The doctors," he said.

"Yes. Their power is very great, but . . ." She dropped her voice. "I believe that drover is beyond their help. His legs are a little better, and the wounds on his face are all but healed, but he has injuries where the doctors cannot reach." She traced a hand across her midsection, suggesting the location of these injuries, if not their nature.

"And me?" Roland asked.

"Ye were ta'en by the green folk," she said. "Ye must have angered them powerfully, for them not to kill ye outright. They roped ye and dragged ye, instead. Tamra, Michela, and Louise were out gathering herbs. They saw the green folk at play with ye, and bade them stop, but—"

"Do the muties always obey you, Sister Jenna?"

She smiled, perhaps pleased he remembered her name. "Not always, but mostly. This time they did, or ye'd have now found the clearing in the trees."

"I suppose so."

"The skin was stripped almost clean off your back—red ye were from nape to waist. Ye'll always bear the scars, but the doctors have gone far toward healing ye. And their singing is passing fair, is it not?"

"Yes," Roland said, but the thought of those black things all over his back, roosting in his raw flesh, still revolted him. "I owe you thanks, and give it freely. Anything I can do for you—"

"Tell me your name, then. Do that."

"I'm Roland of Gilead. A gunslinger. I had revolvers, Sister Jenna. Have you seen them?"

"I've seen no shooters," she said, but cast her eyes aside. The roses bloomed in her cheeks again. She might be a good nurse, and fair, but

Roland thought her a poor liar. He was glad. Good liars were common. Honesty, on the other hand, came dear.

Let the untruth pass for now, he told himself. *She speaks it out of fear, I think.*

"Jenna!" The cry came from the deeper shadows at the far end of the infirmary—today it seemed longer than ever to the gunslinger—and Sister Jenna jumped guiltily. "Come away! Ye've passed words enough to entertain twenty men! Let him sleep!"

"Aye!" she called, then turned back to Roland. "Don't let on that I showed you the doctors."

"Mum is the word, Jenna."

She paused, biting her lip again, then suddenly swept back her wimple. It fell against the nape of her neck in a soft chiming of bells. Freed from its confinement, her hair swept against her cheeks like shadows.

"*Am* I pretty? *Am* I? Tell me the truth, Roland of Gilead—no flattery. For flattery's kind only a candle's length."

"Pretty as a summer night."

What she saw in his face seemed to please her more than his words, because she smiled radiantly. She pulled the wimple up again, tucking her hair back in with quick little finger-pokes. "Am I decent?"

"Decent as fair," he said, then cautiously lifted an arm and pointed at her brow. "One curl's out . . . just there."

"Aye, always that one to devil me." With a comical little grimace, she tucked it back. Roland thought how much he would like to kiss her rosy cheeks . . . and perhaps her rosy mouth, for good measure.

"All's well," he said.

"*Jenna!*" The cry was more impatient than ever. "Meditations!"

"I'm coming just now!" she called, and gathered her voluminous skirts to go. Yet she turned back once more, her face now very grave and very serious. "One more thing," she said in a voice only a step above a whisper. She snatched a quick look around. "The gold medallion ye wear—ye wear it because it's yours. Do'ee understand . . . James?"

"Yes." He turned his head a bit to look at the sleeping boy. "This is my brother."

"If they ask, yes. To say different would be to get Jenna in serious trouble."

How serious he did not ask, and she was gone in any case, seeming to flow along the aisle between all the empty beds, her skirt caught up in one hand. The roses had fled from her face, leaving her cheeks and brow ashy. He remembered the greedy look on the faces of the others, how they had gathered around him in a tightening knot . . . and the way their faces had shimmered.

Six women, five old and one young.

Doctors that sang and then crawled away across the floor when dismissed by jingling bells.

And an improbable hospital ward of perhaps a hundred beds, a ward with a silk roof and silk walls . . .

. . . and all the beds empty save three.

Roland didn't understand why Jenna had taken the dead boy's medallion from his pants pocket and put it around his neck, but he had an idea that if they found out she had done so, the Little Sisters of Eluria might kill her.

Roland closed his eyes, and the soft singing of the doctor-insects once again floated him off into sleep.

IV. A Bowl of Soup. The Boy in the Next Bed. The Night-Nurses.

Roland dreamed that a very large bug (a doctor-bug, mayhap) was flying around his head and banging repeatedly into his nose—collisions which were annoying rather than painful. He swiped at the bug repeatedly, and although his hands were eerily fast under ordinary circumstances, he kept missing it. And each time he missed, the bug giggled.

I'm slow because I've been sick, he thought.

No, ambushed. Dragged across the ground by slow mutants, saved by the Little Sisters of Eluria.

Roland had a sudden, vivid image of a man's shadow growing from the shadow of an overturned freight wagon; heard a rough, gleeful voice cry "Booh!"

He jerked awake hard enough to set his body rocking in its complication of slings, and the woman who had been standing beside his head, giggling as she tapped his nose lightly with a wooden spoon, stepped back so quickly that the bowl in her other hand slipped from her fingers.

Roland's hands shot out, and they were as quick as ever—his frustrated failure to catch the bug had been only part of his dream. He caught the bowl before more than a few drops could spill. The woman—Sister Coquina—looked at him with round eyes.

There was pain all up and down his back from the sudden movement, but it was nowhere near as sharp as it had been before, and there was no sensation of movement on his skin. Perhaps the "doctors" were only sleeping, but he had an idea they were gone.

He held out his hand for the spoon Coquina had been teasing him with (he found he wasn't surprised at all that one of these would tease a sick and sleeping man in such a way; it only would have surprised him if it had been Jenna), and she handed it to him, her eyes still big.

"How speedy ye are!" she said. " 'Twas like a magic trick, and you still rising from sleep!"

"Remember it, sai," he said, and tried the soup. There were tiny bits of chicken floating in it. He probably would have considered it bland under other circumstances, but under these, it seemed ambrosial. He began to eat greedily.

"What do'ee mean by that?" she asked. The light was very dim now, the wall panels across the way a pinkish orange that suggested sunset. In this light, Coquina looked quite young and pretty . . . but it was a glamour, Roland was sure; a sorcerous kind of makeup.

"I mean nothing in particular." Roland dismissed the spoon as too slow, preferring to tilt the bowl itself to his lips. In this way he disposed of the soup in four large gulps. "You have been kind to me—"

"Aye, so we *have*!" she said, rather indignantly.

"—and I hope your kindness has no hidden motive. If it does, Sister, remember that I'm quick. And, as for myself, I have not always been kind."

She made no reply, only took the bowl when Roland handed it back. She did this delicately, perhaps not wanting to touch his fingers. Her eyes dropped to where the medallion lay, once more hidden beneath the breast of his bed-dress. He said no more, not wanting to weaken the implied threat by reminding her that the man who made it was unarmed, next to naked, and hung in the air because his back couldn't yet bear the weight of his body.

"Where's Sister Jenna?" he asked.

"Oooo," Sister Coquina said, raising her eyebrows. "We like her,

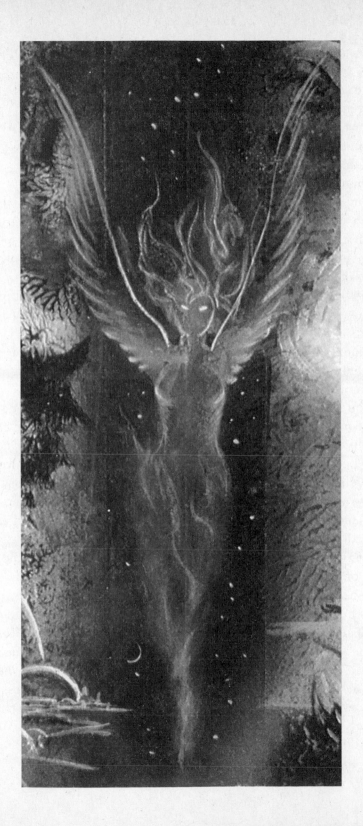

do we? She makes our heart go . . ." She put her hand against the rose on her breast and fluttered it rapidly.

"Not at all, not at all," Roland said, "but she was kind. I doubt she would have teased me with a spoon, as some would."

Sister Coquina's smile faded. She looked both angry and worried. "Say nothing of that to Mary, if she comes by later. Ye might get me in trouble."

"Should I care?"

"I might get back at one who caused me trouble by causing little Jenna trouble," Sister Coquina said. "She's in Big Sister's black books, just now, anyway. Sister Mary doesn't care for the way Jenna spoke to her about ye . . . nor does she like it that Jenna came back to us wearing the Dark Bells."

This was no more out of her mouth before Sister Coquina put her hand over that frequently imprudent organ, as if realizing she had said too much.

Roland, intrigued by what she'd said but not liking to show it just now, only replied, "I'll keep my mouth shut about you, if you keep your mouth shut to Sister Mary about Jenna."

Coquina looked relieved. "Aye, that's a bargain." She leaned forward confidingly. "She's in Thoughtful House. That's the little cave in the hillside where we have to go and meditate when Big Sister decides we've been bad. She'll have to stay and consider her impudence until Mary lets her out." She paused, then said abruptly, "Who's this beside ye? Do ye know?"

Roland turned his head and saw that the young man was awake, and had been listening. His eyes were as dark as Jenna's.

"Know him?" Roland asked, with what he hoped was the right touch of scorn. "Should I not know my own brother?"

"Is he, now, and him so young and you so old?" Another of the sisters materialized out of the darkness: Sister Tamra, who had called herself one-and-twenty. In the moment before she reached Roland's bed, her face was that of a hag who will never see eighty again . . . or ninety. Then it shimmered and was once more the plump, healthy countenence of a thirty-year-old matron. Except for the eyes. They remained yellowish in the corneas, gummy in the corners, and watchful.

"He's the youngest, I the eldest," Roland said. "Betwixt us are seven others, and twenty years of our parents' lives."

"How sweet! And if he's yer brother, then ye'll know his name, won't ye? Know it very well."

Before the gunslinger could flounder, the young man said, "They think you've forgotten such a simple hook as John Norman. What culleens they be, eh, Jimmy?"

Coquina and Tamra looked at the pale boy in the bed next to Roland's, clearly angry . . . and clearly trumped. For the time being, at least.

"You've fed him your muck," the boy (whose medallion undoubtedly proclaimed him 𝔍𝔬𝔥𝔫, 𝓛𝓸𝓿𝓮𝓭 𝓸𝓯 𝓯𝓪𝓶𝓲𝓵𝔂, 𝓛𝓸𝓿𝓮𝓭 𝓸𝓯 𝓖𝓞𝓓) said. "Why don't you go, and let us have a natter?"

"Well!" Sister Coquina huffed. "I like the gratitude around here, so I do!"

"I'm grateful for what's given me," Norman responded, looking at her steadily, "but not for what folk would take away."

Tamra snorted through her nose, turned violently enough for her swirling dress to push a draught of air into Roland's face, and then took her leave. Coquina stayed a moment.

"Be discreet, and mayhap someone ye like better than ye like me will get out of hack in the morning, instead of a week from tonight."

Without waiting for a reply, she turned and followed Sister Tamra.

Roland and John Norman waited until they were both gone, and then Norman turned to Roland and spoke in a low voice. "My brother. Dead?"

Roland nodded. "The medallion I took in case I should meet with any of his people. It rightly belongs to you. I'm sorry for your loss."

"Thankee-sai." John Norman's lower lip trembled, then firmed. "I knew the green men did for him, although these old biddies wouldn't tell me for sure. They did for plenty, and scotched the rest."

"Perhaps the Sisters didn't know for sure."

"They knew. Don't you doubt it. They don't say much, but they know *plenty*. The only one any different is Jenna. That's who the old battle-axe meant when she said 'your friend.' Aye?"

Roland nodded. "And she said something about the Dark Bells. I'd know more of that, if would were could."

"She's something special, Jenna is. More like a princess—someone whose place is made by bloodline and can't be refused—than like the other Sisters. I lie here and look like I'm asleep—it's safer, I think—

but I've heard 'em talking. Jenna's just come back among 'em recently, and those Dark Bells mean something special . . . but Mary's still the one who swings the weight. I think the Dark Bells are only ceremonial, like the rings the old Barons used to hand down from father to son. Was it she who put Jimmy's medal around your neck?"

"Yes."

"Don't take it off, whatever you do." His face was strained, grim. "I don't know if it's the gold or the God, but they don't like to get too close. I think that's the only reason I'm still here." Now his voice dropped all the way to a whisper. "They ain't human."

"Well, perhaps a bit fey and magical, but . . ."

"No!" With what was clearly an effort, the boy got up on one elbow. He looked at Roland earnestly. "You're thinking about hubber-women, or witches. These ain't hubbers, nor witches, either. *They ain't human!*"

"Then what are they?"

"Don't know."

"How came you here, John?"

Speaking in a low voice, John Norman told Roland what he knew of what had happened to him. He, his brother, and four other young men who were quick and owned good horses had been hired as scouts, riding drogue-and-forward, protecting a long-haul caravan of seven freight wagons taking goods—seeds, food, tools, mail, and four ordered brides—to an unincorporated township called Tejuas some two hundred miles farther west of Eluria. The scouts rode fore and aft of the goods-train in turn-and-turn-about fashion; one brother rode with each party because, Norman explained, when they were together they fought like . . . well . . .

"Like brothers," Roland suggested.

John Norman managed a brief, pained smile. "Aye," he said.

The trio of which John was a part had been riding drogue, about two miles behind the freight wagons, when the green mutants had sprung an ambush in Eluria.

"How many wagons did you see when you got there?" he asked Roland.

"Only one. Overturned."

"How many bodies?"

"Only your brother's."

John Norman nodded grimly. "They wouldn't take him because of the medallion, I think."

"The muties?"

"The Sisters. The muties care nothing for gold or God. These bitches, though . . ." He looked into the dark, which was now almost complete. Roland felt lethargy creeping over him again, but it wasn't until later that he realized the soup had been drugged.

"The other wagons?" Roland asked. "The ones not overturned?"

"The muties would have taken them, and the goods, as well," Norman said. "They don't care for gold or God; the Sisters don't care for goods. Like as not they have their own foodstuffs, something I'd as soon not think of. Nasty stuff . . . like those bugs."

He and the other drogue riders galloped into Eluria, but the fight was over by the time they got there. Men had been lying about, some dead but many more still alive. At least two of the ordered brides had still been alive, as well. Survivors able to walk were being herded together by the green folk—John Norman remembered the one in the bowler hat very well, and the woman in the ragged red vest.

Norman and the other two had tried to fight. He had seen one of his pards gutshot by an arrow, and then he saw no more—someone had cracked him over the head from behind, and the lights had gone out.

Roland wondered if the ambusher had cried "Booh!" before he had struck, but didn't ask.

"When I woke up again, I was here," Norman said. "I saw that some of the others—*most* of them—had those cursed bugs on them."

"Others?" Roland looked at the empty beds. In the growing darkness, they glimmered like white islands. "How many were brought here?"

"At least twenty. They healed . . . the bugs healed 'em . . . and then, one by one, they disappeared. You'd go to sleep, and when you woke up there'd be one more empty bed. One by one they went, until only me and that one down yonder was left."

He looked at Roland solemnly.

"And now you."

"Norman," Roland's head was swimming. "I—"

"I reckon I know what's wrong with you," Norman said. He seemed to speak from far away . . . perhaps from all the way around the curve of the earth. "It's the soup. But a man has to eat. A woman, too. If she's a natural woman, anyway. These ones ain't natural. Even Sister Jenna's not natural. Nice don't mean natural." Farther and farther away. "And she'll be like them in the end. Mark me well."

"Can't move." Saying even that required a huge effort. It was like moving boulders.

"No." Norman suddenly laughed. It was a shocking sound, and echoed in the growing blackness which filled Roland's head. "It ain't just sleep medicine they put in their soup; it's can't-move medicine, too. There's nothing much wrong with me, brother . . . so why do you think I'm still here?"

Norman was now speaking not from around the curve of the earth but perhaps from the moon, He said: "I don't think either of us is ever going to see the sun shining on a flat piece of ground again."

You're wrong about that, Roland tried to reply, and more in that vein, as well, but nothing came out. He sailed around to the black side of the moon, losing all his words in the void he found there.

Yet he never quite lost awareness of himself. Perhaps the dose of "medicine" in Sister Coquina's soup had been badly calculated, or perhaps it was just that they had never had a gunslinger to work their mischief on, and did not know they had one now.

Except, of course, for Sister Jenna—*she* knew.

At some point in the night, whispering, giggling voices and lightly chiming bells brought him back from the darkness where he had been biding, not quite asleep or unconscious. Around him, so constant he now barely heard it, were the singing "doctors."

Roland opened his eyes. He saw pale and chancy light dancing in the black air. The giggles and whispers were closer. Roland tried to turn his head and at first couldn't. He rested, gathered his will into a hard blue ball, and tried again. This time his head *did* turn. Only a little, but a little was enough.

It was five of the Little Sisters—Mary, Louise, Tamra, Coquina, Michela. They came up the long aisle of the black infirmary, laughing together like children out on a prank, carrying long tapers in silver holders, the bells lining the forehead-bands of their wimples chiming little silver runs of sound. They gathered about the bed of the bearded man. From within their circle, candleglow rose in a shimmery column that died before it got halfway to the silken ceiling.

Sister Mary spoke briefly. Roland recognized her voice, but not the words—it was neither low speech nor the High, but some other language entirely. One phrase stood out—*can de lach, mi him en tow*—and he had no idea what it might mean.

He realized that now he could hear only the tinkle of bells—the doctor-bugs had stilled.

"*Ras me! On! On!*" Sister Mary cried in a harsh, powerful voice. The candles went out. The light that had shone through the wings of their wimples as they gathered around the bearded man's bed vanished, and all was darkness once more.

Roland waited for what might happen next, his skin cold. He tried to flex his hands or feet, and could not. He had been able to move his head perhaps fifteen degrees; otherwise he was as paralyzed as a fly neatly wrapped up and hung in a spider's web.

The low jingling of bells in the black . . . and then sucking sounds. As soon as he heard them, Roland knew he'd been waiting for them. Some part of him had known what the Little Sisters of Eluria were, all along.

If Roland could have raised his hands, he would have put them to his ears to block those sounds out. As it was, he could only lie still, listening and waiting for them to stop.

For a long time—forever, it seemed—they did not. The women slurped and grunted like pigs snuffling half-liquefied feed up out of a trough. There was even one resounding belch, followed by more whispered giggles (these ended when Sister Mary uttered a single curt word—"*Hais!*"). And once there was a low, moaning cry—from the bearded man, Roland was quite sure. If so, it was his last on this side of the clearing.

In time, the sounds of their feeding began to taper off. As it did, the bugs began to sing again—first hesitantly, then with more confidence. The whispering and giggling recommenced. The candles were relit. Roland was by now lying with his head turned in the other direction. He didn't want them to know what he'd seen, but that wasn't all; he had no urge to see more on any account. He had seen and heard enough.

But the giggles and whispers now came his way. Roland closed his eyes, concentrating on the medallion that lay against his chest. *I don't know if it's the gold or the God, but they don't like to get too close,*

John Norman had said. It was good to have such a thing to remember as the Little Sisters drew nigh, gossiping and whispering in their strange other tongue, but the medallion seemed a thin protection in the dark.

Faintly, at a great distance, Roland heard the cross-dog barking.

As the Sisters circled him, the gunslinger realized he could smell them. It was a low, unpleasant odor, like spoiled meat. And what else *would* they smell of, such as these?

"Such a pretty man it is." Sister Mary. She spoke in a low, meditative tone.

"But such an ugly *sigul* it wears." Sister Tamra.

"We'll have it off him!" Sister Louise.

"And then we shall have kisses!" Sister Coquina.

"Kisses for all!" exclaimed Sister Michela, with such fervent enthusiasm that they all laughed.

Roland discovered that not *all* of him was paralyzed, after all. Part of him had, in fact, arisen from its sleep at the sound of their voices and now stood tall. A hand reached beneath the bed-dress he wore, touched that stiffened member, encircled it, caressed it. He lay in silent horror, feigning sleep, as wet warmth almost immediately spilled from him. The hand remained where it was for a moment, the thumb rubbing up and down the wilting shaft. Then it let him go and rose a little higher. Found the wetness pooled on his lower belly.

Giggles, soft as wind.

Chiming bells.

Roland opened his eyes the tiniest crack and looked up at the ancient faces laughing down at him in the light of their candles—glittering eyes, yellow cheeks, hanging teeth that jutted over lower lips. Sister Michela and Sister Louise appeared to have grown goatees, but of course that wasn't the darkness of hair but of the bearded man's blood.

Mary's hand was cupped. She passed it from Sister to Sister; each licked from her palm in the candlelight.

Roland closed his eyes all the way and waited for them to be gone. Eventually they were.

I'll never sleep again, he thought, and was five minutes later lost to himself and the world.

V. Sister Mary. A Message. A Visit from Ralph. Norman's Fate. Sister Mary Again.

When Roland awoke, it was full daylight, the silk roof overhead a bright white and billowing in a mild breeze. The doctor-bugs were singing contentedly. Beside him on his left, Norman was heavily asleep with his head turned so far to one side that his stubbly cheek rested on his shoulder.

Roland and John Norman were the only ones here. Farther down on their side of the infirmary, the bed where the bearded man had been was empty, its top sheet pulled up and neatly tucked in, the pillow neatly nestled in a crisp white case. The complication of slings in which his body had rested was gone.

Roland remembered the candles—the way their glow had combined and streamed up in a column, illuminating the Sisters as they gathered around the bearded man. Giggling. Their damned bells jingling.

Now, as if summoned by his thoughts, came Sister Mary, gliding along rapidly with Sister Louise in her wake. Louise bore a tray, and looked nervous. Mary was frowning, obviously not in good temper.

To be grumpy after you've fed so well? Roland thought. *Fie, Sister.*

She reached the gunslinger's bed and looked down at him. "I have little to thank ye for, sai," she said with no preamble.

"Have I asked for your thanks?" he responded in a voice that sounded as dusty and little-used as the pages of an old book.

She took no notice. "Ye've made one who was only impudent and restless with her place outright rebellious. Well, her mother was the same way, and died of it not long after returning Jenna to her proper place. Raise your hand, thankless man."

"I can't. I can't move at all."

"Oh, cully! Haven't you heard it said 'fool not your mother 'less she's out of face'? I know pretty well what ye can and can't do. Now raise your hand."

Roland raised his right hand, trying to suggest more effort than it actually took. He thought that this morning he might be strong enough to slip free of the slings . . . but what then? Any real walking would be beyond him for hours yet, even without another dose of "medicine" . . . and behind Sister Mary, Sister Louise was taking the cover from a fresh bowl of soup. As Roland looked at it, his stomach rumbled.

Big Sister heard and smiled a bit. "Even lying in bed builds an appetite in a strong man, if it's done long enough. Wouldn't you say so, Jason, brother of John?"

"My name is James. As you well know, Sister."

"Do I?" She laughed angrily. "Oh, la! And if I whipped your little sweetheart hard enough and long enough—until the blood jumped out her back like drops of sweat, let us say—should I not whip a different name out of her? Or didn't ye trust her with it, during your little talk?"

"Touch her and I'll kill you."

She laughed again. Her face shimmered; her firm mouth turned into something that looked like a dying jellyfish. "Speak not of killing to us, cully; lest we speak of it to you."

"Sister, if you and Jenna don't see eye to eye, why not release her from her vows and let her go her course?"

"Such as us can never be released from our vows, nor be let go. Her mother tried and then came back, her dying and the girl sick. Why, it was we nursed Jenna back to health after her mother was nothing but dirt in the breeze the blows out toward End-World, and how little she thanks us! Besides, she bears the Dark Bells, the *sigul* of our sisterhood. Of our *ka-tet*. Now eat—yer belly says ye're hungry!"

Sister Louise offered the bowl, but her eyes kept drifting to the shape the medallion made under the breast of his bed-dress. *Don't like it, do you?* Roland thought, and then remembered Louise by candlelight, the freighter's blood on her chin, her ancient eyes eager as she leaned forward to lick his spend from Sister Mary's hand.

He turned his head aside. "I want nothing."

"But ye're hungry!" Louise protested. "If'ee don't eat, James, how will'ee get'ee strength back?"

"Send Jenna. I'll eat what she brings."

Sister Mary's frown was black. "Ye'll see her no more. She's been released from Thoughtful House only on her solemn promise to double her time of meditation . . . and to stay out of infirmary. Now eat, James, or whoever ye are. Take what's in the soup, or we'll cut ye with knives and rub it in with flannel poultices. Either way, makes no difference to us. Does it, Louise?"

"Nar," Louise said. She still held out the bowl. Steam rose from it, and the good smell of chicken.

"But it might make a difference to you." Sister Mary grinned humorlessly, baring her unnaturally large teeth. "Flowing blood's risky around here. The doctors don't like it. It stirs them up."

It wasn't just the bugs that were stirred up at the sight of blood, and Roland knew it. He also knew he had no choice in the matter of the soup. He took the bowl from Louise and ate slowly. He would have given much to wipe out the look of satisfaction he saw on Sister Mary's face.

"Good," she said after he had handed the bowl back and she had peered inside to make sure it was completely empty. His hand thumped back into the sling which had been rigged for it, already too heavy to hold up. He could feel the world drawing away again.

Sister Mary leaned forward, the billowing top of her habit touching the skin of his left shoulder. He could smell her, an aroma both ripe and dry, and would have gagged if he'd had the strength.

"Have that foul gold thing off ye when yer strength comes back a little—put it in the pissoir under the bed. Where it belongs. For to be even this close to where it lies hurts my head and makes my throat close."

Speaking with enormous effort, Roland said, "If you want it, take it. How can I stop you, you bitch?"

Once more her frown turned her face into something like a thunderhead. He thought she would have slapped him, if she had dared touch him so close to where the medallion lay. Her ability to touch seemed to end above his waist, however.

"I think you had better consider the matter a little more fully," she said. "I can still have Jenna whipped, if I like. She bears the Dark Bells, but I am the Big Sister. Consider that very well."

She left. Sister Louise followed, casting one look—a strange combination of fright and lust—back over her shoulder.

Roland thought, *I must get out of here—I must.*

Instead, he drifted back to that dark place which wasn't quite sleep. Or perhaps he did sleep, at least for a while; perhaps he dreamed. Fingers once more caressed his fingers, and lips first kissed his ear and then whispered into it: "Look beneath your pillow, Roland . . . but let no one know I was here."

At some point after this, Roland opened his eyes again, half-expecting to see Sister Jenna's pretty young face hovering above him. And that comma of dark hair once more poking out from beneath her wimple. There was no one. The swags of silk overhead were at their brightest, and although it was impossible to tell the hours in here with any real accuracy, Roland guessed it to be around noon. Perhaps three hours since his second bowl of the Sisters' soup.

Beside him, John Norman still slept, his breath whistling out in faint, nasal snores.

Roland tried to raise his hand and slide it under his pillow. The hand wouldn't move. He could wiggle the tips of his fingers, but that was all. He waited, calming his mind as well as he could, gathering his patience. Patience wasn't easy to come by. He kept thinking about what Norman had said—that there had been twenty survivors of the ambush . . . at least to start with. *One by one they went, until only me and that one down yonder was left. And now you.*

The girl wasn't here. His mind spoke in the soft, regretful tone of Alain, one of his old friends, dead these many years now. *She wouldn't dare, not with the others watching. That was only a dream you had.*

But Roland thought perhaps it had been more than a dream.

Some length of time later—the slowly shifting brightness overhead made him believe it had been about an hour—Roland tried his hand again. This time he was able to get it beneath his pillow. This was puffy and soft, tucked snugly into the wide sling that supported the gunslinger's neck. At first he found nothing, but as his fingers worked their slow way deeper, they touched what felt like a stiffish bundle of thin rods.

He paused, gathering a little more strength (every movement was like swimming in glue), and then burrowed deeper. It felt like a dead bouquet. Wrapped around it was what felt like a ribbon.

Roland looked around to make sure the ward was still empty and Norman still asleep, then drew out what was under the pillow. It was six brittle stems of fading green with brownish reed heads at the tops. They gave off a strange, yeasty aroma that made Roland think of early-morning begging expeditions to the Great House kitchens as a child— forays he had usually made with Cuthbert. The reeds were tied with a wide white silk ribbon, and smelled like burned toast. Beneath the ribbon was a fold of cloth. Like everything else in this cursed place, it seemed, the cloth was of silk.

Roland was breathing hard and could feel drops of sweat on his brow. Still alone, though—good. He took the scrap of cloth and un-

folded it. Printed painstakingly in blurred charcoal letters was this message:

NIBBLE HEDS. ONCE EACH HOUR. TOO
MUCH, CRAMPS OR DETH.
TOMORROW NITE. CAN'T BE SOONER.
BE CAREFUL!

No explanation, but Roland supposed none was needed. Nor did he
have any option; if he remained here, he would die. All they had to
do was have the medallion off him, and he felt sure Sister Mary was
smart enough to figure a way to do that.

He nibbled at one of the dry reed heads. The taste was nothing like
the toast they had begged from the kitchen as boys; it was bitter in his
throat and hot in his stomach. Less than a minute after his nibble, his
heart rate had doubled. His muscles awakened, but not in a pleasant
way, as after good sleep; they felt first trembly and then hard, as if
they were gathered into knots. This feeling passed rapidly, and his
heartbeat was back to normal before Norman stirred awake an hour
or so later, but he understood why Jenna's note had warned him not
to take more than a nibble at a time—this was very powerful stuff.

He slipped the bouquet of reeds back under the pillow, being careful
to brush away the few crumbles of vegetable matter which had dropped
to the sheet. Then he used the ball of his thumb to blur the painstaking
charcoaled words on the bit of silk. When he was finished, there was
nothing on the square but meaningless smudges. The square he also
tucked back under his pillow.

When Norman awoke, he and the gunslinger spoke briefly of the
young scout's home—Delain, it was, sometimes known jestingly as
Dragon's Lair, or Liar's Heaven. All tall tales were said to originate
in Delain. The boy asked Roland to take his medallion and that of his
brother home to their parents, if Roland was able, and explain as well
as he could what had happened to James and John, sons of Jesse.

"You'll do all that yourself," Roland said.

"No." Norman tried to raise his hand, perhaps to scratch his nose,
and was unable to do even that. The hand rose perhaps six inches, then
fell back to the counterpane with a small thump. "I think not. It's a

pity for us to have run up against each other this way, you know—I like you."

"And I you, John Norman. Would that we were better met."

"Aye. When not in the company of such fascinating ladies."

He dropped off to sleep again soon after. Roland never spoke with him again . . . although he certainly heard from him. Yes. Roland was lying above his bed, shamming sleep, as John Norman screamed his last.

Sister Michela came with his evening soup just as Roland was getting past the shivery muscles and galloping heartbeat that resulted from his second nibble of brown reed. Michela looked at his flushed face with some concern, but had to accept his assurances that he did not feel feverish; she couldn't bring herself to touch him and judge the heat of his skin for herself—the medallion held her away.

With the soup was a popkin. The bread was leathery and the meat inside it tough, but Roland demolished it greedily, just the same. Michela watched with a complacent smile, hands folded in front of her, nodding from time to time. When he had finished the soup, she took the bowl back from him carefully, making sure their fingers did not touch.

"Ye're healing," she said. "Soon you'll be on yer way, and we'll have just yer memory to keep, Jim."

"Is that true?" he asked quietly.

She only looked at him, touched her tongue against her upper lip, giggled, and departed. Roland closed his eyes and lay back against his pillow, feeling lethargy steal over him again. Her speculative eyes . . . her peeping tongue. He had seen women look at roast chickens and joints of mutton that same way, calculating when they might be done.

His body badly wanted to sleep, but Roland held on to wakefulness for what he judged was an hour, then worked one of the reeds out from under the pillow. With a fresh infusion of their "can't-move medicine" in his system, this took an enormous effort, and he wasn't sure he could have done it at all, had he not separated this one reed from the ribbon holding the others. Tomorrow night, Jenna's note had said. If that meant escape, the idea seemed preposterous. The way he felt now, he might be lying in this bed until the end of the age.

He nibbled. Energy washed into his system, clenching his muscles and racing his heart, but the burst of vitality was gone almost as soon as it came, buried beneath the Sisters' stronger drug. He could only hope . . . and sleep.

When he woke it was full dark, and he found he could move his arms and legs in their network of slings almost naturally. He slipped one of the reeds out from beneath his pillow and nibbled cautiously. She had left half a dozen, and the first two were now almost entirely consumed.

The gunslinger put the stem back under the pillow, then began to shiver like a wet dog in a downpour. *I took too much,* he thought. *I'll be lucky not to convulse—*

His heart, racing like a runaway engine. And then, to make matters worse, he saw candlelight at the far end of the aisle. A moment later he heard the rustle of their gowns and the whisk of their slippers.

Gods, why now? They'll see me shaking, they'll know—

Calling on every bit of his willpower and control, Roland closed his eyes and concentrated on stilling his jerking limbs. If only he had been in bed instead of in these cursed slings, which seemed to tremble as if with their own ague at every movement!

The Little Sisters drew closer. The light of their candles bloomed red within his closed eyelids. Tonight they were not giggling, nor whispering among themselves. It was not until they were almost on top of him that Roland became aware of the stranger in their midst—a creature that breathed through its nose in great, slobbery gasps of mixed air and snot.

The gunslinger lay with his eyes closed, the gross twitches and jumps of his arms and legs under control, but with his muscles still knotted and crampy, thrumming beneath the skin. Anyone who looked at him closely would see at once that something was wrong with him. His heart was larruping away like a horse under the whip, surely they must see—

But it wasn't him they were looking at—not yet, at least.

"Have it off him," Mary said. She spoke in a bastardized version of the low speech Roland could barely understand. "Then t'other 'un. Go on, Ralph."

"U'se has whik-sky?" the slobberer asked, his dialect even heavier than Mary's. "U'se has 'backky?"

"Yes, yes, plenty whiskey and plenty smoke, but not until you have these wretched things off!" Impatient. Perhaps afraid, as well.

Roland cautiously rolled his head to the left and cracked his eyelids open.

Five of the six Little Sisters of Eluria were clustered around the far side of the sleeping John Norman's bed, their candles raised to cast their light upon him. It also cast light upon their own faces, faces which would have given the strongest man nightmares. Now, in the ditch of the night, their glamours were set aside, and they were but ancient corpses in voluminous habits.

Sister Mary had one of Roland's guns in her hand. Looking at her holding it, Roland felt a bright flash of hate for her, and promised himself she would pay for her temerity.

The thing standing at the foot of the bed, strange as it was, looked almost normal in comparison with the Sisters. It was one of the green folk. Roland recognized Ralph at once. He would be a long time forgetting that bowler hat.

Now Ralph walked slowly around to the side of Norman's bed closest to Roland, momentarily blocking the gunslinger's view of the Sisters. The mutie went all the way to Norman's head, however, clearing the hags to Roland's slitted view once more.

Norman's medallion lay exposed—the boy had perhaps wakened enough to take it out of his bed-dress, hoping it would protect him better so. Ralph picked it up in his melted-tallow hand. The Sisters watched eagerly in the glow of their candles as the green man stretched it to the end of its chain . . . and then put it down again. Their faces drooped in disappointment.

"Don't care for such as that," Ralph said in his clotted voice. "Want whik-sky! Want 'backky!"

"You shall have it," Sister Mary said. "Enough for you and all your verminous clan. But first, you must have that horrid thing off him! Off both of them! Do you understand? And you shan't tease us."

"Or what?" Ralph asked. He laughed. It was a choked and gargly sound, the laughter of a man dying from some evil sickness of the throat and lungs, but Roland still liked it better than the giggles of the Sisters. "Or what, Sisser Mary, you'll drink my bluid? My bluid'd drop'ee dead where'ee stand, and glowing in the dark!"

Mary raised the gunslinger's revolver and pointed it at Ralph. "Take that wretched thing, or you die where *you* stand."

"And die after I've done what you want, likely."

Sister Mary said nothing to that. The others peered at him with their black eyes.

Ralph lowered his head, appearing to think. Roland suspected his friend Bowler Hat *could* think, too. Sister Mary and her cohorts might not believe that, but Ralph *had* to be trig to have survived as long as he had. But of course when he came here, he hadn't considered Roland's guns.

"Smasher was wrong to give them shooters to you," he said at last. "Give 'em and not tell me. Did u'se give him whik-sky? Give him 'backky?'"

"That's none o' yours," Sister Mary replied. "You have that gold-piece off the boy's neck right now, or I'll put one of yonder man's bullets in what's left of yer brain."

"All right," Ralph said. "Just as you wish, sai."

Once more he reached down and took the gold medallion in his melted fist. That he did slow; what happened after, happened fast. He snatched it away, breaking the chain and flinging the gold heedlessly into the dark. With his other hand he reached down, sank his long and ragged nails into John Norman's neck, and tore it open.

Blood flew from the hapless boy's throat in a jetting, heart-driven gush more black than red in the candlelight, and he made a single bubbly cry. The women screamed—but not in horror. They screamed as women do in a frenzy of excitement. The green man was forgotten; Roland was forgotten; all was forgotten save the life's blood pouring out of John Norman's throat.

They dropped their candles. Mary dropped Roland's revolver in the same hapless, careless fashion. The last the gunslinger saw as Ralph darted away into the shadows (whiskey and tobacco another time, wily Ralph must have thought; tonight he had best concentrate on saving his own life) was the Sisters bending forward to catch as much of the flow as they could before it dried up.

Roland lay in the dark, muscles shivering, heart pounding, listening to the harpies as they fed on the boy lying in the bed next to his own. It seemed to go on forever, but at last they had done with him. The Sisters relit their candles and left, murmuring.

When the drug in the soup once more got the better of the drug in the reeds, Roland was grateful . . . yet for the first time since he'd come here, his sleep was haunted.

In his dream he stood looking down at the bloated body in the town trough, thinking of a line in the book marked REGISTRY OF MISDEEDS AND REDRESS. *Green folk sent hence*, it had read, and perhaps the green folk *had* been sent hence, but then a worse tribe had come. The

Little Sisters of Eluria, they called themselves. And a year hence, they might be the Little Sisters of Tejuas, or of Kambero, or some other far western village. They came with their bells and their bugs . . . from where? Who knew? Did it matter?

A shadow fell beside his on the scummy water of the trough. Roland tried to turn and face it. He couldn't; he was frozen in place. Then a green hand grasped his shoulder and whirled him about. It was Ralph. His bowler hat was cocked back on his head; John Norman's medallion, now red with blood, hung around his neck.

"Booh!" cried Ralph, his lips stretching in a toothless grin. He raised a big revolver with worn sandalwood grips. He thumbed the hammer back—

—and Roland jerked awake, shivering all over, dressed in skin both wet and icy cold. He looked at the bed on his left. It was empty, the sheet pulled up and tucked about neatly, the pillow resting above it in its snowy sleeve. Of John Norman there was no sign. It might have been empty for years, that bed.

Roland was alone now. Gods help him, he was the last patient of the Little Sisters of Eluria, those sweet and patient hospitalers. The last human being still alive in this terrible place, the last with warm blood flowing in his veins.

Roland, lying suspended, gripped the gold medallion in his fist and looked across the aisle at the long row of empty beds. After a little while, he brought one of the reeds out from beneath his pillow and nibbled at it.

When Mary came fifteen minutes later, the gunslinger took the bowl she brought with a show of weakness he didn't really feel. Porridge instead of soup this time . . . but he had no doubt the basic ingredient was still the same.

"How well ye look this morning, sai," Big Sister said. She looked well herself—there were no shimmers to give away the ancient *wampir* hiding inside her. She had supped well, and her meal had firmed her up. Roland's stomach rolled over at the thought. "Ye'll be on yer pins in no time, I'll warrant."

"That's shit," Roland said, speaking in an ill-natured growl. "Put me on my pins and you'd be picking me up off the floor directly after. I've started to wonder if you're not putting something in the food."

She laughed merrily at that. "La, you lads! Always eager to blame yer weakness on a scheming woman! How scared of us ye are—aye, way down in yer little boys' hearts, how scared ye are!"

"Where's my brother? I dreamed there was a commotion about him in the night, and now I see his bed's empty."

Her smile narrowed. Her eyes glittered. "He came over fevery and pitched a fit. We've taken him to Thoughtful House, which has been home to contagion more than once in its time."

To the grave is where you've taken him, Roland thought. *Mayhap that is a Thoughtful House, but little would you know it, sai, one way or another.*

"I know ye're no brother to that boy," Mary said, watching him eat. Already Roland could feel the stuff hidden in the porridge draining his strength once more. "*Sigul* or no *sigul*, I know ye're no brother to him. Why do you lie? 'Tis a sin against God."

"What gives you such an idea, sai?" Roland asked, curious to see if she would mention the guns.

"Big Sister knows what she knows. Why not 'fess up, Jimmy? Confession's good for the soul, they say."

"Send me Jenna to pass the time, and perhaps I'd tell you much," Roland said.

The narrow bone of smile on Sister Mary's face disappeared like chalk-writing in a rainstorm. "Why would ye talk to such as her?"

"She's passing fair," Roland said. "Unlike some."

Her lips pulled back from her overlarge teeth. "Ye'll see her no more, cully. Ye've stirred her up, so you have, and I won't have that."

She turned to go. Still trying to appear weak and hoping he would not overdo it (acting was never his forte), Roland held out the empty porridge bowl. "Do you not want to take this?"

"Put it on your head and wear it as a nightcap, for all of me. Or stick it in your ass. You'll talk before I'm done with ye, cully—talk till I bid you shut up and then beg to talk some more!"

On this note she swept regally away, hands lifting the front of her skirt off the floor. Roland had heard that such as she couldn't go about in daylight, and that part of the old tales was surely a lie. Yet another part was almost true, it seemed: a fuzzy, amorphous shape kept pace with her, running along the row of empty beds to her right, but she cast no real shadow at all.

VI. Jenna. Sister Coquina. Tamra, Michela, Louise. The Cross-Dog. What Happened in the Sage.

That was one of the longest days of Roland's life. He dozed, but never deeply; the reeds were doing their work, and he had begun to believe that he might, with Jenna's help, actually get out of here. And there was the matter of his guns, as well—perhaps she might be able to help there, too.

He passed the slow hours thinking of old times—of Gilead and his friends, of the riddling he had almost won at one Wide Earth Fair. In the end another had taken the goose, but he'd had his chance, aye. He thought of his mother and father; he thought of Abel Vannay, who had limped his way through a life of gentle goodness, and Eldred Jonas, who had limped his way through a life of evil . . . until Roland had blown him loose of his saddle, one fine desert day.

He thought, as always, of Susan.

If you love me, then love me, she'd said . . . and so he had.

So he had.

In this way the time passed. At rough hourly intervals, he took one of the reeds from beneath his pillow and nibbled it. Now his muscles didn't tremble so badly as the stuff passed into his system, nor his heart pound so fiercely. The medicine in the reeds no longer had to battle the Sisters' medicine so fiercely, Roland thought; the reeds were winning.

The diffused brightness of the sun moved across the white silk ceiling of the ward, and at last the dimness which always seemed to hover at bed-level began to rise. The long room's western wall bloomed with the rose-melting-to-orange shades of sunset.

It was Sister Tamra who brought him his dinner that night—soup and another popkin. She also laid a desert lily beside his hand. She smiled as she did it. Her cheeks were bright with color. All of them were bright with color today, like leeches that had gorged until they were full almost to bursting.

"From your admirer, Jimmy," she said. "She's so sweet on ye! The lily means 'Do not forget my promise.' What has she promised ye, Jimmy, brother of Johnny?"

"That she'd see me again, and we'd talk."

Tamra laughed so hard that the bells lining her forehead jingled.

She clasped her hands together in a perfect ecstasy of glee. "Sweet as honey! Oh, yes!" She bent her smiling gaze on Roland. "It's sad such a promise can never be kept. Ye'll never see her again, pretty man." She took the bowl. "Big Sister has decided." She stood up, still smiling. "Why not take that ugly gold *sigul* off?"

"I think not."

"Yer brother took his off—look!" She pointed, and Roland spied the gold medallion lying far down the aisle, where it had landed when Ralph threw it.

Sister Tamra looked at him, still smiling.

"He decided it was part of what was making him sick, and cast it away. Ye'd do the same, were ye wise."

Roland repeated, "I think not."

"So," she said dismissively, and left him alone with the empty beds glimmering in the thickening shadows.

Roland hung on, in spite of growing sleepiness, until the hot colors bleeding across the infirmary's western wall had cooled to ashes. Then he nibbled one of the reeds and felt strength—real strength, not a jittery, heart-thudding substitute—bloom in his body. He looked toward where the castaway medallion gleamed in the last light and made a silent promise to John Norman: he would take it with the other one to Norman's kin, if *ka* chanced that he should encounter them in his travels.

Feeling completely easy in his mind for the first time that day, the gunslinger dozed. When he awoke it was full dark. The doctor-bugs were singing with extraordinary shrillness. He had taken one of the reeds out from under the pillow and had begun to nibble on it when a cold voice said, "So—Big Sister was right. Ye've been keeping secrets."

Roland's heart seemed to stop dead in his chest. He looked around and saw Sister Coquina getting to her feet. She had crept in while he was dozing and hidden under the bed on his right side to watch him.

"Where did ye get that?" she asked. "Was it—"

"He got it from me."

Coquina whirled about. Jenna was walking down the aisle toward them. Her habit was gone. She still wore her wimple with its forehead-fringe of bells, but its hem rested on the shoulders of a simple checkered shirt. Below this she wore jeans and scuffed desert boots. She had

something in her hands. It was too dark for Roland to be sure, but he thought—

"*You*," Sister Coquina whispered with infinite hate. "When I tell Big Sister—"

"You'll tell no one anything," Roland said.

If he had planned his escape from the slings that entangled him, he no doubt would have made a bad business of it, but, as always, the gunslinger did best when he thought least. His arms were free in a moment; so was his left leg. His right caught at the ankle, however, twisting, hanging him up with his shoulders on the bed and his leg in the air.

Coquina turned on him, hissing like a cat. Her lips pulled back from teeth that were needle-sharp. She rushed at him, her fingers splayed. The nails at the ends of them looked sharp and ragged.

Roland clasped the medallion and shoved it out toward her. She recoiled from it, still hissing, and whirled back to Sister Jenna in a flare of white skirt. "I'll do for ye, ye interfering trull!" she cried in a low, harsh voice.

Roland struggled to free his leg and couldn't. It was firmly caught, the shitting sling actually wrapped around the ankle somehow, like a noose.

Jenna raised her hands, and he saw he had been right: it was his revolvers she had brought, holstered and hanging from the two old gunbelts he had worn out of Gilead after the last burning.

"Shoot her, Jenna! Shoot her!"

Instead, still holding the holstered guns up, Jenna shook her head as she had on the day when Roland had persuaded her to push back her wimple so he could see her hair. The bells rang with a sharpness that seemed to go into the gunslinger's head like a spike.

The Dark Bells. The sigul *of their* ka-tet. *What—*

The sound of the doctor-bugs rose to a shrill, reedy scream that was eerily like the sound of the bells Jenna wore. Nothing sweet about them now. Sister Coquina's hands faltered on their way to Jenna's throat; Jenna herself had not so much as flinched or blinked her eyes.

"No," Coquina whispered. "You *can't!*"

"I *have*," Jenna said, and Roland saw the bugs. Descending from the legs of the bearded man, he'd observed a battalion. What he saw coming from the shadows now was an army to end all armies; had they been men instead of insects, there might have been more than all the men who had ever carried arms in the long and bloody history of Mid-World.

Yet the sight of them advancing down the boards of the aisle was not what Roland would always remember, nor what would haunt his dreams for a year or more; it was the way they coated the *beds*. These were turning black two by two on both sides of the aisle, like pairs of dim rectangular lights going out.

Coquina shrieked and began to shake her own head, to ring her own bells. The sound they made was thin and pointless compared with the sharp ringing of the Dark Bells.

Still the bugs marched on, darkening the floor, blacking out the beds.

Jenna darted past the shrieking Sister Coquina, dropped Roland's guns beside him, then yanked the twisted sling straight with one hard pull. Roland slid his leg free.

"Come," she said. "I've started them, but staying them could be a different thing."

Now Sister Coquina's shrieks were not of horror but of pain. The bugs had found her.

"Don't look," Jenna said, helping Roland to his feet. He thought that never in his life had he been so glad to be upon them. "Come. We must be quick—she'll rouse the others. I've put your boots and clothes aside up the path that leads away from here—I carried as much as I could. How are ye? Are ye strong?"

"Thanks to you." How long he would stay strong Roland didn't know . . . and right now it wasn't a question that mattered. He saw Jenna snatch up two of the reeds—in his struggle to escape the slings, they had scattered all over the head of the bed—and then they were hurrying up the aisle, away from the bugs and from Sister Coquina, whose cries were now failing.

Roland buckled on his guns and tied them down without breaking stride.

They passed only three beds on each side before reaching the flap of the tent . . . and it *was* a tent, he saw, not a vast pavilion. The silk walls and ceiling were fraying canvas, thin enough to let in the light of a three-quarters Kissing Moon. And the beds weren't beds at all, but only a double row of shabby cots.

He turned and saw a black, writhing hump on the floor where Sister

Coquina had been. At the sight of her, Roland was struck by an unpleasant thought.

"I forgot John Norman's medallion!" A keen sense of regret—almost of mourning—went through him like wind.

Jenna reached into the pocket of her jeans and brought it out. It glimmered in the moonlight.

"I picked it up off the floor."

He didn't know which made him gladder—the sight of the medallion or the sight of it in her hand. It meant she wasn't like the others.

Then, as if to dispel that notion before it got too firm a hold on him, she said, "Take it, Roland—I can hold it no more." And, as he took it, he saw unmistakable marks of charring on her fingers.

He took her hand and kissed each burn.

"Thankee-sai," she said, and he saw she was crying. "Thankee, dear. To be kissed so is lovely, worth every pain. Now . . ."

Roland saw her eyes shift, and followed them. Here were bobbing lights descending a rocky path. Beyond them he saw the building where the Little Sisters had been living—not a convent but a ruined *hacienda* that looked a thousand years old. There were three candles; as they drew closer, Roland saw that there were only three sisters. Mary wasn't among them.

He drew his guns.

"Oooo, it's a gunslinger-man he is!" Louise.

"A *scary* man!" Michela.

"And he's found his ladylove as well as his shooters!" Tamra.

"His slut-whore!" Louise.

Laughing angrily. Not afraid . . . at least, not of *his* weapons.

"Put them away," Jenna told him, and when she looked, saw that he already had.

The others, meanwhile, had drawn closer.

"Ooo, see, she cries!" Tamra.

"Doffed her habit, she has!" Michela. "Perhaps it's her broken vows she cries for."

"Why such tears, pretty?" Louise.

"Because he kissed my fingers where they were burned," Jenna said. "I've never been kissed before. It made me cry."

"Ooooo!"

"*Luv*-ly!"

"Next he'll stick his thing in her! Even *luv*-lier!"

Jenna bore their japes with no sign of anger. When they were done, she said, "I'm going with him. Stand aside."

They gaped at her, counterfeit laughter disappearing in shock.

"No!" Louise whispered. "Are ye mad? Ye know what'll happen!"

"No, and neither do you," Jenna said. "Besides, I care not." She half-turned and held her hand out to the mouth of the ancient hospital tent. It was a faded olive-drab in the moonlight, with an old red cross drawn on its roof. Roland wondered how many towns the Sisters had been to with this tent, which was so small and plain on the outside, so huge and gloriously dim on the inside. How many towns and over how many years.

Now, cramming the mouth of it in a black, shiny tongue, were the doctor-bugs. They had stopped their singing. Their silence was somehow terrible.

"Stand aside or I'll have them on ye," Jenna said.

"Ye never would!" Sister Michela cried in a low, horrified voice.

"Aye. I've already set them on Sister Coquina. She's a part of their medicine, now."

Their gasp was like cold wind passing through dead trees. Nor was all of that dismay directed toward their own precious hides. What Jenna had done was clearly far outside their reckoning.

"Then you're damned," Sister Tamra said.

"Such ones to speak of damnation! Stand aside."

They did. Roland walked past them and they shrank away from him . . . but they shrank from her more.

"Damned?" he asked after they had skirted the *hacienda* and reached the path beyond it. The Kissing Moon glimmered above a tumbled scree of rocks. In its light Roland could see a small black opening low on the scarp. He guessed it was the cave the Sisters called Thoughtful House. "What did they mean, damned?"

"Never mind. All we have to worry about now is Sister Mary. I like it not that we haven't seen her."

She tried to walk faster, but he grasped her arm and turned her about. He could still hear the singing of the bugs, but faintly; they were leaving the place of the Sisters behind. Eluria, too, if the compass in his head was still working; he thought the town was in the other direction. The husk of the town, he amended.

"Tell me what they meant."

"Perhaps nothing. Ask me not, Roland—what good is it? 'Tis done, the bridge burned. I can't go back. Nor would if I could." She looked down, biting her lip, and when she looked up again, Roland saw fresh tears falling on her cheeks. "I have supped with them. There were times when I couldn't help it, no more than you could help drinking their wretched soup, no matter if you knew what was in it."

Roland remembered John Norman saying *A man has to eat . . . a woman, too.* He nodded.

"I'd go no further down that road. If there's to be damnation, let it be of my choosing, not theirs. My mother meant well by bringing me back to them, but she was wrong." She looked at him shyly and fearfully . . . but met his eyes. "I'd go beside ye on yer road, Roland of Gilead. For as long as I may, or as long as ye'd have me."

"You're welcome to your share of my way," he said. "And I am—"

Blessed by your company, he would have finished, but before he could, a voice spoke from the tangle of moonshadow ahead of them, where the path at last climbed out of the rocky, sterile valley in which the Little Sisters had practiced their glamours.

"It's a sad duty to stop such a pretty elopement, but stop it I must."

Sister Mary came from the shadows. Her fine white habit with its bright red rose had reverted to what it really was: the shroud of a corpse. Caught, hooded in its grimy folds, was a wrinkled, sagging face from which two black eyes stared. They looked like rotted dates. Below them, exposed by the thing's smile, four great incisors gleamed.

Upon the stretched skin of Sister Mary's forehead, bells tinkled . . . but not the Dark Bells, Roland thought. There was that.

"Stand clear," Jenna said. "Or I'll bring the *can tam* on ye."

"No," Sister Mary said, stepping closer, "ye won't. They'll not stray so far from the others. Shake your head and ring those damned bells until the clappers fall out, and still they'll never come."

Jenna did as bid, shaking her head furiously from side to side. The Dark Bells rang piercingly, but without that extra, almost psychic tone-quality that had gone through Roland's head like a spike. And the doctor-bugs—what Big Sister had called the *can tam*—did not come.

Smiling ever more broadly (Roland had an idea Mary herself hadn't been completely sure they wouldn't come until the experiment was made), the corpse-woman closed in on them, seeming to float above the ground. Her eyes flicked toward him. "And put that away," she said.

Roland looked down and saw that one of his guns was in his hand. He had no memory of drawing it.

"Unless 'tis been blessed or dipped in some sect's holy wet—blood, water, semen—it can't harm such as I, gunslinger. For I am more shade than substance . . . yet still the equal to such as yerself, for all that."

She thought he would try shooting her, anyway; he saw it in her eyes. *Those shooters are all ye have*, her eyes said. *Without 'em, you might as well be back in the tent we dreamed around ye, caught up in our slings and awaiting our pleasure.*

Instead of shooting, he dropped the revolver back into its holster and launched himself at her with his hands out. Sister Mary uttered a scream that was mostly surprise, but it was not a long one; Roland's fingers clamped down on her throat and choked the sound off before it was fairly started.

The touch of her flesh was obscene—it seemed not just alive but *various* beneath his hands, as if it was trying to crawl away from him. He could feel it running like liquid, *flowing*, and the sensation was horrible beyond description. Yet he clamped down harder, determined to choke the life out of her.

Then there came a blue flash (not in the air, he would think later; that flash happened inside his head, a single stroke of lightning as she touched off some brief but powerful brainstorm), and his hands flew away from her neck. For one moment his dazzled eyes saw great wet gouges in her gray flesh—gouges in the shapes of his hands. Then he was flung backward, hitting the scree on his back and sliding, hitting his head on a jutting rock hard enough to provoke a second, lesser, flash of light.

"Nay, my pretty man," she said, grimacing at him, laughing with those terrible dull eyes of hers. "Ye don't choke such as I, and I'll take ye slow for'ee impertinence—cut ye shallow in a hundred places to refresh my thirst. First, though, I'll have this vowless girl . . . and I'll have those damned bells off her, in the bargain."

"Come and see if you can!" Jenna cried in a trembling voice, and shook her head from side to side. The Dark Bells rang mockingly, provokingly.

Mary's grimace of a smile fell away. "Oh, I can," she breathed. Her mouth yawned. In the moonlight, her fangs gleamed in her gums like bone needles poked through a red pillow. "I can and I—"

There was a growl from above them. It rose, then splintered into a volley of snarling barks. Mary turned to her left, and in the moment before the snarling thing left the rock on which it was standing, Roland could clearly read the startled bewilderment on Big Sister's face.

It launched itself at her, only a dark shape against the stars, legs outstretched so it looked like some sort of weird bat, but even before it crashed into the woman, striking her in the chest above her half-raised arms and fastening its own teeth on her throat, Roland knew exactly what it was.

As the shape bore her over onto her back, Sister Mary uttered a gibbering shriek that went through Roland's head like the Dark Bells themselves. He scrambled to his feet, gasping. The shadowy thing tore at her, forepaws on either side of her head, rear paws planted on the grave-shroud above her chest, where the rose had been.

Roland grabbed Jenna, who was looking down at the fallen Sister with a kind of frozen fascination.

"Come on!" he shouted. "Before it decides it wants a bite of you, too!"

The dog took no notice of them as Roland pulled Jenna past. It had torn Sister Mary's head mostly off.

Her flesh seemed to be changing, somehow—decomposing, very likely—but whatever was happening, Roland did not want to see it. He didn't want Jenna to see it, either.

They half-walked, half-ran to the top of the ridge, and when they got there paused for breath in the moonlight, heads down, hands linked, both of them gasping harshly.

The growling and snarling below them had faded, but was still faintly audible when Sister Jenna raised her head and asked him, "What was it? You know—I saw it in your face. And how could it attack her? We all have power over animals, but she has—had—the most."

"Not over that one." Roland found himself recalling the unfortunate boy in the next bed. Norman hadn't known why the medallions kept the Sisters at arms' length—whether it was the gold or the God. Now Roland knew the answer. "It was a dog. Just a town-dog. I saw it in the square, before the green folk knocked me out and took me to the Sisters. I suppose the other animals that could run away *did* run away, but not that one. It had nothing to fear from the Little Sisters of Eluria, and somehow it knew it didn't. It bears the sign of the Jesus-man on its chest. Black fur on white. Just an accident of its birth, I imagine. In any case, it's done for her now. I knew it was lurking around. I heard it barking two or three times."

"Why?" Jenna whispered. "Why would it come? Why would it stay? And why would it take on her as it did?"

Roland of Gilead responded as he ever had and ever would when such useless, mystifying questions were raised: "*Ka*. Come on. Let's get as far as we can from this place before we hide up for the day."

As far as they could turned out to be eight miles at most . . . and probably, Roland thought as the two of them sank down in a patch of sweet-smelling sage beneath an overhang of rock, a good deal less. Five, perhaps. It was him slowing them down; or rather, it was the residue of the poison in the soup. When it was clear to him that he could not go farther without help, he asked her for one of the reeds. She refused, saying that the stuff in it might combine with the unaccustomed exercise to burst his heart.

"Besides," she said as they lay back against the embankment of the little nook they had found, "they'll not follow. Those that are left— Michela, Louise, Tamra—will be packing up to move on. They know to leave when the time comes; that's why the Sisters have survived as long as they have. As *we* have. We're strong in some ways, but weak in many more. Sister Mary forgot that. It was her arrogance that did for her as much as the cross-dog, I think."

She had cached not just his boots and clothes beyond the top of the ridge, but the smaller of his two purses, as well. When she tried to apologize for not bringing his bedroll and the larger purse (she'd tried, she said, but they were simply too heavy), Roland hushed her with a finger to her lips. He thought it a miracle to have as much as he did. And besides (this he did not say, but perhaps she knew it, anyway), the guns were the only things that really mattered. The guns of his father, and his father before him, all the way back to the days of Arthur Eld, when dreams and dragons had still walked the earth.

"Will you be all right?" he asked her as they settled down. The moon had set, but dawn was still at least three hours away. They were surrounded by the sweet smell of the sage. A purple smell, he thought it then . . . and ever after. Already he could feel it forming a kind of magic carpet under him, which would soon float him away to sleep. He thought he had never been so tired.

"Roland, I know not." But even then, he thought she had known. Her mother had brought her back once; no mother would bring her back again. And she had eaten with the others, had taken the communion of the Sisters. *Ka* was a wheel; it was also a net from which none ever escaped.

But then he was too tired to think much of such things . . . and what good would thinking have done, in any case? As she had said, the bridge was burned. Even if they were to return to the valley, Roland guessed they would find nothing but the cave the Sisters had called Thoughtful House. The surviving Sisters would have packed their tent of bad dreams and moved on, just a sound of bells and singing insects moving down the late night breeze.

He looked at her, raised a hand (it felt heavy), and touched the curl which once more lay across her forehead.

Jenna laughed, embarrassed. "That one always escapes. It's wayward. Like its mistress."

She raised her hand to poke it back in, but Roland took her fingers before she could. "It's beautiful," he said. "Black as night and as beautiful as forever."

He sat up—it took an effort; weariness dragged at his body like soft hands. He kissed the curl. She closed her eyes and sighed. He felt her trembling beneath his lips. The skin of her brow was very cool; the dark curve of the wayward curl like silk.

"Push back your wimple, as you did before," he said.

She did it without speaking. For a moment he only looked at her. Jenna looked back gravely, her eyes never leaving his. He ran his hands through her hair, feeling its smooth weight (like rain, he thought, rain with weight), then took her shoulders and kissed each of her cheeks. He drew back for a moment.

"Would ye kiss me as a man does a woman, Roland? On my mouth?"

"Aye."

And, as he had thought of doing as he lay caught in the silken infirmary tent, he kissed her lips. She kissed back with the clumsy sweetness of one who has never kissed before, except perhaps in dreams. Roland thought to make love to her then—it had been long and long, and she was beautiful—but he fell asleep instead, still kissing her.

He dreamed of the cross-dog, barking its way across a great open landscape. He followed, wanting to see the source of its agitation, and soon he did. At the far edge of that plain stood the Dark Tower, its smoky stone outlined by the dull orange ball of a setting sun, its fearful windows rising in a spiral. The dog stopped at the sight of it and began to howl.

Bells—peculiarly shrill and as terrible as doom—began to ring. Dark bells, he knew, but their tone was as bright as silver. At their sound, the dark windows of the Tower glowed with a deadly red light—the red of poisoned roses. A scream of unbearable pain rose in the night.

The dream blew away in an instant, but the scream remained, now unraveling to a moan. That part was real—as real as the Tower, brooding in its place at the very end of End-World. Roland came back to the brightness of dawn and the soft purple smell of desert sage. He had drawn both his guns, and was on his feet before he had fully realized he was awake.

Jenna was gone. Her boots lay empty beside his purse. A little distance from them, her jeans lay as flat as discarded snakeskins. Above them was her shirt. It was, Roland observed with wonder, still tucked into the pants. Beyond them was her empty wimple, with its fringe of bells lying on the powdery ground. He thought for a moment that they were ringing, mistaking the sound he heard at first.

Not bells but bugs. The doctor-bugs. They sang in the sage, sounding a bit like crickets, but far sweeter.

"Jenna?"

No answer . . . unless the bugs answered. For their singing suddenly stopped.

"Jenna?"

Nothing. Only the wind and the smell of the sage.

Without thinking about what he was doing (like playacting, reasoned thought was not his strong suit), he bent, picked up the wimple, and shook it. The Dark Bells rang.

For a moment there was nothing. Then a thousand small dark creatures came scurrying out of the sage, gathering on the broken earth.

Roland thought of the battalion marching down the side of the freighter's bed and took a step back. Then he held his position. As, he saw, the bugs were holding theirs.

He believed he understood. Some of this understanding came from his memory of how Sister Mary's flesh had felt under his hands . . . how it had felt *various*, not one thing but many. Part of it was what she had said: *I have supped with them.* Such as them might never die . . . but they might *change*.

The insects trembled, a dark cloud of them blotting out the white, powdery earth.

Roland shook the bells again.

A shiver ran through them in a subtle wave, and then they began to form a shape. They hesitated as if unsure of how to go on, re-grouped, began again. What they eventually made on the whiteness of the sand there between the blowing fluffs of lilac-colored sage was one of the Great Letters: the letter C.

Except it wasn't really a letter, the gunslinger saw; it was a curl.

They began to sing, and to Roland it sounded as if they were singing his name.

The bells fell from his unnerved hand, and when they struck the ground and chimed there, the mass of bugs broke apart, running in every direction. He thought of calling them back—ringing the bells again might do that—but to what purpose? To what end?

Ask me not, Roland. 'Tis done, the bridge burned.

Yet she had come to him one last time, imposing her will over a thousand various parts that should have lost the ability to think when the whole lost its cohesion . . . and yet she *had* thought, somehow— enough to make that shape. How much effort might that have taken?

They fanned wider and wider, some disappearing into the sage, some trundling up the sides of a rock overhang, pouring into the cracks where they would, mayhap, wait out the heat of the day.

They were gone. *She* was gone.

Roland sat down on the ground and put his hands over his face. He thought he might weep, but in time the urge passed; when he raised his head again, his eyes were as dry as the desert he would eventually come to, still following the trail of Walter, the man in black.

If there's to be damnation, she had said, *let it be of my choosing, not theirs.*

He knew a little about damnation himself . . . and he had an idea that the lessons, far from being done, were just beginning.

She had brought him the purse with his tobacco in it. He rolled a cigarette and smoked it hunkered over his knees. He smoked it down to a glowing roach, looking at her empty clothes the while, remembering the steady gaze of her dark eyes. Remembering the scorch-marks on her fingers from the chain of the medallion. Yet she had picked it up, because she had known he would want it; had dared that pain, and Roland now wore both around his neck.

When the sun was fully up, the gunslinger moved on west. He would find another horse eventually, or a mule, but for now he was content to walk. All that day he was haunted by a ringing, singing sound in his ears, a sound like bells. Several times he stopped and looked around, sure he would see a dark following shape flowing over the ground, chasing after as the shadows of our best and worst memories chase after, but no shape was ever there. He was alone in the low hill country west of Eluria.

Quite alone.

Discworld

———

TERRY PRATCHETT

Granny Weatherwax

Paul Kidby '98

THE COLOUR OF MAGIC (1983)
THE LIGHT FANTASTIC (1988)
EQUAL RITES (1988)
MORT (1989)
SOURCERY (1989)
WYRD SISTERS (1990)
PYRAMIDS (1990)
GUARDS! GUARDS! (1991)
ERIC (1991)
MOVING PICTURES (1992)
REAPER MAN (1992)
WITCHES ABROAD (1994)
SMALL GODS (1994)
LORDS AND LADIES (1994)
INTERESTING TIMES (1995)
SOUL MUSIC (1995)
MASKERADE (1995)
MEN AT ARMS (1996)
FEET OF CLAY (1996)
HOGFATHER (1996)
JINGO (1997)

Discworld is a flat world supported by four elephants standing on top of a huge turtle swimming endlessly through space. Using this classic mythological concept as his starting point, Pratchett cheerfully lampoons a vast range of targets—Shakespeare, Creationism theory, heroic fantasy, etc., etc.—and ventures into such far-flung realms as ancient Egypt, the Aztec Empire, and Renaissance Italy for further raw material. When he is not satirizing historical periods or cultures, Pratchett allows much of the action to center around Ankh-Morpork, a melting pot of a fantasy city that's a mix of Renaissance Florence, Victorian London, and present-day New York.

The series uses fantasy as a fairground mirror, reflecting back at us a distorted but recognizable image of twentieth-century concerns. (For example, equal-opportunity and affirmative-action laws take on new dimensions when you've got vampires, werewolves, and zombies among your citizens. . . .)

The books can be roughly divided into four groups:

In the Rincewind series (*The Colour of Magic, The Light Fantastic, Sourcery, Eric, Interesting Times*), the protagonist is an incompetent, cowardly (or very clear-thinking) magician who is constantly trying to escape some danger only to run into something ten times worse. However unfortunate his misadventures become, in the end he manages to triumph and to restore Discworld to a semblance of order, as order is understood there. The primary satiric target of these books is heroic fantasy, complete with all the genre staples—trolls, wizards, and similar fauna. *Sourcery*, for example, is a parody of the Lovecraftian nether-worlds; *Eric* is a spoof of the Faustian deal-with-the devil theme.

The Granny Weatherwax group (*Equal Rites, Wyrd Systers, Witches Abroad, Lords and Ladies, Maskerade*) introduces one of the most popular characters in the series, a witch of iron constitution, steel mor-als, and reinforced-concrete pride who takes charge in any situation; like a Western hero, she's technically a bad witch who does good. A rewriting of *The Phantom of the Opera* forms the basis for *Maskerade*, and *A Midsummer Night's Dream* is lampooned in *Lords and Ladies* with Shakespeare's more genteel fairies replaced by haughty, vicious elves from Celtic folklore.

The four books composing the Death series (*Mort, Reaper Man, Soul Music, Hogfather*) follow the trials of Death, a humorless entity who secretly harbors a soft spot for humanity, and whose inability to understand these same humans creates real pathos. In *Mort*, Death takes a vacation, leaving his even more softhearted apprentices to carry on while he's gone. *Reaper Man* follows Death when he becomes—temporarily—mortal, and learns what humanity *really* means.

The City Watch books (*Guards! Guards!, Men at Arms, Feet of Clay*) combine fantasy with elements of the police-procedural mystery novel, with appropriately lively results. *Guards! Guards!* finds the grubby but honest Ankh-Morpork Night Watch battling a dragon who wants to assassinate the city's Patrician and install a new puppet ruler. *Men at Arms* tracks a serial killer running amok with Discworld's only gun (designed by Discworld's equivalent of Leonardo da Vinci).

The stand-alone novel *Pyramids* injects some modern thinking into a version of Egypt of the Pharaohs. *Moving Pictures* uses the Discworld toolbox to examine the real magic of the movies. *Small Gods* provides a darkly humorous look at the rise of a religion whose one "truth" is that the Discworld is actually spherical instead of flat.

In "The Sea and Little Fishes" Pratchett offers a new adventure of Granny Weatherwax, a highly competitive spirit who believes that "coming in second" is another term for losing. . . .

The Sea and Little Fishes

TERRY PRATCHETT

Trouble began, and not for the first time, with an apple.

There was a bag of them on Granny Weatherwax's bleached and spotless table. Red and round, shiny and fruity, if they'd known the future they should have ticked like bombs.

"Keep the lot, old Hopcroft said I could have as many as I wanted," said Nanny Ogg. She gave her sister witch a sidelong glance. "Tasty, a bit wrinkled, but a damn good keeper."

"He *named* an *apple* after *you*?" said Granny. Each word was an acid drop on the air.

" 'Cos of my rosy cheeks," said Nanny Ogg. "An' I cured his leg for him after he felt off that ladder last year. An' I made him up some jollop for his bald head."

"It didn't work, though," said Granny. "That wig he wears, that's a terrible thing to see on a man still alive."

"But he was pleased I took an interest."

Granny Weatherwax didn't take her eyes off the bag. Fruit and vegetables grew famously in the mountains' hot summers and cold winters. Percy Hopcroft was the premier grower and definitely a keen man when it came to sexual antics among the horticulture with a camel-hair brush.

"He sells his apple trees all over the place," Nanny Ogg went on.

"Funny, eh, to think that pretty soon thousands of people will be having a bite of Nanny Ogg."

"Thousands more," said Granny, tartly. Nanny's wild youth was an open book, although only available in plain covers.

"Thank you, Esme." Nanny Ogg looked wistful for a moment, and then opened her mouth in mock concern. "Oh, you ain't *jealous*, are you, Esme? You ain't begrudging me my little moment in the sun?"

"Me? Jealous? Why should I be jealous? It's only an *apple*. It's not as if it's anything important."

"That's what I thought. It's just a little frippery to humor an old lady," said Nanny. "So how are things with you, then?"

"Fine. Fine."

"Got your winter wood in, have you?"

"Mostly."

"Good," said Nanny. "Good."

They sat in silence. On the windowpane a butterfly, awoken by the unseasonable warmth, beat a little tattoo in an effort to reach the September sun.

"Your potatoes . . . got them dug, then?" said Nanny.

"Yes."

"We got a good crop off ours this year."

"Good."

"Salted your beans, have you?"

"Yes."

"I expect you're looking forward to the Trials next week?"

"Yes."

"I expects you've been practicing?"

"No."

It seemed to Nanny that, despite the sunlight, the shadows were deepening in the corners of the room. The very air itself was growing dark. A witch's cottage gets sensitive to the moods of its occupant. But she plunged on. Fools rush in, but they are laggards compared to little old ladies with nothing left to fear.

"You coming over to dinner on Sunday?"

"What're you havin'?"

"Pork."

"With apple sauce?"

"Yes—"

"No," said Granny.

There was a creaking behind Nanny. The door had swung open. Someone who wasn't a witch would have rationalized this, would have said that of course it was only the wind. And Nanny Ogg was quite prepared to go along with this, but would have added: *Why* was it only the wind, and how come the wind had managed to lift the latch?

"Oh, well, can't sit here chatting all day," she said, standing up quickly. "Always busy at this time of year, ain't it?"

"Yes."

"So I'll be off, then."

"Goodbye."

The wind blew the door shut again as Nanny hurried off down the path.

It occurred to her that, just possibly, she might have gone a bit too far. But only a bit.

The trouble with being a witch—at least, the trouble with being a witch as far as some people were concerned—was that you got stuck out here in the country. But that was fine by Nanny. Everything she wanted was out here. Everything she'd *ever* wanted was here, although in her youth she'd run out of men a few times. Foreign parts were all right to visit but they weren't really serious. They had interestin' new drinks and the grub was fun, but foreign parts was where you went to do what might need to be done and then you came back here, a place that was real. Nanny Ogg was happy in small places.

Of course, she reflected as she crossed the lawn, she didn't have this view out of her window. Nanny lived down in the town, but Granny could look out across the forest and over the plains and all the way to the great round horizon of the Discworld.

A view like that, Nanny reasoned, could probably suck your mind right out of your head.

They'd told her the world was round and flat, which was common sense, and went through space on the back of four elephants standing on the shell of a turtle, which didn't have to make sense. It was all happening Out There somewhere, and it could continue to do so with Nanny's blessing and disinterest so long as she could live in a personal world about ten miles across, which she carried around with her.

But Esme Weatherwax needed more than this little kingdom could contain. She was the *other* kind of witch.

And Nanny saw it as her job to stop Granny Weatherwax getting bored. The business with the apples was petty enough, a spiteful little triumph when you got down to it, but Esme needed something to make every day worthwhile and if it had to be anger and jealousy then so be it. Granny would now scheme for some little victory, some tiny humiliation that only the two of them would ever know about, and that'd be that. Nanny was confident that she could deal with her friend in a bad mood, but not when she was bored. A witch who is bored might do *anything*.

People said things like "we had to make our own amusements in those days" as if this signaled some kind of moral worth, and perhaps it did, but the last thing you wanted a witch to do was get bored and start making her own amusements, because witches sometimes had famously erratic ideas about what was amusing. And Esme was undoubtedly the most powerful witch the mountains had seen for generations.

Still, the Trials were coming up, and they always set Esme Weatherwax all right for a few weeks. She rose to competition like a trout to a fly.

Nanny Ogg always looked forward to the Witch Trials. You got a good day out and of course there was a big bonfire. Whoever heard of a Witch Trial without a good bonfire afterward?

And afterward you could roast potatoes in the ashes.

The afternoon melted into the evening, and the shadows in corners and under stools and tables crept out and ran together.

Granny rocked gently in her chair as the darkness wrapped itself around her. She had a look of deep concentration.

The logs in the fireplace collapsed into the embers, which winked out one by one.

The night thickened.

The old clock ticked on the mantelpiece and, for some length of time, there was no other sound.

There came a faint rustling. The paper bag on the table moved and then began to crinkle like a deflating balloon. Slowly, the still air filled with a heavy smell of decay.

After a while the first maggot crawled out.

*　　*　　*

Nanny Ogg was back home and just pouring a pint of beer when there was a knock. She put down the jug with a sigh, and went and opened the door.

"Oh, hello, ladies. What're you doing in these parts? And on such a chilly evening, too?"

Nanny backed into the room, ahead of three more witches. They wore the black cloaks and pointy hats traditionally associated with their craft, although this served to make each one look different. There is nothing like a uniform for allowing one to express one's individuality. A tweak here and a tuck there are little details that scream all the louder in the apparent, well, uniformity.

Gammer Beavis' hat, for example, had a very flat brim and a point you could clean your ear with. Nanny liked Gammer Beavis. She might be a bit too educated, so that sometimes it overflowed out of her mouth, but she did her own shoe repairs and took snuff and, in Nanny Ogg's small worldview, things like this meant that someone was All Right.

Old Mother Dismass's clothes had that disarray of someone who, because of a detached retina in her second sight, was living in a variety of times all at once. Mental confusion is bad enough in normal people, but much worse when the mind has an occult twist. You just had to hope it was only her underwear she was wearing on the outside.

It was getting worse, Nanny knew. Sometimes her knock would be heard on the door a few hours before she arrived. Her footprints would turn up several days later.

Nanny's heart sank at the sight of the third witch, and it wasn't because Letice Earwig was a bad women. Quite the reverse, in fact. She was considered to be decent, well-meaning, and kind, at least to less-aggressive animals and the cleaner sort of children. And she would always do you a good turn. The trouble was, though, that she would do you a good turn for your own good even if a good turn wasn't what was good for you. You ended up mentally turned the other way, and that wasn't good.

And she was married. Nanny had nothing against witches being married. It wasn't as if there were *rules*. She herself had had many husbands, and had even been married to three of them. But Mr. Earwig was a retired wizard with a suspiciously large amount of gold, and Nanny suspected that Letice did witchcraft as something to keep herself occupied, in much the same way that other women of a certain class might embroider kneelers for the church or visit the poor.

And she had money. Nanny did not have money and therefore was predisposed to dislike those who did. Letice had a black velvet cloak so fine that it looked as if a hole had been cut out of the world. Nanny did not. Nanny did not *want* a fine velvet cloak and did not aspire to such things. So she didn't see why other people should have them.

"Evening, Gytha. How are you keeping, in yourself?" said Gammer Beavis.

Nanny took her pipe out of her mouth. "Fit as a fiddle. Come on in."

"Ain't this rain dreadful?" said Mother Dismass. Nanny looked at the sky. It was frosty purple. But it was probably raining wherever Mother's mind was at.

"Come along in and dry off, then," she said kindly.

"May fortunate stars shine on this our meeting," said Letice. Nanny nodded understandingly. Letice always sounded as though she'd learned her witchcraft out of a not very imaginative book.

"Yeah, right," she said.

There was some polite conversation while Nanny prepared tea and scones. Then Gammer Beavis, in a tone that clearly indicated that the official part of the visit was beginning, said:

"We're here as the Trials committee, Nanny."

"Oh? Yes?"

"I expect you'll be entering?"

"Oh, yes. I'll do my little turn." Nanny glanced at Letice. There was a smile on that face that she wasn't entirely happy with.

"There's a lot of interest this year," Gammer went on. "More girls are taking it up lately."

"To get boys, one feels," said Letice, and sniffed. Nanny didn't comment. Using witchcraft to get boys seemed a damn good use for it as far as she was concerned. It was, in a way, one of the fundamental uses.

"That's nice," she said. "Always looks good, a big turnout. But."

"I beg your pardon?" said Letice.

"I said 'but,' " said Nanny. " 'Cos someone's going to say 'but,' right? This little chat has got a big 'but' coming up. I can tell."

She knew this was flying in the face of protocol. There should be at least seven more minutes of small talk before anyone got around to the point, but Letice's presence was getting on her nerves.

"It's about Esme Weatherwax," said Gammer Beavis.

"Yes?" said Nanny, without surprise.

"I suppose she's entering?"

"Never known her stay away."

Letice sighed.

"I suppose you . . . couldn't persuade her to . . . not to enter this year?" she said.

Nanny looked shocked.

"With an axe, you mean?" she said.

In unison, the three witches sat back.

"You see—" Gammer began, a bit shamefaced.

"Frankly, Mrs. Ogg," said Letice, "it is very hard to get other people to enter when they know that Miss Weatherwax is entering. She always wins."

"Yes," said Nanny. "It's a competition."

"But she *always* wins!"

"So?"

"In *other* types of competition," said Letice, "one is normally only allowed to win for three years in a row and then one takes a backseat for a while."

"Yeah, but this is witching," said Nanny. "The rules is different."

"How so?"

"There ain't none."

Letice twitched her skirt. "Perhaps it is time there were," she said.

"Ah," said Nanny. "And you just going to go up and tell Esme that? You up for this, Gammer?"

Gammer Beavis didn't meet her gaze. Old Mother Dismass was gazing at last week.

"I understand Miss Weatherwax is a very proud woman," said Letice.

Nanny Ogg puffed at her pipe again.

"You might as well say the sea is full of water," she said.

The other witches were silent for a moment.

"I daresay that was a valuable comment," said Letice, "but I didn't understand it."

"If there ain't no water in the sea, it ain't the sea," said Nanny Ogg.

"It's just a damn great hole in the ground. Thing about Esme is . . ." Nanny took another noisy pull at the pipe. "She's *all* pride, see? She ain't just a proud *person*."

"Then perhaps she should learn to be a bit more humble . . ."

"What's she got to be humble about?" said Nanny sharply.

But Letice, like a lot of people with marshmallow on the outside, had a hard core that was not easily compressed.

"The woman clearly has a natural talent and, really, she should be grateful for—"

Nanny Ogg stopped listening at this point. *The woman*, she thought. So that was how it was going.

It was the same in just about every trade. Sooner or later someone decided it needed organizing, and the one thing you could be sure of was that the organizers weren't going to be the people who, by general acknowledgment, were at the top of their craft. *They* were working too hard. To be fair, it generally wasn't done by the worst, neither. They were working hard, too. They had to.

No, it was done by the ones who had just enough time and inclination to scurry and bustle. And, to be fair again, the world *needed* people who scurried and bustled. You just didn't have to like them very much.

The lull told her that Letice had finished.

"Really? Now, me," said Nanny, "I'm the one who's *nat'rally* talented. Us Oggs've got witchcraft in our blood. I never really had to sweat at it. Esme, now . . . she's got a bit, true enough, but it ain't a lot. She just makes it work harder'n hell. And you're going to tell her she's not to?"

"We were rather hoping you would," said Letice.

Nanny opened her mouth to deliver one or two swearwords, and then stopped.

"Tell you what," she said, "*you* can tell her tomorrow, and I'll come with you to hold her back."

Granny Weatherwax was gathering Herbs when they came up the track.

Everyday herbs of sickroom and kitchen are known as simples. Granny's Herbs weren't simples. They were complicateds or they were nothing. And there was none of the airy-fairy business with a pretty basket and a pair of dainty snippers. Granny used a knife. And a chair held in front of her. And a leather hat, gloves, and apron as secondary lines of defense.

Even she didn't know where some of the Herbs came from. Roots and seed were traded all over the world, and maybe farther. Some had flowers that turned as you passed by, some fired their thorns at passing birds, and several were staked, not so that they wouldn't fall over, but so they'd still be there next day.

Nanny Ogg, who never bothered to grow any herb you couldn't smoke or stuff a chicken with, heard her mutter, "Right, you buggers—"

"Good morning, Miss Weatherwax," said Letice Earwig loudly.

Granny Weatherwax stiffened, and then lowered the chair very carefully and turned around.

"It's Mistress," she said.

"Whatever," said Letice brightly. "I trust you are keeping well?"

"Up till now," said Granny. She nodded almost imperceptibly at the other three witches.

There was a thrumming silence, which appalled Nanny Ogg. They should have been invited in for a cup of something. That was how the ritual went. It was gross bad manners to keep people standing around. Nearly, but not quite, as bad as calling an elderly unmarried witch "Miss."

"You've come about the Trials," said Granny. Letice almost fainted.

"Er, how did—"

" 'Cos you look like a committee. It don't take much reasoning," said Granny, pulling off her gloves. "We didn't used to need a committee. The news just got around and we all turned up. Now suddenly there's folk *arrangin'* things." For a moment Granny looked as though she was fighting some serious internal battle, and then she added in throwaway tones, "Kettle's on. You'd better come in."

Nanny relaxed. Maybe there were some customs even Granny Weatherwax wouldn't defy, after all. Even if someone was your worst enemy, you invited them in and gave them tea and biscuits. In fact, the worser your enemy, the better the crockery you got out and the higher the quality of the biscuits. You might wish black hell on 'em later, but while they were under your roof you'd feed 'em till they choked.

Her dark little eyes noted that the kitchen table gleamed and was still damp from scrubbing.

After cups had been poured and pleasantries exchanged, or at least offered by Letice and received in silence by Granny, the self-elected chairwoman wriggled in her seat and said:

"There's such a lot of interest in the Trials this year, Miss—Mistress Weatherwax."

"Good."

"It does look as though witchcraft in the Ramtops is going through something of a renaissance, in fact."

"A renaissance, eh? There's a thing."

"It's such a good route to empowerment for young women, don't you think?"

Many people could say things in a cutting way, Nanny knew. But Granny Weatherwax could *listen* in a cutting way. She could make something sound stupid just by hearing it.

"That's a good hat you've got there," said Granny. "Velvet, is it? Not made local, I expect."

Letice touched the brim and gave a little laugh.

"It's from Boggi's in Ankh-Morpork," she said.

"Oh? Shop-bought?"

Nanny Ogg glanced at the corner of the room, where a battered wooden cone stood on a stand. Pinned to it were lengths of black calico and strips of willow wood, the foundations for Granny's spring hat.

"*Tailor-made*," said Letice.

"And those hatpins you've got," Granny went on. "All them crescent moons and cat shapes—"

"You've got a brooch that's crescent-shaped, too, ain't that so, Esme?" said Nanny Ogg, deciding it was time for a warning shot. Granny occasionally had a lot to say about jewelry on witches when she was feeling in an acid mood.

"This is true, Gytha. I have a brooch what is shaped like a crescent. That's just the truth of the shape it happens to be. Very practical shape for holding a cloak, is a crescent. But I don't *mean* nothing by it. Anyway, you interrupted just as I was about to remark to Mrs. Earwig how fetchin' her hatpins are. Very *witchy*."

Nanny, swiveling like a spectator at a tennis match, glanced at Letice to see if this deadly bolt had gone home. But the woman was actually *smiling.* Some people just couldn't spot the obvious on the end of a ten-pound hammer.

"On the subject of witchcraft," said Letice, with the born chair-woman's touch for the enforced segue, "I thought I might raise with you the question of your *participation* in the Trials."

"Yes?"

"Do you . . . ah . . . don't you think it is unfair to other people that you win every year?"

Granny Weatherwax looked down at the floor and then up at the ceiling.

"No," she said, eventually. "I'm better'n them."

"You don't think it is a little dispiriting for the other contestants?"

Once again, the floor-to-ceiling search.

"No," said Granny.

"But they start off knowing they're not going to win."

"So do I."

"Oh, no, you surely—"

"I *meant* that I start off knowing they're not goin' to win, too," said Granny witheringly. "And they ought to start off knowing *I'm* not going to win. No wonder they lose, if they ain't getting their minds right."

"It does rather dash their enthusiasm."

Granny looked genuinely puzzled. "What's wrong with 'em striving to come second?" she said.

Letice plunged on.

"What we were hoping to persuade you to do, Esme, is to accept an emeritus position. You would perhaps make a nice little speech of encouragement, present the award, and . . . and possibly even be, er, one of the judges . . ."

"There's going to be judges?" said Granny. "We've never had *judges*. Everyone just used to know who'd won."

"That's true," said Nanny. She remembered the scenes at the end of one or two trials. When Granny Weatherwax won, everyone knew. "Oh, that's very true."

"It would be a very nice gesture," Letice went on.

"Who decided there would be judges?" said Granny.

"Er . . . the committee . . . which is . . . that is . . . a few of us got together. Only to steer things . . ."

"Oh. I see," said Granny. "Flags?"

"Pardon?"

"Are you going to have them lines of little flags? And maybe some-one selling apples on a stick, that kind of thing?"

"Some bunting would certainly be—"

"Right. Don't forget the bonfire."

"So long as it's nice and safe."

"Oh. Right. Things should be nice. And safe," said Granny.

Mrs. Earwig perceptibly sighed with relief. "Well, that's sorted out nicely," she said.

"Is it?" said Granny.

"I thought we'd agreed that—"

"Had we? Really?" She picked up the poker from the hearth and prodded fiercely at the fire. "I'll give matters my consideration."

"I wonder if I may be frank for a moment, Mistress Weatherwax?" said Letice. The poker paused in mid-prod.

"Yes?"

"Times are changing, you know. Now, I think I know why you feel it necessary to be so overbearing and unpleasant to everyone, but be-lieve me when I tell you, as a friend, that you'd find it so much easier if you just relaxed a little bit and tried being nicer, like our sister Gytha here."

Nanny Ogg's smile had fossilized into a mask. Letice didn't seem to notice.

"You seem to have all the witches in awe of you for fifty miles around," she went on. "Now, I daresay you have some valuable skills, but witchcraft isn't about being an old grump and frightening people anymore. I'm telling you this as a friend—"

"Call again whenever you're passing," said Granny.

This was a signal. Nanny Ogg stood up hurriedly.

"I thought we could discuss—" Letice protested.

"I'll walk with you all down to the main track," said Nanny, hauling the other witches out of their seats.

"Gytha!" said Granny sharply, as the group reached the door.

"Yes, Esme?

"You'll come back here afterward, I expect."

"Yes, Esme."

Nanny ran to catch up with the trio on the path.

Letice had what Nanny thought of as a deliberate walk. It had been wrong to judge her by the floppy jowls and the overfussy hair and the silly way she waggled her hands as she talked. She was a witch, after all. Scratch any witch and . . . well, you'd be facing a witch you'd just scratched.

"She is not a nice person," Letice trilled. But it was the trill of some large hunting bird.

"You're right there," said Nanny. "But—"

"It's high time she was taken down a peg or two!"

"We-ell . . ."

"She bullies you most terribly, Mrs. Ogg. A married lady of *your* mature years, too!"

Just for a moment, Nanny's eyes narrowed.

"It's her way," she said.

"A very petty and nasty way, to my mind!"

"Oh, yes," said Nanny simply. "Ways often are. But look, you—"

"Will you be bringing anything to the produce stall, Gytha?" said Gammer Beavis quickly.

"Oh, a couple of bottles, I expect," said Nanny, deflating.

"Oh, homemade wine?" said Letice. "How nice."

"Sort of like wine, yes. Well, here's the path," said Nanny. "I'll just . . . I'll just nip back and say goodnight—"

"It's belittling, you know, the way you run around after her," said Letice.

"Yes. Well. You get used to people. Good night to you."

When she got back to the cottage Granny Weatherwax was standing in the middle of the kitchen floor with a face like an unmade bed and her arms folded. One foot tapped on the floor.

"She married a wizard," said Granny, as soon as her friend had entered. "You can't tell me that's right."

"Well, wizards *can* marry, you know. They just have to hand in the staff and pointy hat. There's no actual law says they can't, so long as they gives up wizarding. They're supposed to be married to the job."

"I should reckon it's a job being married to *her*," said Granny. Her face screwed up in a sour smile.

"Been pickling much this year?" said Nanny, employing a fresh association of ideas around the word "vinegar," which had just popped into her head.

"My onions all got the screwfly."

"That's a pity. You like onions."

"Even screwflies've got to eat," said Granny. She glared at the door. "*Nice*," she said.

"She's got a knitted cover on the lid in her privy," said Nanny.

"Pink?"

"Yes."

"Nice."

"She's not *bad*," said Nanny. "She does good work over in Fiddler's Elbow. People speak highly of her."

Granny sniffed. "Do they speak highly of me?" she said.

"No, they speaks *quietly* of you, Esme."

"Good. Did you see her hatpins?"

"I thought they were rather . . . nice, Esme."

"That's witchcraft today. All jewelry and no drawers."

Nanny, who considered both to be optional, tried to build an embankment against the rising tide of ire.

"You could think of it as an honor, really, them not wanting you to take part," she said.

"That's nice."

Nanny sighed.

"Sometimes nice is worth tryin', Esme," she said.

"I never does anyone a bad turn if I can't do 'em a good one, Gytha, you know that. I don't have to do no frills or fancy labels."

Nanny sighed. Of course, it was true. Granny was an old-fashioned witch. She didn't do good for people, she did right by them. But Nanny knew that people don't always appreciate right. Like old Pollitt the other day, when he fell off his horse. What he wanted was a painkiller. What he *needed* was the few seconds of agony as Granny popped the joint back into place. The trouble was, people remembered the pain.

You got on a lot better with people when you remembered to put frills round it, and took an interest and said things like "How are you?" Esme didn't bother with that kind of stuff because she knew already. Nanny Ogg knew too, but also knew that letting on you knew gave people the serious willies.

She put her head on one side. Granny's foot was still tapping.

"You planning anything, Esme? I know you. You've got that look."

"What look, pray?"

"That look you had when that bandit was found naked up a tree and crying all the time and going on about the horrible thing that was after him. Funny thing, we never found any paw prints. *That* look."

"He deserved more'n that for what he done."

"Yeah . . . well, you had that look just before ole Hoggett was found beaten black and blue in his own pigsty and wouldn't talk about it?"

"You mean old Hoggett the wife beater? Or old Hoggett who won't never lift his hand to a woman no more?" said Granny. The thing her lips had pursed into might have been called a smile.

"And it's the look you had the time all the snow slid down on ole Millson's house just after he called you an interfering old baggage . . ." said Nanny.

Granny hesitated. Nanny was pretty sure that had been natural causes, and also that Granny knew she suspected this, and that pride was fighting a battle with honesty—

"That's as may be," said Granny, noncommittally.

"Like someone who might go along to the Trials and . . . do something," said Nanny.

Her friend's glare should have made the air sizzle.

"Oh? So that's what you think of me? That's what we've come to, have we?"

"Letice thinks we should move with the times—"

"Well? I moves with the times. We ought to move with the times. No one said we ought to give them a *push*. I expect you'll be wanting to be going, Gytha. I want to be alone with my thoughts!"

Nanny's own thoughts, as she scurried home in relief, were that Granny Weatherwax was not an advertisement for witchcraft. Oh, she was one of the *best* at it, no doubt about that. At a certain kind, certainly. But a girl starting out in life might well say to herself, Is this it? You worked hard and denied yourself things and what you got at the end of it was hard work and self-denial?

Granny wasn't exactly friendless, but what she commanded mostly was respect. People learned to respect storm clouds, too. They refreshed the ground. You needed them. But they weren't nice.

Nanny Ogg went to bed in three flannelette nightdresses, because sharp frosts were already pricking the autumn air. She was also in a troubled frame of mind.

Some sort of war had been declared, she knew. Granny could do some terrible things when roused, and the fact that they'd been done to those who richly deserved them didn't make them any the less terrible. She'd be planning something pretty dreadful, Nanny Ogg knew.

She herself didn't like winning things. Winning was a habit that was hard to break and brought you a dangerous status that was hard to defend. You'd walk uneasily through life, always on the lookout for the next girl with a better broomstick and a quicker hand on the frog.

She turned over under the mountain of eiderdowns.

In Granny Weatherwax's worldview was no place for second place. You won, or you were a loser. There was nothing *wrong* with being a loser except for the fact that, of course, you weren't the winner. Nanny had always pursued the policy of being a good loser. People *liked* you when you *almost* won, and bought you drinks. "She only just lost" was a much better compliment than "She only just won."

Runners-up had more fun, she reckoned. But it wasn't a word Granny had much time for.

In her own darkened cottage, Granny Weatherwax sat and watched the fire die.

It was a gray-walled room, the color that old plaster gets not so much from dirt as from age. There was not a thing in it that wasn't useful, utilitarian, earning its keep. Every flat surface in Nanny Ogg's cottage had been pressed into service as a holder for ornaments and potted plants. People gave Nanny Ogg things. Cheap fairground tat, Granny always called it. At least, in public. What she thought of it in the privacy of her own head, she never said.

She rocked gently as the last ember winked out.

It's hard to contemplate, in the gray hours of the night, that probably the only reason people would come to your funeral would be to make sure you're dead.

Next day, Percy Hopcroft opened his back door and looked straight up into the blue stare of Granny Weatherwax.

"Oh my," he said, under his breath.

Granny gave an awkward little cough.

"Mr. Hopcroft, I've come about them apples you named after Mrs. Ogg," she said.

Percy's knees began to tremble, and his wig started to slide off the back of his head to the hoped-for security of the floor.

"I should like to thank you for doing it because it has made her very happy," Granny went on, in a tone of voice which would have struck one who knew her as curiously monotonous. "She has done a lot of fine work and it is about time she got her little reward. It was a very nice thought. And so I have brung you this little token—" Hopcroft jumped backward as Granny's hand dipped swiftly into her apron and produced a small black bottle. "—which is very rare because of the rare herbs in it. What are rare. Extremely rare herbs."

Eventually it crept over Hopcroft that he was supposed to take the bottle. He gripped the top of it very carefully, as if it might whistle or develop legs.

"Uh . . . thank you ver' much," he mumbled.

Granny nodded stiffly.

"Blessings be upon this house," she said, and turned and walked away down the path.

Hopcroft shut the door carefully, and then flung himself against it.

"You start packing right now!" he shouted to his wife, who'd been watching from the kitchen door.

"What? Our whole life's here! We can't just run away from it!"

"Better to run than hop, woman! What's *she* want from me? What's she *want*? She's never *nice*!"

Mrs. Hopcroft stood firm. She just got the cottage looking right and they'd bought a new pump. Some things were hard to leave.

"Let just stop and think, then," she said. "What's in that bottle?"

Hopcroft held it at arm's length. "Do *you* want to find out?"

"Stop shaking, man! She didn't actually threaten, did she?"

"She said 'blessings be upon this house'! Sounds pretty damn threatening to *me*! That was Granny Weatherwax, that was!"

He put the bottle on the table. They stared at it, standing in the cautious leaning position of people who were ready to run if anything began to happen.

"Says 'Haire Reftorer' on the label," said Mrs. Hopcroft.

"I ain't using it!"

"She'll ask us about it later. That's her way."

"If you think for one moment I'm—"

"We can try it out on the dog."

*   *   *

That's a good cow."

William Poorchick awoke from his reverie on the milking stool and looked around the meadow, his hands still working the beast's teats.

There was a black pointy hat rising over the hedge. He gave such a start that he started to milk into his left boot.

"Gives plenty of milk, does she?"

"Yes, Mistress Weatherwax!" William quavered.

"That's good. Long may she continue to do so, that's what I say. Good day to you."

And the pointy hat continued up the lane.

Poorchick stared after it. Then he grabbed the bucket and, squelching at every other step, hurried into the barn and yelled for his son.

"Rummage! You get down here right now!"

His son appeared at the hayloft, pitchfork still in his hand.

"What's up, Dad?"

"You take Daphne down to the market right now, understand?"

"What? But she's our best milker, Dad!"

"*Was*, son, was! Granny Weatherwax just put a curse on her! Sell her now before her horns drop off!"

"What'd she say, Dad?"

"She said . . . she said . . . 'Long may she continue to give milk' . . ." Poorchick hesitated.

"Doesn't sound *awfully* like a curse, Dad." said Rummage. "I mean . . . not like your gen'ral curse. Sounds a bit hopeful, really," said his son.

"Well . . . it was the way . . . she . . . said . . . it . . ."

"What sort of way, Dad?"

"Well . . . like . . . cheerfully."

"You all right, Dad?"

"It was . . . the way . . ." Poorchick paused. "Well, it's not right," he continued. "It's not right! She's got no right to go around being cheerful at people! She's never cheerful! And my *boot* is *full* of *milk*!"

Today Nanny Ogg was taking some time out to tend her secret still in the woods. As a still it was the best kept secret there could be, since everyone in the kingdom knew exactly where it was, and a secret kept by so many people must be very secret indeed. Even the king knew, and knew enough to pretend he didn't know, and that meant he didn't have to ask her for any taxes and she didn't have to refuse. And every year at Hogswatch he got a barrel of what honey might be if only bees weren't teetotal. And everyone understood the situation, no one had to pay any money, and so, in a small way, the world was a happier place. And no one was cursed until their teeth fell out.

Nanny was dozing. Keeping an eye on a still was a day-and-night job. But finally the sound of people repeatedly calling her name got too much for her.

No one would come into the clearing, of course. That would mean admitting that they knew where it was. So they were blundering around in the surrounding bushes. She pushed her way through and was greeted with some looks of feigned surprise that would have done credit to any amateur dramatic company.

"Well, what do you lot want?" she demanded.

"Oh, Mrs. Ogg, we though you might be . . . taking a walk in the woods," said Poorchick, while a scent that could clean glass wafted on the breeze. "You got to do something! It's Mistress Weatherwax!"

"What's she done?"

"You tell 'er, Mr. Hampicker!"

The man next to Poorchick took off his hat quickly and held it respectfully in front of him in the ai-señor-the-banditos-have-raided-our-villages position.

"Well, ma'am, my lad and I were digging for a well and then she come past—"

"Granny Weatherwax?"

"Yes'm, and she said—" Hampicker gulped. " 'You won't find any water there, my good man. You'd be better off looking in the hollow by the chestnut tree'! An' we dug on down anyway and *we never found no water!*"

Nanny lit her pipe. She didn't smoke around the still since that time when a careless spark had sent the barrel she was sitting on a hundred yards into the air. She'd been lucky that a fir tree had broken her fall.

"So . . . *then* you dug in the hollow by the chestnut tree?" she said mildly.

Hampicker looked shocked. "*No*'m! There's no telling *what* she wanted us to find there!"

"And she cursed my cow!" said Poorchick.

"Really? What did she say?"

"She said, may she give a lot of milk!" Poorchick stopped. Once again, now that he came to say it . . .

"Well, it was the way she said it," he added, weakly.

"And what kind of way was that?"

"Nicely!"

"Nicely?"

"Smilin' and everything! I don't dare drink the stuff now!"

Nanny was mystified.

"Can't quite see the problem—"

"You tell that to Mr. Hopcroft's dog," said Poorchick. "Hopcroft daren't leave the poor thing on account of her! The whole family's going mad! There's him shearing, his wife sharpening the scissors, and the two lads out all the time looking for fresh places to dump the hair!"

Patient questioning on Nanny's part elucidated the role the Haire Reftorer had played in this.

"And he gave it—?"

"Half the bottle, Mrs. Ogg."

"Even though Esme writes 'A right small spoonful once a week' on the label? And even then you need to wear roomy trousers."

"He said he was so nervous, Mrs. Ogg! I mean, what's she playing at? Our wives are keepin' the kids indoors. I mean, s'posin' she smiled at them?"

"Well?"

"She's a witch!"

"So'm I, an' I smiles at 'em," said Nanny Ogg. "They're always runnin' after me for sweets."

"Yes, but . . . you're . . . I mean . . . she . . . I mean . . . you don't . . . I mean, well—"

"And she's a good woman," said Nanny. Common sense prompted her to add, "In her own way. I expect there *is* water down in the hollow, and Poorchick's cow'll give good milk, and if Hopcroft won't read the labels on bottles then he deserves a head you can see your face in, and if you think Esme Weatherwax'd curse kids you've got the sense of a earthworm. She'd cuss 'em, yes, all day long. But not curse 'em. She don't aim that low."

"Yes, yes," Poorchick almost moaned, "but it don't *feel* right, that's what we're saying. Her going round being *nice*, a man don't know if he's got a leg to stand on."

"Or hop on," said Hampicker darkly.

"All right, all right, I'll see about it," said Nanny.

"People shouldn't go around not doin' what you expect," said Poorchick weakly. "It gets people on edge."

"And we'll keep an eye on your sti—" Hampicker, and then staggered backward grasping his stomach and wheezing.

"Don't mind him, it's the stress," said Poorchick, rubbing his elbow. "Been picking herbs, Mrs. Ogg?"

"That's right," said Nanny, hurrying away across the leaves.

"So shall I put the fire out for you, then?" Poorchick shouted.

Granny was sitting outside her house when Nanny Ogg hurried up the path. She was sorting through a sack of old clothes. Elderly garments were scattered around her.

And she was humming. Nanny Ogg started to worry. The Granny Weatherwax she knew didn't approve of music.

And she smiled when she saw Nanny, or at least the corner of her mouth turned up. That was *really* worrying. Granny normally only smiled if something bad was happening to someone deserving.

"Why, Gytha, how nice to see you!"

"You all right, Esme?"

"Never felt better, dear." The humming continued.

"Er . . . sorting out rags, are you?" said Nanny. "Going to make that quilt?"

It was one of Granny Weatherwax's firm beliefs that one day she'd make a patchwork quilt. However, it is a task that requires patience, and hence in fifteen years she'd got as far as three patches. But she collected old clothes anyway. A lot of witches did. It was a witch thing. Old clothes had personality, like old houses. When it came to clothes with a bit of wear left in them, a witch had no pride at all.

"It's in here somewhere . . ." Granny mumbled. "Aha, here we are . . ."

She flourished a garment. It was basically pink.

"Knew it was here," she went on. "Hardly worn, either. And about my size, too."

"You're going to *wear* it?" said Nanny.

Granny's piercing blue cut-you-off-at-the-knees gaze was turned upon her. Nanny would have been relieved at a reply like "No, I'm going to eat it, you daft old fool." Instead her friend relaxed and said, a little concerned:

"You don't think it'd suit me?"

There was lace around the collar. Nanny swallowed.

"You usually wear black," she said. "Well, a bit more than usually. More like always."

"And a very sad sight I look too," said Granny robustly. "It's about time I brightened myself up a bit, don't you think?"

"And it's so very . . . pink."

Granny put it aside and to Nanny's horror took her by the hand and said earnestly, "And, you know, I reckon I've been far too dog-in-the-manger about this Trials business, Gytha—"

"Bitch-in-the-manger," said Nanny Ogg, absentmindedly.

For a moment Granny's eyes became two sapphires again.

"What?"

"Er . . . you'd be a bitch-in-the-manger," Nanny mumbled. "Not a dog."

"Ah? Oh, yes. Thank you for pointing that out. Well, I thought, it *is* time I stepped back a bit, and went along and cheered on the younger folks. I mean, I have to say, I . . . really haven't been very nice to people, have I . . ."

"Er . . ."

"I've tried *being* nice," Granny went on. "It didn't turn out like I expected, I'm sorry to say."

"You've never been really . . . *good* at nice," said Nanny.

Granny smiled. Hard though she stared, Nanny was unable to spot anything other than earnest concern.

"Perhaps I'll get better with practice," she said.

She patted Nanny's hand. And Nanny stared at her hand as though something horrible had happened to it.

"It's just that everyone's more used to you being . . . firm," she said.

"I thought I might make some jam and cakes for the produce stall," said Granny.

"Oh . . . good."

"Are there any sick people want visitin'?"

Nanny stared at the trees. It was getting worse and worse. She rummaged in her memory for anyone in the locality sick enough to warrant a ministering visit but still well enough to survive the shock of a ministering visit by Granny Weatherwax. When it came to practical psychology and the more robust type of folk physiotherapy Granny was without equal; in fact, she could even do the latter at a distance, for many a pain-wracked soul had left their bed and walked, nay, run at the news that she was coming.

"Everyone's pretty well at the moment," said Nanny diplomatically.

"Any old folk want cheerin' up?"

It was taken for granted by both women that *old people* did not include them. A witch aged ninety-seven would not have included herself. Old people happened to other people.

"All fairly cheerful right now," said Nanny.

"Maybe I could tell stories to the kiddies?"

Nanny nodded. Granny had done that once before, when the mood had briefly taken her. It had worked pretty well, as far as the children were concerned. They'd listened with openmouthed attention and apparent enjoyment to a traditional old folk legend. The problem had come when they'd gone home afterward and asked the meaning of words like "disemboweled."

"I could sit in a rocking chair while I tell 'em," Granny added. "That's how it's done, I recall. And I could make them some of my special treacle toffee apples. Wouldn't that be nice?"

Nanny nodded again, in a sort of horrified reverie. She realized that only she stood in the way of a wholesale rampage of niceness.

"Toffee," she said. "Would that be the sort you did that shatters like glass, or that sort where our boy Pewsey had to have his mouth levered open with a spoon?"

"I reckon I know what I did wrong last time."

"You know you and sugar don't get along, Esme. Remember them all-day suckers you made?"

"They *did* last all day, Gytha."

"Only 'cos our Pewsey couldn't get it out of his little mouth until we pulled two of his teeth, Esme. You ought to stick to pickles. You and pickles goes well."

"I've got to do *something*, Gytha. I can't be an old grump all the time. I know! I'll help at the Trials. Bound to be a lot that needs doing, eh?"

Nanny grinned inwardly. So *that* was it.

"Why, yes," she said. "I'm sure Mrs. Earwig will be happy to tell you what to do," she said. *And more fool her if she does*, she thought, *because I can tell you're planning something.*

"I shall talk to her," said Granny. "I'm sure there's a million things I could do to help, if I set my mind to it."

"And I'm sure you will," said Nanny heartily. "I've a feelin' you're going to make a big difference."

Granny started to rummage in the bag again.

"You are going to be along as well, aren't you, Gytha?"

"Me?" said Nanny. "I wouldn't miss it for the world."

Nanny got up especially early. If there was going to be any unpleasantness she wanted a ringside seat.

What there was was bunting. It was hanging from tree to tree in terrible brightly colored loops as she walked toward the Trials.

There was something oddly familiar about it, too. It should not technically be possible for anyone with a pair of scissors to be unable to cut out a triangle, but someone had managed it. And it was also obvious that the flags had been made from old clothes, painstakingly cut up. Nanny knew this because not many real flags have collars.

In the Trials field people were setting up stalls and falling over children. The committee were standing uncertainly under a tree, occasionally glancing up at a pink figure at the top of a very long ladder.

"She was here before it was light," said Letice, as Nanny approached. "She said she'd been up all night making the flags."

"Tell her about the cakes," said Gammer Beavis darkly.

"She made *cakes?*" said Nanny. "But she can't cook!"

The committee shuffled aside. A lot of the ladies contributed to the food for the Trials. It was a tradition and an informal competition in its own right. At the center of the spread of covered plates was a large platter piled high with . . . things, of indefinite color and shape. It looked as though a herd of small cows had eaten a lot of raisins and then been ill. They were Ur-cakes, prehistoric cakes, cakes of great weight and presence that had no place among the iced dainties.

"She's never had the knack of it," said Nanny weakly. "Has anyone tried one?"

"Hahaha," said Gammer solemnly.

"Tough, are they?"

"You could beat a troll to death."

"But she was so . . . sort of . . . *proud* of them," said Letice. "And then there's . . . the jam."

It was a large pot. It seemed to be filled with solidified purple lava.

"Nice . . . color," said Nanny. "Anyone tasted it?"

"We couldn't get the spoon out," said Gammer.

"Oh, I'm sure—"

"We only got it in with a hammer."

"What's she planning, Mrs. Ogg? She's got a weak and vengeful nature," said Letice. "You're her friend," she added, her tone suggesting that this was as much an accusation as a statement.

"I don't know what she's thinking, Mrs. Earwig."

"I though she was staying away."

"She said she was going to take an interest and encourage the young 'uns."

"She is planning something," said Letice, darkly. "Those cakes are a plot to undermine my authority."

"No, that's how she always cooks," said Nanny. "She just hasn't got the knack." *Your authority, eh?*

"She's nearly finished the flags," Gammer reported. "Now she's going to try to make herself useful again."

"Well . . . I suppose we could ask her to do the Lucky Dip."

Nanny looked blank. "You mean where kids fish around in a big tub full of bran to see what they can pull out?"

"Yes."

"You're going to let *Granny Weatherwax* do that?"

"Yes."

"Only she's got a funny sense of humor, if you know what I mean."

"Good morning to you all!"

It was Granny Weatherwax's voice. Nanny Ogg had known it for most of her life. But it had that strange edge to it again. It sounded nice.

"We was wondering if you could supervise the bran tub, Miss Weatherwax."

Nanny flinched. But Granny merely said, "Happy to, Mrs. Earwig. I can't wait to see the expressions on their little faces as they pull out the goodies."

Nor can I, Nanny thought.

When the others had scurried off she sidled up to her friend.

"Why're you doing this?" she said.

"I really don't know what you mean, Gytha."

"I seen you face down terrible creatures, Esme. I once seen you catch a unicorn, for goodness' sake. What're you plannin'?"

"I still don't know what you mean, Gytha."

"Are you angry 'cos they won't let you enter, and now you're plannin' horrible revenge?"

For a moment they both looked at the field. It was beginning to fill up. People were bowling for pigs and fighting on the greasy pole. The Lancre Volunteer Band was trying to play a medley of popular tunes, and it was only a pity that each musician was playing a different one. Small children were fighting. It was going to be a scorcher of a day, probably the last one of the year.

Their eyes were drawn to the roped-off square in the center of the field.

"Are you going to enter the Trials, Gytha?" said Granny.

"You never answered my question!"

"What question was that?"

Nanny decided not to hammer on a locked door. "Yes, I am going to have a go, as it happens," she said.

"I certainly hope you win, then. I'd cheer you on, only that wouldn't be fair to the others. I shall merge into the background and be as quiet as a little mouse."

Nanny tried guile. Her face spread into a wide pink grin, and she nudged her friend.

"Right, right," she said. "Only . . . you can tell me, right? I wouldn't like to miss it when it happens. So if you could just give me a little signal when you're going to do *it*, eh?"

"What's it you're referring to, Gytha?"

"Esme Weatherwax, sometimes I could really give you a bloody good slap!"

"Oh dear."

Nanny Ogg didn't often swear, or at least use words beyond the boundaries of what the Lancrastrians thought of as "colorful language." She *looked* as if she habitually used bad words, and had just thought up a good one, but mostly witches are quite careful about what they say. You can never be sure what the words are going to do when they're out of earshot. But now she swore under her breath and caused small brief fires to start in the dry grass.

This put her in just about the right frame of mind for the Cursing.

It was said that once upon a time this had been done on a living, breathing subject, at least at the start of the event, but that wasn't right for a family day out and for several hundred years the Curses had been directed at Unlucky Charlie, who was, however you looked at it, nothing more than a scarecrow. And since curses are generally directed at the mind of the cursed, this presented a major problem, because even "May your straw go moldy and your carrot fall off" didn't make much impression on a pumpkin. But points were given for general style and inventiveness.

There wasn't much pressure for those in any case. Everyone knew what event counted, and it wasn't Unlucky Charlie.

One year Granny Weatherwax had made the pumpkin explode. No one had ever worked out how she'd done it.

Someone would walk away at the end of today and everyone would know that person was the winner, whatever the points said. You could win the Witch with the Pointiest Hat prize and the broomstick dressage, but that was just for the audience. What counted was the Trick you'd been working on all summer.

Nanny had drawn last place, at number nineteen. A lot of witches had turned up this year. News of Granny Weatherwax's withdrawal had got around, and nothing moves faster than news in the occult community, since it doesn't just have to travel at ground level. Many pointy hats moved and nodded among the crowds.

Witches are among themselves generally as sociable as cats but, as also with cats, there are locations and times and neutral grounds where they meet at something like peace. And what was going on was a sort of slow, complicated dance. . . .

The witches walked around saying hello to one another, and rushing to meet newcomers, and innocent bystanders might have believed that here was a meeting of old friends. Which, at one level, it probably was. But Nanny watched through a witch's eyes, and saw the subtle positioning, the careful weighing-up, the little changes of stance, the eye contact finely tuned by intensity and length.

And when a witch was in the arena, especially if she was comparatively unknown, all the others found some excuse to keep an eye on her, preferably without appearing to do so.

It *was* like watching cats. Cats spend a lot of time carefully eyeing one another. When they have to fight, that's merely to rubber-stamp something that's already been decided in their heads.

Nanny knew all this. And she also knew most of the witches to be kind (on the whole), gentle (to the meek), generous (to the deserving; the undeserving got more than they bargained for), and by and large quite dedicated to a life that really offered more kicks than kisses. Not one of them lived in a house made of confectionery, although some of the conscientious younger ones had experimented with various crisp-breads. Even children who deserved it were not slammed into their ovens. Generally they did what they'd always done—smooth the passage of their neighbors into and out of the world, and help them over some of the nastier hurdles in between.

You needed to be a special kind of person to do that. You needed a special kind of ear, because you saw people in circumstances where they were inclined to tell you things, like where the money was buried or who the father was or how come they'd got a black eye again. And you needed a special kind of mouth, the sort that stayed shut. Keeping secrets made you powerful. Being powerful earned you respect. Respect was hard currency.

And within this sisterhood—except that it wasn't a sisterhood, it was a loose assortment of chronic non-joiners; a group of witches wasn't a coven, it was a small war—there was always this awareness of position. It had nothing to do with anything the other world thought of as status. Nothing was ever said. But if an elderly witch died the local witches would attend her funeral for a few last words, and then go solemnly home alone, with the little insistent thought at the back of their minds: *I've moved up one.*

And newcomers were watched very, very carefully.

" 'Morning, Mrs. Ogg," said a voice behind her. "I trust I find you well?"

"How'd'yer do, Mistress Shimmy," said Nanny, turning. Her mental filing system threw up a card: Clarity Shimmy, lives over toward Cut-shade with her old mum, takes snuff, good with animals. "How's your mother keepin'?"

"We buried her last month, Mrs. Ogg."

Nanny Ogg quite liked Clarity, because she didn't see her very often. "Oh dear . . ." she said.

"But I shall tell her you asked after her, anyway," said Clarity. She glanced briefly toward the ring.

"Who's the fat girl on now?" she asked. "Got a backside on her like a bowling ball on a short seesaw."

"That's Agnes Nitt."

"That's a good cursin' voice she's got there. You know you've been cursed with a voice like that."

"Oh yes, she's been blessed with a good voice for cursin'," said Nanny politely. "Esme Weatherwax an' me gave her a few tips," she added.

Clarity's head turned.

At the far edge of the field, a small pink shape sat alone behind the Lucky Dip. It did not seem to be drawing a big crowd.

Clarity leaned closer.

"What's she . . . er . . . doing?"

"I don't know," said Nanny. "I think she's decided to be nice about it."

"Esme? *Nice* about it?"

"Er . . . yes," said Nanny. It didn't sound any better now she was telling someone.

Clarity stared at her. Nanny saw her make a little sign with her left hand, and then hurry off.

The pointy hats were bunching up now. There were little groups of three or four. You could see the points come together, cluster in animated conversation, and then open out again like a flower, and turn toward the distant blob of pinkness. Then a hat would leave that group and head off purposefully to another one, where the process would start all over again. It was a bit like watching very slow nuclear fission. There was a lot of excitement, and soon there would be an explosion.

Every so often someone would turn and look at Nanny, so she hurried away among the sideshows until she fetched up beside the stall of the dwarf Zakzak Stronginthearm, maker and purveyor of occult knickknackery to the more impressionable. He nodded at her cheerfully over the top of a display saying LUCKY HORSESHOES $2 EACH.

"Hello, Mrs. Ogg," he said.

Nanny realized she was flustered.

"What's lucky about 'em?" she said, picking up a horseshoe.

"Well, I get two dollars each for them," said Stronginthearm.

"And that makes them lucky?"

"Lucky for me," said Stronginthearm. "I expect you'll be wanting one too, Mrs. Ogg? I'd have fetched along another box if I'd known they'd be so popular. Some of the ladies've bought two."

There was an inflection to the word "ladies."

"*Witches* have been buying lucky horsehoes?" said Nanny.

"Like there's no tomorrow," said Zakzak. He frowned for a moment. They *had* been witches, after all. "Er . . . there will be . . . won't there?" he added.

"I'm very nearly certain of it," said Nanny, which didn't seem to comfort him.

"Suddenly been doing a roaring trade in protective herbs, too," said Zakzak. And, being a dwarf, which meant that he'd see the Flood as a marvelous opportunity to sell towels, he added, "Can I interest you, Mrs. Ogg?"

Nanny shook her head. If trouble was going to come from the direction everyone had been looking, then a sprig of rue wasn't going to be much help. A large oak tree'd be better, but only maybe.

The atmosphere was changing. The sky was a wide pale blue, but there was thunder on the horizons of the mind. The witches were uneasy and with so many in one place the nervousness was bouncing from one to another and, amplified, rebroadcasting itself to everyone. It meant that even ordinary people who thought that a rune was a dried plum were beginning to feel a deep, existential worry, the kind that causes you to snap at your kids and want a drink.

She peered through a gap between a couple of stalls. The pink figure was still sitting patiently, and a little crestfallen, behind the barrel. There was, as it were, a huge queue of no one at all.

Then Nanny scuttled from the cover of one tent to another until she could see the produce stand. It had already been doing a busy trade but there, forlorn in the middle of the cloth, was the pile of terrible cakes. And the jar of jam. Some wag had chalked up a sign beside it: GET THEE SPOON OUT OF THEE JAR, 3 TRIES FOR A PENNEY!!!

She thought she'd been careful to stay concealed, but she heard the straw rustle behind her. The committee had tracked her down.

"That's your handwriting, isn't it, Mrs. Earwig?" she said. "That's cruel. That ain't . . . nice."

"We've decided you're to go and talk to Miss Weatherwax," said Letice. "She's got to stop it."

"Stop what?"

"She's doing something to people's heads! She's come here to put the 'fluence on us, right? Everyone knows she does head magic. We can all feel it! She's spoiling it for everyone!"

"She's only sitting there," said Nanny.

"Ah, *yes*, but *how* is she sitting there, we may ask?"

Nanny peered around the stall again.

"Well . . . like normal. You know . . . bent in the middle and the knees . . ."

Letice waved a finger sternly.

"Now you listen to me, Gytha Ogg—"

"If you want her to go away, you go and tell her!" snapped Nanny. "I'm fed up with—"

There was the piercing scream of a child.

The witches stared at one another, and then ran across the field to the Lucky Dip.

A small boy was writhing on the ground, sobbing.

It was Pewsey, Nanny's youngest grandchild.

Her stomach turned to ice. She snatched him up, and glared into Granny's face.

"What have you done to him, you—" she began.

"Don't*wanna*dolly! Don't*wanna*dolly! Wanna*soljer!* Wannawanna-wanna*SOLJER!*"

Now Nanny looked down at the rag doll in Pewsey's sticky hand, and the expression of affronted tearful rage on such of his face as could be seen around his screaming mouth—

"Oi*wannawanna*SOLJER!*"

—and then at the other witches, and at Granny Weatherwax's face, and felt the horrible cold shame welling up from her boots.

"I said he could put it back and have another go," said Granny meekly. "But he just wouldn't listen."

"—*wannawanna*SOL—"

"Pewsey Ogg, if you don't shut up right this minute Nanny will—"

Nanny Ogg began, and dredged up the nastiest punishment she could think of: "Nanny won't give you a sweetie ever again!"

Pewsey closed his mouth, stunned into silence by this unimaginable threat. Then, to Nanny's horror, Letice Earwig drew herself up and said, "Miss Weatherwax, we would prefer it if you left."

"Am I being a bother?" said Granny. "I hope I'm not being a bother. I don't *want* to be a bother. He just took a lucky dip and—"

"You're . . . upsetting people."

Any minute now, Nanny thought. Any minute now she's going to raise her head and narrow her eyes and if Letice doesn't take two steps backward she'll be a lot tougher than me.

"I can't stay and watch?" Granny said quietly.

"I know your game," said Letice. "You're planning to spoil it, aren't you? You can't stand the thought of being beaten, so you're intending something nasty."

Three steps back, Nanny thought. Else there won't anything left but bones. Any minute now . . .

"Oh, I wouldn't like anyone to think I was spoiling anything," said Granny. She sighed, and stood up. "I'll be off home . . ."

"No you won't!" snapped Nanny Ogg, pushing her back down onto the chair. "What do *you* think of this, Beryl Dismass? And you, Letty Parkin?"

"They're all—" Letice began.

"I weren't talking to you!"

The witches behind Mrs. Earwig avoided Nanny's gaze.

"Well, it's not that . . . I mean, we don't think . . ." began Beryl awkwardly. "That is . . . I've always had a lot of respect for . . . but . . . well, it *is* for everyone . . ."

Her voice trailed off. Letice looked triumphant.

"Really? I think we *had* better be going after all, then," said Nanny sourly. "I don't like the comp'ny in these parts." She looked around. "Agnes? You give me a hand to get Granny home . . ."

"I really don't need . . ." Granny began, but the other two each took an arm and gently propelled her through the crowd, which parted to let them through and turned to watch them go.

"Probably the best for all concerned, in the circumstances," said Letice. Several of the witches tried not to look at her face.

*   *   *

There were scraps of material all over the floor in Granny's kitchen, and gouts of congealed jam had dripped off the edge of the table and formed an immovable mound on the floor. The jam saucepan had been left in the stone sink to soak, although it was clear that the iron would rust away before the jam ever softened.

There was a row of empty pickle jars beside them.

Granny sat down and folded her hands in her lap.

"Want a cup of tea, Esme?" said Nanny Ogg.

"No, dear, thank you. You get on back to the Trials. Don't you worry about me," said Granny.

"You sure?"

"I'll just sit here quiet. Don't you worry."

"I'm not going back!" Agnes hissed, as they left. "I don't like the way Letice smiles . . ."

"You once told me you didn't like the way Esme *frowns*," said Nanny.

"Yes, but you can trust a frown. Er . . . you don't think she's losing it, do you?"

"No one'll be able to find it if she has," said Nanny. "No, you come on back with me. I'm *sure* she's planning . . . something." *I wish the hell I knew what it is*, she thought. *I'm not sure I can take any more waiting*.

She could feel the mounting tension before they reached the field. Of course, there was *always* tension, that was part of the Trials, but this kind had a sour, unpleasant taste. The sideshows were still going on but ordinary folk were leaving, spooked by sensations they couldn't put their finger on which nevertheless had them under their thumb. As for the witches themselves, they had that look worn by actors about two minutes from the end of a horror movie, when they know the monster is about to make its final leap and now it's only a matter of which door.

Letice was surrounded by witches. Nanny could hear raised voices. She nudged another witch, who was watching gloomily.

"What's happening, Winnie?"

"Oh, Reena Trump made a pig's ear of her piece and her friends say she ought to have another go because she was so nervous."

"That's a shame."

"And Virago Johnson ran off 'cos her weather spell went wrong."

"Left under a bit of a cloud, did she?"

"And I was all thumbs when I had a go. You could be in with a chance, Gytha."

"Oh, I've never been one for prizes, Winnie, you know me. It's the fun of taking part that counts."

The other witch gave her a skewed look.

"You almost made that sound believable," she said.

Gammer Beavis hurried over. "On you go, Gytha," she said. "Do your best, eh? The only contender so far is Mrs. Weavitt and her whistling frog, and it wasn't as if it could even carry a tune. Poor thing was a bundle of nerves."

Nanny Ogg shrugged, and walked out into the roped-off area. Somewhere in the distance someone was having hysterics, punctuated by an occasional worried whistle.

Unlike the magic of wizards, the magic of witches did not usually involve the application of much raw power. The difference is between hammers and levers. Witches generally tried to find the small point where a little changes made a lot of result. To make an avalanche you can either shake the mountain, or maybe you can just find exactly the right place to drop a snowflake.

This year Nanny had been idly working on the Man of Straw. It was an ideal trick for her. It got a laugh, it was a bit suggestive, it was a lot easier than it looked but showed she was joining in, and it was unlikely to win.

Damn! She'd been relying on that frog to beat her. She'd heard it whistling quite beautifully on the summer evenings.

She concentrated.

Pieces of straw rustled through the stubble. All she had to do was use the little bits of wind that drifted across the field, allowed to move *here* and *here*, spiral up and—

She tried to stop her hands from shaking. She'd done this a hundred times, she could tie the damn stuff in *knots* by now. She kept seeing the face of Esme Weatherwax, and the way she'd just sat there, looking puzzled and hurt, while for a few seconds Nanny had been ready to kill—

For a moment she managed to get the legs right, and a suggestion of arms and head. There was a smattering of applause from the watchers. Then an errant eddy caught the thing before she could concentrate on its first step, and it spun down, just a lot of useless straw.

She made some frantic gestures to get it to rise again. It flopped about, tangled itself, and lay still.

There was a bit more applause, nervous and sporadic.

"Sorry . . . don't seem to be able to get the hang of it today," she muttered, walking off the field.

The judges went into a huddle.

"I reckon that frog did *really well*," said Nanny, more loudly than was necessary.

The wind, so contrary a little while ago, blew sharper now. What might be called the psychic darkness of the event was being enhanced by real twilight.

The shadow of the bonfire loomed on the far side of the field. No one as yet had the heart to light it. Almost all of the non-witches had gone home. Anything good about the day had long drained away.

The circle of judges broke up and Mrs. Earwig advanced on the nervous crowd, her smile only slightly waxen at the corners.

"Well, *what* a difficult decision it has been," she said brightly. "But what a marvelous turnout, too! It really *has* been a *most* tricky choice—"

Between me and a frog that lost its whistle and got its foot stuck in its banjo, thought Nanny. She looked sidelong at the faces of her sister witches. She'd known some of them for sixty years. If she'd ever read books, she'd have been able to read the faces just like one.

"We all know who won, Mrs. Earwig," she said, interrupting the flow.

"What *do* you mean, Mrs. Ogg?"

"There's not a witch here who could get her mind right today," said Nanny. "And most of 'em have bought lucky charms, too. Witches? Buying lucky charms?" Several women stared at the ground.

"I don't know why everyone seems so afraid of Miss Weatherwax! I certainly am not! You think she's put a spell on you, then?"

"A pretty sharp one, by the feel of it," said Nanny. "Look, Mrs. Earwig, no one's won, not with the stuff we've managed today. We all know it. So let's just all go home, eh?"

"Certainly not! I paid ten dollars for this cup and I mean to present it—"

The dying leaves shivered on the trees.

The witches drew together.

Branches rattled.

"It's the *wind*," said Nanny Ogg. "That's all . . ."

And then Granny was simply *there*. It was as if they'd just not noticed that she'd been there all the time. She had the knack of fading out of the foreground.

"I jus' thought I'd come to see who won," she said. "Join in the applause, and so on . . ."

Letice advanced on her, wild with rage.

"Have you been getting into people's heads?" she shrieked.

"An' how could I do that, Mrs. Earwig?" said Granny meekly. "Past all them lucky charms?"

"You're lying!"

Nanny Ogg heard the indrawn breaths, and hers was loudest. Witches lived by their words.

"I don't lie, Mrs. Earwig."

"Do you *deny* that you set out to ruin my day?"

Some of the witches at the edge of the crowd started to back away.

"I'll grant my jam ain't to everyone's taste but I never—" Granny began, in a modest little tone.

"You've been putting a 'fluence on everyone!"

"—I just set out to help, you can ask anyone—"

"You did! Admit it!" Mrs. Earwig's voice was as shrill as a gull's.

"—and I certainly didn't do any—"

Granny's head turned as the slap came.

For the moment no one breathed, no one moved.

She lifted a hand slowly and rubbed her cheek.

"You know you could have done it easily!"

It seemed to Nanny that Letice's scream echoed off the mountains.

The cup dropped from her hands and crunched on the stubble.

Then the tableau unfroze. A couple of her sister witches stepped forward, put their hands on Letice's shoulders, and she was pulled, gently and unprotesting, away.

Everyone else waited to see what Granny Weatherwax would do. She raised her head.

"I hope Mrs. Earwig is all right," she said. "She seemed a bit . . . distraught."

There was silence. Nanny picked up the abandoned cup and tapped it with a forefinger.

"Hmm," she said. "Just plated, I reckon. If she paid ten dollars for it, the poor woman was robbed." She tossed it to Gammer Beavis, who fumbled it out of the air. "Can you give it back to her tomorrow, Gammer?"

Gammer nodded, trying not to catch Granny's eye.

"Still, we don't have to let it spoil everything," Granny said pleasantly. "Let's have the proper ending to the day, eh? Traditional, like. Roast potatoes and marshmallows and old stories round the fire. And forgiveness. And let's let bygones be bygones."

Nanny could feel the sudden relief spreading out like a fan. The witches seemed to come alive, at the breaking of the spell that had never actually been there in the first place. There was a general straightening up and the beginnings of a bustle as they headed for the saddlebags on their broomsticks.

"Mr. Hopcroft gave me a whole sack of spuds," said Nanny, as conversation rose around them. "I'll go and drag 'em over. Can you get the fire lit, Esme?"

A sudden change in the air made her look up. Granny's eyes gleamed in the dusk.

Nanny knew enough to fling herself to the ground.

Granny Weatherwax's hand curved through the air like a comet and the spark flew out, crackling.

The bonfire exploded. A blue-white flame shot up through the stacked branches and danced into the sky, etching shadows on the forest. It blew off hats and overturned tables and formed figures and castles and scenes from famous battles and joined hands and danced in a ring. It left a purple image on the eye that burned into the brain—

And settled down, and was just a bonfire.

"I never said nothin' about *forgettin'*," said Granny.

When Granny Weatherwax and Nanny Ogg walked home through the dawn, their boots kicked up the mist. It had, on the whole, been a good night.

After some while, Nanny said, "That wasn't nice, what you done."

"I done nothin'."

"Yeah, well . . . it wasn't nice, what you didn't do. It was like pullin' away someone's chair when they're expecting to sit down . . ."

"People who don't look where they're sitting should stay stood up," said Granny.

There was a brief pattering on the leaves, one of those very brief showers you get when a few raindrops don't want to bond with the group.

"Well, all right," Nanny conceded. "But it was a little bit cruel."

"Right," said Granny.

"And some people might think it was a little bit nasty."

"Right."

Nanny shivered. The thoughts that'd gone through her head in those few seconds after Pewsey had screamed—

"I gave you no cause," said Granny. "I put *nothin'* in anyone's head that weren't there already."

"Sorry, Esme."

"Right."

"But . . . Letice didn't *mean* to be cruel, Esme. I mean, she's spiteful and bossy and silly, but—"

"You've known me since we was girls, right?" Granny interrupted. "Through thick and thin, good and bad?"

"Yes, of course, but—"

"And you never sank to sayin' 'I'm telling you this as a friend,' did you?"

Nanny shook her head. It was a telling point. No one even remotely friendly would say a thing like that.

"What's empowerin' about witchcraft anyway?" said Granny. "It's a daft sort of a word."

"Search me," said Nanny. "I *did* start out in witchcraft to get boys, to tell you the truth."

"Think I don't know that?"

"What did you start out to get, Esme?"

Granny stopped, and looked up at the frosty sky and then down at the ground.

"Dunno," she said, at last. "Even, I suppose."

And that, Nanny thought, was that.

Deer bounded away as they arrived at Granny's cottage.

There was a stack of firewood piled up neatly by the back door, and a couple of sacks on the doorstep. One contained a large cheese.

"Looks like Mr. Hopcroft and Mr. Poorchick have been here," said Nanny.

"Hmph." Granny looked at the carefully yet badly written piece of paper attached to the second sack: " 'Dear Mis*f*tres*f* Weatherwax, I

woud be moſt grateful if you woud let me name thiſ new champi-
onſhip Variety "Eſme Weatherwax." Yours in hopefully good health,
Percy Hopcroft.' Well, well, *well*. I wonder what gave him that idea?"

"Can't imagine," said Nanny.

"I would just bet you can't," said Granny.

She sniffed suspiciously, tugged at the sack's string, and pulled out
an Esme Weatherwax.

It was rounded, very slightly flattened, and pointy at one end. It was
an onion.

Nanny Ogg swallowed. "I *told* him not—"

"I'm sorry?"

"Oh . . . nothing . . ."

Granny Weatherwax turned the onion round and round, while the
world, via the medium of Nanny Ogg, awaited its fate. Then she
seemed to reach a decision she was comfortable with.

"A very useful vegetable, the onion," she said, at last. "Firm.
Sharp."

"Good for the system," said Nanny.

"Keeps well. Adds flavor."

"Hot and spicy," said Nanny, losing track of the metaphor in the
flood of relief. "Nice with cheese—"

"We don't need to go that far," said Granny Weatherwax, putting
it carefully back in the sack. She sounded almost amicable. "You
comin' in for a cup of tea, Gytha?"

"Er . . . I'd be getting along—"

"Fair enough."

Granny started to close the door, and then stopped and opened it
again. Nanny could see one blue eye watching her through the crack.

"I was *right* though, wasn't I," said Granny. It wasn't a question.
Nanny nodded.

"Right," she said.

"That's nice."

The Sword of Truth

—

TERRY GOODKIND

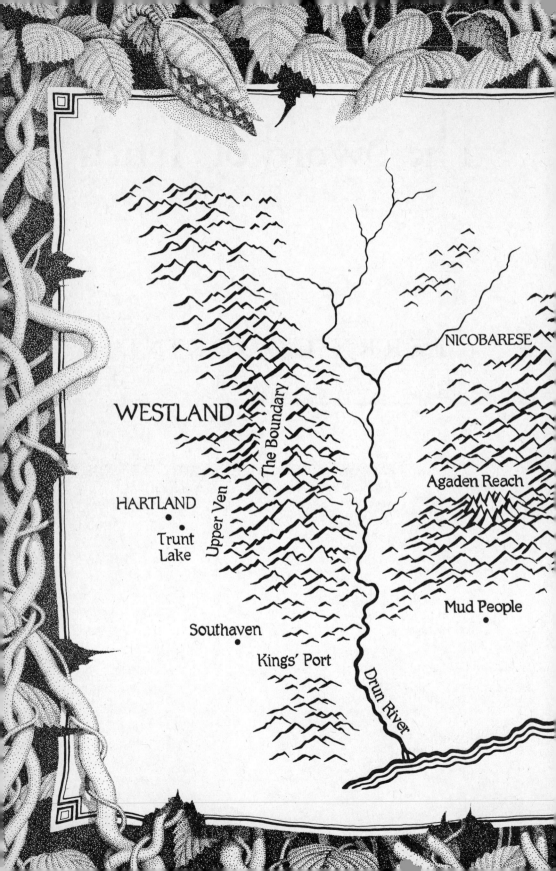

WESTLAND

NICOBARESE

HARTLAND

Trunt
Lake

Upper Ven

The Boundary

Agaden Reach

Mud People

Southaven

Kings' Port

Drun River

WIZARD'S FIRST RULE (1994)
STONE OF TEARS (1995)
BLOOD OF THE FOLD (1996)
TEMPLE OF THE WINDS (1997)

Terry Goodkind burst onto the fantasy scene in 1994 with the publication of *Wizard's First Rule*, which tells the story of Richard Cypher, a young man who learns that he is the key to defeating the evil sorcerer Darken Rahl, who threatens to subjugate all lands and peoples. Three succeeding novels in the series have brought Goodkind to the best-seller lists.

Little does Richard know when he happens across Kahlan, an alluring but secretive woman being chased by four assassins, that his life as a woods guide is about to be forever altered. Richard, a man with his own troubling secrets, helps Kahlan find the wizard she seeks but, as the boundary between the lands begins to fail, discovers himself caught up not only in a strange new world, but in Kahlan's quest for a way to stop Darken Rahl, the charismatic and cunning leader of the far-off land of D'Hara. Darken Rahl has launched a war of arms as well as persuasion against the people of the Midlands as he searches for the power to control them entirely. Richard and Kahlan are running out of time to find the repository of this power before Darken Rahl can impose a merciless fate on them. Richard, who comes to care deeply for Kahlan, must confront timeless lessons about the encroachment of evil on an unsuspecting world. The series becomes an inner quest as much as it is a struggle for destiny and freedom. In the course of obtaining the essential weapon—the Sword of Truth—he learns that the stakes are higher than simple life and death, and that the dividing line between moral choices and evil ones is often shrouded by apathy, ignorance, and greed.

In *Stone of Tears*, Richard strives to master the magic power that is his birthright, but finds that the effort of wielding such magic threatens his life. To save him, Kahlan, in desperation, sends him away with the Sisters of the Light. The Sisters, who promise to teach him to control his power, spirit him away beyond the Valley of the Lost to the Palace of the Prophets in the Old World. Kahlan undertakes an arduous journey to find their friend and mentor, Zedd, the First Wizard. Along the way she discovers the people of a city that has been attacked by the Imperial Order, and must forge an army of young recruits into a force that will not only stop this new threat to the Midlands but will extract vengeance. Richard's teachers turn out to include some who are sworn to the Keeper of the Underworld and intend to use Richard to free their master. Richard has already unwittingly helped them by using his gift, which tore the veil that separates the realm of the dead from the world of the living. Richard's only hope to save everyone is to find the Stone of Tears, but to do that, he must escape his imprisonment at the Palace of the Prophets. And to have any hope of escape, he must learn to use his gift before the Sisters of the Dark, who would destroy him, can turn him to their purposes.

In *Blood of the Fold*, the third novel, the emperor of the Imperial Order in the Old World lusts to conquer the Midlands. To that end, he tries to use an army of anti-magic zealots to purge the Midlands of those born with the gift of magic. The emperor, a dream-walker with magic of his own, captures the Sisters of the Dark and uses them against Richard and Kahlan, while the people who call themselves the Blood of the Fold plot their own conquest of the Midlands. Unless Richard can seize power and mold the fragmented Midlands into one, the Imperial Order will sweep across the land, shadowing the Midlands in an age of slavery, and freedom's last flames will die forever.

In *Temple of the Winds*, Emperor Jagang sends an assassin to kill Richard, and in the process unleashes a deadly plague. The conflagration of disease claims more people with each passing day as Richard and Kahlan desperately search for a cure. Trust and love are tested in a twisting trail of devotion and betrayal. With hundreds and then thousands of their people perishing each day, Richard and Kahlan must find the Temple of the Winds, and then decide if they will pay the terrible price required to enter.

The present story takes place a number of years prior to the events of *Wizard's First Rule*.

Debt of Bones

TERRY GOODKIND

"What do you got in the sack, dearie?"

Abby was watching a distant flock of whistling swans, graceful white specks against the dark soaring walls of the Keep, as they made their interminable journey past ramparts, bastions, towers, and bridges lit by the low sun. The sinister specter of the Keep had seemed to be staring back the whole of the day as Abby had waited. She turned to the hunched old woman in front of her.

"I'm sorry, did you ask me something?"

"I asked what you got in your sack." As the woman peered up, she licked the tip of her tongue through the slot where a tooth was missing. "Something precious?"

Abby clutched the burlap sack to herself as she shrank a little from the grinning woman. "Just some of my things, that's all."

An officer, trailed by a troop of assistants, aides, and guards, marched out from under the massive portcullis that loomed nearby. Abby and the rest of the supplicants waiting at the head of the stone bridge moved tighter to the side, even though the soldiers had ample room to pass. The officer, his grim gaze unseeing as he swept by, didn't return the salute as the bridge guards clapped fists to the armor over their hearts.

All day soldiers from different lands, as well as the Home Guard from the vast city of Aydindril below, had been coming and going from

the Keep. Some had looked travel-sore. Some wore uniforms still filthy with dirt, soot, and blood from recent battles. Abby had even seen two officers from her homeland of Pendisan Reach. They had looked to her to be little more than boys, but boys with the thin veneer of youth shedding too soon, like a snake casting off its skin before its time, leaving the emerging maturity scarred.

Abby had also seen such an array of important people as she could scarcely believe: sorceresses, councilors, and even a Confessor had come up from the Confessor's Palace down in the city. On her way up to the Keep, there was rarely a turn in the winding road that hadn't offered Abby a view of the sprawling splendor in white stone that was the Confessor's Palace. The alliance of the Midlands, headed by the Mother Confessor herself, held council in the palace, and there, too, lived the Confessors.

In her whole life, Abby had seen a Confessor only once before. The woman had come to see Abby's mother and Abby, not ten years at the time, had been unable to keep from staring at the Confessor's long hair. Other than her mother, no woman in Abby's small town of Coney Crossing was sufficiently important to have hair long enough to touch the shoulders. Abby's own fine, dark brown hair covered her ears but no more.

Coming through the city on the way to the Keep, it had been hard for her not to gape at noblewomen with hair to their shoulders and even a little beyond. But the Confessor going up to the Keep, dressed in the simple, satiny black dress of a Confessor, had hair that reached halfway down her back.

She wished she could have had a better look at the rare sight of such long luxuriant hair and the woman important enough to possess it, but Abby had gone to a knee with the rest of the company at the bridge, and like the rest of them feared to raise her bowed head to look up lest she meet the gaze of the other. It was said that to meet the gaze of a Confessor could cost you your mind if you were lucky, and your soul if you weren't. Even though Abby's mother had said that it was untrue, that only the deliberate touch of such a woman could effect such a thing, Abby feared, this day of all days, to test the stories.

The old woman in front of her, clothed in layered skirts topped with one dyed with henna, and mantled with a dark draping shawl, watched the soldiers pass and then leaned closer. "Do better to bring a bone, dearie. I hear that there be those in the city who will sell a bone such as you need—for the right price. Wizards don't take no salt pork for a need. They got salt pork." She glanced past Abby to the others to see them occupied with their own interests. "Better to sell your things and hope you have enough to buy a bone. Wizards don't want what some country girl brung 'em. Favors from wizards don't come easy." She glanced to the backs of the soldiers as they reached the far side of the bridge. "Not even for those doing their bidding, it would seem."

"I just want to talk to them. That's all."

"Salt pork won't get you a talk, neither, as I hear tell." She eyed Abby's hand trying to cover the smooth round shape beneath the burlap. "Or a jug you made. That what it is, dearie?" Her brown eyes, set in a wrinkled leathery mask, turned up, peering with sudden, humorless intent. "A jug?"

"Yes," Abby said. "A jug I made."

The woman smiled her skepticism and fingered a lick of short gray hair back under her wool head wrap. Her gnarled fingers closed around the smocking on the forearm of Abby's crimson dress, pulling the arm up a bit to have a look.

"Maybe you could get the price of a proper bone for your bracelet."

Abby glanced down at the bracelet made of two wires twisted together in interlocking circles. "My mother gave me this. It has no value but to me."

A slow smile came to the woman's weather-cracked lips. "The spirits believe that there is no stronger power than a mother's want to protect her child."

Abby gently pulled her arm away. "The spirits know the truth of that."

Uncomfortable under the scrutiny of the suddenly talkative woman, Abby searched for a safe place to settle her gaze. It made her dizzy to look down into the yawning chasm beneath the bridge, and she was weary of watching the Wizard's Keep, so she pretended that her attention had been caught as an excuse to turn back toward the collection of people, mostly men, waiting with her at the head of the bridge. She busied herself with nibbling on the last crust of bread from the loaf she had bought down in the market before coming up to the Keep.

Abby felt awkward talking to strangers. In her whole life she had never seen so many people, much less people she didn't know. She knew every person in Coney Crossing. The city made her apprehensive, but not as apprehensive as the Keep towering on the mountain above it, and that not as much as her reason for being there.

She just wanted to go home. But there would be no home, at least nothing to go home to, if she didn't do this.

All eyes turned up at the rattle of hooves coming out under the portcullis. Huge horses, all dusky brown or black and bigger than any Abby had ever seen, came thundering toward them. Men bedecked with polished breastplates, chain mail, and leather, and most carrying lances or poles topped with long flags of high office and rank, urged their mounts onward. They raised dust and gravel as they gathered speed crossing the bridge, in a wild rush of color and sparkles of light from metal flashing past. Sandarian lancers, from the descriptions Abby had heard. She had trouble imagining the enemy with the nerve to go up against men such as these.

Her stomach roiled. She realized she had no need to imagine, and no reason to put her hope in brave men such as those lancers. Her only hope was the wizard, and that hope was slipping away as she stood waiting. There was nothing for it but to wait.

Abby turned back to the Keep just in time to see a statuesque woman in simple robes stride out through the opening in the massive stone wall. Her fair skin stood out all the more against straight dark hair parted in the middle and readily reaching her shoulders. Some of the men had been whispering about the sight of the Sanderian officers, but at the sight of the woman, everyone fell to silence. The four soldiers at the head of the stone bridge made way for the woman as she approached the supplicants.

"Sorceress," the old woman whispered to Abby.

Abby hardly needed the old woman's counsel to know it was a sorceress. Abby recognized the simple flaxen robes, decorated at the neck with yellow and red beads sewn in the ancient symbols of the profession. Some of her earliest memories were of being held in her mother's arms and touching beads like those she saw now.

The sorceress bowed her head to the people and then offered a smile. "Please forgive us for keeping you waiting out here the whole of the day. It is not from lack of respect or something we customarily do, but with the war on our hands such precautions are regrettably unavoidable. We hope none took offense at the delay."

The crowd mumbled that they didn't. Abby doubted there was one among them bold enough to claim otherwise.

"How goes the war?" a man behind asked.

The sorceress's even gaze turned to him. "With the blessings of the good spirits, it will end soon."

"May the spirits will that D'Hara is crushed," beseeched the man.

Without response, the sorceress appraised the faces watching her, waiting to see if anyone else would speak or ask a question. None did.

"Please, come with me, then. The council meeting has ended, and a couple of the wizards will take the time to see you all."

As the sorceress turned back to the Keep and started out, three men strode up along the supplicants and put themselves at the head of the line, right in front of the old woman. The woman snatched a velvet sleeve.

"Who do you think you are," she snapped, "taking a place before me, when I've been here the whole of the day?"

The oldest of the three, dressed in rich robes of dark purple with contrasting red sewn inside the length of the slits up the sleeves, looked to be a noble with his two advisors, or perhaps guards. He turned a glare on the woman. "You don't mind, do you?"

It didn't sound at all to Abby like a question.

The old woman took her hand back and fell mute.

The man, the ends of his gray hair coiled on his shoulders, glanced at Abby. His hooded eyes gleamed with challenge. She swallowed and remained silent. She didn't have any objection, either, at least none she was willing to voice. For all she knew, the noble was important enough to see to it that she was denied an audience. She couldn't afford to take that chance now that she was this close.

Abby was distracted by a tingling sensation from the bracelet. Blindly, her fingers glided over the wrist of the hand holding the sack. The wire bracelet felt warm. It hadn't done that since her mother had died. In the presence of so much magic as was at a place such as this, it didn't really surprise her. The crowd moved out to follow the sorceress.

"Mean, they are," the woman whispered over her shoulder. "Mean as a winter night, and just as cold."

"Those men?" Abby whispered back.

"No." The woman tilted her head. "Sorceresses. Wizards, too. That's who. All those born with the gift of magic. You better have something important in that sack, or the wizards might turn you to dust for no other reason than that they'd enjoy it."

Abby pulled her sack tight in her arms. The meanest thing her mother had done in the whole of her life was to die before she could see her granddaughter.

Abby swallowed back the urge to cry and prayed to the dear spirits that the old woman was wrong about wizards, and that they were as understanding as sorceresses. She prayed fervently that this wizard would help her. She prayed for forgiveness, too—that the good spirits would understand.

Abby worked at holding a calm countenance even though her insides were in turmoil. She pressed a fist to her stomach. She prayed for strength. Even in this, she prayed for strength.

The sorceress, the three men, the old woman, Abby, and then the rest of the supplicants passed under the huge iron portcullis and onto the Keep grounds. Inside the massive outer wall Abby was surprised to discover the air warm. Outside it had been a chill autumn day, but inside the air was spring-fresh and pleasant.

The road up the mountain, the stone bridge over the chasm, and then the opening under the portcullis appeared to be the only way into the Keep, unless you were a bird. Soaring walls of dark stone with high windows surrounded the gravel courtyard inside. There were a number of doors around the courtyard, and ahead a roadway tunneled deeper into the Keep.

Despite the warmth of the air, Abby was chilled to the bone by the place. She wasn't sure that the old woman wasn't right about wizards. Life in Coney Crossing was far removed from matters of wizards.

Abby had never seen a wizard before, nor did she know anyone who had, except for her mother, and her mother had never spoken of them except to caution that where wizards were concerned, you couldn't trust even what you saw with your own eyes.

The sorceress led them up four granite steps worn smooth over the ages by countless footsteps, through a doorway set back under a lintel of pink-flecked black granite, and into the Keep proper. The sorceress lifted an arm into the darkness, sweeping it to the side. Lamps along the wall sprang to flame.

It had been simple magic—not a very impressive display of the gift—but several of the people behind fell to worried whispering as they passed on through the wide hall. It occurred to Abby that if this little bit of conjuring would frighten them, then they had no business going to see wizards.

They wended their way across the sunken floor of an imposing anteroom the likes of which Abby could never even have imagined. Red marble columns all around supported arches below balconies. In the center of the room a fountain sprayed water high overhead. The water fell back to cascade down through a succession of ever larger scalloped bowls. Officers, sorceresses, and a variety of others sat about on white marble benches or huddled in small groups, all engaged in seemingly earnest conversation masked by the sound of the water.

In a much smaller room beyond, the sorceress gestured for them to be seated at a line of carved oak benches along one wall. Abby was bone-weary and relieved to sit at last.

Light from windows above the benches lit three tapestries hanging on the high far wall. The three together covered nearly the entire wall and made up one scene of a grand procession through a city. Abby had never seen anything like it, but with the way her dreads careered through her thoughts, she could summon little pleasure in seeing even such a majestic tableau.

In the center of the cream-colored marble floor, inset in brass lines, was a circle with a square inside it, its corners touching the circle. Inside the square sat another circle just large enough to touch the insides of the square. The center circle held an eight-pointed star. Lines radiated out from the points of the star, piercing all the way through both circles, every other line bisecting a corner of the square.

The design, called a Grace, was often drawn by those with the gift. The outer circle represented the beginnings of the infinity of the spirit world out beyond. The square represented the boundary separating the spirit world—the underworld, the world of the dead—from the inner circle, which represented the limits of the world of life. In the center of it all was the star, representing the Light—the Creator.

It was a depiction of the continuum of the gift: from the Creator, through life, and at death crossing the boundary to eternity with the spirits in the Keeper's realm of the underworld. But it represented a hope, too—a hope to remain in the Creator's Light from birth, through life, and beyond, in the underworld.

It was said that only the spirits of those who did great wickedness in life would be denied the Creator's Light in the underworld. Abby knew she would be condemned to an eternity with the Keeper of darkness in the underworld. She had no choice.

The sorceress folded her hands. "An aide will come to get you each in turn. A wizard will see each of you. The war burns hot; please keep your petition brief." She gazed down the line of people. "It is out of a sincere obligation to those we serve that the wizards see supplicants, but please try to understand that individual desires are often detrimental to the greater good. By pausing to help one, then many are denied help. Thus, denial of a request is not a denial of your need, but acceptance of greater need. In times of peace it is rare for wizards to grant the narrow wants of supplicants. At a time like this, a time of a great war, it is almost unheard of. Please understand that it has not to do with what we would wish, but is a matter of necessity."

She watched the line of supplicants, but saw none willing to abandon their purpose. Abby certainly would not.

"Very well then. We have two wizards able to take supplicants at this time. We will bring you each to one of them."

The sorceress turned to leave. Abby rose to her feet.

"Please, mistress, a word if I may?"

The sorceress settled an unsettling gaze on Abby. "Speak."

Abby stepped forward. "I must see the First Wizard himself. Wizard Zorander."

One eyebrow arched. "The First Wizard is a very busy man."

Abby reached into her sack and pulled out the neck band from her mother's robes. She stepped into the center of the Grace and kissed the red and yellow beads on the neck band.

"I am Abigail, born of Helsa. On the Grace and my mother's soul, I must see Wizard Zorander. Please. It is no trivial journey I have made. Lives are at stake."

The sorceress watched the beaded band being returned to the sack. "Abigail, born of Helsa." Her gaze rose to meet Abby's. "I will take your words to the First Wizard."

"Mistress." Abby turned to see the old woman on her feet. "I would be well pleased to see the First Wizard, too."

The three men rose up. The oldest, the one apparently in charge of the three, gave the sorceress a look so barren of timidity that it bordered on contempt. His long gray hair fell forward over his velvet robes as he glanced down the line of seated people, seeming to dare them to stand. When none did, he returned his attention to the sorceress.

"I will see Wizard Zorander."

The sorceress appraised those on their feet and then looked down the line of supplicants on the bench. "The First Wizard has earned a name: the wind of death. He is feared no less by many of us than by our enemies. Anyone else who would bait fate?"

None of those on the bench had the courage to gaze into her fierce stare. To the last they all silently shook their heads. "Please wait," she said to those seated. "Someone will shortly be out to take you to a wizard." She looked once more to the five people standing. "Are you all very, very sure of this?"

Abby nodded. The old woman nodded. The noble glared.

"Very well then. Come with me."

The noble and his two men stepped in front of Abby. The old woman seemed content to take a station at the end of the line. They were led deeper into the Keep, through narrow halls and wide corridors, some dark and austere and some of astounding grandeur. Everywhere there were soldiers of the Home Guard, their breastplates or chain mail covered with red tunics banded around their edges in black. All were heavily armed with swords or battle-axes, all had knives, and many additionally carried pikes tipped with winged and barbed steel.

At the top of a broad white marble stairway the stone railings spiraled at the ends to open wide onto a room of warm oak paneling. Several of the raised panels held lamps with polished silver reflectors. Atop a three-legged table sat a double-bowl cut-glass lamp with twin chimneys, their flames adding to the mellow light from the reflector lamps. A thick carpet of ornate blue patterns covered nearly the entire wood floor.

To each side of a double door stood one of the meticulously dressed Home Guard. Both men were equally huge. They looked to be men more than able to handle any trouble that might come up the stairs.

The sorceress nodded toward a dozen thickly tufted leather chairs set in four groups. Abby waited until the others had seated themselves in two of the groupings and then sat by herself in another. She placed the sack in her lap and rested her hands over its contents.

The sorceress stiffened her back. "I will tell the First Wizard that he has supplicants who wish to see him."

A guard opened one of the double doors for her. As she was swallowed into the great room beyond, Abby was able to snatch a quick glimpse. She could see that it was well lighted by glassed skylights. There were other doors in the gray stone of the walls. Before the door closed, Abby was also able to see a number of people, men and women both, all rushing hither and yon.

Abby sat turned away from the old woman and the three men as with one hand she idly stroked the sack in her lap. She had little fear that the men would talk to her, but she didn't want to talk to the woman; it was a distraction. She passed the time going over in her mind what she planned to say to Wizard Zorander.

At least she tried to go over it in her mind. Mostly, all she could think about was what the sorceress had said, that the First Wizard was called the wind of death, not only by the D'Harans, but also by his own people of the Midlands. Abby knew it was no tale to scare off supplicants from a busy man. Abby herself had heard people whisper of their great wizard, "The wind of death." Those whispered words were uttered in dread.

The lands of D'Hara had sound reason to fear this man as their enemy; he had destroyed countless of their troops, from what Abby had heard. Of course, if they hadn't invaded the Midlands, bent on conquest, they would not have felt the hot wind of death.

Had they not invaded, Abby wouldn't be sitting there in the Wizard's Keep—she would be at home, and everyone she loved would be safe.

Abby marked again the odd tingling sensation from the bracelet. She ran her fingers over it, testing its unusual warmth. This close to a person of such power it didn't surprise her that the bracelet was warming. Her mother had told her to wear it always, and that someday it would be of value. Abby didn't know how, and her mother had died without ever explaining.

Sorceresses were known for the way they kept secrets, even from their own daughters. Perhaps if Abby had been born gifted . . .

She sneaked a peek over her shoulder at the others. The old woman was leaning back in her chair, staring at the doors. The noble's attendants sat with their hands folded as they casually eyed the room.

The noble was doing the oddest thing. He had a lock of sandy-colored hair wound around a finger. He stroked his thumb over the lock of hair as he glared at the doors.

Abby wanted the wizard to hurry up and see her, but time stubbornly dragged by. In a way, she wished he would refuse. No, she told herself, that was unacceptable. No matter her fear, no matter her revulsion, she must do this. Abruptly, the door opened. The sorceress strode out toward Abby.

The noble surged to his feet. "I will see him first." His voice was cold threat. "That is not a request."

"It is our right to see him first," Abby said without forethought. When the sorceress folded her hands, Abby decided she had best go on. "I've waited since dawn. This woman was the only one waiting before me. These men came at the last of the day."

Abby started when the old woman's gnarled fingers gripped her forearm. "Why don't we let these men go first, dearie? It matters not who arrived first, but who has the most important business."

Abby wanted to scream that her business was important, but she realized that the old woman might be saving her from serious trouble in accomplishing her business. Reluctantly, she gave the sorceress a nod. As the sorceress led the three men through the door, Abby could feel the old woman's eyes on her back. Abby hugged the sack against the burning anxiety in her abdomen and told herself that it wouldn't be long, and then she would see him.

As they waited, the old woman remained silent, and Abby was glad for that. Occasionally, she glanced at the door, imploring the good spirits to help her. But she realized it was futile; the good spirits wouldn't be disposed to help her in this.

A roar came from the room beyond the doors. It was like the sound of an arrow zipping through the air, or a long switch whipping, but much louder, intensifying rapidly. It ended with a shrill crack accompanied by a flash of light coming under the doors and around their edges. The doors shuddered on their hinges.

Sudden silence rang in Abby's ears. She found herself gripping the arms of the chair.

Both doors opened. The noble's two attendants marched out, followed by the sorceress. The three stopped in the waiting room. Abby sucked a breath.

One of the two men was cradling the noble's head in the crook of an arm. The wan features of the face were frozen in a mute scream. Thick strings of blood dripped onto the carpet.

"Show them out," the sorceress hissed through gritted teeth to one of the two guards at the door.

The guard dipped his pike toward the stairs, ordering them ahead, and then followed the two men down. Crimson drops splattered onto the white marble of the steps as they descended. Abby sat in stiff, wide-eyed shock.

The sorceress wheeled back to Abby and the old woman.

The woman rose to her feet. "I believe that I would rather not bother the First Wizard today. I will return another day, if need be."

She hunched lower toward Abby. "I am called Mariska." Her brow drew down. "May the good spirits grant that you succeed."

She shuffled to the stairs, rested a hand on the marble railing, and started down. The sorceress snapped her fingers and gestured. The remaining guard rushed to accompany the woman, as the sorceress turned back to Abby.

"The First Wizard will see you now."

Abby gulped air, trying to get her breath as she lurched to her feet.

"What happened? Why did the First Wizard do that?"

"The man was sent on behalf of another to ask a question of the First Wizard. The First Wizard gave his answer."

Abby clutched her sack to herself for dear life as she gaped at the blood on the floor. "Might that be the answer to my question, if I ask it?"

"I don't know the question you would ask." For the first time, the sorceress's expression softened just a bit. "Would you like me to see you out? You could see another wizard or, perhaps, after you've given more thought to your petition, return another day, if you still wish it."

Abby fought back tears of desperation. There was no choice. She shook her head. "I must see him."

The sorceress let out a deep breath. "Very well." She put a hand under Abby's arm as if to keep her on her feet. "The First Wizard will see you now."

Abby hugged the contents of her sack as she was led into the chamber where waited the First Wizard. Torches in iron sconces were not yet burning. The late-afternoon light from the glassed roof windows was still strong enough to illuminate the room. It smelled of pitch, lamp oil, roasted meat, wet stone, and stale sweat.

Inside, confusion and commotion reigned. There were people everywhere, and they all seemed to be talking at once. Stout tables set about the room in no discernible pattern were covered with books, scrolls, maps, chalk, unlit oil lamps, burning candles, partially eaten meals, sealing wax, pens, and a clutter of every sort of odd object, from balls of knotted string to half-spilled sacks of sand. People stood about the tables, engaged in conversations or arguments, as others tapped passages in books, pored over scrolls, or moved little painted weights about on maps. Others rolled slices of roasted meat plucked from platters and nibbled as they watched or offered opinions between swallows.

The sorceress, still holding Abby under her arm, leaned closer as they proceeded. "You will have the First Wizard's divided attention. There will be other people talking to him at the same time. Don't be distracted. He will be listening to you as he also listens to or talks to others. Just ignore the others who are speaking and ask what you have come to ask. He will hear you."

Abby was dumbfounded. "While he's talking to other people?"

"Yes." Abby felt the hand squeeze her arm ever so slightly. "Try to be calm, and not to judge by what has come before you."

The killing. That was what she meant. That a man had come to speak to the First Wizard, and he had been killed for it. She was simply supposed to put that from her thoughts? When she glanced down, she saw that she was walking through a trail of blood. She didn't see the headless body anywhere.

Her bracelet tingled and she looked down at it. The hand under her arm halted her. When Abby looked up, she saw a confusing knot of people before her. Some rushed in from the sides as others rushed away. Some flailed their arms as they spoke with great conviction. So many were talking that Abby could scarcely understand a word of it. At the same time, others were leaning in, nearly whispering. She felt as if she were confronting a human beehive.

Abby's attention was snagged by a form in white to the side. The instant she saw the long fall of hair and the violet eyes looking right at her, Abby went rigid. A small cry escaped her throat as she fell to her knees and bowed over until her back protested. She trembled and shuddered, fearing the worst.

In the instant before she dropped to her knees, she had seen that the elegant, satiny white dress was cut square at the neck, the same as the black dresses had been. The long flag of hair was unmistakable. Abby had never seen the woman before, but without doubt knew who she was. There could be no mistaking this woman. Only one of them wore the white dress.

It was the Mother Confessor herself.

She heard muttering above her, but feared to listen, lest it was death being summoned.

"Rise, my child," came a clear voice.

Abby recognized it as the formal response of the Mother Confessor to one of her people. It took a moment for Abby to realize that it represented no threat, but simple acknowledgment. She stared at a smear of blood on the floor as she debated what to do next. Her mother had never instructed her as to how to conduct herself should she ever meet the Mother Confessor. As far as she knew, no one from Coney Crossing had ever seen the Mother Confessor, much less met her. Then again, none of them had ever seen a wizard, either.

Overhead, the sorceress whispered a growl. "Rise."

Abby scrambled to her feet, but kept her eyes to the floor, even though the smear of blood was making her sick. She could smell it, like a fresh butchering of one of their animals. From the long trail, it looked as if the body had been dragged away to one of the doors in the back of the room.

The sorceress spoke calmly into the chaos. "Wizard Zorander, this is Abigail, born of Helsa. She wishes a word with you. Abigail, this is First Wizard Zeddicus Zu'l Zorander."

Abby dared to cautiously lift her gaze. Hazel eyes gazed back.

To each side before her were knots of people: big, forbidding officers—some of them looked as if they might be generals; several old men in robes, some simple and some ornate; several middle-aged men, some in robes and some in livery; three women—sorceresses all; a variety of other men and women; and the Mother Confessor.

The man at the center of the turmoil, the man with the hazel eyes, was not what Abby had been expecting. She had expected some grizzled, gruff old man. This man was young—perhaps as young as she. Lean but sinewy, he wore the simplest of robes, hardly better made than Abby's burlap sack—the mark of his high office.

Abby had not anticipated this sort of man in such an office as that of First Wizard. She remembered what her mother had told her—not to trust what your eyes told you where wizards were concerned.

All about, people spoke to him, argued at him, a few even shouted, but the wizard was silent as he looked into her eyes. His face was pleasing enough to look upon, gentle in appearance, even though his wavy brown hair looked ungovernable, but his eyes . . . Abby had never seen the likes of those eyes. They seemed to see all, to know all, to understand all. At the same time they were bloodshot and weary-looking, as if sleep eluded him. They had, too, the slightest glaze of distress. Even so, he was calm at the center of the storm. For that moment that his attention was on her, it was as if no one else were in the room.

The lock of hair Abby had seen around the noble's finger was now held wrapped around the First Wizard's finger. He brushed it to his lips before lowering his arm.

"I am told you are the daughter of a sorceress." His voice was placid water flowing through the tumult raging all about. "Are you gifted, child?"

"No, sir . . ."

Even as she answered, he was turning to another who had just finished speaking. "I told you, if you do, we chance losing them. Send word that I want him to cut south."

The tall officer to whom the wizard spoke threw his hands up. "But he said they've reliable scouting information that the D'Harans went east on him."

"That's not the point," the wizard said. "I want that pass to the south sealed. That's where their main force went; they have gifted among them. They are the ones we must kill."

The tall officer was saluting with a fist to his heart as the wizard turned to an old sorceress. "Yes, that's right, three invocations before attempting the transposition. I found the reference last night."

The old sorceress departed to be replaced by a man jabbering in a foreign tongue as he opened a scroll and held it up for the wizard to see. The wizard squinted toward it, reading a moment before waving the man away, while giving orders in the same foreign language.

The wizard turned to Abby. "You're a skip?"

Abby felt her face heat and her ears burn. "Yes, Wizard Zorander."

"Nothing to be ashamed of, child," he said while the Mother Confessor herself was whispering confidentially in his ear.

But it *was* something to be ashamed of. The gift hadn't passed on to her from her mother—it had skipped her.

The people of Coney Crossing had depended on Abby's mother. She helped with those who were ill or hurt. She advised people on matters of community and those of family. For some she arranged marriages. For some she meted out discipline. For some she bestowed favors available only through magic. She was a sorceress; she protected the people of Coney Crossing.

She was revered openly. By some, she was feared and loathed privately.

She was revered for the good she did for the people of Coney Crossing. By some, she had been feared and loathed because she had the gift—because she wielded magic. Others wanted nothing so much as to live their lives without any magic about.

Abby had no magic and couldn't help with illness or injury or shapeless fears. She dearly wished she could, but she couldn't. When Abby had asked her mother why she would abide all the thankless resentment, her mother told her that helping was its own reward and you should not expect gratitude for it. She said that if you went through life expecting gratitude for the help you provided, you might end up leading a miserable life.

When her mother was alive, Abby had been shunned in subtle ways; after her mother died, the shunning became more overt. It had been expected by the people of Coney Crossing that she would serve as her mother had served. People didn't understand about the gift, how it often wasn't passed on to an offspring; instead they thought Abby selfish.

The wizard was explaining something to a sorceress about the casting of a spell. When he finished, his gaze swept past Abby on its way to someone else. She needed his help, now.

"What is it you wanted to ask me, Abigail?"

Abby's fingers tightened on the sack. "It's about my home of Coney Crossing." She paused while the wizard pointed in a book being held out to him. He rolled his hand at her, gesturing for her to go on as a man was explaining an intricacy to do with inverting a duplex spell. "There's terrible trouble there," Abby said. "D'Haran troops came through the Crossing . . ."

The First Wizard turned to an older man with a long white beard. By his simple robes, Abby guessed him to be a wizard, too.

"I'm telling you, Thomas, it can be done," Wizard Zorander insisted. "I'm not saying I agree with the council, I'm just telling you what I found and their unanimous decision that it be done. I'm not claiming to understand the details of just how it works, but I've studied it; it can be done. As I told the council, I can activate it. I have yet to decide if I agree with them that I should."

The man, Thomas, wiped a hand across his face. "You mean what I heard is true, then? That you really do think it's possible? Are you out of your mind, Zorander?"

"I found it in a book in the First Wizard's private enclave. A book from before the war with the Old World. I've seen it with my own eyes. I've cast a whole series of verification webs to test it." He turned his attention to Abby. "Yes, that would be Anargo's legion. Coney Crossing is in Pendisan Reach."

"That's right," Abby said. "And so then this D'Haran army swept through there and—"

"Pendisan Reach refused to join with the rest of the Midlands under central command to resist the invasion from D'Hara. Standing by their sovereignty, they chose to fight the enemy in their own way. They have to live with the consequences of their actions."

The old man was tugging on his beard. "Still, do you know if it's real? All proven out? I mean, that book would have to be thousands of years old. It might have been conjecture. Verification webs don't always confirm the entire structure of such a thing."

"I know that as well as you, Thomas, but I'm telling you, it's real," Wizard Zorander said. His voice lowered to a whisper. "The spirits preserve us, it's genuine."

Abby's heart was pounding. She wanted to tell him her story, but she couldn't seem to get a word in. He had to help her. It was the only way.

An army officer rushed in from one of the back doors. He pushed his way into the crowd around the First Wizard.

"Wizard Zorander! I've just gotten word! When we unleashed the horns you sent, they worked! Urdland's force turned tail!"

Several voices fell silent. Others didn't.

"At least three thousand years old," the First Wizard said to the man with the beard. He put a hand on the newly arrived officer's shoulder and leaned close. "Tell General Brainard to hold short at the Kern River. Don't burn the bridges, but hold them. Tell him to split his men. Leave half to keep Urdland's force from changing their mind; hopefully they won't be able to replace their field wizard. Have Brainard take the rest of his men north to help cut Anargo's escape route; that's where our concern lies, but we may still need the bridges to go after Urdland."

One of the other officers, an older man looking possibly to be a general himself, went red in the face. "Halt at the river? When the horns have done their job, and we have them on the run? But why! We can take them down before they have a chance to regroup and join up with another force to come back at us!"

Hazel eyes turned toward the man. "And do you know what waits over the border? How many men will die if Panis Rahl has something waiting that the horns can't turn away? How many innocent lives has it already cost us? How many of our men will die to bleed them on their own land—land we don't know as they do?"

"And how many of our people will die if we don't eliminate their ability to come back at us another day! We must pursue them. Panis Rahl will never rest. He'll be working to conjure up something else to gut us all in our sleep. We must hunt them down and kill every last one!"

"I'm working on that," the First Wizard said cryptically.

The old man twisted his beard and made a sarcastic face. "Yes, he thinks he can unleash the underworld itself on them."

Several officers, two of the sorceresses, and a couple of the men in robes paused to stare in open disbelief.

The sorceress who had brought Abby to the audience leaned close. "You wanted to talk to the First Wizard. Talk. If you have lost your nerve, then I will see you out."

Abby wet her lips. She didn't know how she could talk into the middle of such a roundabout conversation, but she knew she must, so she just started back in.

"Sir, I don't know anything about what my homeland of Pendisan Reach has done. I know little of the king. I don't know anything about the council, or the war, or any of it. I'm from a small place, and I only know that the people there are in grave trouble. Our defenders were overrun by the enemy. There is an army of Midlands men who drive toward the D'Harans."

She felt foolish talking to a man who was carrying on a half dozen conversations all at once. Mostly, though, she felt anger and frustration. Those people were going to die if she couldn't convince him to help.

"How many D'Harans?" the wizard asked.

Abby opened her mouth, but an officer spoke in her place. "We're not sure how many are left in Anargo's legion. They may be wounded, but they're an enraged wounded bull. Now they're in sight of their homeland. They can only come back at us, or escape us. We've got Sanderson sweeping down from the north and Mardale cutting up from the southwest. Anargo made a mistake going into the Crossing; in there he must fight us or run for home. We have to finish them. This may be our only chance."

The First Wizard drew a finger and thumb down his smooth jaw. "Still, we aren't sure of their numbers. The scouts were dependable, but they never returned. We can only assume they're dead. And why would Anargo do such a thing?"

"Well," the officer said, "it's the shortest escape route back to D'Hara."

The First Wizard turned to a sorceress to answer a question she had just finished. "I can't see how we can afford it. Tell them I said no. I'll not cast that kind of web for them and I'll not give them the means to it for no more offered than a 'maybe.'"

The sorceress nodded before rushing off.

Abby knew that a web was the spell cast by a sorceress. Apparently the spell cast by a wizard was called the same.

"Well, if such a thing is possible," the bearded man was saying, "then I'd like to see your exegesis of the text. A three-thousand-year-old book is a lot of risk. We've no clue as to how the wizards of that time could do most of what they did."

The First Wizard, for the first time, cast a hot glare toward the man. "Thomas, do you want to see exactly what I'm talking about? The spell-form?"

Some of the people had fallen silent at the tone in his voice. The First Wizard threw open his arms, urging everyone back out of his way. The Mother Confessor stayed close behind his left shoulder. The sorceress beside Abby pulled her back a step.

The First Wizard motioned. A man snatched a small sack off the table and handed it to him. Abby noticed that some of the sand on the tables wasn't simply spilled, but had been used to draw symbols. Abby's mother had occasionally drawn spells with sand, but mostly used a variety of other things, from ground bone to dried herbs. Abby's mother used sand for practice; spells, real spells, had to be drawn in proper order and without error.

The First Wizard squatted down and took a handful of sand from the sack. He drew on the floor by letting the sand dribble from the side of his fist.

Wizard Zorander's hand moved with practiced precision. His arm swept around, drawing a circle. He returned for a handful of sand and drew an inner circle. It appeared he was drawing a Grace.

Abby's mother had always drawn the square second; everything in order inward and then the rays back out. Wizard Zorander drew the eight-pointed star inside the smaller circle. He drew the lines radiating outward, through both circles, but left one absent.

He had yet to draw the square, representing the boundary between worlds. He was the First Wizard, so Abby guessed that it wasn't improper to do it in a different order than a sorceress in a little place like Coney Crossing did. But several of the men Abby took as wizards, and the two sorceress behind him, were turning grave glances to one another.

Wizard Zorander laid down the lines of sand for two sides of the square. He scooped up more sand from the sack and began the last two sides.

Instead of a straight line, he drew an arc that dipped well into the edge of the inner circle—the one representing the world of life. The arc, instead of ending at the outer circle, crossed it. He drew the last side, likewise arced, so that it too crossed into the inner circle. He brought the line to meet the other where the ray from the Light was missing. Unlike the other three points of the square, this last point ended outside the larger circle—in the world of the dead.

People gasped. A hush fell over the room for a moment before worried whispers spread among those gifted.

Wizard Zorander rose. "Satisfied, Thomas?"

Thomas's face had gone as white as his beard. "The Creator preserve us." His eyes turned to Wizard Zorander. "The council doesn't truly understand this. It would be madness to unleash it."

Wizard Zorander ignored him and turned toward Abby. "How many D'Harans did you see?"

"Three years past, the locust swarms came. The hills of the Crossing were brown with them. I think I saw more D'Harans than I saw locusts."

Wizard Zorander grunted his discontent. He looked down at the Grace he had drawn. "Panis Rahl won't give up. How long, Thomas? How long until he finds something new to conjure and sends Anargo back on us?" His gaze swept among the people around him. "How many years have we thought we would be annihilated by the invading horde from D'Hara? How many of our people have been killed by Rahl's magic? How many thousands have died of the fevers he sent? How many thousands have blistered and bled to death from the touch of the shadow people he conjured? How many villages, towns, and cities has he wiped from existence?"

When no one spoke, Wizard Zorander went on.

"It has taken us years to come back from the brink. The war has finally turned; the enemy is running. We now have three choices. The first choice is to let him run for home and hope he never comes back to again visit us with his brutality. I think it would only be a matter of time until he tried again. That leaves two realistic options. We can either pursue him into his lair and kill him for good at the cost of tens, perhaps hundreds of thousands of our men—or I can end it."

Those gifted among the crowd cast uneasy glances to the Grace drawn on the floor.

"We still have other magic," another wizard said. "We can use it to the same effect without unleashing such a cataclysm."

"Wizard Zorander is right," another said, "and so is the council. The enemy has earned this fate. We must set it upon them."

The room fell again to arguing. As it did, Wizard Zorander looked into Abby's eyes. It was a clear instruction to finish her supplication.

"My people—the people in Coney Crossing—have been taken by the D'Harans. They have others, too, who they've captured. They have a sorceress holding the captives with a spell. Please, Wizard Zorander, you must help me.

"When I was hiding, I heard the sorceress talking to their officers. The D'Harans plan to use the captives as shields. They will use the captives to blunt the deadly magic you send against them, or to blunt the spears and arrows the Midlands army sends against them. If they decide to turn and attack, they plan to drive the captives ahead. They called it 'dulling the enemies' weapons on their own women and children.' "

No one looked at her. They were all once again engaged in their mass talking and arguing. It was as if the lives of all those people were beneath their consideration.

Tears stung at Abby's eyes. "Either way all those innocent people will die. Please, Wizard Zorander, we must have your help. Otherwise they'll all die."

He looked her way briefly. "There is nothing we can do for them."

Abby panted, trying to hold back the tears. "My father was captured, along with others of my kin. My husband is among the captives. My daughter is among them. She is not yet five. If you send magic, they will be killed. If you attack, they will be killed. You must rescue them, or hold the attack."

He looked genuinely saddened. "I'm sorry. I can't help them. May the good spirits watch over them and take their souls to the Light." He began turning away.

"No!" Abby screamed. Some of the people fell silent. Others only glanced her way as they went on. "My child! You can't!" She thrust a hand into the sack. "I have a bone—"

"Doesn't everyone," he grumbled, cutting her off. "I can't help you."

"But you must!"

"We would have to abandon our cause. We must take the D'Haran force down—one way or another. Innocent though those people are, they are in the way. I can't allow the D'Harans to succeed in such a scheme or it would encourage its widespread use, and then even more innocents would die. The enemy must be shown that it will not deter us from our course."

"NO!" Abby wailed. "She's only a child! You're condemning my baby to death! There are other children! What kind of monster are you?"

No one but the wizard was even listening to her any more as they all went on with their talking.

The First Wizard's voice cut through the din and fell on her ears as clearly as the knell of death. "I am a man who must make choices such as this one. I must deny your petition."

Abby screamed with the agony of failure. She wasn't even to be allowed to show him.

"But it's a debt!" she cried. "A solemn debt!"

"And it cannot be paid now."

Abby screamed hysterically. The sorceress began pulling her away. Abby broke from the woman and ran out of the room. She staggered down the stone steps, unable to see through the tears.

At the bottom of the steps she buckled to the floor in helpless sobbing. He wouldn't help her. He wouldn't help a helpless child. Her daughter was going to die.

Abby, convulsing in sobs, felt a hand on her shoulder. Gentle arms pulled her closer. Tender fingers brushed back her hair as she wept into a woman's lap. Another person's hand touched her back and she felt the warm comfort of magic seeping into her.

"He's killing my daughter," she cried. "I hate him."

"It's all right, Abigail," the voice above said. "It's all right to weep for such a pain as this."

Abby wiped at her eyes, but couldn't stop the tears. The sorceress was there, beside her, at the bottom of the steps.

Abby looked up at the woman in whose arms she lay. It was the Mother Confessor herself. She could do her worst, for all Abby cared. What did it matter, what did any of it matter, now?

"He's a monster," she sobbed. "He is truly named. He is the ill wind of death. This time it's my baby he's killing, not the enemy."

"I understand why you feel that way, Abigail," the Mother Confessor said, "but it is not true."

"How can you say that! My daughter has not yet had a chance to live, and he will kill her! My husband will die. My father, too, but he has had a chance to live a life. My baby hasn't!"

She fell to hysterical wailing again, and the Mother Confessor once again drew her into comforting arms. Comfort was not what Abby wanted.

"You have just the one child?" the sorceress asked.

Abby nodded as she sucked a breath. "I had another, a boy, but he died at birth. The midwife said I will have no more. My little Jana is all I will ever have." The wild agony of it ripped through her. "And he will kill her. Just as he killed that man before me. Wizard Zorander is a monster. May the good spirits strike him dead!"

With a poignant expression, the sorceress smoothed Abby's hair back from her forehead "You don't understand. You see only a part of it. You don't mean what you say."

But she did. "If you had—"

"Delora understands," the Mother Confessor said, gesturing toward the sorceress. "She has a daughter of ten years, and a son, too."

Abby peered up at the sorceress. She gave Abby a sympathetic smile and a nod to confirm the truth of it.

"I, too, have a daughter," the Mother Confessor said. "She is twelve. Delora and I both understand your pain. So does the First Wizard."

Abby's fists tightened. "He couldn't! He's hardly more than a boy himself, and he wants to kill my baby. He is the wind of death and that's all he cares about—killing people!"

The Mother Confessor patted the stone step beside her. "Abigail, sit up here beside me. Let me tell you about the man in there."

Still weeping, Abby pushed herself up and slid onto the step. The Mother Confessor was older by maybe twelve or fourteen years, and pleasant-looking, with those violet eyes. Her mass of long hair reached her waist. She had a warm smile. It had never occurred to Abby to think of a Confessor as a woman, but that was what she saw now. She didn't fear this woman as she had before; nothing she did could be worse than what already had been done.

"I sometimes minded Zeddicus when he was but a toddler and I was still coming into womanhood." The Mother Confessor gazed off with a wistful smile. "I swatted his bottom when he misbehaved, and later twisted his ear to make him sit at a lesson. He was mischief on two legs, driven not by guile but by curiosity. He grew into a fine man.

"For a long time, when the war with D'Hara started, Wizard Zorander wouldn't help us. He didn't want to fight, to hurt people. But in the end, when Panis Rahl, the leader of D'Hara, started using magic to slaughter our people, Zedd knew that the only hope to save more lives in the end was to fight.

"Zeddicus Zu'l Zorander may look young to you, as he did to many of us, but he is a special wizard, born of a wizard and a sorceress. Zedd was a prodigy. Even those other wizards in there, some of them his teachers, don't always understand how he is able to unravel some of the enigmas in the books or how he uses his gift to bring so much power to bear, but we do understand that he has heart. He uses his heart, as well as his head. He was named First Wizard for all these things and more."

"Yes," Abby said, "he is very talented at being the wind of death."

The Mother Confessor smiled a small smile. She tapped her chest. "Among ourselves, those of us who really know him call him the trickster. The trickster is the name he has truly earned. We named him the wind of death for others to hear, so as to strike terror into the hearts of the enemy. Some people on our side take that name to heart. Perhaps, since your mother was gifted, you can understand how people sometimes unreasonably fear those with magic?"

"And sometimes," Abby argued, "those with magic really are monsters who care nothing for the life they destroy."

The Mother Confessor appraised Abby's eyes a moment, and then held up a cautionary finger. "In confidence, I am going to tell you about Zeddicus Zu'l Zorander. If you ever repeat this story, I will never forgive you for betraying my confidence."

"I won't, but I don't see—"

"Just listen."

After Abby remained silent the Mother Confessor began. "Zedd married Erilyn. She was a wonderful woman. We all loved her very much, but not as much as did he. They had a daughter."

Abby's curiosity got the best of her. "How old is she?"

"About the age of your daughter," Delora said.

Abby swallowed. "I see."

"When Zedd became First Wizard, things were grim. Panis Rahl had conjured the shadow people."

"I'm from Coney Crossing. I've never heard of such a thing."

"Well, the war had been bad enough, but then Panis Rahl taught his wizards to conjure shadow people." The Mother Confessor sighed at the anguish of retelling the story. "They are so called because they. are like shadows in the air. They have no precise shape or form. They are not living, but created out of magic. Weapons have no more effect on them than they would have on smoke.

"You can't hide from the shadow people. They drift toward you across fields, or through the woods. They find you.

"When they touch someone, the person's whole body blisters and swells until their flesh splits open. They die in screaming agony. Not even the gift can heal one touched by a shadow person.

"As the enemy attacked, their wizards would send the shadow people out ahead. In the beginning whole battalions of our brave young soldiers were found killed to a man. We saw no hope. It was our darkest hour."

"And Wizard Zorander was able to stop them?" Abby asked.

The Mother Confessor nodded. "He studied the problem and then conjured battle horns. Their magic swept the shadow people away like smoke in the wind. The magic coming from the horns also traced its way back through the spell, to seek out the one who cast it, and kill them. The horns aren't foolproof, though, and Zedd must constantly alter their magic to keep up with the way the enemy changes their conjuring.

"Panis Rahl summoned other magic, too: fevers and sickness, wasting illnesses, fogs that caused blindness—all sorts of horrors. Zedd worked day and night, and managed to counter them all. While Panis Rahl's magic was being checked, our troops were once again able to fight on even terms. Because of Wizard Zorander, the tide of battle turned."

"Well, that much of it is good, but—"

The Mother Confessor again lifted her finger, commanding silence. Abby held her tongue as the woman lowered her hand and went on.

"Panis Rahl was enraged at what Zedd had done. He tried and failed to kill him, so he instead sent a quad to kill Erilyn."

"A quad? What's a quad?"

"A quad," the sorceress answered, "is a unit of four special assassins sent with the protection of a spell from the one who sent them: Panis Rahl. It is their assignment not only to kill the victim, but to make it unimaginably torturous and brutal."

171

Abby swallowed. "And did they . . . murder his wife?"

The Mother Confessor leaned closer. "Worse. They left her, her legs and arms all broken, to be found still alive."

"Alive?" Abby whispered. "Why would they leave her alive, if it was their mission to kill her?"

"So that Zedd would find her all broken and bleeding and in inconceivable agony. She was able only to whisper his name in love." The Mother Confessor leaned even closer. Abby could feel the breath of the woman's whispered words against her own face. "When he used his gift to try to heal her, it activated the worm spell."

Abby had to force herself to blink. "Worm spell . . . ?"

"No wizard would have been able to detect it." The Mother Confessor clawed her fingers and, in front of Abby's stomach, spread her hands outward, in a tearing gesture. "The spell ripped her insides apart. Because he had used his loving touch of magic, she died in screaming pain as he knelt helpless beside her."

Wincing, Abby touched her own stomach, almost feeling the wound. "That's terrible."

The Mother Confessor's violet eyes held an iron look. "The quad also took their daughter. Their daughter, who had seen everything those men had done to her mother."

Abby felt tears burning her eyes again. "They did that to his daughter, too?"

"No," the Mother Confessor said. "They hold her captive."

"Then she still lives? There is still hope?"

The Mother Confessor's satiny white dress rustled softly as she leaned back against the white marble balustrade and nested her hands in her lap. "Zedd went after the quad. He found them, but his daughter had been given to others, and they passed her on to yet others, and so on, so they had no idea who had her, or where she might be."

Abby looked to the sorceress and back to the Mother Confessor. "What did Wizard Zorander do to the quad?"

"No less than I myself would have done." The Mother Confessor stared back through a mask of cold rage. "He made them regret ever being born. For a very long time he made them regret it."

Abby shrank back. "I see."

As the Mother Confessor drew a calming breath, the sorceress took up the story. "As we speak, Wizard Zorander uses a spell that none of us understands; it holds Panis Rahl at his palace in D'Hara. It helps blunt the magic Rahl is able to conjure against us, and enables our men to drive his troops back whence they came.

"But Panis Rahl is consumed with wrath for the man who has thwarted his conquest of the Midlands. Hardly a week passes that an attempt is not made on Wizard Zorander's life. Rahl sends dangerous and vile people of all sort. Even the Mord-Sith."

Abby's breath caught. That was a word she had heard. "What are Mord-Sith?"

The sorceress smoothed back her glossy black hair as she glared with a venomous expression. "Mord-Sith are women who, along with their red leather uniform, wear a single long braid as the mark of their profession. They are trained in the torture and killing of those with the gift. If a gifted person tries to use their magic against a Mord-Sith, she is able to capture their magic and use it against them. There is no escaping a Mord-Sith."

"But surely, a person as strong in the gift as Wizard Zorander—"

"Even he would be lost if he tried to use magic against a Mord-Sith," the Mother Confessor said. "A Mord-Sith can be defeated with common weapons—but not with magic. Only the magic of a Confessor works against them. I have killed two.

"In part because of the brutal nature of the training of Mord-Sith, they have been outlawed for as long as anyone knows, but in D'Hara the ghastly tradition of taking young women to be indoctrinated as Mord-Sith continues to this day. D'Hara is a distant and secretive land. We don't know much about it, except what we have learned through unfortunate experience.

"Mord-Sith have captured several of our wizards and sorceresses. Once captured, they cannot kill themselves, nor can they escape. Before they die, they give over everything they know. Panis Rahl knows of our plans.

"We, in turn, have managed to get our hands on several high-ranking D'Harans, and through the touch of Confessors we know the extent of how we have been compromised. Time works against us."

Abby wiped the palms of her hands on her thighs. "And that man who was killed just before I went in to see the First Wizard, he couldn't have been an assassin; the two with him were allowed to leave."

"No, he was not an assassin." The Mother Confessor folded her hands. "I believe Panis Rahl knows of the spell Wizard Zorander discovered, that it has the potential to obliterate all of D'Hara. Panis Rahl is desperate to rid himself of Wizard Zorander."

The Mother Confessor's violet eyes seemed to glisten with a keen intellect. Abby looked away and picked at a stray thread on her sack. "But I don't see what this has to do with denying me help to save my daughter. He has a daughter. Wouldn't he do anything to get her back? Wouldn't he do whatever he must to have his daughter back and safe?"

The Mother Confessor's head lowered and she stroked her fingers over her brow, as if trying to rub at a grievous ache. "The man who came before you was a messenger. His message had been passed through many hands so that it could not be traced back to its source."

Abby felt cold goose bumps running up her arms. "What was the message?"

"The lock of hair he brought was from Zedd's daughter. Panis Rahl offered the life of Zedd's daughter if Zedd would surrender himself to Panis Rahl to be executed."

Abby clutched a her sack. "But wouldn't a father who loved his daughter do even this to save her life?"

"At what cost?" the Mother Confessor whispered. "At the cost of the lives of all those who will die without his help?

"He couldn't do such a selfish thing, even to save the life of one he loves more than any other. Before he denied your daughter help, he had just refused the offer, thus sentencing his own innocent daughter to death."

Abby felt her hopes again tumbling into blackness. The thought of Jana's terror, of her being hurt, made Abby dizzy and sick. Tears began running down her cheeks again.

"But I'm not asking him to sacrifice everyone else to save her."

The sorceress gently touched Abby's shoulder. "He believes that sparing those people harm would mean letting the D'Harans escape to kill more people in the end."

Abby snatched desperately for a solution. "But I have a bone."

The sorceress sighed. "Abigail, half the people who come to see a wizard bring a bone. Hucksters convince supplicants that they are true bones. Desperate people, just like you, buy them."

"Most of them come seeking a wizard to somehow give them a life free of magic," the Mother Confessor said. "Most people fear magic, but I'm afraid that with the way it's been used by D'Hara, they now want nothing so much as to never again see magic. An ironic reason to buy a bone, and doubly ironic that they buy sham bones, thinking they have magic, in order to petition to be free of magic."

Abby blinked. "But I bought no bone. This is a debt true. On my mother's deathbed she told me of it. She said it was Wizard Zorander himself bound in it."

The sorceress squinted her skepticism. "Abigail, true debts of this nature are exceedingly rare. Perhaps it was a bone she had and you only thought . . ."

Abby held her sack open for the sorceress to see. The sorceress glanced in and fell silent. The Mother Confessor looked in the sack for herself.

"I know what my mother told me," Abby insisted. "She also told me that if there was any doubt, he had but to test it; then he would know it true, for the debt was passed down to him from his father."

The sorceress stroked the beads at her throat. "He could test it. If it is true, he would know. Still, solemn debt though it may be, that doesn't mean that the debt must be paid now."

Abby leaned boldly toward the sorceress. "My mother said it is a debt true, and that it had to be paid. Please, Delora, you know the nature of such things. I was so confused when I met with him, with all those people shouting. I foolishly failed to press my case by asking that he test it." She turned and clutched the Mother Confessor's arm. "Please, help me? Tell him what I have and ask that he test it?"

The Mother Confessor considered behind a blank expression. At last she spoke. "This involves a debt bound in magic. Such a thing must be considered seriously. I will speak to Wizard Zorander on your behalf and request that you be given a private audience."

Abby squeezed her eyes shut as tears sprang anew. "Thank you." She put her face in both hands and began to weep with relief at the flame of hope rekindled.

The Mother Confessor gripped Abby's shoulders. "I said I will try. He may deny my request."

The sorceress snorted a humorless laugh. "Not likely. I will twist his ear, too. But Abigail, that does not mean that we can convince him to help you—bone or no bone."

Abby wiped her cheek. "I understand. Thank you both. Thank you both for understanding."

With a thumb, the sorceress wiped a tear from Abby's chin. "It is said that the daughter of a sorceress is a daughter to all sorceresses."

The Mother Confessor stood and smoothed her white dress. "Delora, perhaps you could take Abigail to a rooming house for women travelers. She should get some rest. Do you have money, child?"

"Yes, Mother Confessor."

"Good. Delora will take you to a room for the night. Return to the Keep just before sunrise. We will meet you and let you know if we were able to convince Zedd to test your bone."

"I will pray to the good spirits that Wizard Zorander will see me and help my daughter," Abby felt sudden shame at her own words. "And I will pray, too, for his daughter."

The Mother Confessor cupped Abby's cheek. "Pray for all of us, child. Pray that Wizard Zorander unleashes the magic against D'Hara, before it is too late for all the children of the Midlands—old and young alike."

On their walk down to the city, Delora kept the conversation from Abby's worries and hopes, and what magic might contribute to either. In some ways, talking with the sorceress was reminiscent of talking with her mother. Sorceresses evaded talk of magic with one not gifted, daughter or not. Abby got the feeling that it was as uncomfortable for them as it had been for Abby when Jana asked how a mother came to have a child in her tummy.

Even though it was late, the streets were teeming with people. Worried gossip of the war floated to Abby's ears from every direction. At one corner a knot of women murmured tearfully of menfolk gone for months with no word of their fate.

Delora took Abby down a market street and had her buy a small loaf of bread with meats and olives baked right inside. Abby wasn't really hungry. The sorceress made her promise that she would eat. Not wanting to do anything to cause disfavor, Abby promised.

The rooming house was up a side street among tightly packed buildings. The racket of the market carried up the narrow street and flittered around buildings and through tiny courtyards with the ease of a chickadee through a dense wood. Abby wondered how people could stand to live so close together and with nothing to see but other houses and people. She wondered, too, how she was going to be able to sleep with all the strange sounds and noise, but then, sleep had rarely come since she had left home, despite the dead-quiet nights in the countryside.

The sorceress bid Abby a good night, putting her in the hands of a sullen-looking woman of few words who led her to a room at the end of a long hall and left her to her night's rest, after collecting a silver coin. Abby sat on the edge of the bed and, by the light of a single lamp sitting on a shelf by the bed, eyed the small room as she nibbled at the loaf of bread. The meat inside was tough and stringy, but had an agreeable flavor, spiced with salt and garlic.

Without a window, the room wasn't as noisy as Abby had feared it might be. The door had no bolt, but the woman who kept the house had said in a mumble for her not to fret, that no men were allowed in the establishment. Abby set the bread aside and, at a basin atop a simple stand two strides across the room, washed her face. She was surprised at how dirty it left the water.

She twisted the lever stem on the lamp, lowering the wick as far as it would go without snuffing the flame; she didn't like sleeping in the dark in a strange place. Lying in bed, staring up at the water-stained ceiling, she prayed earnestly to the good spirits, despite knowing that they would ignore a request such as she made. She closed her eyes and prayed for Wizard Zorander's daughter, too. Her prayers were fragmented by intruding fears that felt as if they clawed her insides raw.

She didn't know how long she had lain in the bed, wishing for sleep to take her, wishing for morning to come, when the door slowly squeaked open. A shadow climbed the far wall.

Abby froze, eyes wide, breath held tight, as she watched a crouched figure move toward the bed. It wasn't the woman of the house. She would be taller. Abby's fingers tightened on the scratchy blanket, thinking that maybe she could throw it over the intruder and then run for the door.

"Don't be alarmed, dearie. I've just come to see if you had success up at the Keep."

Abby gulped air and she sat up in the bed. "Mariska?" It was the old woman who had waited with her in the keep all day. "You frightened the wits out of me!"

The small flame from the lamp reflected in a sharp shimmer in the woman's eye as she surveyed Abby's face. "Worse things to fear than your own safety."

"What do you mean?"

Mariska smiled. It was not a reassuring smile. "Did you get what you wanted?"

"I saw the First Wizard, if that's what you mean."

"And what did he say, dearie?"

Abby swung her feet down off the bed. "That's my business."

The sly smile widened. "Oh, no, dearie, it's our business."

"What do you mean by that?"

"Answer the question. You've not much time left. Your family has not much time left."

Abby shot to her feet. "How do you—"

The old woman seized Abby's wrist and twisted until Abby was forced to sit. "What say the First Wizard?"

"He said he couldn't help me. Please, that hurts. Let me go."

"Oh, dearie, that's too bad, it is. Too bad for your little Jana."

"How . . . how do you know about her? I never—"

"So, Wizard Zorander denied your petition. Such sad news." She clicked her tongue. "Poor, unfortunate, little Jana. You were warned. You knew the price of failure."

She released Abby's wrist and turned away. Abby's mind raced in hot panic as the woman shuffled toward the door.

"No! Please! I'm to see him again, tomorrow. At sunrise."

Mariska peered back over her shoulder. "Why? Why would he agree to see you again, after he has denied you? Lying will buy your daughter no more time. It will buy her nothing."

"It's true. I swear it on my mother's soul. I talked to the sorceress, the one who took us in. I talked to her and the Mother Confessor, after Wizard Zorander denied my petition. They agreed to convince him to give me a private audience."

Her brow bunched. "Why would they do this?"

Abby pointed to her sack sitting on the end of the bed. "I showed them what I brought."

With one gnarled finger, Mariska lifted open the sack. She looked for a moment and then glided closer to Abby.

"You have yet to show this to Wizard Zorander?"

"That's right. They will get me an audience with him. I'm sure of it. Tomorrow, he will see me."

From her bulky waist band, Mariska drew a knife. She waved it slowly back and forth before Abby's face. "We grow weary of waiting for you."

Abby licked her lips. "But I—"

"In the morning I leave for Coney Crossing. I leave to see your frightened little Jana." Her hand slid behind Abby's neck. Fingers like oak roots gripped Abby's hair, holding her head fast. "If you bring him right behind me, she will go free, as you were promised."

Abby couldn't nod. "I will. I swear. I'll convince him. He is bound by a debt."

Mariska put the point of the knife so close to Abby's eye that it brushed her eyelashes. Abby feared to blink.

"Arrive late, and I will stab my knife in little Jana's eye. Stab it through. I will leave her the other so that she can watch as I cut out her father's heart, just so that she will know how much it will hurt when I do her. Do you understand, dearie?"

Abby could only whine that she did, as tears streamed down her cheeks.

"There's a good girl," Mariska whispered from so close that Abby was forced to breathe the spicy stink of the woman's sausage dinner. "If we even suspect any tricks, they will all die."

"No tricks. I'll hurry. I'll bring him."

Mariska kissed Abby's forehead. "You're a good mother." She released Abby's hair. "Jana loves you. She cries for you day and night."

After Mariska closed the door, Abby curled into a trembling ball in the bed and wept against her knuckles.

Delora leaned closer as they marched across the broad rampart. "Are you sure you're all right, Abigail?"

Wind snatched at her hair, flicking it across her face. Brushing it from her eyes, Abby looked out at the sprawl of the city below beginning to coalesce out of the gloom. She had been saying a silent prayer to her mother's spirit.

"Yes. I just had a bad night. I couldn't sleep."

The Mother Confessor's shoulder pressed against Abby's from the other side. "We understand. At least he agreed to see you. Take heart in that. He's a good man, he really is."

"Thank you," Abby whispered in shame. "Thank you both for helping me."

The people waiting along the rampart—wizards, sorceresses, officers, and others—all momentarily fell silent and bowed toward the Mother Confessor as the three women passed. Among several people she recognized from the day before, Abby saw the wizard Thomas, grumbling to himself and looking hugely impatient and vexed as he shuffled through a handful of papers covered in what Abby recognized as magical symbols.

At the end of the rampart they came to the stone face of a round turret. A steep roof overhead protruded down low above a round-topped door. The sorceress rapped on the door and opened it without waiting for a reply. She caught the twitch of Abby's brow.

"He rarely hears the knock," she explained in a hushed tone.

The stone room was small, but had a cozy feel to it. A round window to the right overlooked the city below, and another on the opposite side looked up on soaring walls of the Keep, the distant highest ones glowing pink in the first faint rays of dawn. An elaborate iron candelabrum held a small army of candles that provided a warm glow to the room.

Wizard Zorander, his unruly wavy brown hair hanging down around his face as he leaned on his hands, was absorbed in studying a book lying open on the table. The three women came to a halt.

"Wizard Zorander," the sorceress announced, "we bring Abigail, born of Helsa."

"Bags, woman," the wizard grouched without looking up, "I heard your knock, as I always do."

"Don't you curse at me, Zeddicus Zu'l Zorander," Delora grumbled back.

He ignored the sorceress, rubbing his smooth chin as he considered the book before him. "Welcome, Abigail."

Abby's fingers fumbled at the sack. But then she remembered herself and curtsied. "Thank you for seeing me, Wizard Zorander. It is of vital importance that I have your help. As I've already told you, the lives of innocent children are at stake."

Wizard Zorander finally peered up. After appraising her a long moment he straightened. "Where does the line lie?"

Abby glanced to the sorceress on one side of her and then the Mother Confessor on the other side. Neither looked back.

"Excuse me, Wizard Zorander? The line?"

The wizard's brow drew down. "You imply a higher value to a life because of a young age. The line, my dear child, across which the value of life becomes petty. Where is the line?"

"But a child—"

He held up a cautionary finger. "Do not think to play on my emotions by plying me with the value of the life of a child, as if a higher value can be placed on life because of age. When is life worth less? Where is the line? At what age? Who decides?

"All life is of value. Dead is dead, no matter the age. Don't think to produce a suspension of my reason with a callous, calculated twisting of emotion, like some slippery officeholder stirring the passions of a mindless mob."

Abby was struck speechless by such an admonition. The wizard turned his attention to the Mother Confessor.

"Speaking of bureaucrats, what did the council have to say for themselves?"

The Mother Confessor clasped her hands and sighed. "I told them your words. Simply put, they didn't care. They want it done."

He grunted his discontent. "Do they, now?" His hazel eyes turned to Abby. "Seems the council doesn't care about the lives of even children, when the children are D'Haran." He wiped a hand across his tired-looking eyes. "I can't say I don't comprehend their reasoning, or that I disagree with them, but dear spirits, they are not the ones to do it. It is not by their hand. It will be by mine."

"I understand, Zedd," the Mother Confessor murmured.

Once again he seemed to notice Abby standing before him. He considered her as if pondering some profound notion. It made her fidget. He held out his hand and waggled his fingers. "Let me see it, then."

Abby stepped closer to the table as she reached in her sack.

"If you cannot be persuaded to help innocent people, then maybe this will mean something more to you."

She drew her mother's skull from the sack and placed it in the wizard's upturned palm. "It is a debt of bones. I declare it due."

One eyebrow lifted. "It is customary to bring only a tiny fragment of bone, child."

Abby felt her face flush. "I didn't know," she stammered. "I wanted to be sure there was enough to test . . . to be sure you would believe me."

He smoothed a gentle hand over the top of the skull. "A piece smaller than a grain of sand is enough." He watched Abby's eyes. "Didn't your mother tell you?"

Abby shook her head. "She said only that it was a debt passed to you from your father. She said the debt must be paid if it was called due."

"Indeed it must," he whispered.

Even as he spoke, his hand was gliding back and forth over the skull. The bone was dull and stained by the dirt from which Abby had pulled it, not at all the pristine white she had fancied it would be. It had horrified her to have to uncover her mother's bones, but the alternative horrified her more.

Beneath the wizard's fingers, the bone of the skull began to glow with soft amber light. Abby's breathing nearly stilled when the air hummed, as if the spirits themselves whispered to the wizard. The sorceress fussed with the beads at her neck. The Mother Confessor chewed her lower lip. Abby prayed.

Wizard Zorander set the skull on the table and turned his back on them. The amber glow faded away.

When he said nothing, Abby spoke into the thick silence. "Well? Are you satisfied? Did your test prove it a debt true?"

"Oh yes," he said quietly without turning toward them. "It is a debt of bones true, bound by the magic invoked until the debt is paid."

Abby's fingers worried at the frayed edge of her sack. "I told you. My mother wouldn't have lied to me. She told me that if not paid while she was alive, it became a debt of bones upon her death."

The wizard slowly rounded to face her. "And did she tell you anything of the engendering of the debt?"

"No." Abby cast a furtive, sidelong glance at Delora before going on. "Sorceresses hold secrets close, and reveal only that which serves their purposes."

With a slight, fleeting smile, he grunted his concurrence.

"She said only that it was your father and she who were bound in it, and that until paid it would continue to pass on to the descendants of each."

"Your mother spoke the truth. But that does not mean that it must be paid now."

"It is a solemn debt of bones." Abby's frustration and fear erupted with venom. "I declare it due! You will yield to the obligation!"

Both the sorceress and the Mother Confessor gazed off at the walls, uneasy at a woman, an ungifted woman, raising her voice to the First Wizard himself. Abby suddenly wondered if she might be struck dead for such insolence. But if he didn't help her, it wouldn't matter.

The Mother Confessor diverted the possible results of Abby's outburst with a question. "Zedd, did your reading tell you of the nature of the engendering of the debt?"

"Indeed it did," he said. "My father, too, told me of a debt. My test has proven to me that this is the one of which he spoke, and that the woman standing before me carries the other half of the link."

"So, what was the engendering?" the sorceress asked.

He turned his palms up. "It seems to have slipped my mind. I'm sorry; I find myself to be more forgetful than usual of late."

Delora sniffed. "And you dare to call sorceresses taciturn?"

Wizard Zorander silently considered her a moment and then turned a squint on the Mother Confessor. "The council wants it done, do they?" He smiled a sly smile. "Then it shall be done."

The Mother Confessor cocked her head. "Zedd ... are you sure about this?"

"About what?" Abby asked. "Are you going to honor the debt or not?"

The wizard shrugged. "You have declared the debt due." He plucked a small book from the table and slipped it into a pocket in his robe. "Who am I to argue?"

"Dear spirits," the Mother Confessor whispered to herself. "Zedd, just because the council—"

"I am just a wizard," he said, cutting her off, "serving the wants and wishes of the people."

"But if you travel to this place you would be exposing yourself to needless danger."

"I must be near the border—or it will claim parts of the Midlands, too. Coney Crossing is as good a place as any other to ignite the conflagration."

Beside herself with relief, Abby was hardly hearing anything else he said. "Thank you, Wizard Zorander. Thank you."

He strode around the table and gripped her shoulder with sticklike fingers of surprising strength.

"We are bound, you and I, in a debt of bones. Our life paths have intersected." His smile looked at once sad and sincere. His powerful fingers closed around her wrist, around her bracelet, and he put her mother's skull in her hands. "Please, Abby, call me Zedd."

Near tears, she nodded. "Thank you, Zedd."

Outside, in the early light, they were accosted by the waiting crowd. Wizard Thomas, waving his papers, shoved his way through.

"Zorander! I've been studying these elements you've provided. I have to talk to you."

"Talk, then," the First Wizard said as he marched by. The crowd followed in his wake.

"This is madness."

"I never said it wasn't."

Wizard Thomas shook the papers as if for proof. "You can't do this, Zorander!"

"The council has decided that it is to be done. The war must be ended while we have the upper hand and before Panis Rahl comes up with something we won't be able to counter."

"No, I mean I've studied this thing, and you won't be able to do it. We don't understand the power those wizards wielded. I've looked over the elements you've shown me. Even trying to invoke such a thing will create intense heat."

Zedd halted and put his face close to Thomas. He lifted his eyebrows in mock surprise. "Really, Thomas? Do you think? Igniting a light spell that will rip the fabric of the world of life might cause an instability in the elements of the web field?"

Thomas charged after as Zedd stormed off. "Zorander! You won't be able to control it! If you were able to invoke it—and I'm not saying I believe you can—you would breach the Grace. The invocation uses heat. The breach feeds it. You won't be able to control the cascade. No one can do such a thing!"

"I can do it," the First Wizard muttered.

Thomas shook the fists of papers in a fury. "Zorander, your arrogance will be the end of us all! Once parted, the veil will be rent and all life will be consumed. I demand to see the book in which you found this spell. I demand to see it myself. The whole thing, not just parts of it!"

The First Wizard paused and lifted a finger. "Thomas, if you were meant to see the book, then you would be First Wizard and have access to the First Wizard's private enclave. But you are not, and you don't."

Thomas's face glowed scarlet above his white beard. "This is a fool-hardy act of desperation!"

Wizard Zorander flicked the finger. The papers flew from the old wizard's hand and swirled up into a whirlwind, there to ignite, flaring into ashes that lifted away on the wind.

"Sometimes, Thomas, all that is left to you is an act of desperation. I am First Wizard, and I will do as I must. That is the end of it. I will hear no more." He turned and snatched the sleeve of an officer. "Alert the lancers. Gather all the cavalry available. We ride for Pendisan Reach at once."

The man thumped a quick salute to his chest before dashing off. Another officer, older and looking to be of much higher rank, cleared his throat.

"Wizard Zorander, may I know of your plan?"

"It is Anargo," the First Wizard said, "who is the right hand of Panis Rahl, and in conjunction with Rahl conjures death to stalk us. Quite simply put, I intend to send death back at them."

"By leading the lancers into Pendisan Reach?"

"Yes. Anargo holds at Coney Crossing. We have General Brainard driving north toward Pendisan Reach, General Sanderson sweeping south to join with him, and Mardale charging up from the southwest. We will go in there with the lancers and whoever of the rest of them is able to join with us."

"Anargo is no fool. We don't know how many other wizards and gifted he has with him, but we know what they're capable of. They've bled us time and time again. At last we have dealt them a blow." The officer chose his words carefully. "Why do you think they wait? Why wouldn't they simply slip back into D'Hara?"

Zedd rested a hand on the crenellated wall and gazed out on the dawn, out on the city below.

"Anargo relishes the game. He performs it with high drama; he wants us to think them wounded. Pendisan Reach is the only terrain in all those mountains that an army can get through with any speed. Coney Crossing provides a wide field for battle, but not wide enough to let us maneuver easily, or flank them. He is trying to bait us in."

The officer didn't seem surprised. "But why?"

Zedd looked back over his shoulder at the officer. "Obviously, he believes that in such terrain he can defeat us. I believe otherwise. He knows that we can't allow the menace to remain there, and he knows our plans. He thinks to draw me in, kill me, and end the threat I alone hold over them."

"So . . ." the officer reasoned aloud, "you are saying that for Anargo, it is worth the risk."

Zedd stared out once more at the city below the Wizard's Keep. "If Anargo is right, he could win it all at Coney Crossing. When he has finished me, he will turn his gifted loose, slaughter the bulk of our forces all in one place, and then, virtually unopposed, cut out the heart of the Midlands: Aydindril.

"Anargo plans that before the snow flies, he will have killed me, annihilated our joint forces, have the people of the Midlands in chains, and be able to hand the whip to Panis Rahl."

The officer stared, dumbfounded. "And you plan to do as Anargo is hoping and go in there to face him?"

Zedd shrugged. "What choice have I?"

"And do you at least know how Anargo plans to kill you, so that we might take precautions? Take countermeasures?"

"I'm afraid not." Vexed, he waved his hand, dismissing the matter. He turned to Abby. "The lancers have swift horses. We will ride hard. We will be to your home soon—we will be there in time—and then we'll see to our business."

Abby only nodded. She couldn't put into words the relief of her petition granted, nor could she express the shame she felt to have her prayer answered. But most of all, she couldn't utter a word of her horror at what she was doing, for she knew the D'Harans' plan.

Flies swarmed around dried scraps of viscera, all that was left of Abby's prized bearded pigs. Apparently, even the breeding stock, which Abby's parents had given her as a wedding gift, had been slaughtered and taken.

Abby's parents, too, had chosen Abby's husband. Abby had never met him before: he came from the town of Lynford, where her mother and father bought the pigs. Abby had been beside herself with anxiety over who her parents would choose for her husband. She had hoped for a man who would be of good cheer—a man to bring a smile to the difficulties of life.

When she first saw Philip, she thought he must be the most serious man in all the world. His young face looked to her as if it had never once smiled. That first night after meeting him, she had cried herself to sleep over thoughts of sharing her life with so solemn a man. She thought her life caught up on the sharp tines of grim fate.

Abby came to find that Philip was a hardworking man who looked out at life through a great grin. That first day she had seen him, she only later learned, he had been putting on his most sober face so that his new family would not think him a slacker unworthy of their daughter. In a short time, Abby had come to know that Philip was a man upon whom she could depend. By the time Jana had been born, she had come to love him.

Now Philip, and so many others, depended upon her.

Abby brushed her hands clean after putting her mother's bones to rest once more. The fences Jana had watched Philip so often mend, she saw, were all broken down. Coming back around the house, she noticed that barn doors were missing. Anything an animal or human could eat was gone. Abby could not recall having ever seen her home looking so barren.

It didn't matter, she told herself. It didn't matter, if only Jana would be returned to her. Fences could be mended. Pigs could be replaced, somehow, someday. Jana could never be replaced.

"Abby," Zedd asked as he peered around at the ruins of her home, "how is it that you weren't taken, when your husband and daughter and everyone else were?"

Abby stepped through the broken doorway, thinking that her home had never looked so small. Before she had gone to Aydindril, to the Wizard's Keep, her home had seemed as big as anything she could imagine. Here, Philip had laughed and filled the simple room with his comfort and conversation. With charcoal he had drawn animals on the stone hearth for Jana.

Abby pointed. "Under that door is the root cellar. That's where I was when I heard the things I told you about."

Zedd ran the toe of his boot across the knothole used as a fingerhold to lift the hatch. "They were taking your husband, and your daughter, and you stayed down there? While your daughter was screaming for you, you didn't run up to help her?"

Abby summoned her voice. "I knew that if I came up, they would have me, too. I knew that the only chance my family had was if I waited and then went for help. My mother always told me that even a sorceress was no more than a fool if she acted one. She always told me to think things through, first."

"Wise advice." Zedd set down a ladle that had been bent and holed. He rested a gentle hand on her shoulder. "It would have been hard to leave your daughter crying for you, and do the wise thing."

Abby could only manage a whisper. "You speak the spirits' own truth." She pointed through the window on the side wall. "That way— across the Coney River—lies town. They took Jana and Philip with them as they went on to take all the people from town. They had others, too, that they had already captured. The army set up camp in the hills beyond."

Zedd stood at the window, gazing out at the distant hills. "Soon, I hope, this war will be ended. Dear spirits, let it end."

Remembering the Mother Confessor's admonition not to repeat the story she told, Abby never asked about the wizard's daughter or murdered wife. When on their swift journey back to Coney Crossing she spoke of her love for Jana, it must have broken his heart to think of his own daughter in the brutal hands of the enemy, knowing that he had left her to death lest many more die.

Zedd pushed open the bedroom door. "And back here?" he asked as he put his head into the room beyond.

Abby looked up from her thoughts. "The bedroom. In the rear is a door back to the garden and the barn."

Though he never once mentioned his dead wife or missing daughter, Abby's knowledge of them ate away at her as a swelling spring river ate at a hole in the ice.

Zedd stepped back in from the bedroom as Delora came silently slipping in through the front doorway. "As Abigail said, the town across the river has been sacked," the sorceress reported. "From the looks of it, the people were all taken."

Zedd brushed back his wavy hair. "How close is the river?"

Abby gestured out the window. Night was falling. "Just there. A walk of five minutes."

In the valley, on its way to join the Kern, the Coney River slowed and spread wide, so that it became shallow enough to cross easily. There was no bridge; the road simply led to the river's edge and took up again on the other side. Though the river was near to a quarter mile across in most of the valley, it was in no place much more than knee-deep. Only in the spring melt was it occasionally treacherous to cross. The town of Coney Crossing was two miles beyond, up on the rise of hills, safe from spring floods, as was the knoll where Abby's farmyard stood.

Zedd took Delora by the elbow. "Ride back and tell everyone to hold station. If anything goes wrong . . . well, if anything goes wrong, then they must attack. Anargo's legion must be stopped, even if they have to go into D'Hara after them."

Delora did not look pleased. "Before we left, the Mother Confessor made me promise that I would be sure that you were not left alone. She told me to see to it that gifted were always near if you needed them."

Abby, too, had heard the Mother Confessor issue the orders. Looking back at the Keep as they had crossed the stone bridge, Abby had seen the Mother Confessor up on a high rampart, watching them leave. The Mother Confessor had helped when Abby had feared all was lost. She wondered what would become of the woman.

Then she remembered that she didn't have to wonder. She knew.

The wizard ignored what the sorceress had said. "As soon as I help Abby, I'll send her back, too. I don't want anyone near when I unleash the spell."

Delora gripped his collar and pulled him close. She looked as if she might be about to give him a heated scolding. Instead she drew him into an embrace.

"Please, Zedd," she whispered, "don't leave us without you as First Wizard."

Zedd smoothed back her dark hair. "And abandon you all to Thomas?" He smirked. "Never."

The dust from Delora's horse drifted away into the gathering darkness as Zedd and Abby descended the slope toward the river. Abby led him along the path through the tall grasses and rushes, explaining that the path would offer them better concealment than the road. Abby was thankful that he didn't argue for the road.

Her eyes darted from the deep shadows on one side to the shadows on the other as they were swallowed into the brush. Her pulse raced. She flinched whenever a twig snapped underfoot.

It happened as she feared it would, as she knew it would.

A figure enfolded in a long hooded cloak darted out of nowhere, knocking Abby aside. She saw the flash of a blade as Zedd flipped the attacker into the brush. He squatted, putting a hand back on Abby's shoulder as she lay in the grass panting.

"Stay down," he whispered urgently.

Light gathered at his fingers. He was conjuring magic. That was what they wanted him to do.

Tears welled, burning her eyes. She snatched his sleeve. "Zedd, don't use magic." She could hardly speak past the tightening pain in her chest. "Don't—"

The figure sprang again from the gloom of the bushes. Zedd threw up a hand. The night lit with a flash of hot light that struck the cloaked figure.

Rather than the assailant going down, it was Zedd who cried out and crumpled to the ground. Whatever he had thought to do to the attacker, it had been turned back on him, and he was in the grip of the most terrible anguish, preventing him from rising, or speaking. That was why they had wanted him to conjure magic: so they could capture him.

The figure standing over the wizard glowered at Abby. "Your part here is finished. Go."

Abby scuttled into the grass. The woman pushed the hood back, and cast off her cloak. In the near darkness, Abby could see the woman's long braid and red leather uniform. It was one of the women Abby had been told about, the women used to capture those with magic: the Mord-Sith.

The Mord-Sith watched with satisfaction as the wizard at her feet writhed in choking pain. "Well, well. Looks like the First Wizard himself has just made a very big mistake."

The belts and straps of her red leather uniform creaked as she leaned down toward him, grinning at his agony. "I have been given the whole night to make you regret ever having lifted a finger to resist us. In the morning I'm to allow you to watch as our forces annihilate your people. Afterward, I am to take you to Lord Rahl himself, the man who ordered the death of your wife, so you can beg him to order me to kill you, too." She kicked him. "So you can beg Lord Rahl for your death, as you watch your daughter die before your eyes."

Zedd could only scream in horror and pain.

On her hands and knees, Abby crabbed her way farther back into the weeds and rushes. She wiped at her eyes, trying to see. She was horrified to witness what was being done to the man who had agreed to help her for no more reason than a debt to her mother. By contrast, these people had coerced her service by holding hostage the life of her child.

As she backed away, Abby saw the knife the Mord-Sith had dropped when Zedd had thrown her into the weeds. The knife was a pretext, used to provoke him to act; it was magic that was the true weapon. The Mord-Sith had used his own magic against him—used it to cripple and capture him, and now used it to hurt him.

It was the price demanded. Abby had complied. She had had no choice.

But what toll was she imposing on others?

How could she save her daughter's life at the cost of so many others? Would Jana grow up to be a slave to people who would do this? With a mother who would allow it? Jana would grow up to learn to bow to Panis Rahl and his minions, to submit to evil, or worse, grow up to become a willing part in the scourge, never tasting liberty or knowing the value of honor.

With dreadful finality, everything seemed to fall to ruin in Abby's mind.

She snatched up the knife. Zedd was wailing in pain as the Mord-Sith bent, doing some foul thing to him. Before she had time to lose her resolve, Abby was moving toward the woman's back.

Abby had butchered animals. She told herself that this was no different. These were not people, but animals. She lifted the knife.

A hand clamped over her mouth. Another seized her wrist.

Abby moaned against the hand, against her failure to stop this madness when she had had the chance. A mouth close to her ear urged her to hush.

Struggling against the figure in hooded cloak that held her, Abby turned her head as much as she could, and in the last of the daylight saw violet eyes looking back. For a moment she couldn't make sense of it, couldn't make sense of how the woman could be there when Abby had seen her remain behind. But it truly was her.

Abby stilled. The Mother Confessor released her and, with a quick hand signal, urged her back. Abby didn't question; she scurried back into the rushes as the Mother Confessor reached out toward the woman in red leather. The Mord-Sith was bent over, intent on her grisly business with the screaming wizard.

In the distance, bugs chirped and clicked. Frogs called with insistent croaks. Not far away the river sloshed and burbled as it always did—a familiar, comforting sound of home.

And then there came a sudden, violent concussion to the air. Thunder without sound. It drove the wind from Abby's lungs. The wallop nearly knocked her senseless, making every joint in her body burn in sharp pain.

There was no flash of light—just that pure and flawless jolt to the air. The world seemed to stop in its terrible splendor.

Grass flattened as if in a wind radiating out in a ring from the Mord-Sith and the Mother Confessor. Abby's senses returned as the pain in her joints thankfully melted away.

Abby had never seen it done before, and had never expected to see it in the whole of her life, but she knew without doubt that she had just witnessed a Confessor unleashing her power. From what Abby's mother had told her, it was the destruction of a person's mind so complete that it left only numb devotion to the Confessor. She had but to ask and they would confess any truth, no matter the crime they had previously attempted to conceal or deny.

"Mistress," the Mord-Sith moaned in piteous lamentation.

Abby, first staggered by the shock of the soundless thunder of the Mother Confessor's power, and now stunned by the abject anguish of the woman crumpled on the ground, felt a hand grip her arm. It was the wizard.

With the back of his other hand he wiped blood from his mouth. He labored to get his breath. "Leave her to it."

"Zedd . . . I . . . I'm so sorry. I tried to tell you not to use magic, but I didn't call loud enough for you to hear."

He managed to smile through obvious pain. "I heard you."

"But why then did you use your gift?"

"I thought that in the end, you would not be the kind of person to do such a terrible thing, and that you would show your true heart." He pulled her away from the cries. "We used you. We wanted them to think they had succeeded."

"You knew what I was going to do? You knew I was to bring you to them so that they could capture you?"

"I had a good idea. From the first there seemed more to you than you presented. You are not very talented at being a spy and a traitor. Since we arrived here you've been watching the shadows and jumping at the chirp of every bug."

The Mother Confessor rushed up. "Zedd, are you all right?"

He put a hand on her shoulder. "I'll be fine." His eyes still held the glaze of terror. "Thank you for not being late. For a moment, I feared . . ."

"I know." The Mother Confessor offered a quick smile. "Let us hope your trick was worth it. You have until dawn. She said they expect her to torture you all night before bringing you to them in the morning. Their scouts alerted Anargo to our troops' arrival."

Back in the rushes the Mord-Sith was screaming as though she were being flayed alive.

Shivers ran through Abby's shoulders. "They'll hear her and know what's happened."

"Even if they could hear at this distance, they will think it is Zedd, being tortured by her." The Mother Confessor took the knife from Abby's hand. "I am glad that you rewarded my faith and in the end chose not to join with them."

Abby wiped her palms on her skirts, shamed by all she had done, by what she had intended to do. She was beginning to shake. "Are you going to kill her?"

The Mother Confessor, despite looking bone-weary after having touched the Mord-Sith, still had iron resolve in her eyes. "A Mord-Sith is different from anyone else. She does not recover from the touch of a Confessor. She would suffer in profound agony until she died, sometime before morning." She glanced back toward the cries. "She has told us what we need to know, and Zedd must have his power back. It is the merciful thing to do."

"It also buys me time to do what I must do." Zedd's fingers turned

Abby's face toward him, away from the shrieks. "And time to get Jana back. You will have until morning."

"I will have until morning? What do you mean?"

"I'll explain. But we must hurry if you are to have enough time. Now, take off your clothes."

Abby was running out of time.

She moved through the D'Haran camp, holding herself stiff and tall, trying not to look frantic, even though that was how she felt. All night long she had been doing as the wizard had instructed: acting haughty. To anyone who noticed her, she directed disdain. To anyone who looked her way, thinking to speak to her, she growled.

Not that many, though, so much as dared to catch the attention of what appeared to be a red-leather-clad Mord-Sith. Zedd had told her, too, to keep the Mord-Sith's weapon in her fist. It looked like nothing more than a small red leather rod. How it worked, Abby had no idea—the wizard had said only that it involved magic, and she wouldn't be able to call it to her aid—but it did have an effect on those who saw it in her hand: it made them melt back into the darkness, away from the light of the campfires, away from Abby.

Those who were awake, anyway. Although most people in the camp were sleeping, there was no shortage of alert guards. Zedd had cut the long braid from the Mord-Sith who had attacked him, and tied it into Abby's hair. In the dark, the mismatch of color wasn't obvious. When the guards looked at Abby they saw a Mord-Sith, and quickly turned their attention elsewhere.

By the apprehension on people's faces when they saw her coming, Abby knew she must look fearsome. They didn't know how her heart pounded. She was thankful for the mantle of night so that the D'Harans couldn't see her knees trembling. She had seen only two real Mord-Sith, both sleeping, and she had kept far away from them, as Zedd had warned her. Real Mord-Sith were not likely to be fooled so easily.

Zedd had given her until dawn. Time was running out. He had told her that if she wasn't back in time, she would die.

Abby was thankful she knew the lay of the land, or long since she would have become lost among the confusion of tents, campfires, wagons, horses, and mules. Everywhere pikes and lances were stacked upright in circles with their points leaning together. Men—farriers, fletchers, blacksmiths, and craftsmen of all sorts—worked through the night.

The air was thick with woodsmoke and rang with the sound of metal being shaped and sharpened and wood being worked for everything from bows to wagons. Abby didn't know how people could sleep through the noise, but sleep they did.

Shortly the immense camp would wake to a new day—a day of battle, a day the soldiers went to work doing what they did best. They were getting a good night's sleep so they would be rested for the killing of the Midlands army. From what she had heard, D'Haran soldiers were very good at their job.

Abby had searched relentlessly, but she had been unable to find her father, her husband, or her daughter. She had no intention of giving up. She had resigned herself to the knowledge that if she didn't find them, she would die with them.

She had found captives tied together and staked to trees, or the ground, to keep them from running. Many more were chained. Some she recognized, but many more she didn't. Most were kept in groups and under guard.

Abby never once saw a guard asleep at his post. When they looked her way, she acted as if she were looking for someone, and she wasn't going to go easy on them when she found them. Zedd had told her that her safety, and the safety of her family, depended on her playing the part convincingly. Abby thought about these people hurting her daughter, and it wasn't hard to act angry.

But she was running out of time. She couldn't find them, and she knew that Zedd would not wait. Too much was at stake; she understood that, now. She was coming to appreciate that the wizard and the Mother Confessor were trying to stop a war; that they were people resolved to the dreadful task of weighing the lives of a few against the lives of many.

Abby lifted another tent flap, and saw soldiers sleeping. She squatted and looked at the faces of prisoners tied to wagons. They stared back with hollow expressions. She bent to gaze at the faces of children pressed together in nightmares. She couldn't find Jana. The huge camp sprawled across the hilly countryside; there were a thousand places she could be.

As she marched along a crooked line of tents, she scratched at her wrist. Only when she went farther did she notice that it was the bracelet warming that made her wrist itch. It warmed yet more as she proceeded, but then the warmth began fading. Her brow twitched. Out of curiosity, she turned and went back the way she had come.

Where a pathway between tents turned off, her bracelet tingled again with warmth. Abby paused a moment, looking off into the darkness. The sky was just beginning to color with light. She took the path between the tents, following until the bracelet cooled, then backtracked to where it warmed again and took a new direction where it warmed yet more.

Abby's mother had given her the bracelet, telling her to wear it always, and that someday it would be of value. Abby wondered if somehow the bracelet had magic that would help her find her daughter. With dawn nearing, this seemed the only chance she had left. She hurried onward, wending where the warmth from the bracelet directed.

The bracelet led her to an expanse of snoring soldiers. There were no prisoners in sight. Guards patrolled the men in bedrolls and blankets. There was one tent set among the big men—for an officer, she guessed.

Not knowing what else to do, Abby strode among the sleeping men. Near the tent, the bracelet sent tingling heat up her arm.

Abby saw that sentries hung around the small tent like flies around meat. The canvas sides glowed softly, probably from a candle inside. Off to the side, she noticed a sleeping form different from the men. As she got closer, she saw that it was a woman; Mariska.

The old woman breathed with a little raspy whistle as she slept. Abby stood paralyzed. Guards looked up at her.

Needing to do something before they asked any questions, Abby scowled at them and marched toward the tent. She tried not to make any noise; the guards might think she was a Mord-Sith, but Mariska would not long be fooled. A glare from Abby turned the guards' eyes to the dark countryside.

Her heart pounding nearly out of control, Abby gripped the tent flap. She knew Jana would be inside. She told herself that she must not cry out when she saw her daughter. She reminded herself that she must put a hand over Jana's mouth before she could cry out with joy, lest they be caught before they had a chance to escape.

The bracelet was so hot it felt as if it would blister her skin. Abby ducked into the low tent.

A trembling little girl huddled in a tattered wool cloak sat in blankets on the ground. She stared up with big eyes that blinked with the terror of what might come next. Abby felt a stab of anguish. It was not Jana.

They stared at each other, this little girl and Abby. The child's face was lit clearly by the candle set to the side, as Abby's must be. In those big gray eyes that looked to have beheld unimaginable terrors, the little girl seemed to reach a judgment.

Her arms stretched up in supplication.

Instinctively, Abby fell to her knees and scooped up the little girl, hugging her small trembling body. The girl's spindly arms came out from the tattered cloak and wrapped around Abby's neck, holding on for dear life.

"Help me? Please?" the child whimpered in Abby's ear.

Before she had picked her up she had seen the face in the candlelight. There was no doubt in Abby's mind. It was Zedd's daughter.

"I've come to help you," Abby comforted. "Zedd sent me."

The child moaned expectantly.

Abby held the girl out at arm's length. "I'll take you to your father, but you mustn't let these people know I'm rescuing you. Can you play along with me? Can you pretend that you're my prisoner, so that I can get you away?"

Near tears, the girl nodded. She had the same wavy hair as Zedd, and the same eyes, although they were an arresting gray, not hazel.

"Good," Abby whispered, cupping a chilly cheek, almost lost in those gray eyes. "Trust me, then, and I will get you away."

"I trust you," came the small voice.

Abby snatched up a rope lying nearby and looped it around the girl's neck. "I'll try not to hurt you, but I must make them think you are my prisoner."

The girl cast a worried look at the rope, as if she knew the rope well, and then nodded that she would go along.

Abby stood, once outside the tent, and by the rope pulled the child out after her. The guards looked her way. Abby started out.

One of them scowled as he stepped close. "What's going on?"

Abby stomped to a halt and lifted the red leather rod, pointing it at the guard's nose. "She has been summoned. And who are you to question? Get out of my way or I'll have you gutted and cleaned for my breakfast!"

The man paled and hurriedly stepped aside. Before he had time to reconsider, Abby charged off, the girl in tow at the end of the rope, dragging her heels, making it look real.

No one followed. Abby wanted to run, but she couldn't. She wanted to carry the girl, but she couldn't. It had to look as if a Mord-Sith were taking a prisoner away.

Rather than take the shortest route back to Zedd, Abby followed the hills upriver to a place where the trees offered concealment almost to the water's edge. Zedd had told her where to cross, and warned her not to return by a different way; he had set traps of magic to prevent the D'Harans from charging down from the hills to stop whatever it was he was going to do.

Closer to the river she saw, downstream a ways, a bank of fog hanging close to the ground. Zedd had emphatically warned her not to go near any fog. She suspected that it was a poison cloud of some sort that he had conjured.

The sound of the water told her she was close to the river. The pink sky provided enough light to finally see it when she reached the edge of the trees. Although she could see the massive camp on the hills in the distance behind her, she saw no one following.

Abby took the rope from the child's neck. The girl watched her with those big round eyes. Abby lifted her and held her tight.

"Hold on, and keep quiet."

Pressing the girl's head to her shoulder, Abby ran for the river.

There was light, but it was not the dawn. They had crossed the frigid water and made the other side when she first noticed it. Even as she ran along the bank of the river, before she could see the source of the light, Abby knew that magic was being called there that was unlike any magic she had ever seen before. A sound, low and thin, whined up the river toward her. A smell, as if the air itself had been burned, hung along the riverbank.

The little girl clung to Abby, tears running down her face, afraid to speak—afraid, it seemed, to hope that she had at last been rescued, as if asking a question might somehow make it all vanish like a dream, upon waking. Abby felt tears coursing down her own cheeks.

When she rounded a bend in the river, she spotted the wizard. He stood in the center of the river, on a rock that Abby had never before seen. The rock was just large enough to clear the surface of the water by a few inches, making it almost appear as if the wizard stood on the surface of the water.

Before him as he faced toward distant D'Hara, shapes, dark and wavering, floated in the air. They curled around, as if confiding in him, conversing, warning, tempting him with floating arms and reaching fingers that wreathed like smoke.

Animate light twisted up around the wizard. Colors both dark and wondrous glimmered about him, cavorting with the shadowy forms undulating through the air. It was at once the most enchanting and the most frightening thing Abby had ever seen. No magic her mother conjured had ever seemed . . . aware.

But the most frightening thing by far was what hovered in the air before the wizard. It appeared to be a molten sphere, so hot it glowed from within, its surface a crackling of fluid dross. An arm of water from the river magically turned skyward in a fountain spray and poured down over the rotating silvery mass.

The water hissed and steamed as it hit the sphere, leaving behind clouds of white vapor to drift away in the gentle dawn wind. The molten form blackened at the touch of the water cascading over it, and yet the intense inner heat melted the glassy surface again as fast as the water cooled it, making the whole thing bubble and boil in midair, a pulsing sinister menace.

Transfixed, Abby let the child slip to the silty ground.

The little girl's arms stretched out. "Papa."

He was too far away to hear her, but he heard.

Zedd turned, at once larger than life in the midst of magic Abby could see but not begin to fathom, yet at the same time small with the frailty of human need. Tears filled his eyes as he gazed at his daughter standing beside Abby. This man who seemed to be consulting with spirits looked as if for the first time he were seeing a true apparition.

Zedd leaped off the rock and charged through the water. When he reached her and took her up in the safety of his arms, she began to wail at last with the contained terror released.

"There, there, dear one," Zedd comforted. "Papa is here now."

"Oh, Papa," she cried against his neck, "they hurt Mama. They were wicked. They hurt her so . . ."

He hushed her tenderly. "I know, dear one. I know."

For the first time, Abby saw the sorceress and the Mother Confessor standing off to the side, watching. They, too, shed tears at what they were seeing. Though Abby was glad for the wizard and his daughter, the sight only intensified the pain in her chest at what she had lost. She was choked with tears.

"There, there, dear one," Zedd was cooing. "You're safe, now. Papa won't let anything happen to you. You're safe now."

Zedd turned to Abby. By the time he had smiled his tearful appreciation, the child was asleep.

"A little spell," he explained when Abby's brow twitched with surprise. "She needs to rest. I need to finish what I am doing."

He put his daughter in Abby's arms. "Abby, would you take her up to your house where she can sleep until I'm finished here? Please, put her in bed and cover her up to keep her warm. She will sleep for now."

Thinking about her own daughter in the hands of the brutes across the river, Abby could only nod before turning to the task. She was happy for Zedd, and even felt pride at having rescued his little girl, but as she ran for her home, she was near to dying with grief over her failure to recover her own family.

Abby settled the dead weight of the sleeping child into her bed. She drew the curtain across the small window in her bedroom and, unable to resist, smoothed back silky hair and pressed a kiss to the soft brow before leaving the girl to her blessed rest.

With the child safe at last and asleep, Abby raced back down the knoll to the river. She thought to ask Zedd to give her just a little more time so she could return to look for her own daughter. Fear for Jana had her heart pounding wildly. He owed her a debt, and had not yet seen it through.

Wringing her hands, Abby came to a panting halt at the water's edge. She watched the wizard up on his rock in the river, light and shadow coursing up around him. She had been around magic enough to have the sense to fear approaching him. She could hear his chanted words; though they were words she had never heard before, she recognized the idiosyncratic cadence of words spoken in a spell, words calling together frightful forces.

On the ground beside her was the strange Grace she had seen him draw before, the one that breached the worlds of life and death. The Grace was drawn with a sparkling, pure white sand that stood out in stark relief against the dark silt. Abby shuddered even to look upon it, much less contemplate its meaning. Around the Grace, carefully drawn with the same sparkling white sand, were geometric forms of magical invocations.

Abby lowered her fists, about to call out to the wizard, when Delora leaned close. Abby flinched in surprise.

"Not now, Abigail," the sorceress murmured. "Don't disturb him in the middle of this part."

Reluctantly, Abby heeded the sorceress's words. The Mother Confessor was there, too. Abby chewed her bottom lip as she watched the wizard throw up his arms. Sparkles of colored light curled up along twisting shafts of shadows. "But I must. I haven't been able to find my family. He must help me. He must save them. It's a debt of bones that must be satisfied."

The other two women shared a look. "Abby," the Mother Confessor said, "he gave you a chance, gave you time. He tried. He did his best, but he has everyone else to think of, now."

The Mother Confessor took up Abby's hand, and the sorceress put an arm around Abby's shoulders as she stood weeping on the riverbank. It wasn't supposed to end this way, not after all she had been through, not after all she had done. Despair crushed her.

The wizard, his arms raised, called forth more light, more shadows, more magic. The river roiled around him. The hissing thing in the air grew as it slowly slumped closer to the water. Shafts of light shot from the hot, rotating bloom of power.

The sun was rising over the hills behind the D'Harans. This part of the river wasn't as wide as elsewhere, and Abby could see the activity in the trees beyond. Men moved about, but the fog hanging on the far bank kept them wary, kept them in the trees.

Also across the river, at the edge of the tree-covered hills, another wizard had appeared to conjure magic. He too stood atop a rock as his arms launched sparkling light up into the air. Abby thought that the strong morning sun might outshine the conjured illuminations, but it didn't.

Abby could stand it no longer. "Zedd!" she called out across the river. "Zedd! Please, you promised! I found your daughter! What about mine? Please don't do this until she is safe!"

Zedd turned and looked at her as if from a great distance, as if from another world. Arms of dark forms caressed him. Fingers of dark smoke dragged along his jaw, urging his attention back to them, but he gazed instead at Abby.

"I'm so sorry." Despite the distance, Abby could clearly hear his whispered words. "I gave you time to try to find them. I can spare no more, or countless other mothers will weep for their children—mothers still living, and mothers in the spirit world."

Abby cried out in an anguished wail as he turned back to the ensorcellment. The two women tried to comfort her, but Abby was not to be comforted in her grief.

Thunder rolled through the hills. A clacking clamor from the spell around Zedd rose to echo up and down the valley. Shafts of intense light shot upward. It was a disorienting sight, light shining up into sunlight.

Across the river, the counter to Zedd's magic seemed to spring forth. Arms of light twisted like smoke, lowering to tangle with the light radiating up around Zedd. The fog along the riverbank diffused suddenly.

In answer, Zedd spread his arms wide. The glowing tumbling furnace of molten light thundered. The water sluicing over it roared as it boiled and steamed. The air wailed as if in protest.

Behind the wizard, across the river, the D'Haran soldiers were pouring out of the trees, driving their prisoners before them. People cried out in terror. They quailed at the wizard's magic, only to be driven onward by the spears and swords at their backs.

Abby saw several who refused to move fall to the blades. At the mortal cries, the rest rushed onward, like sheep before wolves.

If whatever Zedd was doing failed, the army of the Midlands would then charge into this valley to confront the enemy. The prisoners would be caught in the middle.

A figure worked its way up along the opposite bank, dragging a child behind. Abby's flesh flashed icy cold with sudden frigid sweat. It was

Mariska. Abby shot a quick glance back over her shoulder. It was impossible. She squinted across the river.

"Nooo!" Zedd called out.

It was Zedd's little girl that Mariska had by the hair.

Somehow, Mariska had followed and found the child sleeping in Abby's home. With no one there to watch over her as she slept, Mariska had stolen the child back.

Mariska held the child out before herself, for Zedd to see. "Cease and surrender, Zorander, or she dies!"

Abby tore away from the arms holding her and charged into the water. She struggled to run against the current, to reach the wizard. Part way there, he turned to stare into her eyes.

Abby froze. "I'm sorry." Her own voice sounded to her like a plea before death. "I thought she was safe."

Zedd nodded in resignation. It was out of his hands. He turned back to the enemy. His arms lifted to his sides. His fingers spread, as if commanding all to stop—magic and men alike.

"Let the prisoners go!" Zedd called across the water to the enemy wizard. "Let them go, Anargo, and I'll give you all your lives!"

Anargo's laugh rang out over the water.

"Surrender," Mariska hissed, "or she dies."

The old woman pulled the knife she kept in the wrap around her waist. She pressed the blade to the child's throat. The girl was screaming in terror, her arms reaching to her father, her little fingers clawing the air.

Abby struggled ahead into the water. She called out, begging Mariska to let Zedd's daughter go free. The woman paid no more heed to Abby than to Zedd.

"Last chance!" Mariska called.

"You heard her," Anargo growled out across the water. "Surrender now or she will die."

"You know I can't put myself above my people!" Zedd called back. "This is between us, Anargo! Let them all go!"

Anargo's laugh echoed up and down the river. "You are a fool, Zorander! You had your chance!" His expression twisted to rage. "Kill her!" he screamed to Mariska.

Fists at his side, Zedd shrieked. The sound seemed to split the morning with its fury.

Mariska lifted the squealing child by her hair. Abby gasped in disbelief as the woman sliced the little girl's throat.

The child flailed. Blood spurted across Mariska's gnarly fingers as she viciously sawed the blade back and forth. She gave a final, mighty yank of the knife. The blood-soaked body dropped in a limp heap. Abby felt vomit welling up in the back of her throat. The silty dirt of the riverbank turned a wet red.

Mariska held the severed head high with a howl of victory. Strings of flesh and blood swung beneath it. The mouth hung in a slack, silent cry.

Abby threw her arms around Zedd's legs. "Dear spirits, I'm sorry! Oh, Zedd, forgive me!"

She wailed in anguish, unable to gather her senses at witnessing a sight so grisly.

"And now, child," Zedd asked in a hoarse voice from above, "what would you have me do? Would you have me let them win, to save your daughter from what they have done to mine? Tell me, child, what should I do?"

Abby couldn't beg for the life of her family at a cost of such people rampaging unchecked across the land. Her sickened heart wouldn't allow it. How could she sacrifice the lives and peace of everyone else just so her loved ones would live?

She would be no better than Mariska, killing innocent children.

"Kill them all!" Abby screamed up at the wizard. She threw her arm out, pointing at Mariska and the hateful wizard Anargo. "Kill the bastards! Kill them all!"

Zedd's arms flung upward. The morning cracked with a peal of thunder. As if he had loosed it, the molten mass before him plunged into the water. The ground shook with a jolt. A huge geyser of water exploded forth. The air itself quaked. All around the most dreadful rumbling whipped the water into froth.

Abby, squatted down with the water to her waist, felt numb not only from the cold, but also from the cold knowledge that she'd been forsaken by the good spirits she had always thought would watch over her. Zedd turned and snatched her arm, dragging her up on the rock with him.

It was another world.

The shapes around them called to her, too. They reached out, bridging the distance between life and death. Searing pain, frightful joy, profound peace, spread through her at their touch. Light moved up through her body, filling her like air filled her lungs, and exploded in showers of sparks in her mind's eye. The thick howl of the magic was deafening.

Green light ripped through the water. Across the river, Anargo had been thrown to the ground. The rock atop which he had stood had shattered into needle-like shards. The soldiers called out in fright as the air all about danced with swirling smoke and sparks of light.

"Run!" Mariska screamed. "While you have the chance! Run for your lives!" Already she was racing toward the hills. "Leave the prisoners to die! Save yourselves! Run!"

The mood across the river suddenly galvanized with a single determination. The D'Harans dropped their weapons. They cast aside the ropes and chains holding the prisoners. They kicked up dirt as they turned and ran. In a single instant, the whole of an army that had a moment before stood grimly facing them were all, as if of a single fright, running for their lives.

From the corner of her eye, Abby saw the Mother Confessor and the sorceress struggling to run into the water. Although the water was hardly above their knees, it bogged them down in their rush nearly as much as would mud.

Abby watched it all as if in a dream. She floated in the light surrounding her. Pain and rapture were one within her. Light and dark, sound and silence, joy and sorrow, all were one, everything and nothing together in a caldron of raging magic.

Across the river, the D'Haran army had vanished into the woods. Dust rose above the trees, marking their horses, wagons, and footfalls racing away, while at the riverbank the Mother Confessor and the sorceress were shoving people into the water, screaming at them, though Abby didn't hear the words, so absorbed was she by the strange harmonious trills twisting her thoughts into visions of dancing color overlaying what her eyes were trying to tell her.

She thought briefly that surely she was dying. She thought briefly that it didn't matter. And then her mind was swimming again in the cold color and hot light, the drumming music of magic and worlds meshing. The wizard's embrace made her feel as if she were being held in her mother's arms again. Maybe she was.

Abby was aware of the people reaching the Midlands side of the river and running ahead of the Mother Confessor and sorceress. They vanished into the rushes and then Abby saw them far away, beyond the tall grass, running uphill, away from the sublime sorcery erupting from the river.

The world thundered around her. A subterranean thump brought sharp pain deep in her chest. A whine, like steel being shredded, tore through the morning air. All around the water danced and quaked.

Hot steam felt as if it would scald Abby's legs. The air went white with it. The noise hurt her ears so much that she squeezed her eyes shut. She saw the same thing with her eyes closed as she saw with them open—shadowy shapes swirling through the green air. Everything was going crazy in her mind, making no sense. Green fury tore at her body and soul.

Abby felt pain, as if something inside her tore asunder. She gasped and opened her eyes. A horrific wall of green fire was receding away from them, toward the far side of the river. Founts of water lashed upward, like a thunderstorm in reverse. Lightning laced together above the surface of the river.

As the conflagration reached the far bank, the ground beneath it rent apart. Shafts of violet light shot up from the ripping wounds in the earth, like the blood of another realm.

Worse, though, than any of it were the howls. Howls of the dead, Abby was sure. It felt as if her own soul moaned in sympathy with the agony of cries filling the air. From the receding green wall of glimmering fire, the shapes twisted and turned, calling, begging, trying to escape the world of the dead.

She understood now that that was what the wall of green fire was—death, come to life.

The wizard had breached the boundary between worlds.

Abby had no idea how much time passed; in the grip of the strange light in which she swam there seemed to be no time, any more than there was anything solid. There was nothing familiar about any of the sensations upon which to hang understanding.

It seemed to Abby that the wall of green fire had halted its advance in the trees on the far hillside. The trees over which it had passed, and those she could see embraced by the shimmering curtain, had been blackened and shriveled by the profound touch of death itself. Even the grass over which the grim presence had passed looked to have been baked black and crisp by a high summer sun.

As Abby watched the wall, it dulled. As she stared, it seemed to waver in and out of her vision, sometimes a glimmering green gloss, like molten glass, and sometimes no more than a pale hint, like a fog just now passed from the air.

To each side, it was spreading, a wall of death raging across the world of life.

Abby realized she heard the river again, the comfortable, common, sloshing, lapping, burbling sounds that she lived her life hearing but most of the time didn't notice.

Zedd hopped down from the rock. He took her hand and helped her down. Abby gripped his hand tightly to brace against the dizzying sensations swimming through her head.

Zedd snapped his fingers, and the rock upon which they had just stood leaped into the air, causing her to gasp in fright. In an instant so brief that she doubted she had seen it, Zedd caught the rock. It had become a small stone, smaller than an egg. He winked at her as he slipped it into a pocket. She thought the wink the oddest thing she could imagine, odder even than the boulder now a stone in his pocket.

On the bank, the Mother Confessor and the sorceress waited. They took her arms, helping her out of the water.

The sorceress looked grim. "Zedd, why isn't it moving?"

It sounded to Abby more like an accusation than a question. Either way, Zedd ignored it.

"Zedd," Abby mumbled, "I'm so sorry. It's my fault. I shouldn't have left her alone. I should have stayed. I'm so sorry."

The wizard, hardly hearing her words, was looking off to the wall of death on the other side of the river. He brought his clawed fingers up past his chest, calling something forth from within himself.

With a sudden thump to the air, fire erupted between his hands. He held it out as he would hold an offering. Abby threw an arm up in front of her face at the heat.

Zedd lifted the roiling ball of liquid fire. It grew between his hands, tumbling and turning, roaring and hissing with rage.

The three women backed away. Abby had heard of such fire. She had once heard her mother name it in a hushed tone: wizard's fire. Even then, not seeing or knowing its like, those whispered words forming a picture in Abby's mind as her mother recounted it, had sent a chill through Abby. Wizard's fire was the bane of life, called forth to scourge an enemy. This could be nothing else.

"For killing my love, my Erilyn, the mother of our daughter, and all the other innocent loved ones of innocent people," Zedd whispered, "I send you, Panis Rahl, the gift of death."

The wizard opened his arms outward. The liquid blue and yellow fire, bidden by its master, tumbled forward, gathering speed, roaring away toward D'Hara. As it crossed the river, it grew like angry lightning blooming forth, wailing with wrathful fury, reflecting in glimmering points from the water in thousands of bright sparkles.

The wizard's fire shot across the growing wall of green, just catching the upper edge. At the contact, green flame flared forth, some of it tearing away, caught up behind the wizard's fire, trailing after like smoke behind flame. The deadly mix howled toward the horizon. Everyone stood transfixed, watching, until all trace of it had vanished in the distance.

When Zedd, pale and drawn, turned back to them, Abby clutched his robes. "Zedd, I'm so sorry. I shouldn't—"

He put his fingers to her lips to silence her. "There is someone waiting for you."

He tilted his head. She turned. Back by the rushes, Philip stood holding Jana's hand. Abby gasped with a jolt of giddy joy. Philip grinned his familiar grin. At his other side, her father smiled and nodded his approval to her.

Arms reaching, Abby ran to them. Jana's face wrinkled. She backed against Philip. Abby fell to her knees before her.

"It's Mama," Philip said to Jana. "She just has herself some new clothes."

Abby realized Jana was frightened by the red leather outfit she was wearing. Abby grinned through her tears.

"Mama!" Jana cried at seeing the smile.

Abby threw her arms around her daughter. She laughed and hugged Jana so hard the child squeaked in protest. Abby felt Philip's hand on her shoulder in loving greeting. Abby stood and threw an arm around him, tears choking her voice. Her father put a comforting hand to her back while she squeezed Jana's hand.

Zedd, Delora, and the Mother Confessor gathered them and herded them up the hill toward the people waiting at the top. Soldiers, mostly officers, some that Abby recognized, a few other people from Aydindril, and the wizard Thomas waited with the freed prisoners. Among the people liberated were those of Coney Crossing; people who held Abby, the daughter of a sorceress, in no favor. But they were her people, the people from her home, the people she had wanted saved.

Zedd rested a hand on Abby's shoulder. Abby was shocked to see that his wavy brown hair was now partly snow white. She knew without a looking glass that hers had undergone the same transformation in the place beyond the world of life, where, for a time, they had been.

"This is Abigail, born of Helsa," the wizard called out to the people gathered. "She is the one who went to Aydindril to seek my help. Though she does not have magic, it is because of her that you people are all free. She cared enough to beg for your lives."

Abby, with Philip's arm around her waist and Jana's hand in hers, looked from the wizard to the sorceress, and then to the Mother Confessor. The Mother Confessor smiled. Abby thought it a coldhearted thing to do in view of the fact that Zedd's daughter had been murdered before their eyes not long before. She whispered as much.

The Mother Confessor's smile widened. "Don't you remember?" she asked as she leaned close. "Don't you remember what I told you we call him?"

Abby, confused by everything that had happened, couldn't imagine what the Mother Confessor was talking about. When she admitted she didn't, the Mother Confessor and the sorceress shepherded her onward, past the grave where Abby had reburied her mother's skull upon her return, and into the house.

With a hand, the Mother Confessor eased back the door to Abby's bedroom. There, on the bed where Abby had placed her, was Zedd's daughter, still sleeping. Abby stared in disbelief.

"The trickster," the Mother Confessor said. "I told you that was our name for him."

"And not a very flattering one," Zedd grumbled as he stepped up behind them.

"But . . . how?" Abby pressed her fingers to her temples. "I don't understand."

Zedd gestured. Abby saw, for the first time, the body lying just beyond the door out the back. It was Mariska.

"When you showed me the room when we first came here," Zedd told her, "I laid a few traps for those intent on harm. That woman was killed by those traps because she came here intent on taking my daughter from where she slept."

"You mean it was all an illusion?" Abby was dumbfounded. "Why would you do such a cruel thing? How could you?"

"I am the object of vengeance," the wizard explained. "I didn't want my daughter to pay the price her mother has already paid. Since my spell killed the woman as she tried to harm my daughter, I was able to use a vision of her to accomplish the deception. The enemy knew the woman, and that she acted for Anargo. I used what they expected to see to convince them and to frighten them into running and leaving the prisoners.

"I cast the death spell so that everyone would think they saw my daughter being killed. This way, the enemy thinks my daughter dead, and will have no reason to hunt her or ever again try to harm her. I did it to protect her from the unforeseen."

The sorceress scowled at him. "If it were any but you, Zeddicus, and for any reason but the reason you had, I'd see you brought up on charges for casting such a web as a death spell." She broke into a grin. "Well done, First Wizard."

Outside, the officers all wanted to know what was happening.

"No battle today," Zedd told them. "I've just ended the war."

They cheered with genuine joy. Had Zedd not been the First Wizard, Abby suspected they would have hoisted him on their shoulders. It seemed that there was no one more glad for peace than those whose job it was to fight for it.

Wizard Thomas, looking more humble than Abby had ever seen him, cleared his throat. "Zorander, I . . . I . . . I simply can't believe what my own eyes have seen." His face finally took on its familiar scowl. "But we have people already in near revolt over magic. When news of this spreads, it is only going to make it worse. The demands for relief from magic grow every day and you have fed the fury. With this, we're liable to have revolt on our hands."

"I still want to know why it isn't moving," Delora growled from behind. "I want to know why it's just sitting there, all green and still."

Zedd ignored her and directed his attention to the old wizard. "Thomas, I have a job for you."

He motioned several officers and officials from Aydindril forward, and passed a finger before all their faces, his own turning grim and determined. "I have a job for all of you. The people have reason to fear magic. Today we have seen magic deadly and dangerous. I can understand those fears.

"In appreciation of these fears, I shall grant their wish."

"What!" Thomas scoffed. "You can't end magic, Zorander! Not even you can accomplish such a paradox."

"Not end it," Zedd said. "But give them a place without it. I want you to organize an official delegation large enough to travel all the Midlands with the offer. All those who would quit a world with magic are to move to the lands to the west. There they shall set up new lives free of any magic. I shall insure that magic cannot intrude on their peace."

Thomas threw up his hands. "How can you make such a promise!"

Zedd's arm lifted to point off behind him, to the wall of green fire growing toward the sky. "I shall call up a second wall of death, through which none can pass. On the other side of it shall be a place free of magic. There, people will be able to live their lives without magic.

"I want you all to see that the word is passed through the land. People have until spring to emigrate to the lands west. Thomas, you will warrant that none with magic make the journey. We have books we can use to insure that we purge a place of any with a trace of magic. We can assure that there will be no magic there.

"In the spring, when all who wish have gone to their new homeland, I will seal them off from magic. In one fell swoop, I will satisfy the large majority of the petitions come to us; they will have lives without magic. May the good spirits watch over them, and may they not come to regret their wish granted."

Thomas pointed heatedly at the thing Zedd had brought into the world. "But what about that? What if people go wandering into it in the dark? They will be walking into death."

"Not only in the dark," Zedd said. "Once it has stabilized, it will be hard to see at all. We will have to set up guards to keep people away. We will have to set aside land near the boundary and have men guard the area to keep people out."

"Men?" Abby asked. "You mean you will have to start a corps of boundary wardens?"

"Yes," Zedd said, his eyebrows lifting, "that's a good name for them. Boundary wardens."

Silence settled over those leaning in to hear the wizard's words. The mood had changed and was now serious with the grim matter at hand. Abby couldn't imagine a place without magic, but she knew how vehemently some wished it.

Thomas finally nodded. "Zedd, this time I think you've gotten it right. Sometimes, we must serve the people by not serving them." The others mumbled their agreement, though, like Abby, they thought it a bleak solution.

Zedd straightened. "Then it is decided."

He turned and announced to the crowd the end of the war, and the division to come in which those who had petitioned for years would finally have their petition granted; for those who wished it, a land outside the Midlands, without magic, would be created.

While everyone was chattering about such a mysterious and exotic thing as a land without magic, or cheering and celebrating the end of the war, Abby whispered to Jana to wait with her father a moment. She kissed her daughter and then took the opportunity to pull Zedd aside.

"Zedd, may I speak with you? I have a question."

Zedd smiled and took her by the elbow, urging Abby into her small home. "I'd like to check on my daughter. Come along."

Abby cast caution to the winds and took the Mother Confessor's hand in one of hers, Delora's in the other, and pulled them in with her. They had a right to hear this, too.

"Zedd," Abby asked once they were away from the crowd in her yard, "may I please know the debt your father owed my mother?"

Zedd lifted an eyebrow. "My father owed your mother no debt."

Abby frowned. "But it was a debt of bones, passed down from your father to you, and from my mother to me."

"Oh, it was a debt all right, but not owed to your mother, but by your mother."

"What?" Abby asked in stunned confusion. "What do you mean?"

Zedd smiled. "When your mother was giving birth to you, she was in trouble. You both were dying in the labor. My father used magic to save her. Helsa begged him to save you, too. In order to keep you in the world of the living and out of the Keeper's grasp, without thought to his own safety, he worked far beyond the endurance anyone would expect of a wizard.

"Your mother was a sorceress, and understood the extent of what was involved in saving your life. In appreciation of what my father had done, she swore a debt to him. When she died, the debt passed to you."

Abby, eyes wide, tried to reconcile the whole thing in her mind. Her mother had never told her the nature of the debt.

"But . . . but you mean that it is I who owe the debt to you? You mean that the debt of bones is my burden?"

Zedd pushed open the door to the room where his daughter slept, smiling as he looked in. "The debt is paid, Abby. The bracelet your mother gave you had magic, linking you to the debt. Thank you for my daughter's life."

Abby glanced to the Mother Confessor. Trickster indeed. "But why would you help me, if it was really not a debt of bones you owed me? If it was really a debt I owed you?"

Zedd shrugged. "We reap a reward merely in the act of helping others. We never know how, or if, that reward will come back to us. Helping is the reward; none other is needed nor better."

Abby watched the beautiful little girl sleeping in the room beyond. "I am thankful to the good spirits that I could help keep such a life in this world. I may not have the gift, but I can foresee that she will go on to be a person of import, not only for you, but for others."

Zedd smiled idly as he watched his daughter sleeping. "I think you may have the gift of prophecy, my dear, for she is already a person who has played a part in bringing a war to an end, and in so doing, saved the lives of countless people."

The sorceress pointed out the window. "I still want to know why that thing isn't moving. It was supposed to pass over D'Hara and purge it of all life, to kill them all for what they have done." Her scowl deepened. "Why is it just sitting there?"

Zedd folded his hands. "It ended the war. That is enough. The wall is a part of the underworld itself, the world of the dead. Their army will not be able to cross it and make war on us for as long as such a boundary stands."

"And how long will that be?"

Zedd shrugged. "Nothing remains forever. For now, there will be peace. The killing is ended."

The sorceress did not look to be satisfied. "But they were trying to kill us all!"

"Well, now they can't. Delora, there are those in D'Hara who are innocent, too. Just because Panis Rahl wished to conquer and subjugate us, that does not mean that all the D'Haran people are evil. Many good people in D'Hara have suffered under harsh rule. How could I kill everyone there, including all the people who have caused no harm, and themselves wish only to live their lives in peace?"

Delora wiped a hand across her face. "Zeddicus, sometimes I don't know about you. Sometimes, you make a lousy wind of death."

The Mother Confessor stood staring out the window, toward D'Hara. Her violet eyes turned back to the wizard.

"There will be those over there who will be your foes for life because of this, Zedd. You have made bitter enemies with this. You have left them alive."

"Enemies," the wizard said, "are the price of honor."

Tales of
Alvin Maker

—

ORSON SCOTT CARD

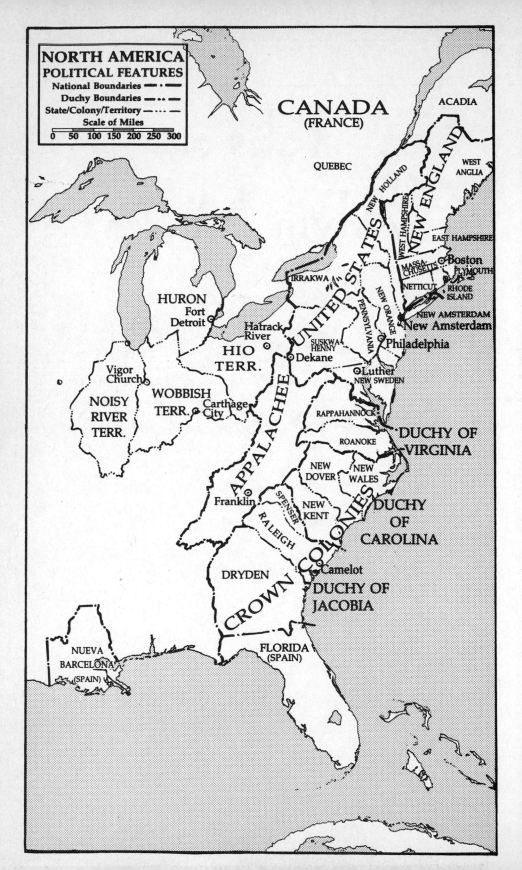

NORTH AMERICA
POLITICAL FEATURES
National Boundaries ——·—
Duchy Boundaries ——··—
State/Colony/Territory —···—
Scale of Miles
0   50 100 150 200 250 300

CANADA
(FRANCE)

ACADIA

QUEBEC

WEST
ANGLIA

NEW HOLLAND

NEW ENGLAND

WEST HAMPSHIRE

EAST HAMPSHIRE

●Boston

MASSA-
CHUSETTS

PLYMOUTH

IRRAKWA

NETTICUT

RHODE
ISLAND

UNITED STATES

NEW ORANGE

NEW AMSTERDAM

New Amsterdam

HURON

Fort
Detroit

PENNSYLVANIA

Hatrack
River

SUSKWA-
HENNY

Philadelphia

HIO
TERR.

Dekane

Vigor
Church

●Luther
NEW SWEDEN

NOISY
RIVER
TERR.

WOBBISH
TERR.

Carthage
City

APPALACHEE

RAPPAHANNOCK

ROANOKE

DUCHY OF
VIRGINIA

NEW
DOVER

NEW
WALES

Franklin

SPENSER

NEW
KENT

DUCHY
OF
CAROLINA

RALEIGH

CROWN COLONIES

DRYDEN

●Camelot

DUCHY OF
JACOBIA

NUEVA
BARCELONA
(SPAIN)

FLORIDA
(SPAIN)

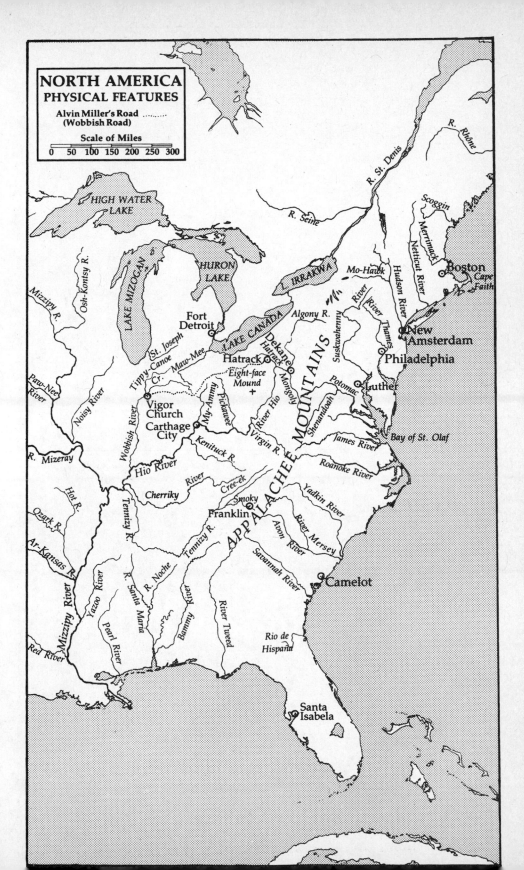

NORTH AMERICA
PHYSICAL FEATURES

Alvin Miller's Road ....
(Wobbish Road)

Scale of Miles

0 50 100 150 200 250 300

HIGH WATER LAKE

R. Rhone

R. St. Denis

Scoggin

R. Seine

Merrimack

Netticut River

Boston

Cape Faith

HURON LAKE

LAKE MIZOGAN

L. IRRAKWA

Mo-Hawk

Hudson River

Algony R.

River

River Thames

New Amsterdam

Fort Detroit

St. Joseph

LAKE CANADA

Dekane

Hatrack

Suskwahenny

Philadelphia

Tippy-Canoe

Maw-Mee

Hatrack

Eight-face Mound

Mongoly

Potomac

Luther

Cr.

Pickawee

River Hio

Shenandoah

Bay of St. Olaf

Noisy River

My-Ammy

Virgin R.

James River

Vigor Church

Carthage City

Wobbish River

Kenituck R.

Roanoke River

R. Mizeray

Hio River

River

Cree-ek

Yadkin River

Cherriky

Smoky

River Mersey

Hot R.

Tennizy R.

Franklin

Avon River

Ozark R.

Tennizy R.

Savannah River

Ar-Kansas R.

R. Noche

Bammy

River Tweed

Camelot

Mizzipy River

Yazoo River

R. Santa Maria

Rio de Hispana

Red River

Pearl River

Santa Isabela

APPALACHEE MOUNTAINS

THE TALES OF ALVIN MAKER:
BOOK ONE: SEVENTH SON (1987)
BOOK TWO: RED PROPHET (1988)
BOOK THREE: PRENTICE ALVIN (1989)
BOOK FOUR: ALVIN JOURNEYMAN (1996)
BOOK FIVE: HEARTFIRE (1998)

In the Tales of Alvin Maker series, an alternate-history view of an America that never was, Orson Scott Card postulated what the world might have been like if the Revolutionary War had never happened, and if folk magic actually worked.

America is divided into several provinces, with the Spanish and French still having a strong presence in the New World. The emerging scientific revolution in Europe has led many people with "talent," that is, magical ability, to emigrate to North America, bringing their prevailing magic with them. The books chronicle the life of Alvin, the seventh son of a seventh son—a fact that marks him right away as a person of great power. It is Alvin's ultimate destiny to become a Maker, an adept being of a kind that has not existed for a thousand years. However, there exists an Unmaker for every Maker—a being of great supernatural evil—who is Alvin's adversary, and strives to use Alvin's brother Calvin against him.

During the course of his adventures, Alvin explores the world around him and encounters such problems as slavery and the continued enmity between the settlers and the Native Americans who control the western half of the continent. The series appears to be heading toward an ultimate confrontation between Alvin and the Unmaker, with the fate of the entire continent, perhaps even the world, hinging on the outcome.

Grinning Man

ORSON SCOTT CARD

The first time Alvin Maker ran across the grinning man was in the steep woody hills of eastern Kenituck. Alvin was walking along with his ward, the boy Arthur Stuart, talking either deep philosophy or the best way for travelers to cook beans, I can't bring to mind now which, when they come upon a clearing where a man was squatting on his haunches looking up into a tree. Apart from the unnatural grin upon his face, there wasn't all that much remarkable about him, for that time and place. Dressed in buckskin, a cap made of coonhide on his head, a musket lying in the grass ready to hand—plenty of men of such youth and roughness walked the game trails of the unsettled forest in those days.

Though come to think of it, eastern Kenituck wasn't all that unsettled by then, and most men gave up buckskin for cotton during summer, less they was too poor to get them none. So maybe it *was* partly his appearance that made Alvin stop up short and look at the fellow. Arthur Stuart, of course, he did what he saw Alvin do, till he had some good reason to do otherwise, so he stopped at the meadow's edge too, and fell silent too, and watched.

The grinning man had his gaze locked on the middle branches of a scruffy old pine that was getting somewhat choked out by slower-growing flat-leaf trees. But it wasn't no tree he was grinning at. No sir, it was the bear.

There's bears and there's bears, as everyone knows. Some little old brown bears are about as dangerous as a dog—which means if you beat it with a stick you deserve what you get, but otherwise it'll leave you alone. But some black bears and some grizzlies, they have a kind of bristle to the hair on their backs, a kind of spikiness like a porcupine that tells you they're just spoiling for a fight, hoping you'll say a cross word so's they can take a swipe at your head and suck your lunch back up through your neck. Like a likkered-up riverman.

This was that kind of bear. A little old, maybe, but as spiky as they come, and it wasn't up that tree cause it was afraid, it was up there for honey, which it had plenty of, along with bees that were now so tired of trying to sting through that matted fur that they were mostly dead, all stung out. There was no shortage of buzzing, though, like a choir of folks as don't know the words to the hymn so they just hum, only the bees was none too certain of the tune, neither.

But there sat that man, grinning at the bear. And there sat the bear, looking down at him with its teeth showing.

Alvin and Arthur stood watching for many a minute while nothing in the tableau changed. The man squatted on the ground, grinning up; the bear squatted on a branch, grinning down. Neither one showed the slightest sign that he knew Alvin and Arthur was even there.

So it was Alvin broke the silence. "I don't know who started the ugly contest, but I know who's going to win."

Without breaking his grin, through clenched teeth the man said, "Excuse me for not shaking your hands but I'm a-busy grinning this bear."

Alvin nodded wisely—it certainly seemed to be a truthful statement. "And from the look of it," says Alvin, "that bear thinks he's grinning you, too."

"Let him think what he thinks," said the grinning man. "He's coming down from that tree."

Arthur Stuart, being young, was impressed. "You can do that just by grinning?"

"Just hope I never turn my grin on *you*," said the man. "I'd hate to have to pay your master the purchase price of such a clever blackamoor as you."

It was a common mistake, to take Arthur Stuart for a slave. He was half-Black, wasn't he? And south of the Hio was all slave country then, where a Black man either was, or used to be, or sure as shooting was bound to become somebody's property. In those parts, for safety's sake, Alvin didn't bother correcting the assumption. Let folks think Arthur Stuart already had an owner, so folks didn't get their hearts set on volunteering for the task.

"That must be a pretty strong grin," said Alvin Maker. "My name's Alvin. I'm a journeyman blacksmith."

"Ain't much call for a smith in these parts. Plenty of better land farther west, more settlers, you ought to try it." The fellow was still talking through his grin.

"I might," said Alvin. "What's your name?"

"Hold still now," says the grinning man. "Stay right where you are. He's a-coming down."

The bear yawned, then clambered down the trunk and rested on all fours, his head swinging back and forth, keeping time to whatever music it is that bears hear. The fur around his mouth was shiny with honey and dotted with dead bees. Whatever the bear was thinking, after a while he was done, whereupon he stood on his hind legs like a man, his paws high, his mouth open like a baby showing its mama it swallowed its food.

The grinning man rose up on *his* hind legs, then, and spread *his* arms, just like the bear, and opened his mouth to show a fine set of teeth for a human, but it wasn't no great shakes compared to bear teeth. Still, the bear seemed convinced. It bent back down to the ground and ambled away without complaint into the brush.

"That's my tree now," said the grinning man.

"Ain't much of a tree," said Alvin.

"Honey's about all et up," added Arthur Stuart.

"My tree and all the land round about," said the grinning man.

"And what you plan to do with it? You don't look to be a farmer."

"I plan to sleep here," said the grinning man. "And my intention was to sleep without no bear coming along to disturb my slumber. So I had to tell him who was boss."

"And that's all you do with that knack of yours?" asked Arthur Stuart. "Make bears get out of the way?"

"I sleep under bearskin in winter," said the grinning man. "So when I grin a bear, it stays grinned till I done what I'm doing."

"Don't it worry you that someday you'll meet your match?" asked Alvin mildly.

"I got no match, friend. My grin is the prince of grins. The king of grins."

"The emperor of grins," said Arthur Stuart. "The Napoleon of grins!"

The irony in Arthur's voice was apparently not subtle enough to escape the grinning man. "Your boy got him a mouth."

"Helps me pass the time," said Alvin. "Well, now you done us the favor of running off that bear, I reckon this is a good place for us to stop and build us a canoe."

Arthur Stuart looked at him like he was crazy. "What do we need a canoe for?"

"Being a lazy man," said Alvin, "I mean to use it to go downstream."

"Don't matter to me," said the grinning man. "Float it, sink it, wear it on your head, or swallow it for supper, you ain't building nothing right here." The grin was still on his face.

"Look at that, Arthur," said Alvin. "This fellow hasn't even told us his name, and he's a-grinning *us*."

"Ain't going to work," said Arthur Stuart. "We been grinned at by politicians, preachers, witchers, and lawyers, and you ain't got teeth enough to scare us."

With that, the grinning man brought his musket to bear right on Alvin's heart. "I reckon I'll stop grinning then," he said.

"I think this ain't canoe-building country," said Alvin. "Let's move along, Arthur."

"Not so fast," said the grinning man. "I think maybe I'd be doing all my neighbors a favor if I kept you from ever moving away from this spot."

"First off," said Alvin, "you got no neighbors."

"All mankind is my neighbor," said the grinning man. "Jesus said so."

"I recall he specified Samaritans," said Alvin, "and Samaritans got no call to fret about me."

"What I see is a man carrying a poke that he hides from my view."

That was true, for in that sack was Alvin's golden plow, and he always tried to keep it halfway hid behind him so folks wouldn't get troubled if they happened to see it move by itself, which it was prone to do from time to time. Now, though, to answer the challenge, Alvin moved the sack around in front of him.

"I got nothing to hide from a man with a gun," said Alvin.

"A man with a poke," said the grinning man, "who *says* he's a blacksmith but his only companion is a boy too scrawny and stubby to be learning his trade. But the boy is just the right size to skinny his way through an attic window or the eaves of a loose-made house. So I says to myself, this here's a second-story man, who lifts his boy up with those big strong arms so he can sneak into houses from above and open the door to the thief. So shooting you down right now would be a favor to the world."

Arthur Stuart snorted. "Burglars don't get much trade in the woods."

"I never said you-all looked smart," said the grinning man.

"Best point your gun at somebody else now," said Arthur Stuart quietly. "Iffen you want to keep the use of it."

The grinning man's answer was to pull the trigger. A spurt of flame shot out as the barrel of the gun exploded, splaying into iron strips like the end of a worn-out broom. The musket ball rolled slowly down the barrel and plopped out into the grass.

"Look what you done to my gun," said the grinning man.

"Wasn't me as pulled the trigger," said Alvin. "And you was warned."

"How come you still grinning?" asked Arthur Stuart.

"I'm just a cheerful sort of fellow," said the grinning man, drawing his big old knife.

"Do you like that knife?" asked Arthur Stuart.

"Got it from my friend Jim Bowie," said the grinning man. "It's took the hide off six bears and I can't count how many beavers."

"Take a look at the barrel of your musket," said Arthur Stuart, "and then look at the blade of that knife you like so proud, and think real hard."

The grinning man looked at the gun barrel and then at the blade. "Well?" asked the man.

"Keep thinking," said Arthur Stuart. "It'll come to you."

"You let him talk to White men like that?"

"A man as fires a musket at me," said Alvin, "I reckon Arthur Stuart here can talk to him any old how he wants."

The grinning man thought that over for a minute, and then, though no one would have believed it possible, he grinned even wider, put away his knife, and stuck out his hand. "You got some knack," he said to Alvin.

Alvin reached out and shook the man's hand. Arthur Stuart knew what was going to happen next, because he'd seen it before. Even though Alvin was announced as a blacksmith and any man with eyes could see the strength of his arms and hands, this grinning man just had to brace foot-to-foot against him and try to pull him down.

Not that Alvin minded a little sport. He let the grinning man work himself up into quite a temper of pulling and tugging and twisting and wrenching. It would have looked like quite a contest, except that Alvin could've been fixing to nap, he looked so relaxed.

Finally Alvin got interested. He squished down hard and the grinning man yelped and dropped to his knees and began to beg Alvin to give him back his hand. "Not that I'll ever have the use of it again," said the grinning man, "but I'd at least like to have it so I got a place to store my second glove."

"I got no plan to keep your hand," said Alvin.

"I know, but it crossed my mind you might be planning to leave it here in the meadow and send me somewheres else," said the grinning man.

"Don't you ever stop grinning?" asked Alvin.

"Don't dare try," said the grinning man. "Bad stuff happens to me when I don't smile."

"You'd be doing a whole lot better if you'd've frowned at me but kept your musket pointed at the ground and your hands in your pockets," said Alvin.

"You got my fingers squished down to one, and my thumb's about to pop off," said the grinning man. "I'm willing to say uncle."

"Willing is one thing. Doing's another."

"Uncle," said the grinning man.

"Nope, that won't do," said Alvin. "I need two things from you."

"I got no money and if you take my traps I'm a dead man."

"What I want is your name, and permission to build a canoe here," said Alvin.

"My name, if it don't become 'One-handed Davy,' is Crockett, in memory of my daddy," said the grinning man. "And I reckon I was wrong about this tree. It's your tree. Me and that bear, we're both far from home and got a ways to travel before nightfall."

"You're welcome to stay," said Alvin. "Room for all here."

"Not for me," said Davy Crockett. "My hand, should I get it back, is going to be mighty swoll up, and I don't think there's room enough for it in this clearing."

"I'll be sorry to see you go," said Alvin. "A new friend is a precious commodity in these parts." He let go. Tears came to Davy's eyes as he gingerly felt the sore palm and fingers, testing to see if any of them was about to drop off.

"Pleased to meet you, Mr. Journeyman Smith," said Davy. "You too, boy." He nodded cheerfully, grinning like an innkeeper. "I reckon you couldn't possibly be no burglar. Nor could you possibly be the famous Prentice Smith what stole a golden plow from his master and run off with the plow in a poke."

"I never stole nothing in my life," said Alvin. "But now you ain't got a gun, what's in my poke ain't none of your business."

"I'm pleased to grant you full title to this land," said Davy, "and all the rights to minerals under the ground, and all the rights to rain and sunlight on top of it, plus the lumber and all hides and skins."

"You a lawyer?" asked Arthur Stuart suspiciously.

Instead of answering, Davy turned tail and slunk out of the clearing just like that bear done, and in the same direction. He kept on slinking, too, though he probably wanted to run; but running would have made his hand bounce and that would hurt too much.

"I think we'll never see *him* again," said Arthur Stuart.

"I think we will," said Alvin.

"Why's that?"

"Cause I changed him deep inside, to be a little more like the bear. And I changed that bear to be a little bit more like Davy."

"You shouldn't go messing with people's insides like that," said Arthur Stuart.

"The Devil makes me do it," said Alvin.

"You don't believe in the Devil."

"Do so," said Alvin. "I just don't think he looks the way folks say he does."

"Oh? What does he look like then?" demanded the boy.

"Me," said Alvin. "Only smarter."

Alvin and Arthur set to work making them a dugout canoe. They cut down a tree just the right size—two inches wider than Alvin's hips—and set to burning one surface of it, then chipping out the ash and burning it deeper. It was slow, hot work, and the more they did of it, the more puzzled Arthur Stuart got.

"I reckon you know your business," he says to Alvin, "but we don't need no canoe."

"*Any* canoe," says Alvin. "Miss Larner'd be right peeved to hear you talking like that."

"First place," says Arthur Stuart, "you learned from Tenskwa-Tawa how to run like a Red man through the forest, faster than any canoe can float, and with a lot less work than this."

"Don't feel like running," said Alvin.

"Second place," Arthur Stuart continued, "water works against you every chance it gets. The way Miss Larner tells it, water near killed you sixteen times before you was ten."

"It wasn't the water, it was the Unmaker, and these days he's about give up on using water against me. He mostly tries to kill me now by making me listen to fools with questions."

"Third," says Arthur Stuart, "in case you're keeping count, we're supposed to be meeting up with Mike Fink and Verily Cooper, and making this canoe ain't going to help us get there on time."

"Those are two boys as need to learn patience," says Alvin calmly.

"Fourth," says Arthur Stuart, who was getting more and more peevish with every answer Alvin gave, "*fourth* and final reason, you're a *Maker,* dagnabbit, you could just think this tree hollow and float it over to the water light as a feather, so even if you had a reason to make this canoe, which you don't, and a safe place to float it, which you don't, you sure don't have to put me through this work to make it by hand!"

"You working too hard?" asked Alvin.

"Harder than is needed is always too hard," said Arthur.

"Needed by whom and for what?" asked Alvin. "You're right that I'm not making this canoe because we need to float down the river, and I'm not making it because it'll hurry up our travel."

"Then why? Or have you give up altogether on doing things for reasons?"

"I'm not making a canoe at all," says Alvin.

There knelt Arthur Stuart, up to his elbows in a hollowed-out log, scraping ash. "This sure ain't a house!"

"Oh, *you're* making a canoe," said Alvin. "And we'll float in that canoe down that river over there. But *I'm* not making a canoe."

Arthur Stuart kept working while he thought this over. After a few minutes he said, "I know what you're making."

"Do you?"

"You're making *me* do what you want."

"Close."

"You're making me make this tree into something, but you're also using this tree to make me into something."

"And what would I be trying to make *you* into?"

"Well, I think *you* think you're making me into a maker," said Arthur Stuart. "But all you're making me into is a *canoe*-maker, which ain't the same thing as being an all-around all-purpose Maker like yourself."

"Got to start somewhere."

"You didn't," says Arthur. "You was born knowing how to make stuff."

"I was born with a knack," says Alvin. "But I wasn't born knowing how to use it, or when, or why. I learned to love making for its own sake. I learned to love the feel of the wood and the stone under my hands, and from that I learned to see inside it, to feel how it felt, to know how it worked, what held it together, and how to help it come apart in just the right way."

"But I'm not learning any of that," says Arthur.

"Yet."

"No sir," says Arthur Stuart. "I'm not seeing inside nothing, I'm not feeling inside nothing except how my back aches and my whole body's pouring off sweat and I'm getting more and more annoyed at being made to labor on a job you could do with a wink of your eye."

"Well, that's something," says Alvin. "At least you're learning to see inside yourself."

Arthur Stuart fumed a little more, chipping away burnt wood as he did. "Someday I'm going to get fed up with your smugness," he says to Alvin, "and I won't follow you anymore."

Alvin shook his head. "Arthur Stuart, I tried to get you not to follow me this time, if you'll recall."

"Is *that* what this is about? You're punishing me for following you when you told me not to?"

"You said you wanted to learn everything about being a Maker," says Alvin. "And when I try to teach you, all I get is pissing and moaning."

"You also get work from me," says Arthur. "I never stopped working the whole time we talked."

"That's true," says Alvin.

"And here's something you didn't consider," says Arthur Stuart. "All the time we're making a canoe, we're also *un*making a tree."

Alvin nodded. "That's how it's done. You never make something out of nothing. You always make it out of something else. When it becomes the new thing, it ceases to be what it was before."

"So every time you do a making, you do an unmaking, too," says Arthur Stuart.

"Which is why the Unmaker always knows where I am and what I'm doing," says Alvin. "Because along with doing my work, I'm also doing a little bit of his."

That didn't sound right or true to Arthur Stuart, but he couldn't figure out an argument to answer it, and while he was trying to think one up, they kept on a-burning and a-chipping and lo and behold, they had them a canoe. They dragged it to the stream and put it in and got inside it and it tipped them right over. Spilled them into the water three times, till Alvin finally gave up and used his knack to feel the balance of the thing and then reshape it just enough that it had a good balance to it.

Arthur Stuart had to laugh at him then. "What lesson am I supposed to learn from *this*? How to make a *bad* canoe?"

"Shut up and row," said Alvin.

"We're going downstream," said Arthur Stuart, "and I don't have to row. Besides which all I've got is this stick, which is no kind of paddle."

"Then use it to keep us from running into the bank," said Alvin, "which we're about to do thanks to your babbling."

Arthur Stuart fended the canoe away from the bank of the stream, and they kept on floating down until they joined a larger stream, and a larger, and then a river. All the time, Arthur kept coming back to the things Alvin said to him, and what he was trying to teach, and as usual Arthur Stuart despaired of learning it. And yet he couldn't help but think he had learned *something*, even if he had no idea at present what the thing he learned might be.

Because folks build towns on rivers, when you float down a river you're likely as not to come upon a town, which they did one morning with mist still on the river and sleep still in their eyes. It wasn't much of a town, but then it wasn't much of a river, and they weren't in much of a boat. They put in to shore and dragged the canoe onto the bank, and Alvin shouldered his poke with the plow inside and they trudged on into town just as folks was getting up and about their day.

First thing they looked for was a roadhouse, but the town was too small and too new. Only a dozen houses, and the road so little traveled that grass was growing from one front door to the next. But that didn't mean there was no hope of breakfast. If there's light in the sky, some-body's up, getting a start on the day's work. Passing one house with a barn out back, they heard the ping-ping-ping of a cow getting milked into a tin pail. At another house, a woman was coming in with the night's eggs from a chicken coop. That looked promising.

"Got anything for a traveler?" asked Alvin.

The woman looked them up and down. Without a word she walked on into her house.

"If you wasn't so ugly," said Arthur Stuart, "she would have asked us in."

"Whereas looking at you is like seeing an angel," said Alvin.

They heard the front door of the house opening.

"Maybe she was just hurrying in to cook them eggs for us," said Arthur Stuart.

But it wasn't the woman who came out. It was a man, looking like he hadn't had much time to fasten his clothing. In fact, his trousers were kind of droopy, and they might have started laying bets on how quick they'd drop to the porch if he hadn't been aiming a pretty capable-looking blunderbuss at them.

"Move along," the man said.

"We're moving," said Alvin. He hoisted his poke to his back and started walking across in front of the house. The barrel of the shotgun followed them. Sure enough, just as they were about even with the front door, the trousers dropped. The man looked embarrassed and angry. The barrel of the blunderbuss dipped. The loose birdshot rolled out of the barrel, dozens of tiny lead balls hitting the porch like rain. The man looked confused now.

"Got to be careful loading up a big-barrel gun like that," Alvin said. "I always wrap the shot in paper so it don't do that."

The man glared at him. "I did."

"Why, I know you did," said Alvin.

But there sat the shot on the porch, a silent refutation. Nevertheless, Alvin was telling the simple truth. The paper was still in the barrel, as a matter of fact, but Alvin had persuaded it to break open at the front, freeing the shot.

"Your pants is down," said Arthur Stuart.

"Move along," said the man. His face was turning red. His wife was watching from the doorway behind him.

"Well, you know, we was already planning to," said Alvin, "but as long as you can't quite kill us, for the moment at least, can I ask you a couple of questions?"

"No," said the man. He set down the gun and pulled up his trousers.

"First off, I'd like to know the name of this town. I reckon it must be called 'Friendly' or 'Welcome.' "

"It ain't."

"Well, that's two down," said Alvin. "We got to keep guessing, or you think you can just tell us like one fellow to another?"

"How about 'Pantsdown Landing'?" murmured Arthur Stuart.

"This here is Westville, Kenituck," said the man. "Now move along."

"My second question is, seeing as how you folks don't have enough to share with a stranger, is there somebody who's prospering a bit more and might have something to spare for travelers as have a bit of silver to pay for it?"

"Nobody here got a meal for the likes of you," said the man.

"I can see why this road got grass growing on it," said Alvin. "But your graveyard must be full of strangers as died of hunger hoping for breakfast here."

On his knees picking up loose shot, the man didn't answer, but his wife stuck her head out the door and proved she had a voice after all. "We're as hospitable as anybody else, except to known burglars and thieving prentices."

Arthur Stuart let out a low whistle. "What you want to bet Davy Crockett came this way?" he said softly.

"I never stole a thing in my life," said Alvin.

"What you got in that poke, then?" demanded the woman.

"I wish I could say it was the head of the last man who pointed a gun at me, but unfortunately I left it attached to his neck, so he could come here and tell lies about me."

"So you're ashamed to show the golden plow you stole?"

"I'm a blacksmith, ma'am," said Alvin, "and I got my tools here. You're welcome to look, if you want."

He turned to address the other folks who were gathering, out on their porches or into the street, a couple of them armed.

"I don't know what you folks heard tell," said Alvin, setting down his poke, "but you're welcome to look at my tools." He drew open the mouth of the poke and let the sides drop so his hammer, tongs, bellows, and nails lay exposed in the street. Not a sign of a plow.

Everyone looked closely, as if taking inventory.

"Well, maybe you ain't the one we heared tell of," said the woman.

"No, ma'am, I'm the exact one, if it was a certain trapper in a coonskin cap named Davy Crockett who was telling the tale."

"So you confess to being that Prentice Smith who stole the plow? And a burglar?"

"No, ma'am, I just confess to being a fellow as got himself on the wrong side of a trapper who talks a man harm behind his back." He gathered up his bag over the tools and drew the mouth closed. "Now, if you-all want to turn me away, go ahead, but don't go thinking you turned away a thief, because it ain't so. You pointed a gun at me and turned me away without a bite to eat for me or this hungry boy, without so much as a trial or a scrap of evidence, just on the word of a traveler who was as much a stranger here as me."

The accusation made them all sheepish. One old woman, though, wasn't having any of it. "We know Davy, I reckon," she said. "It's you we never set eyes on."

"And never will again, I promise you," said Alvin. "You can bet

I'll tell this tale wherever I travel—Westville, Kenituck, where a stranger can't get a bite to eat, and a man is guilty before he even hears the accusation."

"If there's no truth to it," said the old woman, "how did you know it was Davy Crockett a-telling the tale?"

The others nodded and murmured as if this were a telling point.

"Cause Davy Crockett accused me of it to my face," said Alvin, "and he's the only one who ever looked at me and my boy and thought of burglaring. I'll tell you what I told him. If we're burglars, why ain't we in a big city with plenty of fine houses to rob? A burglar could starve to death, trying to find something to steal in a town as poor as this one."

"We ain't poor," said the man on the porch.

"You got no food to spare," said Alvin. "And there ain't a house here with a door that even locks."

"See?" cried the old woman. "He's already checked our doors to see how easy they'll be to break into!"

Alvin shook his head. "Some folks see sin in sparrows and wickedness in willow trees." He took Arthur Stuart by the shoulder and turned to head back out of town the way they came.

"Hold, stranger!" cried a man behind them. They turned to see a large man on horseback approaching slowly along the road. The people parted to make way for him.

"Quick, Arthur," Alvin murmured. "Who do you reckon this is?"

"The miller," said Alvin Stuart.

"Good morning to you, Mr. Miller!" cried Alvin in greeting.

"How did you know my trade?" asked the miller.

"The boy here guessed," said Alvin.

The miller rode nearer, and turned his gaze to Arthur Stuart. "And how did you guess such a thing?"

"You spoke with authority," said Arthur Stuart, "and you're riding a horse, and people made way for you. In a town this size, that makes you the miller."

"And in a bigger town?" asked the miller.

"You'd be a lawyer or a politician," said Arthur Stuart.

"The boy's a clever one," said the miller.

"No, he just runs on at the mouth," said Alvin. "I used to beat him but I plumb gave out the last time. Only thing I've found that shuts him up is a mouthful of food, preferably pancakes, but we'd settle for eggs, boiled, scrambled, poached, or fried."

The miller laughed. "Come along to my house, not three rods beyond the commons and down the road toward the river."

"You know," said Alvin, "my father's a miller."

The miller cocked his head. "Then how does it happen you don't follow his trade?"

"I'm well down the list of eight boys," said Alvin. "Can't all be millers, so I got put out to a smith. I've got a ready hand with mill equipment, though, in case you'll let me help you to earn our breakfast."

"Come along and we'll see how much you know," said the miller. "As for these folks, never mind them. If some wanderer came through and told them the sun was made of butter, you'd see them all trying to spread it on their bread." His mirth at this remark was not widely appreciated among the others, but that didn't faze him. "I've got a shoeing shed, too, so if you ain't above a little farrier work, I reckon there's horses to be shod."

Alvin nodded his agreement.

"Well, go on up to the house and wait for me," said the miller. "I won't be long. I come to pick up my laundry." He looked at the woman that Alvin had first spoken to. Immediately she ducked back inside the house to fetch the clothes the miller had come for.

On the road to the mill, once they were out of sight of the villagers, Alvin began to chuckle.

"What's so funny?" asked Arthur Stuart.

"That fellow with his pants around his ankles and birdshot dribbling out of his blunderbuss."

"I don't like that miller," said Arthur Stuart.

"Well, he's giving us breakfast, so I reckon he can't be all bad."

"He's just showing up the town folks," said Arthur Stuart.

"Well, excuse me, but I don't think that'll change the flavor of the pancakes."

"I don't like his voice."

That made Alvin perk up and pay attention. Voices were part of Arthur Stuart's knack. "Something wrong with the way he talks?"

"There's a meanness in him," said Arthur Stuart.

"May well be," said Alvin. "But his meanness is better than hunting for nuts and berries again, or taking another squirrel out of the trees."

"Or another fish." Arthur made a face.

"Millers get a name for meanness sometimes," he said. "People need their grain milled, all right, but they always think the miller takes too much. So millers are used to having folks accuse them. Maybe that's what you heard in his voice."

"Maybe," said Arthur Stuart. Then he changed the subject. "How'd you hide the plow when you opened your poke?"

"I kind of opened up a hole in the ground under the poke," said Alvin, "and the plow sank down out of sight."

"You going to teach me how to do things like *that*?"

"I'll do my best to teach," said Alvin, "if you do your best to learn."

"What about making shot spill out of a gun that's pointed at you?"

"My knack opened the paper, but his own trousers, that's what made the barrel dip and spill out the shot."

"And you didn't make his trousers fall?"

"If he'd pulled up his suspenders, his pants would've stayed up just fine," said Alvin.

"It's all Unmaking though, isn't it?" said Arthur Stuart. "Spilling shot, dropping trousers, making them folks feel guilty for not taking you in."

"So I should've let them drive us away without breakfast?"

"I've skipped breakfasts before."

"Well, aren't you the prissy one," said Alvin. "Why are you suddenly so critical of the way I do things?"

"You're the one made me dig out a canoe with my own hands," said Arthur Stuart. "To teach me Making. So I keep looking to see how much Making *you* do. And all I see is how you Unmake things."

Alvin took that a little hard. Didn't get mad, but he was kind of thoughtful and didn't speak much the rest of the way to the miller's house.

So nearly a week later, there's Alvin working in a mill for the first time since he left his father's place in Vigor Church and set out to be a Prentice smith in Hatrack River. At first he was happy, running his hands over the machinery, analyzing how the gears all meshed. Arthur Stuart, watching him, could see how each bit of machinery he touched

236

ran a little smoother—a little less friction, a little tighter fit—so more and more of the power from the water flowing over the wheel made it to the rolling millstone. It ground faster and smoother, less inclined to bind and jerk. Rack Miller, for that was his name, also noticed, but since he hadn't been watching Alvin work, he assumed that he'd done something with tools and lubricants. "A good can of oil and a keen eye do wonders for machinery," said Rack, and Alvin had to agree.

But after those first few days, Alvin's happiness faded, for he began to see what Arthur Stuart had noticed from the beginning: Rack was one of the reasons why millers had a bad name. It was pretty subtle. Folks would bring in a sack of corn to be ground into meal, and Rack would cast it in handfuls onto the millstone, then brush the corn flour into a tray and back into the same sack they brought it in. That's how all millers did it. No one bothered with weighing before and after, because everyone knew there was always some corn flour lost on the millstone.

What made Rack's practice a little different was the geese he kept. They had free rein in the millhouse, the yard, the millrace, and—some folks said—Rack's own house at night. Rack called them his daughters, though this was a perverse kind of thing to say, seeing as how only a few laying geese and a gander or two ever lasted out the winter. What Arthur Stuart saw at once, and Alvin finally noticed when he got over his love scene with the machinery, was how those geese were fed. It was expected that a few kernels of corn would drop; couldn't be helped. But Rack always took the sack and held it, not by the top, but by the shank of the sack, so kernels of corn dribbled out the whole way to the millstone. The geese were on that corn like—well, like geese on corn. And then he'd take big sloppy handfuls of corn to throw onto the millstone. A powerful lot of kernels hit the side of the stone instead of the top, and of course they dropped and ended up in the straw on the floor, where the geese would have them up in a second.

"Sometimes as much as a quarter of the corn," Alvin told Arthur Stuart.

"You counted the kernels? Or are you weighing corn in your head now?" asked Arthur.

"I can tell. Never less than a tenth."

"I reckon he figures he ain't stealing, it's the geese doing it," said Arthur Stuart.

"Miller's supposed to keep his tithe of the ground corn, not double or triple it or more in gooseflesh."

"I don't reckon it'll do much good for me to point out to you that this ain't none of our business," said Arthur Stuart.

"I'm the adult here, not you," said Alvin.

"You keep saying that, but the things you do, I keep wondering," said Arthur Stuart. "I'm not the one gallivanting all over creation while my pregnant wife is resting up to have the baby back in Hatrack River. I'm not the one keeps getting himself throwed in jail or guns pointed at him."

"You're telling me that when I see a thief I got to keep my mouth shut?"

"You think these folks are going to thank you?"

"They might."

"Put their miller in jail? Where they going to get their corn ground then?"

"They don't put the *mill* in jail."

"Oh, you going to stay here, then? You going to run this mill for them, till you taught the whole works to a prentice? How about me? You can bet they'll love paying their miller's tithe to a free half-Black prentice. What are you *thinking?*"

Well, that was always the question, wasn't it? Nobody ever knew, really, what Alvin was thinking. When he talked, he pretty much told the truth, he wasn't much of a one for fooling folks. But he also knew how to keep his mouth shut so you didn't know what was in his head. Arthur Stuart knew, though. He might've been just a boy, though more like a near-man these days, height coming on him kind of quick, his hands and feet getting big even faster than his legs and arms was getting long, but Arthur Stuart was an expert, he was a bona fide certified scholar on one subject, and that was Alvin, journeyman blacksmith, itinerant all-purpose dowser and doodlebug, and secret maker of golden plows and reshaper of the universe. He knew Alvin had him a plan for putting a stop to this thievery without putting anybody in jail.

Alvin picked his time. It was a morning getting on toward harvest time, when folks was clearing out a lot of last year's corn to make room for the new. So a lot of folks, from town and the nearby farms, was queued up to have their grain ground. And Rack Miller, he was downright exuberant in sharing that corn with the geese. But as he was handing the sack of corn flour to the customer, less about a quarter of its weight in goose fodder, Alvin scoops up a fine fat gosling and hands it to the customer right along with the grain.

The customer and Rack just looks at him like he's crazy, but Alvin pretends not to notice Rack's consternation at all. It's the customer he talks to. "Why, Rack Miller told me it was bothering him how much corn these geese've been getting, so this year he was giving out his goslings, one to each regular customer, as long as they last, to make up for it. I think that shows Rack to be a man of real honor, don't you?"

Well, it showed *something*, but what could Rack say after that? He just grinned through clenched teeth and watched as Alvin gave away gosling after gosling, making the same explanation, so everybody, wide-eyed and happy as clams, gave profuse thanks to the provider of their Christmas feast about four months off. Them geese would be monsters by then, they were already so big and fat.

Of course, Arthur Stuart noticed how, as soon as Rack saw how things was going, suddenly he started holding the sacks by the top, and taking smaller handfuls, so most of the time not a kernel fell to the ground. Why, that fellow had just learned himself a marvelous species of efficiency, returning corn to the customer diminished by nought but the true miller's tithe. It was plain enough that Rack Miller wasn't about to feed no corn to geese that somebody else was going to be feasting on that winter!

And when the day's work ended, with every last gosling gone, and only two ganders and five layers left, Rack faced Alvin square on and said, "I won't have no liar working for me."

"Liar?" asked Alvin.

"Telling them fools I meant to give them goslings!"

"Well, when I first said it, it wasn't true *yet*, but the minute you didn't raise your voice to argue with me, it became true, didn't it?" Alvin grinned, looking for all the world like Davy Crockett grinning him a bear.

"Don't chop no logic with me," said Rack. "You know what you was doing."

"I sure do," said Alvin. "I was making your customers happy with you for the first time since you come here, and making an honest man out of you in the meantime."

"I already *was* an honest man," said Rack. "I never took but what I was entitled to, living in a godforsaken place like this."

"Begging your pardon, my friend, but God ain't forsaken this place, though now and then a soul around here might have forsaken *Him*."

"I'm done with your help," said Rack icily. "I think it's time for you to move on."

"But I haven't even looked at the machinery you use for weighing the corn wagons," said Alvin. Rack hadn't been in a hurry for Alvin to check them over—the heavy scales out front was only used at harvest time, when farmers brought in whatever corn they meant to sell. They'd roll the wagons onto the scales, and through a series of levers the scale would be balanced with much lighter weights. Then the wagon would be rolled back on empty and weighed, and the difference between the two weights was the weight of the corn. Later on the buyers would come, roll on their empty wagons and weigh them, then load them up and weigh them again. It was a clever bit of machinery, a scale like that, and it was only natural that Alvin wanted to get his hands on it.

But Rack wasn't having none of it. "My scales is my business, stranger," he says to Alvin.

"I've et at your table and slept in your house," says Alvin. "How am I a stranger?"

"Man who gives away my geese, he's a stranger here forever."

"Well, then, I'll be gone from here." Still smiling, Alvin turned to his young ward. "Let's be on our way, Arthur Stuart."

"No sir," says Rack Miller. "You owe me for thirty-six meals these last six days. I didn't notice this Black boy eating one whit less than you. So you owe me in service."

"I gave you due service," says Alvin. "You said yourself that your machinery was working smooth."

"You didn't do nought but what I could have done myself with an oilcan."

"But the fact is I did it, and you didn't, and that was worth our keep. The boy's worked, too, sweeping and fixing and cleaning and hefting."

"I want six days' labor out of your boy. Harvest is upon us, and I need an extra pair of hands and a sturdy back. I've seen he's a good worker and he'll do."

"Then take three days' service from me *and* the boy. I won't give away any more geese."

"I don't have any more geese to give, except the layers. Anyway I don't want no miller's son, I just want the boy's labor."

"Then we'll pay you in silver money."

"What good is silver money here? Ain't nothing to spend it on. Nearest city of any size is Carthage, across the Hio, and hardly anybody goes there."

"I don't use Arthur Stuart to discharge my debts. He's not my—"

Well, long before those words got to Alvin's lips, Arthur Stuart knew what he was about to do—he was going to declare that Arthur wasn't his slave. And that would be about as foolish a thing as Alvin could do. So Arthur Stuart spoke right up before the words could get away. "I'm happy to work off the debt," he says. "Except I don't think it's possible. In six days I'll eat eighteen more meals and then I'll owe another three days, and in those three days I'll eat nine meals and I'll owe a day and a half, and at that rate I reckon I'll never pay off that debt."

"Ah yes," says Alvin. "Zeno's paradox."

"And you told me there was never any practical use for that 'bit of philosophical balderdash,' as I recall you saying," says Arthur Stuart. It was an argument from the days they both studied with Miss Larner, before she became Mrs. Alvin Smith.

"What the Sam Hill you boys talking about?" asked Rack Miller.

Alvin tried to explain. "Each day that Arthur Stuart works for you, he'll build up half again the debt that he pays off by his labor. So he only covers half the distance toward freedom. Half and half and half again, only he never quite gets to the goal."

"I don't get it," says Rack. "What's the joke?"

By this point, though, Arthur Stuart had another idea in mind. Mad as Rack Miller was about the goslings, if he truly needed help at harvest time he'd keep Alvin on for it, unless there was some other reason for getting rid of him. There was something Rack Miller planned to do that he didn't want Alvin to see. What he didn't reckon on was that this half-Black "servant" boy was every bit smart enough to figure it out himself. "I'd like to stay and see how we solve the paradox," says Arthur Stuart.

Alvin looks at him real close. "Arthur, I got to go see a man about a bear."

Well, that tore Arthur Stuart's resolve a bit. If Alvin was looking for Davy Crockett, to settle things, there might be scenes that Arthur wanted to see. At the same time, there was a mystery here at the millhouse, too, and with Alvin gone Arthur Stuart had a good chance at solving it all by himself. The one temptation was greater than the other. "Good luck," said Arthur Stuart. "I'll miss you."

Alvin sighed. "I don't plan to leave you here at the tender mercy of a man with a peculiar fondness for geese."

"What does *that* mean?" Rack said, growing more and more certain that they were making fun of him underneath all their talk.

"Why, you call them your daughters and then cook them and eat them," says Alvin. "What woman would ever marry you? She wouldn't dare leave you alone with the children!"

"Get out of my millhouse!" Rack bellowed.

"Come on, Arthur Stuart," said Alvin.

"I *want* to stay," Arthur Stuart insisted. "It can't be no worse than the time you left me with that schoolmaster." (Which is another story, not to be told right here.)

Alvin looked at Arthur Stuart real steady. He was no Torch, like his wife. He couldn't look into Arthur's heartfire and see a blame thing. But somehow he saw something that let him make up his mind the way Arthur Stuart wanted him to. "I'll go for now. I'll be back, though, in six days, and I'll have an accounting with you. You don't raise a hand or a stick against this boy, and you feed him and treat him proper."

"What do you think I am?" asked Rack.

"A man who gets what he wants," said Alvin.

"I'm glad you recognize that about me," said Rack.

"Everybody knows that about you," said Alvin. "It's just that you aren't too good at picking what you ought to be wanting." With another grin, Alvin tipped his hat and left Arthur Stuart.

Well, Rack was as good as his word. He worked Arthur Stuart hard, getting ready for the harvest. A late-summer rain delayed the corn in the field, but they put the time to good account, and Arthur was given plenty to eat and a good night's rest, though it was the millhouse loft he slept in now, and not the house; he had only been allowed inside as Alvin's personal servant, and with Alvin gone, there was no excuse for a half-Black boy sleeping in the house.

What Arthur noticed was that all the customers were in good cheer when they came to the millhouse for whatever business they had, especially during the rain when there wasn't no field work to be done. The story of the goslings had spread far and wide, and folks pretty much believed that it really had been Rack's idea, and not Alvin's doing at all. So instead of being polite but distant, the way folks usually was with a miller, they gave him hail-fellow-well-met and he heard the kind of jokes and gossip that folks shared with their friends. It was a new experience for Rack, and Arthur Stuart could see that this change was one Rack Miller didn't mind.

Then, the last day before Alvin was due to return, the harvest started up, and farmers from miles around began to bring in their corn wagons. They'd line up in the morning, and the first would pull his wagon onto the scale. The farmer would unhitch the horses and Rack would weigh the whole wagon. Then they'd hitch up the horses, pull the wagon to the dock, the waiting farmers would help unload the corn sacks—of course they helped, it meant they'd be home all the sooner themselves—and then back the wagon onto the scale and weigh it again, empty. Rack would figure the difference between the two weighings, and that difference was how many pounds of corn the farmer got credit for.

Arthur Stuart went over the figures in his head, and Rack wasn't cheating them with his arithmetic. He looked carefully to see if Rack was doing something like standing on the scale when the empty wagon was being weighed, but no such thing.

Then, in the dark of that night, he remembered something one of the farmers grumbled as they were backing an empty wagon onto the scale. "Why didn't he build this scale right at the loading dock, so we could unload the wagon and reweigh it without having to move the durn thing?" Arthur Stuart didn't know the mechanism of it, but he thought back over the day and remembered that another time a farmer had asked if he could get his full wagon weighed while the previous farmer's wagon was being unloaded. Rack glared at the man. "You want to do things your way, go build your own mill."

Yes sir, the only thing Rack cared about was that every wagon get two weighings, right in a row. And the same system would work just as well in reverse when the buyers came with their empty wagons to haul corn east for the big cities. Weigh the empty, load it, and weigh it again.

When Alvin got back, Arthur Stuart would be ready with the mystery mostly solved.

Meanwhile, Alvin was off in the woods, looking for Davy Crockett, that grinning man who was single-handedly responsible for getting two separate guns pointed at Alvin's heart. But it wasn't vengeance that was on Alvin's mind. It was rescue.

For he knew what he'd done to Davy and the bear, and kept track of their heartfires. He couldn't see into heartfires the way Margaret could, but he could see the heartfires themselves, and keep track of who was who. In fact, knowing that no gun could shoot him and no jail could hold him, Alvin had deliberately come to the town of Westville because he knew Davy Crockett had come through that town, the bear not far behind him, though Davy wouldn't know that, not at the time.

He knew it now, though. What Alvin saw back in Rack's millhouse was that Davy and the bear had met again, and this time it might come out a little different. For Alvin had found the place deep in the particles of the body where knacks were given, and he had taken the bear's best knack and given as much to Davy, and Davy's best knack and given the same to the bear. They were evenly matched now, and Alvin figured he had some responsibility to see to it that nobody got hurt. After all, it was partly Alvin's fault that Davy didn't have a gun to defend himself. Mostly it was Davy's fault for pointing it at him, but Alvin hadn't had to wreck the gun the way he did, making the barrel blow apart.

Running lightly through the woods, leaping a stream or two, and stopping to eat from a fine patch of wild strawberries on a riverbank, Alvin got to the place well before nightfall, so he had plenty of time to reconnoiter. There they were in the clearing, just as Alvin expected, Davy and the bear, not five feet apart, both of them a-grinning, staring each other down, neither one budging. That bear was all spiky, but he couldn't get past Davy's grin; and Davy matched the bear's single-minded tenacity, oblivious to pain, so even though his butt was already sore and he was about out of his mind with sleepiness, he didn't break his grin.

Just as the sun set, Alvin stepped out into the clearing behind the bear. "Met your match, Davy?" he asked.

Davy didn't have an ounce of attention to spare for chat. He just kept grinning.

"I think this bear don't mean to be your winter coat this year," said Alvin.

Davy just grinned.

"In fact," said Alvin, "I reckon the first one of you to fall asleep, that's who the loser is. And bears store up so much sleep in the winter, they just flat out don't need as much come summertime."

Grin.

"So there you are barely keeping your eyelids up, and there's the bear just happy as can be, grinning at you out of sincere love and devotion."

Grin. With maybe a little more desperation around the eyes.

"But here's the thing, Davy," said Alvin. "Bears is better than people, mostly. You got your bad bears, sometimes, and your good people, but on average, I'd trust a bear to do what he thinks is right before I'd trust a human. So now what you got to wonder is, what does that bear think will be the right thing to do with you, once he's grinned you down?"

Grin grin grin.

"Bears don't need no coats of human skin. They do need to pile on the fat for winter, but they don't generally eat meat for that. Lots of fish, but you ain't a swimmer and the bear knows that. Besides, that bear don't think of you as meat, or he wouldn't be grinning you. He thinks of you as a rival. He thinks of you as his equal. What *will* he do. Don't you kind of wonder? Don't you have some speck of curiosity that just wants to know the answer to that question?"

The light was dimming now, so it was hard to see much more of either Davy or the bear than their white, white teeth. And their eyes.

"You've already stayed up one whole night," said Alvin. "Can you do it again? I don't think so. I think pretty soon you're going to understand the mercy of bears."

Only now, in his last desperate moments before succumbing to sleep, did Davy dare to speak. "Help me," he said.

"And how would I do that?" asked Alvin.

"Kill that bear."

Alvin walked up quietly behind the bear and gently rested his hand on the bear's shoulder. "Why would I do that? This bear never pointed no gun at me."

"I'm a dead man," Davy whispered. The grin faded from his face. He bowed his head, then toppled forward, curled up on the ground, and waited to be killed.

But it didn't happen. The bear came up, nosed him, snuffled him all over, rolled him back and forth a little, all the time ignoring the little whimpering sounds Davy was making. Then the bear lay down beside the man, flung one arm over him, and dozed right off to sleep.

Unbelieving, Davy lay there, terrified yet hopeful again. If he could just stay awake a little longer.

Either the bear was a light sleeper in the summertime, or Davy made his move too soon, but no sooner did his hand slide toward the knife at his waist than the bear was wide awake, slapping more or less playfully at Davy's hand.

"Time for sleep," said Alvin. "You've earned it, the bear's earned it, and come morning you'll find things look a lot better."

"What's going to happen to me?" asked Davy.

"Don't you think that's kind of up to the bear?"

"You're controlling him somehow," said Davy. "This is all your doing."

"He's controlling himself," said Alvin, careful not to deny the second charge, seeing how it was true. "And he's controlling you. Because that's what grinning is all about—deciding who is master. Well, that bear is master here, and I reckon tomorrow we'll find out what bears do with domesticated humans."

Davy started to murmur a prayer.

The bear laid a heavy paw on Davy's mouth.

"Prayers are done," intoned Alvin. "Gone the sun. Shadows creep. Go to sleep."

That's how it came about that when Alvin returned to Westville, he did it with two friends along—Davy Crockett and a big old grizzly bear. Oh, folks was alarmed when that bear come into town, and ran for their guns, but the bear just grinned at them and they didn't shoot. And when the bear gave Davy a little poke, why, he'd step forward and say a few words. "My friend here doesn't have much command of the American language," said Davy, "but he'd just as soon you put that gun away and didn't go pointing it at him. Also, he'd be glad of a bowl of corn mush or a plate of corn bread, if you've got any to spare."

Why, that bear plumb ate his way through Westville, setting down to banquets without raising a paw except to poke at Davy Crockett, and folks didn't even mind it, it was such a sight to see a man serve gruel and corn bread to a bear. And that wasn't all, either. Davy Crockett spent a good little while picking burrs out of the bear's fur, especially in the rumpal area, and singing to the bear whenever it crooned in a high-pitched tone. Davy sang pert near every song that he ever heard, even if he only heard it once, or didn't hear the whole thing, for there's nothing to bring back the memory of tunes and lyrics like having an eleven-foot bear poking you and whining to get you to sing, and when he flat out couldn't remember, why, he made it something up, and since the bear wasn't altogether particular, the song was almost always good enough.

As for Alvin, he'd every now and then pipe up and ask Davy to mention whether it was true that Alvin was a burglar and a plow-stealing prentice, and each time Davy said no, it wasn't true, that was just a made-up lie because Davy was mad at Alvin and wanted to get even. And whenever Davy told the truth like that, the bear rumbled its approval and stroked Davy's back with his big old paw, which Davy was just barely brave enough to endure without wetting himself much.

Only when they'd gone all through the town and some of the outlying houses did this parade come to the millhouse, where the horses naturally complained a little at the presence of a bear. But Alvin spoke to each of them and put them at ease, while the bear curled up and took him a nap, his belly being full of corn in various forms. Davy didn't go far, though, for the bear kept sniffing, even in his sleep, to make sure Davy was close by.

Davy was putting the best face on things, though. He had his pride. "A man does things for a friend, and this here bear's my friend," said Davy. "I'm done with trapping, as you can guess, so I'm looking for a line of work that can help my friend get ready for the winter. What I mean is, I got to earn some corn, and I hope some of you have jobs for me to do. The bear just watches, I promise, he's no danger to your livestock.''

Well, they heard him out, of course, because one tends to listen for a while at least to a man who's somehow got himself hooked up as a servant to a grizzly bear. But there wasn't a chance in hell that they were going to let no bear anywhere near their pigsties, nor their chicken coops, especially not when the bear clearly showed no disposition to earn its food honestly. If it would beg, they figured, it would steal, and they'd have none of it.

Meanwhile, as the bear napped and Davy talked to the farmers, Alvin and Arthur had their reunion, with Arthur Stuart telling him what he'd figured out. "Some mechanism in the scale makes it weigh light when the wagon's full, and heavy when it's empty, so the farmers get short weight. But then, without changing a thing, it'll weight light on the buyers' empty wagons, and heavy when they're full, so Rack gets extra weight when he's selling the same corn.''

Alvin nodded. "You find out if this theory is actually true?''

"The only time he ain't watching me is in the dark, and in the dark I can't sneak down and see a thing. I'm not crazy enough to risk getting myself caught sneaking around the machinery in the dark, anyway.''

"Glad to know you got a brain.''

"Says the man who keeps getting himself put in jail.''

Alvin made a face at him, but in the meantime he was sending out his doodlebug to probe the machinery of the scale underground. Sure enough, there was a ratchet that engaged on one weighing, causing the levering to shift a little, making short weight; and on the next weighing, the ratchet would disengage and the levers would move back, giving long weight. No wonder Rack didn't want Alvin looking over the machinery of the scale.

The solution, as Alvin saw it, was simple enough. He told Arthur Stuart to stand near the scale but not to step on it. Rack wrote down the weight of the empty wagon, and while it was being pulled off the scale, he stood there calculating the difference. The moment the wagon was clear of the scale, Alvin rounded on Arthur Stuart, speaking loud enough for all to hear.

"Fool boy! What were you doing! Didn't you see you was standing on that scale?''

"I wasn't!'' Arthur Stuart cried.

"I don't think he was," said a farmer. "I worried about that, he was so close, so I looked."

"And I say I saw him stand on it," said Alvin. "This farmer shouldn't be out the cost of a boy's weight in corn, I think!"

"I'm sure the boy didn't stand on the scale," Rack said, looking up from his calculation.

"Well, there's a simple enough test," said Alvin. "Let's get that empty wagon back onto the scale."

Now Rack grew alarmed. "Tell you what," he said to the farmer, "I'll just *give* you credit for the boy's weight."

"Is this scale sensitive enough to weigh the boy?" asked Alvin.

"Well, I don't know," said Rack. "Let's just estimate."

"No!" cried Alvin. "This farmer doesn't want any more than his fair credit, and it's not right for him to receive any less. Haul the wagon back on and let's weigh it again."

Rack was about to protest again, when Alvin said, "Unless there's something wrong with the scale. There wouldn't be something wrong with the scale, now, would there?"

Rack got a sick look on his face. He couldn't very well confess. "Nothing wrong with the scale," he said gruffly.

"Then let's weigh this wagon and see if my boy's weight made any difference."

Well, you guessed it. As soon as the wagon was back on the scale, it showed near a hundred pounds lighter than it did the first time. The other witnesses were flummoxed. "Could have sworn the boy never stepped on that scale," said one. And another said, "I don't know as I would have guessed that boy to weigh a hundred pounds."

"Heavy bones," says Alvin.

"No sir, it's my brain that weighs heavy," said Arthur Stuart, winning a round of laughter.

And Rack, trying to put a good face on it, pipes up, "No, it's the food he's been eating at my table—that's fifteen pounds of it right there!"

In the meantime, though, the farmer's credit was being adjusted by a hundred pounds.

And the next wagon to come on the scale was a full one, while the scale was set to read heavy. In vain did Rack try to beg off early—Alvin simply offered to keep on weighing for him, with the farmers as witnesses so he wrote down everything square. "You don't want any of these men to have to wait an extra day to sell you their market grain, do you?" Alvin said. "Let's weigh it all!"

And weigh it all they did, thirty wagons before the day was done, and the farmers was all remarking to each other about what a good corn year it was, the kernels heavier than usual. Arthur Stuart did hear one man start to grumble that his wagon seemed to be lighter this year than in any previous year, but Arthur immediately spoke up loud enough for all to hear. "It don't matter if the scale is weighing light or heavy—it's the difference between the full weight and the empty weight that matters, and as long as it's the same scale, it's going to be correct." The farmers thought that over and it sounded right to them, while Rack couldn't very well explain.

Arthur Stuart figured it all out in his head and he realized that Alvin hadn't exactly set things to rights. On the contrary, this year Rack was getting cheated royally, recording credits for these farmers that were considerably more than the amount of corn they actually brought in. He could bear such losses for one day; and by tomorrow, Alvin and Arthur both knew, Rack meant to have the scale back in its regular pattern—light for the full wagons, heavy for the empty ones.

Still, Alvin and Arthur cheerfully bade Rack farewell, not even commenting on the eagerness he showed to be rid of them.

That night, Rack Miller's lantern bobbed across the yard between his house and the mill. He closed the mill door behind him and headed for the trapdoor leading down to the scale mechanism. But to his surprise, there was something lying on top of that trapdoor. A bear. And nestled in to sleep with the bear wrapped around him was Davy Crockett.

"I hope you don't mind," said Davy, "but this here bear took it into his head to sleep right here, and I'm not inclined to argue with him."

"Well, he can't, so that's that," said the miller.

"You tell him," said Davy. "He just don't pay no heed to my advice."

The miller argued and shouted, but the bear paid no mind. Rack got him a long stick and poked at the bear, but the bear just opened one eye, slapped the stick out of Rack's hand, then took it in his mouth and crunched it up like a cracker. Rack Miller proposed to bring a gun out, but Davy drew his knife then. "You'll have to kill me along with the bear," he said, "cause if you harm him, I'll carve you up like a Christmas goose."

"I'll be glad to oblige you," said Rack.

"But then you'll have to explain how I came to be dead. If you manage to kill the bear with one shot, that is. Sometimes these bears can take a half-dozen balls into their bodies and still swipe a man's head clean off and then go fishing for the afternoon. Lots of fat, lots of muscle. And how's your aim, anyway?"

So it was that next morning, the scale still weighed opposite to Rack's intent, and so it went day after day until the harvest was over. Every day the bear and his servant ate their corn mush and corn bread and drank their corn likker and lay around in the shade, with onlookers gathering and lingering to see the marvel. The result was that witnesses were around all day and not far off at night. And it went on just the same when the buyers started showing up to haul away the corn.

Stories about the bear who had tamed a man brought more than just onlookers, too. More farmers than usual came to Rack Miller to sell their corn, so they could see the sight; and more buyers went out of their way to come to buy, so there was maybe half again as much business as usual. At the end of the whole harvest season, there was Rack Miller with a ledger book showing a huge loss. He wouldn't be paid enough by the buyers to come close to making good on what he owed the farmers. He was ruined.

He went through a few jugs of corn likker and took some long walks, but by late October he'd given up all hope. One time his despair led him to point a pistol at his head and fire, but the powder for some reason wouldn't ignite, and when Rack tried to hang himself he couldn't tie a knot that didn't slip. Since he couldn't even succeed at killing himself, he finally gave up even that project and took off in the dead of night, abandoning mill and ledger and all. Well, he didn't mean to abandon it—he meant to burn it. But the fires he started kept blowing out, so that was yet another project he failed at. In the end, he left with the clothes on his back and two geese tucked under his arms, and they honked so much he turned them loose before he was out of town.

*   *   *

When it was clear Rack wasn't just off on a holiday, the town's citizens and some of the more prominent farmers from round about met in Rack Miller's abandoned house and went over his ledger. What they learned there told them clear enough that Rack Miller was unlikely to return. They divided up the losses evenly among the farmers, and it turned out that nobody lost a thing. Oh, the farmers got paid less than Rack Miller's ledger showed, but they'd get a good deal more than they had in previous years, so it was still a good year for them. And when they got to inspecting the property, they found the ratchet mechanism in the scale and then the picture was crystal clear.

All in all, they decided, they were well rid of Rack Miller, and a few folks had suspicions that it was that Alvin Smith and his half-Black boy who'd turned the tables on this cheating miller. They even tried to find out where he might be, to offer him the mill in gratitude. Someone had heard tell he came from Vigor Church up in Wobbish, and a letter there did bring results—a letter in reply, from Alvin's father. "My boy thought you might make such an offer, and he asked me to give you a better suggestion. He says that since a man done such a bad job as miller, maybe you'd be better off with a bear, especially if the bear has him a manservant who can keep the books."

At first they laughed off the suggestion, but after a while they began to like it, and when they proposed it to Davy and the bear, they cottoned to it, too. The bear got him all the corn he wanted without ever lifting a finger, except to perform a little for folks at harvest time, and in the winter he could sleep in a warm dry place. The years he mated, the place was a little crowded with bearflesh, but the cubs were no trouble and the mama bears, though a little suspicious, were mostly tolerant, especially because Davy was still a match for any of *them*, and could grin them into docility when the need arose.

As for Davy, he kept true books, and fixed the scale so it didn't ratchet anymore, giving honest weight every time. As time went on, he was so well liked that folks talked about running him for mayor of Westville. He refused, of course, since he wasn't his own man. But he allowed as how, if they elected the bear, he'd be glad to serve as the bear's secretary and interpreter, and that's what they did. After a year or two of having a bear as mayor, they up and changed the name to Bearsville, and the town prospered. Years later, when Kentuck joined the United States of America, it's not hard to guess who got elected to Congress from that part of the state, which is how it happened that for seven terms of Congress a bear put its hand on the Bible right along with the other congressmen, and then proceeded to sleep through every session it attended, while its clerk, one Davy Crockett, cast all its votes for it and gave all its speeches, every one of which ended with the sentence "Or at least that's how it looks to one old grizzly bear."

Majipoor

ROBERT SILVERBERG

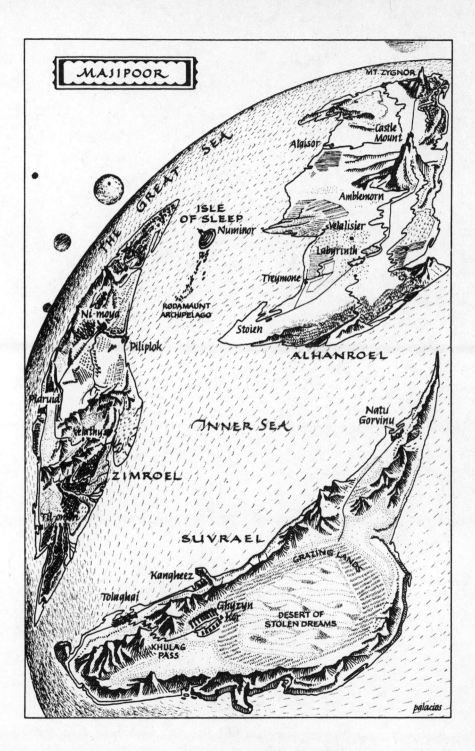

LORD VALENTINE'S CASTLE (1980)
MAJIPOOR CHRONICLES (1981)
VALENTINE PONTIFEX (1983)
THE MOUNTAINS OF MAJIPOOR (1995)
SORCERERS OF MAJIPOOR (1997)
LORD PRESTIMION (1999)

The giant world of Majipoor, with a diameter at least ten times as great as our own planet's, was settled in the distant past by colonists from Earth, who made a place for themselves amid the Piurivars, the intelligent native beings, whom the intruders from Earth called Shapeshifters or Metamorphs because of their ability to alter their bodily forms. Majipoor is an extraordinarily beautiful planet, with a largely benign climate, and is a place of astonishing zoological, botanical, and geographical wonders. Everything on Majipoor is large-scale—fantastic, marvelous.

Over the course of thousands of years, friction between the human colonists and the Piurivars eventually led to a lengthy war and the defeat of the natives, who were penned up in huge reservations in remote regions of the planet. During those years, also, species from various other worlds came to settle on Majipoor—the tiny gnomish Vroons, the great shaggy four-armed Skandars, the two-headed Su-Suheris race, and several more. Some of these—notably the Vroons and the Su-Suheris—were gifted with extrasensory mental powers that permitted them to practice various forms of wizardry. But throughout the thousands of years of Majipoor history the humans remained the dominant species. They flourished and expanded and eventually the human population of Majipoor came to number in the billions, mainly occupying huge and distinctive cities of ten to twenty million people.

The governmental system that evolved over those years was a kind of nonhereditary dual monarchy. The senior ruler, known as the Pontifex, selects his own junior ruler, the Coronal, when he comes to power. Technically the Coronal is regarded as the adoptive son of the Pontifex, and upon the death of the Pontifex takes his place on the senior throne, naming a new Coronal as his own successor. Both of these rulers make their homes on Alhanroel, the largest and most populous of Majipoor's three continents. The imperial residence of the Pontifex is in the lowest level of a vast subterranean city called the Labyrinth, from which he emerges only at rare intervals. The Coronal, by contrast, lives in an enormous castle at the summit of Castle Mount, a thirty-mile-high peak whose atmosphere is maintained in an eternal springtime by elaborate machinery. From time to time the Coronal descends from the opulence of the Castle to travel across the face of the world in a Grand Processional, an event designed to remind Majipoor of the might and power of its rulers. Such a journey, which in Majipoor's vast distances could take several years, invariably brings the Coronal to Zimroel, the second continent, a place of gigantic cities interspersed among tremendous rivers and great unspoiled forests. More rarely he goes to the torrid third continent in the south, Suvrael, largely a wasteland of Sahara-like deserts.

Two other functionaries became part of the Majipoor governmental system later on. The development of a method of worldwide telepathic communication made possible nightly sendings of oracular advice and occasional therapeutic counsel, which became the responsibility of the mother of the incumbent Coronal, under the title of Lady of the Isle of Sleep. Her headquarters are situated on an island of continental size midway between Alhanroel and Zimroel. Later, a second telepathic authority, the King of Dreams, was set in place. He employs more powerful telepathic equipment in order to monitor and chastise criminals and other citizens whose behavior deviates from accepted Majipoor norms. This office is the hereditary property of the Barjazid family of Suvrael.

The first of the Majipoor novels, *Lord Valentine's Castle*, tells of a conspiracy that succeeds in overthrowing the legitimate Coronal, Lord Valentine, and replacing him with an impostor. Valentine, stripped of all his memories, is set loose in Zimroel to live the life of a wandering juggler, but gradually regains an awareness of his true role and launches a successful campaign to reclaim his throne. In the sequel, *Valentine Pontifex*, the now mature Valentine, a pacifist at heart, must deal with an uprising among the Metamorphs, who are determined to drive the hated human conquerors from their world at last. Valentine defeats them and restores peace with the help of the giant maritime beasts known as sea-dragons, whose intelligent powers were not previously suspected on Majipoor.

The story collection *Majipoor Chronicles* depicts scenes from many eras and social levels of Majipoor life, providing detailed insight into a number of aspects of the giant world not described in the novels. The short novel *The Mountains of Majipoor*, set five hundred years after Valentine's reign, carries the saga into the icy northlands, where a separate barbaric civilization has long endured. And the most recent of the Majipoor books, *Sorcerers of Majipoor*, begins a new trilogy set a thousand years prior to Valentine's time, in which the powers of sorcery and magic have become rife on Majipoor. The Coronal Lord Prestimion, after being displaced from his throne by the usurping son of the former Coronal with the assistance of mages and warlocks, leads his faction to victory in a civil war in which he too makes use of necromantic powers. The sequel, *Lord Prestimion*, shows him struggling to deal with the day-by-day problems of kingship in a world that has been immensely altered by the wizardry employed at the climax of the war.

The story presented here offers an episode from a period late in Valentine's reign as Pontifex, when the war against the Metamorphs has been over for some years but the process of reconciliation is still incomplete.

The Seventh Shrine

ROBERT SILVERBERG

One last steep ridge of the rough, boulder-strewn road lay between
the royal party and the descent into Velalisier Plain. Valentine, who
was leading the way, rode up over it and came to a halt, looking down
with amazement into the valley. The land that lay before him seemed
to have undergone a bewildering transformation since his last visit.
"Look there," the Pontifex said, bemused. "This place is always full
of surprises, and here is ours."

The broad shallow bowl of the arid plain spread out below them.
From this vantage point, a little way east of the entrance to the archaeological site, they should easily have been able to see a huge field
of sand-swept ruins. There had been a mighty city here once, that
notorious Shapeshifter city where, in ancient times, so much dark history had been enacted, such monstrous sacrilege and blasphemy. But—
surely it was just an illusion?—the sprawling zone of fallen buildings
at the center of the plain was almost completely hidden now by a
wondrous rippling body of water, pale pink along its rim and pearly
gray at its middle: a great lake where no lake ever had been.

Evidently the other members of the royal party saw it too. But did
they understand that it was simply a trick? Some fleeting combination
of sunlight and dusty haze and the stifling midday heat must have created a momentary mirage above dead Velalisier, so that it seemed as

if a sizable lagoon, of all improbable things, had sprung up in the midst of this harsh desert to engulf the dead city.

It began just a short distance beyond their vantage point and extended as far as the distant gray-blue wall of great stone monoliths that marked the city's western boundary. Nothing of Velalisier could be seen. None of the shattered and timeworn temples and palaces and basilicas, or the red basalt blocks of the arena, the great expanses of blue stone that had been the sacrificial platforms, the tents of the archaeologists who had been at work here at Valentine's behest since late last year. Only the six steep and narrow pyramids that were the tallest surviving structures of the prehistoric Metamorph capital were visible—their tips, at least, jutting out of the gray heart of the ostensible lake like a line of daggers fixed point-upward in its depths.

"Magic," murmured Tunigorn, the oldest of Valentine's boyhood friends, who held the post now of Minister of External Affairs at the Pontifical court. He drew a holy symbol in the air. Tunigorn had grown very superstitious, here in his later years.

"I think not," said Valentine, smiling. "Just an oddity of the light, I'd say."

And, just as though the Pontifex had conjured it up with some countermagic of his own, a lusty gust of wind came up from the north and swiftly peeled the haze away. The lake went with it, vanishing like the phantom it had been. Valentine and his companions found themselves now beneath a bare and merciless iron-blue sky, gazing down at the true Velalisier—that immense dreary field of stony rubble, that barren and incoherent tumble of dun-colored fragments and drab threadbare shards lying in gritty beds of wind-strewn sand, which was all that remained of the abandoned Metamorph metropolis of long ago.

"Well, now," said Tunigorn, "perhaps you were right, majesty. Magic or no, though, I liked it better the other way. It was a pretty lake, and these are ugly stones."

"There's nothing here to like at all, one way or another," said Duke Nascimonte of Ebersinul. He had come all the way from his great estate on the far side of the Labyrinth to take part in this expedition. "This is a sorry place and always has been. If I were Pontifex in your stead, your majesty, I'd throw a dam across the River Glayge and send a raging torrent this way, that would bury this accursed city and its whole history of abominations under two miles of water for all time to come."

Some part of Valentine could almost see the merit of that. It was easy enough to believe that the somber spells of antiquity still hovered here, that this was a territory where ominous enchantments held sway.

But of course Valentine could hardly take Nascimonte's suggestion seriously. "Drown the Metamorphs' sacred city, yes! By all means, let's do that," he said lightly. "Very fine diplomacy, Nascimonte. What a splendid way of furthering harmony between the races that would be!"

Nascimonte, a lean and hard-bitten man of eighty years, with keen sapphire eyes that blazed like fiery gems in his broad furrowed forehead, said pleasantly, "Your words tell us what we already know, majesty: that it's just as well for the world that you are Pontifex, not I. I lack your benign and merciful nature—especially, I must say, when it comes to the filthy Shapeshifters. I know you love them and would bring them up out of their degradation. But to me, Valentine, they are vermin and nothing but vermin. Dangerous vermin at that."

"Hush," said Valentine. He was still smiling, but he let a little annoyance show as well. "The Rebellion's long over. It's high time we put these old hatreds to rest forever."

Nascimonte's only response was a shrug.

Valentine turned away, looking again toward the ruins. Greater mysteries than that mirage awaited them down there. An event as grim and terrible as anything out of Velalisier's doleful past had lately occurred in this city of long-dead stones: a murder, no less.

Violent death at another's hands was no common thing on Majipoor. It was to investigate that murder that Valentine and his friends had journeyed to ancient Velalisier this day.

"Come," he said. "Let's be on our way."

He spurred his mount forward, and the others followed him down the stony road into the haunted city.

The ruins appeared much less dismal at close range than they had on either of Valentine's previous two visits. This winter's rains must have been heavier than usual, for wildflowers were blooming everywhere amidst the dark, dingy waste of ashen dunes and overturned building blocks. They dappled the gray gloominess with startling little bursts of yellow and red and blue and white that were almost musical in their

emphatic effect. A host of fragile bright-winged kelebekkos flitted about among the blossoms, sipping at their nectar, and multitudes of tiny gnatlike ferushas moved about in thick swarms, forming broad misty patches in the air that glistened like silvery dust.

But more was happening here than the unfolding of flowers and the dancing of insects. As he made his descent into Velalisier, Valentine's imagination began to teem suddenly with strangenesses, fantasies, marvels. It seemed to him that inexplicable flickers of sorcery and wonder were arising just beyond the periphery of his vision. Sprites and visitations, singing wordlessly to him of Majipoor's infinite past, drifted upward from the broken edge-tilted slabs and capered temptingly about him, leaping to and fro over the porous, limy soil of the site's surface with frantic energy. A subtle shimmer of delicate jade-green iridescence that had not been apparent at a distance rose above everything, tinting the air: some effect of the hot noontime light striking a luminescent mineral in the rocks, he supposed. It was a wondrous sight all the same, whatever its cause.

These unexpected touches of beauty lifted the Pontifex's mood. Which, ever since the news had reached him the week before of the savage and perplexing death of the distinguished Metamorph archaeologist Huukaminaan amidst these very ruins, had been uncharacteristically bleak. Valentine had had such high hopes for the work that was being done here to uncover and restore the old Shapeshifter capital; and this murder had stained everything.

The tents of his archaeologists came into view now, lofty ones gaily woven from broad strips of green, maroon, and scarlet cloth, billowing atop a low sandy plateau in the distance. Some of the excavators themselves, he saw, were riding toward him down the long rock-ribbed avenues on fat plodding mounts: about half a dozen of them, with chief archaeologist Magadone Sambisa at the head of the group.

"Majesty," she said, dismounting, making the elaborate sign of respect that one would make before a Pontifex. "Welcome to Velalisier."

Valentine hardly recognized her. It was only about a year since Magadone Sambisa had come before him in his chambers at the Labyrinth. He remembered a dynamic, confident, bright-eyed woman, sturdy and strapping, with rounded cheeks florid with life and vigor and glossy cascades of curling red hair tumbling down her back. She seemed oddly diminished now, haggard with fatigue, her shoulders slumped, her eyes dull and sunken, her face sallow and newly lined and no longer full. That great mass of hair had lost its sheen and bounce. He let his amazement show, only for an instant, but long enough for her to see it. She pulled herself upright immediately, trying, it seemed, to project some of her former vigor.

Valentine had intended to introduce her to Duke Nascimonte and Prince Mirigant and the rest of the visiting group. But before he could do it, Tunigorn came officially forward to handle the task.

There had been a time when citizens of Majipoor could not have any sort of direct conversation with the Pontifex. They were required then to channel all intercourse through the court official known as the High Spokesman. Valentine had quickly abolished that custom, and many another stifling bit of imperial etiquette. But Tunigorn, by nature conservative, had never been comfortable with those changes. He did whatever he could to preserve the traditional aura of sanctity in which Pontifices once had been swathed. Valentine found that amusing and charming and only occasionally irritating.

The welcoming party included none of the Metamorph archaeologists connected with the expedition. Magadone Sambisa had brought just five human archaeologists and a Ghayrog with her. That seemed odd, to have left the Metamorphs elsewhere. Tunigorn formally repeated the archaeologists' names to Valentine, getting nearly every one garbled in the process. Then, and only then, did he step back and allow the Pontifex to have a word with her.

"The excavations," he said. "Tell me, have they been going well?"

"Quite well, majesty. Splendidly, in fact, until—*until*—" She made a despairing gesture: grief, shock, incomprehension, helplessness, all in a single poignant movement of her head and hands.

The murder must have been like a death in the family for her, for all of them here. A sudden and horrifying loss.

"*Until*, yes. I understand."

Valentine questioned her gently but firmly. Had there, he asked, been any important new developments in the investigation? Any clues discovered? Claims of responsibility for the killing? Were there any suspects at all? Had the archaeological party received any threats of further attacks?

But there was nothing new at all. Huukaminaan's murder had been an isolated event, a sudden, jarring, and unfathomable intrusion into the serene progress of work at the site. The slain Metamorph's body had been turned over to his own people for interment, she told him, and a shudder that she made an ineffectual effort to hide ran through the entire upper half of her body as she said it. The excavators were attempting now to put aside their distress over the killing and get on with their tasks.

The whole subject was plainly an uncomfortable one for her. She escaped from it as quickly as she could. "You must be tired from your journey, your majesty. Shall I show you to your quarters?"

Three new tents had been erected to house the Pontifex and his entourage. They had to pass through the excavation zone itself to reach them. Valentine was pleased to see how much progress had been made in clearing away the clusters of pernicious little ropy-stemmed weeds and tangles of woody vines that for so many centuries had been patiently at work pulling the blocks of stone one from another.

Along the way Magadone Sambisa poured forth voluminous streams of information about the city's most conspicuous features as though Valentine were a tourist and she his guide. Over here, the broken but still awesome aqueduct. There, the substantial jagged-sided oval bowl of the arena. And there, the grand ceremonial boulevard, paved with sleek greenish flagstones.

Shapeshifter glyphs were visible on those flagstones even after the lapse of twenty thousand years, mysterious swirling symbols, carved deep into the stone. Not even the Shapeshifters themselves were able to decipher them now.

The rush of archaeological and mythological minutia came gushing from her with scarcely a pause for breath. There was a certain frantic, even desperate, quality about it all, a sign of the uneasiness she must feel in the presence of the Pontifex of Majipoor. Valentine was accustomed enough to that sort of thing. But this was not his first visit to Velalisier and he was already familiar with much of what she was telling him. And she looked so weary, so depleted, that it troubled him to see her expending her energy in such needless outpourings.

But she would not stop. They were passing, now, a huge and very dilapidated edifice of gray stone that appeared ready to fall down if anyone should sneeze in its vicinity. "This is called the Palace of the Final King," she said. "Probably an erroneous name, but that's what the Piurivars call it, and for lack of a better one we do too."

Valentine noted her careful use of the Metamorphs' own name for themselves. *Piurivars*, yes. University people tended to be very formal about that, always referring to the aboriginal folk of Majipoor that way, never speaking of them as Metamorphs or Shapeshifters, as ordinary people tended to do. He would try to remember that.

As they came to the ruins of the royal palace she offered a disquisition on the legend of the mythical Final King of Piurivar antiquity, he who had presided over the atrocious act of defilement that had brought about the Metamorphs' ancient abandonment of their city. It was a story with which all of them were familiar. Who did not know that dreadful tale?

But they listened politely as she told of how, those many thousands of years ago, long before the first human settlers had come to live on Majipoor, the Metamorphs of Velalisier had in some fit of blind madness hauled two living sea-dragons from the ocean: intelligent beings of mighty size and extraordinary mental powers, whom the Metamorphs themselves had thought of as gods. Had dumped them down on these platforms, had cut them to pieces with long knives, had burned their flesh on a pyre before the Seventh Pyramid as a crazed offering to some even greater gods in whom the King and his subjects had come to believe.

When the simple folk of the outlying provinces heard of that orgy of horrendous massacre, so the legend ran, they rushed upon Velalisier and demolished the temple at which the sacrificial offering had been made. They put to death the Final King and wrecked his palace, and drove the wicked citizens of the city forth into the wilderness, and smashed its aqueduct and put dams across the rivers that had supplied it with water, so that Velalisier would be thenceforth a deserted and accursed place, abandoned through all eternity to the lizards and spiders and jakkaboles of the fields.

Valentine and his companions moved on in silence when Magadone Sambisa was done with her narrative. The six sharply tapering pyramids that were Velalisier's best-known monuments came now into view, the nearest rising just beyond the courtyard of the Final King's palace, the other five set close together in a straight line stretching to the east. "There was a seventh, once," Magadone Sambisa said. "But the Piurivars themselves destroyed it just before they left here for the last time. Nothing was left but scattered rubble. We were about to start work there early last week, but that was when—when—" She faltered and looked away.

"Yes," said Valentine softly. "Of course."

The road now took them between the two colossal platforms fashioned from gigantic slabs of blue stone that were known to the modern-day Metamorphs as the Tables of the Gods. Even though they were abutted by the accumulated debris of two hundred centuries, they still rose nearly ten feet above the surrounding plain, and the area of their flat-topped surfaces would have been great enough to hold hundreds of people at a time.

In a low sepulchral tone Magadone Sambisa said, "Do you know what these are, your majesty?"

Valentine nodded. "The sacrificial altars, yes. Where the Defilement was carried out."

Magadone Sambisa said, "Indeed. It was also at this site that the murder of Huukaminaan happened. I could show you the place. It would take only a moment."

She indicated a staircase a little way down the road, made of big square blocks of the same blue stone as the platforms themselves. It gave access to the top of the western platform. Magadone Sambisa dismounted and scrambled swiftly up. She paused on the highest step to extend a hand to Valentine as though the Pontifex might be having difficulty in making the ascent, which was not the case. He was still almost as agile as he had been in his younger days. But he reached for her hand for courtesy's sake, just as she—deciding, maybe, that it would be impermissible for a commoner to make contact with the flesh of a Pontifex—began to pull it anxiously back. Valentine, grinning, leaned forward and took the hand anyway, and levered himself upward.

Old Nascimonte came bounding swiftly up just behind him, followed by Valentine's cousin and close counselor, Prince Mirigant, who had the little Vroonish wizard Autifon Deliamber riding on his shoulder. Tunigorn remained below. Evidently this place of ancient sacrilege and infamous slaughter was not for him.

The surface of the altar, roughened by time and pockmarked everywhere by clumps of scruffy weeds and encrustations of red and green lichen, stretched on and on before them, a stupendous expanse. It was hard to imagine how even a great multitude of Shapeshifters, those slender and seemingly boneless people, could ever have hauled so many tremendous blocks of stone into place.

Magadone Sambisa pointed to a marker of yellow tape in the form of a six-pointed star that was affixed to the stone a dozen feet or so away. "We found him here," she said. "Some of him, at any rate. And some here." There was another marker off to the left, about twenty feet farther on. "And here." A third star of yellow tape.

"They dismembered him?" Valentine said, appalled.

"Indeed. You can see the bloodstains all about." She hesitated for an instant. Valentine noticed that she was trembling now.

"All of him was here except his head. We discovered that far away, over in the ruins of the Seventh Pyramid."

"They know no shame," said Nascimonte vehemently. "They are worse than beasts. We should have eradicated them all."

"Who do you mean?" asked Valentine.

"You know who I mean, majesty. You know quite well."

"So you think this was Shapeshifter work, this crime?"

"Oh, no, majesty, no!" Nascimonte said, coloring the words with heavy scorn. "Why would I think such a thing? One of our own archaeologists must have done it, no doubt. Out of professional jealousy, let's say, because the dead Shapeshifter had come upon on some important discovery, maybe, and our own people wanted to take credit for it.—Is that what you think, Valentine? Do you believe any human being would be capable of this sort of loathsome butchery?"

"That's what we're here to discover, my friend," said Valentine amiably. "We are not quite ready for arriving at conclusions, I think."

Magadone Sambisa's eyes were bulging from her head, as though Nascimonte's audacity in upbraiding a Pontifex to his face was a spectacle beyond her capacity to absorb. "Perhaps we should continue on to your tents now," she said.

It felt very odd, Valentine thought, as they rode on down the rubble-bordered roadway that led to the place of encampment, to be here in this forlorn and eerie zone of age-old ruins once again. But at least he was not in the Labyrinth. So far as he was concerned, any place at all was better than the Labyrinth.

This was his third visit to Velalisier. The first had been long ago when he had been Coronal, in the strange time of his brief overthrow by the usurper Dominin Barjazid. He had stopped off here with his little handful of supporters—Carabella, Nascimonte, Sleet, Ermanar, Deliamber, and the rest—during the course of his northward march to Castle Mount, where he was to reclaim his throne from the false Coronal in the War of Restoration.

Valentine had still been a young man, then. But he was young no longer. He had been Pontifex of Majipoor, senior monarch of the realm, for nine years now, following upon the fourteen of his service as Coronal Lord. There were a few strands of white in his golden hair, and though he still had an athlete's trim body and easy grace he was starting to feel the first twinges of the advancing years.

He had vowed, that first time at Velalisier, to have the weeds and vines that were strangling the ruins cleared away, and to send in archaeologists to excavate and restore the old toppled buildings. And he had intended to allow the Metamorph leaders to play a role in that work, if they were willing. That was part of his plan for giving those once-despised and persecuted natives of the planet a more significant place in Majipoori life; for he knew that Metamorphs everywhere were smoldering with barely contained wrath, and could no longer be shunted into the remote reservations where his predecessors had forced them to live.

Valentine had kept that vow. And had come back to Velalisier years later to see what progress the archaeologists had made.

But the Metamorphs, bitterly resenting Valentine's intrusion into their holy precincts, had shunned the enterprise entirely. That was something he had not expected.

He was soon to learn that although the Shapeshifters were eager to see Velalisier rebuilt, they meant to do the job themselves—after they had driven the human settlers and all other offworld intruders from Majipoor and taken control of their planet once more. A Shapeshifter uprising, secretly planned for many years, erupted just a few years after Valentine had regained the throne. The first group of archaeologists that Valentine had sent to Velalisier could achieve nothing more at the site than some preliminary clearing and mapping before the War of the Rebellion broke out; and then all work there had had to be halted indefinitely.

The war had ended with victory for Valentine's forces. In designing the peace that followed it he had taken care to alleviate as many of the grievances of the Metamorphs as he could. The Danipiur—that was the title of their queen—was brought into the government as a full Power of the Realm, placing her on an even footing with the Pontifex and the Coronal. Valentine had, by then, himself moved on from the Coronal's throne to that of the Pontifex. And now he had revived the idea of restoring the ruins of Velalisier once more; but he had made certain that it would be with the full cooperation of the Metamorph, and that Metamorph archaeologists would work side by side with the scholars from the venerable University of Arkilon in the north to whom he had assigned the task.

In the year just past great things had been done toward rescuing the ruins from the oblivion that had been encroaching on them for so long. But he could take little joy in any of that. The ghastly death that had befallen the senior Metamorph archaeologist atop this ancient altar argued that sinister forces still ran deep in this place. The harmony that he thought his reign had brought to the world might be far shallower than he suspected.

Twilight was coming on by the time Valentine was settled in his tent. By a custom that even he was reluctant to set aside, he would stay in it alone, since his consort Carabella had remained behind in the Labyrinth on this trip. Indeed, she had tried very strongly to keep him from going himself. Tunigorn, Mirigant, Nascimonte, and the Vroon would share the second tent; the third was occupied by the security forces that had accompanied the Pontifex to Velalisier.

He stepped out into the gathering dusk. A sprinkling of early stars had begun to sparkle overhead, and the Great Moon's bright glint could be seen close to the horizon. The air was parched and crisp, with a brittle quality to it, as though it could be torn in one's hands like dry paper and crumbled to dust between one's fingers. There was a strange stillness in it, an eerie hush.

But at least he was out-of-doors, here, gazing up at actual stars, and the air he breathed here, dry as it was, was *real* air, not the manufactured stuff of the Pontifical city. Valentine was grateful for that.

By rights he had no business being out and abroad in the world at all.

As Pontifex, his place was in the Labyrinth, hidden away in his secret imperial lair deep underground beneath all those coiling levels of subterranean settlement, shielded always from the view of ordinary mortals. The Coronal, the junior king who lived in the lofty castle of forty thousand rooms atop the great heaven-piercing peak that was Castle Mount, was meant to be the active figure of governance, the visible representative of royal majesty on Majipoor. But Valentine loathed the dank Labyrinth where his lofty rank obliged him to dwell. He relished every opportunity he could manufacture to escape from it.

And in fact this one had been thrust unavoidably upon him. The killing of Huukaminaan was serious business, requiring an inquiry on the highest levels; and the Coronal Lord Hissune was many months' journey away just now, touring the distant continent of Zimroel. And so the Pontifex was here in the Coronal's stead.

"You love the sight of the open sky, don't you?" said Duke Nascimonte, emerging from the tent across the way and limping over to stand by Valentine's side. A certain tenderness underlay the harshness of his rasping voice. "Ah, I understand, old friend. I do indeed."

"I see the stars so infrequently, Nascimonte, in the place where I must live."

The duke chuckled. "*Must* live! The most powerful man in the world, and yet he's a prisoner! How ironic that is! How sad!"

"I knew from the moment I became Coronal that I'd have to live in the Labyrinth eventually," Valentine said. "I've tried to make my peace with that. But it was never my plan to be Coronal in the first place, you know. If Voriax had lived—"

"Ah, yes, Voriax—" Valentine's brother, the elder son of the High Counselor Damiandane: the one who had been reared from childhood to occupy the throne of Majipoor. Nascimonte gave Valentine a close look. "It was a Metamorph, was it not, who struck him down in the forest? That has been proven now?"

Uncomfortably Valentine said, "What does it matter now who killed him? He died. And the throne came to me, because I was our father's other son. A crown I had never dreamed of wearing. Everyone knew that Voriax was the one who was destined for it."

"But he had a darker destiny also. Poor Voriax!"

Poor Voriax, yes. Struck down by a bolt out of nowhere while hunting in the forest eight years into his reign as Coronal, a bolt from the bow of some Metamorph assassin skulking in the trees. By accepting his dead brother's crown, Valentine had doomed himself inevitably to descend into the Labyrinth someday, when the old Pontifex died and it became the Coronal's turn to succeed to the greater title, and to the cheerless obligation of underground residence that went with it.

"As you say, it was the decision of fate," Valentine replied, "and now I am Pontifex. Well, so be it, Nascimonte. But I won't hide down there in the darkness all the time. I can't."

"And why should you? The Pontifex can do as he pleases."

"Yes. Yes. But only within our law and custom."

"You shape law and custom to suit yourself, Valentine. You always have."

Valentine understood what Nascimonte was saying. He had never been a conventional monarch. For much of the time during his exile from power in the period of the usurpation he had wandered the world earning a humble living as an intinerant juggler, kept from awareness of his true rank by the amnesia that the usurping faction had induced in him. Those years had transformed him irreversibly; and after his restoration to the royal heights of Castle Mount he had comported himself in a way that few Coronals ever had before—mingling openly with the populace, spreading a cheerful gospel of peace and love even as the Shapeshifters were making ready to launch their long-cherished campaign of war against the conquerors who had taken their world from them.

And then, when the events of that war made Valentine's succession to the Pontificate unavoidable, he had held back as long as possible before relinquishing the upper world to his protégé Lord Hissune, the new Coronal, and descending into the subterranean city that was so alien to his sunny nature.

In his nine years as Pontifex he had found every excuse to emerge from it. No Pontifex in memory had come forth from the Labyrinth more than once a decade or so, and then only to attend high rites at the castle of the Coronal; but Valentine popped out as often as he could, riding hither and thither through the land as though he were still obliged to undertake the formal grand processionals across the countryside that a Coronal must make. Lord Hissune had been very patient with him on each of those occasions, though Valentine had no doubt that the young Coronal was annoyed by the senior monarch's insistence on coming up into public view so frequently.

"I change what I think needs changing," Valentine said. "But I owe it to Lord Hissune to keep myself out of sight as much as possible."

"Well, here you are above ground today, at any rate!"

"It seems that I am. This is one time, though, when I would gladly have forgone the chance to come forth. But with Hissune off in Zim-roel—"

"Yes. Clearly you had no choice. You had to lead this investigation yourself." They fell silent. "A nasty mess, this murder," Nascimonte said, after a time. "Pfaugh! Pieces of the poor bastard strewn all over the altar like that!"

"Pieces of the government's Metamorph policy, too, I think," said the Pontifex, with a rueful grin.

"You think there's something political in this, Valentine?"

"Who knows? But I fear the worst."

"You, the eternal optimist!"

"It would be more accurate to call me a realist, Nascimonte. A realist."

The old duke laughed. "As you prefer, majesty." There was another pause, a longer one than before. Then Nascimonte said, more quietly now, "Valentine, I need to ask your forgiveness for an earlier fault. I spoke too harshly, this afternoon, when I talked of the Shapeshifters as vermin who should be exterminated. You know I don't truly believe that. I'm an old man. Sometimes I speak so bluntly that I amaze even myself."

Valentine nodded, but made no other reply.

"—And telling you so dogmatically that it had to be one of his fellow Shapeshifters who killed him, too. As you said, it's out of line for us to be jumping to conclusions that way. We haven't even started to collect evidence yet. At this point we have no justification for as-suming—"

"On the contrary. We have *every* reason to assume it, Nascimonte."

The duke stared at Valentine in bewilderment. "Majesty!"

"Let's not play games, old friend. There's no one here right now but you and me. In privacy we're free to speak unvarnished truths, are we not? And you said it truly enough this afternoon. I did tell you then that we mustn't jump to conclusions, yes, but sometimes a con-clusion is so obvious that it comes jumping right at *us*. There's no rational reason why one of the human archaeologists—or one of the

Ghayrogs, for that matter—would have murdered one of his colleagues. I don't see why anyone else would have done it, either. Murder is such a very rare crime, Nascimonte. We can hardly even begin to understand the motivations of someone who'd be capable of doing it. But someone did."

"Yes."

"Well, and which race's motivations are hardest for us to understand, eh? To my way of thinking the killer almost certainly would have to be a Shapeshifter—either a member of the archaeological team, or one who came in from outside for the particular purpose of carrying out the assassination."

"So one might assume. But what possible purpose could a Shapeshifter have for killing one of his own kind?"

"I can't imagine. Which is why we're here as investigators," said Valentine. "And I have a nasty feeling that I'm not going to like the answer when we find it."

At dinner that night in the archaeologists' open-air mess hall, under a clear black sky ablaze now with swirling streams of brilliant stars that cast cold dazzling light on the mysterious humps and mounds of the surrounding ruins, Valentine made the acquaintance of Magadone Sambisa's entire scientific team. There were seventeen in all: six other humans, two Ghayrogs, eight Metamorphs. They seemed, every one of them, to be gentle, studious creatures. Not by the greatest leap of the imagination could Valentine picture any of these people slaying and dismembering their venerable colleague Huukaminaan.

"Are these the only persons who have access to the archaeological zone?" he asked Magadone Sambisa.

"There are the day laborers also, of course."

"Ah. And where are they just now?"

"They have a village of their own, over beyond the last pyramid. They go to it at sundown and don't come back until the start of work the next day."

"I see. How many are there altogether? A great many?"

Magadone Sambisa looked across the table toward a pale and long-faced Metamorph with strongly inward-sloping eyes. He was her site supervisor, Kaastisiik by name, responsible for each day's deployment of diggers. "What would you say? About a hundred?"

"One hundred twelve," said Kaastisiik, and clamped his little slit of a mouth in a way that demonstrated great regard for his own precision.

"Mostly Piurivar?" Valentine asked.

"Entirely Piurivar," said Magadone Sambisa. "We thought it was best to use only native workers, considering that we're not only excavating the city but to some extent rebuilding it. They don't appear to have any problem with the presence of non-Piurivar archaeologists, but having humans taking part in the actual reconstruction work would very likely be offensive to them."

"You hired them all locally, did you?"

"There are no settlements of any kind in the immediate vicinity of the ruins, your majesty. Nor are there many Piurivars living anywhere in the surrounding province. We had to bring them in from great distances. A good many from Piurifayne itself, in fact."

Valentine raised an eyebrow at that. From *Piurifayne?*

Piurifayne was a province of far-off Zimroel, an almost unthinkable distance away on the other side of the Inner Sea. Eight thousand years before, the great conqueror Lord Stiamot—he who had ended for all time the Piurivars' hope of remaining independent on their own world— had driven those Metamorphs who had survived his war against them into Piurifayne's humid jungles and had penned them up in a reservation there. Though the old restrictions had long since been lifted and Metamorphs now were permitted to settle wherever they pleased, more of them still lived in Piurifayne than anywhere else; and it was in the subtropical glades of Piurifayne that the revolutionary Faraataa had founded the underground movement that had sent the War of the Rebellion forth upon peaceful Majipoor like a river of seething lava.

Tunigorn said, "You've questioned them all, naturally? Established their comings and goings at the time of the murder?"

Magadone Sambisa seemed taken aback. "You mean, treat them as though they were suspects in the killing?"

"They *are* suspects in the killing," said Tunigorn.

"They are simple diggers and haulers of burdens, nothing more, Prince Tunigorn. There are no murderers among them, that much I know. They *revered* Dr. Huukaminaan. They regarded him as a guardian of their past—almost a sacred figure. It's inconceivable that any one of them could have carried out such a dreadful and hideous crime. Inconceivable!"

"In this very place some twenty thousand years ago," Duke Nascimonte said, looking upward as if he were speaking only to the air, "the King of the Shapeshifters, as you yourself reminded us earlier today, caused two enormous sea-dragons to be butchered alive atop those huge stone platforms back there. It was clear from your words this afternoon that the Shapeshifters of those days must have regarded sea-dragons with even more reverence than you say your laborers had for Dr. Huukaminaan. They called them 'water-kings,' am I not right, and gave them names, and thought of them as holy elder brothers, and addressed prayers to them? Yet the bloody sacrifice took place here in Velalisier even so, the thing that to this very day the Shapeshifters themselves speak of as the Defilement. Is this not true? Permit me to suggest, then, that if the King of the Shapeshifters could have done such a thing back then, it isn't all that inconceivable that one of your own hired Metamorphs here could have found some reason to perpetrate a similar atrocity last week upon the unfortunate Dr. Huukaminaan on the very same altar."

Magadone Sambisa appeared stunned, as though Nascimonte had struck her in the face. For a moment she could make no reply. Then she said hoarsely, "How can you use an ancient myth, a fantastic legend, to cast suspicion on a group of harmless, innocent—"

"Ah, so it's a myth and a legend when you want to protect these harmless and innocent diggers and haulers of yours, and absolute historical truth when you want us to shiver with rapture over the significance of these piles of old jumbled stones?"

"Please," Valentine said, glaring at Nascimonte. "*Please*." To Magadone Sambisa he said, "What time of day did the murder take place?"

"Late at night. Past midnight, it must have been."

"I was the last to see Dr. Huukaminaan," said one of the Metamorph archaeologists, a frail-looking Piurivar whose skin had an elegant emerald hue. Vo-Siimifon was his name; Magadone Sambisa had introduced him as an authority on ancient Piurivar script. "We sat up late in our tent, he and I, discussing an inscription that had been found the day before. The lettering was extremely minute; Dr. Huukaminaan complained of a headache, and said finally that he was going out for a walk. I went to sleep. —Dr. Huukaminaan did not return."

"It's a long way," Mirigant observed, "from here to the sacrificial platforms. *Quite* a long way. It would take at least half an hour to walk there, I'd guess. Perhaps more, for someone his age. He was an old man, I understand."

"But if someone happened to encounter him just outside the camp, though," Tunigorn suggested, "and *forced* him to go all the way down to the platform area—"

Valentine said, "Is a guard posted here at the encampment at night?"

"No. There seemed to be no purpose in doing that."

"And the dig site itself? It's not fenced off, or protected in any way?"

"No."

"Then anyone at all could have left the day laborers' village as soon as it grew dark," Valentine said, "and waited out there in the road for Dr. Huukaminaan to come out." He glanced toward Vo-Siimifon. "Was Dr. Huukaminaan in the habit of taking a walk before bedtime?"

"Not that I recall."

"And if he *had* chosen to go out late at night for some reason, would he have been likely to take so long a walk?"

"He was quite a robust man, for his age," said the Piurivar. "But even so that would have been an unusual distance to go just for a stroll before bedtime."

"Yes. So it would seem." Valentine turned again to Magadone Sambisa. "It'll be necessary, I'm afraid, for us to question your laborers. And each member of your expedition, too. You understand that at this point we can't arbitrarily rule anyone out."

Her eyes flashed. "Am I under suspicion too, your majesty?"

"At this point," said Valentine, "nobody here is under suspicion. And everyone is. Unless you want me to believe that Dr. Huukaminaan committed suicide by dismembering himself and distributing parts of himself all over the top of that platform."

The night had been cool, but the sun sprang into the morning sky with incredible swiftness. Almost at once, early as it was in the day, the air began to throb with desert warmth. It was necessary to get a quick start at the site, Magadone Sambisa had told them, since by midday the intense heat would make work very difficult.

Valentine was ready for her when she called for him soon after dawn. At her request he would be accompanied only by some members of his security detachment, not by any of his fellow lords. Tunigorn grumbled about this, as did Mirigant. But she said—and would not yield on the point—that she preferred that the Pontifex alone come with her today, and after he had seen what she had to show him he could make his own decisions about sharing the information with the others.

She was taking him to the Seventh Pyramid. Or what was left of it, rather, for nothing now remained except the truncated base, a square structure about twenty feet long on each side and five or six feet high, constructed from the same reddish basalt from which the great arena and some of the other public buildings had been made. East of that stump the fragments of the pyramid's upper section, smallish broken blocks of the same reddish stone, lay strewn in the most random way across a wide area. It was as though some angry colossus had contemptuously given the western face of the pyramid one furious slap with the back of his ponderous hand and sent it flying into a thousand pieces. On the side of the stump away from the debris Valentine could make out the pointed summit of the still-intact Sixth Pyramid about five hundred feet away, rising above a copse of little contorted trees, and beyond it were the other five, running onward one after another to the edge of the royal palace itself.

"According to Piurivar lore," Magadone Sambisa said, "the people of Velalisier held a great festival every thousand years, and constructed a pyramid to commemorate each one. So far as we've been able to confirm by examining and dating the six undamaged ones, that's correct. This one, we know, was the last in the series. If we can believe the legend"—and she gave Valentine a meaningful look—"it was built to mark the very festival at which the Defilement took place. And had just been completed when the city was invaded and destroyed by those who had come here to punish its inhabitants for what they had done."

She beckoned to him, leading him around toward the northern side of the shattered pyramid. They walked perhaps fifty feet onward from the stump. Then she halted. The ground had been carefully cut away here. Valentine saw a rectangular opening just large enough for a man to enter, and the beginning of a passageway leading underground and heading back toward the foundations of the pyramid.

A star-shaped marker of bright yellow tape was fastened to a good-sized boulder just to the left of the excavation.

"That's where you found the head, is it?" he asked.

"Not there. Below." She pointed into the opening. "Will you follow me, your majesty?"

Six members of Valentine's security force had gone with Valentine to the pyramid site that morning: the giant warrior-woman Lisamon Hultin, his personal bodyguard, who had accompanied him on all his travels since his juggling days; two shaggy hulking Skandars; a couple of Pontifical officials whom he had inherited from his predecessor's staff; and even a Metamorph, one Aarisiim, who had defected to Valentine's forces from the service of the arch-rebel Faraataa in the final hours of the War of the Rebellion and had been with the Pontifex ever since. All six stepped forward now as if they meant to go down into the excavation with him, though the Skandars and Lisamon Hultin were plainly too big to fit into the entrance. But Magadone Sambisa shook her head fiercely; and Valentine, smiling, signaled to them all to wait for him above.

The archaeologist, lighting a hand torch, entered the opening in the ground. The descent was steep, via a series of precisely chiseled earthen steps that took them downward nine or ten feet. Then, abruptly, the subterranean passageway leveled off. Here there was a flagstone floor made of broad slabs hewn from some glossy green rock. Magadone Sambisa flashed her light at one and Valentine saw that it bore carved glyphs, runes of some kind, reminiscent of those he had seen in the paving of the grand ceremonial boulevard that ran past the royal palace.

"This is our great discovery," she said. "There are shrines, previously unknown and unsuspected, under each of the seven pyramids. We were working near the Third Pyramid about six months ago, trying to stabilize its foundation, when we stumbled on the first one. It had been plundered, very probably in antiquity. But it was an exciting find all the same, and immediately we went looking for similar shrines beneath the other five intact pyramids. And found them: also plundered. For the time being we didn't bother to go digging for the shrine of the Seventh Pyramid. We assumed that there was no hope of finding anything interesting there, that it must have been looted at the time the pyramid was destroyed. But then Huukaminaan and I decided that we might as well check it out too, and we put down this trench that we've been walking through. Within a day or so we reached this flagstone paving. Come."

They went deeper in, entering a carefully constructed tunnel just about wide enough for four people to stand in it abreast. Its walls were fashioned of thin slabs of black stone laid sideways like so many stacked books, leading upward to a vaulted roof of the same stone that tapered into a series of pointed arches. The craftsmanship was very fine, and distinctly archaic in appearance. The air in the tunnel was hot and musty and dry, ancient air, lifeless air. It had a stale, dead taste in Valentine's nostrils.

"We call this kind of underground vault a processional hypogeum," Magadone Sambisa explained. "Probably it was used by priests carrying offerings to the shrine of the pyramid."

Her torch cast a spreading circlet of pallid light that allowed Valentine to perceive a wall of finely dressed white stone blocking the path just ahead of them. "Is that the foundation of the pyramid we're looking at?" he asked.

"No. What we see here is the wall of the shrine, nestling against the pyramid's base. The pyramid itself is on the far side of it. The other shrines were located right up against their pyramids in the same way. The difference is that all the others had been smashed open. This one has apparently never been breached."

Valentine whistled softly. "And what do you think is inside it?"

"We don't have any idea. We were putting off opening it, waiting for Lord Hissune to return from his processional in Zimroel, so that you and he could be on hand when we broke through the wall. But then—the murder—"

"Yes," Valentine said soberly. And, after a moment: "How strange that the destroyers of the city demolished the Seventh Pyramid so thoroughly, but left the shrine beneath it intact! You'd think they would have made a clean sweep of the place."

"Perhaps there was something walled up in the shrine that they didn't want to go near, eh? It's a thought, anyway. We may never know the truth, even after we open it. *If* we open it."

"If?"

"There may be problems about that, majesty. Political problems, I mean. We need to discuss them. But this isn't the moment for that."

Valentine nodded. He indicated a row of small indented apertures, perhaps nine inches deep and about a foot high, that had been chiseled in the wall some eighteen inches above ground level. "Were those for putting offerings in?"

"Exactly." Magadone Sambisa flashed the torch across the row from right to left. "We found microscopic traces of dried flowers in several of them, and potsherds and colored pebbles in others—you can still see them there, actually. And some animal remains." She hesitated. "And then, in the alcove on the far left—"

The torch came to rest on a star of yellow tape attached to the shallow alcove's back wall.

Valentine gasped in shock. "*There*?"

"Huukaminaan's head, yes. Placed very neatly in the center of the alcove, facing outward. An offering of some sort, I suppose."

"To whom? To what?"

The archaeologist shrugged and shook her head.

Then, abruptly, she said, "We should go back up now, your majesty. The air down here isn't good to spend a lot of time in. I simply wanted you to see where the shrine was situated. And where we found the missing part of Dr. Huukaminaan's body."

Later in the day, with Nascimonte and Tunigorn and the rest now joining him, Magadone Sambisa showed Valentine the site of the expedition's other significant discovery: the bizarre cemetery, previously unsuspected, where the ancient inhabitants of Velalisier had buried their dead.

Or, more precisely, had buried certain fragments of their dead. "There doesn't appear to be a complete body anywhere in the whole graveyard. In every interment we've opened, what we've found is mere tiny bits—a finger here, an ear there, a lip, a toe. Or some internal organ, even. Each item carefully embalmed, and placed in a beautiful stone casket and buried beneath one of these gravestones. The part for the whole: a kind of metaphorical burial."

Valentine stared in wonder and astonishment.

The twenty-thousand-year-old Metamorph cemetery was one of the strangest sights he had seen in all his years of exploring the myriad wondrous strangenesses that Majipoor had to offer.

It covered an area hardly more than a hundred feet long and sixty feet wide, off in a lonely zone of dunes and weeds a short way beyond the end of one of the north-south flagstone boulevards. In that small plot of land there might have been ten thousand graves, all jammed together. A small stela of brown sandstone, a hand's-width broad and about fifteen inches high, jutted upward from each of the grave plots. And each of them crowded in upon the ones adjacent to it in a higgledy-piggledy fashion so that the cemetery was a dense agglomeration of slender close-set gravestones, tilting this way and that in a manner that utterly befuddled the eye.

At one time every stone must have lovingly been set in a vertical position above the casket containing the bit of the departed that had been chosen for interment here. But the Metamorphs of Velalisier had evidently gone on jamming more and more burials into this little funereal zone over the course of centuries, until each grave overlapped the next in the most chaotic manner. Dozens of them were packed into every square yard of terrain.

As the headstones continued to be crammed one against another without heed for the damage that each new burial was doing to the tombs already in place, the older ones were pushed out of perpendicular by their new neighbors. The slender stones all leaned precariously one way and another, looking the way a forest might after some monstrous storm had passed through, or after the ground beneath it had been bent and buckled by the force of some terrible earthquake. They all stood at crazy angles now, no two slanting in the same direction.

On each of these narrow headstones a single elegant glyph was carved precisely one-third of the way from the top, an intricately patterned whorl of the sort found in other zones of the city. No symbol seemed like any other one. Did they represent the names of the deceased? Prayers to some long-forgotten god?

"We hadn't any idea that this was here," Magadone Sambisa said. "This is the first burial site that's ever been discovered in Velalisier."

"I'll testify to that," Nascimonte said, with a great jovial wink. "I did a little digging here myself, you know, long ago. Tomb-hunting, looking for buried treasure that I might be able to sell somewhere, during the time I was forced from my land in the reign of the false Lord Valentine and living like a bandit in this desert. But not a single grave did any of us come upon then. Not one."

"Nor did we detect any, though we tried," said Magadone Sambisa.

"When we found this place it was only by sheer luck. It was hidden deep under the dunes, ten, twelve, twenty feet below the surface of the sand. No one suspected it was here. But one day last winter a terrific whirlwind swept across the valley and hovered right up over this part of the city for half an hour, and by the time it was done whirling the whole dune had been picked up and tossed elsewhere and this amazing collection of gravestones lay exposed. Here. Look."

She knelt and brushed a thin coating of sand away from the base of a gravestone just in front of her. In moments the upper lid of a small box made of polished gray stone came into view. She pried it free and set it to one side.

Tunigorn made a sound of disgust. Valentine, peering down, saw a thing like a curling scrap of dark leather lying within the box.

"They're all like this," said Magadone Sambisa. "Symbolic burial, taking up a minimum of space. An efficient system, considering what a huge population Velalisier must have had in its prime. One tiny bit of the dead person's body buried here, preserved so artfully that it's still in pretty good condition even after all these thousands of years. The rest of it exposed on the hills outside town, for all we know, to be consumed by natural processes of decay. A Piurivar corpse would decay very swiftly. We'd find no traces, after all this time."

"How does that compare with present-day Shapeshifter burial practices?" Mirigant asked.

Magadone Sambisa looked at him oddly. "We know next to nothing about present-day Piurivar burial practices. They're a pretty secretive race, you know. They've never chosen to tell us anything about such things and evidently we've been too polite to ask, because there's hardly a thing on record about it. Hardly a thing."

"You have Shapeshifter scientists on your own staff," Tunigorn said. "Surely it wouldn't be impolite to consult your own associates about something like that. What's the point of training Shapeshifters to be archaeologists if you're going to be too sensitive of their feelings to make any use of their knowledge of their own people's ways?"

"As a matter of fact," said Magadone Sambisa, "I did discuss this find with Dr. Huukaminaan not long after it was uncovered. The layout of the place, the density of the burials, seemed pretty startling to him. But he didn't seem at all surprised by the concept of burial of body parts instead of entire bodies. He gave me to understand what had been done here wasn't all that different in some aspects from things the Piurivars still do today. There wasn't time just then for him to go into further details, though, and we both let the subject slip. And now—now—"

Once more she displayed that look of stunned helplessness, of futility and confusion in the face of violent death, that came over her whenever the topic of the murder of Huukaminaan arose.

Not all that different in some aspects from things the Piurivars still do today, Valentine repeated silently.

He considered the way Huukaminaan's body had been cut apart, the sundered pieces left in various places atop the sacrificial platform, the head carried down into the tunnel beneath the Seventh Pyramid and carefully laid to rest in one of the alcoves of the underground shrine.

There was something implacably alien about that grisly act of dismemberment that brought Valentine once again to the conclusion, mystifying and distasteful but seemingly inescapable, that had been facing him since his arrival here. *The murderer of the Metamorph archaeologist must have been a Metamorph himself.* As Nascimonte had suggested earlier, there seemed to be a ritual aspect to the butchery that had all the hallmarks of Metamorph work.

But still it made no sense. Valentine had difficulty believing that the old man could have been killed by one of his own people.

"What was Huukaminaan like?" he asked Magadone Sambisa. "I never met him, you know. Was he contentious? Cantankerous?"

"Not in the slightest. A sweet, gentle person. A brilliant scholar. There was no one, Piurivar or human, who didn't love and admire him."

"There must have been one person, at least," said Nascimonte wryly.

Perhaps Nascimonte's theory was worth exploring. Valentine said, "Could there have been some sort of bitter professional disagreement? A dispute over the credit for a discovery, a battle over some piece of theory?"

Magadone Sambisa stared at the Pontifex as though he had gone out of his mind. "Do you think we kill each other over such things, your majesty?"

"It was a foolish suggestion," Valentine said, with a smile. "Well, then," he went on, "suppose Huukaminaan had come into possession of some valuable artifact in the course of his work here, some priceless treasure that would fetch a huge sum in the antiquities market. Might that not have been sufficient cause for murdering him?"

Again the incredulous stare. "The artifacts we find here, majesty, are of the nature of simple sandstone statuettes, and bricks bearing inscriptions, not golden tiaras and emeralds the size of gihorna eggs. Everything worth looting was looted a long, long time ago. And we would no more dream of trying to make a private sale of the little things that we find here than we would—would—than, well, than we would of murdering each other. Our finds are divided equally between the university museum in Arkilon and the Piurivar treasury at Ilirivoyne. In any case—no, no, it's not even worth discussing. The idea's completely absurd." Instantly her cheeks turned flame-red. "Forgive me, majesty, I meant no disrespect."

Valentine brushed the apology aside. "What I'm doing, you see, is groping for some plausible explanation of the crime. A place to begin our investigation, at least."

"*I'll* give you one, Valentine," Tunigorn said suddenly. His normally open and genial face was tightly drawn in a splenetic scowl that brought his heavy eyebrows together into a single dark line. "The basic thing that we need to keep in mind all the time is that there's a curse on this place. You know that, Valentine. A *curse*. The Shapeshifters themselves put the dark word on the city, the Divine knows how many thousands of years ago, when they smashed it up to punish those who had chopped up those two sea-dragons. They intended the place to be shunned forever. Only ghosts have lived here ever since. By sending these archaeologists of yours in here, Valentine, you're disturbing those ghosts. Making them angry. And so they're striking back. Killing old Huukaminaan was the first step. There'll be more, mark my words!"

"And you think, do you, that ghosts are capable of cutting someone into five or six pieces and scattering the parts far and wide?"

Tunigorn was not amused. "I don't know what sorts of things ghosts may or may not be capable of doing," he said staunchly. "I'm just telling you what has crossed my mind."

"Thank you, my good old friend," said Valentine pleasantly. "We'll give the thought the examination it deserves." And to Magadone Sambisa he said, "I must tell you what has crossed *my* mind, based on what you've shown me today, here and at the pyramid shrine. Which is that the killing of Huukaminaan strikes me as a ritual murder, and the ritual involved is some kind of Piurivar ritual. I don't say that that's what it was; I just say that it certainly looks that way."

"And if it does?"

"Then we have our starting point. It's time now to move to the next phase of our work, I think. Please have the kindness to call your entire group of Piurivar archaeologists together this afternoon. I want to speak with them."

"One by one, or all together?"

"All of them together at first," said Valentine. "After that, we'll see."

But Magadone Sambisa's people were scattered all over the huge archaeological zone, each one involved with some special project, and she begged Valentine not to have them called in until the working day was over. It would take so long to reach them all, she said, that the worst of the heat would have descended by the time they began their return to camp, and they would be compelled to trek across the ruins in the full blaze of noon, instead of settling in some dark cavern to await the cooler hours that lay ahead. Meet with them at sundown, she implored him. Let them finish their day's tasks.

That seemed only reasonable. He said that he would.

But Valentine himself was unable to sit patiently by until dusk. The murder had jarred him deeply. It was one more symptom of the strange new darkness that had come over the world in his lifetime. Huge as it was, Majipoor had long been a peaceful place where there was comfort and plenty for all, and crime of any sort was an extraordinary rarity. But, even so, just in this present generation there had been the assassination of the Coronal Lord Voriax, and then the diabolically contrived usurpation that had pushed Voriax's successor—Valentine—from his throne for a time.

The Metamorphs, everyone knew now, had been behind both of those dire acts.

And after Valentine's recovery of the throne had come the War of the Rebellion, organized by the embittered Metamorph Faraataa, bringing with it plagues, famines, riots, a worldwide panic, great destruction everywhere. Valentine had ended that uprising, finally, by reaching out himself to take Faraataa's life—a deed that the gentle Valentine had regarded with horror, but which he had carried out all the same, because it had to be done.

Now, in this new era of worldwide peace and harmony that Valentine, reigning as Pontifex, had inaugurated, an admirable and beloved old Metamorph scholar had been murdered in the most brutal way. Murdered here in the holy city of the Metamorphs themselves, while he was in the midst of archaeological work that Valentine had instituted as one way of demonstrating the newfound respect of the human people of Majipoor for the aboriginal people they had displaced. And there was every indication, at least at this point, that the murderer was himself a Metamorph.

But that seemed insane.

Perhaps Tunigorn was right, that all of this was merely the working out of some ancient curse. That was a hard thing for Valentine to swallow. He had little belief in such things as curses. And yet—yet—

Restlessly he stalked the ruined city all through the worst heat of the day, heedless of the discomfort, pulling his hapless companions along. The sun's great golden-green eye stared unrelentingly down. Heat shimmers danced in the air. The leathery-leaved little shrubs that grew all over the ruins seemed to fold in upon themselves to hide from those torrid blasts of light. Even the innumerable skittering lizards that infested these rocks grew reticent as the temperature climbed.

"I would almost think we had been transported to Suvrael," said Tunigorn, panting in the heat as he dutifully labored along beside the Pontifex. "This is the climate of the miserable southland, not of our pleasant Alhanroel."

Nascimonte gave him a sardonic squinting smirk. "Just one more example of the malevolence of the Shapeshifters, my lord Tunigorn. In the days when the city was alive there were green forests all about this place, and the air was cool and mild. But then the river was turned aside, and the forests died, and nothing was left here but the bare rock that you see, which soaks up the heat of noon and holds it like a sponge. Ask the archaeologist lady, if you don't believe me. This province was deliberately turned into a desert, for the sake of punishing those who had committed great sins in it."

"All the more reason for us to be somewhere else," Tunigorn muttered. "But no, no, this is our place, here with Valentine, now and ever."

Valentine scarcely paid attention to what they were saying. He wandered aimlessly onward, down one weedy byway and another, past fallen columns and shattered façades, past the empty shells of what might once have been shops and taverns, past the ghostly outlines marking the foundation of vanished dwellings that must once have been palatial in their grandeur. Nothing was labeled, and Magadone Sambisa was not with him, now, to bend his ear with endless disquisitions about the former identities of these places. They were bits and pieces of lost Velalisier, that was all he knew: skeletonic remnants of this ancient metropolis.

It was easy enough, even for him, to imagine this place as the lair of ancient phantoms. A glassy glimmer of light shining out of some tumbled mass of broken columns—odd scratchy sounds that might have been those of creatures crawling about where no creatures could be seen—the occasional hiss and slither of shifting sand, sand that moved, so it would appear, of its own volition—

"Every time I visit these ruins," he said to Mirigant, who was walking closest to him now, "I'm astounded by the antiquity of it all. The weight of history that presses down on it."

"History that no one remembers," Mirigant said.

"But its weight remains."

"Not our history, though."

Valentine shot his cousin a scornful look. "So you may believe. But it's Majipoor's history, and what is that if not ours?"

Mirigant shrugged and made no answer.

Was there any meaning, Valentine wondered, in what he had just said? Or was the heat addling his brain?

He pondered it. Into his mind there came, with a force almost like that of an explosion, a vision of the totality of vast Majipoor. Its great continents and overwhelming rivers and immense shining seas, its dense moist jungles and great deserts, its forests of towering trees and mountains rich with strange and wonderful creatures, its multitude of sprawling cities with their populations of many millions. His soul was flooded with an overload of sensation, the perfume of a thousand kinds of flowers, the aromas of a thousand spices, the savory tang of a thousand wondrous meats, the bouquet of a thousand wines. It was a world of infinite richness and variety, this Majipoor of his.

And by a fluke of descent and his brother's bad luck he had come first to be Coronal and now Pontifex of that world. Twenty billion people hailed him as their emperor. His face was on the coinage; the world resounded with his praises; his name would be inscribed forever on the roster of monarchs in the House of Records, an imperishable part of the history of this world.

But once there had been a time when there were no Pontifices and Coronals here. When such wondrous cities as Ni-Moya and Alaisor and the fifty great urban centers of Castle Mount did not exist. And in that time before human settlement had begun on Majipoor, this city of Velalisier already was.

What right did he have to appropriate this city, already thousands of years dead and desolate when the first colonists arrived from space, into the flow of human history here? In truth there was a discontinuity so deep between *their* Majipoor and *our* Majipoor, he thought, that it might never be bridged.

In any case he could not rid himself of the feeling that this place's great legion of ghosts, in whom he did not even believe, were lurking all around him, and that their fury was still unappeased. Somehow he would have to deal with that fury, which had broken out now, so it seemed, in the form of a terrible act that had cost the life of a studious and inoffensive old man. The logic that infused every aspect of Valentine's soul balked at any comprehension of such a thing. But his own fate, he knew, and perhaps the fate of the world, might depend on his finding a solution to the mystery that had exploded here.

"You will pardon me, good majesty," said Tunigorn, breaking in on Valentine's broodings just as a new maze of ruined streets opened out before them. "But if I take another step in this heat, I will fall down gibbering like a madman. My very brain is melting."

"Why, then, Tunigorn, you should certainly seek refuge quickly, and cool it off! You can ill afford to damage what's left of it, can you, old friend?" Valentine pointed in the direction of the camp. "Go back. Go. But I will continue, I think."

He was not sure why. But something drove him grimly forward

across this immense bedraggled sprawl of sand-choked sun-blasted ruins, seeking he knew not what. One by one his other companions dropped away from him, with this apology or that, until only the indefatigable Lisamon Hultin remained. The giantess was ever-faithful. She had protected him from the dangers of Mazadone Forest in the days before his restoration to the Coronal's throne. She had been his guardian in the belly of the sea-dragon that had swallowed them both in the sea off Piliplok, that time when they were shipwrecked sailing from Zimroel to Alhanroel, and she had cut him free and carried him up to safety. She would not leave him now. Indeed she seemed willing to walk on and on with him through the day and the night and the day that followed as well, if that was what he required of her.

But eventually even Valentine had had enough. The sun had long since moved beyond its noon height. Sharp-edged pools of shadow, rose and purple and deepest obsidian, were beginning to reach out all about him. He was feeling a little light-headed now, his head swimming a little and his vision wavering from the prolonged strain of coping with the unyielding glare of that blazing sun, and each street of tumbled-down buildings had come to look exactly like its predecessor. It was time to go back. Whatever penance he had been imposing on himself by such an exhausting journey through this dominion of death and destruction must surely have been fulfilled by now. He leaned on Lisamon Hultin's arm now and again as they made their way toward the tents of the encampment.

Magadone Sambisa had assembled her eight Metamorph archaeologists. Valentine, having bathed and rested and had a little to eat, met with them just after sundown in his own tent, accompanied only by the little Vroon, Autifon Deliamber. He wanted to form his opinions of the Metamorphs undistracted by the presence of Nascimonte and the rest; but Deliamber had certain Vroonish wizardly skills that Valentine prized highly, and the small many-tentacled being might well be able to perceive things with those huge and keen golden eyes of his that would elude Valentine's own human vision.

The Shapeshifters sat in a semicircle with Valentine facing them and the tiny wizened old Vroon at his left hand. The Pontifex ran his glance down the group, from the site boss Kaastisiik at one end to the paleographer Vo-Siimifon on the other. They looked back at him calmly, almost indifferently, these seven rubbery-faced slope-eyed Piurivars, as he told them of the things he had seen this day, the cemetery and the shattered pyramid and the shrine beneath it, and the alcove where Huukaminaan's severed head had been so carefully placed by his murderer.

"There was, wouldn't you say, a certain formal aspect to the murder?" Valentine said. "The cutting of the body into pieces? The carrying of the head down to the shrine, the placement in the alcove of offerings?" His gaze fastened on Thiuurinen, the ceramics expert, a lithe, diminutive Metamorph woman with lovely jade-green skin. "What's your reading on that?" he asked her.

Her expression was wholly impassive. "As a ceramicist I have no opinion at all."

"I don't want your opinion as a ceramicist, just as a member of the expedition. A colleague of Dr. Huukaminaan. Does it seem to you that putting the head there meant that some kind of offering was being made?"

"It is only conjecture that those alcoves were places of offering," said Thiuurinen primly. "I am not in a position to speculate."

Nor would she. Nor would any of them. Not Kaastisiik, not Vo-Siimifon, not the stratigrapher Pamikuuk, not Hieekraad, the custodian of material artifacts, nor Driismiil, the architectural specialist, nor Klel-liin, the authority on Piurivar paleotechnology, nor Viitaal-Twuu, the specialist in metallurgy.

Politely, mildly, firmly, unshakably, they brushed aside Valentine's hypotheses about ritual murder. Was the gruesome dismemberment of Dr. Huukaminaan a hearkening-back to the funereal practices of ancient Velalisier? Was the placing of his head in that alcove likely to have been any kind of propitiation of some supernatural being? Was there anything in Piurivar tradition that might countenance killing someone in that particular fashion? They could not say. They would not say. Nor, when he inquired as to whether their late colleague might have had an enemy here at the site, did they provide him with any information.

And they merely gave him the Piurivar equivalent of a shrug when he wondered out loud whether there could have been some struggle over the discovery of a valuable artifact that might have led to Huukaminaan's murder; or even a quarrel of a more abstract kind, a fierce disagreement over the findings or goals of the expedition. Nobody showed any sign of outrage at his implication that one of them might have killed old Huukaminaan over such a matter. They behaved as though the whole notion of doing such a thing were beyond their comprehension, a concept too alien even to consider.

During the course of the interview Valentine took the opportunity to aim at least one direct question at each of them. But the result was always the same. They were unhelpful without seeming particularly evasive. They were unforthcoming without appearing unusually sly or secretive. There was nothing overtly suspicious about their refusal to cooperate. They seemed to be precisely what they claimed to be: scientists, studious scholars, devoted to uncovering the buried mysteries of their race's remote past, who knew nothing at all about the mystery that had erupted right here in their midst. He did not feel himself to be in the presence of murderers here.

And yet—and yet—

They were Shapeshifters. He was the Pontifex, the emperor of the race that had conquered them, the successor across eight thousand years of the half-legendary soldier-king Lord Stiamot, who had deprived them of their independence for all time. Mild and scholarly though they might be, these eight Piurivars before him surely could not help but feel anger, on some level of their souls, toward their human masters. They had no reason to cooperate with him. They would not see themselves under any obligation to tell him the truth. And—was this only his innate and inescapable racial prejudices speaking, Valentine wondered?—intuition told him to take nothing at face value among these people. Could he really trust the impression of apparent innocence that they gave? Was it possible ever for a human to read the things that lay hidden behind a Metamorph's cool impenetrable features?

"What do you think?" he asked Deliamber, when the seven Shapeshifters had gone. "Murderers or not?"

"Probably not," the Vroon replied. "Not these. Too soft, too citified. But they were holding something back. I'm certain of that."

"You felt it too, then?"

"Beyond any doubt. What I sensed, your majesty—do you know what the Vroon word *hsirthiir* means?"

"Not really."

"It isn't easy to translate. But it has to do with questioning someone who doesn't intend to tell you any lies but isn't necessarily going to tell you the truth, either, unless you know exactly how to call it forth. You pick up a powerful perception that there's an important layer of meaning hidden somewhere beneath the surface of what you're being told, but that you won't be allowed to elicit that hidden meaning unless you ask precisely the right question to unlock it. Which means, essentially, that you already have to know the information that you're looking for before you can ask the question that would reveal it. It's a very frustrating sensation, *hsirthiir*: almost painful, in fact. It is like hitting one's beak against a stone wall. I felt myself placed in a state of *hsirthiir* just now. Evidently so did you, your majesty."

"Evidently I did," said Valentine.

There was one more visit to make, though. It had been a long day and a terrible weariness was coming over Valentine now. But he felt some inner need to cover all the basic territory in a single sweep; and so, once darkness had fallen, he asked Magadone Sambisa to conduct him to the village of the Metamorph laborers.

She was unhappy about that. "We don't usually like to intrude on them after they've finished their day's work and gone back there, your majesty."

"You don't usually have murders here, either. Or visits from the Pontifex. I'd rather speak with them tonight than disrupt tomorrow's digging, if you don't mind."

Deliamber accompanied him once again. At her own insistence, so did Lisamon Hultin. Tunigorn was too tired to go—his hike through the ruins at midday had done him in—and Mirigant was feeling feverish from a touch of sunstroke; but formidable old Duke Nascimonte readily agreed to ride with the Pontifex, despite his great age. The final member of the party was Aarisiim, the Metamorph member of Valentine's security staff, whom Valentine brought with him not so much for protection—Lisamon Hultin would look after that—as for the *hsirthiir* problem.

Aarisiim, turncoat though he once had been, seemed to Valentine to be as trustworthy as any Piurivar was likely to be: he had risked his own life to betray his master Faraataa to Valentine in the time of the Rebellion, when he had felt that Faraataa had gone beyond all decency by threatening to slay the Metamorph queen. He could be helpful now, perhaps, detecting things that eluded even Deliamber's powerful perceptions.

The laborers' village was a gaggle of meager wickerwork huts outside the central sector of the dig. In its flimsy makeshift look it reminded Valentine of Ilirivoyne, the Shapeshifter capital in the jungle of Zimroel, which he had visited so many years before. But this place was even sadder and more disheartening than Ilirivoyne. There, at least, the Metamorphs had had an abundance of tall straight saplings and jungle vines with which to build their ramshackle huts, whereas the only construction materials available to them here were the gnarled and twisted desert shrubs that dotted the Velalisier plain. And so their huts were miserable little things, dismally warped and contorted.

They had had advance word, somehow, that the Pontifex was coming. Valentine found them arrayed in groups of eight or ten in front of their shacks, clearly waiting for his arrival. They were a pitiful starved-looking bunch, gaunt and shabby and ragged, very different from the urbane and cultivated Metamorphs of Magadone Sambisa's archaeological team. Valentine wondered where they found the strength to do the digging that was required of them in this inhospitable climate.

As the Pontifex came into view they shuffled forward to meet him, quickly surrounding him and the rest of his party in a way that caused Lisamon Hultin to hiss sharply and put her hand to the hilt of her vibration-sword.

But they did not appear to mean any harm. They clustered excitedly around him and to his amazement offered homage in the most obsequious way, jostling among themselves for a chance to kiss the hem of his tunic, kneeling in the sand before him, even prostrating themselves. "No," Valentine cried, dismayed. "This isn't necessary. It isn't right." Already Magadone Sambisa was ordering them brusquely to get back, and Lisamon Hultin and Nascimonte were shoving the ones closest to Valentine away from him. The giantess was doing it calmly, unhurriedly, efficiently, but Nascimonte was prodding them more truculently, with real detestation apparent in his fiery eyes. Others came pressing forward as fast as the first wave retreated, though, pushing in upon him in frantic determination.

So eager were these weary toil-worn people to show their obeisance to the Pontifex, in fact, that he could not help regarding their enthusiasm as blatantly false, an ostentatious overdoing of whatever might have been appropriate. How likely was it, he wondered, that any group of Piurivars, however lowly and simple, would feel great unalloyed joy at the sight of the Pontifex of Majipoor? Or would, of their own accord, stage such a spontaneous demonstration of delight?

Some, men and women both, were even allowing themselves to mimic the forms of the visitors by way of compliment, so that half a dozen blurry distorted Valentines stood before him, and a couple of Nascimontes, and a grotesque half-sized imitation of Lisamon Hultin. Valentine had experienced that peculiar kind of honor before, in his Ilirivoyne visit, and he had found it disturbing and even chilling then. It distressed him again now. Let them shift shapes if they wished—they had that capacity, to use as they pleased—but there was something almost sinister about this appropriation of the visages of their visitors.

And the jostling began to grow even wilder and more frenzied. Despite himself Valentine started to feel some alarm. There were more than a hundred villagers, and the visitors numbered only a handful. There could be real trouble if things got out of control.

Then in the midst of the hubbub a powerful voice called out, "Back! Back!" And at once the whole ragged band of Shapeshifters shrank away from Valentine as though they had been struck by whips. There was a sudden stillness and silence. Out of the now motionless throng there stepped a tall Metamorph of unusually muscular and powerful build. He made a deep gesticulation and announced, in a dark rumbling tone quite unlike that of any Metamorph voice Valentine had ever heard before, "I am Vathiimeraak, the foreman of these workers. I beg you to feel welcome here among us, Pontifex. We are your servants."

But there was nothing servile about him. He was plainly a man of presence and authority. Briskly he apologized for the uncouth behavior of his people, explaining that they were simple peasants astounded by the presence of a Power of the Realm among them, and this was merely their way of showing respect.

"I know this man," murmured Aarisiim into Valentine's left ear.

But there was no opportunity just then to find out more; for Vathiimeraak, turning away, made a signal with one upraised hand and instantly the scene became one of confusion and noise once again. The villagers went running off in a dozen different directions, some returning almost at once with platters of sausages and bowls of wine for their guests, others hauling lopsided tables and benches from the huts. Platoons of them came crowding in once more on Valentine and his companions, this time urging them to sample the delicacies they had to offer.

"They're giving us their own dinners!" Magadone Sambisa protested. And she ordered Vathiimeraak to call off the feast. But the foreman replied smoothly that it would offend the villagers to refuse their hospitality, and in the end there was no help for it: they must sit down at table and partake of all that the villagers brought for them.

"If you will, majesty," said Nascimonte, as Valentine reached for a bowl of wine. The duke took it from him and sipped it first; and only after a moment did he return it. He insisted also on tasting Valentine's sausages for him, and the scraps of boiled vegetables that went with them.

It had not occurred to Valentine that the villagers would try to poison him. But he allowed old Nascimonte to enact his charming little rite of medieval chivalry without objection. He was too fond of the old man to want to spoil his gesture.

Vathiimeraak said, when the feasting had gone on for some time, "You are here, your majesty, about the death of Dr. Huukaminaan, I assume?"

The foreman's bluntness was startling. "Could it not be," Valentine said good-humoredly, "that I just wanted to observe the progress being made at the excavations?"

Vathiimeraak would have none of that. "I will do whatever you may require of me in your search for the murderer," he said, rapping the table sharply to underscore his words. For an instant the outlines of his broad, heavy-jowled face rippled and wavered as if he were on the verge of undergoing an involuntary metamorphosis. Among the Piurivar, Valentine knew, that was a sign of being swept by some powerful emotion. "I had the greatest respect for Dr. Huukaminaan. It was a privilege to work beside him. I often dug for him myself, when I felt the site was too delicate to entrust to less skillful hands. He thought that that was improper, at first, that the foreman should dig, but I said, No, no, Dr. Huukaminaan, I beg you to allow me this glory, and he understood, and permitted me. —How may I help you to find the perpetrator of this dreadful crime?"

He seemed so solemn and straightforward and open that Valentine could not help but find himself immediately on guard. Vathiimeraak's strong, booming voice and overly formal choice of phrase had an overly theatrical quality. His elaborate sincerity seemed much like the extreme effusiveness of the villagers' demonstration, all that kneeling and kissing of his hem: unconvincing because it was so excessive.

You are too suspicious of these people, he told himself. *This man is simply speaking as he thinks a Pontifex should be spoken to. And in any case I think he can be useful.*

He said, "How much do you know of how the murder was committed?"

Vathiimeraak responded without hesitation, as if he had been holding a well-rehearsed reply in readiness. "I know that it happened late at night, the week before this, somewhere between the Hour of the Gihorna and the Hour of the Jackal. A person or persons lured Dr. Huukaminaan from his tent and led him to the Tables of the Gods, where he was killed and cut into pieces. We found the various segments of his body the next morning atop the western platform, all but his head. Which we discovered later that day in one of the alcoves along the base of the Shrine of the Downfall."

Pretty much the standard account, Valentine thought. Except for one small detail.

"The Shrine of the Downfall? I haven't heard that term before."

"The shrine of the Seventh Pyramid is what I mean," said Vathiimeraak. "The unopened shrine that Dr. Magadone Sambisa found. The name that I used is what we call it among ourselves. You notice that I do not say she 'discovered' it. We have always known that it was there, adjacent to the broken pyramid. But no one ever asked us, and so we never spoke of it."

Valentine glanced across at Deliamber, who nodded ever so minutely. *Hsirthiir* again, yes.

Something was not quite right, though. Valentine said, "Dr. Magadone Sambisa told me that she and Dr. Huukaminaan came upon the seventh shrine jointly, I think. She indicated that he was just as surprised at finding it there as she had been. Are you claiming that you knew of its existence, but he didn't?"

"There is no Piurivar who does not know of the existence of the Shrine of the Downfall," said Vathiimeraak stolidly. "It was sealed at the time of the Defilement and contains, we believe, evidence of the Defilement itself. If Dr. Magadone Sambisa formed the impression that Dr. Huukaminaan was unaware that it was there, that was an incorrect impression." Once again the edges of the foreman's face flickered and wavered. He looked worriedly toward Magadone Sambisa and said, "I mean no offense in contradicting you, Dr. Magadone Sambisa."

"None taken," she said, a little stiffly. "But if Huukaminaan knew of the shrine before the day we found it, he never said a thing about it to me."

"Perhaps he had hoped it would not be found," Vathiimeraak replied.

This brought a show of barely concealed consternation from Magadone Sambisa; and Valentine himself sensed that there was something here that needed to be followed up. But they were drifting away from the main issue.

"What I need you to do," said Valentine to the foreman, "is to determine the whereabouts of every single one of your people during the hours when the murder was committed." He saw Vathiimeraak's reaction beginning to take form, and added quickly, "I'm not suggesting that we believe at this point that anyone from the village killed Dr. Huukaminaan. No one at all is under suspicion at this point. But we do need to account for everybody who was present in or around the excavation zone that night."

"I will do what I can to find out."

"Your help will be invaluable, I know," Valentine said.

"You will also want to enlist the aid of our khivanivod," Vathiimeraak said. "He is not among us tonight. He has gone off on a spiritual retreat into the farthest zone of the city to pray for the purification of the soul of the killer of Dr. Huukaminaan, whoever that may be. I will send him to you when he returns."

Another little surprise.

A khivanivod was a Piurivar holy man, something midway between a priest and a wizard. They were relatively uncommon in modern Metamorph life, and it was remarkable that there should be one in residence at this scruffy out-of-the-way village. Unless, of course, the high religious leaders of the Piurivars had decided that it was best to install one at Velalisier for the duration of the dig, to insure that everything was done with the proper respect for the holy places. It was odd that Magadone Sambisa hadn't mentioned to him that a khivanivod was present here.

"Yes," said Valentine, a little uneasily. "Send him to me, yes. By all means."

As they rode away from the laborers' village Nascimonte said, "Well, Valentine, I'm pained to confess that I find myself once again forced to question your judgment."

"You do suffer much pain on my behalf," said Valentine, with a twinkling smile. "Tell me, Nascimonte: where have I gone amiss this time?"

"You enlisted that man Vathiimeraak as your ally in the investigation. You treated him, in fact, as though he were a trusted constable of police."

"He seems steady enough to me. And the villagers are terrified of him. What harm is there in asking him to question them for us? If we interrogate them ourselves, they'll just shut up like clams—or at best they'll tell us all kinds of fantastic stories. Whereas Vathiimeraak might just be able to bully the truth out of them. Some useful fraction of it, anyway."

"Not if he's the murderer himself," said Nascimonte.

"Ah, is that it? You've solved the crime, my friend? Vathiimeraak did it?"

"That could very well be."

"Explain, if you will, then."

Nascimonte gestured to Aarisiim. "Tell him."

The Metamorph said, "Majesty, I remarked to you when I first saw Vathiimeraak that I thought I knew that man from somewhere. And indeed I do, though it took me a little while more to place him. He is a kinsman of the rebel Faraataa. In the days when I was with Faraataa in Piurifayne, this Vathiimeraak was often by our side."

That was unexpected. But Valentine kept his reaction to himself. Calmly he said, "Does that matter? What of our amnesty, Aarisiim? All rebels who agreed to keep the peace after the collapse of Faraataa's campaign have been forgiven and restored to full civil rights. I should hardly need to remind you, of all people, of that."

"It doesn't mean they all turned into good citizens overnight, does it, Valentine?" Nascimonte demanded. "Surely it's possible that this

Vathiimeraak, a man of Faraataa's own blood, still harbors powerful feelings of—"

Valentine looked toward Magadone Sambisa. "Did you know he was related to Faraataa when you hired him as foreman?"

She seemed embarrassed. "No, majesty, I certainly did not. But I was aware that he had been in the Rebellion and had accepted the amnesty. And he came with the highest recommendation. We're supposed to believe that the amnesty has some meaning, doesn't it? That the Rebellion's over and done with, that those who took part in it and repented deserve to be allowed—"

"And has he truly repented, do you think?" Nascimonte asked. "Can anyone know, really? I say he's a fraud from top to toe. That big booming voice! That high-flown style of speaking! Those expressions of profound reverence for the Pontifex! Phony, every bit of it. And as for killing Huukaminaan, just look at him! Do you think it could have been easy to cut the poor man up in pieces that way? But Vathiimeraak's built like a bull bidlak. In that village of thin flimsy folk he stands out the way a dwikka tree would in a flat meadow."

"Because he has the strength for the crime doesn't yet prove that he's guilty of it," said Valentine in some annoyance. "And this other business, of his being related to Faraataa—what possible motive does that give him for slaughtering that harmless old Piurivar archaeologist? No, Nascimonte. No. No. No. You and Tunigorn between you, I know, would take about five minutes to decree that the man should be locked away for life in the Sangamor vaults that lie deep under the Castle. But we need a little evidence before we proclaim anyone a murderer." To Magadone Sambisa he said, "What about this khivanivod, now? Why weren't we told that there's a khivanivod living in this village?"

"He's been away since the day after the murder, your majesty," she said, looking at Valentine apprehensively. "To be perfectly truthful, I forgot all about him."

"What kind of person is he? Describe him for me."

A shrug. "Old. Dirty. A miserable superstition-monger, like all these tribal shamans. What can I say? I dislike having him around. But it's the price we pay for permission to dig here, I suppose."

"Has he caused any trouble for you?"

"A little. Constantly sniffing into things, worrying that we'll commit some sort of sacrilege. *Sacrilege*, in a city that the Piurivars themselves destroyed and put a curse on! What possible harm could we do here, after what they've already inflicted on it?"

. "This was their capital," said Valentine. "They were free to do with it as they pleased. That doesn't mean they're glad to have us come in here and root around in its ruins. —But has he actually tried to halt any part of your work, this khivanivod?"

"He objects to our unsealing the Shrine of the Downfall."

"Ah. You did say there was some political problem about that. He's filed a formal protest, has he?" The understanding by which Valentine had negotiated the right to send archaeologists into Velalisier included a veto power for the Piurivars over any aspect of the work that was not to their liking.

"So far he's simply told us he doesn't want us to open the shrine," said Magadone Sambisa. "He and I and Dr. Huukaminaan were supposed to have a meeting about it last week and try to work out a compromise, although what kind of middle ground there can be between opening the shrine and *not* opening it is hard for me to imagine. In any event the meeting never happened, for obvious tragic reasons. Now that you're here, perhaps you'll adjudicate the dispute for us when Torkkinuuminaad gets back from wherever he's gone off to."

"Torkkinuuminaad?" Valentine said. "Is that the khivanivod's name?"

"Torkkinuuminaad, yes."

"These jawbreaking Shapeshifter names," Nascimonte said grumpily. "Torkkinuuminaad! Vathiimeraak! Huukaminaan!" He glowered at Aarisiim. "By the Divine, fellow, was it absolutely necessary for you people to give yourself names that are so utterly impossible to pronounce, when you could just as easily have—"

"The system is very logical," Aarisiim replied serenely. "The doubling of the vowels in the first part of a name implies—"

"Save this discussion for some other time, if you will," said Valentine, making a chopping gesture with his hand. To Magadone Sambisa he said, "Just out of curiosity, what was the khivanivod's relationship with Dr. Huukaminaan like? Difficult? Tense? Did he think it was sacrilegious to pull the weeds off these ruins and set some of the buildings upright again?"

"Not at all," Magadone Sambisa said. "They worked hand in glove.

They had the highest respect for each other, though the Divine only knows why Dr. Huukaminaan tolerated that filthy old savage for half a minute. —Why? Are you suggesting that *Torkkinuuminaad* could have been the murderer?"

"Is that so unlikely? You haven't had a single good thing to say about him yourself."

"He's an irritating nuisance and in the matter of the shrine, at least, he's certainly made himself a serious obstacle to our work. But a murderer? Even I wouldn't go that far, your majesty. Anyone could see that he and Huukaminaan had great affection for each other."

"We should question him, all the same," said Nascimonte.

"Indeed," said Valentine. "Tomorrow, I want messengers sent out through the archaeological zone in search of him. He's somewhere around the ruins, right? Let's find him and bring him in. If that interrupts his spiritual retreat, so be it. Tell him that the Pontifex commands his presence."

"I'll see to it," said Magadone Sambisa.

"The Pontifex is very tired, now," said Valentine. "The Pontifex is going to go to sleep."

Alone in his grand royal tent at last after the interminable exertions of the busy day, he found himself missing Carabella with surprising intensity: that small and sinewy woman who had shared his destiny almost from the beginning of the strange time when he had found himself at Pidruid, at the other continent's edge, bereft of all memory, all knowledge of self. It was she, loving him only for himself, all unknowing that he was in fact a Coronal in baffled exile from his true identity, who had helped him join the juggling troupe of Zalzan Kavol; and gradually their lives had merged; and when he had commenced his astounding return to the heights of power she had followed him to the summit of the world.

He wished she were with him now. To sit beside him, to talk with him as they always talked before bedtime. To go over with him the twisting ramifications of all that had been set before him this day. To help him make sense out of the tangled mysteries this dead city posed for him. And simply to *be* with him.

But Carabella had not followed him here to Velalisier. It was a foolish waste of his time, she had argued, for him to go in person to investigate this murder. Send Tunigorn; send Mirigant; send Sleet; send any one of a number of high Pontifical officials. But why go yourself?

"Because I must," Valentine had replied. "Because I've made myself responsible for integrating the Metamorphs into the life of this world. The excavations at Velalisier are an essential part of that enterprise. And the murder of the old archaeologist leads me to think that conspirators are trying to interfere with those excavations."

"This is very far-fetched," said Carabella, then.

"And if it is, so be it. But you know how I long for a chance to free myself of the Labyrinth, if only for a week or two. So I will go to Velalisier."

"And I will not. I loathe that place, Valentine. It's a horrid place of death and destruction. I've seen it twice, and its charm isn't growing on me. If you go, you'll go without me."

"I mean to go, Carabella."

"Go, then. If you must." And she kissed him on the tip of the nose, for they were not in the custom of quarreling, or even of disagreeing greatly. But when he went, it was indeed without her. She was in their royal chambers in the Labyrinth tonight, and he was here, in his grand but solitary tent, in this parched and broken city of ancient ghosts.

They came to him that night in his dreams, those ghosts.

They came to him with such intensity that he thought he was having a sending—a lucid and purposeful direct communication in the form of a dream.

But this was like no sending he had ever had. Hardly had he closed his eyes but he found himself wandering in his sleep among the cracked and splintered buildings of dead Velalisier. Eerie ghost-light, mystery-light, came dancing up out of every shattered stone. The city glowed lime-green and lemon-yellow, pulsating with inner luminescence. Glowing faces, ghost-faces, grinned mockingly at him out of the air. The sun itself swirled and leaped in wild loops across the sky.

A dark hole leading into the ground lay open before him, and unquestioningly he entered it, descending a long flight of massive lichen-encrusted stone steps with archaic twining runes carved in them. Every movement was arduous for him. Though he was going steadily lower, the effort was like that of climbing. Struggling all the way, he made his way ever deeper, but he felt constantly as though he were traveling upward against a powerful pull, ascending some inverted pyramid, not a slender one like those above ground in this city, but one of unthinkable mass and diameter. He imagined himself to be fighting his way up the side of a mountain; but it was a mountain that pointed downward, deep into the world's bowels. And the path was carrying him down, he knew, into some labyrinth far more frightful than the one in which he dwelled in daily life.

The whirling ghost-faces flashed dizzyingly by him and went spinning away. Cackling laughter floated backward to him out of the darkness. The air was moist and hot and rank. The pull of gravity was oppressive. As he descended, traveling through level after endless level, momentary flares of dizzying yellow light showed him caverns twisting away from him on all sides, radiating outward at incomprehensible angles that were both concave and convex.

And now there was sudden numbing brightness. The throbbing fire of an underground sun streamed upward toward him from the depths ahead of him, a harsh, menacing glare.

Valentine found himself drawn helplessly toward that terrible light; and then, without perceptible transition, he was no longer underground at all, but out in the vastness of Velalisier Plain, standing atop one of the great platforms of blue stone known as the Tables of the Gods.

There was a long knife in his hand, a curving scimitar that flashed like lightning in the brilliance of the noon sun.

And as he looked out across the plain he saw a mighty procession coming toward him from the east, from the direction of the distant sea: thousands of people, hundreds of thousands, like an army of ants on the march. No, two armies; for the marchers were divided into two great parallel columns. Valentine could see, at the end of each column far off near the horizon, two enormous wooden wagons mounted on titanic wheels. Great hawsers were fastened to them, and the marchers, with mighty groaning tugs, were hauling the wagons slowly forward, a foot or two with each pull, into the center of the city.

Atop each of the wagons a colossal water-king lay trussed, a sea-dragon of monstrous size. The great creatures were glaring furiously at their captors but were unable, even with a sea-dragon's prodigious strength, to free themselves from their bonds, strain as they might. And with each tug on the hawsers the wagons bearing them carried them closer to the twin platforms called the Tables of the Gods.

The place of the sacrifice.

The place where the terrible madness of the Defilement was to happen. Where Valentine the Pontifex of Majipoor waited with the long gleaming blade in his hand.

Majesty? Majesty?"

Valentine blinked and came groggily awake. A Shapeshifter stood above him, extremely tall and greatly attenuated of form, his eyes so sharply slanted and narrowed that it seemed at first glance that he had none at all. Valentine began to jump up in alarm; and then, recognizing the intruder after a moment as Aarisiim, he relaxed.

"You cried out," the Metamorph said. "I was on my way to you to tell you some strange news I have learned, and when I was outside your tent I heard your voice. Are you all right, your majesty?"

"A dream, only. A very nasty dream." Which still lingered disagreeably at the edges of his mind. Valentine shivered and tried to shake himself free of its grasp. "What time is it, Aarisiim?"

"The Hour of the Haigus, majesty."

Past the middle of the night, that was. Well along toward dawn.

Valentine forced himself the rest of the way into wakefulness. Eyes fully open now, he stared up into the practically featureless face. "There's news, you say? What news?"

The Metamorph's color deepened from pale green to a rich chartreuse, and his eye slits fluttered swiftly three or four times. "I have had a conversation this night with one of the archaeologists, the woman Hieekraad, she who keeps the records of the discovered artifacts. The foreman of the diggers brought her to me, the man Vathiimeraak, from the village. He and this Hieekraad are lovers, it seems."

Valentine stirred impatiently. "Get to the point, Aarisiim."

"I approach it, sir. The woman Hieekraad, it seems, has revealed things to the man Vathiimeraak about the excavations that a mere foreman might otherwise not have known. He has told those things to me this evening."

"Well?"

"They have been lying to us, majesty—all the archaeologists, the whole pack of them, deliberately concealing something important. Something *quite* important, a major discovery. Vathiimeraak, when he learned from this Hieekraad that we had been deceived in this way, made the woman come with him to me, and compelled her to reveal the whole story to me."

"Go on."

"It was this," said Aarisiim. He paused a moment, swaying a little as though he were about to plunge into a fathomless abyss. "Dr. Huukaminaan, two weeks before he died, uncovered a burial site that had never been detected before. This was in an otherwise desolate region out at the western edge of the city. Magadone Sambisa was with him. It was a post-abandonment site, dating from the historic era. From a time not long after Lord Stiamot, actually."

"But how could that be?" said Valentine, frowning. "Completely aside from the little matter that there was a curse on this place and no Piurivar would have dared to set foot in it after it was destroyed, there weren't any Piurivars living on this continent at that time anyway. Stiamot had sent them all into the reservations on Zimroel. You know that very well, Aarisiim. Something's wrong here."

"This was not a Piurivar burial, your majesty."

"What?"

"It was the tomb of a human," Aarisiim said. "The tomb of a *Pontifex*, according to the woman Hieekraad."

Valentine would not have been more surprised if Aarisiim had set off an explosive charge. "A Pontifex?" he repeated numbly. "The tomb of a Pontifex, here in Velalisier?"

"So did this Hieekraad say. A definite identification. The symbols on the wall of the tomb—the Labyrinth sign, and other things of that sort—the ceremonial objects found lying next to the body—inscriptions—everything indicated that this was a Pontifex's grave, thousands of years old. So she said; and I think she was telling the truth. Vathiimeraak was standing over her, scowling, as she spoke. She was too frightened of him to have uttered any falsehoods just then."

Valentine rose and paced fiercely about the tent. "By the Divine, Aarisiim! If this is true, it's something that should have been brought to my attention as soon as it came to light. Or at least mentioned to me upon my arrival here. The tomb of some ancient Pontifex, and they hide it from me? Unbelievable. Unbelievable!"

"It was Magadone Sambisa herself who ordered that all news of the discovery was to be suppressed. There would be no public announcement whatever. Not even the diggers were told what had been uncovered. It was to be a secret known to the archaeologists of the dig, only."

"This according to Hieekraad also?"

"Yes, majesty. She said that Magadone Sambisa gave those orders the very day the tomb was found. This Hieekraad furthermore told me that Dr. Huukaminaan disagreed strenuously with Magadone Sambisa's decision, that indeed they had a major quarrel over it. But in the end he gave in. And when the murder happened, and word came that you were going to visit Velalisier, Magadone Sambisa called a meeting of the staff and reiterated that nothing was to be said to you about it. Everyone involved with the dig was specifically told to keep all knowledge of it from you."

"Absolutely incredible," Valentine muttered.

Earnestly Aarisiim said, "You must protect the woman Hieekraad, majesty, as you investigate this thing. She will be in great trouble if Magadone Sambisa learns that she's the one who let the story of the tomb get out."

"Hieekraad's not the only one who's going to be in trouble," Valentine said. He slipped from his nightclothes and started to dress.

"One more thing, majesty. The khivanivod—Torkkinuuminaad? He's at the tomb site right now. That's where he went to make his prayer retreat. I have this information from the foreman Vathiimeraak."

"Splendid," Valentine said. His head was whirling. "The village khivanivod mumbling Piurivar prayers in the tomb of a Pontifex! Beautiful! Wonderful! —Get me Magadone Sambisa, right away, Aarisiim."

"Majesty, the hour is very early, and—"

"Did you hear me, Aarisiim?"

"Majesty," said the Shapeshifter, more subserviently this time. He bowed deeply. And went out to fetch Magadone Sambisa.

An ancient Pontifex's tomb, Magadone Sambisa, and no announcement is made? An ancient Pontifex's tomb, and when the current Pontifex comes to inspect your dig, you go out of your way to keep him from learning about it? This is all extremely difficult for me to believe, let me assure you."

Dawn was still an hour away. Magadone Sambisa, called from her bed for this interview, looked even paler and more haggard than she had yesterday, and now there might have been a glint of fear in her eyes as well. But for all that, she still was capable of summoning some of the unrelenting strength that had propelled her to the forefront of her profession: there was even a steely touch of defiance in her voice as she said, "Who told you about this tomb, your majesty?"

Valentine ignored the sally. "It was at your order, was it, that the story was suppressed?"

"Yes."

"Over Dr. Huukaminaan's strong objections, so I understand."

Now fury flashed across her features. "They've told you everything, haven't they? Who was it? Who?"

"Let me remind you, lady, that I am the one asking the questions here. —It's true, then, that Huukaminaan disagreed with you about concealing the discovery?"

"Yes." In a very small voice.

"Why was that?"

"He saw it as a crime against the truth," Magadone Sambisa said, still speaking very quietly now. "You have to understand, majesty, that Dr. Huukaminaan was utterly dedicated to his work. Which was, as it is for us all, the recovery of the lost aspects of our past through rigorous application of formal archaeological disciplines. He was totally committed to this, a true and pure scientist."

"Whereas you are not committed quite so totally?"

Magadone Sambisa reddened and glanced shamefacedly to one side. "I admit that my actions may make it seem that way. But sometimes even the pursuit of truth has to give way, at least for a time, before tactical realities. Surely you, a Pontifex, would not deny that. And I had reasons, reasons that seemed valid enough to me, for not wanting to let news of this tomb reach the public. Dr. Huukaminaan didn't agree with my position; and he and I battled long and hard over it. It was the only occasion in our time as co-leaders of this expedition that we disagreed over anything."

"And finally it became necessary, then, for you to have him murdered? Because he yielded to you only grudgingly, and you weren't sure he really would keep quiet?"

"*Majesty!*" It was a cry of almost inexpressible shock.

"A motive for the killing can be seen there. Isn't that so?"

She looked stunned. She waved her arms helplessly about, the palms of her hands turned outward in appeal. A long moment passed before she could bring herself to speak. But she had recovered much of her composure when she did.

"Majesty, what you have just suggested is greatly offensive to me. I am guilty of hiding the tomb discovery, yes. But I swear to you that I had nothing to do with Dr. Huukaminaan's death. I can't possibly tell you how much I admired that man. We had our professional differences, but—" She shook her head. She looked drained. Very quietly she said, "I didn't kill him. I have no idea who did."

Valentine chose to accept that, for now. It was hard for him to believe that she was merely playacting her distress.

"Very well, Magadone Sambisa. But now tell me why you decided to conceal the finding of that tomb."

"I would have to tell you, first, an old Piurivar legend, a tale out of their mythology, one that I heard from the khivanivod Torkkinuuminaad on the day that we found the tomb."

"Must you?"

"I must, yes."

Valentine sighed. "Go ahead, then."

Magadone Sambisa moistened her lips and drew a deep breath.

"There once was a Pontifex, so the story goes," she said, "who lived in the years soon after the conquest of the Piurivars by Lord Stiamot. This Pontifex had fought in the War of the Conquest himself when he was a young man, and had had charge over a camp of Piurivar prisoners, and had listened to some of their campfire tales. Among which was the story of the Defilement at Velalisier—the sacrifice by the Final King of the two sea-dragons, and the destruction of the city that followed it. They told him also of the broken Seventh Pyramid, and of the shrine beneath it, the Shrine of the Downfall, as they called it. In which, they said, certain artifacts dating from the day of the Defilement had been buried—artifacts that would, when properly used, grant their wielder godlike power over all the forces of space and time. This story stayed with him, and many years later when he had become Pontifex he came to Velalisier with the intention of locating the shrine of the Seventh Pyramid, the Shrine of the Downfall, and opening it."

"For the purpose of bringing forth these magical artifacts, and using them to gain godlike power over the forces of space and time?"

"Exactly," said Magadone Sambisa.

"I think I see where this is heading."

"Perhaps you do, majesty. We are told that he went to the site of the shattered pyramid. He drove a tunnel into the ground; he came upon the stone passageway that leads to the wall of the shrine. He found the wall and made preparations for breaking through it."

"But the seventh shrine, you told me, is intact. Since the time of the abandonment of the city no one has ever entered it. Or so you believe."

"No one ever has. I'm sure of that."

"This Pontifex, then—?"

"Was just at the moment of breaching the shrine wall when a Piurivar who had hidden himself in the tunnel overnight rose up out of the darkness and put a sword through his heart."

"Wait a moment," said Valentine. Exasperation began to stir in him. "A Piurivar popped out of nowhere and killed him, you say? A *Piurivar?* I've just gone through this same thing with Aarisiim. Not only weren't there any Piurivars anywhere in Alhanroel at that time, because Stiamot had locked them all up in reservations over in Zimroel, but there was supposed to be a curse on this place that would have prevented members of their race from going near it."

"Except for the guardians of the shrine, who were exempted from the curse," said Magadone Sambisa.

"Guardians?" Valentine said. "What guardians? I've never heard anything about Piurivar guardians here."

"Nor had I, until Torkkinuuminaad told me this story. But at the time of the city's destruction and abandonment, evidently, a decision was made to post a small band of watchmen here, so that nobody would be able to break into the seventh shrine and gain access to whatever's in there. And that guard force remained on duty here throughout the centuries. There were still guardians here when the Pontifex came to loot the shrine. One of them tucked himself away in the tunnel and killed the Pontifex just as he was about to chop through the wall."

"And his people buried him *here*? Why in the world would they do that?"

Magadone Sambisa smiled. "To hush things up, of course. Consider, majesty: A Pontifex comes to Velalisier in search of forbidden mystical knowledge, and is assassinated by a Piurivar who has been sneaking around undetected in the supposedly abandoned city. If word of that got around, it would make everyone look bad."

"I suppose that it would."

"The Pontifical officials certainly wouldn't have wanted to let it be known that their master had been struck down right under their noses. Nor would they be eager to advertise the story of the secret shrine, which might lead others to come here looking for it too. And surely they'd never want anyone to know that the Pontifex had died at the hand of a Piurivar, something that could reopen all the wounds of the War of the Conquest and perhaps touch off some very nasty reprisals."

"And so they covered everything up," said Valentine.

"Exactly. They dug a tomb off in a remote corner of the ruins and buried the Pontifex in it with some sort of appropriate ritual, and went back to the Labyrinth with the news that his majesty had very suddenly been stricken down at the ruins by an unknown disease and it had seemed unwise to bring his body back from Velalisier for the usual kind of state funeral. —Ghorban, was his name. There's an inscription in the tomb that names him. Ghorban Pontifex, three Pontifexes after Stiamot. He really existed. I did research in the House of Records. You'll see him listed there."

"I'm not familiar with the name."

"No. He's not exactly one of the famous ones. But who can remember them all, anyway? Hundreds and hundreds of them, across all those thousands of years. Ghorban was Pontifex only a short while, and the only event of any importance that occurred during his reign was something that was carefully obliterated from the records. I'm speaking of his visit to Velalisier."

Valentine nodded. He had paused by the great screen outside the Labyrinth's House of Records often enough, and many times had stared at that long list of his predecessors, marveling at the names of all-but-forgotten monarchs, Meyk and Spurifon and Heslaine and Kandibal and dozens more. Who must have been great men in their day, but their day was thousands of years in the past. No doubt there was a Ghorban on the list, if Magadone Sambisa said there had been: who had reigned in regal grandeur for a time as the Coronal Lord Ghorban atop Castle Mount, and then had succeeded to the Pontificate in the fullness of his years, and for some reason had paid a visit to this accursed city of Velalisier, where he died, and was buried, and fell into oblivion.

"A curious tale," Valentine said. "But what is there in it that would have made you want to suppress the discovery of this Ghorban's tomb?"

"The same thing that made those ancient Pontifical officials suppress the real circumstances of his death," replied Magadone Sambisa. "You surely know that most ordinary people already are sufficiently afraid of this city. The horrible story of the Defilement, the curse, all the talk of ghosts lurking in the ruins, the general spookiness of the place— well, you know what people are like, your majesty. How timid they can be in the face of the unknown. And I was afraid that if the Ghorban story came out—the secret shrine, the search for mysterious magical lore by some obscure ancient Pontifex, the murder of that Pontifex by a Piurivar—there'd be such public revulsion against the whole idea of excavating Velalisier that the dig would be shut down. I didn't want that to happen. That's all it was, your majesty. I was trying to preserve my own job, I suppose. Nothing more than that."

It was a humiliating confession. Her tone, which had been vigorous enough during the telling of the tale, now was flat, weary, almost lifeless. To Valentine it had the sound of complete sincerity.

"And Dr. Huukaminaan didn't agree with you that revealing the discovery of the tomb could be a threat to the continuation of your work here?"

"He saw the risk. He didn't care. For him the truth came first and foremost, always. If public opinion forced the dig to be shut down, and nobody worked here again for fifty or a hundred or five hundred years, that was all right with him. His integrity wouldn't permit hiding a startling piece of history like that, not for any reason. So we had a big battle and finally I pushed him into giving in. You've seen how stubborn I can be. But I didn't kill him. If I had wanted to kill anybody, it wouldn't have been Dr. Huukaminaan. It would have been the khivanivod, who actually *does* want the dig shut down."

"He does? You said he and Huukaminaan worked hand in glove."

"In general, yes. As I told you yesterday, there was one area where he and Huukaminaan diverged: the issue of opening the shrine. Huukaminaan and I, you know, were planning to open it as soon as we could arrange for you and Lord Hissune to be present at the work. But the khivanivod was passionately opposed. The rest of our work here was acceptable to him, but not that. The Shrine of the Downfall, he kept saying, is the holy of holies, the most sacred Piurivar place."

"He might just have a point there," Valentine said.

"You also don't think we should look inside that shrine?"

"I think that there are certain important Piurivar leaders who might very much not want that to happen."

"But the Danipiur herself has given us permission to work here! Not only that, but she and all the rest of the Piurivar leaders understand that we've come here to restore the city—that we hope to undo as much as we can of the harm that thousands of years of neglect have caused. They have no quarrel with that. But just to be completely certain that our work would give no offense to the Piurivar community, we all agreed that the expedition would consist of equal numbers of Piurivar and non-Piurivar archaeologists, and that Dr. Huukaminaan and I would share the leadership on a co-equal basis."

"Although you turned out to be somewhat more co-equal than he was when there happened to be a significant disagreement between the two of you, didn't you?"

"In that one instance of the Ghorban tomb, yes," said Magadone Sambisa, looking just a little out of countenance. "But only that one. He and I were in complete agreement at all times on everything else. On the issue of opening the shrine, for example."

"A decision which the khivanivod then vetoed."

"The khivanivod has no power to veto anything, majesty. The understanding we had was that any Piurivar who objected to some aspect of our work on religious grounds could appeal to the Danipiur, who would then adjudicate the matter in consultation with you and Lord Hissune."

"Yes. I wrote that decree myself, actually."

Valentine closed his eyes a moment and pressed the tips of his fingers against them. He should have realized, he told himself, that problems like these would inevitably crop up. This city had too much tragic history. Terrible things had happened here. The mysterious aura of Piurivar sorcery still hovered over the place, thousands of years after its destruction.

He had hoped to dispel some of that aura by sending in these scientists. Instead he had only enmeshed himself in its dark folds.

After a time he looked up and said, "I understand from Aarisiim that where your khivanivod has gone to make his spiritual retreat is in fact the Ghorban tomb that you've taken such pains to hide from me, and that he's there at this very moment. Is that true?"

"I believe it is."

The Pontifex walked to the tent entrance and peered outside. The first bronze streaks of the desert dawn were arching across the great vault of the sky.

"Last night," he said, "I asked you to send messengers out looking for him, and you said that you would. You didn't, of course, tell me that you knew where he was. But since you do know, get your messengers moving. I want to speak with him first thing this morning."

"And if he refuses to come, your majesty?"

"Then have him brought."

The khivanivod Torkkinuuminaad was every bit as disagreeable as Magadone Sambisa had led Valentine to expect, although the fact that it had been necessary for Valentine's security people to threaten to drag him bodily from the Ghorban tomb must not have improved his temper. Lisamon Hultin was the one who had ordered him out of there, heedless of his threats and curses. Piurivar witcheries and spells held little dread for her, and she let him know that if he didn't go to Valentine more or less willingly on his own two feet, she would carry him to the Pontifex herself.

The Shapeshifter shaman was an ancient, emaciated man, naked but for some wisps of dried grass around his waist and a nasty-looking amulet, fashioned of interwoven insect legs and other such things, that dangled from a frayed cord about his neck. He was so old that his green skin had faded to a faint gray, and his slitted eyes, bright with rage, glared balefully at Valentine out of sagging folds of rubbery skin.

Valentine began on a conciliatory note. "I ask your pardon for interrupting your meditations. But certain urgent matters must be dealt with before I return to the Labyrinth, and your presence was needed for that."

Torkkinuuminaad said nothing.

Valentine proceeded regardless. "For one thing, a serious crime has been committed in the archaeological zone. The killing of Dr. Huukaminaan is an offense not only against justice but against knowledge itself. I'm here to see that the murderer is identified and punished."

"What does this have to do with me?" asked the khivanivod, glowering sullenly. "If there has been a murder, you should find the murderer and punish him, yes, if that is what you feel you must do. But why must a servant of the Gods That Are be compelled by force to break off his sacred communion like this? Because the Pontifex of Majipoor commands it?" Torkkinuuminaad laughed harshly. "The Pontifex! Why should the commands of the Pontifex mean anything to me? I serve only the Gods That Are."

"You also serve the Danipiur," said Valentine in a calm, quiet tone. "And the Danipiur and I are colleagues in the government of Majipoor." He indicated Magadone Sambisa and the other archaeologists, both human and Metamorph, who stood nearby. "These people are at work in Velalisier this day because the Danipiur has granted her permission for them to be here. You yourself are here at the Danipiur's request, I believe. To serve as spiritual counselor for those of your people who are involved in the work."

"I am here because the Gods That Are require me to be here, and for no other reason."

"Be that as it may, your Pontifex stands before you, and he has questions to ask you, and you will answer."

The shaman's only response was a sour glare.

"A shrine has been discovered near the ruins of the Seventh Pyramid," Valentine went on. "I understand that the late Dr. Huukaminaan intended to open that shrine. You had strong objections to that, am I correct?"

"You are."

"Objections on what grounds?"

"That the shrine is a sacred place not to be disturbed by profane hands."

"How can there be a sacred place," asked Valentine, "in a city that had a curse pronounced on it?"

"The shrine is sacred nevertheless," the khivanivod said obdurately.

"Even though no one knows what may be inside it?"

"*I* know what is inside it," said the khivanivod.

"You? How?"

"I am the guardian of the shrine. The knowledge is handed down from guardian to guardian."

Valentine felt a chill traveling along his spine. "Ah," he said. "The guardian. Of the shrine." He was silent a moment. "As the officially designated successor, I suppose, of the guardian who murdered a Pontifex here once thousands of years ago. The place where you were found praying just now, so I've been told, was the tomb of that very Pontifex. Is that so?"

"It is."

"In that case," said Valentine, allowing a little smile to appear at the corners of his mouth, "I need to ask my guards to keep very careful watch on you. Because the next thing I'm going to do, my friend, is to instruct Magadone Sambisa and her people to proceed at once with the opening of the seventh shrine. And I see now that that might place me in some danger at your hands."

Torkkinuuminaad looked astounded. Abruptly the Metamorph shaman began to go through a whole repertoire of violent changes of form, contracting and elongating wildly, the borders of his body blurring and recomposing with bewildering speed.

But the archaeologists too, both the human ones and the two Ghayrogs and the little tight-knit group of Shapeshifters, were staring at Valentine as though he had just said something beyond all comprehension. Even Tunigorn and Mirigant and Nascimonte were flabbergasted. Tunigorn turned to Mirigant and said something, to which Mirigant replied only with a shrug, and Nascimonte, standing near them, shrugged also in complete bafflement.

Magadone Sambisa said in hoarse choking tones, "Majesty? Do you mean that? I thought you said only a little while ago that the best thing would be to leave the shrine unopened!"

"I said that? I?" Valentine shook his head. "Oh, no. No. How long will it take you to get started on the job?"

"Why—let me see—" He heard her murmur, "The recording devices, the lighting equipment, the masonry drills—" She grew quiet, as if counting additional things off in her mind. Then she said, "We could be ready to begin in half an hour."

"Good. Let's get going, then."

"No! This will not be!" cried Torkkinuuminaad, a wild screech of rage.

"It will," said Valentine. "And you'll be there to watch it. As will I." He beckoned toward Lisamon Hultin. "Speak with him, Lisamon. Tell him in a persuasive way that it'll be much better for him if he remains calm."

Magadone Sambisa said, wonderingly, "Are you serious about all this, Pontifex?"

"Oh, yes. Yes. Very serious indeed."

The day seemed a hundred hours long.

Opening any sealed site for the first time would ordinarily have been a painstaking process. But this one was so important, so freighted with symbolic significance, so potentially explosive in its political implications, that every task was done with triple care.

Valentine himself waited at surface level during the early stages of the work. What they were doing down there had all been explained to him—running cables for illumination and ventilating pipes for the excavators; carefully checking with sonic probes to make sure that opening the shrine wall would not cause the ceiling of the vault to collapse; sonic testing of the interior of the shrine itself to see if there was anything important immediately behind the wall that might be imperiled by the drilling operation.

All that took hours. Finally they were ready to start cutting into the wall.

"Would you like to watch, majesty?" Magadone Sambisa asked.

Despite the ventilation equipment, Valentine found it hard work to breathe inside the tunnel. The air had been hot and stale enough on his earlier visit; but now, with all these people crowded into it, it was thin, feeble stuff, and he had to strain his lungs to keep from growing dizzy.

The close-packed archaeologists parted ranks to let him come forward. Bright lights cast a brilliant glare on the white stone façade of the shrine. Five people were gathered there, three Piurivars, two humans. The actual drilling seemed to be the responsibility of the burly foreman Vathiimeraak. Kaastisiik, the Piurivar archaeologist who was the site boss, was assisting. Just behind them was Driismiil, the Piurivar architectural expert, and a human woman named Shimrayne Gelvoin, who also was an architect, evidently. Magadone Sambisa stood to the rear, quietly issuing orders.

They were peeling the wall back stone by stone. Already an area of the façade perhaps three feet square had been cleared just above the row of offering alcoves. Behind it lay rough brickwork, no more than one course thick. Vathiimeraak, muttering to himself in Piurivar as he worked, now was chiseling away at one of the bricks. It came loose in a crumbling mass, revealing an inner wall made of the same fine black stone slabs as the tunnel wall itself.

A long pause, now, while the several layers of the wall were measured and photographed. Then Vathiimeraak resumed the inward probing. Valentine was at the edge of queasiness in this foul, acrid atmosphere, but he forced it back.

Vathiimeraak cut deeper, halting to allow Kaastisiik to remove some broken pieces of the black stone. The two architects came forward and inspected the opening, conferring first with each other, then with Magadone Sambisa; and then Vathiimeraak stepped toward the breach once again with his drilling tool.

"We need a torch," Magadone Sambisa said suddenly. "Give me a torch, someone!"

A hand torch was passed up the line from the crowd in the rear of the tunnel. Magadone Sambisa thrust it into the opening, peered, gasped.

"Majesty? Majesty, would you come and look?"

By that single shaft of light Valentine made out a large rectangular room, which appeared to be completely empty except for a large square block of dark stone. It was very much like the glossy block of black opal, streaked with veins of scarlet ruby, from which the glorious Confalume Throne at the castle of the Coronal had been carved.

There were things lying on that block. But what they were was impossible to tell at this distance.

"How long will it take to make an opening big enough for someone to enter the room?" Valentine asked.

"Three hours, maybe."

"Do it in two. I'll wait aboveground. You call me when the opening is made. Be certain that no one enters it before me."

"You have my word, majesty."

Even the dry desert air was a delight after an hour or so of breathing the dank stuff below. Valentine could see by the lengthening shadows creeping across the deep sockets of the distant dunes that the afternoon was well along. Tunigorn, Mirigant, and Nascimonte were pacing about amidst the rubble of the fallen pyramid. The Vroon Deliamber stood a little distance apart.

"Well?" Tunigorn asked.

"They've got a little bit of the wall open. There's something inside, but we don't know what, yet."

"Treasure?" Tunigorn asked, with a lascivious grin. "Mounds of emeralds and diamonds and jade?"

"Yes," said Valentine. "All that and more. Treasure. An enormous treasure, Tunigorn." He chuckled and turned away. "Do you have any wine with you, Nascimonte?"

"As ever, my friend. A fine Muldemar vintage."

He handed his flask to the Pontifex, who drank deep, not pausing to savor the bouquet at all, guzzling as though the wine were water.

The shadows deepened. One of the lesser moons crept into the margin of the sky.

"Majesty? Would you come below?"

It was the archaeologist Vo-Siimifon. Valentine followed him into the tunnel.

The opening in the wall was large enough now to admit one person. Magadone Sambisa, her hand trembling, handed Valentine the torch.

"I must ask you, your majesty, to touch nothing, to make no disturbance whatever. We will not deny you the privilege of first entry, but you must bear in mind that this is a scientific enterprise. We have to record everything just as we find it before anything, however trivial, can be moved."

"I understand," said Valentine.

He stepped carefully over the section of the wall below the opening and clambered in.

The shrine's floor was of some smooth glistening stone, perhaps rosy quartz. A fine layer of dust covered it. *No one has walked across this floor for twenty thousand years*, Valentine thought. *No human foot has ever come in contact with it at all.*

He approached the broad block of black stone in the center of the room and turned the torch full on it. Yes, a single dark mass of ruby-streaked opal, just like the Confalume Throne. Atop it, with only the faintest tracery of dust concealing its brilliance, lay a flat sheet of gold, engraved with intricate Piurivar glyphs and inlaid with cabochons of what looked like beryl and carnelian and lapis lazuli. Two long, slender objects that could have been daggers carved from some white stone lay precisely in the center of the gold sheet, side by side.

Valentine felt a tremor of the deepest awe. He knew what those two things were.

"Majesty? Majesty?" Magadone Sambisa called. "Tell us what you see! Tell us, please!"

But Valentine did not reply. It was as though Magadone Sambisa had not spoken. He was deep in memory, traveling back eight years to the climactic hour of the War of the Rebellion.

He had, in that hour, held in his hand a daggerlike thing much like these two, and had felt the strange coolness of it, a coolness that gave a hint of a fiery core within, and had heard a complex far-off music emanating from it into his mind, a turbulent rush of dizzying sound.

It had been the tooth of a sea-dragon that he had been grasping then. Some mystery within that tooth had placed his mind in communion with the mind of the mighty water-king Maazmoorn, a dragon of the distant Inner Sea. And with the aid of the mind of Maazmoorn had Valentine Pontifex reached across the world to strike down the unrepentent rebel Faraataa and bring that sorry uprising to an end.

Whose teeth were these, now?

He thought he knew. This was the Shrine of the Downfall, the Place of the Defilement. Not far from here, long ago, two water-kings had been brought from the sea to be sacrificed on platforms of blue stone. That was no myth. It had actually happened. Valentine had no doubt of that, for the sea-dragon Maazmoorn had shown it to him with the full communion of his mind, in a manner that admitted of no question. He knew their names, even: one was the water-king Niznorn and the other the water-king Domsitor. Was this tooth here Niznorn's, and this one Domsitor's?

Twenty thousand years.

"Majesty? Majesty?"

"One moment," Valentine said, speaking as though from halfway around the world.

He picked up the left-hand tooth. Grasped it tightly. Hissed as its fiery chill stung the palm of his hand. Closed his eyes, allowed his mind to be pervaded by its magic. Felt his spirit beginning to soar outward and outward and outward, toward some waiting dragon of the sea—Maazmoorn again, for all he could know, or perhaps some other one of the giants who swam in those waters out there—while all the time he heard the sounding bells, the tolling music of that sea-dragon's mind.

And was granted a vision of the ancient sacrifice of the two water-kings, the event known as the Defilement.

He already knew, from Maazmoorn in that meeting of minds years ago, that that traditional name was a misnomer. There had been no defilement whatever. It had been a voluntary sacrifice; it had been the formal acceptance by the sea-dragons of the power of That Which Is, which is the highest of all the forces of the universe.

The water-kings had given themselves gladly to those Piurivars of long-ago Velalisier to be slain. The slayers themselves had understood what they were doing, perhaps, but the simple Piurivars of the outlying provinces had not; and so those simpler Piurivars had called it a Defilement, and had put the Final King of Velalisier to death and smashed the Seventh Pyramid and then had wrecked all the rest of this great capital, and had laid a curse on the city forever. But the shrine of these teeth they had not dared to touch.

Valentine, holding the tooth, beheld the sacrifice once more. Not with the bound sea-dragons writhing in fury as they were brought to the knife, the way he had seen it in his nightmare of the previous night. No. He saw it now as a serene and holy ceremony, a benign yielding up of the living flesh. And as the knives flashed, as the great sea-creatures died, as their dark flesh was carried to the pyres for burning, a resounding wave of triumphant harmony went rolling out to the boundaries of the universe.

He put the tooth down and picked up the other one. Grasped. Felt. Surrendered himself to its power.

This time the music was more discordant. The vision that came to him was that of some unknown man of middle years, garbed in a rich costume of antique design, clothing befitting to a Pontifex. He was moving cautiously by the smoky light of a flickering torch down the very passageway outside this room where Magadone Sambisa and her archaeologists now clustered. Valentine watched that Pontifex of long ago approaching the white unsullied wall of the shrine. Saw him press the flat of his hand against it, pushing as though he hoped to penetrate it by his own strength alone. Turning from it, then, beckoning to workmen with picks and spades, indicating that they should start hacking their way through it.

And a figure uncoiling out of the darkness, a Shapeshifter, long and lean and grim-faced, taking one great step forward and in a swift unstoppable lunge driving a knife upward and inward beneath the heart of the man in the brocaded Pontifical robes—

Majesty, I beg you!"

Magadone Sambisa's voice, ripe with anguish.

"Yes," said Valentine, in the distant tone of one who has been lost in a dream. "I'm coming."

He had had enough visions, for the moment. He set the torch down on the floor, aiming it toward the opening in the wall to light his way. Carefully he picked up the two dragon teeth—letting them rest easily on the palms of his hands, taking care not to touch them so tightly as to activate their powers, for he did not want now to open his mind to them—and made his way back out of the shrine.

Magadone Sambisa stared at him in horror. "I asked you, your majesty, not to touch the objects in the vault, not to cause any disturbance to—"

"Yes. I know that. You will pardon me for what I have done."

It was not a request.

The archaeologists melted back out of his way as he strode through their midst, heading for the exit to the upper world. Every eye was turned to the things that rested on Valentine's upturned hands.

"Bring the khivanivod to me here," he said quietly to Aarisiim. The light of day was nearly gone now, and the ruins were taking on the greater mysteriousness that came over them by night, when moonlight's cool gleam danced across the shattered city's ancient stones.

The Shapeshifter went rushing away. Valentine had not wanted the khivanivod anywhere near the shrine while the opening of the wall was taking place; and so, over his violent objections, Torkkinuuminaad had been bundled off to the archaeologists' headquarters in the custody of some of Valentine's security people. The two immense woolly Skandars brought him forth now, holding him by the arms.

Anger and hatred were bubbling up from the shaman like black gas rising from a churning marsh. And, staring into that jagged green wedge of a face, Valentine had a powerful sense of the ancient magic of this world, of mysteries reaching toward him out of the timeless misty Majipoor dawn, when Shapeshifters had moved alone and unhindered through this great planet of marvels and splendors.

The Pontifex held the two sea-dragon teeth aloft.

"Do you know what these are, Torkkinuuminaad?"

The rubbery eye-folds drew back. The narrow eyes were yellow with rage. "You have committed the most terrible of all sacrileges, and you will die in the most terrible of agonies."

"So you do know what they are, eh?"

"They are the holiest of holies! You must return them to the shrine at once!"

"Why did you have Dr. Huukaminaan killed, Torkkinuuminaad?"

The khivanivod's only answer was an even more furiously defiant glare.

He would kill me with his magic, if he could, thought Valentine. *And why not? I know what I represent to Torkkinuuminaad. For I am Majipoor's emperor and therefore I am Majipoor itself, and if one thrust would send us all to our doom he would strike that thrust.*

Yes. Valentine was in his own person the embodiment of the Enemy: of those who had come out of the sky and taken the world away from the Piurivars, who had built their own gigantic sprawling cities over virgin forests and glades, had intruded themselves by the billions into the fragile fabric of the Piurivars' trembling web of life. And so Torkkinuuminaad would kill him, if he could, and by killing the Pontifex kill, by the symbolism of magic, all of human-dominated Majipoor.

But magic can be fought with magic, Valentine thought.

"Yes, look at me," he told the shaman. "Look right into my eyes, Torkkinuuminaad."

And let his fingers close tightly about the two talismans he had taken from the shrine.

The double force of the teeth struck into Valentine with a staggering impact as he closed the mental circuit. He felt the full range of the sensations all at once, not simply doubled, but multiplied many times over. He held himself upright nevertheless; he focused his concentration with the keenest intensity; he aimed his mind directly at that of the khivanivod.

Looked. Entered. Penetrated the khivanivod's memories and quickly found what he was seeking.

Midnight darkness. A sliver of moonlight. The sky ablaze with stars. The billowing tent of the archaeologists. Someone coming out of it, a Piurivar, very thin, moving with the caution of age.

Dr. Huukaminaan, surely.

A slender figure stands in the road, waiting: another Metamorph, also old, just as gaunt, raggedly and strangely dressed.

The khivanivod, that one is. Viewing himself in his own mind's eye.

Shadowy figures moving about behind him, five, six, seven of them. Shapeshifters all. Villagers, from the looks of them. The old archaeologist does not appear to see them. He speaks with the khivanivod; the shaman gestures, points. There is a discussion of some sort. Dr. Huukaminaan shakes his head. More pointing. More discussion. Gestures of agreement. Everything seems to be resolved.

As Valentine watches, the khivanivod and Huukaminaan start off together down the road that leads to the heart of the ruins.

The villagers, now, emerging from the shadows that have concealed them. Surrounding the old man; seizing him; covering his mouth to keep him from crying out. The khivanivod approaches him.

The khivanivod has a knife.

Valentine did not need to see the rest of the scene. Did not *want* to see that monstrous ceremony of dismemberment at the stone platform, nor the weird ritual afterward in the excavation leading to the Shrine of the Downfall, the placing of the dead man's head in that alcove.

He released his grasp on the two sea-dragon teeth and set them down with great care beside him on the ground.

"Now," he said to the khivanivod, whose expression had changed from one of barely controllable wrath to one that might almost have been resignation. "There's no need for further pretending here, I think. Why did you kill Dr. Huukaminaan?"

"Because he would have opened the shrine." The khivanivod's tone was completely flat, no emotion in it at all.

"Yes. Of course. But Magadone Sambisa also was in favor of opening it. Why not kill her instead?"

"He was one of us, and a traitor," said Torkkinuuminaad. "She did not matter. And he was more dangerous to our cause. We know that she might have been prevented from opening the shrine, if we objected strongly enough. But nothing would stop him."

"The shrine was opened anyway, though," Valentine said.

"Yes, but only because you came here. Otherwise the excavations would have been closed down. The outcry over Huukaminaan's death would demonstrate to the whole world that the curse of this place still had power. You came, and you opened the shrine; but the curse will strike you just as it struck the Pontifex Ghorban long ago."

"There is no curse," Valentine said calmly. "This is a city that has seen much tragedy, but there is no curse, only misunderstanding piled on misunderstanding."

"The Defilement—"

"There was no Defilement either, only a sacrifice. The destruction of the city by the people of the provinces was a vast mistake."

"So you understand our history better than we do, Pontifex?"

"Yes," said Valentine. "Yes. I do." He turned away from the sha-man and said, glancing toward the village foreman, "Vathiimeraak, there are murderers living in your settlement. I know who they are. Go to the village now and announce to everyone that if the guilty ones will come forward and confess their crime, they'll be pardoned after they undergo a full cleansing of their souls."

Turning next to Lisamon Hultin, he said, "As for the khivanivod, I want him handed over to the Danipiur's officials to be tried in her own courts. This falls within her area of responsibility. And then—"

"Majesty!" someone called. "Beware!"

Valentine swung around. The Skandar guards had stepped back from the khivanivod and were staring at their own trembling hands as though they had been burned in a fiery furnace. Torkkinuuminaad, freed of their grasp, thrust his face up into Valentine's. His expression was one of diabolical intensity.

"Pontifex!" he whispered. "Look at me, Pontifex! Look at me!"

Taken by surprise, Valentine had no way of defending himself. Al-ready a strange numbness had come over him. The dragon teeth went tumbling from his helpless hands. Torkkinuuminaad was shifting shape, now, running through a series of grotesque changes at a frenzied rate, so that he appeared to have a dozen arms and legs at once, and half a dozen bodies; and he was casting some sort of spell. Valentine was caught in it like a moth in a spider's cunningly woven strands. The air seemed thick and blurred before him, and a wind had come up out of nowhere. Valentine stood perplexed, trying to force his gaze away from the khivanivod's fiery eyes, but he could not. Nor could he find the strength to reach down and seize hold of the two dragon teeth that lay at his feet. He stood as though frozen, muddled, dazed, tottering. There was a burning sensation in his breast and it was a struggle simply to draw breath.

There seemed to be phantoms all around him.

· A dozen Shapeshifters—a hundred, a thousand—

Grimacing faces. Glowering eyes. Teeth; claws; knives. A horde of wildly cavorting assassins surrounded him, dancing, bobbing, gyrating, hissing, mocking him, calling his name derisively—

He was lost in a whirlwind of ancient sorceries.

"Lisamon?" Valentine cried, baffled. "Deliamber? Help me—help—" But he was not sure that the words had actually escaped his lips.

Then he saw that his guardians had indeed perceived his danger. Deliamber, the first to react, came rushing forward, flinging his own many tentacles up hastily in a counterspell, a set of gesticulations and thrusts of mental force intended to neutralize whatever was emanating from Torkkinuuminaad. And then, as the little Vroon began to wrap the Piurivar shaman in his web of Vroonish wizardry, Vathiimeraak advanced on Torkkinuuminaad from the opposite side, boldly seizing the shaman in complete indifference to his spells, forcing him down to the ground, bending him until his forehead was pressing against the soil at Valentine's feet.

Valentine felt the grip of the shaman's wizardry beginning to ebb, then easing further, finally losing its last remaining hold on his soul. The contact between Torkkinuuminaad's mind and his gave way with an almost audible snap.

Vathiimeraak released the khivanivod and stepped back. Lisamon Hultin now came to the shaman's side and stood menacingly over him. But the episode was over. The shaman remained where he was, absolutely still now, staring at the ground, scowling bitterly in defeat.

"Thank you," Valentine said simply to Deliamber and Vathiimeraak. And, with a dismissive gesture: "Take him away."

Lisamon Hultin threw Torkkinuuminaad over her shoulder like a sack of calimbots and went striding off down the road.

A long stunned silence followed. Magadone Sambisa broke it, finally. In a hushed voice she said, "Your majesty, are you all right?"

He answered only with a nod.

"And the excavations," she said anxiously, after another moment. "What will happen to them? Will they continue?"

"Why not?" Valentine replied. "There's still much work to be done." He took a step or two away from her. He touched his hands to his chest, to his throat. He could still almost feel the pressure of those relentless invisible hands.

Magadone Sambisa was not finished with him, though.

"And these?" she asked, indicating the sea-dragon teeth. She spoke more aggressively now, taking charge of things once again, beginning to recover her vigor and poise. "If I may have them now, majesty—"

Angrily Valentine said, "Take them, yes. But put them back in the shrine. And then seal up the hole you made today."

The archaeologist stared at him as though he had turned into a Piurivar himself. With a note of undisguised asperity in her voice she said, "What, your majesty? What? Dr. Huukaminaan died for those teeth! Finding that shrine was the pinnacle of his work. If we seal it up now—"

"Dr. Huukaminaan was the perfect scientist," Valentine said, not troubling to conceal his great weariness now. "His love of the truth cost him his life. Your own love of truth, I think, is less than perfect, and therefore you will obey me in this."

"I beg you, majesty—"

"No. Enough begging. I don't pretend to be a scientist at all, but I understand my own responsibilities. Some things should remain buried. These teeth are not things for us to handle and study and put on display at a museum. The shrine is a holy place to the Piurivars, even if they don't understand its own holiness. It's a sad business for us all that it ever was uncovered. The dig itself can continue, in other parts of the city. But put these back. Seal that shrine and stay away from it. Understood?"

She looked at him numbly, and nodded.

"Good. Good."

The full descent of darkness was settling upon the desert now. Valentine could feel the myriad ghosts of Velalisier hovering around him. It seemed that bony fingers were plucking at his tunic, that eerie whispering voices were murmuring perilous magics in his ears.

Most heartily he yearned to be quit of these ruins. He had had all he cared to have of them for one lifetime.

To Tunigorn he said, "Come, old friend, give the orders, make things ready for our immediate departure."

"Now, Valentine? At this late hour?"

"Now, Tunigorn. Now." He smiled. "Do you know, this place has made the Labyrinth seem almost appealing to me! I feel a great desire to return to its familiar comforts. Come: get everything organized for leaving. We've been here quite long enough."

Earthsea

—

URSULA K. LE GUIN

A WIZARD OF EARTHSEA (1968)
THE TOMBS OF ATUAN (1971)
THE FARTHEST SHORE (1972)
TEHANU THE LAST BOOK OF EARTHSEA (1990)

The island world of Earthsea is inhabited by human beings and by dragons. The dragons are aloof and dangerous creatures, whose native tongue is the Language of the Making. Some events and stories (in *Tehanu*) suggest that there was a time when dragons and human beings were all one kind, but they have long been divided and unfriendly. Among the human beings, magic is a gift with which some people are born, but which must also be learned as an art or science. Essential to the practice of magic is learning at least some words of the Language of the Making, in which things are given their true names. By learning the true name, the witch or wizard gains power over the thing or the person. Power, of course, may be used for good or for ill.

A Wizard of Earthsea opens on Gont Island. Ged, a young peasant boy with a great gift of magic, goes to the School for Wizards on Roke Island. There, attempting to prove his superiority to another boy, he brings a shadow-being from the realm of the dead into the world of the living. This shadow hunts him through the islands, driving him always toward danger and evil. At last, guided by his old teacher Ogion, he turns on it, and pursues it on a desperate course that leads him out of the world across the barrier of death. There Ged and his shadow, confronting each other, find that they are one; and thus Ged's being is healed and made whole.

The Tombs of Atuan is set on one of the four islands of the Kargish people, whose language and customs are different from those of the Archipelagans. A child named Tenar is taken from her parents, renamed Arha, "the Eaten One," and trained as the High Priestess of the Tombs, an ancient desert sanctuary in Atuan, where only women and eunuchs may come. When she is near the end of her training, she comes upon a stranger, a man, in the underground Labyrinth, the heart of the sacred place. This is Ged, now a powerful wizard, seeking the missing half of the Ring of Erreth-Akbe, on which is engraved the broken Rune of Peace. The young priestess's duty is to kill him. Talking with her prisoner, she begins to see that she herself is a prisoner in the Tombs, bound by a meaningless and cruel ritual. Ged gives her back her true name, Tenar. As he has freed her, she frees him: she leads him out of the Labyrinth, and the two escape with the reunited Ring of Peace. Tenar is honored in Havnor, the City of the Kings of Earthsea, but Ged will take her to live and study with his old master Ogion, on Gont.

In *The Farthest Shore*, Ged, now Archmage of Roke and the most powerful man in the Archipelago, goes with young Arren, Prince of Enlad, on a quest to find why magic seems to be losing its power. After strange adventures far in the south, they are led to the dragons' islands; and on Selidor, the westernmost of them all, their quest takes them into the realm of death, the dry land of darkness. There they find the wizard Cob, who, desiring immortality for himself, has breached the wall between life and death. Ged takes Cob's power from him and closes the wound in the world, but it takes all his own power to do so. Arren, who will inherit the throne of Earthsea, empty for five centuries, leads him back into life. The dragon Kalessin carries them both to Roke, where Ged salutes Arren as king; then Kalessin bears him home to Gont Island.

Tehanu, though written seventeen years after *The Farthest Shore*, takes up the story where it ended. Tenar of the Tombs did not stay with Ogion but married a farmer, Flint, had two children, and has lived these thirty years as a farm woman. Dying, Ogion sends for her. She stays on at the old mage's house after his death. With her is her adopted daughter. This girl, Therru, who was raped and burned and left for dead by the men who traveled with her mother, is a silent child full of fear and uncomprehended power. The dragon brings Ged to Gont. Worn out and ill, having lost all his powers of magic, Ged is full of shame, and hides even from Arren, who comes seeking him. Aspen, a disciple of Cob, brews evil magic on Gont; Handy, one of the men who abused the child Therru, keeps hanging around. The young king takes Tenar back to her husband's farm. There Handy and the others try to get at Tenar and the child; Ged comes in time to help her fight them off. That winter Ged stays with Tenar at the farm, and though he has lost his power as a mage, he finds at last his power as a sexual human being. In the spring, Aspen lures Ged and Tenar back to Ogion's house, and since they cannot work magic they have no defense against him. He humiliates and is about to kill them. Now the disfigured, powerless child Therru finds her true name, Tehanu, and her own power. She summons the dragon Kalessin in the dragons' speech, the Language of the Making. The dragon destroys Aspen, and greets Therru as a daughter. She will live with Ged and Tenar now, but will live with the dragons later: "I give you my child," Kalessin says to Ged, "as you will give me yours."

Dragonfly

URSULA K. LE GUIN

1. Iria

Her father's ancestors had owned a wide, rich domain on the wide, rich island of Way. Claiming no title or court privilege in the days of the kings, through all the dark years after Maharion fell they held their land and people with firm hands, putting their gains back into the land, upholding some sort of justice, and fighting off petty tyrants. As order and peace returned to the Archipelago under the sway of the wise men of Roke, for a while yet the family and their farms and villages prospered. That prosperity and the beauty of the meadows and upland pastures and oak-crowned hills made the domain a byword, so that people said, "as fat as a cow of Iria," or, "as lucky as an Irian." The masters and many tenants of the domain added its name to their own, calling themselves Irian. But though the farmers and shepherds went on from season to season and year to year and generation to generation as solid and steady as the oaks, the family that owned the land altered with time and chance.

A quarrel between brothers over their inheritance divided them. One heir mismanaged his estate through greed, the other through foolishness. One had a daughter who married a merchant and tried to run her estate from the city, the other had a son whose sons quarreled again, redividing the divided land. By the time the girl called Dragonfly was born, the domain of Iria, though still one of the loveliest regions of hill and field and meadow in all Earthsea, was a battleground of feuds and litigations. Farmlands went to weeds, farmsteads went unroofed, milking sheds stood unused, and shepherds followed their flocks over the mountain to better pastures. The old house that had been the center of the domain was half in ruins on its hill among the oaks.

Its owner was one of four men who called themselves Master of Iria. The other three called him Master of Old Iria. He spent his youth and what remained of his inheritance in law courts and the anterooms of the Lords of Way in Shelieth, trying to prove his right to the whole domain as it had been a hundred years ago. He came back unsuccessful and embittered and spent his age drinking the hard red wine from his last vineyard and walking his boundaries with a troop of ill-treated, underfed dogs to keep interlopers off his land.

He had married while he was in Shelieth, a woman no one at Iria knew anything about, for she came from some other island, it was said, somewhere in the west, and she never came to Iria, for she died in childbirth there in the city. When he came home he had a three-year-old daughter with him. He turned her over to the housekeeper and forgot about her. When he was drunk sometimes he remembered her. If he could find her, he made her stand by his chair or sit on his knees and listen to all the wrongs that had been done to him and to the house of Iria. He cursed and cried and drank and made her drink, too, pledging to honor her inheritance and be true to Iria. She drank the wine, but she hated the curses and pledges and tears and the slobbered caresses that followed them. She escaped, if she could, and went down to the dogs and the horses and the cattle, and swore to them that she would be loyal to her mother, whom nobody knew or honored or was true to, except herself.

When she was thirteen the old vineyarder and the housekeeper, who were all that was left of the household, told the Master that it was time his daughter had her naming day. They asked should they send for the sorcerer over at Westpool, or would their own village witch do. The Master of Iria fell into a screaming rage. "A village witch? A hex-hag to give Irian's daughter her true name? Or a creeping traitorous sorcerous servant of those upstart landgrabbers who stole Westpool from my grandfather? If that polecat sets foot on my land I'll have the dogs

342

tear out his liver, go tell him that, if you like!" And so on. Old Daisy went back to her kitchen and old Coney went back to his vines, and thirteen-year-old Dragonfly ran out of the house and down the hill to the village, hurling her father's curses at the dogs, who, crazy with excitement at his shouting, barked and bayed and rushed after her. "Get back, you black-hearted bitch!" she yelled. "Home, you crawling traitor!" And the dogs fell silent and went sidling back to the house with their tails down.

Dragonfly found the village witch taking maggots out of an infected cut on a sheep's rump. The witch's use-name was Rose, like a great many women of Way and other islands of the Hardic Archipelago. People who have a secret name that holds their power the way a diamond holds light may well like their public name to be ordinary, common, like other people's names.

Rose was muttering a rote spell, but it was her hands and her little short sharp knife that did most of the work. The ewe bore the digging knife patiently, her opaque, amber, slotted eyes gazing into silence; only she stamped her small left front foot now and then, and sighed. Dragonfly peered close at Rose's work. Rose brought out a maggot, dropped it, spat on it, and probed again. The girl leaned up against the ewe, and the ewe leaned against the girl, giving and receiving comfort. Rose extracted, dropped, and spat on the last maggot, and said, "Just hand me that bucket now." She bathed the sore with salt water. The ewe sighed deeply and suddenly walked out of the yard, heading for home. She had had enough of medicine. "Bucky!" Rose shouted. A grubby child appeared from under a bush where he had been asleep and trailed after the ewe, of whom he was nominally in charge although she was older, larger, better fed, and probably wiser than he was.

"They said you should give me my name," said Dragonfly. "Father fell to raging. So that's that."

The witch said nothing. She knew the girl was right. Once the Master of Iria said he would or would not allow a thing he never changed his mind, priding himself on his intransigeance, since only weak men said a thing and then unsaid it.

"Why can't I give myself my own true name?" Dragonfly asked, while Rose washed the knife and her hands in the salt water.

"Can't be done."

"Why not? Why does it have to be a witch or a sorcerer? What do you *do*?"

"Well," Rose said, and dumped out the salt water on the bare dirt of the small front yard of her house, which, like most witches' houses, stood somewhat apart from the village. "Well," she said, straightening up and looking about vaguely as if for an answer, or a ewe, or a towel. "You have to know something about the power, see," she said at last, and looked at Dragonfly with one eye. Her other eye looked a little off to the side. Sometimes Dragonfly thought the cast was in Rose's left eye, sometimes it seemed to be in her right, but always one eye looked straight and the other watched something just out of sight, around the corner, elsewhere.

"Which power?"

"The one," Rose said. As suddenly as the ewe had walked off, she went into her house. Dragonfly followed her, but only to the door. Nobody entered a witch's house uninvited.

"You said I had it," the girl said into the reeking gloom of the one-roomed hut.

"I said you have a strength in you, a great one," the witch said from the darkness. "And you know it too. What you are to do I don't know, nor do you. That's to find. But there's no such power as to name yourself."

"Why not? What's more yourself than your own true name?"

A long silence.

The witch emerged with a soapstone drop-spindle and a ball of greasy wool. She sat down on the bench beside her door and set the spindle turning. She had spun a yard of greybrown yarn before she answered.

"My name's myself. True. But what's a name, then? It's what another calls me. If there was no other, only me, what would I want a name for?"

"But," said Dragonfly and stopped, caught by the argument. After a while she said, "So a name has to be a gift?"

Rose nodded.

"Give me my name, Rose," the girl said.

"Your dad says not."

"I say to."

"He's the Master here."

"He can keep me poor and stupid and worthless, but he can't keep me nameless!"

The witch sighed, like the ewe, uneasy and constrained.

"Tonight," Dragonfly said. "At our spring, under Iria Hill. What he doesn't know won't hurt him." Her voice was half coaxing, half savage.

"You ought to have your proper name day, your feast and dancing, like any young 'un," the witch said. "It's at daybreak a name should be given. And then there ought to be music and feasting and all. Not sneaking about at night and no one knowing. . . ."

"I'll know. How do you know what name to say, Rose? Does the water tell you?"

The witch shook her iron-grey head once. "I can't tell you." Her "can't" did not mean "won't." Dragonfly waited. "It's the power, like I said. It comes just so." Rose stopped her spinning and looked up with one eye at a cloud in the west; the other looked a little northward of the sky. "You're there in the water, together, you and the child. You take away the child-name. People may go on using that name for a use-name, but it's not her name, nor ever was. So now she's not a child, and she has no name. So then you wait. You open your mind up, like. Like opening the doors of a house to the wind. So it comes. Your tongue speaks it, the name. Your breath makes it. You give it to that child, the breath, the name. You can't think of it. You let it come to you. It must come through you to her it belongs to. That's the power, the way it works. It's all like that. It's not a thing you do. You have to know how to let it do. That's all the mastery."

"Mages can do more than that," the girl said.

"Nobody can do more than that," said Rose.

Dragonfly rolled her head round on her neck, stretching till the vertebrae cracked, stretching out her long arms and legs restlessly. "Will you?" she said.

Rose nodded once.

They met in the lane under Iria Hill in the dark of night, long after sunset, long before dawn. Rose made a dim glow of werelight so that they could find their way through the marshy ground around the spring without falling in a sinkhole among the reeds. In the cold darkness under a few stars and the black curve of the hill, they stripped and waded into the shallow water, their feet sinking deep in velvet mud. The witch touched the girl's hand, saying, "I take your name, child. You are no child. You have no name."

It was utterly still.

In a whisper the witch said, "Woman, be named. You are Irian."

For a moment longer they held still; then the night wind blew across their naked shoulders, and shivering, they waded out, dried themselves as well as they could, struggled barefoot and wretched through the sharp-edged reeds and tangling roots, and found their way back to the lane. And there Dragonfly spoke in a ragged, raging whisper: "How could you name me that!"

The witch said nothing.

"It isn't right. It isn't my true name! I thought my name would make me be me. But this makes it worse. You got it wrong. You're only a witch. You did it wrong. It's *his* name. He can have it. He's so proud of it, his stupid domain, his stupid grandfather. I don't want it. I won't have it. It isn't me. I still don't know who I am. I'm not Irian!" She fell silent abruptly, having spoken the name.

The witch still said nothing. They walked along in the darkness side by side. At last, in a placating, frightened voice, Rose said, "It came so . . ."

"If you ever tell it to anyone I'll kill you," Dragonfly said.

At that, the witch stopped walking. She hissed like a cat. "*Tell* anyone?"

Dragonfly stopped too. She said after a moment, "I'm sorry. But I feel like—I feel like you betrayed me."

"I spoke your true name. It's not what I thought it would be. And I don't feel easy about it. As if I'd left something unfinished. But it is your name. If it betrays you, then that's the truth of it." Rose hesitated and then spoke less angrily, more coldly: "If you want the power to betray me, Irian, I'll give you that. My name is Etaudis."

The wind had come up again. They were both shivering, their teeth chattering. They stood face-to-face in the black lane, hardly able to see where the other was. Dragonfly put out her groping hand and met the witch's hand. They put their arms round each other in a fierce, long embrace. Then they hurried on, the witch to her hut near the village, the heiress of Iria up the hill to her ruinous house, where all the dogs, who had let her go without much fuss, received her back with a clamor and racket of barking that woke everybody for a halfmile round except the Master, sodden drunk by his cold hearth.

2. Ivory

The Master of Iria of Westpool, Birch, didn't own the old house, but he did own the central and richest lands of the old domain. His father, more interested in vines and orchards than in quarrels with his relatives, had left Birch a thriving property. Birch hired men to manage the farms and wineries and cooperage and cartage and all, while he enjoyed his wealth. He married the timid daughter of the younger brother of the Lord of Wayfirth, and took infinite pleasure in thinking that his daughters were of noble blood. The fashion of the time among the nobility was to have a wizard in their service, a genuine wizard with a staff and a grey cloak, trained on the Isle of the Wise, and so the Master of Iria of Westpool got himself a wizard from Roke. He was surprised how easy it was to get one, if you paid the price.

The young man, called Ivory, did not actually have his staff and cloak yet; he explained that he was to be made wizard when he went back to Roke. The Masters had sent him out in the world to gain experience, for all the classes in the School cannot give a man the experience he needs to be a wizard. Birch looked a little dubious at this, and Ivory reassured him that his training on Roke had equipped him with every kind of magic that could be needed in Iria of Westpool on Way. To prove it, he made it seem that a herd of deer ran through the dining hall, followed by a flight of swans, who marvellously soared through the south wall and out through the north wall; and lastly a fountain in a silver basin sprang up in the center of the table, and when the Master and his family cautiously imitated their wizard and filled their cups from it and tasted it, it was a sweet golden wine. "Wine of the Andrades," said the young man with a modest, complacent smile. By then the wife and daughters were entirely won over. And Birch thought the young man was worth his fee, although his own silent preference was for the dry red Fanian of his own vineyards, which got you drunk if you drank enough, while this yellow stuff was just honeywater.

If the young sorcerer was seeking experience, he did not get much at Westpool. Whenever Birch had guests from Kembermouth or from neighboring domains, the herd of deer, the swans, and the fountain of golden wine made their appearance. He also worked up some very pretty fireworks for warm spring evenings. But if the managers of the orchards and vineyards came to the Master to ask if his wizard might put a spell of increase on the pears this year or maybe charm the black rot off the Fanian vines on the south hill, Birch said, "A wizard of Roke doesn't lower himself to such stuff. Go tell the village sorcerer to earn his keep!" And when the youngest daughter came down with a wasting cough, Birch's wife dared not trouble the wise young man about it, but sent humbly to Rose of Old Iria, asking her to come in by the back door and maybe make a poultice or sing a chant to bring the girl back to health. Ivory never noticed that the girl was ailing, nor the pear trees, nor the vines. He kept himself to himself, as a man of craft and learning should. He spent his days riding about the countryside on the pretty black mare that his employer had given him for his use when he made it clear that he had not come from Roke to trudge about on foot in the mud and dust of country byways.

On his rides, he sometimes passed an old house on a hill among great oaks. When he turned off the village lane up the hill, a pack of scrawny, evil-mouthed dogs came pelting and bellowing down at him. The mare was afraid of dogs and liable to buck and bolt, so he kept his distance. But he had an eye for beauty, and liked to look at the old house dreaming away in the dappled light of the early summer afternoons.

He asked Birch about the place. "That's Iria," Birch said—"Old Iria, I mean to say. I own the house by rights. But after a century of feuds and fights over it, my granddad let the place go to settle the quarrel. Though the Master there would still be quarreling with me if he didn't keep too drunk to talk. Haven't seen the old man for years. He had a daughter, I think."

"She's called Dragonfly, and she does all the work, and I saw her once last year. She's tall, and as beautiful as a flowering tree," said the youngest daughter, Rose, who was busy crowding a lifetime of keen observation into the fourteen years that were all she was going to have for it. She broke off, coughing. Her mother shot an anguished, yearning glance at the wizard. Surely he would hear that cough, this time? He smiled at young Rose, and the mother's heart lifted. Surely he wouldn't smile so if Rose's cough was anything serious?

"Nothing to do with us, that lot at the old place," Birch said, displeased. The tactful Ivory asked no more. But he wanted to see the girl as beautiful as a flowering tree. He rode past Old Iria regularly. He tried stopping in the village at the foot of the hill to ask questions, but there was nowhere to stop and nobody would answer questions. A wall-eyed witch took one look at him and scuttled into her hut. If he went up to the house he would have to face the pack of hellhounds and probably a drunk old man. But it was worth the chance, he thought; he was bored out of his wits with the dull life at Westpool, and was never slow to take a risk. He rode up the hill till the dogs were yelling around him in a frenzy, snapping at the mare's legs. She plunged and lashed out her hoofs at them, and he kept her from bolting only by a staying-spell and all the strength in his arms. The dogs were leaping and snapping at his own legs now, and he was about to let the mare have her head when somebody came among the dogs shouting curses and beating them back with a strap. When he got the lathered, gasping mare to stand still, he saw the girl as beautiful as a flowering tree. She was very tall, very sweaty, with big hands and feet and mouth and nose and eyes, and a head of wild dusty hair. She was yelling, "Down! Back to the house, you carrion, you vile sons of bitches!" to the whining, cowering dogs.

Ivory clapped his hand to his right leg. A dog's tooth had ripped his breeches at the calf, and a trickle of blood came through.

"Is she hurt?" the woman said. "Oh, the traitorous vermin!" She was stroking down the mare's right foreleg. Her hands came away covered with blood-streaked horse sweat. "There, there," she said. "The brave girl, the brave heart." The mare put her head down and shivered all over with relief. "What did you keep her standing there in the middle of the dogs for?" the woman demanded furiously. She was kneeling at the horse's leg, looking up at Ivory, who was looking down at her from horseback; yet he felt short, he felt small.

She did not wait for an answer. "I'll walk her up," she said, standing up, and put out her hand for the reins. Ivory saw that he was supposed to dismount. He did so, asking, "Is it very bad?" and peering at the horse's leg, seeing only bright, bloody foam.

"Come on then, my love," the young woman said, not to him. The mare followed her trustfully. They set off up the rough path round the hillside to an old stone and brick stableyard, empty of horses, inhabited only by nesting swallows that swooped about over the roofs calling their quick gossip.

"Keep her quiet," said the young woman, and left him holding the mare's reins in this deserted place. She returned after some time lugging a heavy bucket, and set to sponging off the mare's leg. "Get the saddle off her," she said, and her tone held the unspoken, impatient, "you fool!" Ivory obeyed, half annoyed by this crude giantess and half intrigued. She did not put him in mind of a flowering tree at all, but she was in fact beautiful, in a large, fierce way. The mare submitted to her absolutely. When she said, "Move your foot!" the mare moved her foot. The woman wiped her down all over, put the saddle blanket back on her, and made sure she was standing in the sun. "She'll be all right," she said. "There's a gash, but if you'll wash it with warm salt water four or five times a day, it'll heal clean. I'm sorry." She said the last honestly, though grudgingly, as if she still wondered how he could have let his mare stand there to be assaulted, and she looked straight at him for the first time. Her eyes were clear orange-brown, like dark topaz or amber. They were strange eyes, right on a level with his own.

"I'm sorry too," he said, trying to speak carelessly, lightly.

"She's Irian of Westpool's mare. You're the wizard, then?"

He bowed. "Ivory, of Havnor Great Port, at your service. May I—"

She interrupted. "I thought you were from Roke."

"I am," he said, his composure regained. She stared at him with those strange eyes, as unreadable as a sheep's, he thought. Then she burst out: "You lived there? You studied there? Do you know the Archmage?"

"Yes," he said with a smile. Then he winced and stooped to press his hand against his shin for a moment.

"Are you hurt too?"

"It's nothing," he said. In fact, rather to his annoyance, the cut had stopped bleeding. The woman's gaze returned to his face.

"What is it—what is it like—on Roke?"

Ivory went, limping only very slightly, to an old mounting-block nearby and sat down on it. He stretched his leg, nursing the torn place, and looked up at the woman. "It would take a long time to tell you what Roke is like," he said. "But it would be my pleasure."

*　　*　　*

The man's a wizard, or nearly," said Rose the witch, "a Roke wizard! You must not ask him questions!" She was more than scandalized, she was frightened.

"He doesn't mind," Dragonfly reassured her. "Only he hardly ever really answers."

"Of course not!"

"Why of course not?"

"Because he's a wizard! Because you're a woman, with no art, no knowledge, no learning!"

"You could have taught me! You never would!"

Rose dismissed all she had taught or could teach with a flick of the fingers.

"Well, so I have to learn from him," said Dragonfly.

"Wizards don't teach women. You're besotted."

"You and Broom trade spells."

"Broom's a village sorcerer. This man is a wise man. He learned the High Arts at the Great House on Roke!"

"He told me what it's like," Dragonfly said. "You walk up through the town, Thwil Town. There's a door opening on the street, but it's shut. It looks like an ordinary door." The witch listened, unable to resist the lure of secrets revealed and the contagion of passionate desire. "And a man comes when you knock, an ordinary-looking man. And he gives you a test. You have to say a certain word, a password, before he'll let you in. If you don't know it, you can never go in. But if he lets you in, then from inside you see that the door is entirely different—it's made out of horn, with a tree carved on it, and the frame is made out of a tooth, one tooth of a dragon that lived long, long before Erreth-Akbe, before Morred, before there were people in Earthsea. There were only dragons, to begin with. They found the tooth on Mount Onn, in Havnor, at the center of the world. And the leaves of the tree are carved so thin that the light shines through them, but the door's so strong that if the Doorkeeper shuts it no spell could ever open it. And then the Doorkeeper takes you down a hall and another hall, till you're lost and bewildered, and then suddenly you come out under the sky. In the Court of the Fountain, in the very deepest inside of the Great House. And that's where the Archmage would be, if he was there. . . ."

"Go on," the witch murmured.

"That's all he really told me, yet," said Dragonfly, coming back to the mild, overcast spring day and the infinite familiarity of the village lane, Rose's front yard, her own seven milch-ewes grazing on Iria Hill, the bronze crowns of the oaks. "He's very careful how he talks about the Masters."

Rose nodded.

"But he told me about some of the students."

"No harm in that, I suppose."

"I don't know," Dragonfly said. "To hear about the Great House is wonderful, but I thought the people there would be—I don't know. Of course, they're mostly just boys when they go there. But I thought they'd be . . ." She gazed off at the sheep on the hill, her face troubled. "Some of them are really bad and stupid," she said in a low voice. "They get into the School because they're rich. And they study there just to get richer. Or to get power."

"Well, of course they do," said Rose, "that's what they're there for!"

"But power—like you told me about—that isn't the same as making people do what you want, or pay you—"

"Isn't it?"

"No!"

"If a word can heal, a word can wound," the witch said. "If a hand can kill, a hand can cure. It's a poor cart that goes only one direction."

"But on Roke, they learn to use power well, not for harm, not for gain."

"Everything's for gain some way, I'd say. People have to live. But what do I know? I make my living doing what I know how to do. But I don't meddle with the great arts, the perilous crafts, like summoning the dead," and Rose made the hand-sign to avert the danger spoken of.

"Everything's perilous," Dragonfly said, gazing now through the sheep, the hill, the trees, into still depths, a colorless, vast emptiness like the clear sky before sunrise.

Rose watched her. She knew she did not know who Irian was or what she might be. A big, strong, awkward, ignorant, innocent, angry woman, yes. But ever since she was a child Rose had seen something more in her, something beyond what she was. And when Irian looked away from the world like that, she seemed to enter that place or time or being beyond herself, utterly beyond Rose's knowledge. Then Rose feared her, and feared for her.

"You take care," the witch said, grim. "Everything's perilous, right enough, and meddling with wizards most of all."

Through love, respect, and trust, Dragonfly would never disregard a warning from Rose; but she was unable to see Ivory as perilous. She didn't understand him, but the idea of fearing him, him personally, was not one she could keep in mind. She tried to be respectful, but it was impossible. She thought he was clever and quite handsome, but she didn't think much about him, except for what he could tell her. He knew what she wanted to know and little by little he told it to her, and then it was not really what she had wanted to know, but she wanted to know more. He was patient with her, and she was grateful to him for his patience, knowing he was much quicker than she. Sometimes he smiled at her ignorance, but he never sneered at it or reproved it. Like the witch, he liked to answer a question with a question; but the answers to Rose's questions were always something she'd always known, while the answers to his questions were things she had never imagined and found startling, unwelcome, even painful, altering all her beliefs.

Day by day, as they talked in the old stableyard of Iria, where they had fallen into the habit of meeting, she asked him and he told her more, though reluctantly, always partially; he shielded his Masters, she thought, trying to defend the bright image of Roke, until one day he gave in to her insistence and spoke freely at last.

"There are good men there," he said. "Great and wise the Archmage certainly was. But he's gone. And the Masters . . . Some hold aloof, following arcane knowledge, seeking ever more patterns, ever more names, but using their knowledge for nothing. Others hide their ambition under the grey cloak of wisdom. Roke is no longer where power is in Earthsea. That's the Court in Havnor, now. Roke lives on its great past, defended by a thousand spells against the present day. And inside those spell-walls, what is there? Quarreling ambitions, fear of anything new, fear of young men who challenge the power of the old. And at the center, nothing. An empty courtyard. The Archmage will never return."

"How do you know?" she whispered.

He looked stern. "The dragon bore him away."

"You saw it? You saw that?" She clenched her hands, imagining that flight.

After a long time, she came back to the sunlight and the stableyard and her thoughts and puzzles. "But even if he's gone," she said, "surely some of the Masters are truly wise?"

When he looked up and spoke it was with a hint of a melancholy smile. "All the mystery and wisdom of the Masters, when it's out in the daylight, doesn't amount to so much, you know. Tricks of the trade—wonderful illusions. But people don't want to believe that. They want the mysteries, the illusions. Who can blame them? There's so little in most lives that's beautiful or worthy."

As if to illustrate what he was saying, he had picked up a bit of brick from the broken pavement, and tossed it up in the air, and as he spoke it fluttered about their heads on delicate blue wings, a butterfly. He put out his finger and the butterfly lighted on it. He shook his finger and the butterfly fell to the ground, a fragment of brick.

"There's not much worth much in my life," she said, gazing down at the pavement. "All I know how to do is run the farm, and try to stand up and speak truth. But if I thought it was all tricks and lies even on Roke, I'd hate those men for fooling me, fooling us all. It can't be lies. Not all of it. The Archmage did go into the labyrinth among the Hoary Men and come back with the Ring of Peace. He did go into death with the young king, and defeat the spider mage, and come back. We know that on the word of the king himself. Even here, the harpers came to sing that song, and a teller came to tell it. . . ."

Ivory nodded gravely. "But the Archmage lost all his power in the land of death. Maybe all magery was weakened then."

"Rose's spells work as well as ever," she said stoutly.

Ivory smiled. He said nothing, but she knew how petty the doings of a village witch appeared to him, who had seen great deeds and powers. She sighed and spoke from her heart—"Oh, if only I wasn't a woman!"

He smiled again. "You're a beautiful woman," he said, but plainly, not in the flattering way he had used with her at first, before she showed him she hated it. "Why would you be a man?"

"So I could go to Roke! And see, and learn! Why, why is it only men can go there?"

"So it was ordained by the first Archmage, centuries ago," said Ivory. "But . . . I too have wondered."

"You have?"

"Often. Seeing only boys and men, day after day, in the Great House and all the precincts of the School. Knowing that the towns-women are spell-bound from so much as setting foot on the fields about Roke Knoll. Once in years, perhaps, some great lady is allowed to come briefly into the outer courts. . . . Why is it so? Are all women incapable of understanding? Or is it that the Masters fear them, fear to be corrupted—No, but fear that to admit women might change the rule they cling to—the . . . purity of that rule—"

"Women can live chaste as well as men can," Dragonfly said bluntly. She knew she was blunt and coarse where he was delicate and subtle, but she did not know any other way to be.

"Of course," he said, his smile growing brilliant. "But witches aren't always chaste, are they? . . . Maybe that's what the Masters are afraid of. Maybe celibacy isn't as necessary as the Rule of Roke teaches. Maybe it's not a way of keeping the power pure, but of keeping the power to themselves. Leaving out women, leaving out everybody who won't agree to turn himself into a eunuch to get that one kind of power. . . . Who knows? A she-mage! Now that would change everything, all the rules!"

She could see his mind dance ahead of hers, taking up and playing with ideas, transforming them as he had transformed brick into butterfly. She could not dance with him, she could not play with him, but she watched him in wonder.

"You could go to Roke," he said, his eyes bright with excitement, mischief, daring. Meeting her almost pleading, incredulous silence, he insisted—"You could. A woman you are, but there are ways to change your seeming. You have the heart, the courage, the will of a man. You could enter the Great House. I know it."

"And what would I do there?"

"What all the students do. Live alone in a stone cell and learn to be wise! It might not be what you dream it to be, but that, too, you'd learn."

"I couldn't. They'd know. I couldn't even get in. There's the Door-keeper, you said. I don't know the word to say to him."

"The password, yes. But I can teach it to you."

"You can? Is it allowed?"

355

"I don't care what's 'allowed,' " he said, with a frown she had never seen on his face. "The Archmage himself said, *Rules are made to be broken*. Injustice makes the rules, and courage breaks them. I have the courage, if you do!"

She looked at him. She could not speak. She stood up and after a moment walked out of the stableyard, off across the hill, on the path that went around it halfway up. One of the dogs, her favorite, a big, ugly, heavy-headed hound, followed her. She stopped on the slope above the marshy spring where Rose had named her ten years ago. She stood there; the dog sat down beside her and looked up at her face. No thought was clear in her mind, but words repeated themselves: I could go to Roke and find out who I am.

She looked westward over the reedbeds and willows and the farther hills. The whole western sky was empty, clear. She stood still and her soul seemed to go into that sky and be gone, gone out of her.

There was a little noise, the soft clipclop of the black mare's hoofs, coming along the lane. Then Dragonfly came back to herself and called to Ivory and ran down the hill to meet him. "I will go," she said.

He had not planned or intended any such adventure, but crazy as it was, it suited him better the more he thought about it. The prospect of spending the long grey winter at Westpool sank his spirits like a stone. There was nothing here for him except the girl Dragonfly, who had come to fill his thoughts. Her massive, innocent strength had defeated him absolutely so far, but he did what she pleased in order to have her do at last what he pleased, and the game, he thought, was worth playing. If she ran away with him, the game was as good as won. As for the joke of it, the notion of actually getting her into the School on Roke disguised as a man, there was little chance of pulling it off, but it pleased him as a gesture of disrespect to all the piety and pomposity of the Masters and their toadies. And if somehow it succeeded, if he could actually get a woman through that door, even for a moment, what a sweet revenge it would be!

Money was a problem. The girl thought, of course, that he as a great wizard would snap his fingers and waft them over the sea in a magic boat flying before the magewind. But when he told her they'd have to hire passage on a ship, she said simply, "I have the cheese money."

He treasured her rustic sayings of that kind. Sometimes she frightened him, and he resented it. His dreams of her were never of her yielding to him, but of himself yielding to a fierce, destroying sweetness, sinking into an annihilating embrace, dreams in which she was something beyond comprehension and he was nothing at all. He woke from those dreams shaken and shamed. In daylight, when he saw her big, dirty hands, when she talked like a yokel, a simpleton, he regained his superiority. He only wished there were someone to repeat her sayings to, one of his old friends in the Great Port who would find them amusing. " 'I have the cheese money,' " he repeated to himself, riding back to Westpool, and laughed. "I do indeed," he said aloud. The black mare flicked her ear.

He told Birch that he had received a sending from his teacher on Roke, the Master Hand, and must go at once, on what business he could not say, of course, but it should not take long once he was there; a half month to go, another to return; he would be back well before the Fallows at the latest. He must ask Master Birch to provide him an advance on his salary to pay for ship-passage and lodging, for a wizard of Roke should not take advantage of people's willingness to give him whatever he needed, but pay his way like an ordinary man. As Birch agreed with this, he had to give Ivory a purse for his journey. It was the first real money he had had in his pocket for years: ten ivory counters carved with the Otter of Shelieth on one side and the Rune of Peace on the other in honor of King Lebannen. "Hello, little name-sakes," he told them when he was alone with them. "You and the cheese money will get along nicely."

He told Dragonfly very little of his plans, largely because he made few, trusting to chance and his own wits, which seldom let him down if he was given a fair chance to use them. The girl asked almost no questions. "Will I go as a man all the way?" was one. "Yes," he said, "but only disguised. I won't put a semblance-spell on you till we're on Roke Island."

"I thought it would be a spell of Change," she said.

"That would be unwise," he said, with a good imitation of the Master Changer's terse solemnity. "If need be, I'll do it, of course. But you'll find wizards very sparing of the great spells. For good reason."

"The Equilibrium," she said, accepting all he said in its simplest sense, as always.

"And perhaps because such arts have not the power they once had," he said. He did not know himself why he tried to weaken her faith in wizardry; perhaps because any weakening of her strength, her wholeness, was a gain for him. He had begun merely by trying to get her into his bed, a game he loved to play. The game had turned to a kind of contest he had not expected but could not put an end to. He was determined now not to win her, but to defeat her. He could not let her defeat him. He must prove to her and himself that his dreams were meaningless.

Quite early on, impatient with wooing her massive physical indifference, he had worked up a charm, a sorcerer's seduction-spell of which he was contemptuous even as he made it, though he knew it was effective. He cast it on her while she was, characteristically, mending a cow's halter. The result had not been the melting eagerness it had produced in girls he had used it on in Havnor and Thwil. Dragonfly had gradually become silent and sullen. She ceased asking her endless questions about Roke and did not answer when he spoke. When he very tentatively approached her, taking her hand, she struck him away with a blow to the head that left him dizzy. He saw her stand up and stride out of the stableyard without a word, the ugly hound she favored trotting after her. It looked back at him with a grin.

She took the path to the old house. When his ears stopped ringing he stole after her, hoping the charm was working and that this was only her particularly uncouth way of leading him at last to her bed. Nearing the house, he heard crockery breaking. The father, the drunkard, came wobbling out looking scared and confused, followed by Dragonfly's loud, harsh voice—"Out of the house, you drunken, crawling traitor! You foul, shameless lecher!"

"She took my cup away," the Master of Iria said to the stranger, whining like a puppy, while his dogs yammered around him. "She broke it."

Ivory departed. He did not return for two days. On the third day he rode experimentally past Old Iria, and she came striding down to meet him. "I'm sorry, Ivory," she said, looking up at him with her smoky orange eyes. "I don't know what came over me the other day. I was angry. But not at you. I beg your pardon."

He forgave her gracefully. He did not try a love-charm on her again.

Soon, he thought now, he would not need one. He would have real power over her. He had finally seen how to get it. She had given it into his hands. Her strength and her willpower were tremendous, but fortunately she was stupid, and he was not.

Birch was sending a carter down to Kembermouth with six barrels of ten-year-old Fanian ordered by the wine merchant there. He was glad to send his wizard along as bodyguard, for the wine was valuable, and though the young king was putting things to rights as fast as he could, there were still gangs of robbers on the roads. So Ivory left Westpool on the big wagon pulled by four big carthorses, jolting slowly along, his legs dangling. Down by Jackass Hill an uncouth figure rose up from the wayside and asked the carter for a lift. "I don't know you," the carter said, lifting his whip to warn the stranger off, but Ivory came round the wagon and said, "Let the lad ride, my good man. He'll do no harm while I'm with you."

"Keep an eye on him then, master," said the carter.

"I will," said Ivory, with a wink at Dragonfly. She, well disguised in dirt and a farmhand's old smock and leggings and a loathsome felt hat, did not wink back. She played her part even while they sat side by side dangling their legs over the tailgate, with six great halftuns of wine jolting between them and the drowsy carter, and the drowsy summer hills and fields slipping slowly, slowly past. Ivory tried to tease her, but she only shook her head. Maybe she was scared by this wild scheme, now she was embarked on it. There was no telling. She was solemnly, heavily silent. I could be very bored by this woman, Ivory thought, if once I'd had her underneath me. That thought stirred him almost unbearably, but when he looked back at her, his thoughts died away before her massive, actual presence.

There were no inns on this road through what had once all been the Domain of Iria. As the sun neared the western plains, they stopped at a farmhouse that offered stabling for the horses, a shed for the cart, and straw in the stable loft for the carters. The loft was dark and stuffy and the straw musty. Ivory felt no lust at all, though Dragonfly lay not three feet from him. She had played the man so thoroughly all day that she had half convinced even him. Maybe she'll fool the old men after all! he thought, and grinned at the thought, and slept.

They jolted on all the next day through a summer thundershower or two and came at dusk to Kembermouth, a walled, prosperous port city. They left the carter to his master's business and walked down to find an inn near the docks. Dragonfly looked about at the sights of the city in a silence that might have been awe or disapproval or mere stolidity. "This is a nice little town," Ivory said, "but the only city in the world is Havnor." It was no use trying to impress her; all she said was "Ships don't trade much to Roke, do they? Will it take a long time to find one to take us, do you think?"

"Not if I carry a staff," he said.

She stopped looking about and strode along in thought for a while. She was beautiful in movement, bold and graceful, her head carried high.

"You mean they'll oblige a wizard? But you aren't a wizard."

"That's a formality. We senior sorcerers may carry a staff when we're on Roke's business. Which I am."

"Taking me there?"

"Bringing them a student—yes. A student of great gifts!"

She asked no more questions. She never argued; it was one of her virtues.

That night, over supper at the waterfront inn, she asked with unusual timidity in her voice, "Do I have great gifts?"

"In my judgment, you do," he said.

She pondered—conversation with her was often a slow business— and said, "Rose always said I had power, but she didn't know what kind. And I . . . I know I do, but I don't know what it is."

"You're going to Roke to find out," he said, raising his glass to her. After a moment she raised hers and smiled at him, a smile so tender and radiant that he said spontaneously, "And may what you find be all you seek!"

"If I do, it will be thanks to you," she said. In that moment he loved her for her true heart, and would have forsworn any thought of her but as his companion in a bold adventure, a gallant joke.

They had to share a room at the crowded inn with two other travelers, but Ivory's thoughts were perfectly chaste, though he laughed at himself a little for it.

Next morning he picked a sprig of an herb from the kitchen garden of the inn and spelled it into the semblance of a fine staff, coppershod and his own height exactly. "What is the wood?" Dragonfly asked, fascinated, when she saw it, and when he answered with a laugh, "Rosemary," she laughed too. They set off along the wharves, asking for a ship bound south that might take a wizard and his Prentice to the Isle of the

Wise, and soon enough they found a heavy trader bound for Wathort, whose master would carry the wizard for goodwill and the Prentice for half price. Even half price was half the cheese money, but they would have the luxury of a cabin, for *Sea Otter* was a decked, two-masted ship.

As they were talking with her master a wagon drew up on the dock and began to unload six familiar halftun barrels. "That's ours," Ivory said, and the ship's master said, "Bound for Hort Town," and Dragonfly said softly, "From Iria."

She glanced back at the land then. It was the only time he ever saw her look back.

The ship's weatherworker came aboard just before they sailed, no Roke wizard but a weatherbeaten fellow in a worn sea-cloak. Ivory flourished his staff a little in greeting him. The sorcerer looked him up and down and said, "One man works weather on this ship. If it's not me, I'm off."

"I'm a mere passenger, Master Bagman. I gladly leave the winds in your hands."

The sorcerer looked at Dragonfly, who stood straight as a tree and said nothing.

"Good," he said, and that was the last word he spoke to Ivory.

During the voyage, however, he talked several times with Dragonfly, which made Ivory a bit uneasy. Her ignorance and trustfulness could endanger her and therefore him. What did she and the bagman talk about? he asked, and she answered, "What is to become of us."

He stared.

"Of all of us. Of Way, and Felkway, and Havnor, and Wathort, and Roke. All the people of the islands. He says that when King Lebannen was to be crowned, last autumn, he sent to Gont for the old Archmage to come crown him, and he wouldn't come. And there was no new archmage. So he took the crown himself. And some say that's wrong, and he doesn't rightly hold the throne. But others say the king himself is the new archmage. But he isn't a wizard, only a king. So others say the dark years will come again, when there was no rule of justice, and wizardry was used for evil ends."

After a pause Ivory said, "That old weatherworker says all this?"

"It's common talk, I think," said Dragonfly, with her grave simplicity.

The weatherworker knew his trade, at least. *Sea Otter* sped south;

they met summer squalls and choppy seas, but never a storm or a troublesome wind. They put off and took on cargo at ports on the north shore of O, at Ilien, Leng, Kamery, and O Port, and then headed west to carry the passengers to Roke. And facing the west Ivory felt a little hollow at the pit of his stomach, for he knew all too well how Roke was guarded. He knew neither he nor the weatherworker could do anything at all to turn the Roke-wind if it blew against them. And if it did, Dragonfly would ask why? Why did it blow against them?

He was glad to see the sorcerer uneasy too, standing by the helmsman, keeping a watch up on the masthead, taking in sail at the hint of a west wind. But the wind held steady from the north. A thunder-squall came pelting on that wind, and Ivory went down to the cabin, but Dragonfly stayed up on deck. She was afraid of the water, she had told him. She could not swim; she said, "Drowning must be a horrible thing—Not to breathe the air—" She had shuddered at the thought. It was the only fear she had ever shown of anything. But she disliked the low, cramped cabin, and had stayed on deck every day and slept there on the warm nights. Ivory had not tried to coax her into the cabin. He knew now that coaxing was no good. To have her he must master her; and that he would do, if only they could come to Roke.

He came up on deck again. It was clearing, and as the sun set the clouds broke all across the west, showing a golden sky behind the high dark curve of a hill.

Ivory looked at that hill with a kind of longing hatred.

"That's Roke Knoll, lad," the weatherworker said to Dragonfly, who stood beside him at the rail. "We're coming into Thwil Bay now. Where there's no wind but the wind they want."

By the time they were well into the bay and had let down the anchor it was dark, and Ivory said to the ship's master, "I'll go ashore in the morning."

Down in their tiny cabin Dragonfly sat waiting for him, solemn as ever but her eyes blazing with excitement. "We'll go ashore in the morning," he repeated to her, and she nodded, acceptant. She said, "Do I look all right?"

He sat down on his narrow bunk and looked at her sitting on her narrow bunk; they could not face each other directly, as there was no room for their knees. At O Port she had bought herself a decent shirt and breeches, at his suggestion, so as to look a more probable candidate for the School. Her face was windburned and scrubbed clean. Her hair was braided and the braid clubbed, like Ivory's. She had got her hands clean, too, and they lay flat on her thighs, long strong hands, like a man's.

"You don't look like a man," he said. Her face fell. "Not to me. You'll never look like a man to me. But don't worry. You will to them."

She nodded, with an anxious face.

"The first test is the great test, Dragonfly," he said. Every night as he lay alone in this cabin he had planned this conversation. "To enter the Great House: to go through that door."

"I've been thinking about it," she said, hurried and earnest. "Couldn't I just tell them who I am? With you there to vouch for me— to say even if I am a woman, I have some gift—and I'd promise to take the vow and make the spell of celibacy, and live apart if they wanted me to—"

He was shaking his head all through her speech. "No, no, no, no. Hopeless. Useless. Fatal!"

"Even if you—"

"Even if I argued for you. They won't listen. The Rule of Roke forbids women to be taught any High Art, any word of the Language of the Making. It's always been so. They will not listen. So they must be shown! And we'll show them, you and I. We'll teach them. You must have courage, Dragonfly. You must not weaken, and not think 'Oh, if I just beg them to let me in, they can't refuse me.' They can, and will. And if you reveal yourself, they will punish you. And me." He put a ponderous emphasis on the last word, and inwardly murmured, "Avert."

She gazed at him from her unreadable eyes, and finally said, "What must I do?"

"Do you trust me, Dragonfly?"

"Yes."

"Will you trust me entirely, wholly—knowing that the risk I take for you is greater even than your risk in this venture?"

"Yes."

"Then you must tell me the word you will speak to the Door-keeper."

She stared. "But I thought you'd tell it to me—the password."

"The password he will ask you for is your true name."

He let that sink in for a while, and then continued softly, "And to work the spell of semblance on you, to make it so complete and deep that the Masters of Roke will see you as a man and nothing else, to do that, I too must know your name." He paused again. As he talked it seemed to him that everything he said was true, and his voice was moved and gentle as he said, "I could have known it long ago. But I chose not to use those arts. I wanted you to trust me enough to tell me your name yourself."

She was looking down at her hands, clasped now on her knees. In the faint reddish glow of the cabin lantern her lashes cast very delicate, long shadows on her cheeks. She looked up, straight at him. "My name is Irian," she said.

He smiled. She did not smile.

He said nothing. In fact he was at a loss. If he had known it would be this easy, he could have had her name and with it the power to make her do whatever he wanted, days ago, weeks ago, with a mere pretense at this crazy scheme—without giving up his salary and his precarious respectability, without this sea voyage, without having to go all the way to Roke for it! For he saw the whole plan now was folly. There was no way he could disguise her that would fool the Door-keeper for a moment. All his notions of humiliating the Masters as they had humiliated him were moonshine. Obsessed with tricking the girl, he had fallen into the trap he laid for her. Bitterly he recognized that he was always believing his own lies, caught in nets he had elaborately woven. Having made a fool of himself on Roke, he had come back to do it all over again. A great, desolate anger swelled up in him. There was no good, no good in anything.

"What's wrong?" she asked. The gentleness of her deep, husky voice unmanned him, and he hid his face in his hands, fighting against the shame of tears.

She put her hand on his knee. It was the first time she had ever touched him. He endured it, the warmth and weight of her touch that he had wasted so much time wanting.

He wanted to hurt her, to shock her out of her terrible, ignorant kindness, but what he said when he finally spoke was "I only wanted to make love to you."

"You did?"

"Did you think I was one of their eunuchs? That I'd castrate myself with spells so I could be holy? Why do you think I don't have a staff? Why do you think I'm not at the School? Did you believe everything I said?"

"Yes," she said. "I'm sorry." Her hand was still on his knee. She said, "We can make love if you want."

He sat up, sat still.

"What are you?" he said to her at last.

"I don't know. It's why I wanted to come to Roke. To find out."

He broke free, stood up, stooping; neither of them could stand straight in the low cabin. Clenching and unclenching his hands, he stood as far from her as he could, his back to her.

"You won't find out. It's all lies, shams. Old men playing games with words. I wouldn't play their games, so I left. Do you know what I did?" He turned, showing his teeth in a rictus of triumph. "I got a girl, a town girl, to come to my room. My cell. My little stone celibate cell. It had a window looking out on a back street. No spells—you can't make spells with all their magic going on. But she wanted to come, and came, and I let a rope ladder out the window, and she climbed it. And we were at it when the old men came in! I showed 'em! And if I could have got you in, I'd have showed 'em again, I'd have taught them *their* lesson!"

"Well, I'll try," she said.

He stared.

"Not for the same reasons as you," she said, "but I still want to. And we came all this way. And you know my name."

It was true. He knew her name: Irian. It was like a coal of fire, a burning ember in his mind. His thought could not hold it. His knowledge could not use it. His tongue could not say it.

She looked up at him, her sharp, strong face softened by the shadowy lantern-light. "If it was only to make love you brought me here, Ivory," she said, "we can do that. If you still want to."

Wordless at first, he simply shook his head. After a while he was able to laugh. "I think we've gone on past . . . that possibility . . . ."

She looked at him without regret, or reproach, or shame.

"Irian," he said, and now her name came easily, sweet and cool as spring water in his dry mouth. "Irian, here's what you must do to enter the Great House. . . ."

3. Azver

He left her at the corner of the street, a narrow, dull, somehow sly-looking street that slanted up between featureless walls to a wooden door in a higher wall. He had put his spell on her, and she looked like a man, though she did not feel like one. She and Ivory took each other in their arms, because after all they had been friends, companions, and he had done all this for her. "Courage!" he said, and let her go. She walked up the street and stood before the door. She looked back then, but he was gone.

She knocked.

After a while she heard the latch rattle. The door opened. An ordinary-looking middle-aged man stood there. "What can I do for you?" he said. He did not smile, but his voice was pleasant.

"You can let me into the Great House, sir."

"Do you know the way in?" His almond-shaped eyes were attentive, yet seemed to look at her from miles or years away.

"This is the way in, sir."

"Do you know whose name you must tell me before I let you in?"

"My own, sir. It is Irian."

"Is it?" he said.

That gave her pause. She stood silent. "It's the name the witch Rose of my village on Way gave me, in the spring under Iria Hill," she said at last, standing up and speaking truth.

The Doorkeeper looked at her for what seemed a long time. "Then it is your name," he said. "But maybe not all your name. I think you have another."

"I don't know it, sir."

After another long time she said, "Maybe I can learn it here, sir."

The Doorkeeper bowed his head a little. A very faint smile made crescent curves in his cheeks. He stood aside. "Come in, daughter," he said.

She stepped across the threshold of the Great House.

Ivory's spell of semblance dropped away like a cobweb. She was and looked herself.

She followed the Doorkeeper down a stone passageway. Only at the end of it did she think to turn back to see the light shine through the thousand leaves of the tree carved in the high door in its bone-white frame.

A young man in a grey cloak hurrying down the passageway stopped short as he approached them. He stared at Irian; then with a brief nod he went on. She looked back at him. He was looking back at her.

A globe of misty, greenish fire drifted swiftly down the corridor at eye level, apparently pursuing the young man. The Doorkeeper waved his hand at it, and it avoided him. Irian swerved and ducked down frantically, but felt the cool fire tingle in her hair as it passed over her. The Doorkeeper looked round, and now his smile was wider. Though he said nothing, she felt he was aware of her, concerned for her. She stood up and followed him.

He stopped before an oak door. Instead of knocking he sketched a little sign or rune on it with the top of his staff, a light staff of some greyish wood. The door opened as a resonant voice behind it said, "Come in!"

"Wait here a little, if you please, Irian," the Doorkeeper said, and went into the room, leaving the door wide open behind him. She could see bookshelves and books, a table piled with more books and inkpots and writings, two or three boys seated at the table, and the grey-haired, stocky man the Doorkeeper spoke to. She saw the man's face change, saw his eyes shift to her in a brief, startled gaze, saw him question the Doorkeeper, low-voiced, intense.

They both came to her. "The Master Changer of Roke: Irian of Way," said the Doorkeeper.

The Changer stared openly at her. He was not as tall as she was. He stared at the Doorkeeper, and then at her again.

"Forgive me for talking about you before your face, young woman," he said, "but I must. Master Doorkeeper, you know I'd never question your judgment, but the Rule is clear. I have to ask what moved you to break it and let her come in."

"She asked to," said the Doorkeeper.

"But—" The Changer paused.

"When did a woman last ask to enter the School?"

"They know the Rule doesn't allow them."

"Did you know that, Irian?" the Doorkeeper asked her, and she said, "Yes, sir."

"So what brought you here?" the Changer asked, stern, but not hiding his curiosity.

"Master Ivory said I could pass for a man. Though I thought I should say who I was. I will be as celibate as anyone, sir."

Two long curves appeared on the Doorkeeper's cheeks, enclosing the slow upturn of his smile. The Changer's face remained stern, but he blinked, and after a little thought said, "I'm sure—yes—It was definitely the better plan to be honest. What Master did you speak of?"

"Ivory," said the Doorkeeper. "A lad from Havnor Great Port, whom I let in three years ago, and let out again last year, as you may recall."

"Ivory! That fellow that studied with the Hand?—Is he here?" the Changer demanded of Irian, wrathily. She stood straight and said nothing.

"Not in the School," the Doorkeeper said, smiling.

"He fooled you, young woman. Made a fool of you by trying to make fools of us."

"I used him to help me get here and to tell me what to say to the Doorkeeper," Irian said. "I'm not here to fool anybody, but to learn what I need to know."

"I've often wondered why I let the boy in," said the Doorkeeper. "Now I begin to understand."

At that the Changer looked at him, and after pondering said soberly, "Doorkeeper, what have you in mind?"

"I think Irian of Way may have come to us seeking not only what she needs to know, but also what we need to know." The Doorkeeper's tone was equally sober, and his smile was gone. "I think this may be a matter for talk among the nine of us."

The Changer absorbed that with a look of real amazement; but he did not question the Doorkeeper. He said only, "But not among the students."

The Doorkeeper shook his head, agreeing.

"She can lodge in the town," the Changer said, with some relief.

"While we talk behind her back?"

"You won't bring her into the Council Room?" the Changer said in disbelief.

"The Archmage brought the boy Arren there."

"But—But Arren was King Lebannen—"

"And who is Irian?"

The Changer stood silent, and then he said quietly, with respect, "My friend, what is it you think to do, to learn? What is she, that you ask this for her?"

"Who are we," said the Doorkeeper, "that we refuse her without knowing what she is?"

A woman," said the Master Summoner.

Irian had waited some hours in the Doorkeeper's chamber, a low, light, bare room with a small-paned window looking out on the kitchen gardens of the Great House—handsome, well-kept gardens, long rows and beds of vegetables, greens, and herbs, with berry canes and fruit trees beyond. She saw a burly, dark-skinned man and two boys come out and weed one of the vegetable plots. It eased her mind to watch their careful work. She wished she could help them at it. The waiting and the strangeness were very difficult. Once the Doorkeeper came in, bringing her a plate with cold meat and bread and scallions, and she ate because he told her to eat, but chewing and swallowing was hard work. The gardeners went away and there was nothing to watch out the window but the cabbages growing and the sparrows hopping, and now and then a hawk far up in the sky, and the wind moving softly in the tops of tall trees, on beyond the gardens.

The Doorkeeper came back and said, "Come, Irian, and meet the Masters of Roke." Her heart began to go at a carthorse gallop. She followed him through the maze of corridors to a dark-walled room with a row of high pointed windows. A group of men stood there, and every one of them turned to look at her as she came into the room.

"Irian of Way, my lords," said the Doorkeeper. They were all silent. He motioned her to come farther into the room. "The Master Changer you have met," he said. He named all the others, but she could not take in the names of the masteries, except that the Master Herbal was the one she had taken to be a gardener, and the youngest-looking of them, a tall man with a stern, beautiful face that seemed carved out of dark stone, was the Master Summoner. It was he who spoke, when the Doorkeeper was done. "A woman," he said.

The Doorkeeper nodded once, mild as ever.

"This is what you brought the Nine together for? This and no more?"

369

"This and no more," said the Doorkeeper.

"Dragons have been seen flying above the Inmost Sea. Roke has no Archmage, and the islands no true-crowned king. There is real work to do," the Summoner said, and his voice too was like stone, cold and heavy. "When will we do it?"

There was an uncomfortable silence, as the Doorkeeper did not speak. At last a slight, bright-eyed man who wore a red tunic under his grey wizard's cloak said, "Do you bring this woman into the House as a student, Master Doorkeeper?"

"If I did, it would be up to you all to approve or disapprove," said he.

"Do you?" asked the man in the red tunic, smiling a little.

"Master Hand," said the Doorkeeper, "she asked to enter as a student, and I saw no reason to deny her."

"Every reason," said the Summoner.

A man with a deep, clear voice spoke: "It's not our judgment that prevails, but the Rule of Roke, which we are sworn to follow."

"I doubt the Doorkeeper would defy it lightly," said one of them Irian had not noticed till he spoke, though he was a big man, white-haired, rawboned, and crag-faced. Unlike the others, he looked at her as he spoke. "I am Kurremkarmerruk," he said to her. "As the Master Namer here, I make free with names, my own included. Who named you, Irian?"

"The witch Rose of our village, lord," she answered, standing straight, though her voice came out high-pitched and rough.

"Is she misnamed?" the Doorkeeper asked the Namer.

Kurremkarmerruk shook his head. "No. But . . ."

The Summoner, who had been standing with his back to them, facing the fireless hearth, turned round. "The names witches give each other are not our concern here," he said. "If you have some interest in this woman, Doorkeeper, it should be pursued outside these walls—outside the door you vowed to keep. She has no place here nor ever will. She can bring only confusion, dissension, and further weakness among us. I will speak no longer and say nothing else in her presence. The only answer to conscious error is silence."

"Silence is not enough, my lord," said one who had not spoken before. To Irian's eyes he was very strange-looking, having pale reddish skin, long pale hair, and narrow eyes the color of ice. His speech was also strange, stiff and somehow deformed. "Silence is the answer to everything, and to nothing," he said.

The Summoner lifted his noble, dark face and looked across the room at the pale man, but did not speak. Without a word or gesture he turned away again and left the room. As he walked slowly past Irian, she shrank back from him. It was as if a grave had opened, a winter grave, cold, wet, dark. Her breath stuck in her throat. She gasped a little for air. When she recovered herself she saw the Changer and the pale man both watching her intently.

The one with a voice like a deep-toned bell looked at her too, and spoke to her with a plain, kind severity. "As I see it, the man who brought you here meant to do harm, but you do not. Yet being here, Irian, you do us and yourself harm. Everything not in its own place does harm. A note sung, however well sung, wrecks the tune it isn't part of. Women teach women. Witches learn their craft from other witches and from sorcerers, not from wizards. What we teach here is in a language not for women's tongues. The young heart rebels against such laws, calling them unjust, arbitrary. But they are true laws, founded not on what we want, but on what is. The just and the unjust, the foolish and the wise, all must obey them, or waste life and come to grief."

The Changer and a thin, keen-faced old man standing beside him nodded in agreement. The Master Hand said, "Irian, I am sorry. Ivory was my pupil. If I taught him badly, I did worse in sending him away. I thought him insignificant, and so harmless. But he lied to you and beguiled you. You must not feel shame. The fault was his, and mine."

"I am not ashamed," Irian said. She looked at them all. She felt that she should thank them for their courtesy but the words would not come. She nodded stiffly to them, turned round, and strode out of the room.

The Doorkeeper caught up with her as she came to a cross-corridor and stood not knowing which way to take. "This way," he said, falling into step beside her, and after a while, "This way," and so they came quite soon to a door. It was not made of horn and ivory. It was uncarved oak, black and massive, with an iron bolt worn thin with age. "This is the back door," the mage said, unbolting it. "Medra's Gate, they used to call it. I keep both doors." He opened it. The brightness of the day dazzled Irian's eyes. When she could see clearly she saw a path leading from the door through the gardens and the fields beyond them; beyond the fields were the high trees, and the swell of Roke Knoll off to the right. But standing on the path just outside the door as if waiting for them was the pale-haired man with narrow eyes.

"Patterner," said the Doorkeeper, not at all surprised.

"Where do you send this lady?" said the Patterner in his strange speech.

"Nowhere," said the Doorkeeper. "I let her out as I let her in, at her desire."

"Will you come with me?" the Patterner said to Irian.

She looked at him and at the Doorkeeper and said nothing.

"I don't live in this House. In any house," the Patterner said. "I live there. The Grove. —Ah," he said, turning suddenly. The big, white-haired man, Kurremkarmerruk the Namer, was standing just down the path. He had not been standing there until the other mage said "Ah." Irian stared from one to the other in blank bewilderment.

"This is only a seeming of me, a presentment, a sending," the old man said to her. "I don't live here either. Miles off." He gestured northward. "You might come there when you're done with the Patterner here. I'd like to learn more about your name." He nodded to the other two mages and was not there. A bumblebee buzzed heavily through the air where he had been.

Irian looked down at the ground. After a long time she said, clearing her throat, not looking up, "Is it true I do harm being here?"

"I don't know," said the Doorkeeper.

"In the Grove is no harm," said the Patterner. "Come on. There is an old house, a hut. Old, dirty. You don't care, eh? Stay awhile. You can see." And he set off down the path between the parsley and the bush-beans. She looked at the Doorkeeper; he smiled a little. She followed the pale-haired man.

They walked a half mile or so. The knoll rose up full in the western sun on their right. Behind them the School sprawled grey and many-roofed on its lower hill. The grove of trees towered before them now. She saw oak and willow, chestnut and ash, and tall evergreens. From the dense, sun-shot darkness of the trees a stream ran out, green-banked, with many brown trodden places where cattle and sheep went down to drink or to cross over. They had come through the stile from a pasture where fifty or sixty sheep grazed the short, bright turf, and

now stood near the stream. "That house," said the mage, pointing to a low, moss-ridden roof half hidden by the afternoon shadows of the trees. "Stay tonight. You will?"

He asked her to stay, he did not tell her to. All she could do was nod.

"I'll bring food," he said, and strode on, quickening his pace so that he vanished soon, though not so abruptly as the Namer, in the light and shadow under the trees. Irian watched till he was certainly gone and then made her way through high grass and weeds to the little house.

It looked very old. It had been rebuilt and rebuilt again, but not for a long time. Nor had anyone lived in it for a long time, from the feel of it. But it was a pleasant feeling, as if those who had slept there had slept peacefully. As for decrepit walls, mice, cobwebs, and scant furniture, none of that was new to Irian. She found a bald broom and swept out a bit. She unrolled her blanket on the plank bed. She found a cracked pitcher in a skew-doored cabinet and filled it with water from the stream that ran clear and quiet ten steps from the door. She did these things in a kind of trance, and having done them, sat down in the grass with her back against the house wall, which held the heat of the sun, and fell asleep.

When she woke, the Master Patterner was sitting nearby, and a basket was on the grass between them.

"Hungry? Eat," he said.

"I'll eat later, sir. Thank you," said Irian.

"I am hungry now," said the mage. He took a hardboiled egg from the basket, cracked, shelled, and ate it.

"They call this the Otter's House," he said. "Very old. As old as the Great House. Everything is old, here. We are old—the Masters."

"You're not," Irian said. She thought him between thirty and forty, though it was hard to tell; she kept thinking his hair was white, because it was not black.

"But I came far. Miles can be years. I am Kargish, from Karego. You know?"

"The Hoary Men!" said Irian, staring openly at him. All Daisy's ballads of the Hoary Men who sailed out of the east to lay the land waste and spit innocent babes on their lances, and the story of how Erreth-Akbe lost the Ring of Peace, and the new songs and the King's

Tale about how Archmage Sparrowhawk had gone among the Hoary Men and come back with that ring—

"Hoary?" said the Patterner.

"Frosty. White," she said, looking away, embarrassed.

"Ah." Presently he said, "The Master Summoner is not old." And she got a sidelong look from those narrow, ice-colored eyes.

She said nothing.

"I think you feared him."

She nodded.

When she said nothing, and some time had passed, he said, "In the shadow of these trees is no harm. Only truth."

"When he passed me," she said in a low voice, "I saw a grave."

"Ah," said the Patterner.

He had made a little heap of bits of eggshell on the ground by his knee. He arranged the white fragments into a curve, then closed it into a circle. "Yes," he said, studying his eggshells, then, scratching up the earth a bit, he neatly and delicately buried them. He dusted off his hands. Again his glance flicked to Irian and away.

"You have been a witch, Irian?"

"No."

"But you have some knowledge."

"No. I don't. Rose wouldn't teach me. She said she didn't dare. Because I had power but she didn't know what it was."

"Your Rose is a wise flower," said the mage, unsmiling.

"But I know I have—I have something to do, to be. That's why I wanted to come here. To find out. On the Isle of the Wise."

She was getting used to his strange face now and was able to read it. She thought that he looked sad. His way of speaking was harsh, quick, dry, peaceable. "The men of the Isle are not always wise, eh?" he said. "Maybe the Doorkeeper." He looked at her now, not glancing but squarely, his eyes catching and holding hers. "But there. In the wood. Under the trees. There is the old wisdom. Never old. I can't teach you. I can take you into the Grove." After a minute he stood up. "Yes?"

"Yes," she said uncertainly.

"The house is all right?"

"Yes—"

"Tomorrow," he said, and strode off.

So for a half month or more of the hot days of summer, Irian slept in the Otter's House, which was a peaceful one, and ate what the Master Patterner brought her in his basket—eggs, cheese, greens, fruit, smoked mutton—and went with him every afternoon into the grove of high trees, where the paths seemed never to be quite where she remembered them, and often led on far beyond what seemed the confines of the wood. They walked there in silence, and spoke seldom when they rested. The mage was a quiet man. Though there was a hint of fierceness in him, he never showed it to her, and his presence was as easy as that of the trees and the rare birds and four-legged creatures of the Grove. As he had said, he did not try to teach her. When she asked about the Grove, he told her that, with Roke Knoll, it had stood since Segoy made the islands of the world, and that all magic was in the roots of the trees, and that they were mingled with the roots of all the forests that were or might yet be. "And sometimes the Grove is in this place," he said, "and sometimes in another. But it is always."

She had never seen where he lived. He slept wherever he chose to, she imagined, in these warm summer nights. She asked him where the food they ate came from; what the School did not supply for itself, he said, the farmers round about provided, considering themselves well recompensed by the protections the Masters set on their flocks and fields and orchards. That made sense to her. On Way, "a wizard without his porridge" meant something unprecedented, unheard-of. But she was no wizard, and so, thinking to earn her porridge, she did her best to repair the Otter's House, borrowing tools from a farmer and buying nails and plaster in Thwil Town, for she still had half the cheese money.

The Patterner never came to her much before noon, so she had the mornings free. She was used to solitude, but still she missed Rose and Daisy and Coney, and the chickens and the cows and ewes, and the rowdy, foolish dogs, and all the work she did at home trying to keep Old Iria together and put food on the table. So she worked away unhurriedly every morning till she saw the mage come out from the trees with his sunlight-colored hair shining in the sunlight.

Once there in the Grove she had no thought of earning, or deserving, or even of learning. To be there was enough, was all.

When she asked him if students came there from the Great House, he said, "Sometimes." Another time he said, "My words are nothing.

Hear the leaves." That was all he said that could be called teaching. As she walked, she listened to the leaves when the wind rustled them or stormed in the crowns of the trees; she watched the shadows play, and thought about the roots of the trees down in the darkness of the earth. She was utterly content to be there. Yet always, without discontent or urgency, she felt that she was waiting. And that silent expectancy was deepest and clearest when she came out of the shelter of the woods and saw the open sky.

Once, when they had gone a long way and the trees, dark evergreens she did not know, stood very high about them, she heard a call—a horn blowing, a cry?—remote, on the very edge of hearing. She stood still, listening toward the west. The mage walked on, turning only when he realized she had stopped.

"I heard—" she said, and could not say what she had heard.

He listened. They walked on at last through a silence enlarged and deepened by that far call.

She never went into the Grove without him, and it was many days before he left her alone within it. But one hot afternoon when they came to a glade among a stand of oaks, he said, "I will come back here, eh?" and walked off with his quick, silent step, lost almost at once in the dappled, shifting depths of the forest.

She had no wish to explore for herself. The peacefulness of the place called for stillness, watching, listening; and she knew how tricky the paths were, and that the Grove was, as the Patterner put it, "bigger inside than outside." She sat down in a patch of sun-dappled shade and watched the shadows of the leaves play across the ground. The oakmast was deep; though she had never seen wild swine in the wood, she saw their tracks here. For a moment she caught the scent of a fox. Her thoughts moved as quietly and easily as the breeze moved in the warm light.

Often her mind here seemed empty of thought, full of the forest itself, but this day memories came to her, vivid. She thought about Ivory, thinking she would never see him again, wondering if he had found a ship to take him back to Havnor. He had told her he'd never go back to Westpool; the only place for him was the Great Port, the King's City, and for all he cared the island of Way could sink in the sea as deep as Soléa. But she thought with love of the roads and fields of Way. She thought of Old Iria village, the marshy spring under Iria

Hill, the old house on it. She thought about Daisy singing ballads in the kitchen, winter evenings, beating out the time with her wooden clogs; and old Coney in the vineyards with his razor-edge knife, showing her how to prune the vine "right down to the life in it"; and Rose, her Etaudis, whispering charms to ease the pain in a child's broken arm. I have known wise people, she thought. Her mind flinched away from remembering her father, but the motion of the leaves and shadows drew it on. She saw him drunk, shouting. She felt his prying, tremulous hands on her. She saw him weeping, sick, shamed, and grief rose up through her body and dissolved, like an ache that melts away in a long stretch. He was less to her than the mother she had not known.

She stretched, feeling the ease of her body in the warmth, and her mind drifted back to Ivory. She had had no one in her life to desire. When the young wizard first came riding by so slim and arrogant, she wished she could want him; but she didn't and couldn't, and so she had thought him spell-protected. Rose had explained to her how wizards' spells worked "so that it never enters your head nor theirs, see, because it would take from their power, they say." But Ivory, poor Ivory, had been all too unprotected. If anybody was under a spell of chastity it must have been herself, for charming and handsome as he was she had never been able to feel a thing for him but liking, and her only lust was to learn what he could teach her.

She considered herself, sitting in the deep silence of the Grove. No bird sang; the breeze was down; the leaves hung still. Am I ensorcelled? Am I a sterile thing, not whole, not a woman? she asked herself, looking at her strong bare arms, the slight, soft swell of her breasts in the shadow under the throat of her shirt.

She looked up and saw the Hoary Man come out of a dark aisle of great oaks and come toward her across the glade.

He stopped in front of her. She felt herself blush, her face and throat burning, dizzy, her ears ringing. She sought words, anything to say, to turn his attention away from her, and could find nothing at all. He sat down near her. She looked down, as if studying the skeleton of a last-year's leaf by her hand.

What do I want? she asked herself, and the answer came not in words but throughout her whole body and soul: the fire, a greater fire than that, the flight, the flight burning—

She came back into herself, into the still air under the trees. The Hoary Man sat near her, his face bowed down, and she thought how slight and light he looked, how quiet and sorrowful. There was nothing to fear. There was no harm.

He looked over at her.

"Irian," he said, "do you hear the leaves?"

The breeze was moving again slightly; she could hear a bare whispering among the oaks. "A little," she said.

"Do you hear the words?"

"No."

She asked nothing and he said no more. Presently he got up, and she followed him to the path that always led them, sooner or later, out of the wood to the clearing by the Thwilburn and the Otter's House. When they came there, it was late afternoon. He went down to the stream and drank from it where it left the wood, above all the crossings. She did the same. Then sitting in the cool, long grass of the bank, he began to speak.

"My people, the Kargs, they worship gods. Twin gods, brothers. And the king there is also a god. But before that and after are the streams. Caves, stones, hills. Trees. The earth. The darkness of the earth."

"The Old Powers," Irian said.

He nodded. "There, women know the Old Powers. Here too, witches. And the knowledge is bad—eh?"

When he added that little questioning "eh?" or "neh?" to the end of what had seemed a statement it always took her by surprise. She said nothing.

"Dark is bad," said the Patterner. "Eh?"

Irian drew a deep breath and looked at him eye to eye as they sat there. " 'Only in dark the light,' " she said.

"Ah," he said. He looked away so that she could not see his expression.

"I should go," she said. "I can walk in the Grove, but not live there. It isn't my—my place. And the Master Chanter said I did harm by being here."

"We all do harm by being," said the Patterner.

He did as he often did, made a little design out of whatever lay to hand: on the bit of sand on the riverbank in front of him he set a leaf-steam, a grassblade, and several pebbles. He studied them and rear-ranged them. "Now I must speak of harm," he said.

After a long pause he went on. "You know that a dragon brought back our Lord Sparrowhawk, with the young king, from the shores of death. Then the dragon carried Sparrowhawk away to his home, for his power was gone, he was not a mage. So presently the Masters of Roke met to choose a new Archmage, here, in the Grove, as always. But not as always.

"Before the dragon came, the Summoner too had returned from death, where he can go, where his art can take him. He had seen our lord and the young king there, in that country across the wall of stones. He said they would not come back. He said Lord Sparrowhawk had told him to come back to us, to life, to bear that word. So we grieved for our lord.

"But then came the dragon, Kalessin, bearing him living.

"The Summoner was among us when we stood on Roke Knoll and saw the Archmage kneel to King Lebannen. Then, as the dragon bore our friend away, the Summoner fell down.

"He lay as if dead, cold, his heart not beating, yet he breathed. The Herbal used all his art, but could not rouse him. 'He is dead,' he said. 'The breath will not leave him, but he is dead.' So we mourned him. Then, because there was dismay among us, and all my patterns spoke of change and danger, we met to choose a new Warden of Roke, an Archmage to guide us. And in our council we set the young king in the Summoner's place. To us it seemed right that he should sit among us. Only the Changer spoke against it at first, and then agreed.

"But we met, we sat, and we could not choose. We said this and said that, but no name was spoken. And then I . . ." He paused awhile. "There came on me what my people call the *eduevanu*, the other breath. Words came to me and I spoke them. I said, *Hama Gondun!*— And Kurremkarmerruk told them this in Hardic: 'A woman on Gont.' But when I came back to my own wits, I could not tell them what that meant. And so we parted with no Archmage chosen.

"The king left soon after, and the Master Windkey went with him. Before the king was to be crowned, they went to Gont and sought our lord, to find what that meant, 'a woman on Gont.' Eh? But they did not see him, only my countrywoman Tenar of the Ring. She said she was not the woman they sought. And they found no one, nothing. So Lebannen judged it to be a prophecy yet to be fulfilled. And in Havnor he set his crown on his own head.

"The Herbal, and I too, judged the Summoner dead. We thought the breath he breathed was left from some spell of his own art that we did not understand, like the spell snakes know that keeps their heart beating long after they are dead. Though it seemed terrible to bury a breathing body, yet he was cold, and his blood did not run, and no soul was in him. That was more terrible. So we made ready to bury him. And then, by his grave, his eyes opened. He moved, and spoke. He said, 'I have summoned myself again into life, to do what must be done.'"

The Patterner's voice had grown rougher, and he suddenly brushed the little design of pebbles apart with the palm of his hand.

"So when the Windkey returned, we were nine again. But divided. For the Summoner said we must meet again and choose an Archmage. The king had had no place among us, he said. And 'a woman on Gont,' whoever she may be, has no place among the men on Roke. Eh? The Windkey, the Chanter, the Changer, the Hand, say he is right. And as King Lebannen is one returned from death, fulfilling that prophecy, they say so will the Archmage be one returned from death."

"But—" Irian said, and stopped.

After a while the Patterner said, "That art, summoning, you know, is very . . . terrible. It is . . . always danger. Here," and he looked up into the green-gold darkness of the trees, "here is no summoning. No bringing back across the wall. No wall."

His face was a warrior's face, but when he looked into the trees it was softened, yearning.

"So," he said, "now he makes you his reason for our meeting. But I will not go to the Great House. I will not be summoned."

"He won't come here?"

"I think he will not walk in the Grove. Nor on Roke Knoll. On the Knoll, what is, is so."

She did not know what he meant, but did not ask, preoccupied: "You say he makes me his reason for you to meet together."

"Yes. To send away one woman, it takes nine mages." He very seldom smiled, and when he did it was quick and fierce. "We are to meet to uphold the Rule of Roke. And so to choose an Archmage."

"If I went away—" She saw him shake his head. "I could go to the Namer—"

"You are safer here."

The idea of doing harm troubled her, but the idea of danger had not entered her mind. She found it inconceivable. "I'll be all right," she said. "So the Namer, and you—and the Doorkeeper?—"

"—do not wish Thorion to be Archmage. Also the Master Herbal, though he digs and says little." He saw Irian staring at him in amazement. "Thorion the Summoner speaks his true name," he said. "He died, eh?"

She knew that King Lebannen used his true name openly. He too had returned from death. Yet that the Summoner should do so continued to shock and disturb her as she thought about it.

"And the . . . the students?"

"Divided also."

She thought about the School, where she had been so briefly. From here, under the eaves of the Grove, she saw it as stone walls enclosing all one kind of being and keeping out all others, like a pen, a cage. How could any of them keep their balance in a place like that?

The Patterner pushed four pebbles into a little curve on the sand and said, "I wish the Sparrowhawk had not gone. I wish I could read what the shadows write. But all I can hear the leaves say is Change, change. . . . Everything will change but them." He looked up into the trees again with that yearning look. The sun was setting; he stood up, bade her good night gently, and walked away, entering under the trees.

She sat on awhile by the Thwilburn. She was troubled by what he had told her and by her thoughts and feelings in the Grove, and troubled that any thought or feelings could have troubled her there. She went to the house, set out her supper of smoked meat and bread and summer lettuce, and ate it without tasting it. She roamed restlessly back down the streambank to the water. It was very still and warm in the late dusk, only the largest stars burning through a milky overcast. She slipped off her sandals and put her feet in the water. It was cool, but veins of sunwarmth ran through it. She slid out of her clothes, the man's breeches and shirt that were all she had, and slipped naked into the water, feeling the push and stir of the current all along her body. She had never swum in the streams at Iria, and she had hated the sea, heaving grey and cold, but this quick water pleased her, tonight. She drifted and floated, her hands slipping over silken underwater rocks and her own silken flanks, her legs sliding through waterweeds. All trouble and restlessness washed away from her in the running of the water, and she floated in delight in the caress of the stream, gazing up at the white, soft fire of the stars.

A chill ran through her. The water ran cold. Gathering herself together, her limbs still soft and loose, she looked up and saw on the bank above her the black figure of a man.

She stood straight up in the water.

"Get out!" she shouted. "Get away, you traitor, you foul lecher, or I'll cut the liver out of you!" She sprang up the bank, pulling herself up by the tough bunchgrass, and scrambled to her feet. No one was there. She stood afire, shaking with rage. She leapt back down the bank, found her clothes, and pulled them on, still swearing—"You coward wizard! You traitorous son of a bitch!"

"Irian?"

"He was here!" she cried. "That foul heart, that Thorion!" She strode to meet the Patterner as he came into the starlight by the house. "I was bathing in the stream, and he stood there watching me!"

"A sending—only a seeming of him. It could not hurt you, Irian."

"A sending with eyes, a seeming with seeing! May he be—" She stopped, at a loss suddenly for the word. She felt sick. She shuddered, and swallowed the cold spittle that welled in her mouth.

The Patterner came forward and took her hands in his. His hands were warm, and she felt so mortally cold that she came close up against him for the warmth of his body. They stood so for a while, her face turned from him but their hands joined and their bodies pressed close. At last she broke free, straightening herself, pushing back her lank wet hair. "Thank you," she said. "I was cold."

"I know."

"I'm never cold," she said. "It was him."

"I tell you, Irian, he cannot come here, he cannot harm you here."

"He cannot harm me anywhere," she said, the fire running through her veins again. "If he tries to, I'll destroy him."

"Ah," said the Patterner.

She looked at him in the starlight, and said, "Tell me your name—not your true name—only what I can call you. When I think of you."

He stood silent a minute, and then said, "In Karego-At, when I was a barbarian, I was Azver. In Hardic, that is a banner of war."

"Thank you," she said.

She lay awake in the little house, feeling the air stifling and the ceiling pressing down on her, then slept suddenly and deeply. She woke as suddenly when the east was just getting light. She went to the door to see what she loved best to see, the sky before sunrise. Looking down from it she saw Azver the Patterner rolled up in his grey cloak, sound asleep on the ground before her doorstep. She withdrew noiselessly into the house. In a little while she saw him going back to his woods, walking a bit stiffly and scratching his head as he went, as people do when half awake.

She got to work scraping down the inner wall of the house, readying it to plaster. But before the sun was in the windows, there was a knock at her open door. Outside was the man she had thought was a gardener, the Master Herbal, looking solid and stolid, like a brown ox, beside the gaunt, grim-faced old Namer.

She came to the door and muttered some kind of greeting. They daunted her, these Masters of Roke, and also their presence meant that the peaceful time was over, the days of walking in the silent summer forest with the Patterner. That had come to an end last night. She knew it, but she did not want to know it.

"The Patterner sent for us," said the Master Herbal. He looked uncomfortable. Noticing a clump of weeds under the window, he said, "That's velver. Somebody from Havnor planted it here. Didn't know there was any on the island." He examined it attentively, and put some seedpods into his pouch.

Irian was studying the Namer covertly but equally attentively, trying to see if she could tell if he was what he had called a sending or was there in flesh and blood. Nothing about him appeared insubstantial, but she thought he was not there, and when he stepped into the slanting sunlight and cast no shadow, she knew it.

"Is it a long way from where you live, sir?" she asked.

He nodded. "Left myself halfway," he said. He looked up; the Patterner was coming toward them, wide awake now.

He greeted them and asked, "The Doorkeeper will come?"

"Said he thought he'd better keep the doors," said the Herbal. He closed his many-pocketed pouch carefully and looked around at the others. "But I don't know if he can keep a lid on the anthill."

"What's up?" said Kurremkarmerruk. "I've been reading about dragons. Not paying attention. But all the boys I had studying at the Tower left."

"Summoned," said the Herbal, dryly.

"So?" said the Namer, more dryly.

"I can tell you only how it seems to me," the Herbal said, reluctant, uncomfortable.

"Do that," the old mage said.

The Herbal still hesitated. "This lady is not of our council," he said at last.

"She is of mine," said Azver.

"She came to this place at this time," the Namer said. "And to this place, at this time, no one comes by chance. All any of us knows is how it seems to us. There are names behind names, my Lord Healer."

The dark-eyed mage bowed his head at that, and said, "Very well," evidently with relief at accepting their judgment over his own. "Thorion has been much with the other Masters, and with the young men. Secret meetings, inner circles. Rumors, whispers. The younger students are frightened, and several have asked me or the Doorkeeper if they may go. And we'd let them go. But there's no ship in port, and none has come into Thwil Bay since the one that brought you, lady, and sailed again next day for Wathort. The Windkey keeps the Roke-wind against all. If the king himself should come, he could not land on Roke."

"Until the wind changes, eh?" said the Patterner.

"Thorion says Lebannen is not truly king, since no Archmage crowned him."

"Nonsense! Not history!" said the old Namer. "The first Archmage came centuries after the last king. Roke ruled in the kings' stead."

"Ah," said the Patterner. "Hard for the housekeeper to give up the keys when the owner comes home."

"The Ring of Peace is healed," said the Herbal, in his patient, troubled voice, "the prophecy is fulfilled, the son of Morred is crowned, and yet we have no peace. Where have we gone wrong? Why can we not find the balance?"

"What does Thorion intend?" asked the Namer.

"To bring Lebannen here," said the Herbal. "The young men talk of 'the true crown.' A second coronation, here. By the Archmage Thorion."

"Avert!" Irian blurted out, making the sign to prevent word from becoming deed. None of the men smiled, and the Herbal belatedly made the same gesture.

"How does he hold them all?" the Namer said. "Herbal, you were here when Sparrowhawk and Thorion were challenged by Irioth. His gift was as great as Thorion's, I think. He used it to use men, to control them wholly. Is that what Thorion does?"

"I don't know," the Herbal said. "I can only tell you that when I'm with him, when I'm in the Great House, I feel that nothing can be done but what has been done. That nothing will change. Nothing will grow. That no matter what cures I use, the sickness will end in death." He looked around at them all like a hurt ox. "And I think it is true. There is no way to regain the Equilibrium but by holding still. We have gone too far. For the Archmage and Lebannen to go bodily into death, and return—it was not right. They broke a law that must not be broken. It was to restore the law that Thorion returned."

"What, to send them back into death?" the Namer said, and the Patterner, "Who is to say what is the law?"

"There is a wall," the Herbal said.

"That wall is not as deep rooted as my trees," said the Patterner.

"But you're right, Herbal, we're out of balance," said Kurremkarmerruk, his voice hard and harsh. "When and where did we begin to go too far? What have we forgotten, turned our back on, overlooked?"

Irian looked from one to the other.

"When the balance is wrong, holding still is not good. It must get more wrong," said the Patterner. "Until—" He made a quick gesture of reversal with his open hands, down going up and up down.

"What's more wrong than to summon oneself back from death?" said the Namer.

"Thorion was the best of us all—a brave heart, a noble mind." The Herbal spoke almost in anger. "Sparrowhawk loved him. So did we all."

"Conscience caught him," said the Namer. "Conscience told him he alone could set things right. To do it, he denied his death. So he denies life."

"And who shall stand against him?" said the Patterner. "I can only hide in my woods."

"And I in my tower," said the Namer. "And you, Herbal, and the Doorkeeper, are in the trap, in the Great House. The walls we built to keep all evil out. Or in, as the case may be."

"We are four against him," said the Patterner.

"They are five against us," said the Herbal.

"Has it come to this," the Namer said, "that we stand at the edge of the forest Segoy planted and talk of how to destroy one another?"

"Yes," said the Patterner. "What goes too long unchanged destroys itself. The forest is forever because it dies and dies and so lives. I will not let this dead hand touch me. Or touch the king who brought us hope. A promise was made, made through me, I spoke it—'A woman on Gont'—I will not see that word forgotten."

"Then should we go to Gont?" said the Herbal, caught in Azver's passion. "Sparrowhawk is there."

"Tenar of the Ring is there," said Azver.

"Maybe our hope is there," said the Namer.

They stood silent, uncertain, trying to cherish hope.

Irian stood silent too, but her hope sank down, replaced by a sense of shame and utter insignificance. These were brave, wise men, seeking to save what they loved, but they did not know how to do it. And she had no share in their wisdom, no part in their decisions. She drew away from them, and they did not notice. She walked on, going toward the Thwilburn where it ran out of the wood over a little fall of boulders. The water was bright in the morning sunlight and made a happy noise. She wanted to cry but she had never been good at crying. She stood and watched the water, and her shame turned slowly into anger.

She came back toward the three men, and said, "Azver."

He turned to her, startled, and came forward a little.

"Why did you break your Rule for me? Was it fair to me, who can never be what you are?"

Azver frowned. "The Doorkeeper admitted you because you asked," he said. "I brought you to the Grove because the leaves of the trees spoke your name to me before you ever came here. *Irian*, they said, *Irian*. Why you came I don't know, but not by chance. The Summoner too knows that."

"Maybe I came to destroy him."

He looked at her and said nothing.

"Maybe I came to destroy Roke."

His pale eyes blazed then. "Try!"

A long shudder went through her as she stood facing him. She felt herself larger than he was, larger than she was, enormously larger. She could reach out one finger and destroy him. He stood there in his small, brave, brief humanity, his mortality, defenseless. She drew a long, long breath. She stepped back from him.

The sense of huge strength was draining out of her. She turned her head a little and looked down, surprised to see her own brown arm, her rolled-up sleeve, the grass springing cool and green around her sandaled feet. She looked back at the Patterner and he still seemed a fragile being. She pitied and honored him. She wanted to warn him of the peril he was in. But no words came to her at all. She turned round and went back to the streambank by the little falls. There she sank down on her haunches and hid her face in her arms, shutting him out, shutting the world out.

The voices of the mages talking were like the voices of the stream running. The stream said its words and they said theirs, but none of them were the right words.

4. Irian

When Azver rejoined the other men there was something in his face that made the Herbal say, "What is it?"

"I don't know," he said. "Maybe we should not leave Roke."

"Probably we can't," said the Herbal. "If the Windkey locks the winds against us . . ."

"I'm going back to where I am," Kurremkarmerruk said abruptly. "I don't like leaving myself about like an old shoe. I'll join you this evening." And he was gone.

"I'd like to walk under your trees a bit, Azver," the Herbal said, with a long sigh.

"Go on, Deyala. I'll stay here." The Herbal went off. Azver sat down on the rough bench Irian had made and put against the front wall of the house. He looked upstream at her, crouching motionless on the bank. Sheep in the field between them and the Great House blatted softly. The morning sun was getting hot.

His father had named him Banner of War. He had come west, leaving all he knew behind him, and had learned his true name from the trees of the Immanent Grove, and become the Patterner of Roke. All this year the patterns of the shadows and the branches and the roots, all the silent language of his forest, had spoken of destruction, of transgression, of all things changed. Now it was upon them, he knew. It had come with her.

She was in his charge, in his care, he had known that when he saw her. Though she came to destroy Roke, as she had said, he must serve her. He did so willingly. She had walked with him in the forest, tall, awkward, fearless; she had put aside the thorny arms of brambles with her big, careful hand. Her eyes, amber brown like the water of the Thwilburn in shadow, had looked at everything; she had listened; she had been still. He wanted to protect her and knew he could not. He had given her a little warmth when she was cold. He had nothing else to give her. Where she must go she would go. She did not understand danger. She had no wisdom but her innocence, no armor but her anger. Who are you, Irian? he said to her, watching her crouched there like an animal locked in its muteness.

His friend came back from the woods and sat down beside him on the bench awhile. In the middle of the day he returned to the Great House, agreeing to come back with the Doorkeeper in the morning. They would ask all the other Masters to meet with them in the Grove. "But *he* won't come," Deyala said, and Azver nodded.

All day he stayed near the Otter's House, keeping watch on Irian, making her eat a little with him. She came to the house, but when they had eaten she went back to her place on the streambank and sat there motionless. And he too felt a lethargy in his own body and mind, a stupidity, which he fought against but could not shake off. He thought of the Summoner's eyes, and then it was he that felt cold, cold through, though he was sitting in the full heat of the summer's day. We are ruled by the dead, he thought. The thought would not leave him.

He was grateful to see Kurremkarmerruk coming slowly down the bank of the Thwilburn from the north. The old man waded through the stream barefoot, holding his shoes in one hand and his tall staff in the other, snarling when he missed his footing on the rocks. He sat down on the near bank to dry his feet and put his shoes back on. "When I go back to the Tower," he said, "I'll ride. Hire a carter, buy a mule. I'm old, Azver."

"Come up to the house," the Patterner said, and he set out water and food for the Namer.

"Where's the girl?"

"Asleep." Azver nodded toward where she lay, curled up in the grass above the little falls.

The heat of the day was beginning to lessen and the shadows of the Grove lay across the grass, though the Otter's House was still in sunlight. Kurremkarmerruk sat on the bench with his back against the house wall, and Azver on the doorstep.

"We've come to the end of it," the old man said out of silence.

Azver nodded, in silence.

"What brought you here, Azver?" the Namer asked. "I've often thought of asking you. A long, long way to come. And you have no wizards in the Kargish lands, I think."

"No. But we have the things wizardry is made of. Water, stones, trees, words . . ."

"But not the words of the Making."

"No. Nor dragons."

"Never?"

"Only in some very, very old tales. Before the gods were. Before men were. Before men were men, they were dragons."

"Now that is interesting," said the old scholar, sitting up straighter. "I told you I was reading about dragons. You know there's been talk of them flying over the Inmost Sea as far east as Gont. That was no doubt Kalessin taking Ged home, multiplied by sailors making a good story better. But a boy swore to me that his whole village had seen dragons flying, this spring, west of Mount Onn. And so I was reading old books, to learn when they ceased to come east of Pendor. And in one I came on your story, or something like it. That men and dragons were all one kind, but they quarreled. Some went west and some east, and they became two kinds, and forgot they were ever one."

"We went farthest east," Azver said. "But do you know what the leader of an army is, in my tongue?"

"*Erdan*," said the Namer promptly, and laughed. "Drake. Dragon. . . ."

After a while he said, "I could chase an etymology on the brink of doom. . . . But I think, Azver, that that's where we are. We won't defeat him."

"He has the advantage," Azver said, very dry.

"He does. So. . . . So therefore, admitting it unlikely, admitting it impossible—if we did defeat him—if he went back into death and left us here alive—what would we do? What comes next?"

After a long time, Azver said, "I have no idea."

"Your leaves and shadows tell you nothing?"

"Change, change," said the Patterner. "Transformation."

He looked up suddenly. The sheep, who had been grouped near the stile, were scurrying off, and someone was coming along the path from the Great House.

"A group of young men," said the Herbal, breathless, as he came to them. "Thorion's army. Coming here. To take the girl. To send her away." He stood and drew breath. "The Doorkeeper was speaking with them when I left. I think—"

"Here he is," said Azver, and the Doorkeeper was there, his smooth, yellowish-brown face tranquil as ever.

"I told them," he said, "that if they went out Medra's Gate this day, they'd never go back through it into a house they knew. Some of them were for turning back, then. But the Windkey and the Chanter urged them on. They'll be along soon."

They could hear men's voices in the fields east of the Grove.

Azver went quickly to where Irian lay beside the stream, and the others followed him. She roused up and got to her feet, looking dull and dazed. They were standing around her, a kind of guard, when the group of thirty or more men came past the little house and approached them. They were mostly older students; there were five or six wizard's staffs among the crowd, and the Master Windkey led them. His thin, keen old face looked strained and weary, but he greeted the four mages courteously by their titles. They greeted him, and Azver took the word—"Come into the Grove, Master Windkey," he said, "and we will wait there for the others of the Nine."

"First we must settle the matter that divides us," said the Windkey.

"That is a stony matter," said the Namer.

"The woman with you defies the Rule of Roke," the Windkey said. "She must leave. A boat is waiting at the dock to take her, and the wind, I can tell you, will stand fair for Way."

"I have no doubt of that, my lord," said Azver, "but I doubt she will go."

"My Lord Patterner, will you defy our Rule and our community, that has been one so long, upholding order against the forces of ruin? Will it be you, of all men, who break the pattern?"

"It is not glass, to break," Azver said. "It is breath, it is fire."

It cost him a great effort to speak.

"It does not know death," he said, but he spoke in his own language, and they did not understand him. He drew closer to Irian. He felt the warmth of her body. She stood staring, in that animal silence, as if she did not understand any of them.

"Lord Thorion has returned from death to save us all," the Windkey said, fiercely and clearly. "He will be Archmage. Under his rule Roke will be as it was. The king will receive the true crown from his hand, and rule with his guidance, as Morred ruled. No witches will defile sacred ground. No dragons will threaten the Inmost Sea. There will be order, safety, and peace."

None of the mages answered him. In the silence, the men with him murmured, and a voice among them said, "Let us have the witch."

"No," Azver said, but could say nothing else. He held his staff of willow, but it was only wood in his hand. Of the four of them, only the Doorkeeper moved and spoke. He took a step forward, looking from one young man to the next and the next. He said, "You trusted me, giving me your names. Will you trust me now?"

"My lord," said one of them with a fine, dark face and a wizard's oaken staff, "we do trust you, and therefore ask you to let the witch go, and peace return."

Irian stepped forward before the Doorkeeper could answer.

"I am not a witch," she said. Her voice sounded high, metallic, after the men's deep voices. "I have no art. No knowledge. I came to learn."

"We do not teach women here," said the Windkey. "You know that."

"I know nothing," Irian said. She stepped forward again, facing the mage directly. "Tell me who I am."

"Learn your place, woman," the mage said with cold passion.

"My place," she said, slowly, the words dragging—"my place is on the hill. Where things are what they are. Tell the dead man I will meet him there."

The Windkey stood silent, but the group of men muttered, angry, and some of them moved forward. Azver came between her and them, her words releasing him from the paralysis of mind and body that had held him. "Tell Thorion we will meet him on Roke Knoll," he said. "When he comes, we will be there. Now come with me," he said to Irian. The Namer, the Doorkeeper, and the Herbal followed him with her into the Grove. There was a path for them. But when some of the young men started after them, there was no path.

"Come back," the Windkey said to the men.

They turned back, uncertain. The low sun was still bright on the fields and the roofs of the Great House, but inside the wood it was all shadows.

"Witchery," they said, "sacrilege, defilement."

"Best come away," said the Master Windkey, his face set and somber, his keen eyes troubled. He set off back to the School, and they straggled after him, arguing and debating in frustration and anger.

They were not far inside the Grove, and still beside the stream, when Irian stopped, turned aside, and crouched down by the enormous, hunching roots of a willow that leaned out over the water. The four mages stood on the path.

"She spoke with the other breath," Azver said.

The Namer nodded.

"So we must follow her?" the Herbal asked.

This time the Doorkeeper nodded. He smiled faintly and said, "So it would seem."

"Very well," said the Herbal, with his patient, troubled look; and he went aside a little, and knelt to look at some small plant or fungus on the forest floor.

Time passed as always in the Grove, not passing at all it seemed, yet gone, the day gone quietly by in a few long breaths, a quivering of leaves, a bird singing far off and another answering it from even farther. Irian stood up slowly. She did not speak, but looked down the path, and then walked down it. The four men followed her.

They came out into the calm, open evening air. The west still held some brightness as they crossed the Thwilburn and walked across the fields to Roke Knoll, which stood up before them in a high dark curve against the sky.

"They're coming," the Doorkeeper said. Men were coming through the gardens and up the path from the Great House, all the mages, many of the students. Leading them was Thorion the Summoner, tall in his grey cloak, carrying his tall staff of bone-white wood, about which a faint gleam of werelight hovered.

Where the two paths met and joined to wind up to the heights of the Knoll, Thorion stopped and stood waiting for them. Irian strode forward to face him.

"Irian of Way," the Summoner said in his deep, clear voice, "that there may be peace and order, and for the sake of the balance of all things, I bid you now leave this island. We cannot give you what you ask, and for that we ask your forgiveness. But if you seek to stay here you forfeit forgiveness, and must learn what follows on transgression."

She stood up, almost as tall as he, and as straight. She said nothing for a minute and then spoke out in a high, harsh voice. "Come up onto the hill, Thorion," she said.

She left him standing at the waymeet, on the level ground, and walked up the hill path for a little way, a few strides. She turned and looked back down at him. "What keeps you from the hill?" she said.

The air was darkening around them. The west was only a dull red line, the eastern sky was shadowy above the sea.

The Summoner looked up at Irian. Slowly he raised his arms and the white staff in the invocation of a spell, speaking in the tongue that all the wizards and mages of Roke had learned, the language of their art, the Language of the Making: "Irian, by your name I summon you and bind you to obey me!"

She hesitated, seeming for a moment to yield, to come to him, and then cried out, "I am not only Irian!"

At that the Summoner ran up toward her, reaching out, lunging at her as if to seize and hold her. They were both on the hill now. She towered above him impossibly, fire breaking forth between them, a flare of red flame in the dusk air, a gleam of red-gold scales, of vast wings—then that was gone, and there was nothing there but the woman standing on the hill path and the tall man bowing down before her, bowing slowly down to earth, and lying on it.

Of them all it was the Herbal, the healer, who was the first to move. He went up the path and knelt down by Thorion. "My lord," he said, "my friend."

Under the huddle of the grey cloak his hands found only a huddle of clothes and dry bones and a broken staff.

"This is better, Thorion," he said, but he was weeping.

The old Namer came forward and said to the woman on the hill, "Who are you?"

"I do not know my other name," she said. She spoke as he had spoken, as she had spoken to the Summoner, in the Language of the Making, the tongue the dragons speak.

She turned away and began to walk on up the hill.

"Irian," said Azver the Patterner, "will you come back to us?"

She halted and let him come up to her. "I will, if you call me," she said.

She reached out and touched his hand. He drew his breath sharply.

"Where will you go?" he said.

"To those who will give me my name. In fire not water. My people."

"In the west," he said.

She said, "Beyond the west."

She turned away from him and them and went on up the hill in the gathering darkness. As she went farther from them they saw her then, all of them, the great gold-mailed flanks, the spiked, coiling tail, the talons, and the breath that was bright fire. On the crest of the knoll she paused awhile, her long head turning to look slowly round the Isle of Roke, gazing longest at the Grove, only a blur of darkness in darkness now. Then with a rattle like the shaking of sheets of brass the wide, vaned wings opened and the dragon sprang up into the air, circled Roke Knoll once, and flew.

A curl of fire, a wisp of smoke drifted down through the dark air.

Azver the Patterner stood with his left hand holding his right hand, which her touch had burnt. He looked down at the men who stood silent at the foot of the hill, staring after the dragon. "Well, my friends," he said, "what now?"

Only the Doorkeeper answered. He said, "I think we should go to our house, and open its doors."

Memory, Sorrow and Thorn

—

TAD WILLIAMS

THE DRAGONBONE CHAIR (1988)
STONE OF FAREWELL (1990)
TO GREEN ANGEL TOWER (1993)

Tad Williams' trilogy takes place all across the lands of Osten Ard, from the marshes of the southern Wran to Yiqanuc, the icy northern home of the trolls, but its heart is in the great high keep known as the Hayholt.

The story begins when the death of Prester John, the powerful human king who has been the castle's master for many years, and who has extended his empire out from Erkynland to rule nearly all the nations of Osten Ard, sets in motion a falling-out between his royal sons—a war that eventually brings the entire world to the edge of actual extinction as the undead immortal Ineluki exploits the conflict for his own purposes. Among those caught up in this vast apocalyptic struggle are the scullion Simon Snowlock; Miriamele, the daughter of one of the royal brothers; Binabik the troll; the mysterious witch woman known as Geloë; and several members of Ineluki's own Sithi— the near-immortal people he once gave his life to protect.

Five centuries before Prester John's era, in the failing days of his race's multimillennial empire, Ineluki had been the lord of the Hayholt, known then by its ancient name of Asu'a. As mortals besieged his castle, he had cast a terrible spell, a final and suicidal attempt to defeat the human upstarts. Ineluki and his followers had died in the conflagration, and Asu'a had been largely destroyed, but the mortals who survived merely rebuilt on the ruins of the Sithi's great keep, making it their own. Several mortal kings of different lands claimed the castle over the centuries, among them the Heron King, Holly King, and Fisher King of Osten Ard's legends, but none ever held it long until Prester John began his storied reign.

The Burning Man

TAD WILLIAMS

Years and years later, I still start up in the deepest part of night with his agonized face before me. And always, in these terrible dreams, I am helpless to ease his suffering.

I will tell the tale then, in hope the last ghosts may be put to rest, if such a thing can even happen in this place where there are more ghosts than living souls. But you will have to listen closely—this is a tale that the teller herself does not fully understand.

I will tell you of Lord Sulis, my famous stepfather.

I will tell you what the witch foretold to me.

I will tell you of the love that I had and I lost.

I will tell you of the night I saw the burning man.

*   *   *

Tellarin gifted me with small things, but they were not small to me. My lover brought me sweetmeats, and laughed to see me eat them so greedily.

"Ah, little Breda," he told me. "It is strange and wonderful that a mere soldier should have to smuggle honeyed figs to a king's daughter." And then he kissed me, put his rough face against me and kissed me, and that was a sweeter thing than any fig that God ever made.

But Sulis was not truly a king, nor was I his true daughter.

Tellarin was not wrong about everything. The gladness I felt when

403

I saw my soldier or heard him whistling below the window was strange and wonderful indeed.

My true father, the man from whose loins I sprang, died in the cold waters of the Kingslake when I was very small. His companions said that a great pikefish became caught in the nets and dragged my father Ricwald to a drowning death, but others whispered that it was his companions themselves who murdered him, then weighted his body with stones.

Everyone knew that my father would have been gifted with the standard and spear of Great Thane when all the thanes of the Lake People next met. His father and uncle had both been Great Thane before him, so some whispered that God had struck down my poor father because one family should not hold power so long. Others believed that my father's companions on the boat had simply been paid shame-gold to drown him, to satisfy the ambition of one of the other families.

I know these things only from my mother Cynethrith's stories. She was young when my father died, and had two small children—me, not yet five years old, and my brother Aelfric, two years my elder. Together we went to live in the house of my father's father because we were the last of his line, and among the Lake People of Erkynland it was blood of high renown. But it was not a happy house. Godric, my grandfather, had himself been Great Thane for twice ten years before illness ended his rule, and he had high hopes that my father would follow him, but after my father died, Godric had to watch a man from one of the other families chosen to carry the spear and standard instead. From that moment, everything that happened in the world only seemed to prove to my grandfather that the best days of Erkynland and the Lake People had passed.

Godric died before I reached seven years, but he made those years between my father's death and his own very unhappy ones for my mother, with many complaints and sharp rebukes at how she managed the household and how she raised Aelfric and me, his dead son's only children. My grandfather spent much time with Aelfric, trying to make him the kind of man who would bring the spear and standard back to our family, but my brother was small and timid—it must have been clear he would never rule more than his own household. This Godric blamed on my mother, saying she had taught the boy womanish ways.

Grandfather was less interested in me. He was never cruel to me, only fierce and short-spoken, but he was such a frightening figure, with bristling white beard, growling voice, and several missing fingers, that I could never do anything but shrink from him. If that was another reason he found little savor in life, then I am sorry for it now.

In any case, my mother's widowhood was a sad, bitter time for her. From mistress of her own house, and wife of the Great Thane, she now became only one of three grown daughters in the house of a sour old man, for one of my father's sisters had also lost her husband, and the youngest had been kept at home, unmarried, to care for her father in his dotage.

I believe that had even the humblest of fishermen courted my mother, she would have looked upon him kindly, as long as he had a house of his own and no living relatives. But instead a man who has made the entire age tremble came to call.

"What is he like?" Tellarin once asked me. "Tell me about your stepfather."

"He is your lord and commander." I smiled. "What can I tell you that you do not know?"

"Tell me what he says when he is in his house, at his table, what he does." Tellarin looked at me then, his long face suddenly boyish and surprised. "Hah! It feels like sacrilege even to wonder!"

"He is just a man," I told him, and rolled my eyes. Such silly things men feel about other men—that this one is so large and important, while they themselves are so small! "He eats, he sleeps, he breaks wind. When my mother was alive, she used to say that he took up more room in a bed than any three others might, because he thrashed so, and talked aloud in his sleep." I made my stepfather sound ordinary on purpose, because I did not like it when Tellarin seemed as interested in him as he was in me.

My Nabbanai soldier became serious then. "How it must have grieved him when your mother died. He must have loved her very much."

As if it had not grieved me! I resisted the temptation to roll my eyes again, and instead told him, with all the certainty of youth, "I do not think he loved her at all."

My mother once said that when my stepfather and his household first appeared across the meadowlands, riding north toward the Kingslake, it was as though the heavenly host itself had descended to earth. Trumpets heralded their approach, drawing people from every town as though to witness a pilgrimage passing, or the procession of a saint's relic. The knights' armor and lances were polished to a sparkle, and their lord's heron crest gleamed in gold thread on all the tall banners. Even the horses of the Nabban-men were larger and prouder than our poor Erkynlandish ponies. The small army was followed by sheep and cattle in herds, and by dozens and dozens of wagons and oxcarts, a train so vast that their rutted path is still visible on the face of the land three score years later.

I was a child, though, and saw none of it—not then. Within my grandfather's hall, I heard only rumors, things whispered by my aunts and my mother over their sewing. The powerful lord who had come was a Nabbanai nobleman, they reported, called by many Sulis the Apostate. He claimed that he came in peace, and wanted only to make a home for himself here beside the Kingslake. He was an exile from his own country—a heretic, some claimed, driven forth by the Lector under threat of excommunication because of his impertinent questions about the life of Usires Aedon, our blessed Ransomer. No, he had been forced from his home by the conniving of the escritors, said others. Angering a churchman is like treading on a serpent, they said.

Mother Church still had an unsolid grip on Erkynland in those days, and even though most had been baptized into the Aedonite faith, very few of the Lake People trusted the Sancellan Aedonitis. Many called it "that hive of priests," and said that its chief aim was not God's work, but increasing its own power.

Many still think so, but they no longer speak ill of the church where strangers can hear them.

I know far more of these things today than I did when they happened. I understand much and much, now that I am old and everyone in my story is dead. Of course, I am not the first to have traveled this particular sad path. Understanding always comes too late, I think.

Lord Sulis had indeed fallen out with the Church, and in Nabban the Church and the state were so closely tied, he had made an enemy of the Imperator in the Sancellan Mahistrevis as well, but so powerful and important was the family of my stepfather-to-be that he was not imprisoned or executed, but instead strongly encouraged to leave Nabban. His countrymen thought he took his household to Erkynland because any nobleman could be king in that backward country—my country—but Sulis had his own reasons, darker and stranger than anyone could guess. So it was that he had brought his entire household, his knights and kerns and all their women and children, a small city's worth of folk, the shores of the Kingslake.

For all the sharpness of their swords and strength of their armor, the Nabbanai treated the Lake People with surprising courtesy, and for the first weeks there was trade and much good fellowship between their camp and our towns. It was only when Lord Sulis announced to the thanes of the Lake People that he meant to settle in the High Keep, the deserted castle on the headlands, that the Erkynlanders became uneasy.

Huge and empty, the domain only of wind and shadows, the High Keep had looked down on our lands since the beginnings of the oldest tales. No one remembered who had built it—some said giants, but some swore the fairy-folk had built it themselves. The Northmen from Rimmersgard were said to have held it for a while, but they were long gone, driven out by a dragon from the fortress the Rimmersmen had stolen from the Peaceful Ones. So many tales surrounded that castle! When I was small, one of my mother's bondwomen told me that it was now the haunt of frost-witches and restless ghosts. Many a night I had thought of it standing deserted on the windy clifftop, only a half-day's ride away, and frightened myself so that I could not sleep.

The idea of someone rebuilding the ruined fortress made the thanes uneasy, but not only for fear of waking its spirits. The High Keep held a powerful position, perhaps an impregnable one—even in their crumbling condition, the walls would be almost impossible to storm if armed men held them. But the thanes were in a difficult spot. Though the men of the Lake People might outnumber those of Sulis, the heron knights were better armed, and the discipline of Nabbanai fighting men was well known—a half-legion of the Imperator's Sea Wolves had slaughtered ten times that number of Thrithingsmen in a battle just a few years before. And Osweard, the new Great Thane, was young and untested as a war leader. The lesser thanes asked my grandfather Godric to lend his wisdom, to speak to this Nabbanai lord and see what he could grasp of the man's true intention.

So it was that Lord Sulis came to my grandfather's steading, and saw my mother for the first time.

When I was a little girl, I liked to believe that Sulis fell in love with my mother Cynethrith the moment he saw her, as she stood quietly behind her father-in-law's chair in Godric's great hall. She was beautiful, that I know—before my father died, all the people of the household used to call her Ricwald's Swan, because of her long neck and white shoulders. Her hair was a pale, pale gold, her eyes as green as the summer Kingslake. Any ordinary man would have loved her on sight. But "ordinary" must be the least likely of all the words that could be used to describe my stepfather.

When I was a young woman, and falling in love myself for the first time, I knew for certain that Sulis could not have loved her. How could anyone who loved have been as cold and distant as he was? As heavily polite? Aching then at the mere thought of Tellarin, my secret beloved, I knew that a man who acted as my stepfather had acted toward my mother could not feel anything like love.

Now I am not so sure. So many things are different when I look at them now. In this extremity of age, I am farther away, as though I looked at my own life from a high hilltop, but in some ways it seems I see things much more closely.

Sulis was a clever man, and could not have failed to notice how my grandfather Godric hated the new Great Thane—it was in everything my grandfather said. He could not speak of the weather without mentioning how the summers had been warmer and the winters shorter in the days when he himself had been Great Thane, and had his son been allowed to succeed him, he as much as declared, every day would have been the first day of Maia-month. Seeing this, Sulis made compact with the bitter old man, first by the gifts and subtle compliments he gave him, but soon in the courting of Godric's daughter-in-law as well.

While my grandfather became more and more impressed by this foreign nobleman's good sense, Sulis made his master stroke. Not only did he offer a bride price for my mother—for a widow!—that was greater than would have been paid even for the virgin daughter of a ruling Great Thane, a sizable fortune of swords and proud Nabban horses and gold plate, but Sulis told Godric that he would even leave my brother and myself to be raised in our grandfather's house.

Godric had still not given up all hope of Aelfric, and this idea delighted him, but he had no particular use for me. My mother would be happier, both men eventually decided, if she were allowed to bring at least one of her children to her new home on the headlands.

Thus it was settled, and the powerful foreign lord married into the household of the old Great Thane. Godric told the rest of the thanes that Sulis meant only good, that by this gesture he had proved his honest wish to live in peace with the Lake People. There were priests in Sulis' company who would cleanse the High Keep of any unquiet spirits, Godric explained to the thanes—as Sulis himself had assured my grandfather—and thus, he argued, letting Sulis take the ancient keep for his own would bring our folk a double blessing.

What Osweard and the lesser thanes thought of this, I do not know. Faced with Godric's enthusiasm, with the power of the Nabbanai lord, and perhaps even with their own secret shame in the matter of my father's death, they chose to give in. Lord Sulis and his new bride were gifted with the deserted High Keep, with its broken walls and its ghosts.

Did my mother love her second husband? I cannot answer that any better than I can say what Sulis felt, and they are both so long dead that I am now the only living person who knew them both. When she first saw him in the doorway at Godric's house, he would certainly have been the light of every eye. He was not young—like my mother, he had already lost a spouse, although a decade had passed since his widowing, while hers was still fresh—but he was a great man from the greatest city of all. He wore a mantle of pure white over his armor, held at the shoulder by a lapis badge of his family's heron crest. He had tucked his helmet under his arm when he entered the hall and my mother could see that he had very little hair, only a fringe of curls at the back of his head and over his ears, so that his forehead gleamed in the firelight. He was tall and strongly made, his unwhiskered jaw square, his nose wide and prominent. His strong, heavy features had a deep and contemplative look, but also a trace of sadness—almost, my mother once told me, the sort of face she thought God Himself might show on the Day of Weighing-Out.

He frightened her and he excited her—both of these things I know from the way she spoke of that first meeting. But did she love him, then or in the days to come? I cannot say. Does it matter? So many years later, it is hard to believe that it does.

Her time in her father-in-law's house had been hard, though. Whatever her deepest feelings about him, I do not doubt that she was happy to wed Sulis.

In the month that my mother died, when I was in my thirteenth year, she told me that she believed Sulis had been afraid to love her. She never explained this—she was in her final weakness, and it was difficult for her to speak—and I still do not know what she meant.

The next to the last thing she ever said to me made even less sense. When the weakness in her chest was so terrible that she would lose the strength to breathe for long moments, she still summoned the strength to declare, "I am a ghost."

She may have spoken of her suffering—that she felt she only clung to the world, like a timid spirit that will not take the road to Heaven, but lingers ever near the places it knew. Certainly her last request made it clear that she had grown weary of the circles of this world. But I have wondered since if there might be some other meaning to her words. Did she mean that her own life after my father's death had been nothing more than a ghost-life? Or did she perhaps intend to say that she had become a shade in her own house, something that waited in the dark, haunted corridors of the High Keep for her second husband's regard to give it true life—a regard that would never come from that silent, secret-burdened man?

My poor mother. Our poor, haunted family!

I remember little of the first year of my mother's marriage to Lord Sulis, but I cannot forget the day we took possession of our new home. Others had gone before us to make our arrival as easeful as possible—I know they had, because a great tent had already been erected on the green in the Inner Bailey, which was where we slept for the first months—but to the child I was, it seemed we were riding into a place where no mortals had ever gone. I expected witches or ogres around every corner.

We came up the cliff road beside the Kingslake until we reached the curtain wall and began to circle the castle itself. Those who had gone before had hacked a crude road in the shadow of the walls, so we had a much easier passage than we would have only days earlier. We rode in a tunnel cut between the wall and forest. Where the trees and brush had not been chopped away, the Kingswood grew right to the castle's edge, striving with root and tendril to breach the great stones of the wall.

At the castle's northern gate we found nothing but a cleared place on the hillside, a desolation of tree stumps and burn-blackened grass— the thriving town of Erkynchester that today sprawls all around the castle's feet had not even been imagined. Not all the forest growth had been cleared. Vines still clung to the pillars of the shattered gatehouse, rooted in the cracks of the odd, shiny stone which was all that remained of the original gateway, hanging in great braids across the opening to make a tangled, living arbor.

"Do you see?" Lord Sulis spread his strong arms as if he had designed and crafted the wilderness himself. "We will make our home in the greatest and oldest of all houses."

As he led her across that threshold and into the ruins of the ancient castle, my mother made the sign of the Tree upon her breast.

I know many things now that I did not know on the first day we came to the High Keep. Of all the many tales about the place, some I now can say are false, but others I am now certain are true. For one thing, there is no question that the Northmen lived here. Over the years I have I found many of their coins, struck with the crude *"F"* rune of their King Fingil, and they also left the rotted remains of their wooden longhouses in the Outer Bailey, which my stepfather's workmen found during the course of other diggings. So I came to realize that if the story of the Northmen living here was a true one, it stood to reason that the legend of the dragon might also be true, as well as the terrible tale of how the Northmen slaughtered the castle's immortal inhabitants.

But I did not need such workaday proofs as coins or ruins to show me that our home was full of unquiet ghosts. That I learned for myself beyond all dispute, on the night I saw the burning man.

Perhaps someone who had grown up in Nabban or one of the other large cities of the south would not have been so astonished by their first sight of the High Keep, but I was a child of the Lake People. Before that day, the largest building I had ever approached was the great hall of our town, where the thanes met every spring—a building that could easily have been hidden in any of several parts of the High Keep and then never discovered again. On that first day, it was clear to me that the mighty castle could only have been built by giants.

The curtain wall was impressive enough to a small girl—ten times my own height and made of huge, rough stones that I could not imagine being hauled into place by anything smaller than the grandest of ogres—but the inner walls, in the places where they still stood, were not just vast but also beautiful. They were shaped of shining white stone that had been polished like jewelry, the blocks of equal size to those of the outer wall but with every join so seamless that from a distance each wall appeared to be a single thing, a curving piece of ivory or bone erupting from the hillside.

Many of the keep's original buildings had been burned or torn down, some so that the men from Rimmersgard could pillage the stones to build their own tower, squat as a barrel but very tall. In any other place the Northmen's huge construction would have loomed over the whole landscape and would certainly have been the focus of my amazement. But in any other place, there would not have been the Angel Tower.

I did not know its name then—in fact, it had no name, since the shape at its very peak could scarcely be seen—but the moment I saw it I knew there could be nothing else like it on earth, and for once childish exaggeration was correct. Its entrance was blocked by piles of rubble the Northmen had never finished clearing, and much of the lower part of its façade had cracked and fallen away in some unimaginable cataclysm, so that its base was raw stone, but it still thrust into the sky like a great white fang, taller than any tree, taller than anything mortals have ever built.

Excited but also frightened, I asked my mother whether the tower might not fall down on us. She tried to reassure me, saying it had stood for a longer time than I could imagine, perhaps since before there had even been people living beside the Kingslake, but that only made me feel other, stranger things.

The last words my mother ever spoke to me were "Bring me a dragon's claw."

I thought at first that in the final hours of her illness she was wandering in her thoughts back to our early days at the castle.

The story of the High Keep's dragon, the creature who had driven out the last of the Northmen, was so old it had lost much of its power to frighten, but it was still potent to a little girl. The men of my stepfather's company used to bring me bits of polished stone—I learned after a while that they were shards of crumbled wall carvings from the oldest parts of the castle—and tell me, "See, here is a broken piece of the great red dragon's claw. He lives down in the caves below the castle, but sometimes at night he comes up to sniff around. He is sniffing for little girls to eat!"

The first few times, I believed them. Then, as I grew older and less susceptible, I learned to scorn the very idea of the dragon. Now that I am an old woman, I am plagued by dreams of it again. Sometimes even when I am awake, I think I can sense it down in the darkness below the castle, feel the moments of restlessness that trouble its long, deep sleep.

So on that night long ago, when my dying mother told me to bring her a dragon's claw, I thought she was remembering something from our first year in the castle. I was about to go look for one of the old stones, but her bondwoman Ulca—what the Nabbanai called her handmaiden or body servant—told me that was not what my mother wanted. A dragon's claw, she explained to me, was a charm to help those who suffered find the ease of a swift death. Ulca had tears in her eyes, and I think she was Aedonite enough to be troubled by the idea, but she was a sensible young woman and did not waste time arguing the right or wrong of it. She told me that the only way I could get such a thing swiftly would be from a woman named Xanippa who lived in the settlement that had sprung up just outside the High Keep's walls.

I was barely into womanhood, but I felt very much a child. The idea of even such a short journey outside the walls after dark frightened me, but my mother had asked, and to refuse a deathbed request was a sin long before Mother Church arrived to parcel up and name the rights and wrongs of life. I left Ulca at my mother's side and hurried across the rainy, nightbound castle.

The woman Xanippa had once been a whore, but as she had become older and fatter she had decided she needed another profession, and had developed a name as an herbwife. Her tumbledown hut, which stood against the keep's southeast curtain wall, overlooking the Kingswood, was full of smoke and bad smells. Xanippa had hair like a bird's nest, tied with what had once been a pretty ribbon. Her face might have been round and comely once, but years and fat had turned it into something that looked as though it had been brought up in a fishing net. She was also so large she did not move from her stool by the fire during the time I was there—or on most other occasions, I guessed.

Xanippa was very suspicious of me at first, but when she found out who I was and what I wanted, and saw my face as proof, she accepted the three small coins I gave her and gestured for me to fetch her splintered wooden chest from the fireplace corner. Like its mistress, the chest had clearly once been in better condition and more prettily painted. She set it on the curve of her belly and began to search through it with a painstaking care that seemed at odds with everything else about her.

"Ah, here," she said at last. "Dragon's claw." She held out her hand to show me the curved, black thing. It was certainly a claw, but far too small to belong to any dragon I could imagine. Xanippa saw my hesitation. "It is an owl's toe, you silly girl. 'Dragon's claw' is just a name." She pointed to a tiny ball of glass over the talon's tip. "Do not pull that off or break it. In fact, do not touch it at all. Do you have a purse?"

I showed her the small bag that hung always on a cord around my neck. Xanippa frowned. "The cloth is very thin." She found some rags in one of the pockets of her shapeless robe and wrapped the claw, then dropped it into my purse and tucked it back in my bodice. As she did so, she squeezed my breast so hard that I murmured in pain, then patted my head. "Merciful Rhiap," she growled, "was I ever so young as this? In any case, be careful, my little sweetmeat. This is heartsbane on the tip of this claw, from the marshes of the Wran. If you are careless, this is one prick that will make sure you die a virgin." She laughed. "You don't want that, do you?"

I backed to the door. Xanippa grinned to see my fright. "And you had better give your stepfather a message from me. He will not find what he seeks among the womenfolk here or among the herbwives of the Lake People. Tell him he can believe me, because if I could solve his riddle, I would—and, oh, but I would make him pay dearly for it! No, he will have to find the Witch of the Forest and put his questions to her."

She was laughing again as I got the door open at last and escaped. The rain was even stronger now, and I slipped and fell several times, but still ran all the way back to the Inner Bailey.

When I reached my mother's bed, the priest had already come and gone, as had my stepfather, who Ulca told me had never spoken a word. My mother had died only a short time after I left on my errand. I had failed her—had left her to suffer and die with no family beside her. The shame and sorrow burned so badly that I could not imagine the pain would ever go away. As the other women prepared her for burial, I could do nothing but weep. The dragon's claw dangled next to my heart, all but forgotten.

I spent weeks wandering the castle, lost and miserable. I only remembered the message Xanippa had given me when my mother had been dead and buried almost a month.

I found my stepfather on the wall overlooking the Kingslake, and told him what Xanippa had said. He did not ask me how I came to be carrying messages for such a woman. He did not even signify he had heard me. His eyes were fixed on something in the far distance—on the boats of the fisher-folk, perhaps, dim in the fog.

The first years in the ruined High Keep were hard ones, and not just for my mother and me. Lord Sulis had to oversee the rebuilding, a vast and endlessly complicated task, as well as keep up the spirits of his own people through the first bleak winter.

It is one thing for soldiers, in the initial flush of loyal indignity, to swear they will follow their wronged commander anywhere. It is another thing entirely when that commander comes to a halt, when following becomes true exile. As the Nabbanai troops came to understand that this cold backwater of Erkynland was to be their home forever,

problems began—drinking and fighting among the soldiers, and even more unhappy incidents between Sulis' men and the local people ... *my* people, although it was hard for me to remember that sometimes. After my mother died, I sometimes felt as if I were the true exile, surrounded by Nabbanai names and faces and speech even in the middle of my own land.

If we did not enjoy that first winter, we survived it, and continued as we had begun, a household of the dispossessed. But if ever a man was born to endure that state, it was my stepfather.

When I see him now in my memory, when I picture again that great heavy brow and that stern face, I think of him as an island, standing by himself on the far side of dangerous waters, near but forever unvisited. I was too young and too shy to try to shout across the gulf that separated us, but it scarcely mattered—Sulis did not seem like a man who regretted his own solitude. In the middle of a crowded room his eyes were always on the walls instead of the people, as though he could see through stone to some better place. Even in his happiest and most festive moods, I seldom heard him laugh, and his swift, distracted smiles suggested that the jokes he liked best could never truly be explained to anyone else.

He was not a bad man, or even a difficult man, as my grandfather Godric had been, but when I saw the immense loyalty of his soldiers it was sometimes hard for me to understand it. Tellarin said that when he had joined Avalles' company, the others had told him of how Lord Sulis had once carried two of his wounded bondmen from the field, one trip for each, through a storm of Thrithings arrows. If that is true, it is easy to understand why his men loved him, but there were few opportunities for such obvious sorts of bravery in the High Keep's echoing halls.

While I was still young, Sulis would pat me on the head when we met, or ask me questions that were meant to show a paternal interest, but which often betrayed an uncertainty as to how old I was and what I liked to do. When I began to grow a womanish form, he became even more correct and formal, and would offer compliments on my clothes or my stitchery in the same studied way that he greeted the High Keep's tenants at Aedonmansa, when he called each man by his name—learned from the seneschal's accounting books—as he filed past, and wished each a good year.

Sulis grew even more distant in the year after my mother died, as though losing her had finally untethered him from the daily tasks he had always performed in such a stiff, practiced way. He spent less and less time seeing to the matters of government, and instead sat reading for hours—sometimes all through the night, wrapped in heavy robes against the midnight chill, burning candles faster than the rest of the house put together.

The books that had come with him from his family's great house in Nabban were mostly tomes of religious instruction, but also some military and other histories. He occasionally allowed me to look at one, but although I was learning, I still read only slowly, and could make little of the odd names and devices in the accounts of battle. Sulis had other books that he would never even let me glance at, plainbound volumes that he kept locked in wooden boxes. The first time I ever saw one go back into its chest, I found the memory returning to me for days afterward. What sort of books were they, I wondered, that must be kept sealed away?

One of the locked boxes contained his own writings, but I did not find that out for two more years, until the night of Black Fire was almost upon us.

It was in the season after my mother's death, on a day when I found him reading in the gray light that streamed into the throne room, that Lord Sulis truly looked at me for the one and only time I remember.

When I shyly asked what he was doing, he allowed me to examine the book in his lap, a beautiful illuminated history of the prophet Varris with the heron of Honsa Sulis worked in gilt on the binding. I traced with my finger an illustration of Varris being martyred on the wheel. "Poor, poor man," I said. "How he must have suffered. And all because he stayed true to his God. The Lord must have given him sweet welcome to Heaven."

The picture of Varris in his agony jumped a little—I had startled my stepfather into a flinch. I looked up to find him gazing at me intently, his brown eyes so wide with feelings I could not recognize that for a moment I was terrified that he would strike me. He lifted his huge, broad hand, but gently. He touched my hair, then curled the hand into a fist, never once shifting that burning stare from me.

"They have taken everything from me, Breda." His voice was tight-clenched with a pain I could not begin to understand. "But I will never bend my back. Never."

I held my breath, uncertain and still a little frightened. A moment later my stepfather recovered himself. He brought his fist to his mouth and pretended to cough—he was the least able dissembler I have ever known—and then bade me let him finish his reading while the light still held. To this day I do not know who he believed had taken everything from him—the Imperator and his court in Nabban? The priests of Mother Church? Or perhaps even God and His army of angels?

What I do know was that he tried to tell me of what burned inside him, but could not find the words. What I also know is that at least for that moment, my heart ached for the man.

My Tellarin asked me once, "How could it be possible that no other man has made you his own? You are beautiful, and the daughter of a king."

But as I have said before, Lord Sulis was not my father, nor was he king. And the evidence of the mirror that had once been my mother's suggested that my soldier overspoke my comeliness as well. Where my mother had been fair and full of light, I was dark. Where she was long of neck and limb and ample of hip, I was made small, like a young boy. I have never taken up much space on the earth—nor will I below it, for that matter. Wherever my grave is made, the digging will not shift much soil.

But Tellarin spoke with the words of love, and love is a kind of spell which banishes all sense.

"How can you care for a rough man like me?" he asked me. "How can you love a man who can bring you no lands but the farm a soldier's pension can buy? Who can give your children no title of nobility?"

Because love does not do sums, I should have told him. Love makes choices, and then gives its all.

Had he seen himself as I first saw him, though, he could have had no questions.

It was an early spring day in my fifteenth year, and the sentries had seen the boats coming across the Kingslake at first light of morning. These were no ordinary fishing craft, but barges loaded with more than a dozen men and their warhorses. Many of the castle folk had gathered to see the travelers come in and to learn their news.

After they had brought all their goods ashore on the lakefront, Tellarin and the rest of the company mounted and rode up the hill path and in through the main gates. The gates themselves had only lately been rebuilt—they were crude things of heavy, undressed timbers, but enough to serve in case of war. My stepfather had reason to be cautious, as the delegation that arrived that day was to prove.

It was actually Tellarin's friend Avalles who was called master of these men, because Avalles was an equestrian knight, one of the Sulean family nephews, but it was not hard to see which of the two truly held the soldiers' loyalty. My Tellarin was barely twenty years old on the first day I saw him. He was not handsome—his face was too long and his nose too impudent to grace one of the angels painted in my stepfather's books—but I thought him quite, quite beautiful. He had taken off his helmet to feel the morning sun as he rode, and his golden hair streamed in the wind off the lake. Even my inexperienced eye could see that he was still young for a fighting man, but I could also see that the men who rode with him admired him too.

His eyes found me in the crowd around my father and he smiled as though he recognized me, although we had never seen each other before. My blood went hot inside me, but I knew so little of the world, I did not recognize the fever of love.

My stepfather embraced Avalles, then allowed Tellarin and the others to kneel before him as each swore his fealty in turn, although I am sure Sulis wanted only to be finished with ceremony so he could return to his books.

The company had been sent by my stepfather's family council in Nabban. A letter from the council, carried by Avalles, reported that there had been a resurgence of talk against Sulis in the imperatorial court at Nabban, much of it fanned by the Aedonite priests. A poor man who held odd, perhaps irreligious beliefs was one thing, the council wrote, but when the same beliefs belonged to a nobleman with money, land, and a famous name, many powerful people would consider him a threat. In fear for my stepfather's life, his family had thus sent this carefully picked troop and warnings to Sulis to be more cautious than ever.

Despite the company's grim purpose, news from home was always welcome, and many of the new troop had fought beside other members of my stepfather's army. There were many glad reunions.

When Lord Sulis had at last been allowed to retreat to his reading, but before Ulca could hurry me back indoors, Tellarin asked Avalles if he could be introduced to me. Avalles himself was a dark, heavy-faced youth with a fledgling beard, only a few years Tellarin's elder, but with so much of the Sulean family's gravity in him that he seemed a sort of foolish old uncle. He gripped my hand too tightly and mumbled several clumsy compliments about how fair the flowers grew in the north, then introduced me to his friend.

Tellarin did not kiss my hand, but held me far more firmly with just his bright eyes. He said, "I will remember this day always, my lady," then bowed. Ulca caught my elbow and dragged me away.

Even in the midst of love's fever, which was to spread all through my fifteenth year, I could not help but notice that the changes which had begun in my stepfather when my mother died were growing worse.

Lord Sulis now hardly left his chambers at all, closeting himself with his books and his writings, being drawn out only to attend to the most pressing of affairs. His only regular conversations were with Father Ganaris, the plain-spoken military chaplain who was the sole priest to have accompanied Lord Sulis out of Nabban. Sulis had installed his old battlefield comrade in the castle's newly built chapel, and it was one of the few places the master of the High Keep would still go. His visits did not seem to bring the old chaplain much pleasure, though. Once I watched them bidding each other farewell, and as Sulis turned and shouldered his way through the wind, heading back across the courtyard to our residence, Ganaris sent a look after him that was grim and sad—the expression, I thought, of a man whose old friend has a mortal illness.

Perhaps if I had tried, I could have done something to help my stepfather. Perhaps there could have been some other path than the one that led us to the base of the tree that grows in darkness. But the truth is that although I saw all these signs, I gave them little attention. Tellarin, my soldier, had begun to court me—at first only with glances and greetings, later with small gifts—and all else in my life shrank to insignificance by comparison.

In fact, so changed was everything that a newer, larger sun might have risen into the sky above the High Keep, warming every corner with its light. Even the most workaday tasks took fresh meaning because of my feelings for bright-eyed Tellarin. My catechisms and my reading lessons I now pursued diligently, so that my beloved might not find me lacking in conversation . . . except on those days when I could scarcely attend to them at all for dreaming about him. My walks in the castle grounds became excuses to look for him, to hope for a shared glance across a courtyard or down a hallway. Even the folktales Ulca told me over our stitchery, which before had been only a means to make the time pass pleasantly, now seemed completely new. The princes and princesses who fell in love were Tellarin and me. Their every moment of suffering burned me like fire, their ultimate triumphs thrilled me so deeply that some days I feared I might actually faint.

After a time, Ulca, who guessed but did not know, refused to tell me any tale that had kissing in it.

But I had my own story by then, and I was living it fully. My own first kiss came as we were walking in the sparse, windy garden that lay in the shadow of the Northmen's tower. That ugly building was ever after beautiful to me, and even on the coldest of days, if I could see that tower, it would warm me.

"Your stepfather could have my head," my soldier told me, his cheek touching lightly against mine. "I have betrayed both his trust and my station."

"Then if you are a condemned man," I whispered, "you may as well steal again." And I pulled him back farther into the shadows and kissed him until my mouth was sore. I was alive in a way I had never been, and almost mad with it. I was hungry for him, for his kisses, his breath, the sound of his voice.

He gifted me with small things that could not be found in Lord Sulis' drab and careful household—flowers, sweetmeats, small baubles he found at the markets in the new town of Erkynchester, outside the castle gates. I could hardly bring myself to eat the honeyed figs he bought for me, not because they were too rich for his purse, although they were—he was not wealthy like his friend Avalles—but because they were gifts from him, and thus precious. To do something as destructive as eat them seemed unimaginably wasteful.

"Eat them slowly, then," he told me. "They will kiss your lips when I cannot."

I gave myself to him, of course, completely and utterly. Ulca's dark hints about soiled women drowning themselves in the Kingslake, about brides sent back to their families in disgrace, even about bastardy as the root of a dozen dreadful wars, were all ignored. I offered Tellarin my body as well as my heart. Who would not? And if I were that young girl once more, coming out of the shadows of her sorrowful childhood into that bright day, I would do it again, with equal joy. Even now that I see the foolishness, I cannot fault the girl I was. When you are young and your life stretches so far ahead of you, you are also without patience—you cannot understand that there will be other days, other times, other chances. God has made us this way. Who knows why He chose it so?

As for me, I knew nothing in those days but the fever in my blood. When Tellarin rapped at my door in the dark hours, I brought him to my bed. When he left me, I wept, but not from shame. He came to me again and again as autumn turned to winter, and as winter crept past we built a warm, secret world all our own. I could not imagine a life without him in it every moment.

Again, youth was foolish, for I have now managed to live without him for many years. There has even been much that was pleasing in my life since I lost him, although I would never have been able to believe such a thing then. But I do not think I have ever again lived as deeply, as truly, as in that first year of reckless discovery. It was as though I somehow knew that our time together would be short.

Whether it is called fate, or our weird, or the will of Heaven, I can look back now and see how each of us was set onto the track, how we were all made ready to travel in deep, dark places.

It was a night in late Feyever-month of that year when I began to realize that something more than simple distraction had overtaken my stepfather. I was reeling back down the corridor to my chamber—I had just kissed Tellarin farewell in the great hall, and was mad with the excitement of it—and I nearly stumbled into Lord Sulis. I was first startled, then terrified. My crime, I felt sure, must be as plain as blood on a white sheet. I waited trembling for him to denounce me. Instead he only blinked and held his candle higher.

"Breda?" he said. "What are you doing, girl?

He had not called me "girl" since before my mother died. His fringe of hair was astrew, as though he had just clambered from some assignation of his own, but if that was so, his stunned gaze suggested it had not been a pleasant one. His broad shoulders sagged, and he seemed so tired he could barely hold up his head. The man who had so impressed my mother on that first day in Godric's hall had changed almost beyond recognizing.

My stepfather was wrapped in blankets, but his legs showed naked below the knee. Could this be the same Sulis, I wondered, who as long as I had known him had dressed each day with the same care as he had once used to set his lines of battle? The sight of his pale bare feet was unspeakably disturbing.

"I . . . I was restless and could not sleep, sire. I wished some air."

His glance flicked across me and then began to rove the shadows again. He looked not just confused but actually frightened. "You should not be out of your chamber. It is late, and these corridors are full of . . ." He hesitated, then seemed to stop himself from saying something. "Full of draughts," he said at last. "Full of cold air. Go on with you, girl."

Everything about him made me uneasy. As I backed away, I felt compelled to say, "Good night, sire, and God bless you."

He shook his head—it almost seemed a shudder—then turned and padded away.

A few days later the witch was brought to the High Keep in chains.

I only learned the woman had been brought to the castle when Tellarin told me. As we lay curled in my bed after lovemaking, he suddenly announced, "Lord Sulis has captured a witch."

I was startled. Even with my small experience, I knew this was not the general run of pillow talk. "What do you mean?"

"She is a woman who lives in the Aldheorte forest," he said, pronouncing the Erkylandish name with his usual charming clumsiness. "She comes often to the market in a town down the Ymstrecca, east of here. She is well known there—she makes herbal cures, I think, charms away warts, nonsense such as that. That is what Avalles said, anyway."

I remembered the message that the once-whore Xanippa had bade me give my stepfather on the night my mother died. Despite the warm night, I pulled the blanket up over our damp bodies. "Why should Lord Sulis want her?" I asked.

Tellarin shook his head, unconcerned. "Because she is a witch, I suppose, and so she is against God. Avalles and some of the other soldiers arrested her and brought her in this evening."

"But there are dozens of root peddlers and conjure-women in the town on the lakeshore where I grew up, and more living outside the castle walls. What does he want with her?"

"My lord does not think she is any old harmless conjure-woman," Tellarin said. "He has put her in one of the deep cells underneath the throne room, with chains on her arms and legs."

I had to see, of course, as much out of curiosity as out of worry about what seemed my stepfather's growing madness.

In the morning, while Lord Sulis was still abed, I went down to the cells. The woman was the only prisoner—the deep cells were seldom used, since those kept in them were likely to die from the chill and damp before they had served a length of term instructive to others— and the guard on duty there was perfectly willing to let the stepdaughter of the castle's master gawk at the witch. He pointed me to the last cell door in the underground chamber.

I had to stand on my toes to see through the barred slot in the door. The only light was a single torch burning on the wall behind me, so the witch was mostly hidden in shadows. She wore chains on wrists and ankles, just as Tellarin had said, and sat on the floor near the back of the windowless cell, her hunched shoulders giving her the shape of a rain-soaked hawk.

As I stared, the chains rattled ever so slightly, although she did not look up. "What do you want, little daughter?" Her voice was surprisingly deep.

"Lord . . . Lord Sulis is my stepfather," I said at last, as if it explained something.

Her eyes snapped open, huge and yellow. I had already thought her shaped like a hunting bird—now I almost feared she would fly at me and tear me with sharp talons. "Do you come to plead his case?" she demanded. "I tell you the same thing I told him—there is no answer to his question. None that I can give, anyway."

"What question?" I asked, hardly able to breathe.

The witch peered at me in silence for a moment, then clambered to her feet. I could see that it was a struggle for her to lift the chains. She shuffled forward until the light from the door slot fell on her squarely.

Her dark hair was cut short as a man's. She was neither pretty nor ugly, neither tall nor short, but there was a power about her, and especially in the unblinking yellow lamps of her eyes, that drew my gaze and held it. She was something I had not seen before and did not at all understand. She spoke like an ordinary woman, but she had wildness in her like the crack of distant thunder, like the flash of a deer in flight. I felt so helpless to turn away that I feared she had cast a spell upon me.

At last she shook her head. "I will not involve you in your father's madness, child."

"He is not my father. He married my mother."

Her laugh was almost a bark. "I see."

I moved uneasily from foot to foot, face still pressed against the bars. I did not know why I spoke to the woman at all, or what I wanted from her. "Why are you chained?"

"Because they fear me."

"What is your name?" She frowned but said nothing, so I tried another. "Are you really a witch?"

She sighed. "Little daughter, go away. If you have nothing to do with your stepfather's foolish ideas, then the best you can do is stay far from all this. It does not take a sorceress to see that it will not end happily."

Her words frightened me, but I still could not pull myself away from the cell door. "Is there something you want? Food? Drink?"

She eyed me again, the large eyes almost fever-bright. "This is an even stranger household than I guessed. No, child. What I want is the open sky and my forest, but that is what I will not get from you or anyone. But your father says he has need of me—he will not starve me."

The witch turned her back on me then and shuffled to the rear of the cell, dragging her chains across the stone. I climbed the stairs with my head full to aching—excited thoughts, sorrowful thoughts, frightened thoughts, all were mixed together and full of fluttering confusion, like birds in a sealed room.

My stepfather kept the witch prisoned as Marris-month turned into Avrel and the days of spring paced by. Whatever he wished from her, she would not give it. I visited her many times, but although she was kind enough in her way, she would speak to me only of meaningless things. Often she asked me to describe how the frost on the ground had looked that morning, or what birds were in the trees and what they sang, since in that deep, windowless cell carved into the stone of the headland, she could see and hear nothing of the world outside.

I do not know why I was so drawn to her. Somehow she seemed to hold the key to many mysteries—my stepfather's madness, my mother's sorrow, my own growing fears that the foundations beneath my new happiness were unsolid.

Although my stepfather did feed her, as she had promised he would, and did not allow her to be mistreated in anything beyond the fact of her imprisonment, the witch woman still grew markedly thinner by the day, and dark circles formed like bruises beneath her eyes. She was pining for freedom, and like a wild animal kept in a pen, she was sickening from her unhappiness. It hurt me to see her, as though my own liberty had been stolen. Each time I found her more drawn and weak than the time before, it brought back to me the agony and shame of my mother's last, horrible days. Each time I left the cells, I went to a spot where I could be alone and I wept. Even my stolen hours with Tellarin could not ease the sadness I felt.

I would have hated my stepfather for what he was doing to her, but he too was growing more sickly with each day, as though he were trapped in some mirror version of her dank cell. Whatever the question was that she had spoken of, it plagued Sulis so terribly that he, a decent man, had stolen her freedom—so terribly that he scarcely slept in the nights at all, but sat up until dawn's first light reading and writing and mumbling to himself in a kind of ecstasy. Whatever the question, I began to fear that both he and the witch would die because of it.

The one time that I worked up the courage to ask my stepfather why he had imprisoned her, he stared over my head at the sky, as though it had turned an entirely new color, and told me, "This place has too many doors, girl. You open one, then another, and you find yourself back where you began. I cannot find my way."

If that was an answer, I could make no sense of it.

I offered the witch death and she gave me a prophecy in return.

*　　*　　*

The sentries on the wall of the Inner Bailey were calling the midnight watch when I arose. I had been in my bed for hours, but sleep had never once come near. I wrapped myself in my heaviest cloak and slipped into the hallway. I could hear my stepfather through his door, talking as though to a visitor. It hurt to hear his voice, because I knew he was alone.

At this hour, the only guard in the cells was a crippled old soldier who did not even stir in his sleep when I walked past him. The torch in the wall sconce had burned very low, and at first I could not see the witch's shape in the shadows. I wanted to call to her, but I did not know what to say. The bulk of the great, sleeping castle seemed to press down on me.

At last the heavy chains clinked. "Is that you, little daughter?" Her voice was weary. After a while she stood and shuffled forward. Even in the faint light, she had a terrible, dying look. My hand stole to the purse that hung around my neck. I touched my golden Tree as I said a silent prayer, then felt the curve of that other thing, which I had carried with me since the night of my mother's death. In a moment that seemed to have its own light, quite separate from the flickering glow of the torch, I pulled out the dragon's claw and extended it to her through the bars.

The witch raised an eyebrow as she took it from me. She carefully turned it over in her palm, then smiled sadly. "A poisoned owl's claw. Very appropriate. Is this for me to use on my captors? Or on myself?"

I shrugged helplessly. "You want to be free" was all I could say.

"Not with this, little daughter," she said. "At least, not this time. As it happens, I have already surrendered—or, rather, I have bargained. I have agreed to give your stepfather what he thinks he wants in exchange for my freedom. I must see and feel the sky again." Gently, she handed me back the claw.

I stared at her, almost sick with the need to know things. "Why won't you tell me your name?"

Another sad smile. "Because my true name I give to no one. Because any other name would be a lie."

"Tell me a lie, then."

"A strange household, indeed! Very well. The people of the north call me Valada."

I tried it on my tongue. "Valada. He will set you free now?"

"Soon, if the bargain is honored on both sides."

"What is it, this bargain?"

"A bad one for everyone." She saw my look. "You do not want to know, truly. Someone will die because of this madness—I see it as clearly as I see your face peering through the door."

My heart was a piece of cold stone in my breast. "Someone will die? Who?"

Her expression became weary, and I could see that standing with the weight of her shackles was an effort for her. "I do not know. And in my weariness, I have already told you too much, little daughter. These are not matters for you."

I was dismissed, even more miserable and confused. The witch would be free, but someone else would die. I could not doubt her word—no one could, who had seen her fierce, sad eyes as she spoke. As I walked back to my bedchamber, the halls of the Inner Bailey seemed a place entirely new, a strange and unfamiliar world.

My feelings for Tellarin were still astonishingly strong, but in the days after the witch's foretelling I was so beset with unhappiness that our love was more like a fire that made a cold room habitable than a sun which warmed everything, as it had been. If my soldier had not had worries of his own, he would certainly have noticed.

The cold inside me became a chill like deepest winter when I overheard Tellarin and Avalles speaking about a secret task Lord Sulis had for them, something to do with the witch. It was hard to tell what was intended—my beloved and his friend did not themselves know all that Sulis planned, and they were speaking only to each other, and not for the benefit of their secret listener. I gathered that my stepfather's books had shown him that the time for some important thing had drawn close. They would build or find some kind of fire. It would take them on a short journey by night, but they did not say—or perhaps did not yet know—on what night. Both my beloved and Avalles were clearly disturbed by the prospect.

If I had feared before, when I thought the greatest risk was to my poor, addled stepfather, now I was almost ill with terror. I could barely stumble through the remaining hours of the day, so consumed was I with the thought that something might happen to Tellarin. I dropped my beadwork so many times that Ulca took it away from me at last.

When dark came, I could not get to sleep for hours, and when I did I woke up panting and shuddering from a dream in which Tellarin had fallen into flames and was burning just beyond my reach.

I lay tossing in my bed all the night. How could I protect my beloved? Warning him would do no good. He was stubborn, and also saved his deepest beliefs for those things he could grasp and touch, so I knew he would put little stock in the witch's words. In any case, even if he believed me, what could he do? Refuse an order from Lord Sulis because of a warning from me, his secret lover? No, it would be hopeless to try to persuade Tellarin not to go—he spoke of his loyalty to his master almost as often as he did of his feelings for me.

I was in an agony of fearful curiosity. What did my stepfather plan? What had he read in those books, that he now would risk not just his own life, but that of my beloved as well?

Not one of them would tell me anything, I knew. Even the witch had said that the matter was not for me. Whatever I discovered would be by my own hand.

I resolved to look at my stepfather's books, those that he kept hidden from me and everyone else. Once it would have been all but impossible, but now—because he sat reading and writing and whispering to himself all the night's dark hours—I could trust that when Sulis did sleep, he would sleep like the dead.

I stole into my stepfather's chambers early the next morning. He had sent his servants away weeks before, and the castle-folk no longer dared rap on his doors unless summoned. The rooms were empty but for my stepfather and me.

He lay sprawled across his bed, his head hanging back over the edge of the pallet. Had I not known how moderate most of his habits were, I would have thought from his deep, rough breathing and the way he had disordered the blankets that he had drunk himself stuporous, but Sulis seldom took even a single cup of wine.

The key to the locked boxes was on a cord around his neck. As I tugged it out of his shirt with as much care as I could, I could not help but see how much happier he appeared with the blankness of sleep on him. The furrows on his brow had loosened, and his jaw was no longer clenched in the grimace of distraction that had become his constant expression. In that moment, although I hated what he had done to the witch Valada, I pitied him. Whatever madness had overtaken him of late, he had been a kind man in his way, in his time.

He stirred and made an indistinct sound. Heart beating swiftly, I hurried to draw the cord and key over his head.

When I had found the wooden chests and unlocked them, I began to pull out and examine my stepfather's forbidden books, leafing quickly and quietly through each in turn, with one ear cocked for changes in his breathing. Most of the plainbound volumes were written in tongues I did not know, two or three in characters I could not even recognize. Those of which I could understand a little seemed to contain either tales of the fairy-folk or stories about the High Keep during the time of the Northmen.

A good part of an hour had passed when I discovered a loosely bound book titled *Writings of Vargellis Sulis, Seventh Lord of Honsa Sulis, Now Master of the Sulean House in Exile.* My stepfather's careful hand filled the first pages densely, then grew larger and more imperfect as it continued, until the final pages seemed almost to have been scribed by a child still learning letters.

A noise from the bed startled me, but my stepfather had only grunted and turned on his side. I continued through the book as swiftly as I could. It seemed to be only the most recent of a lifetime's worth of writings—the earliest dates in the volume were from the first year we had lived in the High Keep. The bulk of the pages listed tasks to be performed in the High Keep's rebuilding, and records of important judgments Sulis had made as lord of the keep and its tenant lands. There were other notations of a more personal nature, but they were brief and unelaborated. For that terrible day almost three years earlier, he had written only *"Cynethrith Dead of Chest Fever. She shall be Buried on the Headland."*

The sole mention of me was a single sentence from several months before—*"Breda happy Today."* It was oddly painful to me that my somber stepfather should have noticed that and made a record of it.

The later pages held almost no mention of the affairs of either home or governance, as in daily life Sulis had also lost interest in both. Instead, there were more and more notes that seemed to be about things he had read in other books—one said *"Plesinnen claims that Mortality is consumed in God as a Flame consumes Branch or Bough. How then . . ."* with the rest smudged—one word might have been *"nails,"* and further on I could make out *"Holy Tree."* Another of his notes listed several *"Doorways"* that had been located by someone named Nisses, with explanations next to each that explained nothing at all— *"Shifted,"* read my stepfather's shaky hand beside one, or *"from a Time of No Occupation,"* or even *"Met a Dark Thing."*

It was only on the last two pages that I found references to the woman in the cell below the throne room.

"Have at Last rec'd Word of the woman called Valada," the scrawl stated. *"No one else Living North of Perdruin has Knowledge of the Black Fire. She must be Made to Speak what she knows."* Below that, in another day's even less disciplined hand, was written, *"The Witch balks me, but I cannot have another Failure as on the Eve of Elysia-mansa. Stoning Night will be next Time of Strong Voices beneath the Keep. Walls will be Thin. She will show me the Way of Black Fire or there is no other Hope. Either she will answer, or Death."*

I sat back, trying to make sense of it all. Whatever my stepfather planned, it would happen soon—Stoning Night was the last night of Avrel, only a few days away. I could not tell from his writings if the witch was still in danger—did he mean to kill her if she failed, or only if she tried to cheat his bargain with her?—but I had no doubt that this search for the thing called Black Fire would bring danger to everyone else, most importantly and most frighteningly my soldier, Tellarin. Again my stepfather murmured in his sleep, an unhappy sound. I locked his books away and stole out again.

All that day I felt distracted and feverish, but this time it was not love that fevered me. I was terrified for my lover and fearful for my stepfather and the witch Valada, but what I knew and how I had discovered it I could not tell to anyone. For the first time since my soldier had kissed me, I felt alone. I was full up with secrets, and unlike Sulis, had not even a book to which they could be confided.

I would follow them, I decided at last. I would follow them into the place my stepfather spoke of, the place beneath the keep where the walls were thin and the voices strong. While they searched for the Black Fire, I would watch for danger. I would protect them all. I would be their angel.

* * *

Stoning Night came around at last.

Even had I not read my stepfather's writings, I think I would have known that the hour had come in which they meant to search for Black Fire, because Tellarin was so distracted and full of shadows. Although he admitted nothing to me as we lay together in my bedchamber, I could feel that he was anxious about what would happen that night. But he was bound to my stepfather by honor and blood, and had no choice.

He snapped at me when I kissed his ear and curled my fingers in his hair. "Give a man some peace, girl."

"Why are you a man and I am a girl?" I teased him, pretending a lightness I did not truly feel. "Is there such a difference in our ages? Have I not given to you already that which makes me a woman?"

My soldier was short-tempered and did not hear the love in what I said. "Anybody who will not leave off when she is asked proves herself still a child. And I am a man because I wear a soldier's badge, and because if my master asks, I must give my life."

Tellarin was five years my elder, and in those long-ago days I was almost as impressed by the difference as he was, but I think now that all men are younger than their women, especially when their honor has been touched.

As he stared at the ceiling his face turned from angry to solemn, and I knew he was thinking of what he must do that night. I was frightened too, so I kissed him again, softly this time, and apologized.

When he had gone, full of excuses meant to hide his actual task, I prepared for my own journey. I had hidden my thickest cloak and six fat candles where Ulca and the other serving-women would not find them. When I was dressed and ready, I touched my mother's golden Tree where it lay against my heart, and said a prayer for the safety of all who would go with me into darkness.

Stoning Night—the last night of Avrel, on the eve of Maia-month, the black hours when tales say spirits walk until driven back to their graves by dawn and the crowing cock. The High Keep lay silent around me as I followed my beloved and the others through the dark. It did not feel so much that the castle slept as that the great keep held its breath and waited.

There is a stairwell beneath the Angel Tower, and that was where they were bound. I learned of it for the first time on that night, as I stood wrapped in my dark cloak, listening from the shadows of the wall opposite the tower. Those I followed were four—my stepfather, Tellarin and his friend Avalles, and the woman Valada. Despite the bargain she had made, the witch's arms were still chained. It saddened me to see her restrained like an animal.

The workmen who had been repairing the tower had laid a rough wooden floor over the broken stones of the old one—perhaps to make certain no one fell down one of the many holes, perhaps simply to close off any openings into the castle's deepest places. Some had even suggested that all the old castle floor should be sealed under brick, so that nothing would ever come up that way to trouble the sleep of God-fearing folk.

Because of this wooden floor, I waited a long time before following them through the tower's outer portal, knowing it would take some time for my stepfather and his two bondmen to shift the boards. As I lurked in the shadows by the tower wall while the wind prowled the Inner Bailey, I thought about the Angel who stood at the top of the tower, a figure black with the grime of centuries that no rain could wash away, tipped sideways as though about to lose her balance and fall. Who was she? One of the blessed saints? Was it an omen—did she watch over me as I meant to look over Tellarin and the rest? I looked up, but the tower's high top was invisible in the night.

At last I tried the latch of the tower door and found the bolt had not been shot. I hoped that it meant the Angel was indeed looking out for me.

Inside the tower the moonlight ended, so while still in the doorway I lit my first candle from the hidden touchwood, which had nearly burnt down. My footsteps seemed frighteningly loud in the stony entry hall, but no one appeared from the shadows to demand my business in that place. I heard no sound of my stepfather or the rest.

I paused for a moment in front of the great, upward-winding stair-case, and could not help but wonder what the workmen would find when they cleared the rubble and reached the top—as I still wonder all these years later, with the painstaking work yet unfinished. I suppose I will not see it in my lifetime. Will they discover treasures left by the fairy-folk? Or perhaps only those ancient beings' frail bones?

Even were it not for the things that happened on that fateful night, still the Angel Tower would haunt me, as it haunts this great keep and all the lands beneath its long shadow. No mortals, I think, will ever know its all its secrets.

Once, long ago, I dreamed that my stepfather gave me the Angel herself to clean, but that no matter how I tried, I could not scrub the black muck from her limbs and face. He told me that it was not my fault, that God would have lent me the strength if He truly wanted the Angel's face to be seen, but I still wept at my failure.

I moved from the entry hall to a place where the floor fell away in great broken shards, and tried to imagine what could smash stones so thoroughly and yet leave the tower itself still standing. It was not easy to follow where my stepfather and my beloved had already gone, but I climbed down the rubble, leaning to set my candle before me so that I could have both my hands free. I wished, not for the last time, that I had worn something other than my soft shoes. I clambered down and down, hurting my feet, tearing my dress in several places, until I reached the jumble of smaller broken stones which was the floor, at least a half dozen times my own height below the level of the Inner Bailey. In the midst of this field of shards gaped a great, black hole bigger than the rest, a jagged mouth that waited to swallow me down. As I crunched closer to it, I heard what I knew must be the voices of the others floating up from the depths, although they sounded strange to me.

More stones had been pushed aside to reveal the entrance to the stairwell, a lip of shiny white with steps inside it that vanished into shadow. Another voice floated up, laughing. It belonged to no one I knew.

Even with all that had happened in the previous days, I had never yet felt so frightened, but I knew Tellarin was down there in the dark places. I made the sign of the Tree upon my breast, then stepped onto the stairway.

At first I could find no trace of them.

As I descended, the light of my single candle served only to make the stairwell seem more than ever like a shadowy throat waiting to swallow me, but fear alone could not keep me from my beloved—if anything, it sped my steps. I hurried downward until it seemed I must have gone as far beneath the castle as the Angel Tower loomed above it, but still I had not caught up with them.

Whether it was a trick of sound, or of the winds that are said to blow through the caves of the Kingslake cliffs, I continued to hear unfamiliar voices. Some seemed so close that if I had not had a candle, I would have been certain I could reach out and touch the person who whispered to me, but the flickering light showed me that the stairwell was empty. The voices babbled, and sometimes sang, in a soft, sad tongue I did not understand or even recognize.

I knew I should be too frightened to remain, that I should turn and flee back to moonlight and clean air, but although the bodiless murmurs filled me with dismay, I felt no evil in them. If they were ghosts, I do not think they even knew I was there. It was as though the castle talked to itself, like an old man sitting beside the fire, lost in the memories of days long past.

The stairwell ended in a wide landing with open doorways at either end, and I could not help thinking of the doorways mentioned in my stepfather's book. As I paused to consider which way I should go, I examined the carvings on the walls, delicate vines and flowers whose type I had never seen before. Above one doorframe a nightingale perched on a tree bough. Another tree bough was carved above the far doorway—or rather, I saw as I moved my candle, they were both boughs from one single tree, which had been carved directly above me, spreading across the ceiling of the stairwell as though I myself were the tree's trunk. On the bough above the second doorway twined a slender serpent. I shuddered, and began to move toward the nightingale door, but at that moment words floated up out of the darkness.

"... *if you have lied to me. I am a patient man, but* ..."

It was my stepfather, and even if I had not recognized his faint voice, I would have known him by the words, for that is what he always said. And he spoke the truth—he *was* a patient man. He had always been like one of the stones of the hilltop rings, cool and hard and in no hurry to move, growing warm only after the sun of an entire summer has beat upon him. I had sometimes felt I would like to break a stick upon him, if only to make him turn and truly look at me.

Only once did he ever do that, I had believed—on that day when he told me that "they" had taken everything from him. But now I knew he had looked at me another time, perhaps seen me smile on a day when my lover had given me a gift or a kiss, and had written in his book, *"Breda happy Today."*

My stepfather's words had drifted up through the other doorway. I lit another candle and place it on top of the first, which had burned almost to the holder, then followed the voice of Sulis through the serpent door.

Downward I went, and downward still farther—what seemed a journey of hours, through sloping, long-deserted corridors that twisted like yarn spilled from a sack. The light of the candles showed me stone that, although I knew it was even more ancient, seemed newer and brighter than that which I had seen farther above. In places the passageways opened into rooms choked with dirt and rubble, but which must have been massive, with ceilings as high as any of the greatest halls I have ever heard of in Nabban. The carvings I could see were so delicate, so perfect, that they might have been the actual things of nature—birds, plants, trees—frozen into stone by the sort of magical spells that so often had been part of my mother's and Ulca's stories.

It was astonishing to think that this entire world had lain in its tomb of earth below us as long as we had lived in the High Keep, and for generations before that. I knew I was seeing the ancient home of the fairy-folk. With all the stories, and even with the evidence of the tower itself, I had still never imagined they would have such a way with stone, to make it froth like water and shimmer like ice, to make it stretch overhead in slender arcs like the finest branches of a willow tree. Had the Northmen truly killed them all? For the first time, I understood something of what this meant, and a deep, quiet horror stole over me. The creators of all this beauty, slaughtered, and their houses usurped by their slayers—no wonder the darkness was full of unquiet voices. No wonder the High Keep was a place of haunted sadness for everyone who lived in it. The castle of our day was founded on ancient murder. It was built on death.

It pulled at me, that thought. It became tangled in my mind with the memory of my stepfather's distracted stare, of the witch in chains. Good could not come from evil, I felt sure. Not without sacrifice. Not without blood and atonement.

My fear was growing again.

* * *

The Peaceful Ones might have been gone, but I was learning that their great house remained lively.

As I hurried downward, following the tracks of my stepfather and his company in the dust of centuries, I found suddenly that I had taken a wrong turning. The passage ended in a pile of broken stone, but when I returned to the last cross-corridor, there was no sign of footprints, and the place itself was not familiar, as though the ruins themselves had shifted around me. I closed my eyes, listening for the sound of Tellarin's voice, for I felt sure that my heart would be able to hear him through all the stone in Erkynland. But nothing came to me but the ghost-murmurs, which blew in like an autumn breeze, full of sighing, rustling nonsense.

I was lost.

For the first time it became clear to me what a foolish thing I had done. I had gone into a place where I should not be. Not one person knew I was there, and when my last candle burned out, I would be lost in the darkness.

Tears started in my eyes, but I wiped them away. Weeping had not brought my father back, or my mother. It would do me no good now.

I did my best to retrace my steps, but the voices flittered around me like invisible birds, and before long I was wandering blindly. Confused by the noises in my head and by the flickering shadows, twice I almost tumbled into great crevices in the passageway floor. I kicked a stone into one that fell without hitting anything until I could not bear to listen any longer.

The darkness seemed to be closing on me, and I might have been lost forever—might have become another part of the whispering chorus—but by luck or accident or the hand of fate, I made a turning into a corridor I did not recognize and found myself standing at the lip of another stairwell, listening to the voice of the witch Valada drift up from the deeps.

"... not an army or a noble household that you can order about, Lord Sulis. Those who lived here are dead, but the place is alive. You must take what you are given ..."

It is as though she had heard my very thoughts. Even as I shuddered to hear my forebodings spoken aloud, I hurried toward the sound, terrified that if it faded I would never again hear a familiar voice.

*   *   *

What seemed another hour went by, although I had been so long in the haunted dark that I was no judge. My lover and the rest seemed almost to have become phantoms themselves, floating ahead of me like dandelion seeds, always just beyond my reach.

The stairs continued to curl downward, and as my third and fourth candles burned I could see glimpses of the great spaces through which we all descended, level upon level, as if making a pilgrimage down the tiers of Heaven. At times, as the candles flickered on the wooden base, I thought I could see even more. From the corner of my eye the ruins seemed to take on a sort of life. There were moments when the ghost-voices swelled and the shadows seem to take on form. If I half-closed my eyes, I could almost see these bleak spaces full of bright, laughing folk.

Why did the Northmen kill such beauty? And how could a people who built such a place be defeated by any mortals, however blood-thirsty and battle-hungry?

A light bloomed in the depths, red and yellow, making the polished stone of the stairwell seem to quiver. For a moment I thought it only another wisp of my imagination, but then, from so close it seemed we could kiss if we wished, I heard my beloved's voice.

"Do not trust her, sire," Tellarin said, sounding more than a little fearful. *"She is lying again."*

Intensely happy, but with my caution abruptly restored, I shaded the candle with my palm and hurried down the stairs as quietly as I could. As their voices grew louder, and I saw that the light blooming in the darkness came from their torches, I pinched the flame to extinguish my candle completely. However glad I was to find them, I guessed they would not feel the same about me.

I crept closer to the light, but could not see Tellarin and the others because something like a cloud of smoke blocked my view. It was only when I reached the base of the curving stair and stepped silently onto the floor of the great chamber that I could actually see the four shapes.

They stood in the middle of a room so cavernous that even the torches my lover and Avalles held could not carry light to its highest corners. Before them loomed the thing I had thought was smoke. I still could not see it clearly, despite the torch flames burning only an arm's length from it, but now it seemed a vast tree with black leaves and trunk. A shadow cloaked it and hid all but the broadest outline, a dark shroud like the mist that hid the hills on a winter morning, but it was not mist in which the tree-shape crouched, I felt sure. It was pure Darkness.

"You must decide whether to listen to me or a young soldier," the witch was saying to my stepfather. "I will tell you again—if you cut so much as a leaf, you will mark yourselves as ravagers and it will not go well with you. Can you not feel that?"

"And I think Tellarin is right," Avalles proclaimed, but his voice was less sure than his words. "She seeks to trick us."

My stepfather looked from the tree-shadow to the witch. "If we may not take any wood, then why have you brought us here?" he asked slowly, as though it cost great effort just to speak.

I could hear the sour smile in Valada's answer. "You have held me captive in your damp pile of stones for two moons, seeking my help with your mad questions. If you do not believe that I know what I know, why did you shackle me and bring me here?"

"But the wood . . . ?"

"I did not say you could not take anything to burn, I said that you would be a fool to lift axe or knife to the Great Witchwood. There is deadfall beneath, if you are bold enough to search for it."

Sulis turned to Avalles. "Go and gather some dead wood, nephew."

The young knight hesitated, then handed his torch to my stepfather and walked a little unsteadily toward the great dark tree. He bent beneath the outer branches and vanished from sight. After an interval of silence, Avalles stumbled back out again.

"It is . . . it is too dark to see," he panted. His eyes were showing white around the edges. "And there is something in there—an animal, perhaps. I . . . I can feel it breathing." He turned to my stepfather. "Tellarin's eyes are better than mine . . ."

No! I wanted to scream. The tree-thing sat and waited, cloaked in shadows no torchlight could penetrate. I was ready to burst from hiding and beg my beloved not to go near it, but as if he had heard my silent cry, Lord Sulis cursed and thrust the torch back into Avalles' hand.

"By Pelippa and her bowl!" my stepfather said. "I will do it myself."

Just before he stepped through the branches, I thought I heard the leaves whisper, although there was no wind in the chamber. The quiet hiss and rattle grew louder, perhaps because my stepfather was forcing his way beneath the thick branches. Long moments trudged past; then the rustling became even more violent. At last Sulis emerged, staggering a little, with what seemed a long bar of shadow clasped under each arm. Tellarin and Avalles stepped forward to help him but he waved them off, shaking his head as though he had been dealt a blow. Even in the dark room, I could see that he had gone very pale.

"You spoke the truth, Valada," he said. "No axe, no knife."

While I watched, he bade Avalles and my beloved make a ring on the ground from the broken stones that littered the chamber. He crossed the two pieces of wood he had gathered in the center of the circle, then he used kindling from a pouch on his belt and one of the torches to set the witchwood alight. As the strange fire sputtered into life, the room seemed to become darker, as though the very light from the torches bent toward the firepit and was sucked away. The flames began to rise.

The rustle of the shadowy tree stilled. Everything grew silent—even the flames made no sound. My heart pounded as I leaned closer, almost forgetting to keep myself hidden. It was indeed a Black Fire that burned now in that deep, lost place, a fire that flickered like any blaze, and yet whose flames were wounds in the very substance of the world, holes as darkly empty as a starless sky.

It is hard to believe, but that is what I saw. I could look through the flames of the Black Fire, not to what stood on the other side of the fire, but to *somewhere else*—into nothingness at first, but then color and shape began to expand outward in the space above the firepit, as though something turned the very air inside out.

A face appeared in the fire. It was all I could do not to cry out.

The stranger surrounded by the black flames was like no man I had ever seen. The angles of his face were all somehow wrong, his chin too narrow, the large eyes slanted upward at the corners. His hair was long and white, but he did not look old. He was naked from the waist up, and his pale, glossy skin was marked with dreadful scars, but despite the flames in which he lay, his burns seemed old rather than new.

The Black Fire unshaped even the darkness. All that was around it bent, as though the very world grew stretched and shivery as the reflection on a bubble of river water.

The burning man seemed to slumber in the flames, but it was a horribly unquiet sleep. He pitched and writhed, even brought his hands up before his face, as though to protect himself from some terrible attack. When his eyes at last opened, they were dark as shadow itself, staring at things that I could not see, at shadows far beyond the fire. His mouth stretched in a silent, terrible scream, and despite his alien aspect, despite being so frightened I feared my heart would stop, I still ached to see his suffering. If he was alive, how could his body burn and burn without being consumed? If he was a ghost, why had death not ended his pain?

Tellarin and Avalles backed away from the firepit, wide-eyed and fearful. Avalles made the sign of the Tree.

My stepfather looked at the burning man's writhing mouth and blind eyes, then turned to the witch Valada. "Why does he not speak to us? Do something!"

She laughed her sharp laugh. "You wished to meet one of the Sithi, Lord Sulis—one of the Peaceful Ones. You wished to find a doorway, but some doorways open not on elsewhere, but elsewhen. The Black Fire has found you one of the Fair Folk in his sleep. He is dreaming, but he can hear you across the centuries. Speak to him! I have done what I promised."

Clearly shaken, Sulis turned to the man in the flames. "You!" he called. "Can you understand me?"

The burning man writhed again, but now his dark unseeing eyes turned in my stepfather's direction. "Who is there?" he asked, and I heard his voice in the chamber of my skull rather than in my ears. "Who walks the Road of Dreams?" The apparition lifted a hand as though he might reach through the years and touch us. For a moment, astonishment pushed the agony from his odd face. "You are mortals! But why do you come to me? Why do you disturb the sleep of Hakatri of the House of Year-Dancing?"

"I am Sulis." The tremble in my stepfather's voice made him seem an old, old man. "Called by some 'the Apostate.' I have risked everything I own—have spent years studying—to ask a question which only the Peaceful Ones can answer. Will you help me?"

The burning man did not seem to be listening. His mouth twisted again, and this time his cry of pain had sound. I tried to stop my ears, but it was already inside my head. "Ah, it burns!" he moaned. "Still the worm's blood burns me—even when I sleep. Even when I walk the Road of Dreams!"

"The worm's blood . . . ?" My stepfather was puzzled. "A dragon? What are you saying?"

"She was like a great black snake," Hakatri murmured. "My brother and I, we followed her into her deep place and we fought her and slew her, but I have felt her scorching blood upon me and will never be at peace again. By the Garden, it pains me so!" He made a choking sound, then fell silent for a moment. "Both our swords bit," he said, and it was almost a chant, a song, "but my brother Ineluki was the fortunate one. He escaped a terrible burning. Black, black it was, that ichor, and hotter than even the flames of Making! I fear death itself could not ease this agony . . ."

"Be silent!" Sulis thundered, full of rage and misery. "Witch, is this spell for nothing? Why will he not listen to me?"

"There is no spell, except that which opens the doorway," she replied. "Hakatri perhaps came to that doorway because of how the dragon's blood burned him—there is nothing else in all the world like the blood of the great worms. His wounds keep him always close to the Road of Dreams, I think. Ask him your question, Nabban-man. He is as like to answer it as any other of the immortals you might have found."

I could feel it now—could feel the weird that had brought us here take us all in its grip. I held my breath, caught between a terror that blew like a cold wind inside my head, that screamed at me to leave Tellarin and everything else and run away, and a fierce wondering about what had brought my stepfather to this impossibly strange meeting.

Lord Sulis tilted his chin down toward his chest for a moment, as though now that the time had come, he was uncertain of what he wished to say. At last he spoke, quaveringly at first, but with greater strength as he went on.

"Our Church teaches us that God appeared in this world, wearing the form of Usires Aedon, performing many miracles, singing up cures for the sick and lame, until at last the Imperator Crexis caused him to be hung from the Execution Tree. Do you know of this, Hakatri?"

The burning man's blind eyes rolled toward Sulis again. He did not answer, but he seemed to be listening.

"The promise of Aedon the Ransomer is that all who live will be gathered up—that there will be no death," my stepfather continued.

"And this is proved because he was God made flesh in this world, and that is proved because of the miracles he performed. But I have studied much about your own people, Hakatri. Such miracles as Usires the Aedon performed could have been done by one of your Sithi people, or even perhaps by one of only half-immortal blood." His smile was as bleak as a skull's. "After all, even my fiercest critics in Mother Church agree that Usires had no human father."

Sulis bowed his head again for a moment, summoning up words or strength. I gasped for air—I had forgotten to breathe. Avalles and Tellarin still stared, their fear now mixed with astonishment, but the witch Valada's face was hidden from me in shadow.

"Both my wives have been taken from me by death, both untimely," my stepfather said. "My first wife gave me a son before she died, a beautiful boy named Sarellis who died himself in screaming pain because he stepped on a horseshoe nail—a nail!—and caught a death fever. Young men I have commanded were slaughtered in the hundreds, the thousands, their corpses piled on the battlefield like the husks of locusts, and all for a small stretch of land here or there, or sometimes merely over words. My parents are dead, too, with too much unspoken between us. Everyone I ever truly loved has been stolen from me by death."

His hoarse voice had taken on a disturbing force, a cracked power, as though he meant to shout down the walls of Heaven itself.

"Mother Church tells me to believe that I will be reunited with them," he said. "They preach to me, saying, 'See the works of Usires our Lord and be comforted, for his task was to show death should hold no fear,' they told me. But I cannot be sure—I cannot simply trust! Is the Church right? Will I see those I love again? Will we all live on? The masters of the Church have called me a heretic and declared me apostate because I would not give up doubting the divinity of the Aedon, but I must know! Tell me, Hakatri, was Usires of your folk? Is the story of his godhood simply a lie to keep us happy, to keep priests fat and rich?" He blinked back tears, his stolid face transfigured by rage and pain. "Even if God should damn me forever to hell for it, still I must know—*is our faith a lie?*"

He was shaking so badly now that he took a staggering step back from the fire and almost fell. No one moved except the man in the flames, who followed Sulis with his blank, dark eyes.

I realized that I was weeping too, and silently rubbed the tears away. Seeing my stepfather's true and terrible pain was like a knife twisted inside me, and yet I was angry too. All for this? For such unknowable things he left my mother lonely, and now had nearly destroyed his own life?

After a long time in which all was silent as the stone around us, Hakatri said slowly, "Always you mortals have tortured yourselves." He blinked, and the way his face moved was so alien that I had to turn away and then look at him anew before I could understand what he said. "But you torture yourself most when you seek answers to things that have none."

"No answers?" Sulis was still shaking. "How can that be?"

The burning man raised his long-fingered hands in what I could only guess was a gesture of peace. "Because that which is meant for mortals is not given to the Zida'ya to know, any more than you can know of our Garden, or where we go when we leave this place.

"Listen to me, mortal. What if your messiah were indeed one of the Dawn Children—would that prove somehow that your God had not chosen that to happen? Would that prove your Ransomer's words any the less true?" Hakatri shook his head with the weird, foreign grace of a shorebird.

"Just tell me whether Usires was one of your folk," Sulis demanded raggedly. "Spare me your philosophies and tell me! For I am burning too! I have not been free of the pain in years!"

As the echoes of my stepfather's cry faded, the fairy-lord in his ring of black flames paused, and for the first time he seemed truly to see across the gulf. When he spoke, his voice was full of sadness.

"We Zida'ya know little of the doings of mortals, and there are some of our own blood who have fallen away from us, and whose works are hidden from us as well. I do not think your Usires Aedon was one of the Dawn Children, but more than that I cannot tell you, mortal man, nor could any of my folk." He lifted his hands again, weaving the fingers in an intricate, incomprehensible gesture. "I am sorry."

A great shudder ran through the creature called Hakatri then— perhaps the pain of his burns returning, a pain that he had somehow held at bay while he listened to my stepfather speak. Sulis did not wait to hear more, but stepped forward and kicked the witchwood fire into a cloud of whirling sparks, then dropped to his knees with his hands over his face.

The burning man was gone.

After a march of silence that seemed endless, the witch called out, "Will you honor your bargain with me now, Lord Sulis? You said that if I brought you to one of the immortals, you would free me." Her voice was flat, but there was still a gentleness to it that surprised me.

My stepfather's reply, when it came, was choked and hard to understand. He waved his hand. "Take off her chains, Avalles. I want nothing more from her."

In the midst of this great bleak wilderness of sorrow, I felt a moment of sharp happiness as I realized that despite my foreboding, the witch, my beloved, even my tortured stepfather, all would survive this terrible night. As Avalles began to unlock the witch's shackles, shivering so that he could hardly hold the key, I had a moment to dream that my uncle would return to health, that he would reward my Tellarin for his bravery and loyalty, and that my beloved and I would make a home for ourselves somewhere far away from this ghost-riddled, windswept headland.

My stepfather let out a sudden, startling cry. I turned to see him fall forward onto his belly, his body ashake with weeping. This seizure of grief in stern, quiet Sulis was in some ways the most frightening thing I had yet seen in that long, terrifying night.

Then, even as his cry rebounded in the invisible upper reaches of the chamber and provoked a dim rustle in the leaves of the shadowy tree, something else seized my attention. Two figures were struggling where the witch had stood. At first I thought Avalles and the woman Valada were fighting, but then I saw that the witch had stepped back and was watching the battle, her bright eyes wide with surprise. Instead, it was Avalles and Tellarin who were tangled together, their torches fallen from their hands. Shocked, helpless with surprise, I watched them tumble to the ground. A moment later a dagger rose and fell, then the brief struggle was ended.

I screamed "Tellarin!" and rushed forward.

He stood, brushing the dust from his breeks, and stared at me as I came out of the shadows. The end of his knife was blackened with blood. He had a stillness about him that might have been fear, or simply surprise.

"Breda? What are you doing here?"

"Why did he attack you?" I cried. Avalles lay twisted on the ground in a spreading puddle of black. "He was your friend!"

He said nothing, but leaned to kiss me, then turned and walked to where my stepfather still crouched on the ground in a fit of grief. My beloved put his knee in my stepfather's back, then wrapped his hand in the hair at the back of the older man's head and pulled until his tearstained face was tilted up into the torchlight.

"I did not want to kill Avalles," my soldier explained, in part to me, in part to Sulis. "But he insisted on coming, fearing that I would become closer in his uncle's favor if he were not there too." He shook his head. "Sad. But it is only your death that was my task, Sulis, and I have been waiting long for such a perfect opportunity."

Despite the merciless strain of his position, my stepfather smiled, a ghastly, tight-stretched grin. "Which Sancellan sent you?"

"Does it matter? You have more enemies in Nabban than you can count, Sulis Apostate. You are a heretic and a schismatic, and you are dangerous. You should have known you would not be left here, to build your power in the wilderness."

"I did not come here to build power," my stepfather grunted. "I came here to have my questions answered."

"Tellarin!" I struggled to make sense where there could be none. "What are you doing?"

His voice took on a little of its former gentle tone. "This is nothing to do with you and me, Breda."

"Did you . . . ?" I could scarcely say it. My tears were making the chamber as blurry as the Black Fire ever did. "Did you . . . only pretend love for me? Was it all to help you kill him?"

"No! I had no need of you, girl—I was already one of his most trusted men." He tightened his grip on Sulis then, until I feared my stepfather's neck would break. "What you and I have, little Breda, that is good and real. I will take you back to Nabban with me—I will be rich now, and you will be my wife. You will learn what a true city is, instead of this devilish, backward pile of stone."

"You love me? Truly, you love me?" I wanted very much to believe him. "Then let my stepfather go, Tellarin!"

He frowned. "I cannot. His death is the task I was given to do before I ever met you, and it is a task that needs doing. He is a madman,

Breda! Surely after tonight's horrors, after seeing the demon he called up with forbidden magic, you can see why he cannot be allowed to live."

"Do not kill him, please! I beg you!"

He lifted his hand to still me. "I am sworn to my master in Nabban. This one thing I must do, and then we are both free."

Even an appeal in the name of love could not stop him. Confused and overwhelmed, unable to argue any longer with the man who had brought me so much joy, I turned to the witch, praying that she would do something—but Valada was gone. She had taken her freedom, leaving the rest of us to murder each other if we wished. I thought I saw a movement in the shadows, but it was only some other phantom, some flying thing that drifted above the stairwell on silent wings.

Lord Sulis was silent. He did not struggle against Tellarin's grip, but waited for slaughter like an old bull. When he swallowed, the skin on his neck pulled so tight that watching it made tears spill onto my cheeks once more. My beloved pressed his knife against my stepfather's throat as I stumbled toward them. Sulis looked at me, but still said nothing. Whatever thought was in his eyes, it had gone so deep that I could not even guess what it might be.

"Tell me again that you love me," I asked as I reached his side. As I looked at my soldier's frightened but exultant face, I could not help thinking of the High Keep, a haunted place built on murder, in whose corrupted, restless depths we stood. For a moment I thought the ghost-voices had returned, for my head was full of roaring, rushing noise. "Tell me again, Tellarin," I begged him. "Please."

My beloved did not move the blade from Sulis' throat, but said, "Of course I love you, Breda. We will be married, and all of Nabban will lie at your feet. You will never be cold or lonely again." He leaned forward, and I could feel the beautiful long muscles of his back tense beneath my hand. He hesitated when he heard the click of the glass ball as it fell to the tiles and rattled away.

"What . . . ?" he asked, then straightened suddenly, grabbing at the spot at his waist where the claw had pricked him. I took a few staggering steps and fell, weeping. Behind me, Tellarin began to wheeze, then to choke. I heard his knife clatter to the stone.

I could not look, but the sound of his last rattling breaths will never leave me.

*   *   *

Now that I am old, I know that this secretive keep will be the place I die. When I have breathed my last, I suppose they will bury me on the headland beside my mother and Lord Sulis.

After that long night beneath the castle had ended, the Heron King, as the Lake People called my stepfather, came to resemble once more the man he had been. He reigned over the High Keep for many more years, and gradually even my own brawling, jealous folk acknowledged him as their ruler, although the kingship did not outlive Sulis himself.

My own mark on the world will be even smaller.

I never married, and my brother Aelfric died of a fall from his horse without fathering any children, so although the Lake People still squabble over who should carry the standard and spear of the Great Thane, none of my blood will ever lead them again. Nor, I expect, will anyone stay on in the great castle that Lord Sulis rebuilt after I am dead— there are few enough left of our household now, and those who stay only do so for love of me. When I am gone, I doubt any will remain even to tend our graves.

I cannot say why I chose to keep this bleak place as my home, any more than I could say why I chose my stepfather's life over that of my beautiful, deceitful Tellarin. Because I feared to build something on blood that should have been founded on something better, I suppose. Because love does not do sums, but instead makes choices, and then gives its all.

Whatever the reasons, I have made those choices.

After he carried me out of the depths and back to daylight, my stepfather scarcely ever mentioned that dreadful night again. He was still distant to the end of his days, still full of shadows, but at times I thought I sensed a peace in him that he had not had before. Why that might be, I could not say.

As he lay at last on his deathbed, breath growing fainter and fainter, I sat by his side for hours of every day and spoke to him of all that happened in the High Keep, talking of the rebuilding, which still continued, and of the tenants, and the herds, as if at any moment he might rise to resume his stewardship. But we both knew he would not.

When the last moment came, there was a kind of quiet expectancy on his face—no fear, but something more difficult to describe. As he strained for his final breath of air, I suddenly remembered something I had read in his book, and realized that I had made a mistake on that night so long ago.

"... *She will show me the Way of Black Fire or there is no other Hope,*" he had written. *"Either she will answer, or Death."*

He had not meant that he would kill her if she did not give him what he needed. He had meant that if she could not help him find an answer, then he would have to wait until death came for him before he could learn the truth.

And now he would finally receive an answer to the question that had tormented him for so long.

Whatever that answer might be, Sulis did not return to share it with me. Now I am an old, old woman, and I will find it soon enough myself. It is strange, perhaps, but I find I do not much care. In one year with Tellarin, in those months of fierce love, I lived an entire lifetime. Since then I have lived another one, a long, slow life whose small pleasures have largely balanced the moments of suffering. Surely two lives are enough for anyone—who needs the endless span of the immortals? After all, as the burning man made clear, an eternity of pain would be no gift.

And now that I have told my tale, even the ghosts that sometimes still startle me awake at midnight seem more like ancient friends than things to be feared.

I have made my choices.

I think I am content.

A Song of Ice and Fire

—

GEORGE R. R. MARTIN

The South

Three Sisters

The Fingers

The Kingsroad

Iron Islands

Seagard

Green Fork

VALE OF ARRYN

Pyke

Blue Fork

The Eyrie

Red Fork

The Trident

Bloody Gate

Gulltown

Tumblestone

Riverrun

Bay of Crabs

Golden Tooth

Harrenhal

God's Eye

The Kingsroad

Casterly Rock

Dragonstone

Lannisport

The Goldroad

Blackwater Rush

King's Landing

THE REACH

N

Kingswood

Tarth

The Searoad

The Roseroad

Mander

Storm's End

SHIPBREAKER BAY

Highgarden

The Dornish Marches

Rainwood

Cape Wrath

SEA OF DORNE

Oldtown

Starfall

DORNE

The Broken Arm

Sunspear

The Arbor

Map by
James Sinclair

A GAME OF THRONES (1996)
A CLASH OF KINGS (1998)
A DANCE WITH DRAGONS (FORTHCOMING)
THE WINDS OF WINTER (FORTHCOMING)

One of the most recent of the great multivolume fantasy epics is George R. R. Martin's *A Song of Ice and Fire*, which when complete will span four volumes. This immense saga is set in the world of the Seven Kingdoms, a land where seasons have been thrown out of balance, with summer and winter both lasting for years.

As the first book opens, the reader learns that three noble families had conspired to depose their insane king and take control of the kingdom. The Lannisters, the Baratheons, and the Starks all exist in an uneasy truce that is soon broken when the current king, Robert Baratheon, asks Ned Stark to come down from the northern city of Winterfell and help him to rule, giving him the coveted title of Hand of the King, which makes him the second most powerful man of the Seven Kingdoms. Ned's efforts to solve the murder of his predecessor in that post soon embroil him in conflict with the queen and her brothers. The balance of power among the great families is thus unsettled. As the game of thrones grows deadly, even more sinister forces are stirring in the north, behind the great ice wall that protects the Seven Kingdoms and all the realms of men.

A civil war threatens to sweep the land when the Lannisters kill Robert and attempt to seize power, opposed only by the Starks and Baratheons. Meanwhile, the head of the Targaryen family, Viserys, sells his sister into marriage in return for armies that will help him reconquer the Seven Kingdoms.

The forthcoming volumes of the series will depict the gradual un-folding and resolution of the terrible many-sided conflict that will rack this troubled world.

The story offered here, "The Hedge Knight," takes place about a hundred years prior to the events described in *A Game of Thrones*.

The Hedge Knight
A Tale of the Seven Kingdoms

GEORGE R. R. MARTIN

The spring rains had softened the ground, so Dunk had no trouble digging the grave. He chose a spot on the western slope of a low hill, for the old man had always loved to watch the sunset. "Another day done," he would sigh, "and who knows what the morrow will bring us, eh, Dunk?"

Well, one morrow had brought rains that soaked them to the bones, and the one after had brought wet gusty winds, and the next a chill. By the fourth day the old man was too weak to ride. And now he was gone. Only a few days past, he had been singing as they rode, the old song about going to Gulltown to see a fair maid, but instead of Gulltown he'd sung of Ashford. *Off to Ashford to see the fair maid, heigh-ho, heigh-ho,* Dunk thought miserably as he dug.

When the hole was deep enough, he lifted the old man's body in his arms and carried him there. He had been a small man, and slim; stripped of hauberk, helm, and sword belt, he seemed to weigh no more than a bag of leaves. Dunk was hugely tall for his age, a shambling, shaggy, big-boned boy of sixteen or seventeen years (no one was quite certain which) who stood closer to seven feet than to six, and had only just begun to fill out his frame. The old man had often praised his strength. He had always been generous in his praise. It was all he had to give.

He laid him out in the bottom of the grave and stood over him for a time. The smell of rain was in the air again, and he knew he ought to fill the hole before the rain broke, but it was hard to throw dirt down on that tired old face. *There ought to be a septon here, to say some prayers over him, but he only has me.* The old man had taught Dunk all he knew of swords and shields and lances, but had never been much good at teaching him words.

"I'd leave your sword, but it would rust in the ground," he said at last, apologetic. "The gods will give you a new one, I guess. I wish you didn't die, ser." He paused, uncertain what else needed to be said. He didn't know any prayers, not all the way through; the old man had never been much for praying. "You were a true knight, and you never beat me when I didn't deserve it," he finally managed, "except that one time in Maidenpool. It was the inn boy who ate the widow woman's pie, not me, I told you. It don't matter now. The gods keep you, ser." He kicked dirt in the hole, then began to fill it methodically, never looking at the thing at the bottom. *He had a long life*, Dunk thought. *He must have been closer to sixty than to fifty, and how many men can say that?* At least he had lived to see another spring.

The sun was westering as he fed the horses. There were three; his swaybacked stot, the old man's palfrey, and Thunder, his warhorse, who was ridden only in tourney and battle. The big brown stallion was not as swift or strong as he had once been, but he still had his bright eye and fierce spirit, and he was more valuable than everything else Dunk owned. *If I sold Thunder and old Chestnut, and the saddles and bridles too, I'd come away with enough silver to . . .* Dunk frowned. The only life he knew was the life of a hedge knight, riding from keep to keep, taking service with this lord and that lord, fighting in their battles and eating in their halls until the war was done, then moving on. There were tourneys from time to time as well, though less often, and he knew that some hedge knights turned robber during lean winters, though the old man never had.

I could find another hedge knight in need of a squire to tend his animals and clean his mail, he thought, *or might be I could go to some city, to Lannisport or King's Landing, and join the City Watch. Or else . . .*

He had piled the old man's things under an oak. The cloth purse contained three silver stags, nineteen copper pennies, and a chipped garnet; as with most hedge knights, the greatest part of his worldly wealth had been tied up in his horses and weapons. Dunk now owned a chain-mail hauberk that he had scoured the rust off a thousand times. An iron halfhelm with a broad nasal and a dent on the left temple. A sword belt of cracked brown leather, and a longsword in a wood-and-leather scabbard. A dagger, a razor, a whetstone. Greaves and gorget, an eight-foot war lance of turned ash topped by a cruel iron point, and an oaken shield with a scarred metal rim, bearing the sigil of Ser Arlan of Pennytree: a winged chalice, silver on brown.

Dunk looked at the shield, scooped up the sword belt, and looked at the shield again. The belt was made for the old man's skinny hips. It would never do for him, no more than the hauberk would. He tied the scabbard to a length of hempen rope, knotted it around his waist, and drew the longsword.

The blade was straight and heavy, good castle-forged steel, the grip soft leather wrapped over wood, the pommel a smooth polished black stone. Plain as it was, the sword felt good in his hand, and Dunk knew how sharp it was, having worked it with whetstone and oilcloth many a night before they went to sleep. *It fits my grip as well as it ever fit his,* he thought to himself, *and there is a tourney at Ashford Meadow.*

Sweetfoot had an easier gait than old Chestnut, but Dunk was still sore and tired when he spied the inn ahead, a tall daub-and-timber building beside a stream. The warm yellow light spilling from its windows looked so inviting that he could not pass it by. *I have three silvers,* he told himself, *enough for a good meal and as much ale as I care to drink.*

As he dismounted, a naked boy emerged dripping from the stream and began to dry himself on a roughspun brown cloak. "Are you the stableboy?" Dunk asked him. The lad looked to be no more than eight or nine, a pasty-faced skinny thing, his bare feet caked in mud up to the ankle. His hair was the queerest thing about him. He had none. "I'll want my palfrey rubbed down. And oats for all three. Can you tend to them?"

The boy looked at him brazenly. "I could. If I wanted."

Dunk frowned. "I'll have none of that. I am a knight, I'll have you know."

"You don't look to be a knight."

"Do all knights look the same?"

"No, but they don't look like you, either. Your sword belt's made of rope."

"So long as it holds my scabbard, it serves. Now see to my horses. You'll get a copper if you do well, and a clout in the ear if you don't." He did not wait to see how the stableboy took that, but turned away and shouldered through the door.

At this hour, he would have expected the inn to be crowded, but the common room was almost empty. A young lordling in a fine damask mantle was passed out at one table, snoring softly into a pool of spilled wine. Otherwise there was no one. Dunk looked around uncertainly until a stout, short, whey-faced woman emerged from the kitchens and said, "Sit where you like. Is it ale you want, or food?"

"Both." Dunk took a chair by the window, well away from the sleeping man.

"There's good lamb, roasted with a crust of herbs, and some ducks my son shot down. Which will you have?"

He had not eaten at an inn in half a year or more. "Both."

The woman laughed. "Well, you're big enough for it." She drew a tankard of ale and brought it to his table. "Will you be wanting a room for the night as well?"

"No." Dunk would have liked nothing better than a soft straw mattress and a roof above his head, but he needed to be careful with his coin. The ground would serve. "Some food, some ale, and it's on to Ashford for me. How much farther is it?"

"A day's ride. Bear north when the road forks at the burned mill. Is my boy seeing to your horses, or has he run off again?"

"No, he's there," said Dunk. "You seem to have no custom."

"Half the town's gone to see the tourney. My own would as well, if I allowed it. They'll have this inn when I go, but the boy would sooner swagger about with soldiers, and the girl turns to sighs and giggles every time a knight rides by. I swear I couldn't tell you why. Knights are built the same as other men, and I never knew a joust to change the price of eggs." She eyed Dunk curiously; his sword and shield told her one thing, his rope belt and roughspun tunic quite another. "You're bound for the tourney yourself?"

He took a sip of the ale before he answered. A nut brown color it was, and thick on the tongue, the way he liked it. "Aye," he said. "I mean to be a champion."

"Do you, now?" the innkeep answered, polite enough.

Across the room, the lordling raised his head from the wine puddle. His face had a sallow, unhealthy cast to it beneath a rat's nest of sandy brown hair, and blond stubble crusted his chin. He rubbed his mouth, blinked at Dunk, and said, "I dreamed of you." His hand trembled as he pointed a finger. "You stay away from me, do you hear? You stay *well* away."

Dunk stared at him uncertainly. "My lord?"

The innkeep leaned close. "Never you mind that one, ser. All he does is drink and talk about his dreams. I'll see about that food." She bustled off.

"Food?" The lordling made the word an obscenity. He staggered to his feet, one hand on the table to keep himself from falling. "I'm going to be sick," he announced. The front of his tunic was crusty red with old wine stains. "I wanted a whore, but there's none to be found here. All gone to Ashford Meadow. Gods be good, I need some wine." He lurched unsteadily from the common room, and Dunk heard him climbing steps, singing under his breath.

A sad creature, thought Dunk. *But why did he think he knew me?* He pondered that a moment over his ale.

The lamb was as good as any he had ever eaten, and the duck was even better, cooked with cherries and lemons and not near as greasy as most. The innkeep brought buttered pease as well, and oaten bread still hot from her oven. *This is what it means to be a knight*, he told himself as he sucked the last bit of meat off the bone. *Good food, and ale whenever I want it, and no one to clout me in the head*. He had a second tankard of ale with the meal, a third to wash it down, and a fourth because there was no one to tell him he couldn't, and when he was done he paid the woman with a silver stag and still got back a fistful of coppers.

It was full dark by the time Dunk emerged. His stomach was full and his purse was a little lighter, but he felt good as he walked to the stables. Ahead, he heard a horse whicker. "Easy, lad," a boy's voice said. Dunk quickened his step, frowning.

He found the stableboy mounted on Thunder and wearing the old man's armor. The hauberk was longer than he was, and he'd had to tilt the helm back on his bald head or else it would have covered his eyes. He looked utterly intent, and utterly absurd. Dunk stopped in the stable door and laughed.

The boy looked up, flushed, vaulted to the ground. "My lord, I did not mean—"

"Thief," Dunk said, trying to sound stern. "Take off that armor, and be glad that Thunder didn't kick you in that fool head. He's a warhorse, not a boy's pony."

The boy took off the helm and flung it to the straw. "I could ride him as well as you," he said, bold as you please.

"Close your mouth, I want none of your insolence. The hauberk too, take it off. What did you think you were doing?"

"How can I tell you, with my mouth closed?" The boy squirmed out of the chain mail and let it fall.

"You can open your mouth to answer," said Dunk. "Now pick up that mail, shake off the dirt, and put it back where you found it. And the halfhelm too. Did you feed the horses, as I told you? And rub down Sweetfoot?"

"Yes," the boy said, as he shook straw from the mail. "You're going to Ashford, aren't you? Take me with you, ser."

The innkeep had warned him of this. "And what might your mother say to that?"

"My mother?" The boy wrinkled up his face. "My mother's dead, she wouldn't say anything."

He was surprised. Wasn't the innkeep his mother? Perhaps he was only 'prenticed to her. Dunk's head was a little fuzzy from the ale. "Are you an orphan boy?" he asked uncertainly.

"Are you?" the boy threw back.

"I was once," Dunk admitted. *Till the old man took me in.*

"If you took me, I could squire for you."

"I have no need of a squire," he said.

"Every knight needs a squire," the boy said. "You look as though you need one more than most."

Dunk raised a hand threateningly. "And you look as though you need a clout in the ear, it seems to me. Fill me a sack of oats. I'm off for Ashford . . . alone."

If the boy was frightened, he hid it well. For a moment he stood there defiant, his arms crossed, but just as Dunk was about to give up on him the lad turned and went for the oats.

Dunk was relieved. *A pity I couldn't . . . but he has a good life here at the inn, a better one than he'd have squiring for a hedge knight. Taking him would be no kindness.*

He could still feel the lad's disappointment, though. As he mounted Sweetfoot and took up Thunder's lead, Dunk decided that a copper penny might cheer him. "Here, lad, for your help." He flipped the coin down at him with a smile, but the stableboy made no attempt to catch it. It fell in the dirt between his bare feet, and there he let it lie.

He'll scoop it up as soon as I am gone, Dunk told himself. He turned the palfrey and rode from the inn, leading the other two horses. The trees were bright with moonlight, and the sky was cloudless and speckled with stars. Yet as he headed down the road he could feel the stableboy watching his back, sullen and silent.

The shadows of the afternoon were growing long when Dunk reined up on the edge of broad Ashford Meadow. Three score pavilions had already risen on the grassy field. Some were small, some large; some square, some round; some of sailcloth, some of linen, some of silk; but all were brightly colored, with long banners streaming from their center poles, brighter than a field of wildflowers with rich reds and sunny yellows, countless shades of green and blue, deep blacks and greys and purples.

The old man had ridden with some of these knights; others Dunk knew from tales told in common rooms and round campfires. Though he had never learned the magic of reading or writing, the old man had been relentless when it came to teaching him heraldry, often drilling him as they rode. The nightingales belonged to Lord Caron of the Marches, as skilled with the high harp as he was with a lance. The crowned stag was for Ser Lyonel Baratheon, the Laughing Storm. Dunk picked out the Tarly huntsman, House Dondarrion's purple lightning, the red apple of the Fossoways. There roared the lion of Lannister gold on crimson, and there the dark green sea turtle of the Estermonts swam across a pale green field. The brown tent beneath red stallion could only belong to Ser Otho Bracken, who was called the Brute of Bracken since slaying Lord Quentyn Blackwood three years past during a tourney at King's Landing. Dunk heard that Ser Otho struck so hard with the blunted longaxe that he stove in the visor of Lord Blackwood's helm and the face beneath it. He saw some Blackwood banners as well, on the west edge of the meadow, as distant from Ser Otho as they could be. Marbrand, Mallister, Cargyll, Westerling, Swann, Mullendore, Hightower, Florent, Frey, Penrose, Stokeworth, Darry, Parren, Wylde; it seemed as though every lordly house of the west and south had sent a knight or three to Ashford to see the fair maid and brave the lists in her honor.

Yet however fine their pavilions were to look upon, he knew there was no place there for him. A threadbare wool cloak would be all the shelter he had tonight. While the lords and great knights dined on capons and suckling pigs, Dunk's supper would be a hard, stringy piece of salt beef. He knew full well that if he made his camp upon that gaudy field, he would need to suffer both silent scorn and open mockery. A few perhaps would treat him kindly, yet in a way that was almost worse.

A hedge knight must hold tight to his pride. Without it, he was no more than a sellsword. *I must earn my place in that company. If I fight well, some lord may take me into his household. I will ride in noble company then, and eat fresh meat every night in a castle hall, and raise my own pavilion at tourneys. But first I must do well.* Reluctantly, he turned his back on the tourney grounds and led his horses into the trees.

On the outskirts of the great meadow a good half mile from town and castle he found a place where a bend in a brook had formed a deep pool. Reeds grew thick along its edge, and a tall leafy elm presided over all. The spring grass there was as green as any knight's banner and soft to the touch. It was a pretty spot, and no one had yet laid claim to it. *This will be my pavilion*, Dunk told himself, *a pavilion roofed with leaves, greener even than the banners of the Tyrells and the Estermonts.*

His horses came first. After they had been tended, he stripped and waded into the pool to wash away the dust of travel. "A true knight is cleanly as well as godly," the old man always said, insisting that they wash themselves head to heels every time the moon turned, whether they smelled sour or not. Now that he was a knight, Dunk vowed he would do the same.

He sat naked under the elm while he dried, enjoying the warmth of the spring air on his skin as he watched a dragonfly move lazily among the reeds. *Why would they name it a dragonfly?* he wondered. *It looks nothing like a dragon.* Not that Dunk had ever seen a dragon. The old man had, though. Dunk had heard the story half a hundred times, how Ser Arlan had been just a little boy when his grandfather had taken him to King's Landing, and how they'd seen the last dragon there the year before it died. She'd been a green female, small and stunted, her wings withered. None of her eggs had ever hatched. "Some say King Aegon poisoned her," the old man would tell. "The third Aegon that would be, not King Daeron's father, but the one they named Dragon-bane, or Aegon the Unlucky. He was afraid of dragons, for he'd seen his uncle's beast devour his own mother. The summers have been shorter since the last dragon died, and the winters longer and crueler."

The air began to cool as the sun dipped below the tops of the trees. When Dunk felt gooseflesh prickling his arms, he beat his tunic and breeches against the trunk of the elm to knock off the worst of the dirt, and donned them once again. On the morrow he could seek out the master of the games and enroll his name, but he had other matters he ought to look into tonight if he hoped to challenge.

He did not need to study his reflection in the water to know that he did not look much a knight, so he slung Ser Arlan's shield across his back to display the sigil. Hobbling the horses, Dunk left them to crop the thick green grass beneath the elm as he set out on foot for the tourney grounds.

In normal times the meadow served as a commons for the folk of Ashford town across the river, but now it was transformed. A second town had sprung up overnight, a town of silk instead of stone, larger and fairer than its elder sister. Dozens of merchants had erected their stalls along the edge of the field, selling felts and fruits, belts and boots, hides and hawks, earthenware, gemstones, pewterwork, spices, feathers, and all manner of other goods. Jugglers, puppeteers, and magicians wandered among the crowds plying their trades . . . as did the whores and cutpurses. Dunk kept a wary hand on his coin.

When he caught the smell of sausages sizzling over a smoky fire, his mouth began to water. He bought one with a copper from his pouch, and a horn of ale to wash it down. As he ate he watched a painted wooden knight battle a painted wooden dragon. The puppeteer who worked the dragon was good to watch too; a tall drink of water, with the olive skin and black hair of Dorne. She was slim as a lance with no breasts to speak of, but Dunk liked her face and the way her fingers made the dragon snap and slither at the end of its strings. He would have tossed the girl a copper if he'd had one to spare, but just now he needed every coin.

There were armorers among the merchants, as he had hoped. A Tyroshi with a forked blue beard was selling ornate helms, gorgeous fantastical things wrought in the shapes of birds and beasts and chased with gold and silver. Elsewhere he found a swordmaker hawking cheap steel blades, and another whose work was much finer, but it was not a sword he lacked.

The man he needed was all the way down at the end of the row, a shirt of fine chain mail and a pair of lobstered steel gauntlets displayed on the table before him. Dunk inspected them closely. "You do good work," he said.

"None better." A stumpy man, the smith was no more than five feet tall, yet wide as Dunk about the chest and arms. He had a black beard, huge hands, and no trace of humility.

"I need armor for the tourney," Dunk told him. "A suit of good mail, with gorget, greaves, and greathelm." The old man's halfhelm would fit his head, but he wanted more protection for his face than a nasal bar alone could provide.

The armorer looked him up and down. "You're a big one, but I've armored bigger." He came out from behind the table. "Kneel, I want to measure those shoulders. Aye, and that thick neck o' yours." Dunk knelt. The armorer laid a length of knotted rawhide along his shoulders, grunted, slipped it about his throat, grunted again. "Lift your arm. No, the right." He grunted a third time. "Now you can stand." The inside of a leg, the thickness of his calf, and the size of his waist elicited further grunts. "I have some pieces in me wagon that might do for you," the man said when he was done. "Nothing prettied up with gold nor silver, mind you, just good steel, strong and plain. I make helms that look like helms, not winged pigs and queer foreign fruits, but mine will serve you better if you take a lance in the face."

"That's all I want," said Dunk. "How much?"

"Eight hundred stags, for I'm feeling kindly."

"*Eight hundred?*" It was more than he had expected. "I . . . I could trade you some old armor, made for a smaller man . . . a halfhelm, a mail hauberk . . ."

"Steely Pate sells only his own work," the man declared, "but it might be I could make use of the metal. If it's not too rusted, I'll take it and armor you for six hundred."

Dunk could beseech Pate to give him the armor on trust, but he knew what sort of answer that request would likely get. He had traveled with the old man long enough to learn that merchants were notoriously mistrustful of hedge knights, some of whom were little better than robbers. "I'll give you two silvers now, and the armor and the rest of the coin on the morrow."

The armorer studied him a moment. "Two silvers buys you a day. After that, I sell me work to the next man."

Dunk scooped the stags out of his pouch and placed them in the armorer's callused hand. "You'll get it all. I mean to be a champion here."

"Do you?" Pate bit one of the coins. "And these others, I suppose they all came just to cheer you on?"

The moon was well up by the time he turned his steps back toward his elm. Behind him, Ashford Meadow was ablaze with torchlight. The sounds of song and laughter drifted across the grass, but his own mood was somber. He could think of only one way to raise the coin for his armor. And if he should be defeated . . . "One victory is all I need," he muttered aloud. "That's not so much to hope for."

Even so, the old man would never have hoped for it. Ser Arlan had not ridden a tilt since the day he had been unhorsed by the Prince of Dragonstone in a tourney at Storm's End, many years before. "It is not every man who can boast that he broke seven lances against the finest knight in the Seven Kingdoms," he would say. "I could never hope to do better, so why should I try?"

Dunk had suspected that Ser Arlan's age had more to do with it than the Prince of Dragonstone did, but he never dared say as much. The old man had his pride, even at the last. *I am quick and strong, he always said so, what was true for him need not be true for me,* he told himself stubbornly.

He was moving through a patch of weed, chewing over his chances in his head, when he saw the flicker of firelight through the bushes. *What is this?* Dunk did not stop to think. Suddenly his sword was in his hand and he was crashing through the grass.

He burst out roaring and cursing, only to jerk to a sudden halt at the sight of the boy beside the campfire. "You!" He lowered the sword. "What are you doing here?"

"Cooking a fish," said the bald boy. "Do you want some?"

"I meant, how did you *get* here? Did you steal a horse?"

"I rode in the back of a cart, with a man who was bringing some lambs to the castle for my lord of Ashford's table."

"Well, you'd best see if he's gone yet, or find another cart. I won't have you here."

"You can't make me go," the boy said, impertinent. "I'd had enough of that inn."

"I'll have no more insolence from you," Dunk warned. "I should throw you over my horse right now and take you home."

"You'd need to ride all the way to King's Landing," said the boy. "You'd miss the tourney."

King's Landing. For a moment Dunk wondered if he was being mocked, but the boy had no way of knowing that he had been born in King's Landing as well. *Another wretch from Flea Bottom, like as not, and who can blame him for wanting out of that place?*

He felt foolish standing there with sword in hand over an eight-year-old orphan. He sheathed it, glowering so the boy would see that he would suffer no nonsense. *I ought to give him a good beating at the least,* he thought, but the child looked so pitiful he could not bring himself to hit him. He glanced around the camp. The fire was burning merrily within a neat circle of rocks. The horses had been brushed, and clothes were hanging from the elm, drying above the flames. "What are those doing there?"

"I washed them," the boy said. "And I groomed the horses, made the fire, and caught this fish. I would have raised your pavilion, but I couldn't find one."

"There's my pavilion." Dunk swept a hand above his head, at the branches of the tall elm that loomed above them.

"That's a tree," the boy said, unimpressed.

"It's all the pavilion a true knight needs. I would sooner sleep under the stars than in some smoky tent."

"What if it rains?"

"The tree will shelter me."

"Trees leak."

Dunk laughed. "So they do. Well, if truth be told, I lack the coin for a pavilion. And you'd best turn that fish, or it will be burned on the bottom and raw on the top. You'd never make a kitchen boy."

"I would if I wanted," the boy said, but he turned the fish.

"What happened to your hair?" Dunk asked of him.

"The maesters shaved it off." Suddenly self-conscious, the boy pulled up the hood of his dark brown cloak, covering his head.

Dunk had heard that they did that sometimes, to treat lice or root-worms or certain sicknesses. "Are you ill?"

"No," said the boy. "What's your name?"

"Dunk," he said.

The wretched boy laughed aloud, as if that was the funniest thing he'd ever heard. "*Dunk?*" he said. "Ser Dunk? That's no name for a knight. Is it short for Duncan?"

Was it? The old man had called him just *Dunk* for as long as he could recall, and he did not remember much of his life before. "Duncan, yes," he said. "Ser Duncan of . . ." Dunk had no other name, nor any house; Ser Arlan had found him living wild in the stews and alleys of Flea Bottom. He had never known his father or mother. What was he to say? "Ser Duncan of Flea Bottom" did not sound very knightly. He could take Pennytree, but what if they asked him where it was? Dunk had never been to Pennytree, nor had the old man talked much about it. He frowned for a moment, and then blurted out, "Ser Duncan the Tall." He *was* tall, no one could dispute that, and it sounded puissant.

Though the little sneak did not seem to think so. "I have never heard of any Ser Duncan the Tall."

"Do you know every knight in the Seven Kingdoms, then?"

The boy looked at him boldly. "The good ones."

"I'm as good as any. After the tourney, they'll all know that. Do *you* have a name, thief?"

The boy hesitated. "Egg," he said.

Dunk did not laugh. *His head does look like an egg. Small boys can be cruel, and grown men as well.* "Egg," he said, "I should beat you bloody and send you on your way, but the truth is, I have no pavilion and I have no squire either. If you'll swear to do as you're told, I'll let you serve me for the tourney. After that, well, we'll see. If I decide you're worth your keep, you'll have clothes on your back and food in your belly. The clothes might be roughspun and the food salt beef and salt fish, and maybe some venison from time to time where there are no foresters about, but you won't go hungry. And I promise not to beat you except when you deserve it."

Egg smiled. "Yes, my lord."

"*Ser*," Dunk corrected. "I am only a hedge knight." He wondered if the old man was looking down on him. *I will teach him the arts of battle, the same as you taught me, ser. He seems a likely lad, might be one day he'll make a knight.*

The fish was still a little raw on the inside when they ate it, and the boy had not removed all the bones, but it still tasted a world better than hard salt beef.

Egg soon fell asleep beside the dying fire. Dunk lay on his back nearby, his big hands behind his head, gazing up at the night sky. He could hear distant music from the tourney grounds, half a mile away. The stars were everywhere, thousands and thousands of them. One fell as he was watching, a bright green streak that flashed across the black and then was gone.

A falling star brings luck to him who sees it, Dunk thought. *But the rest of them are all in their pavilions by now, staring up at silk instead of sky. So the luck is mine alone.*

In the morning, he woke to the sound of a cock crowing. Egg was still there, curled up beneath the old man's second-best cloak. *Well, the boy did not run off during the night, that's a start.* He prodded him awake with his foot. "Up. There's work to do." The boy rose quick enough, rubbing his eyes. "Help me saddle Sweetfoot," Dunk told him.

"What about breakfast?"

"There's salt beef. *After* we're done."

"I'd sooner eat the horse," Egg said. "Ser."

"You'll eat my fist if you don't do as you're told. Get the brushes. They're in the saddle sack. Yes, that one."

Together they brushed out the palfrey's sorrel coat, hefted Ser Arlan's best saddle over her back, and cinched it tight. Egg was a good worker once he put his mind to it, Dunk saw.

"I expect I'll be gone most of the day," he told the boy as he mounted. "You're to stay here and put the camp in order. Make sure no *other* thieves come nosing about."

"Can I have a sword to run them off with?" Egg asked. He had blue eyes, Dunk saw, very dark, almost purple. His bald head made them seem huge, somehow.

"No," said Dunk. "A knife's enough. And you had best be here when I come back, do you hear me? Rob me and run off and I'll hunt you down, I swear I will. With dogs."

"You don't have any dogs," Egg pointed out.

"I'll get some," said Dunk. "Just for you." He turned Sweetfoot's head toward the meadow and moved off at a brisk trot, hoping the threat would be enough to keep the boy honest. Save for the clothes on his back, the armor in his sack, and the horse beneath him, everything Dunk owned in the world was back at that camp. *I am a great fool to trust the boy so far, but it is no more than the old man did for me,* he reflected. *The Mother must have sent him to me so that I could pay my debt.*

As he crossed the field, he heard the ring of hammers from the riverside, where carpenters were nailing together jousting barriers and raising a lofty viewing stand. A few new pavilions were going up as well, while the knights who had come earlier slept off last night's revels or sat to break their fasts. Dunk could smell woodsmoke, and bacon as well.

To the north of the meadow flowed the river Cockleswent, a vassal stream to the mighty Mander. Beyond the shallow ford lay town and castle. Dunk had seen many a market town during his journeys with the old man. This was prettier than most; the whitewashed houses with their thatched roofs had an inviting aspect to them. When he was smaller, he used to wonder what it would be like to live in such a place; to sleep every night with a roof over your head, and wake every morning with the same walls wrapped around you. *It may be that soon I'll know. Aye, and Egg too.* It could happen. Stranger things happened every day.

Ashford Castle was a stone structure built in the shape of a triangle, with round towers rising thirty feet tall at each point and thick crenellated walls running between. Orange banners flew from its battlements, displaying the white sun-and-chevron sigil of its lord. Men-at-arms in orange-and-white livery stood outside the gates with halberds, watching people come and go, seemingly more intent on joking with a pretty milkmaid than in keeping anyone out. Dunk reined up in front of the short, bearded man he took for their captain and asked for the master of the games.

"It's Plummer you want, he's steward here. I'll show you."

Inside the yard, a stableboy took Sweetfoot for him. Dunk slung Ser Arlan's battered shield over a shoulder and followed the guards captain back of the stables to a turret built into an angle of the curtain wall. Steep stone steps led up to the wallwalk. "Come to enter your master's name for the lists?" the captain asked as they climbed.

"It's my own name I'll be putting in."

"Is it now?" Was the man smirking? Dunk was not certain. "That door there. I'll leave you to it and get back to my post."

When Dunk pushed open the door, the steward was sitting at a trestle table, scratching on a piece of parchment with a quill. He had thinning grey hair and a narrow pinched face. "Yes?" he said, looking up. "What do you want, man?"

Dunk pulled shut the door. "Are you Plummer the steward? I came for the tourney. To enter the lists."

Plummer pursed his lips. "My lord's tourney is a contest for knights. Are you a knight?"

He nodded, wondering if his ears were red.

"A knight with a name, mayhaps?"

"Dunk." Why had he said *that?* "Ser Duncan. The Tall."

"And where might you be from, Ser Duncan the Tall?"

"Everyplace. I was squire to Ser Arlan of Pennytree since I was five or six. This is his shield." He showed it to the steward. "He was coming to the tourney, but he caught a chill and died, so I came in his stead. He knighted me before he passed, with his own sword." Dunk drew the longsword and laid it on the scarred wooden table between them.

The master of the lists gave the blade no more than a glance. "A sword it is, for a certainty. I have never heard of this Arlan of Pennytree, however. You were his squire, you say?"

"He always said he meant for me to be a knight, as he was. When he was dying he called for his longsword and bade me kneel. He touched me once on my right shoulder and once on my left, and said some words, and when I got up he said I was a knight."

"Hmpf." The man Plummer rubbed his nose. "Any knight can make a knight, it is true, though it is more customary to stand a vigil and be anointed by a septon before taking your vows. Were there any witnesses to your dubbing?"

"Only a robin, up in a thorn tree. I heard it as the old man was saying the words. He charged me to be a good knight and true, to obey the seven gods, defend the weak and innocent, serve my lord faithfully and defend the realm with all my might, and I swore that I would."

"No doubt." Plummer did not deign to call him *ser*, Dunk could not help but notice. "I shall need to consult with Lord Ashford. Will you or your late master be known to any of the good knights here assembled?"

Dunk thought a moment. "There was a pavilion flying the banner of House Dondarrion? The black, with purple lightning?"

"That would be Ser Manfred, of that House."

"Ser Arlan served his lord father in Dorne, three years past. Ser Manfred might remember me."

"I would advise you to speak to him. If he will vouch for you, bring him here with you on the morrow, at this same time."

"As you say, m'lord." He started for the door.

"Ser Duncan," the steward called after him.

Dunk turned back.

"You are aware," the man said, "that those vanquished in tourney forfeit their arms, armor, and horse to the victors, and must needs ransom them back?"

"I know."

"And do you have the coin to pay such ransom?"

Now he *knew* his ears were red. "I won't have need of coin," he said, praying it was true. *All I need is one victory. If I win my first tilt, I'll have the loser's armor and horse, or his gold, and I can stand a loss myself.*

He walked slowly down the steps, reluctant to get on with what he must do next. In the yard, he collared one of the stableboys. "I must speak with Lord Ashford's master of horse."

"I'll find him for you."

It was cool and dim in the stables. An unruly grey stallion snapped at him as he passed, but Sweetfoot only whickered softly and nuzzled his hand when he raised it to her nose. "You're a good girl, aren't you?" he murmured. The old man always said that a knight should never love a horse, since more than a few were like to die under him, but he never heeded his own counsel either. Dunk had often seen him spend his last copper on an apple for old Chestnut or some oats for Sweetfoot and Thunder. The palfrey had been Ser Arlan's riding horse, and she had borne him tirelessly over thousands of miles, all up and down the Seven Kingdoms. Dunk felt as though he were betraying an old friend, but what choice did he have? Chestnut was too old to be worth much of anything, and Thunder must carry him in the lists.

Some time passed before the master of horse deigned to appear. As he waited, Dunk heard a blare of trumpets from the walls, and a voice in the yard. Curious, he led Sweetfoot to the stable door to see what was happening. A large party of knights and mounted archers poured through the gates, a hundred men at least, riding some of the most splendid horses that Dunk had ever seen. *Some great lord has come.* He grabbed the arm of a stableboy as he ran past. "Who are they?"

The boy looked at him queerly. "Can't you see the banners?" He wrenched free and hurried off.

The banners . . . As Dunk turned his head, a gust of wind lifted the black silk pennon atop the tall staff, and the fierce three-headed dragon of House Targaryen seemed to spread its wings, breathing scarlet fire. The banner-bearer was a tall knight in white scale armor chased with gold, a pure white cloak streaming from his shoulders. Two of the other riders were armored in white from head to heel as well. *Kingsguard knights with the royal banner.* Small wonder Lord Ashford and his sons came hurrying out the doors of the keep, and the fair maid too, a short girl with yellow hair and a round pink face. *She does not seem so fair to me*, Dunk thought. The puppet girl was prettier.

"Boy, let go of that nag and see to my horse."

A rider had dismounted in front of the stables. *He is talking to me*, Dunk realized. "I am not a stableboy, m'lord."

"Not clever enough?" The speaker wore a black cloak bordered in scarlet satin, but underneath was raiment bright as flame, all reds and yellows and golds. Slim and straight as a dirk, though only of middling height, he was near Dunk's own age. Curls of silver-gold hair framed a face sculpted and imperious; high brow and sharp cheekbones, straight nose, pale smooth skin without blemish. His eyes were a deep violet color. "If you cannot manage a horse, fetch me some wine and a pretty wench."

"I . . . m'lord, pardons, I'm no serving man either. I have the honor to be a knight."

"Knighthood has fallen on sad days," said the princeling, but then one of the stableboys came rushing up, and he turned away to hand him the reins of his palfrey, a splendid blood bay. Dunk was forgotten in an instant. Relieved, he slunk back inside the stables to wait for the master of horse. He felt ill-at-ease enough around the lords in their pavilions, he had no business speaking to princes.

That the beautiful stripling was a prince he had no doubt. The Targaryens were the blood of lost Valyria across the seas, and their silvergold hair and violet eyes set them apart from common men. Dunk knew Prince Baelor was older, but the youth might well have been one of his sons: Valarr, who was often called "the Young Prince" to set him apart from his father, or Matarys, "the Even Younger Prince," as old Lord Swann's fool had named him once. There were other princelings as well, cousins to Valarr and Matarys. Good King Daeron had four grown sons, three with sons of their own. The line of the dragonkings had almost died out during his father's day, but it was commonly said that Daeron II and his sons had left it secure for all time.

"You. Man. You asked for me." Lord Ashford's master of horse had a red face made redder by his orange livery, and a brusque manner of speaking. "What is it? I have no time for—"

"I want to sell this palfrey," Dunk broke in quickly, before the man could dismiss him. "She's a good horse, sure of foot—"

"I have no time, I tell you." The man gave Sweetfoot no more than a glance. "My lord of Ashford has no need of such. Take her to the town, perhaps Henly will give you a silver or three." That quick, he was turning away.

"Thank you, m'lord," Dunk said before he could go. "M'lord, has the king come?"

The master of horse laughed at him. "No, thank the gods. This infestation of princes is trial enough. Where am I going to find the stalls for all these animals? And fodder?" He strode off shouting at his stableboys.

By the time Dunk left the stable, Lord Ashford had escorted his princely guests into the hall, but two of the Kingsguard knights in their white armor and snowy cloaks still lingered in the yard, talking with the captain of the guard. Dunk halted before them. "M'lords, I am Ser Duncan the Tall."

"Well met, Ser Duncan," answered the bigger of the white knights. "I am Ser Roland Crakehall, and this is my Sworn Brother, Ser Donnel of Duskendale."

The seven champions of the Kingsguard were the most puissant warriors in all the Seven Kingdoms, saving only perhaps the crown prince, Baelor Breakspear himself. "Have you come to enter the lists?" Dunk asked anxiously.

"It would not be fitting for us to ride against those we are sworn to protect," answered Ser Donnel, red of hair and beard.

"Prince Valarr has the honor to be one of Lady Ashford's champions," explained Ser Roland, "and two of his cousins mean to challenge. The rest of us have come only to watch."

Relieved, Dunk thanked the white knights for their kindness, and rode out through the castle gates before another prince should think to accost him. *Three princelings*, he pondered as he turned the palfrey toward the streets of Ashford town. Valarr was the eldest son of Prince Baelor, second in line to the Iron Throne, but Dunk did not know how much of his father's fabled prowess with lance and sword he might have inherited. About the other Targaryen princes he knew even less. *What will I do if I have to ride against a prince? Will I even be allowed to challenge one so highborn?* He did not know the answer. The old man had often said he was thick as a castle wall, and just now he felt it.

Henly liked the look of Sweetfoot well enough until he heard Dunk wanted to sell her. Then all the stableman could see in her were faults. He offered three hundred silvers. Dunk said he must have three thousand. After much arguing and cursing, they settled at seven hundred fifty silver stags. That was a deal closer to Henly's starting price than to Dunk's, which made him feel the loser in the tilt, but the stableman would go no higher, so in the end he had no choice but to yield. A second argument began when Dunk declared that the price did not include the saddle, and Henly insisted that it had.

Finally it was all settled. As Henly left to fetch his coin, Dunk stroked Sweetfoot's mane and told her to be brave. "If I win, I'll come back and buy you again, I promise." He had no doubt that all the palfrey's flaws would vanish in the intervening days, and she would be worth twice what she was today.

The stableman gave him three gold pieces and the rest in silver. Dunk bit one of the gold coins and smiled. He had never tasted gold before, nor handled it. "Dragons," men called the coins, since they were stamped with the three-headed dragon of House Targaryen on one side. The other bore the likeness of the king. Two of the coins Henly gave him had King Daeron's face; the third was older, well worn, and showed a different man. His name was there under his head, but Dunk could not read the letters. Gold had been shaved off its edges too, he saw. He pointed this out to Henly, and loudly. The stableman grumbled, but handed over another few silvers and a fistful of coppers to make up the weight. Dunk handed a few of the coppers right back, and nodded at Sweetfoot. "That's for her," he said. "See that she has some oats tonight. Aye, and an apple too."

With the shield on his arm and the sack of old armor slung over his shoulder, Dunk set out on foot through the sunny streets of Ashford town. The heft of all that coin in his pouch made him feel queer; almost giddy on one hand, and anxious on the other. The old man had never trusted him with more than a coin or two at a time. He could live a year on this much money. *And what will I do when it's gone, sell Thunder?* That road ended in beggary or outlawry. *This chance will never come again, I must risk all.*

By the time he splashed back across the ford to the south bank of the Cockleswent, the morning was almost done and the tourney grounds had come to life once more. The winesellers and sausage makers were doing a brisk trade, a dancing bear was shuffling along to his master's playing as a singer sang "The Bear, the Bear, and the Maiden Fair," jugglers were juggling, and the puppeteers were just finishing another fight.

Dunk stopped to watch the wooden dragon slain. When the puppet knight cut its head off and the red sawdust spilled out onto the grass, he laughed aloud and threw the girl two coppers. "One for last night," he called. She caught the coins in the air and threw him back a smile as sweet as any he had ever seen.

Is it me she smiles at, or the coins? Dunk had never been with a girl, and they made him nervous. Once, three years past, when the old man's purse was full after half a year in the service of blind Lord

Florent, he'd told Dunk the time had come to take him to a brothel and make him a man. He'd been drunk, though, and when he was sober he did not remember. Dunk had been too embarrassed to remind him. He was not certain he wanted a whore anyway. If he could not have a highborn maiden like a proper knight, he wanted one who at least liked him more than his silver.

"Will you drink a horn of ale?" he asked the puppet girl as she was scooping the sawdust blood back into her dragon. "With me, I mean? Or a sausage? I had a sausage last night, and it was good. They're made with pork, I think."

"I thank you, m'lord, but we have another show." The girl rose, and ran off to the fierce fat Dornishwoman who worked the puppet knight while Dunk stood there feeling stupid. He liked the way she ran, though. *A pretty girl, and tall. I would not have to kneel to kiss that one.* He knew how to kiss. A tavern girl had showed him one night in Lannisport, a year ago, but she'd been so short she had to sit on the table to reach his lips. The memory made his ears burn. What a great fool he was. It was jousting he should be thinking about, not kissing.

Lord Ashford's carpenters were whitewashing the waist-high wooden barriers that would separate the jousters. Dunk watched them work awhile. There were five lanes, arrayed north to south so none of the competitors would ride with the sun in his eyes. A three-tiered viewing stand had been raised on the eastern side of the lists, with an orange canopy to shield the lords and ladies from rain and sun. Most would sit on benches, but four high-backed chairs had been erected in the center of the platform, for Lord Ashford, the fair maid, and the visiting princes.

On the eastern verge of the meadow, a quintain had been set up and a dozen knights were tilting at it, sending the pole arm spinning every time they struck the splintered shield suspended from one end. Dunk watched the Brute of Bracken take his turn, and then Lord Caron of the Marches. *I do not have as good a seat as any of them,* he thought uneasily.

Elsewhere, men were training afoot, going at each other with wooden swords while their squires stood shouting ribald advice. Dunk watched a stocky youth try to hold off a muscular knight who seemed lithe and quick as a mountain cat. Both had the red apple of the Fossoways painted on their shields, but the younger man's was soon hacked and chipped to pieces. "Here's an apple that's not ripe yet," the older said as he slammed the other's helm. The younger Fossoway was bruised and bloody by the time he yielded, but his foe was hardly winded. He raised his visor, looked about, saw Dunk, and said, "You there. Yes, you, the big one. Knight of the winged chalice. Is that a longsword you wear?"

"It is mine by rights," Dunk said defensively. "I am Ser Duncan the Tall."

"And I Ser Steffon Fossoway. Would you care me try me, Ser Duncan the Tall? It would be good to have someone new to cross swords with. My cousin's not ripe yet, as you've seen."

"Do it, Ser Duncan," urged the beaten Fossoway as he removed his helm. "I may not be ripe, but my good cousin is rotten to the core. Knock the seeds out of him."

Dunk shook his head. Why were these lordlings involving him in their quarrel? He wanted no part of it. "I thank you, ser, but I have matters to attend." He was uncomfortable carrying so much coin. The sooner he paid Steely Pate and got his armor, the happier he would be.

Ser Steffon looked at him scornfully. "The hedge knight has matters." He glanced about and found another likely opponent loitering nearby. "Ser Grance, well met. Come try me. I know every feeble trick my cousin Raymun has mastered, and it seems that Ser Duncan needs to return to the hedges. Come, come."

Dunk stalked away red-faced. He did not have many tricks himself, feeble or otherwise, and he did not want anyone to see him fight until the tourney. The old man always said that the better you knew your foe, the easier it was to best him. Knights like Ser Steffon had sharp eyes to find a man's weakness at a glance. Dunk was strong and quick, and his weight and reach were in his favor, but he did not believe for a moment that his skills were the equal of these others. Ser Arlan had taught him as best he could, but the old man had never been the greatest of knights even when young. Great knights did not live their lives in the hedges, or die by the side of a muddy road. *That will not happen to me*, Dunk vowed. *I will show them that I can be more than a hedge knight.*

"Ser Duncan." The younger Fossoway hurried to catch him. "I should not have urged you to try my cousin. I was angry with his arrogance, and you are so large, I thought . . . well, it was wrong of me. You wear no armor. He would have broken your hand if he could, or a knee. He likes to batter men in the training yard, so they will be bruised and vulnerable later, should he meet them in the lists."

"He did not break you."

"No, but I am his own blood, though his is the senior branch of the apple tree, as he never ceases to remind me. I am Raymun Fossoway."

"Well met. Will you and your cousin ride in the tourney?"

"He will, for a certainty. As to me, would that I could. I am only a squire as yet. My cousin has promised to knight me, but insists that I am not ripe yet." Raymun had a square face, a pug nose, and short woolly hair, but his smile was engaging. "You have the look of a challenger, it seems to me. Whose shield do you mean to strike?"

"It makes no difference," said Dunk. That was what you were supposed to say, though it made all the difference in the world. "I will not enter the lists until the third day."

"And by then some of the champions will have fallen, yes," Raymun said. "Well, may the Warrior smile on you, ser."

"And you." *If he is only a squire, what business do I have being a knight? One of us is a fool.* The silver in Dunk's pouch clinked with every step, but he could lose it all in a heartbeat, he knew. Even the rules of this tourney worked against him, making it very unlikely that he would face a green or feeble foe.

There were a dozen different forms a tourney might follow, according to the whim of the lord who hosted it. Some were mock battles between teams of knights, others wild melees where the glory went to the last fighter left standing. Where individual combats were the rule, pairings were sometimes determined by lot, and sometimes by the master of the games.

Lord Ashford was staging this tourney to celebrate his daughter's thirteenth nameday. The fair maid would sit by her father's side as the reigning Queen of Love and Beauty. Five champions wearing her favors would defend her. All others must perforce be challengers, but any man who could defeat one of the champions would take his place and stand as a champion himself, until such time as another challenger unseated him. At the end of three days of jousting, the five who remained would determine whether the fair maid would retain the crown of Love and Beauty, or whether another would wear it in her place.

Dunk stared at the grassy lists and the empty chairs on the viewing stand and pondered his chances. One victory was all he needed; then he could name himself one of the champions of Ashford Meadow, if only for an hour. The old man had lived nigh on sixty years and had never been a champion. *It is not too much to hope for, if the gods are good.* He thought back on all the songs he had heard, songs of blind Symeon Star-Eyes and noble Serwyn of the Mirror Shield, of Prince Aemon the Dragonknight, Ser Ryam Redwyne, and Florian the Fool. They had all won victories against foes far more terrible than any he would face. *But they were great heroes, brave men of noble birth, except for Florian. And what am I? Dunk of Flea Bottom? Or Ser Duncan the Tall?*

He supposed he would learn the truth of that soon enough. He hefted the sack of armor and turned his feet toward the merchants' stalls, in search of Steely Pate.

Egg had worked manfully at the campsite. Dunk was pleased; he had been half afraid his squire would run off again. "Did you get a good price for your palfrey?" the boy asked.

"How did you know I'd sold her?"

"You rode off and walked back, and if robbers had stolen her you'd be more angry than you are."

"I got enough for this." Dunk took out his new armor to show the boy. "If you're ever to be a knight, you'll need to know good steel from bad. Look here, this is fine work. This mail is double-chain, each link bound to two others, see? It gives more protection than single-chain. And the helm, Pate's rounded the top, see how it curves? A sword or an axe will slide off, where they might bite through a flat-topped helm." Dunk lowered the greathelm over his head. "How does it look?"

"There's no visor," Egg pointed out.

"There's air holes. Visors are points of weakness." Steely Pate had said as much. "If you knew how many knights have taken an arrow in the eye as they lifted their visor for a suck o' cool air, you'd never want one," he'd told Dunk.

"There's no crest either," said Egg. "It's just plain."

Dunk lifted off the helm. "Plain is fine for the likes of me. See how bright the steel is? It will be your task to keep it that way. You know how to scour mail?"

"In a barrel of sand," said the boy, "but you don't have a barrel. Did you buy a pavilion too, ser?"

"I didn't get *that* good a price." *The boy is too bold for his own good, I ought to beat that out of him.* He knew he would not, though. He liked the boldness. He needed to be bolder himself. *My squire is braver than I am, and more clever.* "You did well here, Egg," Dunk told him. "On the morrow, you'll come with me. Have a look at the tourney grounds. We'll buy oats for the horses and fresh bread for ourselves. Maybe a bit of cheese as well, they were selling good cheese at one of the stalls."

"I won't need to go into the castle, will I?"

"Why not? One day, I mean to live in a castle. I hope to win a place above the salt before I'm done."

The boy said nothing. *Perhaps he fears to enter a lord's hall*, Dunk reflected. *That's no more than might be expected. He will grow out of it in time.* He went back to admiring his armor, and wondering how long he would wear it.

Ser Manfred was a thin man with a sour look on his face. He wore a black surcoat slashed with the purple lightning of House Dondarrion, but Dunk would have remembered him anyway by his unruly mane of red-gold hair. "Ser Arlan served your lord father when he and Lord Caron burned the Vulture King out of the Red Mountains, ser," he said from one knee. "I was only a boy then, but I squired for him. Ser Arlan of Pennytree."

Ser Manfred scowled. "No. I know him not. Nor you, boy."

Dunk showed him the old man's shield. "This was his sigil, the winged chalice."

"My lord father took eight hundred knights and near four thousand foot into the mountains. I cannot be expected to remember every one of them, nor what shields they carried. It may be that you were with us, but . . ." Ser Manfred shrugged.

Dunk was struck speechless for an instant. *The old man took a wound in your father's service, how can you have forgotten him?* "They will not allow me to challenge unless some knight or lord will vouch for me."

"And what is that to me?" said Ser Manfred. "I have given you enough of my time, ser."

If he went back to the castle without Ser Manfred, he was lost. Dunk eyed the purple lightning embroidered across the black wool of Ser Manfred's surcoat and said, "I remember your father telling the camp how your house got its sigil. One stormy night, as the first of your line bore a message across the Dornish Marches, an arrow killed his horse beneath him and spilled him on the ground. Two Dornishmen came out of the darkness in ring mail and crested helms. His sword had broken beneath him when he fell. When he saw that, he thought he was doomed. But as the Dornishmen closed to cut him down, lightning cracked from the sky. It was a bright burning purple, and it split, striking the Dornishmen in their steel and killing them both where they stood. The message gave the Storm King victory over the Dornish, and in thanks he raised the messenger to lordship. He was the first Lord Dondarrion, so he took for his arms a forked purple lightning bolt, on a black field powdered with stars."

If Dunk thought the tale would impress Ser Manfred, he could not have been more wrong. "Every pot boy and groom who has ever served my father hears that story soon or late. Knowing it does not make you a knight. Begone with you, ser."

It was with a leaden heart that Dunk returned to Ashford Castle, wondering what he might say so that Plummer would grant him the right of challenge. The steward was not in his turret chamber, however. A guard told him he might be found in the Great Hall. "Shall I wait here?" Dunk asked. "How long will he be?"

"How should I know? Do what you please."

The Great Hall was not so great, as halls went, but Ashford was a small castle. Dunk entered through a side door, and spied the steward at once. He was standing with Lord Ashford and a dozen other men at the top of the hall. He walked toward them, beneath a wall hung with wool tapestries of fruits and flowers.

"—more concerned if they were *your* sons, I'll wager," an angry man was saying as Dunk approached. His straight hair and square-cut beard were so fair they seemed white in the dimness of the hall, but as he got closer he saw that they were in truth a pale silvery color touched with gold.

"Daeron has done this before," another replied. Plummer was standing so as to block Dunk's view of the speaker. "You should never have commanded him to enter the lists. He belongs on a tourney field no more than Aerys does, or Rhaegel."

"By which you mean he'd sooner ride a whore than a horse," the first man said. Thickly built and powerful, the prince—he was surely a prince—wore a leather brigandine covered with silver studs beneath a heavy black cloak trimmed with ermine. Pox scars marked his cheeks, only partly concealed by his silvery beard. "I do not need to be reminded of my son's failings, brother. He has only eighteen years. He can change. He *will* change, gods be damned, or I swear I'll see him dead."

"Don't be an utter fool. Daeron is what he is, but he is still your blood and mine. I have no doubt Ser Roland will turn him up, and Aegon with him."

"When the tourney is over, perhaps."

"Aerion is here. He is a better lance than Daeron in any case, if it is the tourney that concerns you." Dunk could see the speaker now. He was seated in the high seat, a sheaf of parchments in one hand, Lord Ashford hovering at his shoulder. Even seated, he looked to be a head taller than the other, to judge from the long straight legs stretched out before him. His short-cropped hair was dark and peppered with grey, his strong jaw clean-shaven. His nose looked as though it had been broken more than once. Though he was dressed very plainly, in green doublet, brown mantle, and scuffed boots, there was a weight to him, a sense of power and certainty.

It came to Dunk that he had walked in on something that he ought never have heard. *I had best go and come back later, when they are done,* he decided. But it was already too late. The prince with the silvery beard suddenly took note of him. "Who are you, and what do you mean by bursting in on us?" he demanded harshly.

"He is the knight that our good steward was expecting," the seated man said, smiling at Dunk in a way that suggested he had been aware of him all the time. "You and I are the intruders here, brother. Come closer, ser."

Dunk edged forward, uncertain what was expected of him. He looked at Plummer, but got no help there. The pinch-faced steward who had been so forceful yesterday now stood silent, studying the stones of the floor. "My lords," he said, "I asked Ser Manfred Dondarrion to vouch for me so I might enter the lists, but he refuses. He says he knows me not. Ser Arlan served him, though, I swear it. I have his sword and shield, I—"

"A shield and a sword do not make a knight," declared Lord Ashford, a big bald man with a round red face. "Plummer has spoken to me of you. Even if we accept that these arms belonged to this Ser Arlan of Pennytree, it may well be that you found him dead and stole them. Unless you have some better proof of what you say, some writing or—"

"I remember Ser Arlan of Pennytree," the man in the high seat said quietly. "He never won a tourney that I know, but he never shamed himself either. At King's Landing sixteen years ago, he overthrew Lord Stokeworth and the Bastard of Harrenhal in the melee, and many years before at Lannisport he unhorsed the Grey Lion himself. The lion was not so grey then, to be sure."

"He told me about that, many a time," said Dunk.

The tall man studied him. "Then you will remember the Grey Lion's true name, I have no doubt."

For a moment there was nothing in Dunk's head at all. *A thousand times the old man had told that tale, a thousand times, the lion, the lion, his name, his name, his name . . .* He was near despair when suddenly it came. "Ser Damon Lannister!" he shouted. "The Grey Lion! He's Lord of Casterly Rock now."

"So he is," said the tall man pleasantly, "and he enters the lists on the morrow." He rattled the sheaf of papers in his hand.

"How can you possibly remember some insignificant hedge knight who chanced to unhorse Damon Lannister sixteen years ago?" said the prince with the silver beard, frowning.

"I make it a practice to learn all I can of my foes."

"Why would you deign to joust with a hedge knight?"

"It was nine years past, at Storm's End. Lord Baratheon held a hastilude to celebrate the birth of a grandson. The lots made Ser Arlan my opponent in the first tilt. We broke four lances before I finally unhorsed him."

"*Seven,*" insisted Dunk, "and that was against the Prince of Dragonstone!" No sooner were the words out than he wanted them back. *Dunk the lunk, thick as a castle wall,* he could hear the old man chiding.

"So it was." The prince with the broken nose smiled gently. "Tales grow in the telling, I know. Do not think ill of your old master, but it was four lances only, I fear."

Dunk was grateful that the hall was dim; he knew his ears were red. "My lord." *No, that's wrong too.* "Your Grace." He fell to his knees and lowered his head. "As you say, four, I meant no . . . I never . . . The old man, Ser Arlan, he used to say I was thick as a castle wall and slow as an aurochs."

"And strong as an aurochs, by the look of you," said Baelor Breakspear. "No harm was done, ser. Rise."

Dunk got to his feet, wondering if he should keep his head down or if he was allowed to look a prince in the face. *I am speaking with Baelor Targaryen, Prince of Dragonstone, Hand of the King, and heir apparent to the Iron Throne of Aegon the Conqueror.* What could a hedge knight dare say to such a person? "Y-you gave him back his horse and armor and took no ransom, I remember," he stammered. "The old—Ser Arlan, he told me you were the soul of chivalry, and that one day the Seven Kingdoms would be safe in your hands."

"Not for many a year still, I pray," Prince Baelor said.

"No," said Dunk, horrified. He almost said, *I didn't mean that the king should die*, but stopped himself in time. "I am sorry, m'lord. Your Grace, I mean."

Belatedly he recalled that the stocky man with the silver beard had addressed Prince Baelor as brother. *He is blood of the dragon as well, damn me for a fool.* He could only be Prince Maekar, the youngest of King Daeron's four sons. Prince Aerys was bookish and Prince Rhaegel mad, meek, and sickly. Neither was like to cross half the realm to attend a tourney, but Maekar was said to be a redoubtable warrior in his own right, though ever in the shadow of his eldest brother.

"You wish to enter the lists, is that it?" asked Prince Baelor. "That decision rests with the master of the games, but I see no reason to deny you."

The steward inclined his head. "As you say, my lord."

Dunk tried to stammer out thanks, but Prince Maekar cut him off. "Very well, ser, you are grateful. Now be off with you."

"You must forgive my noble brother, ser," said Prince Baelor. "Two of his sons have gone astray on their way here, and he fears for them."

"The spring rains have swollen many of the streams," said Dunk. "Perhaps the princes are only delayed."

"I did not come here to take counsel from a hedge knight," Prince Maekar declared to his brother.

"You may go, ser," Prince Baelor told Dunk, not unkindly.

"Yes, my lord." He bowed and turned.

But before he could get away, the prince called after him. "Ser. One thing more. You are not of Ser Arlan's blood?"

"Yes, m'lord. I mean, no. I'm not."

The prince nodded at the battered shield Dunk carried, and the winged chalice upon its face. "By law, only a trueborn son is entitled to inherit a knight's arms. You must needs find a new device, ser, a sigil of your own."

"I will," said Dunk. "Thank you again, Your Grace. I will fight bravely, you'll see." *As brave as Baelor Breakspear*, the old man would often say.

The winesellers and sausage makers were doing a brisk trade, and whores walked brazenly among the stalls and pavilions. Some were pretty enough, one red-haired girl in particular. He could not help staring at her breasts, the way they moved under her loose shift as she sauntered past. He thought of the silver in his pouch. *I could have her, if I liked. She'd like the clink of my coin well enough, I could take her back to my camp and have her, all night if I wanted.* He had never lain with a woman, and for all he knew he might die in his first tilt. Tourneys could be dangerous . . . but whores could be dangerous too, the old man had warned him of that. *She might rob me while I slept, and what would I do then?* When the red-haired girl glanced back over her shoulder at him, Dunk shook his head and walked away.

He found Egg at the puppet show, sitting cross-legged on the ground with the hood of his cloak pulled all the way forward to hide his baldness. The boy had been afraid to enter the castle, which Dunk put down to equal parts shyness and shame. *He does not think himself worthy to mingle with lords and ladies, let alone great princes.* It had been the same with him when he was little. The world beyond Flea Bottom had seemed as frightening as it was exciting. *Egg needs time, that's all.* For the present, it seemed kinder to give the lad a few coppers and let him enjoy himself among the stalls than to drag him along unwilling into the castle.

This morning the puppeteers were doing the tale of Florian and Jonquil. The fat Dornishwoman was working Florian in his armor made of motley, while the tall girl held Jonquil's strings. "You are no knight," she was saying as the puppet's mouth moved up and down. "I know you. You are Florian the Fool."

"I am, my lady," the other puppet answered, kneeling. "As great a fool as ever lived, and as great a knight as well."

"A fool *and* a knight?" said Jonquil. "I have never heard of such a thing."

"Sweet lady," said Florian, "all men are fools, and all men are knights, where women are concerned."

It was a good show, sad and sweet both, with a sprightly swordfight at the end, and a nicely painted giant. When it was over, the fat woman went among the crowd to collect coins while the girl packed away the puppets.

Dunk collected Egg and went up to her.

"M'lord?" she said, with a sideways glance and a half-smile. She was a head shorter than he was, but still taller than any other girl he had ever seen.

"That was good," Egg enthused. "I like how you make them move, Jonquil and the dragon and all. I saw a puppet show last year, but they moved all jerky. Yours are more smooth."

"Thank you," she told the boy politely.

Dunk said, "Your figures are well carved too. The dragon, especially. A fearsome beast. You make them yourself?"

She nodded. "My uncle does the carving. I paint them."

"Could you paint something for me? I have the coin to pay." He slipped the shield off his shoulder and turned it to show her. "I need to paint something over the chalice."

The girl glanced at the shield, and then at him. "What would you want painted?"

Dunk had not considered that. If not the old man's winged chalice, what? His head was empty. *Dunk the lunk, thick as a castle wall.* "I don't . . . I'm not certain." His ears were turning red, he realized miserably. "You must think me an utter fool."

She smiled. "All men are fools, and all men are knights."

"What color paint do you have?" he asked, hoping that might give him an idea.

"I can mix paints to make any color you want."

The old man's brown had always seemed drab to Dunk. "The field should be the color of sunset," he said suddenly. "The old man liked sunsets. And the device . . ."

"An elm tree," said Egg. "A big elm tree, like the one by the pool, with a brown trunk and green branches."

"Yes," Dunk said. "That would serve. An elm tree . . . but with a shooting star above. Could you do that?"

The girl nodded. "Give me the shield. I'll paint it this very night, and have it back to you on the morrow."

Dunk handed it over. "I am called Ser Duncan the Tall."

"I'm Tanselle," she laughed. "Tanselle Too-Tall, the boys used to call me."

"You're not too tall," Dunk blurted out. "You're just right for . . ." He realized what he had been about to say, and blushed furiously.

"For?" said Tanselle, cocking her head inquisitively.

"Puppets," he finished lamely.

The first day of the tourney dawned bright and clear. Dunk bought a sackful of foodstuffs, so they were able to break their fast on goose eggs, fried bread, and bacon, but when the food was cooked he found he had no appetite. His belly felt hard as a rock, even though he knew he would not ride today. The right of first challenge would go to knights of higher birth and greater renown, to lords and their sons and champions from other tourneys.

Egg chattered all though their breakfast, talking of this man and that man and how they might fare. *He was not japing me when he said he knew every good knight in the Seven Kingdoms*, Dunk thought ruefully. He found it humbling to listen so intently to the words of a scrawny orphan boy, but Egg's knowledge might serve him should he face one of these men in a tilt.

The meadow was a churning mass of people, all trying to elbow their way closer for a better view. Dunk was as good an elbower as any, and bigger than most. He squirmed forward to a rise six yards from the fence. When Egg complained that all he could see were arses, Dunk sat the boy on his shoulders. Across the field, the viewing stand was filling up with highborn lords and ladies, a few rich townfolk, and a score of knights who had decided not to compete today. Of Prince Maekar he saw no sign, but he recognized Prince Baelor at Lord Ashford's side. Sunlight flashed golden off the shoulder clasp that held his cloak and the slim coronet about his temples, but otherwise he dressed far more simply than most of the other lords. *He does not look a Targaryen in truth, with that dark hair.* Dunk said as much to Egg.

"It's said he favors his mother," the boy reminded him. "She was a Dornish princess."

The five champions had raised their pavilions at the north end of the lists with the river behind them. The smallest two were orange, and the shields hung outside their doors displayed the white sun-and-chevron. Those would be Lord Ashford's sons Androw and Robert, brothers to the fair maid. Dunk had never heard other knights speak of their prowess, which meant they would likely be the first to fall.

Beside the orange pavilions stood one of deep-dyed green, much larger. The golden rose of Highgarden flapped above it, and the same device was emblazoned on the great green shield outside the door. "That's Leo Tyrell, Lord of Highgarden," said Egg.

"I knew that," said Dunk, irritated. "The old man and I served at Highgarden before you were ever born." He hardly remembered that year himself, but Ser Arlan had often spoken of Leo Longthorn, as he was sometimes called; a peerless jouster, for all the silver in his hair. "That must be Lord Leo beside the tent, the slender greybeard in green and gold."

"Yes," said Egg. "I saw him at King's Landing once. He's not one you'll want to challenge, ser."

"Boy, I do not require your counsel on who to challenge."

The fourth pavilion was sewn together from diamond-shaped pieces of cloth, alternating red and white. Dunk did not know the colors, but Egg said they belonged to a knight from the Vale of Arryn named Ser Humfrey Hardyng. "He won a great melee at Maidenpool last year, ser, and overthrew Ser Donnel of Duskendale and the Lords Arryn and Royce in the lists."

The last pavilion was Prince Valarr's. Of black silk it was, with a line of pointed scarlet pennons hanging from its roof like long red flames. The shield on its stand was glossy black, emblazoned with the three-headed dragon of House Targaryen. One of the Kingsguard

knights stood beside it, his shining white armor stark against the black
of the tentcloth. Seeing him there, Dunk wondered whether any of the
challengers would dare to touch the dragon shield. Valarr was the
king's grandson, after all, and son to Baelor Breakspear.

He need not have worried. When the horns blew to summon the
challengers, all five of the maid's champions were called forth to defend
her. Dunk could hear the murmur of excitement in the crowd as the
challengers appeared one by one at the south end of the lists. Heralds
boomed out the name of each knight in turn. They paused before the
viewing stand to dip their lances in salute to Lord Ashford, Prince
Baelor, and the fair maid, then circled to the north end of the field to
select their opponents. The Grey Lion of Casterly Rock struck the
shield of Lord Tyrell, while his golden-haired heir Ser Tybolt Lannister
challenged Lord Ashford's eldest son. Lord Tully of Riverrun tapped
the diamond-patterned shield of Ser Humfrey Hardyng, Ser Abelar
Hightower knocked upon Valarr's, and the younger Ashford was called
out by Ser Lyonel Baratheon, the knight they called the Laughing
Storm.

The challengers trotted back to the south end of the lists to await
their foes: Ser Abelar in silver and smoke colors, a stone watchtower
on his shield, crowned with fire; the two Lannisters all crimson, bearing
the golden lion of Casterly Rock; the Laughing Storm shining in cloth-
of-gold, with a black stag on breast and shield and a rack of iron antlers
on his helm; Lord Tully wearing a striped blue-and-red cloak clasped
with a silver trout at each shoulder. They pointed their twelve-foot
lances skyward, the gusty winds snapping and tugging at the pennons.

At the north end of the field, squires held brightly barded destriers
for the champions to mount. They donned their helms and took up
lance and shield, in splendor the equal of their foes: the Ashfords'
billowing orange silks, Ser Humfrey's red-and-white diamonds, Lord
Leo on his white charger with green satin trappings patterned with
golden roses, and of course Valarr Targaryen. The Young Prince's
horse was black as night, to match the color of his armor, lance, shield,
and trappings. Atop his helm was a gleaming three-headed dragon,
wings spread, enameled in a rich red; its twin was painted upon the
glossy black surface of his shield. Each of the defenders had a wisp of
orange silk knotted about an arm, a favor bestowed by the fair maid.

As the champions trotted into position, Ashford Meadow grew almost still. Then a horn sounded, and stillness turned to tumult in half a heartbeat. Ten pairs of gilded spurs drove into the flanks of ten great warhorses, a thousand voices began to scream and shout, forty iron-shod hooves pounded and tore the grass, ten lances dipped and steadied, the field seemed almost to shake, and champions and challengers came together in a rending crash of wood and steel. In an instant, the riders were beyond each other, wheeling about for another pass. Lord Tully reeled in his saddle but managed to keep his seat. When the commons realized that all ten of the lances had broken, a great roar of approval went up. It was a splendid omen for the success of the tourney, and a testament to the skill of the competitors.

Squires handed fresh lances to the jousters to replace the broken ones they cast aside, and once more the spurs dug deep. Dunk could the feel the earth trembling beneath the soles of his feet. Atop his shoulders, Egg shouted happily and waved his pipestem arms. The Young Prince passed nearest to them. Dunk saw the point of his black lance kiss the watchtower on his foe's shield and slide off to slam into his chest, even as Ser Abelar's own lance burst into splinters against Valarr's breastplate. The grey stallion in the silver-and-smoke trappings reared with the force of the impact, and Ser Abelar Hightower was lifted from his stirrups and dashed violently to the ground.

Lord Tully was down as well, unhorsed by Ser Humfrey Hardyng, but he sprang up at once and drew his longsword, and Ser Humfrey cast aside his lance—unbroken—and dismounted to continue their fight afoot. Ser Abelar was not so sprightly. His squire ran out, loosened his helm, and called for help, and two servingmen lifted the dazed knight by the arms to help him back to his pavilion. Elsewhere on the field, the six knights who had remained ahorse were riding their third course. More lances shattered, and this time Lord Leo Tyrell aimed his point so expertly he ripped the Grey Lion's helm cleanly off his head. Barefaced, the Lord of Casterly Rock raised his hand in salute and dismounted, yielding the match. By then Ser Humfrey had beaten Lord Tully into surrender, showing himself as skilled with a sword as he was with a lance.

Tybolt Lannister and Androw Ashford rode against each other thrice more before Ser Androw finally lost shield, seat, and match all at once. The younger Ashford lasted even longer, breaking no less than nine lances against Ser Lyonel Baratheon, the Laughing Storm. Champion and challenger both lost their saddles on their tenth course, only to rise together to fight on, sword against mace. Finally a battered Ser Robert Ashford admitted defeat, but on the viewing stand his father looked anything but dejected. Both Lord Ashford's sons had been ushered from the ranks of the champions, it was true, but they had acquitted themselves nobly against two of the finest knights in the Seven Kingdoms.

I must do even better, though, Dunk thought as he watched victor and vanquished embrace and walk together from the field. *It is not enough for me to fight well and lose. I must win at least the first challenge, or I lose all.*

Ser Tybolt Lannister and the Laughing Storm would now take their places among the champions, replacing the men they had defeated. Already the orange pavilions were coming down. A few feet away, the Young Prince sat at his ease in a raised camp chair before his great black tent. His helm was off. He had dark hair like his father, but a bright streak ran through it. A servingman brought him a silver goblet and he took a sip. *Water, if he is wise,* Dunk thought, *wine if not.* He found himself wondering if Valarr had indeed inherited a measure of his father's prowess, or whether it had only been that he had drawn the weakest opponent.

A fanfare of trumpets announced that three new challengers had entered the lists. The heralds shouted their names. "*Ser Pearse of House Caron, Lord of the Marches.*" He had a silver harp emblazoned on his shield, though his surcoat was patterned with nightingales. "*Ser Joseth of House Mallister, from Seagard.*" Ser Joseth sported a winged helm; on his shield, a silver eagle flew across an indigo sky. "*Ser Gawen of House Swann, Lord of Stonehelm on the Cape of Wrath.*" A pair of swans, one black and one white, fought furiously on his arms. Lord Gawen's armor, cloak, and horse bardings were a riot of black and white as well, down to the stripes on his scabbard and lance.

Lord Caron, harper and singer and knight of renown, touched the point of his lance to Lord Tyrell's rose. Ser Joseth thumped on Ser Humfrey Hardyng's diamonds. And the black-and-white knight, Lord Gawen Swann, challenged the black prince with the white guardian. Dunk rubbed his chin. Lord Gawen was even older than the old man, and the old man was dead. "Egg, who is the least dangerous of these challengers?" he asked the boy on his shoulders, who seemed to know so much of these knights.

"Lord Gawen," the boy said at once. "Valarr's foe."

"*Prince* Valarr," he corrected. "A squire must keep a courteous tongue, boy."

The three challengers took their places as the three champions mounted up. Men were making wagers all around them and calling out encouragement to their choices, but Dunk had eyes only for the prince. On the first pass he struck Lord Gawen's shield a glancing blow, the blunted point of the lance sliding aside just as it had with Ser Abelar Hightower, only this time it was deflected the other way, into empty air. Lord Gawen's own lance broke clean against the prince's chest, and Valarr seemed about to fall for an instant before he recovered his seat.

The second time through the lists, Valarr swung his lance left, aiming for his foe's breast, but struck his shoulder instead. Even so, the blow was enough to make the older knight lose his lance. One arm flailed for balance and Lord Gawen fell. The Young Prince swung from the saddle and drew his sword, but the fallen man waved him off and raised his visor. "I yield, Your Grace," he called. "Well fought." The lords in the viewing stand echoed him, shouting, *"Well fought! Well fought!"* as Valarr knelt to help the grey-haired lord to his feet.

"It was not either," Egg complained.

"Be quiet, or you can go back to camp."

Farther away, Ser Joseth Mallister was being carried off the field unconscious, while the harp lord and the rose lord were going at each other lustily with blunted longaxes, to the delight of the roaring crowd. Dunk was so intent on Valarr Targaryen that he scarcely saw them. *He is a fair knight, but no more than that,* he found himself thinking. *I would have a chance against him. If the gods were good, I might even unhorse him, and once afoot my weight and strength would tell.*

"Get him!" Egg shouted merrily, shifting his seat on Dunk's back in his excitement. "Get him! Hit him! Yes! He's right there, he's *right there*!" It seemed to be Lord Caron he was cheering on. The harper was playing a different sort of music now, driving Lord Leo back and back as steel sang on steel. The crowd seemed almost equally divided between them, so cheers and curses mingled freely in the morning air. Chips of wood and paint were flying from Lord Leo's shield as Lord

Pearse's axe knocked the petals off his golden rose, one by one, until the shield finally shattered and split. But as it did, the axehead hung up for an instant in the wood . . . and Lord Leo's own axe crashed down on the haft of his foe's weapon, breaking it off not a foot from his hand. He cast aside his broken shield, and suddenly he was the one on the attack. Within moments, the harper knight was on one knee, singing his surrender.

For the rest of the morning and well into the afternoon, it was more of the same, as challengers took the field in twos and threes, and sometimes five together. Trumpets blew, the heralds called out names, warhorses charged, the crowd cheered, lances snapped like twigs, and swords rang against helms and mail. It was, smallfolk and high lord alike agreed, a splendid day of jousting. Ser Humfrey Hardyng and Ser Humfrey Beesbury, a bold young knight in yellow and black stripes with three beehives on his shield, splintered no less than a dozen lances apiece in an epic struggle the smallfolk soon began calling "the Battle of Humfrey." Ser Tybolt Lannister was unhorsed by Ser Jon Penrose and broke his sword in his fall, but fought back with shield alone to win the bout and remain a champion. One-eyed Ser Robyn Rhysling, a grizzled old knight with a salt-and-pepper beard, lost his helm to Lord Leo's lance in their first course, yet refused to yield. Three times more they rode at each other, the wind whipping Ser Robyn's hair while the shards of broken lances flew round his bare face like wooden knives, which Dunk thought all the more wondrous when Egg told him that Ser Robyn had lost his eye to a splinter from a broken lance not five years earlier. Leo Tyrell was too chivalrous to aim another lance at Ser Robyn's unprotected head, but even so Rhysling's stubborn courage (or was it folly?) left Dunk astounded. Finally the Lord of Highgarden struck Ser Robyn's breastplate a solid thump right over the heart and sent him cartwheeling to the earth.

Ser Lyonel Baratheon also fought several notable matches. Against lesser foes, he would often break into booming laughter the moment they touched his shield, and laugh all the time he was mounting and charging and knocking them from their stirrups. If his challengers wore any sort of crest on their helm, Ser Lyonel would strike it off and fling it into the crowd. The crests were ornate things, made of carved wood or shaped leather, and sometimes gilded and enameled or even wrought in pure silver, so the men he beat did not appreciate this habit, though it made him a great favorite of the commons. Before long, only crestless men were choosing him. As loud and often as Ser Lyonel laughed down a challenger, though, Dunk thought the day's honors should go to Ser Humfrey Hardyng, who humbled fourteen knights, each one of them formidable.

Meanwhile the Young Prince sat outside his black pavilion, drinking from his silver goblet and rising from time to time to mount his horse and vanquish yet another undistinguished foe. He had won nine victories, but it seemed to Dunk that every one was hollow. *He is beating old men and upjumped squires, and a few lords of high birth and low skill. The truly dangerous men are riding past his shield as if they do not see it.*

Late in the day, a brazen fanfare announced the entry of a new challenger to the lists. He rode in on a great red charger whose black bardings were slashed to reveal glimpses of yellow, crimson, and orange beneath. As he approached the viewing stand to make his salute, Dunk saw the face beneath the raised visor, and recognized the prince he'd met in Lord Ashford's stables.

Egg's legs tightened around his neck. "Stop that," Dunk snapped, yanking them apart. "Do you mean to choke me?"

"Prince Aerion Brightflame," a herald called, *"of the Red Keep of King's Landing, son of Maekar Prince of Summerhall of House Targaryen, grandson to Daeron the Good, the Second of His Name, King of the Andals, the Rhoynar, and the First Men, and Lord of the Seven Kingdoms."*

Aerion bore a three-headed dragon on his shield, but it was rendered in colors much more vivid than Valarr's; one head was orange, one yellow, one red, and the flames they breathed had the sheen of gold leaf. His surcoat was a swirl of smoke and fire woven together, and his blackened helm was surmounted by a crest of red enamel flames.

After a pause to dip his lance to Prince Baelor, a pause so brief that was almost perfunctory, he galloped to the north end of the field, past Lord Leo's pavilion and the Laughing Storm's, slowing only when he approached Prince Valarr's tent. The Young Prince rose and stood stiffly beside his shield, and for a moment Dunk was certain that Aerion meant to strike it . . . but then he laughed and trotted past, and banged his point hard against Ser Humfrey Hardyng's diamonds.

"Come out, come out, little knight," he sang in a loud clear voice, "it's time you faced the dragon."

Ser Humfrey inclined his head stiffly to his foe as his destrier was brought out, and then ignored him while he mounted, fastened his helm, and took up lance and shield. The spectators grew quiet as the two knights took their places. Dunk heard the *clang* of Prince Aerion dropping his visor. The horn blew.

Ser Humfrey broke slowly, building speed, but his foe raked the red charger hard with both spurs, coming hard. Egg's legs tightened again. "*Kill him!*" he shouted suddenly. "*Kill him, he's right there, kill him, kill him, kill him!*" Dunk was not certain which of the knights he was shouting to.

Prince Aerion's lance, gold-tipped and painted in stripes of red, orange, and yellow, swung down across the barrier. *Low, too low,* thought Dunk the moment he saw it. *He'll miss the rider and strike Ser Humfrey's horse, he needs to bring it up.* Then, with dawning horror, he began to suspect that Aerion intended no such thing. *He cannot mean to . . .*

At the last possible instant, Ser Humfrey's stallion reared away from the oncoming point, eyes rolling in terror, but too late. Aerion's lance took the animal just above the armor that protected his breastbone, and exploded out of the back of his neck in a gout of bright blood. Screaming, the horse crashed sideways, knocking the wooden barrier to pieces as he fell. Ser Humfrey tried to leap free, but a foot caught in a stirrup and they heard his shriek as his leg was crushed between the splintered fence and falling horse.

All of Ashford Meadow was shouting. Men ran onto the field to extricate Ser Humfrey, but the stallion, dying in agony, kicked at them as they approached. Aerion, having raced blithely around the carnage to the end of the lists, wheeled his horse and came galloping back. He was shouting too, though Dunk could not make out the words over the almost human screams of the dying horse. Vaulting from the saddle, Aerion drew his sword and advanced on his fallen foe. His own squires and one of Ser Humfrey's had to pull him back. Egg squirmed on Dunk's shoulders. "Let me down," the boy said. "The poor horse, *let me down.*"

Dunk felt sick himself. *What would I do if such a fate befell Thunder?* A man-at-arms with a poleaxe dispatched Ser Humfrey's stallion, ending the hideous screams. Dunk turned and forced his way through the press. When he came to open ground, he lifted Egg off his shoulders. The boy's hood had fallen back and his eyes were red. "A terrible sight, aye," he told the lad, "but a squire must needs be strong. You'll see worse mishaps at other tourneys, I fear."

"It was no mishap," Egg said, mouth trembling. "Aerion meant to do it. You saw."

Dunk frowned. It had looked that way to him as well, but it was hard to accept that any knight could be so unchivalrous, least of all one who was blood of the dragon. "I saw a knight green as summer grass lose control of his lance," he said stubbornly, "and I'll hear no more of it. The jousting is done for the day, I think. Come, lad."

He was right about the end of the day's contests. By the time the chaos had been set to rights, the sun was low in the west, and Lord Ashford had called a halt.

As the shadows of evening crept across the meadow, a hundred torches were lit along the merchant's row. Dunk bought a horn of ale for himself and half a horn for the boy, to cheer him. They wandered for a time, listening to a sprightly air on pipes and drums and watching a puppet show about Nymeria, the warrior queen with the ten thousand ships. The puppeteers had only two ships, but managed a rousing sea battle all the same. Dunk wanted to ask the girl Tanselle if she had finished painting his shield, but he could see that she was busy. *I'll wait until she is done for the night*, he resolved. *Perhaps she'll have a thirst then.*

"Ser Duncan," a voice called behind him. And then again, "Ser Duncan." Suddenly Dunk remembered that was him. "I saw you among the smallfolk today, with this boy on your shoulders," said Raymun Fossoway as he came up, smiling. "Indeed, the two of you were hard to miss."

"The boy is my squire. Egg, this is Raymun Fossoway." Dunk had to pull the boy forward, and even then Egg lowered his head and stared at Raymun's boots as he mumbled a greeting.

"Well met, lad," Raymun said easily. "Ser Duncan, why not watch from the viewing gallery? All knights are welcome there."

Dunk was at ease among smallfolk and servants; the idea of claiming a place among the lords, ladies, and landed knights made him uncomfortable. "I would not have wanted any closer view of that last tilt."

Raymun grimaced. "Nor I. Lord Ashford declared Ser Humfrey the victor and awarded him Prince Aerion's courser, but even so, he will not be able to continue. His leg was broken in two places. Prince Baelor sent his own maester to tend him."

"Will there be another champion in Ser Humfrey's place?"

"Lord Ashford had a mind to grant the place to Lord Caron, or perhaps the other Ser Humfrey, the one who gave Hardyng such a splendid match, but Prince Baelor told him that it would not be seemly to remove Ser Humfrey's shield and pavilion under the circumstances. I believe they will continue with four champions in place of five."

Four champions, Dunk thought. *Leo Tyrell, Lyonel Baratheon, Tybolt Lannister, and Prince Valarr*. He had seen enough this first day to know how little chance he would stand against the first three. Which left only . . .

A hedge knight cannot challenge a prince. Valarr is second in line to the Iron Throne. He is Baelor Breakspear's son, and his blood is the blood of Aegon the Conqueror and the Young Dragon and Prince Aemon the Dragonknight, and I am some boy the old man found behind a pot shop in Flea Bottom.

His head hurt just thinking about it. "Who does your cousin mean to challenge?" he asked Raymun.

"Ser Tybolt, all things being equal. They are well matched. My cousin keeps a sharp watch on every tilt, though. Should any man be wounded on the morrow, or show signs of exhaustion or weakness, Steffon will be quick to knock on his shield, you may count on it. No one has ever accused him of an excess of chivalry." He laughed, as if to take the sting from his words. "Ser Duncan, will you join me for a cup of wine?"

"I have a matter I must attend to," said Dunk, uncomfortable with the notion of accepting hospitality he could not return.

"I could wait here and bring your shield when the puppet show is over, ser," said Egg. "They're going to do Symeon Star-Eyes later, and make the dragon fight again as well."

"There, you see, your matter is attended to, and the wine awaits," said Raymun. "It's an Arbor vintage, too. How can you refuse me?"

Bereft of excuses, Dunk had no choice but to follow, leaving Egg at the puppet show. The apple of House Fossoway flew above gold-colored pavilion where Raymun attended his cousin. Behind it, two servants were basting a goat with honey and herbs over a small cook-fire. "There's food as well, if you're hungry," Raymun said negligently as he held the flap for Dunk. A brazier of coals lit the interior and made the air pleasantly warm. Raymun filled two cups with wine. "They say Aerion is in a rage at Lord Ashford for awarding his charger to Ser Humfrey," he commented as he poured, "but I'll wager it was his uncle who counseled it." He handed Dunk a wine cup.

"Prince Baelor is an honorable man."

"As the Bright Prince is not?" Raymun laughed. "Don't look so anxious, Ser Duncan, there's none here but us. It is no secret that Aerion is a bad piece of work. Thank the gods that he is well down in the order of succession."

"You truly believe he meant to kill the horse?"

"Is there any doubt of it? If Prince Maekar had been here, it would have gone differently, I promise you. Aerion is all smiles and chivalry so long as his father is watching, if the tales be true, but when he's not . . ."

"I saw that Prince Maekar's chair was empty."

"He's left Ashford to search for his sons, along with Roland Crakehall of the Kingsguard. There's a wild tale of robber knights going about, but I'll wager the prince is just off drunk again."

The wine was fine and fruity, as good a cup as he had ever tasted. He rolled it in his mouth, swallowed, and said, "Which prince is this now?"

"Maekar's heir. Daeron, he's named, after the king. They call him Daeron the Drunken, though not in his father's hearing. The youngest boy was with him as well. They left Summerhall together but never reached Ashford." Raymun drained his cup and set it aside. "Poor Maekar."

"Poor?" said Dunk, startled. "The king's son?"

"The king's *fourth* son," said Raymun, "not quite as bold as Prince Baelor, nor as clever as Prince Aerys, nor as gentle as Prince Rhaegel. And now he must suffer seeing his own sons overshadowed by his brother's. Daeron is a sot, Aerion is vain and cruel, the third son was so unpromising they gave him to the Citadel to make a maester of him, and the youngest—"

"*Ser! Ser Duncan!*" Egg burst in panting. His hood had fallen back, and the light from the brazier shone in his big dark eyes. "You have to run, he's hurting her!"

Dunk lurched to his feet, confused. "Hurting? Who?"

"*Aerion!*" the boy shouting. "He's *hurting* her. The puppet girl. *Hurry.*" Whirling, he darted back out into the night.

Dunk made to follow, but Raymun caught his arm. "Ser Duncan. Aerion, he said. A prince of the blood. Be careful."

It was good counsel, he knew. The old man would have said the same. But he could not listen. He wrenched free of Raymun's hand and shouldered his way out of the pavilion. He could hear shouting off in the direction of the merchants' row. Egg was almost out of sight. Dunk ran after him. His legs were long and the boy's short; he quickly closed the distance.

A wall of watchers had gathered around the puppeteers. Dunk shouldered through them, ignoring their curses. A man-at-arms in the royal livery stepped up to block him. Dunk put a big hand on his chest and shoved, sending the man flailing backward to sprawl on his arse in the dirt.

The puppeteer's stall had been knocked on its side. The fat Dornishwoman was on the ground weeping. One man-at-arms was dangling the puppets of Florian and Jonquil from his hands as another set them afire with a torch. Three more men were opening chests, spilling more puppets on the ground and stamping on them. The dragon puppet was scattered all about them, a broken wing here, its head there, its tail in three pieces. And in the midst of it all stood Prince Aerion, resplendent in a red velvet doublet with long dagged sleeves, twisting Tanselle's arm in both hands. She was on her knees, pleading with him. Aerion ignored her. He forced open her hand and seized one of her fingers. Dunk stood there stupidly, not quite believing what he saw. Then he heard a *crack*, and Tanselle screamed.

One of Aerion's men tried to grab him, and went flying. Three long strides, then Dunk grabbed the prince's shoulder and wrenched him around hard. His sword and dagger were forgotten, along with everything the old man had ever taught him. His fist knocked Aerion off his feet, and the toe of his boot slammed into the prince's belly. When Aerion went for his knife, Dunk stepped on his wrist and then kicked him again, right in the mouth. He might have kicked him to death right then and there, but the princeling's men swarmed over him. He had a man on each arm and another pounding him across the back. No sooner had he wrestled free of one than two more were on him.

Finally they shoved him down and pinned his arms and legs. Aerion was on his feet again. The prince's mouth was bloody. He pushed inside it with a finger. "You've loosened one of my teeth," he complained, "so we'll start by breaking all of yours." He pushed his hair from his eyes. "You look familiar."

"You took me for a stableboy."

Aerion smiled redly. "I recall. You refused to take my horse. Why did you throw your life away? For this whore?" Tanselle was curled up on the ground, cradling her maimed hand. He gave her a shove with the toe of his boot. "She's scarcely worth it. A traitor. The dragon ought never lose."

He is mad, thought Dunk, *but he is still a prince's son, and he means to kill me.* He might have prayed then, if he had known a prayer all the way through, but there was no time. There was hardly even time to be afraid.

"Nothing more to say?" said Aerion. "You bore me, ser." He poked at his bloody mouth again. "Get a hammer and break all his teeth out, Wate," he commanded, "and then let's cut him open and show him the color of his entrails."

"*No!*" a boy's voice said. "Don't hurt him!"

Gods be good, the boy, the brave foolish boy, Dunk thought. He fought against the arms restraining him, but it was no good. "Hold your tongue, you stupid boy. Run away. They'll hurt you!"

"No they won't." Egg moved closer. "If they do, they'll answer to my father. And my uncle as well. Let go of him, I said. Wate, Yorkel, you know me. Do as I say."

The hands holding his left arm were gone, and then the others. Dunk did not understand what was happening. The men-at-arms were backing away. One even knelt. Then the crowd parted for Raymun Fossoway. He had donned mail and helm, and his hand was on his sword. His cousin Ser Steffon, just behind him, had already bared his blade, and with them were a half-dozen men-at-arms with the red apple badge sewn on their breasts.

Prince Aerion paid them no mind. "Impudent little wretch," he said to Egg, spitting a mouthful of blood at the boy's feet. "What happened to your hair?"

"I cut it off, brother," said Egg. "I didn't want to look like you."

The second day of the tourney was overcast, with a gusty wind blowing from the west. *The crowds should be less on a day like this*, Dunk thought. It would have been easier for them to find a spot near the fence to see the jousting up close. *Egg might have sat on the rail, while I stood behind him.*

Instead Egg would have a seat in the viewing box, dressed in silks and furs, while Dunk's view would be limited to the four walls of the tower cell where Lord Ashford's men had confined him. The chamber had a window, but it faced in the wrong direction. Even so, Dunk crammed himself into the window seat as the sun came up, and stared gloomily off across town and field and forest. They had taken his hempen sword belt, and his sword and dagger with it, and they had taken his silver as well. He hoped Egg or Raymun would remember Chestnut and Thunder.

"Egg," he muttered low under his breath. His squire, a poor lad plucked from the streets of King's Landing. Had ever a knight been made such a fool? *Dunk the lunk, thick as a castle wall and slow as an aurochs.*

He had not been permitted to speak to Egg since Lord Ashford's soldiers had scooped them all up at the puppet show. Nor Raymun, nor Tanselle, nor anyone, not even Lord Ashford himself. He wondered if he would ever see any of them again. For all he knew, they meant to keep him in this small room until he died. *What did I think would happen?* he asked himself bitterly. *I knocked down a prince's son and kicked him in the face.*

Beneath these grey skies, the flowing finery of the highborn lords and great champions would not seem quite so splendid as it had the day before. The sun, walled behind the clouds, would not brush their steel helms with brilliance, nor make their gold and silver chasings glitter and flash, but even so, Dunk wished he were in the crowd to watch the jousting. It would be a good day for hedge knights, for men in plain mail on unbarded horses.

He could *hear* them, at least. The horns of the heralds carried well, and from time to time a roar from the crowd told him that someone had fallen, or risen, or done something especially bold. He heard faint hoofbeats too, and once in a great while the clash of swords or the *snap* of a lance. Dunk winced whenever he heard that last; it reminded him of the noise Tanselle's finger had made when Aerion broke it. There were other sounds too, closer at hand: footfalls in the hall outside his door, the stamp of hooves in the yard below, shouts and voices from the castle walls. Sometimes they drowned out the tourney. Dunk supposed that was just as well.

"A hedge knight is the truest kind of knight, Dunk," the old man had told him, a long long time ago. "Other knights serve the lords who keep them, or from whom they hold their lands, but we serve where we will, for men whose causes we believe in. Every knight swears to protect the weak and innocent, but we keep the vow best, I think." Queer how strong that memory seemed. Dunk had quite forgotten those words. And perhaps the old man had as well, toward the end.

The morning turned to afternoon. The distant sounds of the tourney began to dwindle and die. Dusk began to seep into the cell, but Dunk still sat in the window seat, looking out on the gathering dark and trying to ignore his empty belly.

And then he heard footsteps and a jangling of iron keys. He uncoiled and rose to his feet as the door opened. Two guards pushed in, one bearing an oil lamp. A servingman followed with a tray of food. Behind came Egg. "Leave the lamp and the food and go," the boy told them.

They did as he commanded, though Dunk noticed that they left the heavy wooden door ajar. The smell of the food made him realize how ravenous he was. There was hot bread and honey, a bowl of pease porridge, a skewer of roast onions and well-charred meat. He sat by the tray, pulled apart the bread with his hands, and stuffed some into his mouth. "There's no knife," he observed. "Did they think I'd stab you, boy?"

"They didn't tell me what they thought." Egg wore a close-fitting black wool doublet with a tucked waist and long sleeves lined with red satin. Across his chest was sewn the three-headed dragon of House Targaryen. "My uncle says I must humbly beg your forgiveness for deceiving you."

"Your uncle," said Dunk. "That would be Prince Baelor."

The boy looked miserable. "I never meant to lie."

"But you did. About everything. Starting with your name. I never heard of a Prince Egg."

"It's short for Aegon. My brother Aemon named me Egg. He's off at the Citadel now, learning to be a maester. And Daeron sometimes calls me Egg as well, and so do my sisters."

Dunk lifted the skewer and bit into a chunk of meat. Goat, flavored with some lordly spice he'd never tasted before. Grease ran down his chin. "Aegon," he repeated. "Of course it would be Aegon. Like Aegon the Dragon. How many Aegons have been king?"

"Four," the boy said. "Four Aegons."

Dunk chewed, swallowed, and tore off some more bread. "Why did you do it? Was it some jape, to make a fool of the stupid hedge knight?"

"No." The boy's eyes filled with tears, but he stood there manfully. "I was supposed to squire for Daeron. He's my oldest brother. I learned everything I had to learn to be a good squire, but Daeron isn't a very good knight. He didn't want to ride in the tourney, so after we left Summerhall he stole away from our escort, only instead of doubling back he went straight on toward Ashford, thinking they'd never look for us that way. It was him shaved my head. He knew my father would send men hunting us. Daeron has common hair, sort of a pale brown, nothing special, but mine is like Aerion's and my father's."

"The blood of the dragon," Dunk said. "Silver-gold hair and purple eyes, everyone knows that." *Thick as a castle wall, Dunk.*

"Yes. So Daeron shaved it off. He meant for us to hide until the tourney was over. Only then you took me for a stableboy, and . . ." He lowered his eyes. "I didn't care if Daeron fought or not, but I wanted to be *somebody's* squire. I'm sorry, ser. I truly am."

Dunk looked at him thoughtfully. He knew what it was like to want something so badly that you would tell a monstrous lie just to get near it. "I thought you were like me," he said. "Might be you are. Only not the way I thought."

"We're both from King's Landing still," the boy said hopefully.

Dunk had to laugh. "Yes, you from the top of Aegon's Hill and me from the bottom."

"That's not so far, ser."

Dunk took a bite from an onion. "Do I need to call you *m'lord* or *Your Grace* or something?"

"At court," the boy admitted, "but other times you can keep on calling me Egg if you like. Ser."

"What will they do with me, Egg?"

"My uncle wants to see you. After you're done eating, ser."

Dunk shoved the platter aside, and stood. "I'm done now, then. I've already kicked one prince in the mouth, I don't mean to keep another waiting."

Lord Ashford had turned his own chambers over to Prince Baelor for the duration of his stay, so it was to the lord's solar that Egg—no, *Aegon*, he would have to get used to that—conducted him. Baelor sat reading by the light of beeswax candle. Dunk knelt before him. "Rise," the prince said. "Would you care for wine?"

"As it please you, Your Grace."

"Pour Ser Duncan a cup of the sweet Dornish red, Aegon," the prince commanded. "Try not to spill it on him, you've done him sufficient ill already."

"The boy won't spill, Your Grace," said Dunk. "He's a good boy. A good squire. And he meant no harm to me, I know."

"One need not intend harm to do it. Aegon should have come to me when he saw what his brother was doing to those puppeteers. Instead he ran to you. That was no kindness. What you did, ser . . . well, I might have done the same in your place, but I am a prince of the realm, not a hedge knight. It is never wise to strike a king's grandson in anger, no matter the cause."

Dunk nodded grimly. Egg offered him a silver goblet, brimming with wine. He accepted it and took a long swallow.

"I *hate* Aerion," Egg said with vehemence. "And I had to run for Ser Duncan, uncle, the castle was too far."

"Aerion is your brother," the prince said firmly, "and the septons say we must love our brothers. Aegon, leave us now, I would speak with Ser Duncan privately."

The boy put down the flagon of wine and bowed stiffly. "As you will, Your Grace." He went to the door of the solar and closed it softly behind him.

Baelor Breakspear studied Dunk's eyes for a long moment. "Ser Duncan, let me ask you this—how good a knight are you, truly? How skilled at arms?"

Dunk did not know what to say. "Ser Arlan taught me sword and shield, and how to tilt at rings and quintains."

Prince Baelor seemed troubled by that answer. "My brother Maekar returned to the castle a few hours ago. He found his heir drunk in an inn a day's ride to the south. Maekar would never admit as much, but I believe it was his secret hope that his sons might outshine mine in this tourney. Instead they have both shamed him, but what is he to do? They are blood of his blood. Maekar is angry, and must needs have a target for his wrath. He has chosen you."

"Me?" Dunk said miserably.

"Aerion has already filled his father's ear. And Daeron has not helped you either. To excuse his own cowardice, he told my brother that a huge robber knight, chance met on the road, made off with Aegon. I fear you have been cast as this robber knight, ser. In Daeron's tale, he has spent all these days pursuing you hither and yon, to win back his brother."

"But Egg will tell him the truth. Aegon, I mean."

"Egg *will* tell him, I have no doubt," said Prince Baelor, "but the boy has been known to lie too, as you have good reason to recall. Which son will my brother believe? As for the matter of these puppeteers, by the time Aerion is done twisting the tale it will be high treason. The dragon is the sigil of the royal House. To portray one being slain, sawdust blood spilling from its neck... well, it was doubtless innocent, but it was far from wise. Aerion calls it a veiled attack on House Targaryen, an incitement to revolt. Maekar will likely agree. My brother has a prickly nature, and he has placed all his best hopes on Aerion, since Daeron has been such a grave disappointment to him." The prince took a sip of wine, then set the goblet aside. "Whatever my brother believes or fails to believe, one truth is beyond dispute. You laid hands upon the blood of the dragon. For that offense, you must be tried, and judged, and punished."

"Punished?" Dunk did not like the sound of that.

"Aerion would like your head, with or without teeth. He will not have it, I promise you, but I cannot deny him a trial. As my royal father is hundreds of leagues away, my brother and I must sit in judgment of you, along with Lord Ashford, whose domains these are, and Lord Tyrell of Highgarden, his liege lord. The last time a man was found guilty of striking one of royal blood, it was decreed that he should lose the offending hand."

"My *hand?*" said Dunk, aghast.

"And your foot. You kicked him too, did you not?"

Dunk could not speak.

"To be sure, I will urge my fellow judges to be merciful. I am the King's Hand and the heir to the throne, my word carries some weight. But so does my brother's. The risk is there."

"I," said Dunk, "I . . . Your Grace, I . . ." *They meant no treason, it was only a wooden dragon, it was never meant to be a royal prince,* he wanted to say, but his words had deserted him once and all. He had never been any good with words.

"You have another choice, though," Prince Baelor said quietly. "Whether it is a better choice or a worse one, I cannot say, but I remind you that any knight accused of a crime has the right to demand trial by combat. So I ask you once again, Ser Duncan the Tall—how good a knight are you? Truly?"

A trial of seven," said Prince Aerion, smiling. "That is *my* right, I do believe."

Prince Baelor drummed his fingers on the table, frowning. To his left, Lord Ashford nodded slowly. "Why?" Prince Maekar demanded, leaning forward toward his son. "Are you afraid to face this hedge knight alone, and let the gods decide the truth of your accusations?"

"Afraid?" said Aerion. "Of such as this? Don't be absurd, Father. My thought is for my beloved brother. Daeron has been wronged by this Ser Duncan as well, and has first claim to his blood. A trial of seven allows both of us to face him."

"Do me no favors, brother," muttered Daeron Targaryen. The eldest son of Prince Maekar looked even worse than he had when Dunk had encountered him in the inn. He seemed to be sober this time, his red-and-black doublet unstained by wine, but his eyes were bloodshot, and a fine sheen of sweat covered his brow. "I am content to cheer you on as you slay the rogue."

"You are too kind, sweet brother," said Prince Aerion, all smiles, "but it would be selfish of me to deny you the right to prove the truth of your words at the hazard of your body. I must insist upon a trial of seven."

Dunk was lost. "Your Grace, my lords," he said to the dais. "I do not understand. What is this *trial of seven?*"

Prince Baelor shifted uncomfortably in his seat. "It is another form of trial by combat. Ancient, seldom invoked. It came across the narrow sea with the Andals and their seven gods. In any trial by combat, the accuser and accused are asking the gods to decide the issue between them. The Andals believed that if the seven champions fought on each side, the gods, being thus honored, would be more like to take a hand and see that a just result was achieved."

"Or mayhap they simply had a taste for swordplay," said Lord Leo Tyrell, a cynical smile touching his lips. "Regardless, Ser Aerion is within his rights. A trial of seven it must be."

"I must fight *seven men*, then?" Dunk asked hopelessly.

"Not alone, ser," Prince Maekar said impatiently. "Don't play the fool, it will not serve. It must be seven against seven. You must needs find six other knights to fight beside you."

Six knights, Dunk thought. They might as well have told him to find six thousand. He had no brothers, no cousins, no old comrades who had stood beside him in battle. Why would six strangers risk their own lives to defend a hedge knight against two royal princelings? "Your Graces, my lords," he said, "what if no one will take my part?"

Maekar Targaryen looked down on him coldly. "If a cause is just, good men will fight for it. If you can find no champions, ser, it will be because you are guilty. Could anything be more plain?"

Dunk had never felt so alone as he did when he walked out the gates of Ashford Castle and heard the portcullis rattle down behind him. A soft rain was falling, light as dew on his skin, and yet he shivered at the touch of it. Across the river, colored rings haloed the scant few pavilions where fires still burned. The night was half gone, he guessed. Dawn would be on him in few hours. *And with dawn comes death.*

They had given him back his sword and silver, yet as he waded across the ford, his thoughts were bleak. He wondered if they expected him to saddle a horse and flee. He could, if he wished. That would be the end of his knighthood, to be sure; he would be no more than an outlaw henceforth, until the day some lord took him and struck off his head. *Better to die a knight than live like that*, he told himself stubbornly. Wet to the knee, he trudged past the empty lists. Most of the pavilions were dark, their owners long asleep, but here and there a few candles still burned. Dunk heard soft moans and cries of pleasure coming from within one tent. It made him wonder whether he would die without ever having known a maid.

Then he heard the snort of a horse, a snort he somehow knew for Thunder's. He turned his steps and ran, and there he was, tied up with Chestnut outside a round pavilion lit from within by a vague golden glow. On its center pole the banner hung sodden, but Dunk could still make out the dark curve of the Fossoway apple. It looked like hope.

A trial by combat," Raymun said heavily. "Gods be good, Duncan, that means lances of war, morningstars, battle-axes . . . the swords won't be blunted, do you understand that?"

"Raymun the Reluctant," mocked his cousin Ser Steffon. An apple made of gold and garnets fastened his cloak of yellow wool. "You need not fear, cousin, this is a knighty combat. As you are no knight, your skin is not at risk. Ser Duncan, you have one Fossoway at least. The ripe one. I saw what Aerion did to those puppeteers. I am for you."

"And I," snapped Raymun angrily. "I only meant—"

His cousin cut him off. "Who else fights with us, Ser Duncan?"

Dunk spread his hands hopelessly. "I know no one else. Well, except for Ser Manfred Dondarrion. He wouldn't even vouch that I was a knight, he'll never risk his life for me."

Ser Steffon seemed little perturbed. "Then we need five more good men. Fortunately, I have more than five friends. Leo Longthorn, the Laughing Storm, Lord Caron, the Lannisters, Ser Otho Bracken . . . aye, and the Blackwoods as well, though you will never get Blackwood and Bracken on the same side of a melee. I shall go and speak with some of them."

"They won't be happy at being woken," his cousin objected.

"Excellent," declared Ser Steffon. "If they are angry, they'll fight all the more fiercely. You may rely on me, Ser Duncan. Cousin, if I do not return before dawn, bring my armor and see that Wrath is saddled and barded for me. I shall meet you both in the challengers' paddock." He laughed. "This will be a day long remembered, I think." When he strode from the tent, he looked almost happy.

Not so Raymun. "Five knights," he said glumly after his cousin had gone. "Duncan, I am loath to dash your hopes, but . . ."

"If your cousin can bring the men he speaks of . . ."

"Leo Longthorn? The Brute of Bracken? The Laughing Storm?" Raymun stood. "He knows all of them, I have no doubt, but I would be less certain that any of them know *him*. Steffon sees this as a chance for glory, but it means your life. You should find your own men. I'll help. Better you have too many champions than too few." A noise outside made Raymun turn his head. "Who goes there?" he demanded, as a boy ducked through the flap, followed by a thin man in a rain-sodden black cloak.

"Egg?" Dunk got to his feet. "What are you doing here?"

"I'm your squire," the boy said. "You'll need someone to arm you, ser."

"Does your lord father know you've left the castle?"

"Gods be good, I hope not." Daeron Targaryen undid the clasp of his cloak and let it slide from his thin shoulders.

"*You?* Are you mad, coming here?" Dunk pulled his knife from his sheath. "I ought to shove this through your belly."

"Probably," Prince Daeron admitted. "Though I'd sooner you poured me a cup of wine. Look at my hands." He held one out and let them all see how it shook.

Dunk stepped toward him, glowering. "I don't care about your hands. You lied about me."

"I had to say *something* when my father demanded to know where my little brother had gotten to," the prince replied. He seated himself, ignoring Dunk and his knife. "If truth be told, I hadn't even realized Egg was gone. He wasn't at the bottom of my wine cup, and I hadn't looked anywhere else, so . . ." He sighed.

"Ser, my father is going to join the seven accusers," Egg broke in. "I begged him not to, but he won't listen. He says it is the only way to redeem Aerion's honor, and Daeron's."

"Not that I ever asked to have my honor redeemed," said Prince Daeron sourly. "Whoever has it can keep it, so far as I'm concerned. Still, here we are. For what it's worth, Ser Duncan, you have little to fear from me. The only thing I like less than horses are swords. Heavy things, and beastly sharp. I'll do my best to look gallant in the first charge, but after that . . . well, perhaps you could strike me a nice blow to the side of the helm. Make it ring, but not *too* loud, if you take my meaning. My brothers have my measure when it comes to fighting and dancing and thinking and reading books, but none of them is half my equal at lying insensible in the mud."

Dunk could only stare at him, and wonder whether the princeling was trying to play him for a fool. "Why did you come?"

"To warn you of what you face," Daeron said. "My father has commanded the Kingsguard to fight with him."

"The Kingsguard?" said Dunk, appalled.

"Well, the three who are here. Thank the gods Uncle Baelor left the other four at King's Landing with our royal grandfather."

Egg supplied the names. "Ser Roland Crakehall, Ser Donnel of Duskendale, and Ser Willem Wylde."

"They have small choice in the matter," said Daeron. "They are sworn to protect the lives of the king and royal family, and my brothers and I are blood of the dragon, gods help us."

Dunk counted on his fingers. "That makes six. Who is the seventh man?"

Prince Daeron shrugged. "Aerion will find someone. If need be, he will buy a champion. He has no lack of gold."

"Who do you have?" Egg asked.

"Raymun's cousin Ser Steffon."

Daeron winced. "Only one?"

"Ser Steffon has gone to some of his friends."

"I can bring people," said Egg. "Knights. I can."

"Egg," said Dunk, "I will be fighting your own brothers."

"You won't hurt Daeron, though," the boy said. "He *told* you he'd fall down. And Aerion . . . I remember, when I was little, he used to come into my bedchamber at night and put his knife between my legs. He had too many brothers, he'd say, maybe one night he'd make me his sister, then he could marry me. He threw my cat in the well too. He says he didn't, but he always lies."

Prince Daeron gave a weary shrug. "Egg has the truth of it. Aerion's quite the monster. He thinks he's a dragon in human form, you know. That's why he was so wroth at that puppet show. A pity he wasn't born a Fossoway, then he'd think himself an apple and we'd all be a deal safer, but there you are." Bending, he scooped up his fallen cloak and shook the rain from it. "I must steal back to the castle before my father wonders why I'm taking so long to sharpen my sword, but before I go, I would like a private word, Ser Duncan. Will you walk with me?"

Dunk looked at the princeling suspiciously a moment. "As you wish. Your Grace." He sheathed his dagger. "I need to get my shield too."

"Egg and I will look for knights," promised Raymun.

Prince Daeron knotted his cloak around his neck and pulled up the hood. Dunk followed him back out into the soft rain. They walked toward the merchants' wagons.

"I dreamed of you," said the prince.

"You said that at the inn."

"Did I? Well, it's so. My dreams are not like yours, Ser Duncan. Mine are true. They frighten me. *You* frighten me. I dreamed of you and a dead dragon, you see. A great beast, huge, with wings so large they could cover this meadow. It had fallen on top of you, but you were alive and the dragon was dead."

"Did I kill it?"

"That I could not say, but you were there, and so was the dragon. We were the masters of dragons once, we Targaryens. Now they are all gone, but we remain. I don't care to die today. The gods alone know why, but I don't. So do me a kindness if you would, and make certain it is my brother Aerion you slay."

"I don't care to die either," said Dunk.

"Well, I shan't kill you, ser. I'll withdraw my accusation as well, but it won't serve unless Aerion withdraws his." He sighed. "It may be that I've killed you with my lie. If so, I am sorry. I'm doomed to some hell, I know. Likely one without wine." He shuddered, and on that they parted, there in the cool soft rain.

The merchants had drawn up their wagons on the western verge of the meadow, beneath a stand of birch and ash. Dunk stood under the trees and looked helplessly at the empty place where the puppeteers' wagon had been. *Gone.* He had feared they might be. *I would flee as well, if I were not thick as a castle wall.* He wondered what he would do for a shield now. He had the silver to buy one, he supposed, *if* he could find one for sale. . . .

"Ser Duncan," a voice called out of the dark. Dunk turned to find Steely Pate standing behind him, holding an iron lantern. Under a short leather cloak, the armorer was bare from the waist up, his broad chest and thick arms covered with coarse black hair. "If you are come for your shield, she left it with me." He looked Dunk up and down. "Two hands and two feet, I count. So it's to be trial by combat, is it?"

"A trial of seven. How did you know?"

"Well, they might have kissed you and made you a lord, but it didn't seem likely, and if it went t'other way, you'd be short some parts. Now follow me."

His wagon was easy to distinguish by the sword and anvil painted on its side. Dunk followed Pate inside. The armorer hung the lantern on a hook, shrugged out of his wet cloak, and pulled a roughspun tunic down over his head. A hinged board dropped down from one wall to make a table. "Sit," he said, shoving a low stool toward him.

Dunk sat. "Where did she go?"

"They make for Dorne. The girl's uncle, there's a wise man. Well gone is well forgot. Stay and be seen, and belike the dragon remembers. Besides, he did not think she ought see you die." Pate went to the far end of the wagon, rummaged about in the shadows a moment, and returned with the shield. "Your rim was old cheap steel, brittle and rusted," he said. "I've made you a new one, twice as thick, and put some bands across the back. It will be heavier now, but stronger too. The girl did the paint."

She had made a better job of it than he could ever have hoped for. Even by lantern light, the sunset colors were rich and bright, the tree tall and strong and noble. The falling star was a bright slash of paint across the oaken sky. Yet now that Dunk held it in his hands, it seemed all wrong. The star was *falling*, what sort of sigil was that? Would he fall just as fast? And sunset heralds night. "I should have stayed with the chalice," he said miserably. "It had wings, at least, to fly away, and Ser Arlan said the cup was full of faith and fellowship and good things to drink. This shield is all painted up like death."

"The elm's alive," Pate pointed out. "See how green the leaves are? Summer leaves, for certain. And I've seen shields blazoned with skulls and wolves and ravens, even hanged men and bloody heads. They served well enough, and so will this. You know the old shield rhyme? *Oak and iron, guard me well . . ."*

"*. . . or else I'm dead, and doomed to hell,*" Dunk finished. He had not thought of that rhyme in years. The old man had taught it to him, a long time ago. "How much do you want for the new rim and all?" he asked Pate.

"From you?" Pate scratched his beard. "A copper."

The rain had all but stopped as the first wan light suffused the eastern sky, but it had done its work. Lord Ashford's men had removed the barriers, and the tourney field was one great morass of grey-brown mud and torn grass. Tendrils of fog were writhing along the ground like pale white snakes as Dunk made his way back toward the lists. Steely Pate walked with him.

The viewing stand had already begun to fill, the lords and ladies clutching their cloaks tight about them against the morning chill. Small-folk were drifting toward the field as well, and hundreds of them already stood along the fence. *So many come to see me die*, thought Dunk bitterly, but he wronged them. A few steps farther on, a woman called out, "Good fortune to you." An old man stepped up to take his hand and said, "May the gods give you strength, ser." Then a begging brother in a tattered brown robe said a blessing on his sword, and a maid kissed his cheek. *They are for me.* "Why?" he asked Pate. "What am I to them?"

"A knight who remembered his vows," the smith said.

They found Raymun outside the challengers' paddock at the south end of the lists, waiting with his cousin's horse and Dunk's. Thunder tossed restlessly beneath the weight of chinet, chamfron, and blanket of heavy mail. Pate inspected the armor and pronounced it good work, even though someone else had forged it. Wherever the armor had come from, Dunk was grateful.

Then he saw the others: the one-eyed man with the salt-and-pepper beard, the young knight in the striped yellow-and-black surcoat with the beehives on the shield. *Robyn Rhysling and Humfrey Beesbury*, he thought in astonishment. *And Ser Humfrey Hardyng as well.* Hardyng was mounted on Aerion's red charger, now barded in his red-and-white diamonds.

He went to them. "Sers, I am in your debt."

"The debt is Aerion's," Ser Humfrey Hardyng replied, "and we mean to collect it."

"I had heard your leg was broken."

"You heard the truth," Hardyng said. "I cannot walk. But so long as I can sit a horse, I can fight."

Raymun took Dunk aside. "I hoped Hardyng would want another chance at Aerion, and he did. As it happens, the other Humfrey is his brother by marriage. Egg is responsible for Ser Robyn, whom he knew from other tourneys. So you are five."

"Six," said Dunk in wonder, pointing. A knight was entering the paddock, his squire leading his charger behind him. "The Laughing Storm." A head taller than Ser Raymun and almost of a height with Dunk, Ser Lyonel wore a cloth-of-gold surcoat bearing the crowned stag of House Baratheon, and carried his antlered helm under his arm. Dunk reached for his hand. "Ser Lyonel, I cannot thank you enough for coming, nor Ser Steffon for bringing you."

"Ser Steffon?" Ser Lyonel gave him a puzzled look. "It was your squire who came to me. The boy, Aegon. My own lad tried to chase him off, but he slipped between his legs and turned a flagon of wine over my head." He laughed. "There has not been a trial of seven for more than a hundred years, do you know that? I was not about to miss a chance to fight the Kingsguard knights, and tweak Prince Maekar's nose in the bargain."

"Six," Dunk said hopefully to Raymun Fossoway as Ser Lyonel joined the others. "Your cousin will bring the last, surely."

A roar went up from the crowd. At the north end of the meadow, a column of knights came trotting out of the river mist. The three Kingsguard came first, like ghosts in their gleaming white enamel armor, long white cloaks trailing behind them. Even their shields were white, blank and clean as a field of new-fallen snow. Behind rode Prince Maekar and his sons. Aerion was mounted on a dapple grey, orange and red flickering through the slashes in the horse's caparison at each stride. His brother's destrier was a smaller bay, armored in overlapping black and gold scales. A green silk plume trailed from Daeron's helm. It was their father who made the most fearsome appearance, however. Black curved dragon teeth ran across his shoulders, along the crest of his helm, and down his back, and the huge spiked mace strapped to his saddle was as deadly-looking a weapon as any Dunk had ever seen.

"Six," Raymun exclaimed suddenly. "They are only six."

It was true, Dunk saw. *Three black knights and three white. They are a man short as well.* Was it possible that Aerion had not been able to find a seventh man? What would that mean? Would they fight six against six if neither found a seventh?

Egg slipped up beside him as he was trying to puzzle it out. "Ser, it's time you donned your armor."

"Thank you, squire. If you would be so good?"

Steely Pate lent the lad a hand. Hauberk and gorget, greaves and gauntlet, coif and codpiece, they turned him into steel, checking each buckle and each clasp thrice. Ser Lyonel sat sharpening his sword on a whetstone while the Humfreys talked quietly, Ser Robyn prayed, and Raymun Fossoway paced back and forth, wondering where his cousin had got to.

Dunk was fully armored by the time Ser Steffon finally appeared. "Raymun," he called, "my mail, if you please." He had changed into a padded doublet to wear beneath his steel.

"Ser Steffon," said Dunk, "what of your friends? We need another knight to make our seven."

"You need two, I fear," Ser Steffon said. Raymun laced up the back of the hauberk.

"M'lord?" Dunk did not understand. "Two?"

Ser Steffon picked up a gauntlet of fine lobstered steel and slid his left hand into it, flexing his fingers. "I see five here," he said while Raymun fastened his sword belt. "Beesbury, Rhysling, Hardyng, Baratheon, and yourself."

"And you," said Dunk. "You're the sixth."

"I am the seventh," said Ser Steffon, smiling, "but for the other side. I fight with Prince Aerion and the accusers."

Raymun had been about to hand his cousin his helm. He stopped as if struck. "No."

"Yes." Ser Steffon shrugged. "Ser Duncan understands, I am sure. I have a duty to my prince."

"You told him to rely on you." Raymun had gone pale.

"Did I?" He took the helm from his cousin's hands. "No doubt I was sincere at the time. Bring me my horse."

"Get him yourself," said Raymun angrily. "If you think I wish any part of this, you're as thick as you are vile."

"Vile?" Ser Steffon *tsk*ed. "Guard your tongue, Raymun. We're both apples from the same tree. And you are my squire. Or have you forgotten your vows?"

"No. Have you forgotten yours? You swore to be a knight."

"I shall be more than a knight before this day is done. *Lord* Fossoway. I like the sound of that." Smiling, he pulled on his other gauntlet, turned away, and crossed the paddock to his horse. Though the other defenders stared at him with contemptuous eyes, no one made a move to stop him.

Dunk watched Ser Steffon lead his destrier back across the field. His hands coiled into fists, but his throat felt too raw for speech. *No words would move the likes of him anyway.*

"Knight me." Raymun put a hand on Dunk's shoulder and turned him. "I will take my cousin's place. Ser Duncan, knight me." He went to one knee.

Frowning, Dunk moved a hand to the hilt of his longsword, then hesitated. "Raymun, I . . . I should not."

"You must. Without me, you are only five."

"The lad has the truth of it," said Ser Lyonel Baratheon. "Do it, Ser Duncan. Any knight can make a knight."

"Do you doubt my courage?" Raymun asked.

"No," said Dunk. "Not that, but . . ." Still he hesitated.

A fanfare of trumpets cut the misty morning air. Egg came running up to them. "Ser, Lord Ashford summons you."

The Laughing Storm gave an impatient shake of the head. "Go to him, Ser Duncan. I'll give squire Raymun his knighthood." He slid his sword out of his sheath and shouldered Dunk aside. "Raymun of House Fossoway," he began solemnly, touching the blade to the squire's right shoulder, "in the name of the Warrior I charge you to be brave." The sword moved from his right shoulder to his left. "In the name of the Father I charge you to be just." Back to the right. "In the name of the Mother I charge you to defend the young and innocent." The left. "In the name of the Maid I charge you to protect all women. . . ."

Dunk left them there, feeling as relieved as he was guilty. *We are still one short*, he thought as Egg held Thunder for him. *Where will I find another man?* He turned the horse and rode slowly toward the viewing stand, where Lord Ashford stood waiting. From the north end of the lists, Prince Aerion advanced to meet him. "Ser Duncan," he said cheerfully, "it would seem you have only five champions."

"Six," said Dunk. "Ser Lyonel is knighting Raymun Fossoway. We will fight you six against seven." Men had won at far worse odds, he knew.

But Lord Ashford shook his head. "That is not permitted, ser. If you cannot find another knight to take your side, you must be declared guilty of the crimes of which you stand accused."

Guilty, thought Dunk. *Guilty of loosening a tooth, and for that I must die.* "M'lord, I beg a moment."

"You have it."

Dunk rode slowly along the fence. The viewing stand was crowded with knights. *"M'lords,"* he called to them, *"do none of you remember Ser Arlan of Pennytree? I was his squire. We served many of you. Ate at your tables and slept in your halls."* He saw Manfred Dondarrion seated in the highest tier. *"Ser Arlan took a wound in your lord father's service."* The knight said something to the lady beside him, paying no heed. Dunk was forced to move on. *"Lord Lannister, Ser Arlan unhorsed you once in tourney."* The Grey Lion examined his gloved hands, studiedly refusing to raise his eyes. *"He was a good man, and he taught me how to be a knight. Not only sword and lance, but honor. A knight defends the innocent, he said. That's all I did. I need one more knight to fight beside me. One, that's all. Lord Caron? Lord Swann?"* Lord Swann laughed softly as Lord Caron whispered in his ear.

Dunk reined up before Ser Otho Bracken, lowering his voice. "Ser Otho, all know you for a great champion. Join us, I beg you. In the names of the old gods and the new. My cause is just."

"That may be," said the Brute of Bracken, who had at least the grace to reply, "but it is your cause, not mine. I know you not, boy."

Heartsick, Dunk wheeled Thunder and raced back and forth before the tiers of pale cold men. Despair made him shout. *"ARE THERE NO TRUE KNIGHTS AMONG YOU?"*

Only silence answered.

Across the field, Prince Aerion laughed. "The dragon is not mocked," he called out.

Then came a voice. "I will take Ser Duncan's side."

A black stallion emerged from out of the river mists, a black knight on his back. Dunk saw the dragon shield, and the red enamel crest upon his helm with its three roaring heads. *The Young Prince. Gods be good, it is truly him?*

Lord Ashford made the same mistake. "Prince Valarr?"

"No." The black knight lifted the visor of his helm. "I did not think to enter the lists at Ashford, my lord, so I brought no armor. My son was good enough to lend me his." Prince Baelor smiled almost sadly.

The accusers were thrown into confusion, Dunk could see. Prince Maekar spurred his mount forward. "Brother, have you taken leave of your senses?" He pointed a mailed finger at Dunk. "This man attacked my son."

"This man protected the weak, as every true knight must," replied Prince Baelor. "Let the gods determine if he was right or wrong." He gave a tug on his reins, turned Valarr's huge black destrier, and trotted to the south end of the field.

Dunk brought Thunder up beside him, and the other defenders gathered round them; Robyn Rhysling and Ser Lyonel, the Humfreys. *Good men all, but are they good enough?* "Where is Raymun?"

"*Ser* Raymun, if you please." He cantered up, a grim smile lighting his face beneath his plumed helm. "My pardons, ser. I needed to make a small change to my sigil, lest I be mistaken for my dishonorable cousin." He showed them all his shield. The polished golden field remained the same, and the Fossoway apple, but this apple was green instead of red. "I fear I am still not ripe . . . but better green than wormy, eh?"

Ser Lyonel laughed, and Dunk grinned despite himself. Even Prince Baelor seemed to approve.

Lord Ashford's septon had come to the front of the viewing stand and raised his crystal to call the throng to prayer.

"Attend me, all of you," Baelor said quietly. "The accusers will be armed with heavy war lances for the first charge. Lances of ash, eight feet long, banded against splitting and tipped with a steel point sharp enough to drive through plate with the weight of a warhorse behind it."

"We shall use the same," said Ser Humfrey Beesbury. Behind him, the septon was calling on the Seven to look down and judge this dispute, and grant victory to the men whose cause was just.

"No," Baelor said. "We will arm ourselves with tourney lances instead."

"Tourney lances are made to break," objected Raymun.

"They are also made twelve feet long. If our points strike home, theirs cannot touch us. Aim for helm or chest. In a tourney it is a gallant thing to break your lance against a foe's shield, but here it may well mean death. If we can unhorse them and keep our own saddles, the advantage is ours." He glanced to Dunk. "If Ser Duncan is killed, it is considered that the gods have judged him guilty, and the contest is over. If both of his accusers are slain, or withdraw their accusations, the same is true. Elsewise, all seven of one side or the other must perish or yield for the trial to end."

"Prince Daeron will not fight," Dunk said.

"Not well, anyway," laughed Ser Lyonel. "Against that, we have three of the White Swords to contend with."

Baelor took that calmly. "My brother erred when he demanded that the Kingsguard fight for his son. Their oath forbids them to harm a prince of the blood. Fortunately, I am such." He gave them a faint smile. "Keep the others off me long enough, and I shall deal with the Kingsguard."

"My prince, is that chivalrous?" asked Ser Lyonel Baratheon as the septon was finishing his invocation.

"The gods will let us know," said Baelor Breakspear.

A deep expectant silence had fallen across Ashford Meadow.

Eighty yards away, Aerion's grey stallion trumpeted with impatience and pawed the muddy ground. Thunder was very still by comparison; he was an older horse, veteran of half a hundred fights, and he knew what was expected of him. Egg handed Dunk up his shield. "May the gods be with you, ser," the boy said.

The sight of his elm tree and shooting star gave him heart. Dunk slid his left arm through the strap and tightened his fingers around the grip. *Oak and iron, guard me well, or else I'm dead and doomed to hell.* Steely Pate brought his lance to him, but Egg insisted that it must be he who put it into Dunk's hand.

To either side, his companions took up their own lances and spread out in a long line. Prince Baelor was to his right and Ser Lyonel to his left, but the narrow eye slit of the greathelm limited Dunk's vision to what was directly ahead of him. The viewing stand was gone, and likewise the smallfolk crowding the fence; there was only the muddy field,

the pale blowing mist, the river, town, and castle to the north, and the princeling on his grey charger with flames on his helm and a dragon on his shield. Dunk watched Aerion's squire hand him a war lance, eight feet long and black as night. *He will put that through my heart if he can.*

A horn sounded.

For a heartbeat Dunk sat as still as a fly in amber, though all the horses were moving. A stab of panic went through him. *I have forgotten*, he thought wildly, *I have forgotten all, I will shame myself, I will lose everything.*

Thunder saved him. The big brown stallion knew what to do, even if his rider did not. He broke into a slow trot. Dunk's training took over then. He gave the warhorse a light touch of spur and couched his lance. At the same time he swung his shield until it covered most of the left side of his body. He held it at an angle, to deflect blows away from him. *Oak and iron guard me well, or else I'm dead and doomed to hell.*

The noise of the crowd was no more than the crash of distant waves. Thunder slid into a gallop. Dunk's teeth jarred together with the violence of the pace. He pressed his heels down, tightening his legs with all his strength and letting his body become part of the motion of the horse beneath. *I am Thunder and Thunder is me, we are one beast, we are joined, we are one.* The air inside his helm was already so hot he could scarce breathe.

In a tourney joust, his foe would be to his left across the tilting barrier, and he would need to swing his lance across Thunder's neck. The angle made it more likely that the wood would split on impact. But this was a deadlier game they played today. With no barriers dividing them, the destriers charged straight at one another. Prince Baelor's huge black was much faster than Thunder, and Dunk glimpsed him pounding ahead through the corner of his eye slit. He sensed more than saw the others. *They do not matter, only Aerion matters, only him.*

He watched the dragon come. Spatters of mud sprayed back from the hooves of Prince Aerion's grey, and Dunk could see the horse's nostrils flaring. The black lance still angled upward. A knight who holds his lance high and brings it on line at the last moment always risks lowering it too far, the old man had told him. He brought his own point to bear on the center of the princeling's chest. *My lance is part of my arm*, he told himself. *It's my finger, a wooden finger. All I need do is touch him with my long wooden finger.*

He tried not to see the sharp iron point at the end of Aerion's black lance, growing larger with every stride. *The dragon, look at the dragon,* he thought. The great three-headed beast covered the prince's shield, red wings and gold fire. *No, look only where you mean to strike,* he remembered suddenly, but his lance had already begun to slide off line. Dunk tried to correct, but it was too late. He saw his point strike Aerion's shield, taking the dragon between two of its heads, gouging into a gout of painted flame. At the muffled *crack*, he felt Thunder recoil under him, trembling with the force of the impact, and half a heartbeat later something smashed into his side with awful force. The horses slammed together violently, armor crashing and clanging as Thunder stumbled and Dunk's lance fell from his hand. Then he was past his foe, clutching at his saddle in a desperate effort to keep his seat. Thunder lurched sideways in the sloppy mud and Dunk felt his rear legs slip out from under. They were sliding, spinning, and then the stallion's hindquarters slapped down hard. "*Up!*" Dunk roared, lashing out with his spurs. "*Up, Thunder!*" And somehow the old warhorse found his feet again.

He could feel a sharp pain under his rib, and his left arm was being pulled down. Aerion had driven his lance through oak, wool, and steel; three feet of splintered ash and sharp iron stuck from his side. Dunk reached over with his right hand, grasped the lance just below the head, clenched his teeth, and pulled it out of him with one savage yank. Blood followed, seeping through the rings of his mail to redden his surcoat. The world swam and he almost fell. Dimly, through the pain, he could hear voices calling his name. His beautiful shield was useless now. He tossed it aside, elm tree, shooting star, broken lance, and all, and drew his sword, but he hurt so much he did not think he could swing it.

Turning Thunder in a tight circle, he tried to get a sense of what was happening elsewhere on the field. Ser Humfrey Hardyng clung to the neck of his mount, obviously wounded. The other Ser Humfrey lay motionless in a lake of bloodstained mud, a broken lance protruding from his groin. He saw Prince Baelor gallop past, lance still intact, and drive one of the Kingsguard from his saddle. Another of the white knights was already down, and Maekar had been unhorsed as well. The third of the Kingsguard was fending off Ser Robyn Rhysling.

Aerion, where is Aerion? The sound of drumming hooves behind him made Dunk turn his head sharply. Thunder bugled and reared, hooves lashing out futilely as Aerion's grey stallion barreled into him at full gallop.

This time there was no hope of recovery. His longsword went spinning from his grasp, and the ground rose up to meet him. He landed with a bruising impact that jarred him to the bone. Pain stabbed through him, so sharp he sobbed. For a moment it was all he could do to lie there. The taste of blood filled his mouth. *Dunk the lunk, thought he could be a knight.* He knew he had to find his feet again, or die. Groaning, he forced himself to hands and knees. He could not breathe, nor could he see. The eye slit of his helm was packed with mud. Lurching blindly to his feet, Dunk scraped at the mud with a mailed finger. *There, that's . . .*

Through his fingers, he glimpsed a dragon flying, and a spiked morningstar whirling on the end of a chain. Then his head seemed to burst to pieces.

When his eyes opened he was on the ground again, sprawled on his back. The mud had all been knocked from his helm, but now one eye was closed by blood. Above was nothing was dark grey sky. His face throbbed, and he could feel cold wet metal pressing in against cheek and temple. *He broke my head, and I'm dying.* What was worse was the others who would die with him, Raymun and Prince Baelor and the rest. *I've failed them. I am no champion. I'm not even a hedge knight. I am nothing.* He remembered Prince Daeron boasting that no one could lie insensible in the mud as well as he did. *He never saw Dunk the lunk, though, did he?* The shame was worse than the pain.

The dragon appeared above him.

Three heads it had, and wings bright as flame, red and yellow and orange. It was laughing. "Are you dead yet, hedge knight?" it asked. "Cry for quarter and admit your guilt, and perhaps I'll only claim a hand and a foot. Oh, and those teeth, but what are a few teeth? A man like you can live years on pease porridge." The dragon laughed again. "No? Eat *this*, then." The spiked ball whirled round and round the sky, and fell toward his head as fast as a shooting star.

Dunk rolled.

Where he found the strength he did not know, but he found it. He rolled into Aerion's legs, threw a steel-clad arm around his thigh, dragged him cursing into the mud, and rolled on top of him. *Let him swing his bloody morningstar now.* The prince tried forcing the lip of his shield up at Dunk's head, but his battered helm took the brunt of the impact. Aerion was strong, but Dunk was stronger, and larger and heavier as well. He grabbed hold of the shield with both hands and twisted until the straps broke. Then he brought it down on the top of the princeling's helm, again and again and again, smashing the enameled flames of his crest. The shield was thicker than Dunk's had been, solid oak banded with iron. A flame broke off. Then another. The prince ran out of flames long before Dunk ran out of blows.

Aerion finally let go the handle of his useless morningstar and clawed for the poniard at his hip. He got it free of its sheath, but when Dunk whanged his hand with the shield the knife sailed off into the mud.

He could vanquish Ser Duncan the Tall, but not Dunk of Flea Bottom. The old man had taught him jousting and swordplay, but this sort of fighting he had learned earlier, in shadowy wynds and crooked alleys behind the city's winesinks. Dunk flung the battered shield away and wrenched up the visor of Aerion's helm.

A visor is a weak point, he remembered Steely Pate saying. The prince had all but ceased to struggle. His eyes were purple and full of terror. Dunk had a sudden urge to grab one and pop it like a grape between two steel fingers, but that would not be knightly. *"YIELD!"* he shouted.

"I yield," the dragon whispered, pale lips barely moving. Dunk blinked down at him. For a moment he could not credit what his ears had heard. *Is it done, then?* He turned his head slowly from side to side, trying to see. His vision slit was partly closed by the blow that had smashed in the left side of his face. He glimpsed Prince Maekar, mace in hand, trying to fight his way to his son's side. Baelor Breakspear was holding him off.

Dunk lurched to his feet and pulled Prince Aerion up after him. Fumbling at the lacings of his helm, he tore it off and flung it away. At once he was drowned in sights and sounds; grunts and curses, the shouts of the crowd, one stallion screaming while another raced riderless across the field. Everywhere steel rang on steel. Raymun and his cousin were slashing at each other in front of the viewing stand, both afoot. Their shields were splintered ruins, the green apple and the red both hacked to tinder. One of the Kingsguard knights was carrying a wounded brother from the field. They both looked alike in their white armor and white cloaks. The third of the white knights was down, and the Laughing Storm had joined Prince Baelor against Prince Maekar. Mace, battle-axe, and longsword clashed and clanged, ringing against helm and shield. Maekar was taking three blows for every one he landed, and Dunk could see that it would be over soon. *I must make an end to it before more of us are killed.*

Prince Aerion made a sudden dive for his morningstar. Dunk kicked him in the back and knocked him facedown, then grabbed hold of one of his legs and dragged him across the field. By the time he reached the viewing stand where Lord Ashford sat, the Bright Prince was brown as a privy. Dunk hauled him onto his feet and rattled him, shaking some of the mud onto Lord Ashford and the fair maid. "Tell him!"

Aerion Brightflame spit out a mouthful of grass and dirt. "I withdraw my accusation."

Afterward Dunk could not have said whether he walked from the field under his own power or had required help. He hurt everywhere, and some places worse than others. *I am a knight now in truth?* he remembered wondering. *Am I a champion?*

Egg helped him remove his greaves and gorget, and Raymun as well, and even Steely Pate. He was too dazed to tell them apart. They were fingers and thumbs and voices. Pate was the one complaining, Dunk knew. "Look what he's done to me armor," he said. "All dinted and banged and scratched. Aye, I ask you, why do I bother? I'll have to cut that mail off him, I fear."

"Raymun," Dunk said urgently, clutching at his friend's hands. "The others. How did they fare?" He had to know. "Has anyone died?"

"Beesbury," Raymun said. "Slain by Donnel of Duskendale in the first charge. Ser Humfrey is gravely wounded as well. The rest of us are bruised and bloody, no more. Save for you."

"And them? The accusers?"

"Ser Willem Wylde of the Kingsguard was carried from the field insensate, and I think I cracked a few of my cousin's ribs. At least I hope so.".

"And Prince Daeron?" Dunk blurted. "Did he survive?"

"Once Ser Robyn unhorsed him, he lay where he fell. He may have a broken foot. His own horse trod on him while running loose about the field."

Dazed and confused as he was, Dunk felt a huge sense of relief. "His dream was wrong, then. The dead dragon. Unless Aerion died. He didn't though, did he?"

"No," said Egg. "You spared him. Don't you remember?"

"I suppose." Already his memories of the fight were becoming confused and vague. "One moment I feel drunk. The next it hurts so bad I know I'm dying."

They made him lie down on his back and talked over him as he gazed up into the roiling grey sky. It seemed to Dunk that it was still morning. He wondered how long the fight had taken.

"Gods be good, the lance point drove the rings deep into his flesh," he heard Raymun saying. "It will mortify unless . . ."

"Get him drunk and pour some boiling oil into it," someone suggested. "That's how the maesters do it."

"Wine." The voice had a hollow metallic ring to it. "*Not* oil, that will kill him, boiling wine. I'll send Maester Yormwell to have a look at him when he's done tending my brother."

A tall knight stood above him, in black armor dinted and scarred by many blows. *Prince Baelor*. The scarlet dragon on his helm had lost a head, both wings, and most of its tail. "Your Grace," Dunk said, "I am your man. Please. Your man."

"My man." The black knight put a hand on Raymun's shoulder to steady himself. "I need good men, Ser Duncan. The realm . . ." His voice sounded oddly slurred. Perhaps he'd bit his tongue.

Dunk was very tired. It was hard to stay awake. "Your man," he murmured once more.

The prince moved his head slowly from side to side. "Ser Raymun . . . my helm, if you'd be so kind. Visor . . . visor's cracked, and my fingers . . . fingers feel like wood . . ."

"At once, Your Grace." Raymun took the prince's helm in both hands and grunted. "Goodman Pate, a hand."

Steely Pate dragged over a mounting stool. "It's crushed down at the back, Your Grace, toward the left side. Smashed into the gorget. Good steel, this, to stop such a blow."

"Brother's mace, most like," Baelor said thickly. "He's strong." He winced. "That . . . feels queer, I . . ."

"Here it comes." Pate lifted the battered helm away. "Gods be good. *Oh gods oh gods oh gods preserve . . .* "

Dunk saw something red and wet fall out of the helm. Someone was screaming, high and terrible. Against the bleak grey sky swayed a tall tall prince in black armor with only half a skull. He could see red blood and pale bone beneath and something else, something blue-grey and pulpy. A queer troubled look passed across Baelor Breakspear's face, like a cloud passing before a sun. He raised his hand and touched the back of his head with two fingers, oh so lightly. And then he fell.

Dunk caught him. "Up," they say he said, just as he had with Thunder in the melee, "up, up." But he never remembered that afterward, and the prince did not rise.

Baelor of House Targaryen, Prince of Dragonstone, Hand of the King, Protector of the Realm, and heir apparent to the Iron Throne of the Seven Kingdoms of Westeros, went to the fire in the yard of Ashford Castle on the north bank of River Cockleswent. Other great houses might choose to bury their dead in the dark earth or sink them in the cold green sea, but the Targaryens were the blood of the dragon, and their ends were writ in flame.

He had been the finest knight of his age, and some argued that he should have gone to face the dark clad in mail and plate, a sword in his hand. In the end, though, his royal father's wishes prevailed, and Daeron II had a peaceable nature. When Dunk shuffled past Baelor's bier, the prince wore a black velvet tunic with the three-headed dragon picked out in scarlet thread upon his breast. Around his throat was a heavy gold chain. His sword was sheathed by his side, but he did wear a helm, a thin golden helm with an open visor so men could see his face.

Valarr, the Young Prince, stood vigil at the foot of the bier while his father lay in state. He was a shorter, slimmer, handsomer version of his sire, without the twice-broken nose that had made Baelor seem more human than royal. Valarr's hair was brown, but a bright streak of silver-gold ran through it. The sight of it reminded Dunk of Aerion, but he knew that was not fair. Egg's hair was growing back as bright as his brother's, and Egg was a decent enough lad, for a prince.

When he stopped to offer awkward sympathies, well larded with thanks, Prince Valarr blinked cool blue eyes at him and said, "My father was only nine-and-thirty. He had it in him to be a great king, the greatest since Aegon the Dragon. Why would the gods take him, and leave *you*?" He shook his head. "Begone with you, Ser Duncan. Begone."

Wordless, Dunk limped from the castle, down to the camp by the green pool. He had no answer for Valarr. Nor for the questions he asked himself. The maesters and the boiling wine had done their work, and his wound was healing cleanly, though there would be a deep puckered scar between his left arm and his nipple. He could not see the wound without thinking of Baelor. *He saved me once with his sword, and once with a word, even though he was a dead man as he stood there.* The world made no sense when a great prince died so a hedge knight might live. Dunk sat beneath his elm and stared morosely at his foot.

When four guardsmen in the royal livery appeared in his camp late one day, he was sure they had come to kill him after all. Too weak and weary to reach for a sword, he sat with his back to the elm, waiting.

"Our prince begs the favor of a private word."

"Which prince?" asked Dunk, wary.

"This prince," a brusque voice said before the captain could answer. Maekar Targaryen walked out from behind the elm.

Dunk got slowly to his feet. *What would he have of me now?*

Maekar motioned, and the guards vanished as suddenly as they had appeared. The prince studied him a long moment, then turned and paced away from him to stand beside the pool, gazing down at his reflection in the water. "I have sent Aerion to Lys," he announced abruptly. "A few years in the Free Cities may change him for the better."

Dunk had never been to the Free Cities, so he did not know what to say to that. He was pleased that Aerion was gone from the Seven Kingdoms, and hoped he never came back, but that was not a thing you told a father of his son. He stood silent.

Prince Maekar turned to face him. "Some men will say I meant to kill my brother. The gods know it is a lie, but I will hear the whispers till the day I die. And it was my mace that dealt the fatal blow, I have no doubt. The only other foes he faced in the melee were three Kingsguard, whose vows forbade them to do any more than defend themselves. So it was me. Strange to say, I do not recall the blow that broke his skull. Is that a mercy or a curse? Some of both, I think."

From the way he looked at Dunk, it seemed the prince wanted an answer. "I could not say, Your Grace." Perhaps he should have hated Maekar, but instead he felt a queer sympathy for the man. "You swung the mace, m'lord, but it was for me Prince Baelor died. So I killed him too, as much as you."

"Yes," the prince admitted. "You'll hear them whisper as well. The king is old. When he dies, Valarr will climb the Iron Throne in place of his father. Each time a battle is lost or a crop fails, the fools will say, 'Baelor would not have let it happen, but the hedge knight killed him.' "

Dunk could see the truth in that. "If I had not fought, you would have had my hand off. And my foot. Sometimes I sit under that tree there and look at my feet and ask if I couldn't have spared one. How could my foot be worth a prince's life? And the other two as well, the Humfreys, they were good men too." Ser Humfrey Hardyng had succumbed to his wounds only last night.

"And what answer does your tree give you?"

"None that I can hear. But the old man, Ser Arlan, every day at evenfall he'd say, 'I wonder what the morrow will bring.' He never knew, no more than we do. Well, mighten it be that some morrow will come when I'll have need of that foot? When the *realm* will need that foot, even more than a prince's life?"

Maekar chewed on that a time, mouth clenched beneath the silvery-pale beard that made his face seem so square. "It's not bloody likely," he said harshly. "The realm has as many hedge knights as hedges, and all of them have feet."

"If Your Grace has a better answer, I'd want to hear it."

Maekar frowned. "It may be that the gods have a taste for cruel japes. Or perhaps there are no gods. Perhaps none of this had any meaning. I'd ask the High Septon, but the last time I went to him he told me that no man can truly understand the workings of the gods.

Perhaps he should try sleeping under a tree." He grimaced. "My youngest son seems to have grown fond of you, ser. It is time he was a squire, but he tells me he will serve no knight but you. He is an unruly boy, as you will have noticed. Will you have him?"

"Me?" Dunk's mouth opened and closed and opened again. "Egg . . . Aegon, I mean . . . he is a good lad, but, Your Grace, I know you honor me, but . . . I am only a hedge knight."

"That can be changed," said Maekar. "Aegon is to return to my castle at Summerhall. There is a place there for you, if you wish. A knight of my household. You'll swear your sword to me, and Aegon can squire for you. While you train him, my master-at-arms will finish your own training." The prince gave him a shrewd look. "Your Ser Arlan did all he could for you, I have no doubt, but you still have much to learn."

"I know, m'lord." Dunk looked about him. At the green grass and the reeds, the tall elm, the ripples dancing across the surface of the sunlit pool. Another dragonfly was moving across the water, or perhaps it was the same one. *What shall it be, Dunk?* he asked himself. *Dragonflies or dragons?* A few days ago he would have answered at once. It was all he had ever dreamed, but now that the prospect was at hand it frightened him. "Just before Prince Baelor died, I swore to be his man."

"Presumptuous of you," said Maekar. "What did he say?"

"That the realm needed good men."

"That's true enough. What of it?"

"I will take your son as squire, Your Grace, but not at Summerhall. Not for a year or two. He's seen sufficient of castles, I would judge. I'll have him only if I can take him on the road with me." He pointed to old Chestnut. "He'll ride my steed, wear my old cloak, and he'll keep my sword sharp and my mail scoured. We'll sleep in inns and stables, and now and again in the halls of some landed knight or lesser lordling, and maybe under trees when we must."

Prince Maekar gave him an incredulous look. "Did the trial addle your wits, man? Aegon is a prince of the realm. The blood of the dragon. Princes are not made for sleeping in ditches and eating hard salt beef." He saw Dunk hesitate. "What is it you're afraid to tell me? Say what you will, ser."

"Daeron never slept in a ditch, I'll wager," Dunk said, very quietly, "and all the beef that Aerion ever ate was thick and rare and bloody, like as not."

Maekar Targaryen, Prince of Summerhall, regarded Dunk of Flea Bottom for a long time, his jaw working silently beneath his silvery beard. Finally he turned and walked away, never speaking a word. Dunk heard him riding off with his men. When they were gone, there was no sound but the faint thrum of the dragonfly's wings as it skimmed across the water.

The boy came the next morning, just as the sun was coming up. He wore old boots, brown breeches, a brown wool tunic, and an old traveler's cloak. "My lord father says I am to serve you."

"Serve you, *ser*," Dunk reminded him. "You can start by saddling the horses. Chestnut is yours, treat her kindly. I don't want to find you on Thunder unless I put you there."

Egg went to get the saddles. "Where are we going, ser?"

Dunk thought for a moment. "I have never been over the Red Mountains. Would you like to have a look at Dorne?"

Egg grinned. "I hear they have good puppet shows," he said.

Pern

——

ANNE McCAFFREY

DRAGONRIDERS OF PERN TRILOGY:

DRAGONFLIGHT (1969)
DRAGONQUEST (1971)
THE WHITE DRAGON (1978)

HARPER HALL TRILOGY:

DRAGONSONG (1976)
DRAGONSINGER (1977)
DRAGONDRUMS (1978)

OTHER PERN NOVELS:

MORETA, DRAGONLADY OF PERN (1983)
NERILKA'S STORY (1986)
DRAGONSDAWN (1988)
THE RENEGADES OF PERN (1989)
ALL THE WEYRS OF PERN (1991)
THE CHRONICLES OF PERN (1992)
THE DOLPHINS OF PERN (1994)
DRAGONSEYE (1996)
THE MASTERHARPER OF PERN (1998)

Dissatisfied with life on technologically advanced Earth, hundreds of colonists traveled through space to the star Rukbat, which held six planets in orbit around it, five in stable trajectories, and one that looped wildly around the others. The third planet was capable of sustaining life, and the spacefarers settled there, naming it Pern. They cannibalized their spaceships for material and began building their homes.

Pern was ideal for settlement, except for one thing. At irregular intervals, the sixth planet of its system would swing close to it and release swarms of deadly mycorrhizoid spores, which devoured anything organic that they touched and rendered the ground where they landed fallow for years. The colonists immediately began searching for a way to combat the Thread, as the spores were named. For defense, they turned to the dragonets, small flying lizards that the colonists had tamed when they first landed. The fire-breathing ability of these reptiles had been a great help in the first Threadfall. By genetically enhancing and selectively breeding these reptiles through the generations, the colonists created a race of full-sized dragons.

With the dragons and their riders working together, the Pern colonists were able to fight Thread effectively and establish a firm hold on the planet. They settled into a quasi-feudal agricultural society, building Holds for the administrators and field workers, Halls for the craftsmen, and Weyrs for the dragons and riders to inhabit.

Many of the Pern novels detail the politics of the Holds and Weyrs between Threadfalls. The entire line of books spans over twenty-five hundred years, from the first landing of the settlers to their descendants' discovery of the master ship's computer centuries later.

Dragonflight, the first of the Dragonriders of Pern books, tells of a time twenty-five hundred years after the initial landing. The Thread has not been seen in four centuries, and people are starting to be skeptical of the old warnings. Three dragonriders, Lessa, F'lar, and F'nor, believe that the Thread is coming back, and try to mobilize the planetary defenses. Lessa, knowing that there are not enough dragons to combat the Thread effectively, time-travels back four hundred years to a point just after the last Threadfall, when that era's Dragonriders are growing restless and bored from lack of activity. Lessa convinces most of them to come back with her to combat Thread in her time. They arrive and fight off the Thread.

Dragonquest, the second book, picks up seven years after the end of the first book. Relations between the Oldtimers, as the time-traveling dragonriders are called, and the current generation are growing tense. After getting into a fight with one of the old dragonriders, F'nor is sent to Pern's Southern Continent to recover from his wound.

There he discovers a grub that neutralizes the Thread after it burrows into the ground. Realizing they have discovered a powerful new weapon against Thread, F'nor begins planning to seed the grubs over both continents.

Meanwhile, an unexpected Threadfall is the catalyst for a duel between F'lar, the Benden Weyrleader, and T'ron, the leader of the Old-timers. F'lar wins and banishes all dragonriders who will not accept his role as overall Weyrleader. The banished go to the Southern Continent. The book ends with the grubs being bred for distribution over Pern.

The third book, *The White Dragon*, chronicles the trials of young Jaxom as he raises the only white dragon on Pern, a genetic anomaly. Jaxom encounters prejudice and scorn from other dragonriders because his dragon is smaller than the rest. He is also scheduled to take command of one of the oldest Holds on Pern, and there are those who doubt his ability to govern. Both Jaxom and his dragon, Ruth, rise to the challenges and succeed in proving that bigger is not necessarily better. Jaxom commands his Hold, gets the girl, and all is set right with the world.

The Harper Hall trilogy (*Dragonsong, Dragonsinger, Dragondrums*) is aimed at young readers, and deals with a girl named Menolly and her rise from unappreciated daughter to Journeywoman Harper and keeper of fire-lizards.

In many subsequent novels, and in the short novel published here, McCaffrey has examined various other aspects of life on Pern from the earliest days of its colonization by humans.

Runner of Pern

ANNE McCAFFREY

Tenna topped the rise and paused to catch her breath, leaning forward, hands on her knees to ease her back muscles. Then, as she had been taught, she walked along the top on what flat space there was, kicking out her legs and shaking the thigh muscles, breathing through her mouth until she stopped panting. Taking her water bottle from her belt, she allowed herself a swig, swishing it around in her mouth to moisturize the dry tissue. She spat out that mouthful and took another, letting this one slowly trickle down her throat. The night was cool enough to keep her from sweating too heavily. But she wouldn't be standing around long enough to get a chill.

It didn't take long for her breath to return to normal, and she was pleased by that. She was in good shape. She kicked out her legs to ease the strain she had put on them to make the height. Then, settling her belt and checking the message pouch, she started down the hill at a rapid walking pace. It was too dark—Belior had not yet risen above the plain to give her full light for the down side of the hill—to be safe to run in shadows. She only knew this part of the trace by word of mouth, not actually footing it. She'd done well so far during this, her second Turn of running, and had made most of her first Cross by the suggested easy laps. Runners watched out for each other, and no station manager would overtax a novice. With any luck, she'd've made it all the way to the Western Sea in the next sevenday. This was the first big test of her apprenticeship as an express runner. And really she'd only the Western Range left to cross once she got to Fort Hold.

Halfway down from the top of the rise, she met the ridge crest she'd been told about and, with the usual check of the pouch she carried, she picked up her knees and started the ground-eating lope that was the pride of a Pernese runner.

Of course, the legendary "lopers"—the ones who had been able to do a hundred miles in a day—had perished ages ago, but their memory was kept alive. Their endurance and dedication were an example to everyone who ran the traces of Pern. There hadn't been many of them, according to the legend, but they had started the runner stations when the need for the rapid delivery of messages arose, during the First Fall of Thread. Lopers had been able to put themselves in some sort of trance which not only allowed them to run extended distances but kept them warm during snowstorms and in freezing temperatures. They had also planted the original traces, which now were a network crisscrossing the entire continent.

While only Lord Holders and Craftmasters could afford to keep runnerbeasts for their couriers, the average person, wanting to contact crafthalls, relatives, or friends across Pern, could easily afford to express a letter across the continent in runner pouches, carried from station to station. Others might call them "holds," but runners had always had "stations," and station agents, as part of *their* craft history. Drum messages were great for short messages, if the weather was right and the winds didn't interrupt the beat, but as long as folks wanted to send written messages there'd be runners to take them.

Tenna often thought proudly of the tradition she was carrying on. It was a comfort on long solitary journeys. Right now, the running was good: the ground was firm but springy, a surface that had been assiduously maintained since the ancient runners had planted it. Not only did the mossy stuff make running easier but it identified a runner's path. A runner would instantly feel the difference in the surface, if he, or she, strayed off the trace.

Slowly, as full Belior rose behind her, her way became illuminated by the moon's light and she picked up her pace, running easily, breathing freely, her hands carried high, chest height, with elbows tucked in. No need to leave a "handle," as her father called it, to catch the wind and slow the pace. At times like these, with good footing, a fair light, and a cool evening, you felt like you could run forever. If there weren't a sea to stop you.

She ran on, able to see the flow of the ridge, and by the time the trace started to descend again, Belior was high enough to light her way. She saw the stream ahead and slowed cautiously . . . though she'd been told that the ford had a good pebbly surface . . . and splashed through the ankle-high cold water, up onto the bank, veering slightly south, picking up the trace again by its springy surface.

She'd be over halfway now to Fort Hold and should make it by dawn. This was a well-traveled route, southwest along the coast to the farther Holds. Most of what she carried right now was destined for Fort Holders, so it was the end of the line for both the pouch and herself. She'd heard so much about the facilities at Fort that she didn't quite believe it. Runners tended to understatement rather than exaggeration. If a runner told you a trace was dangerous, you believed it! But what they said about Fort was truly amazing.

Tenna came from a running family: father, uncles, cousins, grandfathers, brothers, sisters, and two aunts were all out and about the traces that crisscrossed Pern from Nerat Tip to High Reaches Hook, from Benden to Boll.

"It's bred in us," her mother had said, answering the queries of her younger children. Cesila managed a large runner station, just at the northern Lemos end of the Keroon plains where the immense sky-broom trees began. Strange trees that flourished only in that region of Pern. Trees that, a much younger Tenna had been sure, were where the Benden Weyr dragons took a rest in their flights across the continent. Cesila had laughed at Tenna's notion.

"The dragons of Pern don't need to rest anywhere, dear. They just go *between* to wherever they need to go. You probably saw some of them out hunting their weekly meal."

In her running days, Cesila had completed nine full Crosses a Turn until she'd married another runner and started producing her own bag of runners-to-be.

"Lean we are in the breeding, and leggy, most of us, with big lungs and strong bones. Ah, there now, a few come out who're more for speed than distance but they're handy enough at Gathers, passing the winning line before the others have left the starting ribbon. We have our place on the world same as holders and even Weyrfolk. Each to his, or her, own. Weaver and tanner, and farmer, and fisher, and smith and runner and all."

"That's not the way we was taught to sing the Duty Song," Tenna's younger brother had remarked.

"Maybe," Cesila had said with a grin, "but it's the way I sing it and you can, too. I must have a word with the next harper through here. He can change his words if he wants us to take his messages." And she gave her head one of her emphatic shakes to end that conversation.

As soon as runner-bred children reached full growth, they were tested to see if they'd the right Blood for the job. Tenna's legs had stopped growing by the time she'd reached her fifteenth full Turn. That was when she was assessed by a senior runner of another Bloodline. Tenna had been very nervous, but her mother, in her usual offhanded way, had given her lanky daughter a long knowing look.

"Nine children I've given your father, Fedri, and four are already runners. You'll be one, too, never fear."

"But Sedra's . . ."

Cesila held up her hand. "I know your sister's mated and breeding but she did two Crosses before she found a man she had to have. So she counts, too. Gotta have proper Bloodlines to breed proper runners and it's us who do that." Cesila paused to be sure Tenna would not interrupt again. "I came from a hold with twelve, all of them runners. And all breeding runners. You'll run, girl. Put your mind at ease. You'll run." Then she'd laughed. "It's for how long, not will you, for a female."

Tenna had decided a long time ago—when she had first been considered old enough to mind her younger siblings—that she'd prefer running to raising runners. She'd run until she could no longer lift her knees. She'd an aunt who'd never mated: ran until she was older than Cesila was now and then took over the management of a connecting station down Igen way. Should something happen and she couldn't run any more, Tenna wouldn't mind managing a station. Her mother ran hers proper, always had hot water ready to ease a runner's aching limbs, good food, comfortable beds, and healing skills that rivaled what you could find in any Hold. And it was always exciting, for you never knew who might run in that day, or where they'd be going. Runners crossed the continent regularly, bringing with them news from other parts of Pern. Many had interesting tales to tell of problems on the trace and how to cope with them. You heard all about other Holds and Halls, and the one dragonweyr, as well as what interested runners most specifically: what conditions were like and where traces might need maintenance after a heavy rain or landslide.

She was mightily relieved, however, when her father said he had asked Mallum of the Telgar station to do her assessment. At least Tenna had met the man on those occasions when he'd been through to their place on the edge of Keroon's plains. Like other runners, he was a lanky length of man, with a long face and graying hair that he tied back with his sweatband as most runners did.

Her parents didn't tell her when Mallum was expected, but he turned up one bright morning, handing in a pouch to be logged on the board by the door and then limping to the nearest seat.

"Bruised the heel. We'll have to rock that south trace again. I swear it grows new ones every Turn or two," he said, mopping his forehead with his orange sweatband and thanking Tenna for the cup of water. "Cesila, got some of that sheer magic poultice of yours?"

"I do. Put the kettle to heat the moment I saw you struggling up the trace."

"Was not struggling," Mallum said in jovial denial. "Was careful not to put the heel down was all."

"Don't try to fool me, you spavined gimper," Cesila replied as she was dipping a poultice sack into the heated water, testing it with a finger.

"Who's to run on? Some orders in that need to be got south smartly."

"I'm taking it on," Fedri said, coming out of his room and tying on his sweatband. "How urgent?" His runner's belt was draped over his shoulder. "I've others to add from the morning's eastern run."

"Hmmm. They want to make the Igen Gather."

"Ha! It'll be there betimes," Fedri said, reaching for the pouch and carefully adding the other messages to it before he put it through the belt loops. Settling it in the small of his back with one hand, he chalked up the exchange time with the other. "See you."

Then he was out the door and turning south, settling into his long-distance stride almost as soon as his foot hit the moss of the trace.

Tenna, knowing what was needed, had already pulled a footstool over to Mallum. She looked up at him for permission and, with his nod, unlaced the right shoe, feeling the fine quality of the leather. Mallum made his own footwear and he had set the stitching fine and tight.

Cesila knelt beside her daughter, craning her head to see the bruise.

"Hmmm. Hit it early on, didn'tcha?"

"I did," Mallum said, drawing his breath in with a hiss as Cesila slapped the poultice on. "Oooooh! Shards . . . you didn't get it too hot, didja?"

Cesila sniffed denial in reply as she neatly and deftly tied the packet to his foot.

"And is this the lass of yours as is to be taken for a run?" he asked, relaxing his expression from the grimace he'd made when the poultice was first applied. "Prettiest of the bunch." And he grinned at Tenna.

"Handsome is as handsome does," Cesila said. "Looks is all right but long legs is better. Tenna's her name."

"Handsome's not a bad thing to be, Cesila, and it's obvious your daughter takes after you."

Cesila sniffed again but Tenna could see that her mother didn't mind Mallum's remarks. And Cesila was a handsome woman: lithe still and slender, with graceful hands and feet. Tenna wished she were more like her mother.

"Nice long line of leg," Mallum went on approvingly. He beckoned for Tenna to come closer and had a good look at the lean muscles, then asked to see her bare feet. Runners tended to walk barefooted a lot. Some even ran barefooted. "Good bone. Hmmm. Nice lean frame. Hmm. Not a pick on you, girl. Hope you can keep warm enough in winter like that." That was such an old runner comment, but his jollity was encouraging and Tenna was ever so glad that Mallum was her assessor. He was always pleasant on his short stops at Station 97. "We'll take a short one tomorrow when this foot's eased."

More runners came in so Cesila and Tenna were busy, checking in messages, sorting the packets for the changeovers, serving food, heating water for baths, tending scratched legs. It was spring of the year and most runners only used leggings during the coldest months.

Enough stayed the night so there was good chatter and gossip to entertain. And prevent Tenna from worrying about satisfying her assessor on the morning.

A runner had come in late that night, on her way north, with some messages to be transferred to an eastern route. His heel bruise much eased, Mallum thought he could take those on.

"It's a good testing trot," he said, and gestured for Tenna to slip the message pouch on her belt. "I'll travel light, girl." His grin was teasing, for the pouch weighed little more than the wherhide it was made from. "First, lemme see what you wear on your feet."

She showed him her shoes, the most important part of a runner's gear. She'd used her family's special oils to soften the wherhide and then formed it on the lasts that had been carved for her feet by her uncle who did them for her Bloodline. Her stitches were neat but not as fine as Mallum's. She intended to improve. Meanwhile, this pair wasn't a bad effort and fit her feet like gloves. The spikes were medium length as fit for the present dry trace conditions. Most long-distance runners carried an extra pair with shorter spikes for harder ground, especially during spring and summer. She was working on her winter footwear, hoping she'd need it, for those boots came up to midcalf and required a lot more conditioning. Even they were of lighter weight than the footgear holders would use. But then most holders plodded and the thicker leather was suitable for their tasks as fine soft hide was right for a runner's foot.

Mallum nodded in approval as he handed back her shoes. Now he checked the fit of her belt to be sure it was snug enough not to rub against the small of her back as she ran, and made certain that her short trunks would not pull against her leg and that her sleeveless top covered her backside well below her waist to help prevent her getting a kidney chill. Stopping often from a need to relieve oneself ruined the rhythm of a run.

"We'll go now," Mallum said, having assured himself that she was properly accoutred.

Cesila stood in the door, gave her daughter a reassuring nod, and saw them off, up the eastern trace. Before they were out of sight, she gave the particular runner yodel that stopped them in their tracks. They saw her pointing skyward: at the arrow formation of dragons in the sky, a most unusual sight these days when the dragons of Benden Weyr were so rarely seen.

To see dragons in the sky was the best sort of omen. They were there . . . and then they weren't! She smiled. Too bad runners couldn't just *think* themselves to their destinations the way dragons could. As if he had shared her thought, Mallum grinned back at her and then turned to face the direction in which they were headed, and any nervousness Tenna had had disappeared. When he sprang off again, she was in step with him by the third stride. He nodded again approvingly.

"Running's not just picking up your heels and showing them to those behind you," Mallum said, his eyes watching the trace ahead, though he must have known it as well as Tenna did. "A good bit of proper running is learning to pace yourself and your stride. It's knowing the surfaces of the traces you have to traverse. It's knowing how to save your strength so you'll last the longer hauls. When to ease back to a walk, when and how to drink and eat so's you're not too gutty to run right. It's learning the routes of the various Crosses and what sort of weather you might have to run through . . . and learning to maneuver on snowrunners on the northern Crosses. And, most important, when to take cover and just let the weather have its way with the world and you safe out of it. So's the messages and the packets you carry will get through as soon as possible."

She had responded with a nod of appreciation. Not that she hadn't heard the same lecture time and again in the station from every relative and runner. But this time it was for her benefit and she owed Mallum the courtesy of listening closely. She did watch Mallum's stride, though, to be sure his heel wasn't bothering him. He caught her glance once and gave her a grin.

"Be sure you carry a wedge of that poultice on any long laps, girl. You never know, you know, when you might need it. As I just did." And he grimaced, reminding Tenna that even the best runner can put a foot wrong.

While no runner carries much, the long-tailed orange sweatband that runners invariably wore could be used to strap a strain or sprain. An oiled packet, no larger than the palm of a hand, had a cloth soaked in numbweed which both cleansed and eased the scratches one could acquire from time to time. Simple remedies for the most common problems. A wedge of poultice could be added to such travel gear and be well worth its weight.

Tenna had no trouble making that lap with Mallum even when he picked up the pace on the flat section.

"Running with a pretty girl's not hard to do," he told her when they took one brief pause.

She wished he didn't make so much of her looks. They wouldn't help her run any better or help her become what she wanted to be: a top runner.

By the time they reached Irma's station at midday, she was not even breathing very hard. But the moment Mallum slowed, he limped slightly with his full weight on the heel.

"Hmm. Well, I can wait out the day here with more poultice," he said, pulling the little wedge from one of the pockets of his belt. "See," and he displayed it to Tenna, "handy enough."

She tapped her aid pocket and smiled.

Old Irma came out with a grin on her sun-dried face for them.

"Will she do, Mallum?" the old woman asked, handing each a cup.

"Oh, aye, she'll do. A credit to her Bloodline and not a bother to run with!" Mallum said with a twinkle in his eyes.

"I pass, do I, Mallum?" Tenna asked, needing to have a direct answer.

"Oh, aye," and he laughed, walking about and shaking his legs to get the kinks out even as she was doing. "No fear on that. Any hot water for m'poultice, Irm?"

"Coming up." She ducked back into her station and came out with a bowl of steaming water which she set down on the long bench that was an inevitable fixture of every station. The overhang of the roof provided a shelter from sun and rain. Most runners were obsessed with watching the traces to see who was coming and going. The long bench, its surface smoothed by generations of bums sliding across it, was placed so that it commanded a good view of the four traces linking at Irma's.

Automatically, Tenna pulled a footstool from under the bench and held out her hand to receive Mallum's right foot. She untied the shoe, and placed the now moistened poultice on the bruise while Irma handed her a bandage to fix it in place, taking a good look at the injury in the process.

" 'Nother day'll do it. Shoulda stayed off it this mornin', too."

"Not when I'd a chance to run with such a pretty girl," Mallum said.

"Just like a man," Irma said dismissively.

Tenna felt herself blushing, although she was beginning to believe he wasn't just teasing. No one else had ever commented on her looks.

"It wasn't a taxing leg, Irma. It's level most of the way and a good surface," she said, grinning shyly at Mallum as she tried to divert Irma's criticism.

"Humph! Well, a hill run would've been downright foolish and it is flat this a way."

"Anything for Tenna to take back," Mallum asked, getting back to business, "to make her first round-trip as a runner?"

"Should be," Irma said, winking at Tenna for this informal inclusion into the ranks of Pern runners. "You could eat now . . . soup's ready and so's the bread."

"Wouldn't mind a bit myself," Mallum said, carefully shifting his position as if easing the heat from the poultice, since the heat probably penetrated even the toughened sole of his foot.

By the time Tenna had eaten the light meal, two runners came in: a man she didn't know by sight, on a long leg from Bitra with a pouch to go farther west; and one of Irma's sons.

"I can run it to Ninety-Seven," she said, the official designation of her family's station.

"That'll do," the man said, panting and heaving from his long haul. "That'll do fine." He gasped for more breath. "It's an urgent," he got out. "Your name?"

"Tenna."

"One . . . of . . . Fedri's?" he asked and she nodded. "That's good . . . enough for me. Ready to . . . hit the trace?"

"Sure." She held out her hand for the pouch that he slipped off his belt, pausing only to mark the pass-over time on the flap as he gave it into her keeping. "You are?" she asked, sliding the pouch onto her own belt and settling it in the small of her back.

"Masso," he said, reaching now for the cup of water Irma had hastened to bring him. He whooshed her off to the westward trace. With a final grateful farewell wave to Mallum, she picked up her heels as Mallum cheered her on with the traditional runner's "yo-ho."

She made it home in less time than it had taken her to reach Irma's, and one of her brothers was there to take the pouch on the next westward lap. Silan nodded approval at the pass-over time, marked his own receipt, and was off.

"So, girl, you're official," her mother said, and embraced her. "And no need to sweat it at all, was there?"

"Running's not always as easy," her father said from the bench, "but you made good time and that's a grand way to start. I hadn't expected you back before midafternoon."

Tenna did the short legs all around Station 97 for the first summer and into that winter, building her stamina for longer runs and becoming known at all the connecting stations. She made her longest run to Greystones, on the coast, just ahead of a very bad snowstorm. Then, because she was the only runner available in Station 18 when the exhausted carrier of an urgent message came in, she had to carry it two stations north. A fishing sloop would be delayed back to port until a new mast could be stepped. Since the vessel was overdue, there were those who'd be very glad to get the message she carried.

Such emergency news should have been drummed ahead, but the high winds would tear such a message to nonsense. It was a tough run, with cold as well as wind and snow across a good bit of the low-lying trace. Pacing herself, she did take an hour's rest in one of the Thread shelters that dotted a trace. She made the distance in such good time in those conditions that she got extra stitches on her belt, marking her rise toward journeyman rank.

This run to Fort Hold would be two more stitches on her belt if she finished in good time. And she was sure she would . . . with the comforting sort of certainty that older runners said you began to sense when you'd been traveling the traces awhile. She was also now accustomed to judging how long she had run by the feeling in her legs. There was none of the leaden feeling that accompanied real fatigue, and she was still running easily. So long as she had no leg cramp, she knew she could continue effortlessly at this good pace until she reached Station 300 at Fort. Leg cramp was always a hazard and could strike you without warning. She was careful to renew the tablets a runner chewed to ease off a cramp. And was not too slow about grabbing a handful of any useful herbs she spotted which would help prevent the trouble.

She oughtn't to be letting her mind wander like this, but with an easy stride and a pleasant night in which to travel, it was hard to keep her mind on the job. She would, smartly enough, if there were complications like bad weather or poor light. This was also far too well traveled country for there to be dangers like tunnel snakes, which were about the worst risk that runners encountered—usually at dawn or dusk, when the creatures were out hunting. Of course, renegades, while not as common as tunnel snakes, were more dangerous, since they were human, not animal, but that distinction was often moot. As runners rarely carried marks, they were not as likely to be waylaid as were messengers on runnerbeasts, or other solitary travelers. Tenna hadn't heard of any renegade attacks this far west, but sometimes those people were so vicious that they might pull up a runner just for spite and malice. In the past three turns, there had been two cases—and those up in northern Lemos and Bitra—where runners had been hamstrung out of sheer malevolence.

Once in a while, in a bad winter, a flock of very hungry wherries might attack a runner in the open, but the instances were rare enough. Snakes were the most likely danger encountered, particularly midsummer, when there were newly hatched clutches.

Her father had had injuries two summers back with such a hazard. He'd been amazed at how fast the adult tunnel snake could move when alarmed. Mostly they were torpid creatures, only hunger quickening them. But he'd stepped in the midst of an ill-placed nest and had had the hatchlings swarming up his legs, pricking the skin in innumerable places and even managing to get as high as his crotch. (Her mother had stifled a giggle and remarked that it had been more than her father's pride that had been wounded.) But he'd scars from claw and tooth that he could show.

Moonlit nights like this one were a joy to run in, with the air cool enough to dry the sweat on her face and chest, the trace springy underfoot and clear ahead of her. And her thoughts could wander.

There would be a Gather shortly after she reached her destination; she knew she was carrying some orders for Crafts displaying at Fort Hold. Pouches were invariably fuller going to or coming from a Gather—orders from those unable to attend, wishing to contact a Mastercraftsman. Maybe, if she was lucky, she could stay over for the Gather. She hadn't been to one in a long while and she did want to find well-tanned leathers for a new pair of running shoes. She'd enough money to her credit to give a fair price for the right hides: she'd checked the books her mother kept of her laps. Most Halls were quite willing to take a runner-station chit. She'd one in a belt pocket. If she found just the right skins, she'd a bit of leeway to bargain, above and beyond the surface value of the chit.

A Gather would be fun, too. She loved dancing, and was very good at the toss dance, if she could find someone who could properly partner her in it. Fort was a good Hold. And the music would be special, seeing as how the Harper Hall was right there in Fort.

She ran on, tunes of harper melodies flitting through her mind even if she'd no breath to sing them.

She was running along a long curve now, around an upthrust of rock—most traces were as straight as possible—and brought her mind back to her directions. Just around this curve, she should find a trace turning off to the right, inland, toward Fort. She must pay attention now so she wouldn't have to break stride and backtrack.

Suddenly she could feel vibrations through her feet, though she could see nothing around the vegetation banking the curve. Listening intently, she could now hear an odd *phuff-phuff* sound, coming closer, getting louder. The sound was just enough of a warning for her to move left, out of the center of the trace, where she'd have just that much more of a glimpse of what was making the sound and the vibrations. This was a runner track, not a trail or road. No runner made those sounds, or hit the ground that hard to make vibrations. She saw the dark mass bearing down on her, and flung herself into the undergrowth as runnerbeast and rider came within a finger span of knocking into her. She could feel the wind of their passing and smell the sweat of the beast.

"Stupid!" she shouted after them, getting branches and leaves in her mouth as she fell, feeling needly gouges in the hands she had put out to break her fall. She spent the next minute struggling to her feet and spitting bitter leaves and twigs out of her mouth. They left behind an acrid, drying taste: sticklebush! She'd fallen into a patch of sticklebush. At this time of the Turn, there were no leaves yet to hide the hairlike thorns that coated twig and branch. A nuisance which balanced out their gift of succulent berries in the autumn.

Nor did the rider falter, or even pull up, when the least he could have done was return to be sure she hadn't been injured. Surely he'd seen her? Surely he'd heard her outraged shout. And what was *he* doing, using a runner trace in the first place? There was a good road north for ordinary travelers.

"I'll get you!" she called, shaking her fist with frustration.

She was shaking with reaction to such a near miss. Then she became uncomfortably aware of the scratches on hands, arms, legs, chest, and two on one cheek. Stamping with fury, she got the numbweed from her belt pocket and daubed at the cuts, hissing as the solution stung. But she didn't want the sap to get into her blood. Nor did she want the slivers to work in. She managed to pick the ones out of her hands, daubing the numbweed into those. She couldn't really see the extent of her injuries, some being down the back of her arm. She picked out what slivers she could and carefully pressed in the pad until all the moisture was gone from it. Even if she had avoided infection, she was likely to be teased about falling when she got to the station. Runners were supposed to keep *on* their feet, and in balance. Not that a rider had any business on the trace. Surely that would also help her find out who the rider had been, besides being bold enough to ride a runner trace. And if she wasn't around to give him a fat lip, maybe another runner would give the lesson in her place. Runners were not above complaining to Lord Holders or their stewards if someone abused their rights.

Having done as much as she could then, she stifled her anger: that didn't get the pouch to its destination. And she mustn't let her anger get the better of common sense. The brush with disaster, close as it was, had resulted in very minor problems, she told herself firmly. What were scratches! But she found it hard to regain her stride. She'd been going so smoothly, too, and so close to the end of this lap.

She could have been killed, smacking into a runnerbeast at the speeds they'd both been traveling. If she hadn't thought to move out of the center of the trace . . . where she had every right to be, not him . . . if she hadn't felt the hoofbeats through her shoes and heard the animal's high breathing . . . Why, both sets of messages could have been delayed! Or lost.

Her legs felt tired and heavy and she had to concentrate hard to try to regain the rhythm. Reluctantly she realized that she was unlikely to and settled for conserving her energy.

Running into the end of night, the dawn behind her, was not as much a pleasure as it could have been, and that annoyed Tenna even more. Just wait till she found out who that rider was! She'd tell him a thing or two. Though common sense told her that she was unlikely to encounter him. He was outbound and she was inbound. If he'd been in that much of a hurry, he might be a relay rider, bound for a distant location. Lord Holders could afford such services and the stabling of fast runnerbeasts along the way. But he shouldn't have been on a runner trace. There were roads for beasts! Hooves could tear up the surface of the trace and the station manager might have to spend hours replacing divots torn up by shod hooves. Traces were for runners. She kept returning to that indignant thought. She just hoped any other runner on the trace would hear him in time! *That's one reason you keep your mind on your run, Tenna.* Even if you'd no reason to suspect you weren't alone with the night and the moon on a runner trace.

The runner station was just below the main entrance to Fort Hold. History had it that Fort had started runners as short-distance messengers, hundreds and hundreds of turns ago, even before drum towers were built. Fort Hold had utilized the skills of runners for many tasks, especially during Threadfall, when runners had accompanied all ground crews, vital as couriers in emergencies. The installation of the drum towers and the development of runnerbeasts had not put an end to the need for the runners of Pern. This main connecting hold was the largest ever built just to house and care for runners. Three levels high, she'd been told, and several back into the Fort cliff. It also boasted one of the best bathing facilities on the continent: hot running water in deep tubs that had eased centuries of runner aches and pains. Cesila had highly recommended that Tenna try for Fort when she got that far west. And here she was and right ready to appreciate the accommodations.

She was very weary and not only out of pace but jarring herself with every step down the broader avenue that led to her destination. Her hands stung from the sap and she hoped she hadn't any slivers left in them. But hands were a long way from the feet.

Beastholders, up early to feed stock, gave her cheery waves and smiles, and their courtesies somewhat restored her good humor. She did not care to arrive petulant as well as scratched, not on her first visit here.

Almost as if the manager had a special sensitivity to incoming runners, the double door was thrown open as she came to a rough, gasping halt, hand raised to catch the bell cord.

"Thought I heard someone coming." The man, a welcoming grin on his face, put out both hands to steady her. He was one of the oldest men she had ever seen: his skin was a network of wrinkles and grooves, but his eyes were bright—for this hour—and he looked to be a merry man. "New one, too, at that, for all you look familiar to me. A pretty face is a great sight on a fine morning."

Sucking in breath enough to give her name, Tenna paced into the large entry room. She unbuckled her message pouch as she eased the tension in her leg muscles.

"Tenna passing Two-Oh-Eight with eastern messages. Fort's the destination for all."

"Welcome to Three Hundred, Tenna," he said, taking the pouch from her and immediately chalking up her arrival on the heavy old board to the left of the station door. "All for here, huh?" He passed her a cup before he opened the pouch, to check the recipients.

With cup in hand, she went out again, still flicking her legs to ease the muscles. First she rinsed her mouth, spitting out that first mouthful onto the cobbles. Then she would sip to swallow. Nor was this just water but some sort of fresh-tasting drink that refreshed dry tissues.

"You're a mite the worse for the run," the man said, standing in the door and pointing to the bloody smears on her bare skin. "What'd you run into?"

"Sticklebush," she said through gritted teeth. "Runnerbeast ran me off round the hill curve . . . galloping along a *runner* trace like he must know he shouldn't." She was astonished at the anger in her voice when she'd meant to sound matter-of-fact.

"That'd be Haligon, more'n likely," the station keeper said, nodding with a disapproving scowl. "Saw him peltin' down to the beasthold an hour or so ago. I've warned him myself about using the traces but he says it cuts half an hour off a trip and he's conducting an ex-per-i-ment."

"He might have killed me," she said, her anger thoroughly fanned.

"You'd better tell him. Maybe a pretty runner'll get it through his thick skull because the odd crack or two hasn't."

His reaction made Tenna feel that her anger was righteous. It's one thing to be angry on your own, another to have confirmation of your right to be angry. She felt redeemed. Though she couldn't see why being pretty would be an advantage if you were giving someone what-for. She could hit just as hard as the ugliest runner she'd ever met.

"You'll need a long soak with sticklebush slivers in you. You did have something to put on 'em right then, didn't you?" When she nodded, now annoyed because he implied that she might not have that much sense, he added, "I'll can send m'mate to look at those cuts. Wrong time of the Turn to fall into sticklebush, ya know." And she nodded her head vigorously. "All in all, you made a good time from Two-Oh-Eight," he added, approvingly. "Like that in a young runner. Shows you're not just a pretty face. Now, go up the stairs there, take your first right, go along the corridor, fourth door on the left. No one else's up. Towels on the shelves. Leave your clothes: they'll be washed and dry by evening. You'll want a good feed after a night run and then a good long sleep. We've all for you, runner."

She thanked him, turned to the stairs, and then tried to lift the wooden blocks her legs had become up the steps. Her toes dragged as she made her feet move, and she was grateful for the carpeting that saved the wooden stairs from her spikes. But then this place was for runners, shoes, spikes, and all.

"Fourth door," she murmured to herself, and pushed against a portal that opened into the most spacious bathing room she'd ever seen. And pungent with something pleasantly astringent. Nothing as grand as this even at Keroon Hold. Five tubs ranged along the back wall with curtains to separate them if one needed privacy. There were two massage tables, sturdy, padded, with shelves of oils and salves underneath. They would account for the nice smells. The room was hot and she began to sweat again, a sweat that made her nicks and scratches itch. There were changing cubicles, too, to the right of the door ... and behind her she found oversized towels in stacks higher than her head, and she wasn't short. There were cubbies holding runner pants and shirts for all weathers and the thick anklets that cushioned and warmed weary feet. She took a towel, her fingers feeling the thick, soft nap. It was as big as a blanket.

In the cubicle nearest the tubs, she shucked off her garments, automatically folding them into a neat pile. Then, looping the towel over the hook set by the side of the tub for that purpose, she eased herself into the warm water. The tub was taller than she was and she let herself down to touch a floor, a full hand of water above her head when she did. Amazing!

This was sheer luxury. She wondered how often she could draw a run to Fort Hold. The water made her scratches sting, but that was nothing to the comfort it was giving her tired muscles. Swishing around in the large square tub, her hand connected with a ledge, sort of curved, a few inches below the surface. With a grin she realized that she could rest her head on it and be able to float safely. Which was exactly what she did, arms out to her sides, legs dangling. She hadn't known bathing could be so . . . so splendid. She let every muscle in her body go limp. And lay suspended in the water.

"Tenna?" a woman's voice called gently, as if not to startle the lone bather. "I'm Penda, Torlo's mate. He sent me up. I've some herbs for the bath that'll help those scratches. Wrong time of the Turn to fall into sticklebush."

"I know," Tenna agreed dourly. "Be glad of any help." Tenna didn't really want to open her eyes or move but she politely swished herself across the water to the edge of the tub.

"Lemme see them cuts so's I can see didja get any punctures like. That'd be no good with the sap rising," Penda said. She walked quickly to the tub with a odd sideways gait, so whatever had injured her hip had happened a long time ago and she had learned to cope with it. She grinned at Tenna. "Pretty runner girl, you are. You give Haligon what-for next time you see him."

"How'll I know him?" Tenna asked acerbically, though she dearly wished a confrontation with the rider. "And why is 'pretty' a help?"

"Haligon likes pretty girls." Penda gave an exaggerated wink. "We'll see you stay about long enough to give him what-for. *You* might do some good."

Tenna laughed and, at Penda's gesture, held out her hands and turned her left arm where Penda could see it.

"Hmmm. Mostly surface but there's punctures on the heels of both hands." She ran oddly soft fingers across Tenna's hands, catching on three slivers so that Tenna shivered with the unpleasant sensation. "Soaking'll do the most good. Loosen them up in your skin. Prolly clean 'em all out. Stickle's a clever bush, harming you so, but this'll help," she said, and took a collection of bottles from the deep pocket in her apron and selected one. "Got to leave nothing to chance, ya know," she added as she deftly splashed about twenty drops into the tub water. "Don't worry about emptying the tub, either. It'll run clear and'll be fresh water by the time someone else climbs in. I'll take out the slivers when you've soaked. You want a rub then? Or would you rather sleep first?"

"A bit of a rub would be marvelous, thanks. And before I sleep."

"I'll be back with some food."

Tenna thought of the bathing room in her parents' station and grinned. Nothing to compare to this, though she'd always thought her station was lucky to have a tub so long you could lie out flat in it: even the tallest runners could. But you had to keep the fire going under the tank all the time to be sure there was enough for when a bath was needed. Not like this—the water already hot and you only needing to step into the tub. The herbs scented the steamy water, making it feel softer against her skin. She lay back again.

She was nearly asleep when Penda returned with a tray containing klah, fresh-baked bread, a little pot of, appropriately enough, stickleberry preserve, and a bowl of porridge.

"Messages've already been handed over to them they was sent to, so you can sleep good, knowing the run's well ended."

Tenna consumed her meal, down to the last scrap. Penda was making quite a mixture with the massage oils, and the runner inhaled the scent of them. Then Tenna climbed on the table, letting her body go limp while Penda used a tweezer on the slivers still caught in her flesh. Penda counted as she deposited the wicked hairs. Nine, all told. She applied more medication and the last of the itching and discomfort vanished. Tenna sighed. Then Penda soothed tired muscles and tendons. Her touch was sure but gentle. She did announce that there were more punctures on the backs of Tenna's arms and legs and proceeded go at them with the tweezers to remove the slivers. That done, her motions became more soothing and Tenna relaxed again.

"There y'are. Just go along to the third door down on your left, Tenna," Penda said softly when she had finished.

Tenna roused enough from the delightful, massage-induced stupor and wrapped the big towel tightly around her chest. Like most runner females, she didn't have much of a bust, but that was an advantage.

"Don't forget these," Penda said, shoving the laces of her running shoes at her. "Clothes'll be clean and dry when you wake."

"Thanks, Penda," Tenna said sincerely, astonished that she'd been drowsy enough to forget her precious shoes.

She padded down the hall in the thick anklets that Penda had slipped on her feet and pushed in the third door. Light from the corridor showed her where the bed was, straight across the narrow space, against the wall. Closing the door, she made her way to it in the dark. Dropping the towel, she leaned down to feel for the edge of the quilt she'd seen folded on the foot of the bed. She pulled it over her as she stretched out. Sighed once and fell asleep.

Good-natured laughter and movement down the hall roused her. Someone had half-opened the glowbasket, so she saw her own clothes, clean, dry, and neatly folded on the stool where she'd dropped her running shoes. She realized she hadn't even taken off the anklets before she got into bed. She wriggled her toes in them. No tenderness there. Her hands were stiff but cool, so Penda'd gotten out all the slivers. The skin of her left arm and leg was stiff, though, and she threw back the quilt and tried to see the injuries. She couldn't, but there was a little too much heat in the skin on the back of her left arm for her liking, and her right leg. Five sort-of-sore spots she couldn't really check at all other than identifying them as "sore." And, when she checked her legs, two bad red bumps on her thigh, one in the left calf and two on the fleshy part of her right leg by the shinbone. She had suffered more hurt than she'd realized. And stickle slivers could work their way through your flesh and into your blood. If one got to your heart, you could die from it. She groaned and rose. Shook out her legs, testing the feel of her muscles, and, thanks to Penda's massage, they didn't ache. She dressed and then carefully folded the quilt, placing it just as she'd found it on the bed.

Making her way back to the stairs, she passed the bathing room and heard the hum of masculine voices, then a laugh that was clearly from a female runner. As she came down the stairs, she was aware of the smell of roasting meats. Her stomach rumbled. One long narrow window lit the hall that led to the main room, and she gauged that she had slept most of the day. Perhaps she ought to have had a healer check out the scratches, but Penda knew what to do as well as any Hall-trained healer . . . probably better, since she was a station manager's mate.

"Now, here's a one who's prompt for her supper," Torlo said, calling the attention of the runners sitting around the room to Tenna's appearance. He introduced her. "Had a brush with Haligon early this morning," he added, and Tenna did not fail to note that this brash personage was known to them all from the nods and grimaces on their faces.

"I tol' Lord Groghe myself," one of the older runners said, nodding his head and looking solemn, "that there'd be an accident . . . then what'd he say to that? I asked him. Someone hurt because a wild lad won't respect what's our rights and propitty." Then he nodded directly at Tenna. "You aren't the only one he's knocked aside. Dinncha hear him coming?"

"Met him on the hill curve, she said," Torlo answered before Tenna could open her own mouth.

"Bad place, bad place. Runner can't see around it," a second man said, and nodded his sympathy to her. "See you've scratches? Penda put her good junk on ya?" Tenna nodded. "You'll be right then. I've seen your kin on the traces, haven't I? Betchur one of Fedri and Cesila's, aincha?" He smiled knowingly at the others. "You're prettier than she was and she was some pretty woman."

Tenna decided to ignore the compliment and admitted to her parentage. "Have you been through Station Ninety-Seven?"

"A time or two, a time or two," he said, grinning amiably. His runner's belt was covered with stitches.

Torlo had come up beside her and now took her left arm to peer at the side she couldn't really see well.

"Punctures," he said in a flat tone.

The other runners came to be sure his verdict was correct. They all nodded sagely and resumed their seats.

"Sometimes I wonder if all those berries're worth the risk of them slivers in spring," the veteran runner said.

"Worse time of the Turn to fall into them," she was told again.

"Misler, you run over to Healer Hall," Torlo said to one of them.

"Oh, I don't think that's necessary," Tenna said, because you had to pay healers and she then wouldn't have enough for good leathers.

"Being as how it was the Lord Holder's runnerbeast knocked you in, he'll pay for it," Torlo said, sensing her reluctance and winking at her.

"One of these days he'll have to pay out blood money iffen he doesn't bring that Haligon up short and *make* him quit our traces. Did those shod hooves leave many holes?" another man asked her.

"No," she had to admit. "Surface sprang right back up."

"Hmmm, that's what it's supposed to do."

"But we don't need Haligon galloping up and down like traces was put there for *his* benefit."

Misler departed on his errand and then, after each runner spoke his or her name and home station, a glass of wine was poured for her. She started to demur but Torlo eyed her sternly.

"You're not on the run list this day, girl."

"I need to finish my first Cross," she said wistfully as she took the glass and found an empty seat.

"You will, lass, you will," the first man—Grolly—said so assuredly as he held his glass up that she was heartened. The others all seconded his words.

A few scratches and maybe the three-four punctures were not going to keep her from reaching the western seashore. She sipped her wine.

The runners who'd been bathing descended now and were served their wine by the time Misler came trotting back, a man in healer colors following behind, with a hop and a skip to keep up with his long-legged escort.

Beveny introduced himself and asked for Penda to join him—a nicety that pleased Tenna and gave her a very good opinion of the journeyman. The consultation was conducted right there in the main hall since the injuries were to visible portions of her body. And the other runners were genuinely interested in knowing the worst of her condition and offered suggestions, most of them knowledgeable as to which herbs should be used and how efficacious they had been on such and such an occasion. Beveny kept a grin on his face as if he was well used to runner chaffering. As he probably was.

"I think this one, and the two on your leg, may still have slivers in them," Beveny said at length. "Nothing a poultice won't draw out overnight, I'm sure."

There were approving nods and wise smiles from the audience. Poultices were then discussed again and at length and the appropriate one decided on. During this part of the consultation, Tenna was installed in a comfortable, padded chair, a long stool affair attached to the front of it so her legs could stretch out. She'd never been fussed over so much in her life, but it was a runner thing: she'd seen her mother and father take the same personal care of anyone arriving at their station with an injury. But to be the center of so much attention—and at Fort

Station—was embarrassing in the extreme for Tenna and she kept trying to discount the urgency of such minor wounds. She did offer her
packet of her mother's poultice, and three of the runners remarked
favorably on Cesila's famous poultice, but hers was clearly for bruises,
not infections, so the healer told her to keep it for emergencies.

"Which I hope you won't have, of course," he said, smiling at her
as he mixed—with the hot water Penda fetched—an aromatic concoc-
tion that everyone now in the room had to approve.

Keenly aware that she must be properly modest and forbearing, as
well as brave, Tenna braced herself for the treatment. Hot poultices,
however therapeutic, could be somewhat uncomfortable. Then the mixture was ready. With deft fingers, Healer Beveny deposited neat blobs,
no larger than his thumbnail, on the sore spots. He must have judged
the heat just right, because none were too hot. He made sure to position the patches right over each blob before securing them with bandage strips that Penda had produced. Tenna felt each of the ten hot
spots, but the sensation was not all that unpleasant.

"I'll check tomorrow, Tenna, but I don't think we have to worry
about any of them," Beveny said with such conviction that Tenna was
relieved.

"Nor do you, here at Fort Station with the Healer Hall a stretch
away," said Torlo, and courteously saw Beveny to the door and
watched a polite few moments until the healer was halfway to his Hall.

"Nice fella," he said to anyone listening, and smiled at Tenna. "Ah,
here's the food."

Evidently that meal had been held up for her to be treated, because
now Penda led in the drudge carrying the roast platter with others
behind him, laden with large bowls of steaming food.

"Rosa," she said, pointing to one of the female runners, "get the
board. Spacia, grab a fork and spoon for Tenna. She's not to move.
Grolly, her glass is empty. . . ." As she directed the others to serve the
injured runner, she herself carved fine slices from the roasted ribs of
herdbeast. "The rest of you, get on line."

Tenna's embarrassment returned, waited on as she was by Rosa and
Spacia, who cheerfully performed their assigned tasks. Always she had
been the one to help, so this situation was quite novel. Of course, it
was also a runner thing, to be cosseted in need, but she'd never been
the recipient before.

Two more batches of runners arrived in from south and east. When they came back from bathing, they had to be told all about Haligon's forcing Tenna off the trace and how she had sticklebush punctures that were severe enough to require a healer. She got the distinct impression that almost everyone had had a run-in with this infamous Haligon, or knew someone who had. Eventually the tale had been told to everyone and the conversation changed to talk of the Gather three days hence.

Tenna sighed softly to herself. Three days? She'd be fully recovered by then and have to run on. She really did want to get the extra stitches for her first Cross. A Gather, even one at Fort, was not as important as upgrading herself. Well, nearly. It wasn't as if this were the last Gather she'd ever have a chance to attend, even if it was the first for her at the First Hold on Pern.

This was home station for two girls. Rosa had a cap of very tight dark curls and a pert face with mischievous eyes. Spacia, with long blond hair tied back, runner-wise, had a more dignified way about her although she kept up a wickedly bantering conversation with the younger male runners among others there. Then there was an informal concert for Tenna, some of the newer songs that the Harper Hall was airing. Rosa led, Spacia adding an alto line while three of the other runners joined in, one with a little whistle and the others with their voices. The evening became quite enjoyable, especially as either Grolly or Torlo kept filling Tenna's wineglass.

Rosa and Spacia helped her up the stairs, one on either side of her, with the excuse that the bandages mustn't loosen. They chattered about what they intended to wear to the Gather and who they hoped to dance with.

"We're on line tomorrow," Rosa said as they got her to her bed, "so we'll probably be off before you get down. Those poultices ought to do the trick."

They both wished her a good night's sleep. Her head was spinning as she lay down, but pleasantly, and she drifted into sleep very quickly.

Torlo arrived with a tray of food just as she was waking up.

"Not as sore today?"

"Not all over but my leg . . ." She pulled the quilt back so he could see.

"Hmmm. Need more on that one. Went in at an angle. I'm calling Beveny."

"Oh, really . . . I'd rather . . . Surely Penda knows what the healer made up for me . . ."

"She does, but we want the healer to speak about your injuries to Lord Groghe."

Tenna was dismayed now. A runner didn't go to the Lord Holder without *real* cause for complaint, and her injuries were not that serious.

"Now, see here, young runner," and Torlo waggled a finger at her, "I'm station master and I say we take this to the Lord Holder on account of it shouldna happened at all."

Beveny recommended a long soak in the tub and provided her with an astringent to use in the water.

"I'll leave more poultice with Penda. We want that final sliver out. See . . ." and he pointed to the thin, almost invisible hairs of the stick-lebush which had come from the arm puncture. "We want another of these fellows on the pad, not in you."

Two more had also erupted from the puncture wounds, and he carefully covered all three pads with glass slides, which he tied together.

"Soak at least an hour, Tenna," he told her. "You're to take it very handy today, too. Don't want that sliver to work any further down in your flesh."

She shuddered at the thought of an evil-looking hair loose in her body.

"Don't worry. It'll be out by evening," Beveny said, grinning reassuringly. "And you'll be dancing with us."

"Oh, I'll have to run on as soon as I'm able," she said earnestly.

Beveny's grin broadened. "What? And do me out of my dance with you?" Then his expression turned professional. "I can't release you as fit to run yet, you know. I'd want to see those puncture marks healing. Especially in the shin, where just the dirt and dust of a run could be embedded and cause a repeat infection. The wounds may seem," and he emphasized the word, "insignificant but I've tended a lot of runners and I know the hazards of the trace."

"Oh," Tenna said meekly.

"Right. Oh!" And he grinned again, pressing her shoulder with a kindly squeeze. "You will make your first Cross. Now rest. You runners are a breed apart, you know."

With that reminder, he left her to make her way to the bathing room.

Rosa, Spacia, Grolly—in fact, all the runners at the Fort Station—were in and out, groaning over the special messages that needed to be delivered to the Fort crafthalls, the Lord Holder, the Harper Hall, coming from the "backside of beyond" as Rosa termed it.

"Don't mind us," Rosa said when Tenna began to feel as if she ought to be doing her share. "It's always like this just before a Gather and we always complain, but the Gather makes up for it. Which reminds me, you don't have anything to wear."

"Oh, no, don't worry about me. . . ."

"Nonsense," Spacia said. "We will if we want to and we do." She gave Tenna's long frame an intent look and then shook her head. "Well, nothing we have would fit." Both girls were shorter than Tenna by a full head and, while neither carried much flesh, they were stockier than the eastern girl.

Then both turned to each other in the same instant and snapped their fingers. "Silvina!" they exclaimed in chorus.

"C'mon," Spacia said, and reached for Tenna's hand. "You can walk, can't you?"

"Oh, yes, but . . ."

"On your feet then, runner," Rosa said, and took Tenna's other arm, assisting her to an upright position. "Silvina's headwoman at the Harper Hall and she always has good things. . . ."

"But . . . I . . ." and then Tenna gave up protesting. It was obvious from the determined expressions on the two runners' faces that they would brook no argument.

"You're taking her to Silvina?" Penda asked, sidling out of the kitchen. "Good. I've nothing here to fit her and she's got to look her best when she meets that wretch Haligon."

"Why?" Tenna suspiciously wanted to know. Why would she need to look her best just to give Haligon what-for?

"Why, to maintain the reputation of Fort Station, of course," Rosa said with an impish grin. "We've our pride, you know, and you may be a visitor but you're here, now," and she pointed emphatically to the ground, "and must be presentable."

"Not that you aren't," Spacia hastily added, being slightly more tactful than Rosa, "except we want you more so than ever."

"After all, it *is* your first Fort Gather . . ."

"And you nearly finishing your first Cross, too."

Their chatter was impossible to resist and there was no way Tenna could appear at a Gather in runner gear, which was all she had of her own to wear.

At this evening hour, they found Silvina checking day-records in her office at the Harper Hall and she was more than delighted that she had been approached. She led them down to the storage rooms underneath the Harper Hall.

"We keep quite a few performance dresses in case a soloist wants to wear harper colors. You wouldn't mind wearing blue, would you?" Silvina said as she paused by the second of a line of locked doors. "Actually, I think blue would be a very good color for you." She had such a lovely speaking voice that Tenna was listening more to her tone than what she was saying. "And I've one that I think might be just the thing for you."

She opened a large wardrobe and, from the many there, she brought out a long gown with full sleeves and some fine embroidered trim that made all three girls gasp.

"It's lovely. Oh, I couldn't wear something this valuable," Tenna exclaimed, backing away.

"Nonsense," Silvina said, and gestured for Tenna to slip out of her runner top.

When Tenna carefully slipped on the dress, the softness of the fabric against her skin made her feel . . . special. She tried a little spin and the long skirt swirled about her ankles while the full sleeves billowed about her arms. It was the most flattering dress she'd worn and she examined it thoroughly, committing the details of its design to her mind so that she could reproduce it the next time she had marks enough for a Gather dress. The one she had at home was nowhere near as splendid as this. Could she, should she dance, in something as elegant as this? What if she spilled something on it?

"I'm not sure . . ." she began as she faced her companions.

"Not *sure!*" Rosa was indignant. "Why, that deep blue shows up your lovely skin and your eyes . . . they are blue, aren't they, or is it the dress makes them so? And it fits like it was made for *you*!"

Tenna looked down at the low-cut front of the bodice. Whoever it had been made for had had a lot more breast. She didn't fill it out properly. Silvina was rummaging through another box.

"Here," she said, and stuffed two pads in the front, settling them with such a practiced hand that the adjustment was done before Tenna could protest.

"*There!* That's much better," Spacia said, and then giggled. "I have to pad, too. But it'd be worse for us as runners to be heavy, bumping around all the time."

Tenna tentatively felt her newly improved form but, as she looked at herself in the mirror, she could see that the fit of the top was vastly improved and she looked more ... more ... well, it fit better. The fabric was so smooth to the touch, it was a pleasure just to feel the dress on her. And this shade of blue ...

"This is harper blue," she said with surprise.

"Of course it is," Silvina said with a laugh. "Not that it matters. You'll be wearing runner cords ... though right now," and Silvina's appreciative grin broadened, "you don't look runnerish ... if you'll forgive my frankness."

Tenna couldn't help admiring how much better her figure looked with that little alteration. She had a slim waist and the dress hugged it before flaring out over hips that she knew to be too bony and best covered.

"The pads won't ... pop out ... will they, when I'm dancing?"

"If you'll take off the dress, I'll put a few stitches to secure them where they should stay," Silvina said.

That was done so quickly that Silvina was folding the lovely dress over Tenna's arm before she realized it.

"Now, shoes?" Spacia asked. "She can't wear spikes. . . ."

"She might better wear them," Rosa said dourly, "with some of those louts who come to a Fort Gather. Haligon's not the only one who'll home in on her, looking that way."

Silvina had cast a measuring glance at Tenna's long, narrow feet and now took a long box down from one of the many shelves in this huge storeroom.

"Should have something to fit even narrow runner feet . . ." she murmured, and came up with a pair of soft, ankle-high, black suede boots. "Try these."

They did not fit. But the fourth pair—in dark red—were only slightly too long.

"Wear thick anklets and they'll fit fine," Spacia suggested.

And the three girls left, Tenna carefully transporting the dress to the station. Rose and Spacia insisted on sharing the burden of the boots and the underskirt that Silvina had offered to complete the costume.

The last sliver of sticklebush was on the pad the next morning and Beveny added it to the others, handing the evidence packet over to Torlo, who grinned in satisfaction.

"This'll make Lord Groghe see that we've a legitimate complaint," he said, and nodded emphatically at Tenna. She was about to protest when he added, "But not until after the Gather, for he's too busy to be approached right now. And he'll be in a much better mood after a good Gather." He turned to Tenna. "So you have to stay till after and that's that."

"But I could run short distances now, couldn't I?"

"Mmm," Torlo said, nodding. "Iffen a run comes up. Don't like to be idle, do you, girl?" She shook her head. "Wal, Healer, is she fit?"

"Short run and no hills," Beveny said, "and nowhere Haligon might ride." He grinned mischievously at her and took his leave.

Just before midday, Torlo called her from the front bench where she'd been watching the Gather stalls being erected.

"Run down to the port for me, will you? A ship just was drummed in and has cargo for the Gather. We're to get its manifests." He took her by the arm and showed the route to her on the big map of Fort Hold that displayed local traces and roads. "Straight run . . . downhill all the way to the port. And not too steep on the way back."

It was good to be running again and, though the spring weather had turned chilly, she soon worked up enough heat to keep warm. The captain was muchly relieved to deliver the manifests to her. The cargo was being unloaded and he was anxious to get it up the road to the Hold in time for the Gather. He was equally anxious to receive payment for the deliveries, and she could promise she'd have the manifests in the designated hands before dinnertime.

He also had a pouch of letters from the eastern seacoast on board which were addressed to Fort Hold. So she carried a full belt back.

Her legs felt the slight incline but she didn't decrease her pace despite a slight soreness in the right leg at the shin.

Well, a warm bath in one of those incredible tubs would take care of that. And the Gather was tomorrow.

Fort Station was full that night, with runners coming from other stations for the Gather the next day. Tenna bunked in with Rosa and Spacia and a southern runner, Delfie, took the fourth bed in their room. It was a front room with a window, and you heard the traffic on the road, but Tenna was tired enough to sleep through anything.

"Which is as well because the comings and goings up the main track kept up all night long," Rosa said with cheerful disgust. "Let's eat outside. It's so crowded in here." So they all sat on the front benches to eat.

Spacia gave Tenna a conspiratorial wink as Tenna followed the others outside. There had been a few spare seats but not all together. It would be nicer to eat outside instead of the packed tables. Penda and her drudges had their hands full pouring klah and distributing bread, cheese, and porridge.

Actually, it was much more interesting to sit outside to eat. There was so much going on. Gather wagons kept arriving from both directions and rolled onto the field set aside for their use. Stalls which had been bare boards and uprights last night were being decorated with Hall colors and craft insignia. And more stalls were being erected on the wide court in front of the Hold. The long tongue and groove boards for the dancing surface were being slotted into place in the center and the harpers' platform erected. Tenna wanted to hug herself with delight at all the activity. She'd never actually seen a Gather gathering before . . . especially in such a big Hold as Fort. Since she had run yesterday, she felt a little better about not having made a push to finish her first Cross. And she had the chance to see the dragonriders pop into the air above Fort Hold.

"Oh, they are so beautiful," she said, noticing that Rosa and Spacia were also watching the graceful creatures landing, and the elegantly clad dragonriders dismounting.

"Yes, they are," Rosa said in an odd tone. "I just wish they wouldn't keep going on about Thread coming back." She shuddered.

"You don't think it will?" Tenna said, for she had recently had several runs into the Benden Station and knew that Weyrfolk were certain that Thread would return. Hadn't the Red Star been seen in the Eye Rock at the winter solstice?

Rosa shrugged. "It can for all of me but it's going to interfere with running something fierce."

"I noticed that the Benden Thread halts are all repaired," Tenna said.

Spacia shrugged. "We'd be fools to take any chances, wouldn't we?" Then she grimaced. "I'd really hate to be stuck in one of those boxes with Thread falling all around me. Why, the wardrobe in Silvina's storeroom is larger. What if it got in a crack, Thread got in, and I couldn't get out?" She pantomimed terror and revulsion.

"It'll never come to that," Rosa said confidently.

"Lord Groghe certainly got rid of all the greenery around the Hold," Spacia remarked, gesturing around.

"That was as much for the Gather as because the dragonriders said he had to," Rosa said dismissively. "Oh, here come the Boll runners. . . ." She jumped to her feet, waving at the spearhead of runners who had just appeared on the southern road.

They were running effortlessly, their legs moving as if they had drilled that matched stride. They certainly made a fine sight, Tenna thought, pride swelling in her chest and catching her breath.

"They must have started last night," Rosa said. "Oh, d'you see Cleve, Spacia?"

"Third rank from the rear," Spacia said pointing. "As if anyone could miss *him!*" she added in a slightly derisive tone, winking at Tenna. Then she murmured, behind her hand for Tenna's ears only, "She's been so sure he wouldn't come . . . Ha!"

Tenna grinned, now understanding why Rosa had wanted to sit outside that morning and why she had sent Spacia in when they needed more klah.

Then, all of a sudden, as if the arrival of that contingent had been the signal, the Gather was ready. All stalls were up and furnished, the first shift of harpers on the platform and ready to entertain. Then Rosa pointed to the wide steps leading down from the entrance to the Hold and there were the Lord and Lady, looking exceedingly grand in brown Gather finery, descending to the court to formally open the Gather Square. They were accompanied by the dragonriders as well as a clutch of folk, young and old and all related to the Lord Holder. According to Rosa, Lord Groghe had a large family.

"Oh, let's not miss the opening," Spacia told Tenna. Rosa had accompanied Cleve into the station and was helping Penda serve the Boll group a second breakfast after their long run.

So the two girls had excellent seats to watch the two Lord Holders do the official walk through the Gather.

"There's Haligon," Spacia said, her tone hard, pointing.

"Which one?"

"He's wearing brown," Spacia said.

Tenna was none the wiser. "There are a lot of people wearing brown."

"He's walking just behind Lord Groghe."

"So are a lot of other people."

"He's got the curliest head of hair," Spacia added.

There were two who answered that description, but Tenna decided it was the shorter of the young men, the one who walked with a definite swagger. That had to be Haligon. He was handsome enough, though she liked the appearance of the taller man in brown more: not as attractive perhaps, but with a nicer grin on his face. Haligon obviously thought himself very much the lad, from the smug expression on *his* face.

Tenna nodded. She'd give him what-for, so she would.

"C'mon, we should change before the mob get upstairs," Spacia said, touching Tenna's arm to get her attention.

Now that she had identified Haligon, Tenna was quite ready to be looking her very best. Spacia was also determined to assist and took pains with Tenna's appearance, fluffing her hair so that it framed her face, helping her with lip color and a touch of eye shadow.

"Bring out the blue in 'em, though your eyes are really gray, aren't they?"

"Depends on what I'm wearing." Tenna gave a little twirl in front of the long mirror in the room, watching the bias-cut swirl around her ankles. As Spacia had suggested, the anklets took up the spare room in the toes of the borrowed boots. Nor did they look ungainly on the end of her legs as her long feet usually did. She was really quite pleased with her looks. And had to admit, with a degree of satisfaction, that she look "pretty."

Then Spacia stood beside her, the yellow of her gown an attractive contrast to Tenna's deep blue.

"Ooops, I'd better find you some spare runner cords or everyone'll think you're new in the Harper Hall."

No spare cords were found, though Spacia turned out all the drawers.

"Maybe I should be Harper Hall," Tenna said thoughtfully. "That way I can deal with Haligon as he deserves before he suspects."

"Hmm, that might be the wiser idea, you know," Spacia agreed.

Rosa came rushing in, pulling at her clothes in a rush to change.

"Need any help?" Spacia asked as Rosa pulled her pink, floral-printed Gather dress from its hanger.

"No, no but get down there and keep Felisha from Cleve. She's determined to get him, you know. Waltzed right in before he'd finished eating and started hanging on his arm as if they were espoused." Rosa's voice was muffled as she pulled the dress over her head. They all heard a little tearing and Rosa cried out in protest, standing completely still, the dress half on. "Oh, no, no! What did I rip? What'll I do? How bad is it? Can you see?"

While the seam had only parted a bit, and Spacia was threading a needle to make the repairs, Rosa was so disturbed at the thought of her rival that Tenna volunteered to go down.

"You know which one Cleve is?" Rosa asked anxiously, and Tenna nodded and left the room.

She identified Felisha before she did Cleve. The girl, with a mop of curly black tangles half-covering her face, was flirting outrageously with the tall, lantern-jawed runner. He had an engaging smile, though a trifle absent, as he kept looking toward the stairs. Tenna chuckled to herself. Rosa needn't worry. Cleve was obviously uncomfortable with Felisha's coy looks and the way she kept tossing her hair over her shoulder, letting it flick into his face.

"Cleve?" she asked as she approached them. Felisha glared at her and gave her head a perceptible tilt to indicate to Tenna to move on.

"Yes?" Cleve moved a step closer to Tenna, and farther from Felisha, who then altered her stance to put her arm through his in a proprietary fashion that obviously annoyed Cleve.

"Rosa told me that you'd had a run-in with Haligon, too?"

"Yes, I did," Cleve said, seizing on the subject and trying to disentangle himself. "Ran me down on the Boll trace six sevendays ago. Got a nasty sprain out of it. Rosa mentioned he pushed you into sticklebush and you had some mean slivers. Caught you on the hill curve, did he?"

Tenna turned up her hands to show the mottled sliver pricks still visible from that encounter.

"How terrible!" Felisha said insincerely. "That boy's far too reckless."

"Indeed," Tenna said, not liking this girl at all, though she smiled amiably. Surely she was too heavyset to be a runner. Her mop of hair covered whatever Hall or Hold cords she might be wearing. Tenna turned to Cleve. "Spacia told me that you know a lot about the local leathers and I need new shoes."

"Don't they tan hides wherever you come from?" Felisha asked snidely.

"Station Ninety-Seven, isn't it?" Cleve said, grinning. "Come, I've a mind to look for new leathers myself and the bigger the Gather the more chance at a good price, right?" He brushed free of Felisha and, taking Tenna by the arm, propelled her across to the door.

Tenna had a brief glance at the furious look on Felisha's face as they made their escape.

"Thank *you*, Tenna," Cleve said, exhaling with exaggeration as they strode across the court to the Gather Square. "That girl's a menace."

"Is she a Boll runner? She didn't introduce herself."

Cleve chuckled. "No, she's Weaver Hall," he said dismissively, "but my station runs messages for her Craftmaster." He grimaced.

"Tenna?" Torlo called from the door, and they both stopped, allowing him to catch up with them.

"Anyone point out Haligon to you yet?" he asked.

"Yes, Rosa and Spacia did. He was behind the Lord Holder. I'll have a word with him when we meet."

"Good girl, good girl," Torlo said, pressing her arm firmly in encouragement, and then he returned to the station.

"Will you?" Cleve asked, eyes wide with surprise.

"Will I what? Give him what-for? Indeed I will," Tenna said, firming her mind with purpose. "A bit of what he gave me."

"I thought it was sticklebushes you fell into?" Cleve asked, taking it all literally. "There're none of those in a Square."

"Measuring his length on a Gather floor will do nicely, I think," she replied. It ought to be rather easy to trip someone up with such a crowd around. And she had committed herself rather publicly to giving this Haligon a visible lesson. Even Healer Beveny was helping her. She was obliged to act. She certainly didn't wish to lose respect in the station. She took a deep breath. Would tripping him be sufficient? At least on the personal level. There'd still be the charge of reckless behavior leveled against him with the healer-verified proof of her injuries. These had certainly kept her from running for three days—loss of income.

"Oh!" she said, seeing the display for fabrics draped on the Weaver Hall booth: brilliant colors, and floral prints, as well as stripes in both bold and muted colors. She put her hands behind her back because the temptation to finger the cloth was almost irresistible.

Cleve wrinkled his nose. "That's Felisha's Hall's stuff."

"Oh, that red is amazing. . . ."

"Yeah, it's a good Hall. . . ."

"In spite of her?" Tenna chuckled at his reluctant admission.

"Yes . . ." and he grinned ruefully.

They passed the Glasscraft display: mirrors with ornate frames and plain wood, goblets and drinking glasses in all shapes and colors, pitchers in all sizes.

Tenna caught a reflection and almost didn't recognize herself except for that fact that there was Cleve beside her. She straightened her shoulders and smiled back at the unfamiliar girl in the glass.

The next stand was a large Tailor Hall display with finished goods in tempting array: dresses, shirts, trousers, and more intimate garments—enticing merchandise, to be sure, and this one was already packed out with buyers.

"What's keeping Rosa?" Cleve asked, glancing back over his shoulder toward the station, which would be visible until they turned the corner.

"Well, she wanted to look extra nice for you," Tenna said.

Cleve grinned. "She always looks nice." And he blushed suddenly.

"She's a very kind and thoughtful person," Tenna said sincerely.

"Ah, here we are," he said, pointing to the hides displayed at the stall on the corner of the square. "Though I think there are several stalls. Fort Gathers're big enough to attract a lot of crafthalls. Let's see what's available everyplace. Are you good at haggling? If you're not, we can leave it to Rosa. She's very good. And they'd know she means business. You being unknown, they might think they could put one over on you."

Tenna grinned slyly. "I plan to get the most for my mark, I assure you."

"I shouldn't teach you how to run traces, then, should I?" Cleve said with a tinge of rueful apology in his voice.

Tenna smiled back and began to saunter aimlessly past the leather stall. Just then Rosa caught up with them, giving Tenna a kiss as if they hadn't parted company fifteen minutes before. Cleve threw one arm about Rosa's shoulders and whispered in her ear, making her giggle. Other shoppers walked around the three, standing in the middle of the wide aisle. Tenna didn't object to the chance to examine the leather goods without appearing to do so. The journeyman behind the counter pretended not to see her not looking at his wares. She was also trying to see if she could spot Haligon among those promenading about the Square.

By the time the three of them had done their first circuit of the Gather, it was almost impossible to move for the crowds. But a goodly crowd also added to the "Gather feeling," and the trio of runners were exhilarated by the atmosphere. They spent so many hours in work that was solitary and time-consuming, often at hours when most other folk had finished their labors and were enjoying companionship and family life. True, they had the constant satisfaction of knowing that they provided an important service, but you didn't think of that running through a chilling rain or battling against a fierce gale. You thought more of what you *didn't* have and what you were missing.

Refreshment stalls displayed all kinds of drink and finger edibles. So, when they had finished their circuit, they bought food and drink and sat at the tables about the dance square.

"There he is!" Rosa said suddenly, pointing across the square to where a group of young men were surveying girls parading in their Gather finery. It was a custom to take a Gather partner, someone with whom to spend the occasion—which could include the day, the evening meal, the dancing, and whatever else was mutually decided. Everyone recognized the limitation and made sure that the details were arranged ahead of time so that there wouldn't be a misunderstanding of intent.

This would be an ideal situation in which to make Haligon suffer indignity. The area where he was standing with his friends was at the roadside, dusty and spotted with droppings from all the draft animals pulling Gather wagons past it. He'd looked silly, his good clothes mussed. With any luck, she could get his fancy Gather clothing soiled as well as dusty.

"Excuse me," Tenna said, putting down her drink. "I've a score to settle."

"Oh!" Rosa's eyes went wide but an encouraging "yo-ho" followed Tenna as she cut diagonally across the wooden dancing floor.

Haligon was still in the company of the taller man, laughing at something said and eyeing the girls who were parading conspicuously along that side of the Gather Square. Yes, this was the time to repay him for her fall.

Tenna went right up to him, tapped him on the shoulder, and when he turned around in response, the arch smile on his face turned to one of considerable interest at her appearance, his eyes lighting as he gave her a sweeping look of appreciation. He was looking so boldly that he did not see Tenna cock her right arm. Putting her entire body into the swing, she connected her fist smartly to his chin. He dropped like a felled herd-beast, flat on his back and unconscious. And right on top of some droppings. Although the impact of her fist on his chin had rocked her back on her heels, she brushed her hands together with great satisfaction and, pivoting on the heel of her borrowed red shoe, retraced her steps.

She was halfway back to Rosa and Cleve when she heard someone rapidly overtaking her. So she was ready when her arm was seized and her progress halted.

"What was that all about?" It was the tall lad in brown who pulled her about, a look of genuine surprise on his face. And his eyes, too, surveyed her in her formfitting blue dress.

"I thought he ought to have a little of what he deals out so recklessly," she said, and proceeded.

"Wait a minute. What was he supposed to have done to you? I've never seen you around Fort before and he's never mentioned meeting someone like you. And he would!" His eyes glinted with appreciation.

"Oh?" Tenna cocked her head at him. They were nearly at eye level. "Well, he pushed me into sticklebushes." She showed him her hands and his expression altered to one of real concern.

"Sticklebushes? They're dangerous at this season."

"I do know that . . . the hard way," she replied caustically.

"But where? When?"

"That doesn't matter. I've evened the score."

"Indeed," and his grin was respectful. "But are you sure it was my brother?"

"Do you know all Haligon's friends?"

"Haligon?" He blinked. After a pause in which his eyes reflected a rapid series of considerations, he said, "I thought I did." And he laughed nervously. Then he gestured for her to continue on her way. She could see that he was being careful not to annoy her, and that provided her with further amused satisfaction.

"There is a lot about Haligon that he would want kept quiet," she said. "He's a reckless sort."

"And you're the one to teach him manners?" He had to cover his mouth, but she could see that his eyes were brimming with laughter.

"Someone has to."

"Oh? Just what offense did he give you? It's not often . . . Haligon . . . measures his length. Couldn't you have found a less public spot to deliver your lesson? You've ruined his Gather clothes with muck."

"Actually, I chose the spot deliberately. Let him feel what it's like to be flattened unexpectedly."

"Yes, I'm sure. But where did he you encounter him?"

"He was using a runner trace, at a gallop, in the middle of the night. . . ."

"Oh," and he stopped dead in his tracks, an odd, almost guilty look on his face. "When was this?" he asked, all amusement gone.

"Four nights ago, at the hill curve."

"And?"

"I was knocked into sticklebushes." With those words, she held out her right leg and pulled her skirt up high enough to expose the red dots of the healing injuries. And again displayed her free hand and its healing rack of punctures.

"They got infected?" He was really concerned now and obviously knew the dangers of the sticklebush.

"I've saved the slivers," she said in a firm tone. "Healer Beveny has them for proof. I wasn't able to continue working and I've been laid up three days."

"I'm sorry to hear that." And he sounded sincere, his expression somber. Then he gave his head a little shake and smiled at her, a trifle warily, but there was a look in his eyes that told her he found her attractive. "If you promise not to drop me, may I say that you don't look at all like most runners I've met." His eyes lingered only briefly on her bodice, and then he hastily cleared his throat. "I'd better get back and see . . . if Haligon's come to."

Tenna spared a glance at the little knot of people clustered around her victim and, giving him a gracious nod, continued on her way back to Rosa and Cleve.

They were looking pale and shocked.

"There! Honor is satisfied," she said, slipping into her seat.

Rosa and Cleve exchanged looks.

"No," Rosa said, and leaned toward her, one hand on her forearm. "It wasn't Haligon you knocked down."

"It wasn't? But that's the fellow you pointed out to me. He's in brown . . ."

"So is Haligon. He's the one followed you across the dance floor. The one you were talking to, and I don't think you were giving him any what-for."

"Oh." Tenna slumped weakly against the back of her chair. "I hit the wrong man?"

"Uh-huh," Rosa said as both she and Cleve nodded their heads.

"Oh dear," and she made a start to get up but Rosa hastily put out a restraining hand.

"I don't think apologies will help."

"No? Who did I hit?"

"His twin brother, Horon, who's bad enough in his own way."

"Quite likely, with the lewd look he gave me." Tenna was halfway to convincing herself that she had at least hit someone who needed a put-down.

"Horon's a bit of a bully and nice girls won't have anything to do with him. Especially at a Gather." Then Rosa giggled, covering her mouth with her hand. "He was sure looking you up and down. That's why we thought you'd hit him."

Remembering the force of her punch, Tenna rubbed her sore knuckles.

"You may have done someone a favor," Cleve said, grinning. "That was some punch."

"My brothers taught me how," Tenna said absently, watching the group across the Square. She was a trifle relieved when Horon was helped to his feet. And pleased that he staggered and needed assistance. Then, as the group around Horon moved about, she saw Haligon's figure striding up to the station. "Uh-oh. Why's he going to the station?"

"I wouldn't worry about that," Rosa said, standing up. "Torlo would love to remind him of all the harm he's been doing runners."

"Even if they weren't as pretty as you are," Cleve said. "Let's see about your leathers."

They took their empty glasses back to the refreshment stand. Tenna managed one more look at the station but there was no sign of Haligon or Torlo, though there was a lot of coming and going. There would be, on a Gather day. Would she have to knock Haligon down, too? To satisfy runner honor? It wouldn't be as easy, for he had been wary enough of her when he had caught up with her on the dance floor.

After a second round of the Gather stalls, they all decided to find out what prices were being asked. At the first tanner's stall, Cleve did more of the talking so that the real buyer was protected from the blandishments of the tanner journeyman, a man named Ligand.

"Blue for a harper singer?" Ligand had begun, glancing at Tenna. "Thought I saw you eyeing the stall earlier."

"I'm runner," Tenna said.

"She just happens to look her best in blue," Rosa said quickly in case Tenna might be embarrassed to admit she wore a borrowed gown.

"She does indeed," Ligand said, "I'd never have guessed her for a runner."

"Why not?" Rosa asked, bridling.

"Because she's wearing blue," Ligand said deferentially. "So what color is your delight this fine Gather day?"

"I'd like a dark green," and Tenna pointed to a stack of hides dyed various shades of that color in the shelves behind him.

"Good choice for a runner," he said and, with a deft lift, transferred the heavy stack of hides to the front counter. Then he moved off to the other end of his stall, where two holders were examining heavy belts.

"Not that trace moss leaves stains," Rosa remarked as Tenna began flipping through the pile, fingering the leather as she went along.

"We go for the reddy-browns in Boll," Cleve said. "So much of the soil down in Boll is that shade. And trace moss doesn't do as well in the heat as it does in the north."

"Does fine in Igen," Tenna said, having run trace there.

"So it does," Cleve said reflectively. "I like that one," he added, spreading his hand over the hide before Tenna could flip to the next one. "Good deep emerald green."

Tenna had also been considering it. "Enough here for boots. I only need enough for summer shoes. He wouldn't want to divide it."

"Ah, and you've found one you like, huh? Good price on that." Ligand was obviously aware of all that went on at his booth. He flipped up the hide to see the markings on the underside. "Give it to you for nine marks."

Rosa gasped. "At five it's robbery." Then she looked chagrined to have protested when Tenna was the prospective purchaser.

"I'd agree with that," Tenna said, having only four to spend. She gave the skin one more pat and, smiling courteously at Ligand, walked off, her companions hastily following her.

"You won't find better quality anywhere," Ligand called after them.

"It was good quality," Tenna murmured as they walked away. "But four marks is my limit."

"Oh, we should be able to find a smaller hide for that much, though maybe not the same green," Rosa said airily.

However, by the time they had done a third circuit and seen all the green hides available, they had not found either the same green or the same beautifully softened hide.

"I just don't have five, even if we could bargain him down to that price," Tenna said. "That brown at the third stand would be all right. Shall we try that?"

"Oho," Rosa said, stopping in her tracks, her expression alarmed.

Cleve, too, was stopped, and Tenna couldn't see what caused their alarm until suddenly a man appeared out of the crowd and stood directly in their path. She recognized the tall, white-haired man from the morning's ceremony as Lord Holder Groghe.

"Runner Tenna?" he asked formally. But the expression in his wide-set eyes was pleasant.

"Yes," she said, raising her chin slightly. Was he about to give *her* what-for for punching his son Horon? She certainly couldn't admit to having hit the wrong one.

"Shall we sit over here, with your friends?" Lord Groghe said, gesturing toward a free table. He put a hand on her elbow and guided her gently in that direction, away from the stream of folk.

Tenna thought confusedly that neither his expression not his tone were peremptory. He was unexpectedly gracious. A heavyset man with a full face and the beginning of jowls, he smiled to everyone as they made their way to the table, for there were many curious glances at the four of them. He caught the eye of the wineman and held up four fingers. The wineman nodded and hastened to serve them.

"I have an apology to make to you, Runner Tenna." He kept his voice low and for their ears alone.

"You do?" And, at Rosa's startled expression, Tenna added courteously with only a short hesitation, "Lord Groghe?"

"I have verified that my son, Haligon, ran you down four nights ago and you were sufficiently injured so that you were unable to run." Groghe's brows met in a scowl that was for the circumstances, not her part in them. "I confess that I have heard rumors of other complaints about his use of runner traces. Station Master Torlo informed me of several near-collisions. You may be sure that, from now on, Haligon will leave the traces for the runners who made them. You're from Station Ninety-Seven? Keroon Hold?"

Tenna could only nod. She couldn't believe this was happening. A Lord Holder was apologizing to her?

"My son, Haligon, had no idea that he had nearly run you down the other night. He may be reckless," and Groghe smiled somewhat indulgently, "but he would never knowingly cause injury."

Rosa prodded Tenna in the ribs, and Tenna realized that she must make as much as she could of this opportunity, not just for herself but for all runners.

"Lord Groghe, I . . . we all," and she included Rosa and Cleve, "would be grateful to know that we may run the traces without interference. I had only the briefest warning that someone else was using the path. The hill hid his approach and there was wind, too, covering the sound. I could have been severely injured. Traces are not wide, you know." He nodded, and she went on boldly. "And they were made for runners, not riders." He nodded again. "I think Fort Station would be grateful for your help in keeping just runners on the traces."

Then she couldn't think of anything else to say. And just sat there, smiling with nervous twitches in the corners of her mouth.

"I have been well and truly told off, Runner Tenna." He smiled back at her, his eyes dropping for a split second to her bodice. "You're a very pretty girl. Blue becomes you." He reached over and gave her hand a pat before he rose. "I've told Torlo that the incursions will cease." Then, in his usual booming voice, he added, "Enjoy the Gather, runners, and the wine."

With that he rose and walked off, nodding and smiling as he went, leaving the three runners stunned. Rosa was the first to recover. She took a good swig of the wine.

"Torlo was right. You did it," Rosa said. "And this is *good* wine."

"What else would they serve Lord Groghe?" Cleve said, and surreptitiously eased the glass left at the Lord Holder's seat closer to his. The level of wine had not been much reduced by the sip that Lord Groghe had taken. "We can split this one."

"I can't believe that Lord Holder apologized to . . ." Tenna shook her head, hand on her chest. ". . . me. Tenna."

"You were the one injured, weren't you?" Rosa said.

"Yes, but . . ."

"How did Lord Groghe know?" Cleve finished for Tenna, who was puzzling such an answer.

"We all saw Haligon go up to the station," Rosa said before taking another sip of the wine. She rolled her eyes in appreciation of the taste. "But Lord Groghe's a fair man, even if he usually thinks women are half-wits. But he's fair." Then she giggled again. "And he said how pretty you are, so that helped, you know. Haligon likes his girls pretty. So does Lord Groghe but he only looks."

The three runners had been so intent on their own conversation that they did not notice Haligon's approach until he unrolled the green hide from Ligand's stall in front of Tenna.

"In apology, Runner Tenna, because I really didn't know there was someone on the curve of the trace the other night," Haligon said, and gave a courteous bow, his eyes fixed on Tenna's face. Then his contrite expression altered to chagrin. "The station master gave me what-for in triples. So did my father."

"Oh, didn't you believe Tenna?" Rosa asked him pertly.

"How could I doubt the injuries she showed me?" Haligon said. Now he waved for the wineman to serve their table.

Cleve gestured for him to be seated.

"Is . . . your brother all right?" Tenna asked, a question she hadn't quite dared ask Lord Groghe.

Haligon's eyes twinkled with merriment. "You have taught him a lesson, too, you know."

"I don't usually go around knocking people down," Tenna began, and received another surreptitious jab in her ribs from Rosa, sitting beside her. "Except when they need it." She leaned forward, away from Rosa. "I meant to hit *you*."

Haligon rubbed his jaw. "I'm as glad enough you didn't. When Master Torlo told me that you'd been kept from running for three days, I knew I was very much at fault. Then he told me of the other near-misses. Will you accept this leather in compensation, with my apology?"

"Your father has already apologized."

"I make my own, Runner Tenna," he said with an edge to his voice and a solemn expression.

"I accept, but . . ." She was about to refuse the leather when, once again, Rosa jabbed her. She'd have sore ribs at this rate. "I accept."

"Good, for I should have a miserable Gather without your forgiveness," Haligon said, his expression lightening. Lifting the glass he had just been served, he tilted it in her direction and drank. "Will you save me a dance?"

Tenna pretended to consider. But she was secretly thrilled, for despite their first encounter, there was something about Haligon that she found very attractive. Just in case, she shifted in her chair, moving her upper body away from Rosa to avoid another peremptory jab.

"I was hoping to be able to do the toss dance," she began and, when Haligon eagerly opened his mouth to claim that, she added, "but my right leg isn't entirely sound."

"But sound enough surely for the quieter dances?" Haligon asked. "You seemed to be walking well enough."

"Yes, walking's no strain for me . . ." and Tenna hesitated a little longer, "but I would enjoy having a partner." Which allowed him to ask for more than one dance.

"The slow ones, then?"

"Beveny asked for one, remember," Rosa said casually.

"When does the dancing start?" Tenna asked.

"Not until full dark, after the meal," Haligon said. "Would you be my supper partner?"

She heard Rosa inhale sharply but she really did find him an agreeable sort. Certainly the invitation was acceptable. "I would be delighted to," she said graciously.

It was so arranged and Haligon toasted the agreement with the last of his wine, rose, bowed to them all, and left the table.

"Yo-ho, Tenna," Rosa murmured as they watched his tall figure disappear in the Gather crowd.

Cleve, too, grinned. "Neatly done. Do hope you'll be back on another Cross soon in case we have some more problems you can help us with."

"Oh, run off, will you?" Tenna replied flippantly. Now she allowed herself to finger the dark green leather hide. "Was he watching us, do you suppose? How'd he know?"

"Oh, no one's ever said Haligon was a dimwit," Rosa said. "Though he is, riding runner traces like he has."

"*He* must have told his father, then," Cleve said. "Owning up to all that shows an honest nature. I might end up liking him after all."

"Proper order," Rosa said. "Though he never admitted using the traces before when Torlo braced him on that." She grinned at Tenna. "It's sure true that a pretty girl gets more attention than a plain one like me."

"You are not plain," Cleve said indignantly and realized he had fallen into Rosa's neatly laid trap to elicit a compliment from him.

"I'm not?" she replied, smiling archly.

"Oh, you!" he said with the wordless disgust of the well-baited. Then he laughed and carefully split Groghe's glass between their glasses. "Much too good to waste."

Tenna returned to the station long enough to put away the beautiful leather. And long enough to get many requests for dances and to be supper partner from other runners who congratulated her.

"Told ya so, dinnit I?" Penda said, catching Tenna's arm as she was leaving. The woman was grinning from ear to ear. "Pretty girl's always heard, ya know."

Tenna laughed. "And Haligon's going to stay off the traces."

"So his father promised," Penda said, "but we'll have to see does he."

"I'll see that he does," Tenna promised airily and returned to the Gather Square. She'd never had such a marvelous time before.

The supper lines were now forming down the road at the roasting pits and she began to wonder if Haligon had just been funning her and had never intended, Lord Holder's son that he was, to honor his invitation. Then he appeared beside her, offering his arm.

"I didn't forget," he murmured, taking her by the arm..

Being partnered with a Holder's son allowed them to patronize a different line at the roasting pits and so they were served well before Cleve and Rosa. The wine Haligon ordered was more of the excellent one she'd sampled in the afternoon so Tenna was quite merry and relaxed by the time the dancing began.

What surprised her, because she'd given the first dance to Grolly— as much because he didn't expect to get any dances from such a pretty girl as because he asked her first—was that Haligon did not dance it with someone else. He waited at the table for a breathless Grolly to bring her back. It was a sprightly enough tune for dancing but not as fast or complicated as the toss was. The next dance was at a slower tempo and she held out her hand to Haligon, despite the fact that half the male runners at the Gather were now crowding about for a chance to dance with her.

He pulled her into his arms with a deft movement and they were suddenly cheek to cheek. He was only a little taller than she was so their steps matched effortlessly. One circuit of the room and she had perfect confidence in his leading.

Since they were dancing cheek to cheek—he was only a little taller than she was—she could feel his face muscles lifting in a smile. And he gave her a quick pressure with both hands.

"Do you know when you're running again?"

"I've already had a short leg, down to the port," she said. "Enough for a good warm-up."

"How *do* you manage such long distances on your own legs?" he asked, holding her out slightly to see her face in the light of the glow-baskets that lined the dance floor. He really wanted to know, too.

"Part of it's training, of course. Part that my Blood is bred to produce runners."

"Could you have done anything else with your life?"

"I could but I like running. There's a sort of . . . magic to it. Sometimes you feel you could run round the world. And I like night running. You feel like you're the only one awake and alive and moving."

"Quite likely you are, save for dimwits on mounts on traces they shouldn't be using," he said in a wry tone. "How long *have* you been running?"

He sounded genuinely interested. She had thought perhaps she had made a mistake, being sentimental about something as commonplace as running.

"Almost two whole Turns. This is my first Cross."

"And I was a dimglowed idiot who interrupted it," he said in an apologetic tone.

Tenna was almost embarrassed at his continued references to his mistake.

"How often do I have to say I've forgiven you?" she said, putting her lips closer to his ear. "That green leather is going to make fine shoes for me. By the way, how'd you know that was the hide I wanted? Were you following us about?"

"Father said I had to make amends in some way more personal than handing you marks . . ."

"You didn't give Tanner Ligand what he asked for, did you?" Her query was sharp, because she didn't want him to have had to spend more than she felt necessary. And she leaned away from his guiding arm enough so that she could see his face as he answered

"I won't tell you how much, Tenna, but we struck a fair bargain. Trouble was," and now Haligon's voice was rueful, "he knew just how much I needed that particular hide. It's the talk of the Gather, you know."

Tenna suspected that it was and she hoped she could tell it to her own station before they heard rumor, which always exaggerated.

"Hmmm. I should have expected that," she said. "I shall be able to make two pairs of summer shoes out of that much leather and I'll think of you every time I wear them." She grinned up at him.

"Fair enough." Evidently satisfied by this exchange, he resettled his arms about her, drawing her just that much closer. "You didn't seem as interested in any other hide, you know. So I'd got off more lightly than I thought I might. I didn't know runners made their own foot-wear."

"We do and it's much better to make them for yourself. Then you've only yourself to blame if you've blisters."

"Blisters? They would be bad for a runner."

"Almost as bad as sticklebush slivers."

He groaned. "Will I ever be able to live that down?"

"You can try." Maybe she could get him to dance with her all night. He was possibly the best partner she'd ever had. Not that she ever lacked for them. But he was subtly different. In his dancing, too, for he seemed to know many combinations of the dance steps and she really had to keep her attention on her feet and following his lead. Maybe it was him being a Holder's son.

"Maybe it's being a runner," and his remark startled her, it being near what she'd just been thinking, "but you're the lightest thing on your feet." He reset his hands more firmly about her, drawing her as close as he could.

They were both silent, each concentrating on the complexities of the dance. It ended all too soon for Tenna. She didn't really wish to release him. Nor he, her. So they stood on the dance floor, arms at their sides but not with much distance between them. The music began again, a faster dance, and before she could say a word, Haligon had swung her into his arms and moved off in the rhythm of this tune. This time they had to concentrate not only on the steps but also to avoid collisions with more erratic dancers whirling about the floor.

Three dances to a set and Haligon whisked her off the floor during the change of musicians on the pretext of needing a drink. With glasses of chilled white wine, he guided her into the shadow of a deserted stall.

She smiled to herself, rehearsing a number of deft rejections if she needed them.

"I don't think you're at all lame, Tenna," he said conversationally. "Especially if the station master let you take a run down to the port. Care to have a go at the first toss dance after all?"

His expression dared her.

"We'll see."

Pause.

"So, will you run on tomorrow?"

"I'll be careful with the wine in case I do," she said, half warning him as she lifted the glass.

"Will you make it to the sea from here in one run?"

"Quite likely. It's spring and there'd be no snow on the pass trace."

"Would you still go if there were?"

"No one said anything about snow on the pass trace at the station."

"Keep your ears open, don't you?"

"A runner always needs to know conditions on the trace." She gave him a stern look.

"All right, I've got the message."

"Fair enough."

Pause.

"You're not at all what I expected, you know," Haligon said respectfully.

"I can quite candidly say the same of you, Haligon," she replied.

The new musicians played the first bar of the next song, to acquaint people with a sample of the dance to come.

So, when Tenna felt his arm about her shoulders, she did not resist the pressure. Nor did she when both arms enfolded her and his mouth found hers. It was a nice kiss, not sloppy as others had been, but well placed on her lips, as if he knew what he was about in kissing. His arms about her were sure, too, not crushing her needlessly against him. Respectful, she thought . . . and then, as the kiss deepened with her cooperation, she didn't think of anything but enjoying the experience.

Haligon monopolized her all evening, rather deftly, she realized. Always whisking her off the dance floor before any one else could find her. They kissed quite a bit between dances. He was far more respectful of her person than she expected. And said so.

"With the punch you can deliver, my girl," he answered, "you can bet your last mark I'm not about to risk my brother's fate."

He also found other chilled drinks for her to drink instead of more wine. She appreciated that even more. Especially when the music of the toss dance began. The floor cleared of all save a few hardy couples.

"Shall we?" and Haligon's grin was all the challenge she needed.

The ache in her right shin was really minor and her confidence in his partnering had grown throughout the evening; otherwise she would not have taken his dare.

During the pattern of the dance, the female partner was to be swung as high as possible, and if she was very clever, she would twirl in midair before being caught by the male. It would be a dangerous dance, but it was ever so much fun. Tenna's older brother had taught her and given her enough practice so that she was well able to make the turns. It had insured her partners at any Gather in the east once it was known how light she was and what a good dancer.

From the very first toss, she knew that Haligon was the best partner she'd ever had. There was great cheering for them when she managed a full two turns in the air before he caught her. In one of the rare close movements of the dance, he whispered swift instructions so that she was prepared for the final toss. And able to execute it, sure he would be there to keep her from crashing on the floor. She was close enough to being missed so that the spectators gasped just as he caught her half a handspan above the floor. Another girl was not so lucky but suffered no more than the indignity of the fall.

Cleve, Rosa, Spacia, Grolly, and most of the station crowded about them when they left the dance floor, congratulating them on such a performance. They were offered drinks, meat rolls, and other delicacies.

"Upholding the honor of the station," Cleve loudly proclaimed. "And the Hold, of course," he magnanimously added, bowing to Haligon.

"Tenna's the best partner I've ever had," Haligon replied sincerely, mopping his face.

Then Torlo reached through the crowd and tapped Tenna's shoulder.

"You're on the run list, Tenna," he said, emphasizing the warning with a nod.

"To the coast?"

"Aye, as you wished." Torlo gave Haligon a severe look.

"I'll escort you to the station, then, Tenna?" Haligon asked.

The harpers had struck up another slow dance. Rosa and Spacia were looking intensely at Tenna but she couldn't interpret their glances. She also knew her duty as a runner.

"This is the last dance then." And she took Haligon by the arm and led him to the floor.

Haligon tucked her in against him and she let her body relax against his and to his leading. She had never had such a Gather in her life. She could almost be glad that he'd run her off the trace and so started the events that had culminated in this lovely night.

They said nothing, both enjoying the flow of the dance and the sweet music. When it ended, Haligon led her from the floor, holding her right hand in his, and toward the station, its glowbasket shining at the door.

"So, Runner Tenna, you finish your first Cross. It won't be your last, will it?" Haligon asked as they paused just beyond the circle of light. He lifted his hand and lightly brushed back the curls.

"No, it's unlikely to. I'm going to run as long as I'm able."

"But you'll be Crossing often, won't you?" he asked, and she nodded. "So, if sometime in the future, when I've got my own holding . . . I'm going to breed runners . . . beasts, that is," he qualified hastily, and she almost laughed at his urgent correction. "I've been trying to find the strain I want to breed, you see, and used the traces as sort of the best footing for comparison. I mean, is there any chance you might . . . possibly . . . consider running more often on this side of the world?"

Tenna cocked her head at him, surprised by the intensity and roughness in his pleasant voice.

"I might." She smiled up at him. This Haligon was more of a temptation to her than he knew.

Now he smiled back at her, a challenge sparkling in his eyes. "We'll just have to see, won't we?"

"Yes, I guess we will."

With that answer, she gave him a quick kiss on the cheek and ducked into the station before she could say more than she ought right now after such a limited acquaintance. But maybe raising runners— both kinds, four-legged and two—in the west wasn't a bad idea at all.

The Riftwar Saga

RAYMOND E. FEIST

THE RIFTWAR SAGA:

MAGICIAN (1982, REVISED EDITION 1992)
SILVERTHORN (1985)
A DARKNESS IN SETHANON (1986)

THE EMPIRE TRILOGY (WITH JANNY WURTS):

DAUGHTER OF THE EMPIRE (1989)
SERVANT OF THE EMPIRE (1990)
MISTRESS OF THE EMPIRE (1992)

STAND-ALONE RIFTWAR-RELATED BOOKS:

PRINCE OF THE BLOOD (1989)
THE KING'S BUCCANEER (1992)

THE SERPENTWAR SAGA:

SHADOW OF A DARK QUEEN (1994)
RISE OF A MERCHANT PRINCE (1995)
RAGE OF A DEMON KING (1997)
SHARDS OF A BROKEN CROWN (1998)

Raymond E. Feist's Riftwar fantasy series begins with the adventures of two boys, Pug and Tomas, each wishing to rise above his lowly station in life. Pug desires to become a magician, Tomas a great warrior. Each achieves his dream through outside agencies and his own natural abilities; Pug is kidnapped during the Riftwar, discovered to have magic abilities, and trained to greatness. Tomas stumbles upon a dying dragon who gives him a suit of armor imbued with an ancient magic, turning him into a warrior of legendary might.

As Pug and Tomas undergo their transformations and become more adept at controlling the powers that have been granted them, the scope of the novel expands to reveal more about the two worlds upon which the conflict known as the Riftwar takes place: Midkemia and Kelewan. Midkemia is a young world, vibrant and conflict-ridden, while Kelewan is ancient and tradition-bound, but no freer of conflict. The militaristic Tsurani, from Kelewan, have invaded the Kingdom of the Isles on Midkemia to expand their domain and seize metals common on Midkemia but rare at home. The only way open between these worlds is a magic Rift, and through that portal in space-time the invaders have established a foothold in the Kingdom. Gradually Tomas learns that he has become invested with the power of a Valheru, one of the mystical creatures who are legends in Midkemia. The Dragon Lords were near-godlike beings who once warred with the gods themselves. The action in the first trilogy comes to a climax in *A Darkness at Sethanon*, with the resolution of the war between the Kingdom and the invading Tsurani, Tomas gaining control over the ancient magic that sought to conquer him, and Pug returning to the homeland of his youth.

The Empire Trilogy concerns itself with conflict back on the Tsurani home world, where for much of the first and second book we see "the other side of the Riftwar." Lady Mara of the Acoma, a girl of seventeen in the first book, is thrust into a murderous game of politics and ritual, and only through her own genius and ability to improvise does she weather unrelenting attacks on all sides. Aided by a loyal group of followers, including a Kingdom slave named Kevin, whom she comes to love more than any other, Mara rises to dominate the Empire of Tsuranuanni, even facing down the mighty Great Ones, the magicians who are outside the law.

The latest series, the SerpentWar saga, is the story of Erik, the bastard son of a noble, and Roo, a street boy who is his best friend. The Kingdom again faces invaders, but this time from across the sea. The story of the two young men is set against the Kingdom's hurried preparation for and resistance against a huge army under the banner of the Emerald Queen, a woman who is another agent of dark forces seeking dominion over the world of Midkemia. More of the cosmic nature of the battle between good and evil is revealed and Pug and Tomas again have to take a hand in the struggle.

Feist sees Midkemia as an objective, virtual world, though a fictional one. He regards all the tales set in Midkemia as historical novels and stories of this fantastic realm. "The Wood Boy" is a tale from the early days of the Riftwar, when the Tsurani first were establishing their foothold in the Kingdom.

The Wood Boy

A Tale from the Riftwar

RAYMOND E. FEIST

The Duke looked up.

Borric, Duke of Crydee and commander of the Armies of the West, acknowledged the captain at the door of his command tent. "Your Grace, if you have a minute and could come outside?"

Borric stood up, envying his old friend Brucal, who was now probably sitting before a warm fire somewhere in LaMut while he wrote long letters of complaint to the Prince of Krondor about supplies.

The war was leaving its second winter and a stable front had been established, with Borric's headquarters camp located ten miles behind the lines. The Duke was a seasoned campaigner, having fought against goblins and the Brotherhood of the Dark Path—the dark elves—since boyhood, and every bone in his body told him that this was going to be a long war.

The Duke donned his heavy cloak, and wrapped it around him. He exited his tent and a strange tableau greeted him.

In the distance, a group of figures could barely be seen as they approached the camp. Through the swirling snow Borric could see them slowly take shape. Grey figures against the dull white, surrounded by a haze of snowflakes, they approached at a steady rate. Finally, the figures resolved themselves into a patrol escorting someone.

The soldiers marched slowly, for the figure they surrounded was pulling a heavy sled, plodding along unfalteringly despite what appeared a considerable burden. As they came close, Borric could see that it was a peasant boy who labored to haul the sled to the camp. He moved with steady purpose, coming at last to stand before the commander of the King's Armies in the West.

Borric looked at the lad, who had obviously been through an ordeal. He was bareheaded, his blond hair encrusted with ice crystals. About his neck and face he wore a heavy jacket scarf wrapped several times around. He wore a heavy jacket and trousers, and thick sturdy boots. His simple wool coat was stained dark with blood.

The sled he had been pulling was laden with odd cargo. A large sack had been secured with ropes atop the sled, and over that two bodies had been lashed down. A dead man stared up at the sky with empty eyes, his lashes sparkling with frozen tears. He had been a fighter, from the look of him, and he wore leather armor. His scabbard hung empty at his side and his left glove was missing. Beside him lay a girl, under blankets, so that it appeared she was sleeping. She had been a pretty girl in life, but in death her features were almost porcelain, near perfection in their pale whiteness.

"Who are you, boy?"

The boy said, "I am the Wood Boy." His voice was faint and his eyes were vacant, as if he stared inward, though they were fixed on Borric.

"What did you say?" asked the Duke.

The boy seemed to gather his wits. "Sir, my name is Dirk. I am the servant of Lord Paul of White Hill. It's the estate on the other side of the Kakisaw Valley." He pointed to the west. "Three days' walk from here. I carry firewood."

Borric nodded. "I know the estate. I've visited Lord Paul many times over the years. That's thirty-five miles from here, and twenty behind enemy lines." Pointing to the sled, he asked, "What is this?"

Weary, the boy said, "It is my master's treasure. She is his daughter. The man is a murderer. He was once my friend."

"You'd better come inside and tell me your story," said Borric. He motioned for two soldiers to take the ropes that the boy used as a harness to pull the sled out of the way, and indicated that another man should help the exhausted youth.

The Duke led the boy inside and let him know it was permissible to sit. He signaled for an orderly to get the boy a cup of hot tea and something to eat, and as the soldier hurried to obey, Borric said, "Why don't you start at the beginning, Dirk?"

Spring brought the Tsurani. They had been reported in the Grey Tower Mountains the year before, bringing dire warnings of invasion from both the Kingdom rulers on the other side of the mountains and some of the more important merchants and nobles in the other Free Cities. But the tales that accompanied the warning, of fierce warriors appearing out of nowhere by some magic means, had been met with skepticism and disbelief. And the fighting seemed distant, up in the mountains between Borric of Crydee's soldiers, the dwarves, and the invaders.

Until the first warning by the Rangers of Natal—who had quickly ridden on to warn others—followed a day later by a column of short men in their brightly colored armor who appeared on the road approaching the estate at White Hill.

Lord Paul had ordered his bodyguards to stand ready, but to offer no resistance unless provoked. Dirk and the rest of the household stood behind the Lord of White Hill and his armed guards.

Dirk glanced back at his master and saw that he stood alone, his daughter still in the house. Dirk wondered what extra protection the master thought that afforded his young daughter.

Dirk found the master's pose admirable. The stories of Tsurani fierceness had trickled down from the early fighting, and the Free Cities would be wholly dependent upon the Kingdom for defense. Areas like White Hill and the other estates around Walinor were simply on their own. Yet Lord Paul stood motionless, without any sign of fear, in his formal robe, the scarlet one with the ermine collar. No hereditary title had been conferred on any citizen since the Empire of Great Kesh had abandoned its northern colonies a century before, yet those families with ancient titles used them with pride. Like other nobles in the Free Cities, he held in disdain other men's claims on title while treasuring his own.

As the invaders calmly marched into view, it was obvious that any resistance would have been quickly crushed. Paul had a personal bodyguard and a score of hired mercenaries who acted as wagon guards and protection against roving bandits. But they were a poor band of hired cutthroats next to the highly disciplined command that marched across the estate. The Tsurani wore bright orange and black armor, looking like lacquered hide or wood, nothing remotely like the metal armor worn by the officers of the Natal Defense Force.

Paul repeated the order that no resistance was to be mounted, and when the Tsurani commander presented himself, Paul offered something that resembled a formal salute. Then, with the aid of a man in a black robe, the leader of the invaders gave his demands. The property of White Hill, as well as the surrounding countryside, was now under Tsurani rule, specifically an entity named Minwanabi. Dirk wondered if that was a person or a place, like a Kingdom Duchy. But he was too frightened to imagine voicing the question.

The leader of this group of Tsurani—all short, tough-looking veteran soldiers—could be differentiated from his men only by a slightly more ornate helm, graced with what Dirk took to be some creature's hair. The black fall reached the officer's shoulders.

Dirk tried to guess what the role of the black-robed man might be; the officer seemed extremely polite and deferential to him as he translated the officer's words for him.

The officer was called Chapka, and his rank was Hit Leader or Strike Leader, Dirk wasn't sure which.

He shouted orders and the black robe said, "Only the noble of this house may bear arms, and his personal man." Dirk took that to mean a bodyguard. That would be Hamish. "All others put weapons here."

The estate guards looked at Lord Paul, who nodded. They stepped forward and put their weapons in a pile, slowly, and when they were done they stepped back. "Any other weapons?" asked the man in black.

One of the guards looked at his companions, then came forward and took a small blade from his boot, throwing it in the pile. He stepped back into line.

The officer shouted an order. A dozen Tsurani soldiers ran forward, each searching the now unarmed guards. One Tsurani stood, holding up a knife he had found in a guard's boot, and the officer indicated that the man be brought forward. He spoke rapidly to the man in black, who said, "This man disobeyed. He hid a weapon. He will be punished."

Lord Paul slowly said, "What shall you do with him?"

"The sword is too honorable a death for a disobedient slave. He will be hanged."

The man turned pale. "It was just a small one; I forgot I had it!"

The man was struck hard from behind and collapsed. Dirk watched in dread fascination as two other Tsurani guards dragged the guard—a man Dirk hardly knew, named Jackson—to the entrance to the barn. A hoist hung over the small door to the hayloft—there was one at each end of the barn—from which a long rope dangled. The unconscious man had the rope tied around his neck and was hoisted quickly up. He never regained consciousness, though his body twitched twice before it went still.

Dirk had seen dead men before; the town of Walinor, where he grew up, had known a few raids by bandits and the Brotherhood of the Dark Path, and once he had stumbled across a drunk who had frozen to death in the gutter outside an inn. But this hanging made his stomach twist, and he knew it was as much from fear over his own safety as from any revulsion over Jackson's death.

The black-robed man said, "Any slave with weapon—we hang."

Then the officer shouted an order, and Tsurani warriors ran off in all directions, a half-dozen into the master's house, others into the outbuildings, and still others to the springhouse, the barn, and the root cellar. Efficient to a degree that astonished Dirk, the Tsurani returned in short order and started reporting. Dirk couldn't understand them, but from the rapidity of the exchanges, he was certain they were listing what they found for their officer.

Others returned from the barn and kitchen carrying dozens of commonplace items. The officer, with the aid of the black-robed man, began interrogating Lord Paul about the nature of various common household items. As the master of the estate explained the use of such common tools as a leather punch or iron skillet, the Tsurani officer indicated one of two piles, one on a large canvas tarp. When two of the same items were displayed, one instantly went into one pile, while the other might join it or be separated.

Old William, the gardener and groundskeeper, said, "Look at that," as two Tsurani soldiers picked up the tarp, securing the larger of the two piles, and carried it off.

"What is it?" whispered Dirk, barely loud enough for the old man to hear.

"They're queer for metal," softly said the old man with a knowing nod. "Look at their armor and weapons."

Dirk did so, and then it struck him. Nowhere on any Tsurani could a glint of sunlight on metal be seen. Their armor and weapons all appeared to be hide or wood cleverly fashioned and lacquered, but there were no buckles, blades, or fasteners of metal in evidence. From their cross-gartered sandals to the top of their large flared helmets, the Tsurani appeared devoid of any metal artifacts.

"What's it mean?" whispered Dirk.

"I don't know, but I'm sure we'll find out," said the old man.

The Tsurani continued their investigation of Lord Paul's household, until almost sundown, then they were ordered to gather their personal belongings and move them into the barn or kitchen, as the Tsurani would be occupying the servants' quarters. In a move that puzzled Dirk, the Tsurani officer stayed in the same building with his men, leaving Paul and his daughter alone in the big house.

It was but the first of many things that would puzzle Dirk over the coming year.

Alex lay curled up, his face a mask of pain while Hamish shouted, "Don't get up!"

The Tsurani soldier who had struck the young man in the stomach stood over him, his hand a scant inch from the hilt of his sword. Alex groaned and again Hamish shouted to the young man to remain still.

Dirk stood near the entrance to the barn while those servants nearby stood anxiously watching, expecting the worst at any moment. The Tsurani had revealed themselves as strict but fair masters in the two months since arriving at White Hill, but there was occasionally some breach of etiquette or honor that took the residents of White Hill by surprise, often with bloody consequences. An old farmer by the name of Samuel had gotten drunk on fermented corncob squeeze a month earlier and had struck out at a Tsurani who had ordered him back into his home. Samuel had been beaten senseless and hanged as his wife and children looked on in horror.

Alex continued to groan but did as he was bid by Hamish until the Tsurani soldier seemed satisfied that he wasn't going to move. The soldier said something in his alien language, spat in contempt upon the workman, turned, and walked away.

Hamish hesitated a moment; then he and Dirk hurried over to help Alex to his feet. "What happened?" asked Dirk.

"I don't know," said Alex. "I just looked at the man."

"It's how you looked at him," said Hamish. "You smirked at him. If you'd looked at me that way, I'd have done the same." The burly old soldier inspected Alex. "I had my fill of smirking boys in the army and knocked down a few in my time before I retired. Show these murderers some respect, lad, or they'll hang you just because they can and it's a slow day for amusements."

Rubbing his side, Alex said, "I won't do that again, you can bet."

"See that you don't," said Hamish. The old soldier motioned for Drogen, his senior guard, to come over. "Pass the word that the bastards seem touchy. Must have something to do with the war. Just make sure the lads know to keep polite and do whatever they're told."

Drogen nodded and ran off. Hamish turned to inspect Alex again, then said, "Get off with you. You'll live."

Dirk helped Alex for a few steps. Then the man's legs seemed to steady and Dirk let go of his arm. "They don't seem to take kindly to any sort of greeting," said Dirk.

"I think keeping your eyes down or some such is what they want."

Dirk said nothing. He was scared most of the time when he was around the Tsurani and didn't look at them for that reason. That was probably a wise choice, he judged.

"Can you take the wood?" asked Alex.

"Sure," said Dirk before he realized that he was being asked to carry wood to the Tsurani quarters. Dirk picked up the fallen bundle and wrestled with it a moment before getting the unwieldy load under control. He moved to the door of the outbuilding and hesitated, then rolled the wood back on his chest and reached out to pull the latch rope.

The door opened slightly and Dirk pushed it open with his foot. He entered, blinking a moment to get his eyes used to the darkness inside.

A half-dozen Tsurani warriors sat on their beds, speaking in quiet conversation as they tended their arms and armor. Upon seeing the serving boy enter, they fell silent. Dirk went to the woodbox next to the fireplace, situated in the center of the rear wall, and deposited his load there.

The Tsurani watched him with impassive expressions. He quickly left the room. Closing the door behind him, he could hardly believe that just weeks before the bed in the farthest corner had been his own. He and the other workers had been turned out to the barn, except for the house staff, who now slept on the floor in Lord Paul's kitchen.

There was little need for wood save for cooking, as the warm nights of summer made sleeping fires unnecessary. The Tsurani used their fires primarily for cooking their alien food, filling the area nearby with strange yet intriguing aromas.

Dirk paused a moment and glanced around, taking in the images of White Hill; familiar, yet cast in alien shadow by the invaders. Mikia and Torren, a young couple engaged the week before at the Midsummer's festival, were approaching the milking shed, hand in hand, and the invaders could be invisible for all the distraction they provided the young lovers.

From the kitchen, voices and the clatter of pots heralded the advent of the noon meal. Dirk realized he was hungry. Still, he needed to carry firewood to the other buildings before breaking to eat, and he decided the sooner started, the sooner done. As he turned to the woodshed, he caught a glimpse of a soldier in black and orange moving toward the barn. He idly wondered if the time would come when the invaders would be driven from White Hill. It seemed unlikely, for there was no news of the war, and the Tsurani were settling in at White Hill as if they were never leaving.

Reaching the woodshed, Dirk opened the door and saw Alex in back of the shed cutting more wood. The still-bruised man said, "You can carry, lad. I'll cut."

Dirk nodded and went in the shed, to get another armful of firewood. Dirk sighed. As youngest boy in service, the worst jobs fell to him, and this would just be another task added to his burden, one which would not free him from any other.

Before coming to White Hill, Dirk had been nothing, the youngest son of a stonecutter who had two sons already to apprentice. His father had cut the stone for Lord Paul's home, and had used that slight acquaintanceship to gain Dirk a position in Paul's household.

With that position was the promise that eventually he would have some sort of rank on the estate, perhaps a groundsman, a kennel master, or a herdsman. Or he might gain a farm to work, with a portion of his crops going to his landlord, even eventually earning the rank of Franklin, one who owned his own lands free of service to any lord. He had even dared to imagine meeting a girl and marrying, raising sons and daughter of his own. And perhaps, despite the Tsurani, he still might.

Reminding himself that he had much to be thankful for, he lifted the next load of wood destined for the fireplaces of the invaders.

Fall brought a quick change in the weather, with sunny but cool days and cold nights. Apples were harvested and the juice presses were busy. The Tsurani found the juice a wonderful delicacy and commanded a large portion for themselves. A portion was put aside for fermenting, and the air around the kitchen was spicy with the smell of warm pies.

Dirk had gotten used to hauling wood to the Tsurani, and now was the one designated to keep all the woodboxes on the property filled, while Alex still did most of the chopping. Everyone began calling him "Wood Boy," rather than his name.

Dirk also worked the woodpile, and the constant work was broadening his shoulders and putting muscle on him by the week. He could now lift as much as the older boys and some of the men.

He found that as the nights cooled his workload increased, for now he had to help plan for the coming winter. The sheep pens were repaired. The herd needed to be kept close, as starving predators would come down from the mountain to hunt. The cattle would be brought down from the higher meadows as well.

Fences needed repairing and the root cellar and springhouse needed stocking. The winters in the foothills of Yabon came quickly and the snow was often deep after the first fall, lasting until the thaw of spring.

Dirk worked hard and enjoyed those infrequent moments he could steal to relax, joke with the older boys and young men, and talk to Litia, an old woman who had once been in charge of the poultry and lambs. She was kind to the awkward boy and told him things that helped him understand the world that seemed to be changing around him by the day.

Dirk now was faced with the realization that life's choices were down to a precious few. Before the Tsurani's arrival, he had stood a chance of learning to be a herdsman or farmer, and perhaps meeting a girl and starting a family on the edge of Lord Paul's estates, having land and a share of the harvest. Or he might save the tiny sum allotted him over and above his keep and someday attempt to start a trade of his own; he knew the rudiments of cutting stone and perhaps might pay a mason to apprentice him.

But now he feared that he was doomed to be a servant until death took him. There was no payment of wages above his keep; the Tsurani had taken all of Lord Paul's wealth—though it was rumored that he had two parts in three safely hidden from the Tsurani. Even if the rumor was true, he wasn't about to risk hanging to pay a lowly servant boy his back wages.

And there were no girls his own age on the estates, save Lord Paul's daughter.

The Midwinter's festival was supposed to be the time to meet the girls from town or the nearby estates, but the Tsurani had forbidden such travel for the Midsummer's festival, and Dirk doubted they would change their minds for the winter festival. Lord Paul's household had celebrated Banapis on Midsummer's Day by themselves, with little enthusiasm, because of the poor food and drink, and the isolation.

At least, thought Dirk, Midwinter's Day was likely to be a little livelier, as there was a good supply of fermenting applejack laid in. Then, remembering how morose his father could get when drinking, Dirk wondered if that was a good thing. Hamish had been known to drink himself into a dark and blind rage in the depths of winter.

Putting aside his own misery, he attacked the tasks the day put before him and was judged a hardworking if unremarkable boy by those of the household.

The festival was a pale shadow of its former self.

Traditionally the towns turned out, with those living on the neighboring estates coming in for the parties. A townsman would be selected to play the part of Old Man Winter, who would come into town on a sled pulled by wolves—usually a motley collection of dogs pressed into playing the part, often to comic results. He would pass out sweets to the children, and the adults would exchange small gifts and tokens. Then everyone would eat too much food and many would drink too much wine and ale.

And many young couples would be married.

This year the Tsurani had forbidden travel, and Dirk stood at the edge of a small crowd in the barnyard watching Mikia and Torren getting married under the watchful eyes of Lord Paul and his daughter. The Tsurani had let Dirk travel to the shrine of Dala and return with a priest of that order, so that the wedding could be conducted.

The couple looked happy despite the frigid surroundings, made slightly more bearable by the large bonfire Dirk and the others had built earlier in the day. It roared and warmed whichever side was facing it, but otherwise it was a cold and bitter day for a wedding, with low grey skies and a constant wind off the mountains.

The meal was the best that could be managed under the circumstances, and Dirk had his first encounter with too much to drink, consuming far too much applejack and discovering that his stomach would inform him of its limits before any of his friends would. The other boys stood around in amusement as Dirk stood against the wall behind the barn, sick beyond belief, his head swimming and his pulse pounding in his temples as his stomach tried to throw up drink no longer there.

He had somehow managed to find his way back to the loft in which he now slept. Because he was the youngest boy in the household, he got the worst pallet, next to the hay door, which meant a drafty, frigid night's rest. He passed out and risked freezing to death without the other boys' warmth nearby.

Late that night, he stirred as a shout from outside rang through the silent darkness. Dirk stirred as did the other boys, and Hemmy said, "What's that?"

Dirk pushed open the hay door. In the moonlight a drunken figure stood waving a sword with his right hand, while holding a jug of applejack with the left. He shouted words that the boys couldn't understand, but Hemmy said, "He's fighting some old battle, for sure."

Suddenly Alex said, "The Tsurani! If Hamish wakes them with all that shouting, they'll kill him. We've got to get him to shut up."

"You want to go and try to talk to him while he's waving that sword around," said Hemmy, "you go ahead. I'll take my chances up here. I've seen him drunk before. Puts him in a dangerous dark temper, it does."

"We've got to do something," said Dirk.

"What?" asked Hemmy.

"I don't know," admitted Dirk.

Then two Tsurani ran into view and stopped when they saw the drunken old soldier in the moonlight, his breath forming clouds of steam in the frigid night air.

"You stinkin' bastards!" shouted Hamish. "You come on and I'll show you how to use a sword."

The two Tsurani slowly drew weapons, and one spoke to the other. The second man nodded and stepped back, putting his sword away. He turned and ran off.

"They're going to get some help," whispered Dirk, afraid to be overheard by the Tsurani.

"Maybe they'll just make him put up his sword and go to bed," said Hemmy.

"Maybe," echoed Dirk.

Then a half-dozen Tsurani, led by the officer, came into view. The officer shouted at Hamish, who grinned like a grizzly wolf in the stark white moonlight. "Come and sing to me, you sons of dogs!" shouted the drunken old man.

The Tsurani officer seemed more irritated by the display than anything else, and said something briefly to the men. He turned and walked off without a glance back.

"Maybe they're going to let him alone," said Hemmy.

Suddenly an arrow sped through the darkness and struck old Hamish in the chest. He looked down in disbelief and sank to his knees. Then he fell off to the right, still holding his sword and jug of applejack.

"Gods!" whispered Dirk.

The Tsurani turned as one and walked away, leaving the dead bodyguard lying in the moonlight, a black figure against the white snow.

"What do we do?" whispered Dirk to the older boys.

"Nothing," said Alex. "Until the Tsurani tell us to get out tomorrow and bury him, we do nothing."

"But it's not right," said Dirk, fighting back tears of frustration and fear.

"Nothing is right these days," said Hemmy, reaching out to shut the hay doors.

Dirk lay in the loft, huddled against a cold far more bitter than winter's night.

* * *

Let me help you with that," said Drogen, as Dirk tried to close the kitchen door with a kick. The wind outside howled and this had been Dirk's fifth trip to the woodbox.

Dirk said, "Shut the door, please."

The new bodyguard to Lord Paul did as Dirk asked, and Dirk said, "Thanks. I've got to get this to the great hall." He hurried with the heavy bundle of wood and made his way through the big house. He entered the great hall, where Lord Paul ate dinner with his daughter Anika.

Dirk was very deliberate in arranging the new firewood, as it gave him a moment to watch Anika from beside the fireplace. She was a year younger than Dirk. Fifteen last Midsummer's day, she was perfection embodied to the young kitchen boy. She had delicate features, a small bow of a mouth, wide-set blue eyes, and hair of pale gold. Her skin held a faint touch of the sun in summer and was flawless pink in winter. Her figure was ripening, yet not voluptuous like the kitchen women, still possessing a grace when she moved that set Dirk's heart to beating.

Dirk knew she didn't even know his name, but he dreamed of somehow earning rank and fame someday, and winning her love. Her imaged filled his mind every waking moment of the day.

"Is something wrong, Wood Boy?" asked Lord Paul.

"No, sir!" said the boy, standing up and striking his head on the mantel. The girl covered her mouth as she laughed, and he blushed furiously. "I was just putting the wood away. I'm done, sir."

"Then get back to the kitchen, lad," said the Lord of the house.

Lord Paul was an Elector of the City. Before the Tsurani had come, Lord Paul had voted on every important matter confronting Walinor and had once been the delegate from the city to the General Council of Electors for the Free Cities of Natal. He was by any measure one of the wealthiest men in the city. He had ships plying the Bitter Sea and farms and holdings throughout the west, as well as investments in both the Kingdom of the Isles and the Empire of Great Kesh.

And Dirk was now hopelessly in love with his daughter.

It didn't matter that she didn't know his name, or even notice he was there, he just couldn't stop thinking of her. For the last two weeks, since Hamish's death, he had found his mind turning constantly to thoughts of Anika. Her smile, how she moved, the tilt of her chin when she was listening to something her father was saying.

She wore only the finest clothing and her hair was always put up with combs of fine bone or shell from the Bitter Sea, or left down with ringlets that softly framed her face. She was always polite, even to the servants, and had the sweetest voice Dirk had ever heard.

Getting back to the kitchen, Jenna the old stout cook said, "Getting a peek at the girl, were we?"

Drogen laughed and Dirk blushed. His infatuation with Lord Paul's daughter was a well-known source of amusement in the kitchen. Dirk prayed Jenna said nothing to any of the other boys, for if it became obvious to the boys in the barn, Dirk's already miserable existence would become even blacker than it presently was.

"She's a pretty girl," said Drogen with a smile at Dirk. "Most men would look more than once."

Dirk liked Drogen. He had been just one of Lord Paul's men-at-arms until Hamish had been killed for disturbing the Tsuranis on Midwinter's Night. Since then he had become a fixture in the main house and Dirk had gotten several chances to talk to him. Unlike Hamish, who had been given to bouts of ill-humor, Drogen was a quiet fellow, saying little unless answering a direct question. Easygoing, he was reputed to be one of the best men with a sword in the Free Cities, and he had an open and friendly manner. He was handsome in a dark fashion, and Dirk had heard gossip that more than one of the serving-women had snuck off with him on a thin pretext, and there were several tavern girls in the city who waited for his next visit. Dirk thought the man a nice enough fellow, though Jenna often had acid comments on Drogen's inability to think of much besides women.

Dirk stood and said, "I have to get more wood over to the Tsurani." He left the warm kitchen and, back out in the cold, wished he hadn't. He hurried to the woodpile.

Dirk picked up a large pile of wood and moved to the first of the three buildings. He pushed open the door and found the Tsurani as he always did. Quietly they rested between patrols or other duties which might take as much as half the garrison away for days, even weeks at a time. Occasionally they would return carrying their wounded. When resting they slept in their bunks, tended their odd, black-and-orange-colored armor, and talked quietly. Some played what appeared to be a gambling game of some sort involving sticks and rocks, and others played what looked to be chess.

Most were off on some mission for their master, leaving less than a dozen in residence at White Hill. They looked on impassively as he filled the woodbox. He left and serviced the other two woodboxes. When he was finished, he sighed audibly in relief. No matter how many times being the Wood Boy forced him to enter the buildings occupied by the Tsurani, having witnessed their capacity for ruthless murder brought Dirk to the edge of blind panic when he encountered them alone. When he knew he had done with them for another night, he felt as if he was entering a safe place for some hours to come.

Done with his outside chores for the night, he returned to the kitchen and ate his meager supper, a watery stew and coarse bread. The very best of the foodstuffs not taken by the invaders was served to Lord Paul and his daughter. He had overheard Anika complain about the food, only to hear her father reply that it wasn't too bad, all things considered. Dirk thought that by the standards he was used to it was a feast. Drogen and the other workers in the house got the pick of leftovers and there was never anything for a mere Wood Boy.

Dirk returned to the barn and ignored the moaning that came from under a blanket in the first stall. Mikia and Torren seemed unconcerned that their privacy was nonexistent. Still, Dirk reasoned, they were dairy people, a herdsman and a milkmaid, and he found farm people far more earthy and unconcerned with modesty than townspeople.

Litia sat in the corner of the next stall, her slight form shivering under a blanket as she sat on the dirt floor, huddled close to the warmth of a small fire. Dirk waved and she returned a toothless smile. He went over and said, "How are you?"

"Well enough," she said, and her voice was barely more than a whisper.

Dirk was concerned that the old woman might not last the winter, given the scant food and warmth, but others in the household seemed indifferent. You got old, then you died, they always said.

"What gossip?" asked the old woman. She lived for tidbits of news or rumors. Dirk always kept his ears open for something to enliven the old woman's evening.

"Nothing new, sorry to say," he replied.

With a wide, gummy grin, the old woman said, "And has the master's daughter favored you with a glance yet, my young buck?"

Dirk felt his face flush and he said, "I don't know what you mean, Litia."

"Yes you do," she chided him playfully. "It's all right, lad. She's the only girl your age here and it wouldn't be natural if you didn't feel a tug toward her. If those heathens who took our beds relent and let us visit with neighbors in the spring, the first young farm lass you meet will get your mind off my lord's wicked child."

"Wicked child?" said Dirk. "What do you mean?"

Litia said, "Nothing, sweet boy. She's a willful girl who always gets what she wants, is all. What you need is a good strong lass, a farm girl with broad hips who can bear you sons who will take care of you in your old age."

The bitterness in Litia's words was not lost on Dirk, even if he was young. He knew that her only son had died years before in a drowning accident and that she had no one left to care for her. Dirk said, "I'll try to get you another blanket from the house tomorrow."

"Don't get yourself into trouble on my account," said the woman, but her expression showed she appreciated the offer.

Dirk left her and climbed the ladder to the loft, where the young men slept. He was the youngest up there, for the boys younger than he stayed with their families. Alex, Hans, and Leonard were already resting. Hemmy and Petir would be up shortly. Dirk wished for another blanket himself, but knew that he would have to depend upon the ones allotted to him. At least one side of him would be warm at a time, as he would huddled next to Hemmy, the next older boy. He would turn a few times in the night to ward off the freezing air.

And spring was but two months away. Hemmy and Petir climbed up and took their places in the loft, and Dirk snuggled down as best he could in his blankets and went to sleep.

It was an odd sound, and Dirk couldn't quite make sense of it as he came awake in the dark. Then it registered: someone had cried out. It had been a muffled sound, but it had been a cry. Dirk listened for a moment, but the sound wasn't repeated. He tried to go back to sleep.

Just as he was drowsy again, he heard a creak and the sound of someone moving in the barn. A dull thud and a strange gurgling noise made him lift himself up on his right elbow, listening in the dark. He strained to hear something, but he couldn't make out the sounds. Assuming it was Mikia and Torren again, he rolled over and tried to go back to sleep.

Again he was almost dozing when he realized something was wrong. As he turned over, he saw something moving rapidly toward him in the gloom, a large dark shape. He sat up, reflexively pulling away from what was coming toward him.

Two things happened at once. Someone slashed at him, a blade cutting into the fabric of his coat below his collarbone, and he struck the hay door with his back. He choked out an inarticulate cry, unable to speak for the terror which overwhelmed him. Then another body slammed into him with a strangled cry and he felt the door latch behind him give.

Never too sturdy, the latch parted as the weight of two bodies struck it, and with a muffled cry, Dirk fell out the hay door, down to the snow-covered ground below. He landed with a thud that drove the breath out of him.

Then the other body landed on him, and Dirk was knocked senseless.

He awoke as the sky was lightening. He was freezing and barely able to breathe. His left eye seemed glued shut and something on top of him held him firmly to the ground.

Dirk tried to move, and discovered that Hemmy lay atop him. "Hey, get off!" he said, but his voice was weak and strangled. A burning pain below his throat caused him to gasp when he moved.

His legs were numb from the cold, and he lay in a hole in the snow. He wiggled his bottom and managed to work his way upright and realized Hemmy was dead. The older boy's face was white, and his throat was cut. Terror galvanized Dirk and he lifted the corpse enough to get out from beneath him, forcing numb legs to do his bidding.

He pulled himself out of the snow and his muscles screamed at being forced to move. He climbed out of the hole and saw he was drenched in blood, Hemmy's blood.

"What happened?" he whispered.

As he staggered toward the barn he saw that the morning sun was still an hour from cresting the eastern horizon. His legs became wobbly and he leaned against the barn, looking up to see the rear hay door still opened. He paused a moment to get control over his frozen, stiff legs, walked around to the front, and looked at the large doors thrown open to the cold. He glanced down at the snow before the door and saw no unusual number of footprints. But off to the south side of the entrance, where snow remained unclear, he saw a single set of footprints and the parallel impression left by a sled's runners. Someone had pulled the large sled out of the barn. The depth of the runner tracks in the snow told him it was heavily loaded. The horses were long gone, having been eaten by the Tsurani the winter before, so whoever had moved the sled was pulling it.

Dirk went inside the barn and saw Mikia and Torren lying in each other's arms, their throats cut. Old Litia also lay dead in her own blood, her eyes open wide. Everywhere he looked, he saw death.

Who did this? Dirk wondered in panicked confusion. Had the Tsurani who occupied Lord Paul's estate gone mad and killed everyone? But if they had, there would have been footprints in abundance outside in the snow, and there were none. Most of them were gone on some mission or another, leaving only a few in the outbuildings this week. Then Dirk thoughts turned to the manor house. "Anika!" he said in a hoarse whisper.

He hurried through the predawn gloom to the kitchen and found the door open. He stared in mute horror at the carnage in the room. Everyone who slept in the kitchen was as dead as those in the barn.

He hurried up stairs and, without knocking, entered Anika's room. Her bed lay empty. He peered under it, afraid she might have crawled under it to die. Then he realized there was no blood in the room.

He got up and ran to her father's room, and pushed open the door. Lord Paul lay in a sea of blood, on his bed, Dirk didn't need to see if he lived. Beside the bed a secret door was opened, a door painted to look like a section of the wall. Dirk looked through the door into the small hiding place and realized that here was where his master had kept his wealth. The invaders had demanded every gold, silver, and copper coin held by those living in the occupied region, yet it was well documented that they had no concept of wealth on this planet. The servants had speculated that Lord Paul had turned over only one part in three of his wealth and the rest had remained hidden. Perhaps they had found he had hidden wealth and this was their way of punishing everyone. If the Tsurani had gone on a rampage—

"No," he said softly to himself. The Tsurani hanged those without honor. The blade was for honorable foes. Whoever did the killing had moved with stealth, as if afraid to raise an alarm and be overwhelmed, and had cautiously killed all the servants one at a time. The killer had been armed. . . .

Drogen!

Only Drogen and the Lord of the House, of all those who weren't Tsurani, were permitted arms. Dirk closed the secret door, too stunned to appreciate how clever it was. Once closed, it appeared indistinguishable from the wall.

He hurried down to the large dining hall and saw over the fireplace the two swords hung there, heirlooms of Lord Paul's family. He considered taking one down, then remembered that should the Tsurani find him with a sword in his possession, he would be hanged without any opportunity to explain.

He returned to the kitchen and took a large boning knife from the butcher's block next to the stove. That was something he had handled many times before, and the familiarity of the handle was reassuring to him.

He had to do something about finding Anika, but he didn't know what. Drogen must have taken her with the gold. He ran back to the barn to see if anyone else might have survived. Within minutes he knew that only he and Anika had survived.

And the Tsurani, of course.

Panic struck Dirk. He knew that if one of them stuck his head outside one of the huts he would be hanged for carrying a kitchen knife, no matter what the reason.

He put the knife in his tunic, and climbed into the loft. He went to the canvas bag that served as his closet, holding his few belongings. He removed his only coat, and saw a long cut below the collar. Drogen had lashed out at him first, because he had awakened. He must have thought Dirk's throat cut. Then he had killed Hemmy, pushing him atop Dirk, causing them to fall through the hay door. Only the darkness and the fall had saved Dirk's life, he knew. Had he not fallen out of the barn, Drogen would certainly have insured the boy was dead.

Dirk put on his extra shirt for warmth, ignoring the sticky blood soaked into his undershirt and the shirt he already wore. Wearing the extra layers of clothing might be the difference between life and death. He considered pulling a tunic off one of the other boys, but he couldn't bring himself to touch the bodies of his dead friends.

He again donned his coat and took his only pair of gloves from the bag, along with a large woolen scarf Litia had knitted for him the year before. He put them on and checked the bag for his other belongings: there was nothing else there he could imagine would help him.

He hurried down the ladder. The only thing he could think of doing was following the murderer. He was terrified of waking the Tsurani, and not certain they would care about the murder of people they obviously felt were inferior to themselves. They might blame Dirk and hang him, he feared.

Drogen. He had to find Drogen and rescue Anika and get the gold back for her. The boy knew that without gold the girl would be at the mercy of the town's people. She would be forced to depend on the generosity of relatives or friends. But he was terrified enough he couldn't move. He stood in the barn aisle, rooted with indecision.

After a time he heard a shout from across the compound. The Tsurani were up and one had seen something. A confusion of voices sounded from outside, and Dirk knew they would be in the barn in moments.

He hid himself in the darkest corner of the stall most removed from the door, and lay shivering in fear and cold as men came into the barn, speaking rapidly in their odd language. Two walked past where Dirk lay, once casting a quick glance in his direction. He must have simply assumed Dirk was another dead boy, for he said nothing to his companion, who climbed the ladder to the hayloft. After a moment, he shouted down, and the other responded. He heard the man return down the ladder and the two of them leave the barn. Dirk waited until it grew quiet again, then got out of the straw. He hurried to the door and peered out. From his vantage point he saw one Tsurani instructing others to search the area.

Uncertain of what to do next, Dirk waited. A Tsurani he knew to be of some rank came out and pointed to the tracks in the snow. There was some sort of debate, and the man who had sent the others searching seemed to be indicating that someone should follow the murderer.

Then the leader spoke in commanding tones and the other man

bowed slightly and turned away. Dirk realized that no one was going to follow Drogen. He was going to get away with killing more than two dozen people and kidnapping Anika and taking all of Lord Paul's gold. The Tsurani soldier in charge seemed content to leave this matter to his own officer, when the bulk of the command returned from their mission.

Dirk knew that if anyone was to save Anika, it would have to be him. Dirk slipped out of the barn and around the side, and when he was certain no one was nearby, he went down the hill behind the barn and made his way into the woods. He hurried along through the birch and pines until he found the sled tracks. He turned to follow them.

Dirk slogged his way through the snow, his breath a white cloud before him. His feet were numb and he felt weak and hungry, but he was determined to overtake Drogen. The landscape was white and green— the boughs of pines and firs peering out from mantles of snow. A stand of bare trees stood a short distance away, and Dirk knew he had left the boundary of Lord Paul's estate.

The murderer was making good time, despite having to pull the heavy sled. He knew that he gained on Drogen each time he had to pull the sled up a hill, but each time he went down the next slope, Drogen probably gained some of that time back.

Dirk stopped to rest a moment, His best chance of finding the murderer, he knew was to catch him at night. Dirk glanced around. He had no idea how much time had passed; a good part of the day, he realized, but he couldn't tell from the grey sky where the sun was and when darkness would arrive.

A rabbit poked its head above a nearby ridge and sniffed. Dirk wished he had some sort of weapon, or the time to rig a snare, for a rabbit cooked over an open fire would be welcome, but he knew such wishes would go ungranted.

He continued on.

It began to snow as darkness came, and it came quickly. Dirk's plan of following through the night vanished along with the sled tracks. Dirk tried to follow the tracks, but there was no light. It was the blackest night he could remember, and he was terrified.

He found a small clump of trees overhung by a large pine bower thick with snow that acted like a roof, and he crawled in for the meager shelter it provided. He built up a low snow wall around him, having been taught as a boy that such a wall would shelter him from the wind. He dozed but didn't sleep.

A soft sound woke him. He heard it again. He poked his head out from under the pine bower and saw that snow had fallen from a branch in a large clump.

He crawled out and looked for tracks. There were places where the snow had fallen lightly, and he could barely see the tracks, but they were there, and they pointed the way.

Dirk began again to hunt down the murderer.

At sundown he saw the light of the fire, high on a ridge to the east. Drogen was making his way toward the city of Natal. It was free of the Tsurani invaders. Once there, Drogen could make his way to Ylith and from there anywhere in the world, the Kingdom, Kesh, or the Island Empire of Queg. How Drogen was going to cross the frontier, Dirk didn't know, but he assumed the man had a plan. Maybe he just counted on the Tsurani holding tight to their campfires and not having too many men in the field in the dead of winter. From what he had heard, there had been almost no fighting between them and the Free Cities and Kingdom forces since the first heavy snow of winter.

Dirk slogged his way toward the fire.

He finally reached a place from where he could get a glimpse of the site. Slowly approaching as quietly as he could, Dirk saw a single man resting on the sled, warming his hands on the fire. Drogen must have thought himself free of pursuit, for he had taken no pains to hide his whereabouts. At his feet, Anika lay in a bundle of furs. Dirk had aired them out every fall after fetching them out of storage, so he knew the girl was well protected from the cold. She appeared to be asleep— probably exhausted from terror, Dirk thought.

Dirk stopped, again rooted by fear. He had no idea how to proceed. He made up and discarded a dozen plans to attack the murderer. He couldn't imagine how to attack a trained warrior, one who was paid to fight.

Dirk stood freezing on his feet, watching the fire grow dimmer. Drogen ate, and still Dirk remained motionless. Cold, exposure, hunger, and fear were on the verge of reducing him to tears.

Then Drogen threw more wood on the fire and wrapped a blanket around himself. He lay down on the ground between the sled and Anika, who moved, but didn't awake. He was going to sleep!

Dirk knew that he could only rescue Anika and regain Lord Paul's gold by sneaking up on Drogen and killing him as he slept. Dirk had no compunctions about the act; Drogen had killed everyone Dirk had known since leaving his family to work at the master's estate, in their sleep, and he deserved no more than they got. Dirk just feared he wouldn't be up to the task, or would inadvertently wake up the killer.

Dirk moved his legs, trying to regain circulation in the freezing night, and eventually he judged it safe to approach the camp. Stiff legs and an inability to catch his breath drove Dirk to a heart-pounding frenzy. He found his hands shaking so badly he could barely manage to get the heavy knife out from within his jacket.

The familiar handle was suddenly an alien thing that resisted fitting comfortably in his palm. He crept forward and tried not to let panic overwhelm him.

He stopped on the other side of the sled, uncertain which way to approach. He decided that he'd approach Drogen's head.

Dirk held the knife high, and crept around the sled, slowly, moving as carefully as he could so as not to make noise. When he was just a few feet away, Drogen moved, shifting the blanket around his shoulders. He snuggled down behind Anika, who didn't move.

Fear overwhelmed Dirk. He knew if he didn't move now, he would never move. He struck down hard with the knife and felt the point dig into the murderer's shoulder.

Drogen shouted in pain and convulsed, almost pulling the knife out of Dirk's hard. Dirk yanked it back, and struck out again as Drogen tried to rise. The point again dug deep into his shoulder, and he howled in pain.

Anika awoke with a scream and kicked off the furs, then leaped to her feet, spinning around and trying to understand what was happening. Dirk pulled the blade out and was ready for a third strike, but Drogen charged, driving his shoulder into Dirk, knocking him aside.

The boy rolled on the ground and found Drogen sitting atop Dirk's chest, his hand poised to deliver a blow. "You!" he said as he saw the boy's face in the dim light of the dying fire. Drogen hesitated.

Dirk lashed out with his knife and struck Drogen in the face, cutting deeply. Drogen reared back, his hand to his cheek as he cried out in pain. Dirk acted without thought. He pushed hard with his knife, driving it deep into Drogen, just under his rib cage.

Drogen loomed above Dirk in the dim light, his eyes wide in silent astonishment. His left hand dropped from where it had momentarily touched his cheek. With his right hand he grabbed Dirk's tunic, as if he were going to pull him upright to ask him something. Then he slowly toppled backward. He didn't release his grip on Dirk's coat and he pulled the boy upright, then forward.

Dirk's legs were pinned under Drogen, and he was forced to bend forward.

Dirk frantically pried the dying man's fingers from his coat. He fell back and the pain in his side was a searing agony. He saw the blade of the knife protruding from his coat and his head swam. Using his elbows, he pulled himself back and got his legs free of Drogen's weight. Dimly he was aware of a sobbing voice saying, "No."

Dirk was in a fog as he reached down and pulled out the knife from Drogen's body. He turned as a girl's voice again said, "No!"

"You killed him!" screamed Anika as she rushed toward Dirk. The disoriented boy stood uncertain of what was occurring. He tried to focus his eyes as his head swam from pain. "I—" he began, but the girl seemed to fly at him.

"You killed him!" she screamed again as she fell upon him. He stepped back, his heel striking Drogen's body and he fell, the girl suddenly atop him. She landed heavily upon Dirk, her eyes wide in shock. She pushed herself up from atop Dirk and looked down between them.

Dirk followed her gaze and saw that the knife was still in his hand. Anika had impaled herself upon the blade. Confusion beset her features and she gazed at his face and at last said, softly, "The Wood Boy?"

She fell atop Dirk. He moved her aside, but held her in his arms, and he sank to the snow, holding her. She looked up at the sky, eyes glassy, and he gently closed them.

Then Dirk felt a hot stabbing pain in his side and bile rose in his throat as he realized somehow he had been cut. He touched the wound and hot pain shot through his body, and his eyes seemed unwilling to focus. He knew that he couldn't move with the blade there, and reached up to grip the handle again. Mustering all the resolve he could, he pulled the knife from his side, and screamed at the agony of it. After a moment, the pain subsided and was replaced by a throbbing torment, but one that didn't make him feel as if he was going to die. He slowly stood, and turned to confront the girl.

Then he passed out.

Borric said, "She helped him kill her father and the rest?"

"I don't think so, sir." Sadly Dirk said, "I think Drogen tricked her, convinced her to elope with him to gain the secret of where her father's gold was. She was an innocent girl and he was a rake known to have wooed many women. If he killed everyone without awakening her, then bundled her up in those furs and carried her straight to the sled, she wouldn't have seen. Once away from the Free Cities, she might never have known." He looked as if he was about to cry, but held his tone steady as he said, "She fell upon me in a fright, and without knowing what had occurred at home. Else she wouldn't have been so frantic over Drogen's death, I'm certain. Her death was an accident, but it was all my fault."

"There was no fault in you, lad. It was, as you say, an accident." After a moment, Borric nodded. "Yes, it's better to think of it that way. Lad, why did you come here?"

"I didn't know what else to do. I thought if Drogen planned on coming this way, I would, too. I knew the Tsurani would take my master's gold and hang me as likely as not . . . it was all I could think of."

"You did well," said Borric softly.

Dirk put the cup down and said, "That was good. Thank you, sir." He moved and winced.

"You're hurt?"

"I bound the wounds as best I could, sir."

Borric called for an orderly and instructed him to take the boy to the healers' tent and have the wound treated.

After Dirk had left, the captain said, "That was quite a story, Your Grace."

Borric agreed. "The boy has special courage."

"Did the girl know?" asked the Captain.

"Of course she knew," said Borric. "I knew Paul of White Hill; I've done enough business with him through my agent in Bordon, Talbot Kilrane. I've been to his home, and he's been to Crydee.

"And I knew the daughter." Borric sighed, as if what he thought tired him. "She's the same age as my Carline. And they're as different as two children could be. Anika was born scheming." Borric sighed. "I have no doubt she planned this, though we'll never know if she anticipated all the murders; she may have only suggested to the body-guard they steal the gold and flee. With her father behind Tsurani lines and all that gold in her possession . . . she could have cut quite a social figure for herself back in Krondor or even in Rillanon. She easily could have disposed of the bodyguard—he clearly couldn't admit to anyone his part in this, could he? And if word of the killings reached us, we would assume the Tsurani murdered the household on some pretext." Borric was silent. Then he said, "In my bones I know the girl was the one behind all this . . . but we'll never know, for certain, will we?"

"No, Your Grace," agreed the captain. "What of the bodies?"

"Bury them. We have no means to return the girl to her family in Walinor."

The captain said, "I'll detail men to the digging. It'll take a while to dig through the frozen ground." He then asked, "And the gold?"

Borric said, "It's confiscated. The Tsurani would have taken it anyway, and we've an army to feed. Send it under guard to Brucal in LaMut." He paused a moment, then said, "Send the boy, too. I'll pen a note to Brucal asking the boy be found some service there at head-quarters. He's a resourceful lad and as he said, he has nowhere else to go."

"Very well, Your Grace."

As the captain turned to go, Borric said, "And Captain."

"Yes, Your Grace?"

"Keep what I said to yourself. The boy doesn't need to know."

"As you wish, Your Grace," said the captain as he departed.

Borric sat forward and tried to return his attention to the business at hand, but he found his mind returning to the boy's story. He tried to imagine what Dirk had felt, alone, armed only with the kitchen knife, and afraid. He had been a trained warrior for most of his life, but he remembered what it was to be uncertain. He recognized the boy's act for what it had been, an unusual and rare act of heroism. The image of a lovestruck, frightened boy trudging through the snow at night to confront a murderer and rescue a damsel lingered with the Duke, and he decided it was best that the boy be left with that one shred of illusion about the girl. He had earned that much, at least.

The Wheel of Time

—

ROBERT JORDAN

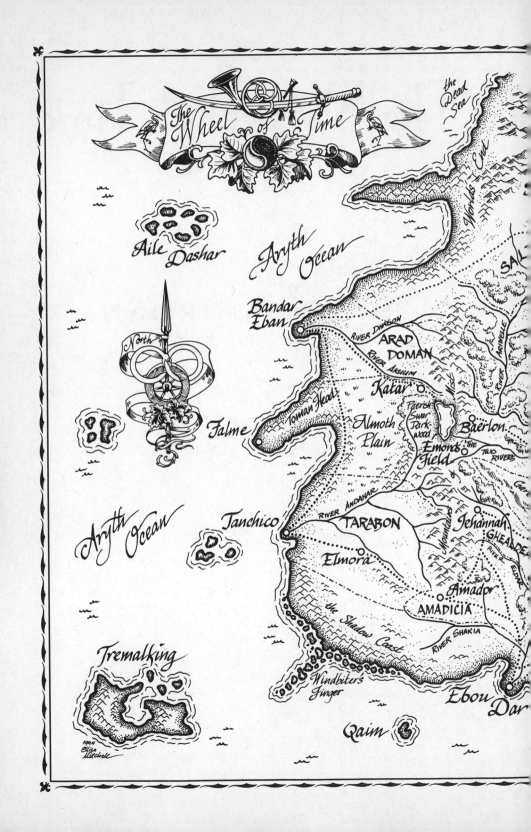

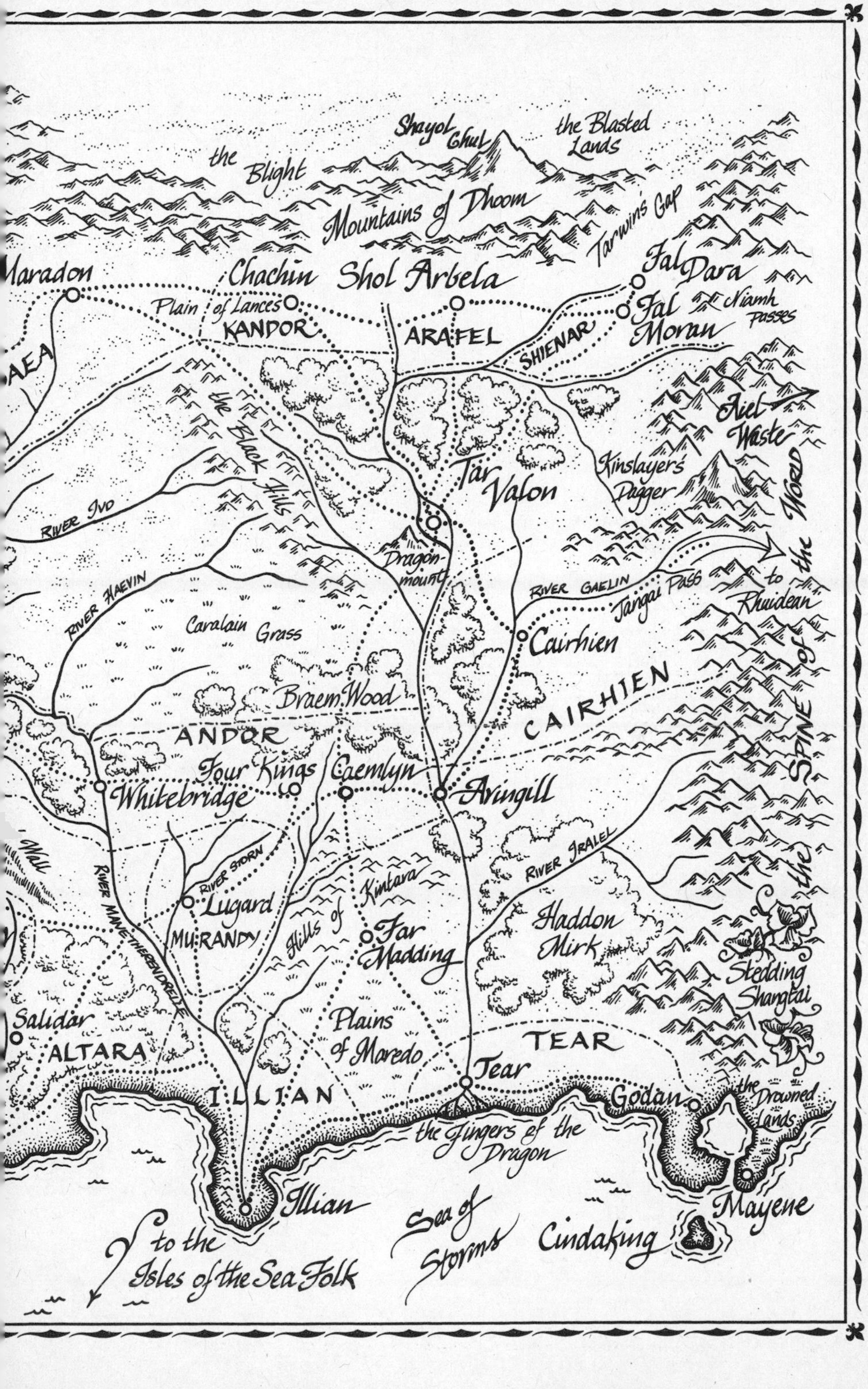

Shayol Ghul
the Blasted Lands
the Blight
Mountains of Dhoom
Tarwin's Gap
Maradon
Chachin
Shol Arbela
Fal Dara
Fal Moran
Niamh Passes
Plain of Lances
KANDOR
ARAFEL
SHIENAR
Aiel Waste
the Black Hills
Tar Valon
Kinslayer's Dagger
River Ivo
Dragonmount
River Haevin
River Gaelin
Jangai Pass
to Rhuidean
Caralain Grass
Cairhien
Braem Wood
CAIRHIEN
ANDOR
Four Kings
Caemlyn
Whitebridge
Aringill
Spine of the World
River Storn
River Iralell
Hills of Kintara
River Manetherendrelle
Lugard
MURANDY
Far Madding
Haddon Mirk
Stedding Shangtai
Salidar
ALTARA
Plains of Maredo
TEAR
Tear
ILLIAN
Godan
the Drowned Lands
the Fingers of the Dragon
Illian
Mayene
Sea of Storms
Cindaking
to the Isles of the Sea Folk

The world of Robert Jordan's *The Wheel of Time* lies both in our future and our past, a world of kings and queens and Aes Sedai, women who can tap the True Source and wield the One Power, which turns the Wheel and drives the universe: a world where the war between the Light and the Shadow is fought every day.

At the moment of Creation, the Creator bound the Dark One away from the world of humankind, but more than three thousand years ago Aes Sedai, then both men and women, unknowingly bored into that prison outside of time. The Dark One was able to touch the world only lightly, and the hole was eventually sealed over, but the Dark One's taint settled on *saidin*, the male half of the Power. Eventually every male Aes Sedai went mad, and in the Breaking of the World they destroyed civilization and changed the very face of the earth, sinking mountains beneath the sea and bringing new seas where land had been.

Now only women bear the title Aes Sedai. Commanded by their Amyrlin Seat and divided into seven Ajahs named by color, they rule the great island city of Tar Valon, where their White Tower is located, and are bound by the Three Oaths, fixed into their bones with *saidar*, the female half of the Power: To speak no word that is not true, to make no weapon for one man to kill another, and never to use the One Power except as a weapon against Shadowspawn or in the last extreme of defending her own life, or that of her Warder or another sister.

Men still are born who can learn to channel the Power, or worse, who will channel one day whether they try to or not. Doomed to madness, destruction, and death by the taint on *saidin*, they are hunted down by Aes Sedai and gentled, cut off forever from the Power for the safety of the world. No man goes to this willingly. Even if they survive the hunt, they seldom survive long after gentling.

For more than three thousand years, while nations and empires rose and fell, nothing has been so feared as a man who can channel. But for all those three thousand years there have been the Prophecies of the Dragon, that the seals on the Dark One's prison will weaken and he will touch the world once more, and that the Dragon, who sealed up that hole, will be Reborn to face the Dark One again. A child, born in sight of Tar Valon on the slopes of Dragonmount, will grow up to be the Dragon Reborn, the only hope of humanity in the Last Battle— a man who can channel. Few people know more than scraps of the Prophecies, and few want to know more.

A world of kings and queens, nations and wars, where the White Tower rules only Tar Valon but even kings and queens are wary of Aes Sedai machinations. A world where the Shadow and the Prophecies loom together.

The present story takes place before the first volume of the series. The succeeding books should be read in order.

New Spring

ROBERT JORDAN

The air of Kandor held the sharpness of new spring when Lan returned to the lands where he had always known he would die. Trees bore the first red of new growth, and a few scattered wildflowers dotted winter-brown grass where shadows did not cling to patches of snow, yet the pale sun offered little warmth after the south, a gusting breeze cut through his coat, and gray clouds hinted at more than rain. He was almost home. Almost.

A hundred generations had beaten the wide road nearly as hard as the stone of the surrounding hills, and little dust rose, though a steady stream of ox-carts was leaving the morning farmers' markets in Can-luum and merchant trains of tall wagons, surrounded by mounted guards in steel caps and bits of armor, flowed toward the city's high gray walls. Here and there the chains of the Kandori merchants' guild spanned a chest or an Arafellin wore bells, a ruby decorated this man's ear, a pearl brooch that woman's breast, but for the most part the traders' clothes were as subdued as their manner. A merchant who flaunted too much profit discovered it hard to find bargains. By con-trast, farmers showed off their success when they came to town. Bright embroidery decorated the striding country men's baggy breeches, the women's wide trousers, their cloaks fluttering in the wind. Some wore colored ribbons in their hair, or a narrow fur collar. They might have been dressed for the coming Bel Tine dances and feasting. Yet country folk eyed strangers as warily as any guard, eyed them and hefted spears or axes and hurried along. The times carried an edge in Kandor, maybe all along the Borderlands. Bandits had sprung up like weeds this past year, and more troubles than usual out of the Blight. Rumor even spoke of a man who channeled the One Power, but then, rumor often did.

Leading his horse toward Canluum, Lan paid as little attention to the stares he and his companion attracted as he did to Bukama's scowls and carping. Bukama had raised him from the cradle, Bukama and other men now dead, and he could not recall seeing anything but a glower on that weathered face, even when Bukama spoke praise. This time his mutters were for a stone-bruised hoof that had him afoot, but he could always find something.

They did attract attention, two very tall men walking their mounts and a packhorse with a pair of tattered wicker hampers, their plain clothes worn and travel-stained. Their harness and weapons were well tended, though. A young man and an old, hair hanging to their shoulders and held back by a braided leather cord around the temples. The *hadori* drew eyes. Especially here in the Borderlands, where people had some idea what it meant.

"Fools," Bukama grumbled. "Do they think we're bandits? Do they think we mean to rob the lot of them, at midday on the high road?" He glared and shifted the sword at his hip in a way that brought considering stares from a number of merchants' guards. A stout farmer prodded his ox wide of them.

Lan kept silent. A certain reputation clung to Malkieri who still wore the *hadori,* though not for banditry, but reminding Bukama would only send him into a black humor for days. His mutters shifted to the chances of a decent bed that night, of a decent meal before. Bukama seldom complained when there actually was no bed or no food, only about prospects and the inconsequential. He expected little, and trusted to less.

Neither food nor lodging entered Lan's thoughts, despite the distance they had traveled. His head kept swinging north. He remained aware of everyone around him, especially those who glanced his way more than once, aware of the jingle of harness and the creak of saddles, the clop of hooves, the snap of wagon canvas loose on its hoops. Any sound out of place would shout at him. That had been the first lesson

Bukama and his friends had imparted in his childhood: Be aware of everything, even when asleep. Only the dead could afford oblivion. Lan remained aware, but the Blight lay north. Still miles away across the hills, yet he could feel it, feel the twisted corruption.

Just his imagination, but no less real for that. It had pulled at him in the south, in Cairhien and Andor, even in Tear, almost five hundred leagues distant. Two years away from the Borderlands, his personal war abandoned for another, and every day the tug grew stronger. The Blight meant death to most men. Death and the Shadow, a rotting land tainted by the Dark One's breath, where anything at all could kill. Two tosses of a coin had decided where to begin anew. Four nations bordered the Blight, but his war covered the length of it, from the Aryth Ocean to the Spine of the World. One place to meet death was as good as another. He was almost home. Almost back to the Blight.

A drymoat surrounded Canluum's wall, fifty paces wide and ten deep, spanned by five broad stone bridges with towers at either end as tall as those that lined the wall itself. Raids out of the Blight by Trollocs and Myrddraal often struck much deeper into Kandor than Canluum, but none had ever made it inside the city's wall. The Red Stag waved above every tower. A proud man was Lord Varan, the High Seat of House Marcasiev; Queen Ethenielle did not fly so many of her own banners even in Chachin itself.

The guards at the outer towers, in helmets with Varan's antlered crest and the Red Stag on their chests, peered into the backs of wagons before allowing them to trundle onto the bridge, or occasionally motioned someone to push a hood further back. No more than a gesture was necessary; the law in every Borderland forbade hiding your face inside village or town, and no one wanted to be mistaken for one of the Eyeless trying to sneak into the city. Hard gazes followed Lan and Bukama onto the bridge. Their faces were clearly visible. And their *hadori*. No recognition lit any of those watching eyes, though. Two years was a long time in the Borderlands. A great many men could die in two years.

Lan noticed that Bukama had gone silent, always a bad sign, and cautioned him. "I never start trouble," the older man snapped, but he did stop fingering his sword hilt.

The guards on the wall above the open iron-plated gates and those on the bridge wore only back- and breast-plates for armor, yet they were no less watchful, especially of a pair of Malkieri with their hair tied back. Bukama's mouth grew tighter at every step.

"Al'Lan Mandragoran! The Light preserve us, we heard you were dead fighting the Aiel at the Shining Walls!" The exclamation came from a young guard, taller than the rest, almost as tall as Lan. Young, perhaps a year or two less than he, yet the gap seemed ten years. A lifetime. The guard bowed deeply, left hand on his knee. *"Tai'shar Malkier!"* True blood of Malkier. "I stand ready, Majesty."

"I am not a king," Lan said quietly. Malkier was dead. Only the war still lived. In him, at least.

Bukama was not quiet. "You stand ready for *what,* boy?" The heel of his bare hand struck the guard's breastplate right over the Red Stag, driving the man upright and back a step. "You cut your hair short and leave it unbound!" Bukama spat the words. "You're sworn to a Kandori lord! By what right do you claim to be Malkieri?"

The young man's face reddened as he floundered for answers. Other guards started toward the pair, then halted when Lan let his reins fall. Only that, but they knew his name, now. They eyed his bay stallion, standing still and alert behind him, almost as cautiously as they did him. A warhorse was a formidable weapon, and they could not know Cat Dancer was only half-trained yet.

Space opened up as people already through the gates hurried a little distance before turning to watch, while those still on the bridge pressed back. Shouts rose in both directions from people wanting to know what was holding traffic. Bukama ignored it all, intent on the red-faced guard. He had not dropped the reins of the packhorse or his yellow roan gelding.

An officer appeared from the stone guardhouse inside the gates, crested helmet under his arm, but one hand in a steel-backed gauntlet resting on his sword hilt. A bluff, graying man with white scars on his face, Alin Seroku had soldiered forty years along the Blight, yet his eyes widened slightly at the sight of Lan. Plainly he had heard the tales of Lan's death, too.

"The Light shine upon you, Lord Mandragoran. The son of el'Leanna and al'Akir, blessed be their memories, is always welcome." Seroku's eyes flickered toward Bukama, not in welcome. He planted his feet in the middle of the gateway. Five horsemen could have passed easily on either side, but he meant himself for a bar, and he was. None of the guards shifted a boot, yet every one had hand on sword hilt. All but the young man meeting Bukama's glares with his own. "Lord Marcasiev has commanded us to keep the peace strictly," Seroku went on, half in apology. But no more than half. "The city is on edge. All these tales of a man channeling are bad enough, but there have been murders in the street this last month and more, in broad daylight, and strange accidents. People whisper about Shadowspawn loose inside the walls."

Lan gave a slight nod. With the Blight so close, people always muttered of Shadowspawn when they had no other explanation, whether for a sudden death or unexpected crop failure. He did not take up Cat Dancer's reins, though. "We intend to rest here a few days before riding north."

For a moment he thought Seroku was surprised. Did the man expect pledges to keep the peace, or apologies for Bukama's behavior? Either would shame Bukama, now. A pity if the war ended here. Lan did not want to die killing Kandori.

His old friend turned from the young guard, who stood quivering, fists clenched at his sides. "All fault here is mine," Bukama announced to the air in a flat voice. "I had no call for what I did. By my mother's name, I will keep Lord Marcasiev's peace. By my mother's name, I will not draw sword inside Canluum's walls." Seroku's jaw dropped, and Lan hid his own shock with difficulty.

Hesitating only a moment, the scar-faced officer stepped aside, bowing and touching sword hilt, then heart. "There is always welcome for Lan Mandragoran Dai Shan," he said formally. "And for Bukama Marenellin, the hero of Salmarna. May you both know peace, one day."

"There is peace in the mother's last embrace," Lan responded with equal formality, touching hilt and heart.

"May she welcome us home, one day," Seroku finished. No one really wished for the grave, but that was the only place to find peace in the Borderlands.

Face like iron, Bukama strode ahead pulling Sun Lance and the packhorse after him, not waiting for Lan. This was not well.

Canluum was a city of stone and brick, its paved streets twisting around tall hills. The Aiel invasion had never reached the Borderlands, but the ripples of war always diminished trade a long way from any battles, and now that fighting and winter were both finished, the city had filled with people from every land. Despite the Blight practically on the city's doorstep, gemstones mined in the surrounding hills made Canluum wealthy. And, strangely enough, some of the finest clockmakers anywhere. The cries of hawkers and shopkeepers shouting their wares rose above the hum of the crowd even away from the terraced market squares. Colorfully dressed musicians, or jugglers, or tumblers performed at every intersection. A handful of lacquered carriages swayed through the mass of people and wagons and carts and barrows, and horses with gold- or silver-mounted saddles and bridles picked their way through the throng, their riders' garb embroidered as ornately as the animals' tack and trimmed with fox or marten or ermine. Hardly a foot of street was left bare anywhere. Lan even saw several Aes Sedai, women with serene, ageless faces. Enough people recognized them on sight that they created eddies in the crowd, swirls to clear a way. Respect or caution, awe or fear, there were sufficient reasons for a king to step aside for a sister. Once you might have gone a year without seeing an Aes Sedai even in the Borderlands, but the sisters seemed to be everywhere since their old Amyrlin Seat died a few months earlier. Maybe it was those tales of a man channeling; they would not let him run free long, if he existed. Lan kept his eyes away from them. The *hadori* could be enough to attract the interest of a sister seeking a Warder.

Shockingly, lace veils covered many women's faces. Thin lace, sheer enough to reveal that they had eyes, and no one had ever heard of a female Myrddraal, but Lan had never expected law to yield to mere fashion. Next they would take down the oil lamps lining the streets and let the nights grow black. Even more shocking than the veils, Bukama looked right at some of those women and did not open his mouth. Then a jut-nosed man named Nazar Kurenin rode in front of Bukama's eyes, and he did not blink. The young guard surely had been born after the Blight swallowed Malkier, but Kurenin, his hair cut short and wearing a forked beard, was twice Lan's age. The years had not erased the marks of his *hadori* completely. There were many like Kurenin, and the sight of him should have set Bukama spluttering. Lan eyed his friend worriedly.

They had been moving steadily toward the center of the city, climbing toward the highest hill, Stag's Stand. Lord Marcasiev's fortress-like palace covered the peak, with those of lesser lords and ladies on the terraces below. Any threshold up there offered warm welcome for al'Lan Mandragoran. Perhaps warmer than he wanted now. Balls and hunts, with nobles invited from as much as fifty miles away, including from across the border with Arafel. People avid to hear of his "adventures." Young men wanting to join his forays into the Blight, and old men to compare their experiences there with his. Women eager to share the bed of a man whom, so fool stories claimed, the Blight could not kill. Kandor and Arafel were as bad as any southland at times; some of those women would be married. And there would be men like Kurenin, working to submerge memories of lost Malkier, and women who no longer adorned their foreheads with the *ki'sain* in pledge that they would swear their sons to oppose the Shadow while they breathed. Lan could ignore the false smiles while they named him al'Lan Dai Shan, diademed battle lord and uncrowned king of a nation betrayed while he was in his cradle. In his present mood, Bukama might do murder. Or worse, given his oaths at the gate. He would keep those to the death.

"Varan Marcasiev will hold us a week or more with ceremony," Lan said, turning down a narrower street that led away from the Stand. "With what we've heard of bandits and the like, he will be just as happy if I don't appear to make my bows." True enough. He had met the High Seat of House Marcasiev only once, years past, but he remembered a man given entirely to his duties.

Bukama followed without complaint about missing a palace bed or the feasts the cooks would prepare. It was worrying.

No palaces rose in the hollows toward the north wall, only shops and taverns, inns and stables and wagon yards. Bustle surrounded the factors' long warehouses, but no carriages came to the Deeps, and most streets were barely wide enough for carts. They were just as jammed with people as the wide ways, though, and every bit as noisy. Here, the street performers' finery was tarnished, yet they made up for it by being louder, and buyers and sellers alike bellowed as if trying to be heard in the next street. Likely some of the crowd were cutpurses, slipfingers, and other thieves, finished with a morning's business higher up or headed there for the afternoon. It would have been a wonder otherwise, with so many merchants in town. The second time unseen fingers brushed his coat in the crowd, Lan tucked his purse under his shirt. Any banker would advance him more against the Shienaran estate he had been granted on reaching manhood, but loss of the gold on hand meant accepting the hospitality of Stag's Stand.

At the first three inns they tried, slate-roofed cubes of gray stone with bright signs out front, the innkeepers had not a cubbyhole to offer. Lesser traders and merchants' guards filled them to the attics. Bukama began to mutter about making a bed in a hayloft, yet he never mentioned the feather mattresses and linens waiting on the Stand. Leaving their horses with ostlers at a fourth inn, The Blue Rose, Lan entered determined to find some place for them if it took the rest of the day.

Inside, a graying woman, tall and handsome, presided over a crowded common room where talk and laughter almost drowned out the slender girl singing to the music of her zither. Pipesmoke wreathed the ceiling beams, and the smell of roasting lamb floated from the kitchens. As soon as the innkeeper saw Lan and Bukama, she gave her blue-striped apron a twitch and strode toward them, dark eyes sharp.

Before Lan could open his mouth, she seized Bukama's ears, pulled his head down, and kissed him. Kandori women were seldom retiring, but even so it was a remarkably thorough kiss in front of so many eyes. Pointing fingers and snickering grins flashed among the tables.

"It's good to see you again, too, Racelle," Bukama murmured with a small smile when she finally released him. "I didn't know you had an inn here. Do you think—?" He lowered his gaze rather than meeting her eyes rudely, and that proved a mistake. Racelle's fist caught his jaw so hard that his hair flailed as he staggered.

"Six years without a word," she snapped. "Six years!" Grabbing his ears again, she gave him another kiss, longer this time. Took it rather than gave. A sharp twist of his ears met every attempt to do anything besides standing bent over and letting her do as she wished. At least she would not put a knife in his heart if she was kissing him. Perhaps not.

"I think Mistress Arovni might find Bukama a room somewhere," a man's familiar voice said dryly behind Lan. "And you, too, I suppose."

Turning, Lan clasped forearms with the only man in the room beside Bukama of a height with him, Ryne Venamar, his oldest friend except for Bukama. The innkeeper still had Bukama occupied as Ryne led Lan to a small table in the corner. Five years older, Ryne was Malkieri too, but his hair fell in two long bell-laced braids, and more silver bells lined the turned-down tops of his boots and ran up the sleeves of his yellow coat. Bukama did not exactly dislike Ryne—not exactly—yet in his present mood, only Nazar Kurenin could have had a worse effect.

While the pair of them were settling themselves on benches, a serving maid in a striped apron brought hot spiced wine. Apparently Ryne had ordered as soon as he saw Lan. Dark-eyed and full-lipped, she stared Lan up and down openly as she set his mug in front of him, then whispered her name, Lira, in his ear, and an invitation, if he was staying the night. All he wanted that night was sleep, so he lowered his gaze, murmuring that she honored him too much. Lira did not let him finish. With a raucous laugh, she bent to bite his ear, hard, then announced that by tomorrow's sun she would have honored him till his knees would not hold him up. More laughter flared at the tables around them.

Ryne forestalled any possibility of righting matters, tossing her a fat coin and giving her a slap on the bottom to send her off. Lira offered him a dimpled smile as she slipped the silver into the neck of her dress, but she left sending smoky glances over her shoulder at Lan that made him sigh. If he tried to say no now, she might well pull a knife over the insult.

"So your luck still holds with women, too." Ryne's laugh had an edge. Perhaps he fancied her himself. "The Light knows, they can't find you handsome; you get uglier every year. Maybe I ought to try some of that coy modesty, let women lead me by the nose."

Lan opened his mouth, then took a drink instead of speaking. He should not have to explain, but Ryne's father had taken him to Arafel the year Lan turned ten. The man wore a single blade on his hip instead of two on his back, yet he was Arafellin to his toenails. He actually started conversations with women who had not spoken to him first. Lan, raised by Bukama and his friends in Shienar, had been surrounded by a small community who held to Malkieri ways.

A number of people around the room were watching their table, sidelong glances over mugs and goblets. A plump copper-skinned woman wearing a much thicker dress than Domani women usually did made no effort to hide her stares as she spoke excitedly to a fellow with curled mustaches and a large pearl in his ear. Probably wondering whether there would be trouble over Lira. Wondering whether a man wearing the *hadori* really would kill at the drop of a pin.

"I didn't expect to find you in Canluum," Lan said, setting the wine mug down. "Guarding a merchant train?" Bukama and the innkeeper were nowhere to be seen.

Ryne shrugged. "Out of Shol Arbela. The luckiest trader in Arafel, they say. Said. Much good it did him. We arrived yesterday, and last night footpads slit his throat two streets over. No return money for me this trip." He flashed a rueful grin and took a deep pull at his wine, perhaps to the memory of the merchant or perhaps to the lost half of his wages. "Burn me if I thought to see you here, either."

"You shouldn't listen to rumors, Ryne. I've not taken a wound worth mentioning since I rode south." Lan decided to twit Bukama if they did get a room, about whether it was already paid for and how. Indignation might take him out of his darkness.

"The Aiel," Ryne snorted. "I never thought *they* could put paid to you." He had never faced Aiel, of course. "I expected you to be wherever Edeyn Arrel is. Chachin, now, I hear."

That name snapped Lan's head back to the man across the table. "Why should I be near the Lady Arrel?" he demanded softly. Softly, but emphasizing her proper title.

"Easy, man," Ryne said. "I didn't mean . . ." Wisely, he abandoned that line. "Burn me, do you mean to say you haven't heard? She's raised the Golden Crane. In your name, of course. Since the year turned, she's been from Fal Moran to Maradon, and coming back now." Ryne shook his head, the bells in his braids chiming faintly. "There must be two or three hundred men right here in Canluum ready to follow her. You, I mean. Some you'd not believe. Old Kurenin wept when he heard her speak. All ready to carve Malkier out of the Blight again."

"What dies in the Blight is gone," Lan said wearily. He felt more than cold inside. Suddenly Seroku's surprise that he intended to ride north took on new meaning, and the young guard's assertion that he stood ready. Even the looks here in the common room seemed different. And Edeyn was part of it. Always she liked standing in the heart of the storm. "I must see to my horse," he told Ryne, scraping his bench back.

Ryne said something about making a round of the taverns that night, but Lan hardly heard. He hurried through the kitchens, hot from iron stoves and stone ovens and open hearths, into the cool of the stableyard, the mingled smells of horse and hay and woodsmoke. A graylark warbled on the edge of the stable roof. Graylarks came even before robins in the spring. Graylarks had been singing in Fal Moran when Edeyn first whispered in his ear.

The horses had already been stabled, bridles and saddles and pack-saddle atop saddle blankets on the stall doors, but the wicker hampers were gone. Plainly Mistress Arovni had sent word to the ostlers that he and Bukama were being given accommodation.

There was only a single groom in the dim stable, a lean, hard-faced woman mucking out. Silently she watched him check Cat Dancer and the other horses as she worked, watched him begin to pace the length of the straw-covered floor. He tried to think, but Edeyn's name kept spinning though his head. Edeyn's face, surrounded by silky black hair that hung below her waist, a beautiful face with large dark eyes that could drink a man's soul even when filled with command.

After a bit the groom mumbled something in his direction, touching her lips and forehead, and hurriedly shoved her half-filled barrow out of the stable, glancing over her shoulder at him. She paused to shut the doors, and did that hurriedly, too, sealing him in shadow broken only by a little light from open hay doors in the loft. Dust motes danced in the pale golden shafts.

Lan grimaced. Was she that afraid of a man wearing the *hadori*? Did she think his pacing a threat? Abruptly he became aware of his hands running over the long hilt of his sword, aware of the tightness in his own face. Pacing? No, he had been in the walking stance called Leopard in High Grass, used when there were enemies on all sides. He needed calm.

Seating himself cross-legged on a bale of straw, he formed the image of a flame in his mind and fed emotion into it, hate, fear, everything, every scrap, until it seemed that he floated in emptiness. After years of practice, achieving *ko'di*, the oneness, needed less than a heartbeat. Thought and even his own body seemed distant, but in this state he was more aware than usual, becoming one with the bale beneath him, the stable, the scabbarded sword folded behind him. He could "feel" the horses, cropping at their mangers, and flies buzzing in the corners. They were all part of him. Especially the sword. This time, though, it was only the emotionless void that he sought.

From his belt pouch he took a heavy gold signet ring worked with a flying crane and turned it over and over in his fingers. The ring of Malkieri kings, worn by men who had held back the Shadow nine hundred years and more. Countless times it had been remade as time wore it down, always the old ring melted to become part of the new. Some particle might still exist in it of the ring worn by the rulers of Rhamdashar, that had lived before Malkier, and Aramaelle that had been before Rhamdashar. That piece of metal represented over three thousand years fighting the Blight. It had been his almost as long as he had lived, but he had never worn it. Even looking at the ring was a labor, usually. One he disciplined himself to every day. Without the emptiness, he did not think he could have done so today. In *ko'di*, thought floated free, and emotion lay beyond the horizon.

In his cradle he had been given four gifts. The ring in his hands and the locket that hung around his neck, the sword on his hip and an oath sworn in his name. The locket was the most precious, the oath the heaviest. "To stand against the Shadow so long as iron is hard and stone abides. To defend the Malkieri while one drop of blood remains. To avenge what cannot be defended." And then he had been anointed with oil and named Dai Shan, consecrated as the next King of Malkier, and sent away from a land that knew it would die. Twenty men began that journey; five survived to reach Shienar.

Nothing remained to be defended now, only a nation to avenge, and he had been trained to that from his first step. With his mother's gift at his throat and his father's sword in his hand, with the ring branded on his heart, he had fought to avenge Malkier from his sixteenth nameday. But never had he led men into the Blight. Bukama had ridden with him, and others, but he would not lead men there. That war was his alone. The dead could not be returned to life, a land any more than a man. Only, now, Edeyn Arrel wanted to try.

Her name echoed in the emptiness within him. A hundred emotions loomed like stark mountains, but he fed them into the flame until all was still. Until his heart beat time with the slow stamping of the stalled horses, and the flies' wings beat rapid counterpoint to his breath. She was his *carneira*, his first lover. A thousand years of tradition shouted that, despite the stillness that enveloped him.

He had been fifteen, Edeyn more than twice that, when she gathered the hair that had still hung to his waist in her hands and whispered her intentions. Women had still called him beautiful then, enjoying his blushes, and for half a year she had enjoyed parading him on her arm and tucking him into her bed. Until Bukama and the other men gave him the *hadori*. The gift of his sword on his tenth nameday had made him a man by custom along the Border, though years early for it, yet among Malkieri, that band of braided leather had been more important. Once that was tied around his head, he alone decided where he went, and when, and why. And the dark song of the Blight had become a howl that drowned every other sound. The oath that had murmured so long in his heart became a dance his feet had to follow.

Almost ten years past now that Edeyn had watched him ride away from Fal Moran, and been gone when he returned, yet he still could recall her face more clearly than that of any woman who had shared his bed since. He was no longer a boy, to think that she loved him just because she had chosen to become his first lover, yet there was an old saying among Malkieri men. *Your* carneira *wears part of your soul as a ribbon in her hair forever.* Custom strong as law made it so.

One of the stable doors creaked open to admit Bukama, coatless, shirt tucked raggedly into his breeches. He looked naked without his sword. As if hesitant, he carefully opened both doors wide before coming all the way in. "What are you going to do?" he said finally. "Racelle told me about . . . about the Golden Crane."

Lan tucked the ring away, letting emptiness drain from him. Edeyn's face suddenly seemed everywhere, just beyond the edge of sight. "Ryne says even Nazar Kurenin is ready to follow," he said lightly. "Wouldn't that be a sight to see?" An army could die trying to defeat the Blight. Armies had died trying. But the memories of Malkier already were dying. A nation was memory as much as land. "That boy at the gates might let his hair grow and ask his father for the *hadori*." People were forgetting, trying to forget. When the last man who bound his hair was gone, the last woman who painted her forehead, would Malkier truly be gone, too? "Why, Ryne might even get rid of those braids." Any trace of mirth dropped from his voice as he added, "But is it worth the cost? Some seem to think so." Bukama snorted, yet there had been a pause. He might be one of those who did.

Striding to the stall that held Sun Lance, the older man began to fiddle with his roan's saddle as though suddenly forgetting why he had moved. "There's always a cost for anything," he said, not looking up. "But there are costs, and costs. The Lady Edeyn . . ." He glanced at

Lan, then turned to face him. "She was always one to demand every right and require the smallest obligation be met. Custom ties strings to you, and whatever you choose, she will use them like a set of reins unless you find a way to avoid it."

Carefully Lan tucked his thumbs behind his sword belt. Bukama had carried him out of Malkier tied to his back. The last of the five. Bukama had the right of a free tongue even when it touched Lan's *carneira*. "How do you suggest I avoid my obligations without shame?" he asked more harshly than he had intended. Taking a deep breath, he went on in a milder tone. "Come; the common room smells much better than this. Ryne suggested a round of the taverns tonight. Unless Mistress Arovni has claims on you. Oh, yes. How much will our rooms cost? Good rooms? Not too dear, I hope."

Bukama joined him on the way to the doors, his face going red. "Not too dear," he said hastily. "You have a pallet in the attic, and I . . . ah . . . I'm in Racelle's rooms. I'd like to make a round, but I think Racelle. . . . I don't think she means to let me. . . . I. . . . Young whelp!" he growled. "There's a lass named Lira in there who's letting it be known you won't be using that pallet tonight, *or* getting much sleep, so don't think you can—!" He cut off as they walked into the sunlight, bright after the dimness inside. The graylark still sang of spring.

Six men were striding across the otherwise empty yard. Six ordinary men with swords at their belts, like any men on any street in the city. Yet Lan knew before their hands moved, before their eyes focused on him and their steps quickened. He had faced too many men who wanted to kill him not to know. And at his side stood Bukama, bound by oaths that would not let him raise a hand even had he been wearing his blade. If they both tried to get back inside the stable, the men would be on them before they could haul the doors shut. Time slowed, flowed like cool honey.

"Inside and bar the doors!" Lan snapped as his hand went to his hilt. "Obey me, armsman!"

Never in his life had he given Bukama a command in that fashion, and the man hesitated a heartbeat, then bowed formally. "My life is yours, Dai Shan," he said in a thick voice. "I obey."

As Lan moved forward to meet his attackers, he heard the bar drop inside with a muffled thud. Relief was distant. He floated in *ko'di*, one with the sword that came smoothly out of its scabbard. One with the men rushing at him, boots thudding on the hard-packed ground as they bared steel.

A lean heron of a fellow darted ahead of the others, and Lan danced the forms. Time like cool honey. The graylark sang, and the lean man shrieked as Cutting the Clouds removed his right hand at the wrist, and Lan flowed to one side so the rest could not all come at him together, flowed from form to form. Soft Rain at Sunset laid open a fat man's face and took his left eye, and a ginger-haired young splinter drew a gash across Lan's ribs with Black Pebbles on Snow. Only in stories did one man face six without injury. The Rose Unfolds sliced down a bald man's left arm, and ginger-hair nicked the corner of Lan's eye. Only in stories did one man face six and survive. He had known that from the start. Duty was a mountain, death a feather, and his duty was to Bukama, who had carried an infant on his back. For this moment he lived, though, so he fought, kicking ginger-hair in the head, dancing his way toward death, danced and took wounds, bled and danced the razor's edge of life. Time like cool honey, flowing from form to form, and there could only be one ending. Thought was distant. Death was a feather. Dandelion in the Wind slashed open the now one-eyed fat man's throat—he had barely paused when his face was ruined—and a fork-bearded fellow with shoulders like a blacksmith gasped in surprise as Kissing the Adder put Lan's steel through his heart.

And suddenly Lan realized that he alone stood, with six men sprawled across the width of the stableyard. The ginger-haired youth thrashed his heels on the ground one last time, and then only Lan of the seven still breathed. He shook blood from his blade, bent to wipe the last drops off on the blacksmith's too-fine coat, sheathed his sword as formally as if he were in the training yard under Bukama's eye.

Abruptly people flooded out of the inn, cooks and stablemen, maids and patrons shouting to know what all the noise was about, staring at the dead men in astonishment. Ryne was the very first, sword already in hand, his face blank as he came to stand by Lan. "Six," he muttered, studying the bodies. "You really do have the Dark One's own flaming luck."

Dark-eyed Lira reached Lan only moments before Bukama, the pair of them gently parting slashes in his clothes to examine his injuries.

She shivered delicately as each was revealed, but she discussed whether an Aes Sedai should be sent for to give Healing and how much stitching was needed in as calm a tone as Bukama, and disparagingly dismissed his hand on the needle in favor of her own. Mistress Arovni stalked about, holding her skirts up out of patches of bloody mud, glaring at the corpses littering her stableyard, complaining in a loud voice that gangs of footpads would never be wandering in daylight if the Watch was doing its job. The Domani woman who had stared at Lan inside agreed just as loudly, and for her pains received a sharp command from the innkeeper to fetch them, along with a shove to start her on her way. It was a measure of Mistress Arovni's shock that she treated one of her patrons so, a measure of everyone's shock that the Domani woman went running without complaint. The innkeeper began organizing men to drag the bodies out of sight, still going on about footpads.

Ryne looked from Bukama to the stable as though he did not understand—perhaps he did not, at that—but what he said was, "Not footpads, I think." He pointed to the fellow who looked like a blacksmith. "That one listened to Edeyn Arrel when she was here, and he liked what he heard. One of the others did, too, I think." Bells chimed as he shook his head. "It's peculiar. The first she said of raising the Golden Crane was after we heard you were dead outside the Shining Walls. Your name brings men, but with you dead, she could be el'Edeyn." He spread his hands at the looks Lan and Bukama shot him. "I make no accusations," he said hastily. "I'd never accuse the Lady Edeyn of any such thing. I'm sure she is full of all a woman's tender mercy." Mistress Arovni gave a grunt like a fist, and Lira murmured half under her breath that the pretty Arafellin did not know much about women.

Lan shook his head. Edeyn might decide to have him killed if it suited her purposes, she might have left orders here and there in case the rumors about him proved false, but if she had, that was still no reason to speak her name in connection with this, especially in front of strangers.

Bukama's hands stilled, holding open a slash down Lan's sleeve. "Where do we go from here?" he asked quietly.

"Chachin," Lan said after a moment. There was always a choice, but sometimes every choice was grim. "You'll have to leave Sun Lance.

I mean to depart at first light tomorrow." His gold would stretch to a new mount for the man.

"Six!" Ryne growled, sheathing his sword with considerable force. "I think I'll ride with you. I'd as soon not go back to Shol Arbela until I'm sure Ceiline Noreman doesn't lay her husband's death at my boots. And it will be good to see the Golden Crane flying again."

Lan nodded. To put his hand on the banner and abandon what he had promised himself all those years ago, or to stop her, if he could. Either way, he had to face Edeyn. The Blight would have been much easier.

Chasing after prophecy, Moiraine had decided by the end of the first month, involved very little adventure and a great deal of saddlesoreness and frustration. The Three Oaths still made her skin feel too tight. The wind rattled the shutters, and she shifted on the hard wooden chair, hiding impatience behind a sip of honeyless tea. In Kandor, comforts were kept to a minimum in a house of mourning. She would not have been overly surprised to see frost on the leaf-carved furniture or the metal clock above the cold hearth.

"It was all so strange, my Lady," Mistress Najima sighed, and for the tenth time hugged her daughters. Perhaps thirteen or fourteen, standing close to their mother's chair, Colar and Eselle had her long black hair and large blue eyes still full of loss. Their mother's eyes seemed big, too, in a face shrunken by tragedy, and her plain gray dress appeared made for a larger woman. "Josef was always careful with lanterns in the stable," she went on, "and he never allowed any kind of open flame. The boys must have carried little Jerid out to see their father at his work, and . . ." Another hollow sigh. "They were all trapped. How could the whole stable be ablaze so fast? It makes no sense."

"Little is ever senseless," Moiraine said soothingly, setting her cup on the small table at her elbow. She felt sympathy, but the woman had begun repeating herself. "We cannot always see the reason, yet we can take some comfort in knowing there is one. The Wheel of Time weaves us into the Pattern as it wills, but the Pattern is the work of the Light."

Hearing herself, she suppressed a wince. Those words required dignity and weight her youth failed to supply. If only time could pass faster. At least for the next five years or so. Five years should give her

her full strength and provide all the dignity and weight she would ever need. But then, the agelessness that came after working long enough with the One Power would only have made her present task more difficult. The last thing she could afford was anyone connecting an Aes Sedai to her visits.

"As you say, my Lady," the other woman murmured politely, though an unguarded shift of pale eyes spoke her thoughts. This outlander was a foolish child. The small blue stone of a kesiera dangling from a fine golden chain onto Moiraine's forehead and a dark green dress with six slashes of color across the breast, far fewer than she was entitled to, made Mistress Najima think her merely a Cairhienin noblewoman, one of many wandering since the Aiel ruined Cairhien. A noblewoman of a minor House, named Alys not Moiraine, making sympathy calls in mourning for her own king, killed by the Aiel. The fiction was easy to maintain, though she did not mourn her uncle in the least.

Perhaps sensing that her thoughts had been too clear, Mistress Najima started up again, speaking quickly. "It's just that Josef was always so lucky, my Lady. Everyone spoke of it. They said if Josef Najima fell down a hole, there'd be opals at the bottom. When he answered the Lady Kareil's call to go fight the Aiel, I worried, but he never took a scratch. When camp fever struck, it never touched us or the children. Josef gained the Lady's favor without trying. Then it seemed the Light truly did shine on us. Jerid was born safe and whole, and the war ended, all in a matter of days, and when we came home to Canluum, the Lady gave us the livery stable for Josef's service, and . . . and . . ." She swallowed tears she would not shed. Colar began to weep, and her mother pulled her closer, whispering comfort.

Moiraine rose. More repetition. There was nothing here for her. Jurine stood, too, not a tall woman, yet almost a hand taller than she. Either of the girls could look her in the eyes. She had grown accustomed to that since leaving Cairhien. Forcing herself to take time, she murmured more condolences and tried to press a washleather purse on the woman as the girls brought her fur-lined cloak and gloves. A small purse. Obtaining coin meant visits to the bankers and a clear trail. Not that the Aiel had left her estates in a condition to provide much money for some years yet. And not that anyone was likely to be looking for her. Still, discovery might be decidedly unpleasant.

The woman's stiff-necked refusal to take the purse irritated Moiraine. No, that was not the real reason. She understood pride, and besides, Lady Kareil had provided. The real irritant was her own desire to be gone. Jurine Najima had lost her husband and three sons in one fiery morning, but her Jerid had been born in the wrong place by almost twenty miles. The search continued. Moiraine did not like feeling relief in connection with the death of an infant. Yet she did.

Outside under a gray sky, she gathered her cloak tightly. Ignoring the cold was a simple trick, but anyone who went about the streets of Canluum with open cloak would draw stares. Any outlander, at least, unless clearly Aes Sedai. Besides, not allowing the cold to touch you did not make you unaware of it. How these people could call this "new spring" without a hint of mockery was beyond her.

Despite the near-freezing wind that gusted over the rooftops, the winding streets were packed, requiring her to pick her way through a milling mass of people and carts and wagons. The world had certainly come to Canluum. A Taraboner with heavy mustaches pushed past her muttering a hasty apology, and an olive-skinned Altaran woman who scowled at Moiraine, then an Illianer with a beard that left his upper lip bare, a very pretty fellow and not too tall.

Another day she might have enjoyed the sight of him, in another city. Now, he barely registered. It was women she watched, especially those well dressed, in silks or fine woolens. If only so many were not veiled. Twice she saw Aes Sedai strolling through the crowds, neither a woman she had ever met. Neither glanced in her direction, but she kept her head down and stayed to the other side of the street. Perhaps she should put on a veil. A stout woman brushed by, features blurred behind lace. Sierin Vayu herself could have passed unrecognized at ten feet in one of those.

Moiraine shivered at the thought, ridiculous at it was. If the new Amrylin learned what she was up to. . . . Inserting herself into secret plans, unbidden and unannounced, would not go unpunished. No matter that the Amrylin who had made them was dead in her sleep and another woman sat on the Amrylin Seat. Being sequestered on a farm until the search was done was the least she could expect.

It was not just. She and her friend Siuan had helped gather the names, in the guise of offering assistance to any woman who had given birth during the days when the Aiel threatened Tar Valon itself. Of all the women involved in that gathering, just they two knew the real reason. They had winnowed those names for Tamra. Only children born outside the city's walls had really been important, though the promised aid went to every woman found, of course. Only boys born on the west bank of the River Erinin, boys who might have been born on the slopes of Dragonmount.

Behind her a woman shouted shrilly, angrily, and Moiraine jumped a foot before she realized it was a wagon driver, brandishing her whip at a hawker to hustle his pushcart of steaming meat pies out of her way. Light! A farm was the *least* she could expect! A few men around Moiraine laughed raucously at her leap, and one, a dark-faced Tairen in a striped cloak, made a rude joke about the cold wind curling under her skirts. The laughter grew.

Moiraine stalked ahead stiffly, cheeks crimson, hand tight on the silver hilt of her belt knife. Unthinking, she embraced the True Source, and the One Power flooded her with joyous life. A single glance over her shoulder was all she needed; with *saidar* in her, smells became sharper, colors truer. She could have counted the threads in the cloak the Tairen was letting flap while he laughed. She channeled fine flows of the Power, of Air, and the fellow's baggy breeches dropped to his turned-down boots, the laces undone. Bellowing, he snatched his cloak around him amid gales of renewed mirth. Let him see how *he* liked cold breezes and rowdy jokes!

Satisfaction lasted as long as it took to release the Source. Impetuous impulse and a quick temper had always been her downfall. Any woman able to channel would have seen her weaving if close enough, seen the glow of *saidar* surround her. Even those thin flows could have been felt at thirty paces by the weakest sister in the Tower. A fine way to hide.

Quickening her step, she put distance between herself and the incident. Too little too late, but all she could do now. She stroked the small book in her belt pouch, tried to focus on her task. With only one hand, keeping her cloak closed proved impossible. It whipped about in the wind, and after a moment, she let herself feel the knifing chill. Sisters who took on penances at every turn were foolish, yet a penance could serve many purposes, and maybe she needed a reminder. If she could not remember to be careful, she might as well return to the White Tower now and ask where to start hoeing turnips.

Mentally she drew a line through the name of Jurine Najima. Other names in the book already had real lines inked through them. The mothers of five boys born in the wrong place. The mothers of three girls. An army of almost two hundred thousand men had gathered to face the Aiel outside the Shining Walls, and it still astonished her how many women followed along, how many were with child. An older sister had had to explain. The war had not been short, and men who knew they might die tomorrow wanted to leave part of themselves behind. Women who knew their men might die tomorrow wanted that part of them to keep.

Hundreds had given birth during the key ten days, and in that sort of gathering, with soldiers from nearly every land, too often there was only rumor as to exactly where or when a child had been born. Or to where the parents had gone, with the war ended and the Coalition army melting away along with the Coalition. There were too many entries like "Saera Deosin. Husband Eadwin. From Murandy. A son?" A whole country to search, only a pair of names to go by, and no certainty the woman had borne a boy. Too many like "Kari al'Thor. From Andor? Husband Tamlin, Second Captain of the Illianer Companions, took discharge." That pair might have gone anywhere in the world, and there was doubt she had had a child at all. Sometimes only the mother was listed, with six or eight variations on the name of a home village that might lie in one of two or three countries. The list of those easy to find was growing shorter rapidly.

But the child had to be found. An infant who would grow to manhood and wield the tainted male half of the One Power. Moiraine shuddered at the thought despite herself. That was why this search was so secret, why Moiraine and Siuan, still only Accepted when they learned of the child's birth by accident, had been shunted aside and kept in as much ignorance as Tamra could manage. This was a matter for experienced sisters. But who could she trust with the news that the birth of the Dragon Reborn had been Foretold, and more, that somewhere he already suckled at his mother's breast? Had she had the sort of nightmares that had wakened Moiraine and Siuan so many nights? Yet this boychild would grow to manhood and save the world, so the Prophecies of the Dragon said. If he was not found by a Red sister; the Red Ajah's main purpose was hunting down men who could channel, and Moiraine was sure Tamra had not trusted any of them, even with a child. Could a Red be trusted to remember that he would be humankind's salvation while remembering what else he would be? The day suddenly seemed colder to Moiraine, for remembering.

The inn where she had a small room was called The Gates of Heaven, four sprawling stories of green-roofed stone, Canluum's best and largest. Nearby shops catered to the lord and ladies on the Stand, looming behind the inn. She would not have stopped in it had there been another room to be found in the city. Taking a deep breath, she hurried inside. Neither the sudden warmth from fires on four large hearths nor the good smells of cooking from the kitchens eased her tight shoulders.

The common room was large, and every table beneath the bright red ceiling beams was taken. By plainly dressed merchants for the most part, and a sprinkling of well-to-do craftsfolk with rich embroidery covering colorful shirts or dresses. She hardly noticed them. No fewer than five sisters were staying at The Gates of Heaven, and all sat in the common room when she walked in. Master Helvin, the innkeeper, would always make room for an Aes Sedai even when he had to force other patrons to double up. The sisters kept to themselves, barely acknowledging one another, and people who might not have recognized an Aes Sedai on sight knew them now, knew enough not to intrude. Every other table was jammed, yet where any man sat with an Aes Sedai, it was her Warder, a hard-eyed man with a dangerous look about him however ordinary he might seem otherwise. One of the sisters sitting alone was a Red; Reds took no Warder.

Tucking her gloves behind her belt and folding her cloak over her arm, Moiraine started toward the stone stairs at the back of the room. Not too quickly, but not dawdling, either. Looking straight ahead. She did not need to see an ageless face or glimpse the golden serpent biting its own tail encircling a finger to know when she passed close to another sister. Each time, she felt the other woman's ability to channel, felt her strength. No one here matched her. She could sense their ability, and they could sense hers. Their eyes following her seemed the touch of fingers. Not quite grasping. None spoke to her.

Then, just as she reached the staircase, a woman did speak behind her. "Well, now. This is a surprise."

Turning quickly, Moiraine kept her face smooth with an effort as she made a brief curtsy suitable for a minor noblewoman to an Aes

Sedai. To two Aes Sedai. She did not think she could have encountered two worse than this pair in sober silks.

The white wings in Larelle Tarsi's long hair emphasized her serene, copper-skinned elegance. She had taught Moiraine in several classes, as both novice and Accepted, and she had a way of asking the last question you wanted to hear. Worse was Merean Redhill, plump and so motherly that hair more gray than not, and gathered at the nape of her neck, almost submerged the agelessness of her features. She had been Mistress of Novices under Tamra, and she made Larelle seem blind when it came to discovering just what you most wanted to hide. Both wore their vine-embroidered shawls, Merean's fringed blue. Blue was Moiraine's Ajah, too. That might count for something. Or not. It was a surprise to see them together; she had not thought they particularly liked one another.

Both were stronger in the Power than she, unfortunately, though she would stand above them eventually, but the gap was only wide enough that she had to defer, not obey. In any case, they had no right to interfere in anything she might be doing. Custom held very strongly on that. Unless they were part of Tamra's search and had been told about her. An Amyrlin's commands superseded the strongest custom, or at least altered it. But if either said the wrong thing here, word that Moiraine Damodred was wandering about in disguise would spread with the sisters in the room, and it would reach the wrong ears as surely as peaches were poison. That was the way of the world. A summons back to Tar Valon would find her soon after. She opened her mouth hoping to forestall the chance, but someone else spoke first.

"No need trying that one," a sister alone at a table nearby said, twisting around on her bench. Felaana Bevaine, a slim yellow-haired Brown with a raspy voice, had been the first to corner Moiraine when she arrived. "Says she has no interest in going to the Tower. Stubborn as stone about it. Secretive, too. You would think we'd have heard about a wilder popping up in even a lesser Cairhienin House, but this child likes to keep to herself."

Larelle and Merean looked at Moiraine, Larelle arching a thin eyebrow, Merean apparently trying to suppress a smile. Most sisters disliked wilders, women who managed to survive teaching themselves to channel without going to the White Tower.

"It is quite true, Aes Sedai," Moiraine said carefully, relieved that someone else had laid a foundation. "I have no desire to enroll as a novice, and I will not."

Felaana fixed her with considering eyes, but she still spoke to the others. "Says she's twenty-two, but that rule has been bent a time or two. A woman says she's eighteen, and that's how she's enrolled. Unless it's too obvious a lie, anyway, and this girl—"

"Our rules were not made to be broken," Larelle said sharply, and Merean added in a wry voice, "I don't believe this young woman will lie about her age. She doesn't want to be a novice, Felaana. Let her go her way." Moiraine almost let out a relieved sigh.

Enough weaker than they to accept being cut off, Felaana still began to rise, plainly meaning to continue the argument. Halfway to her feet she glanced up the stairs behind Moiraine, her eyes widened, and abruptly she sat down again, focusing on her plate of black peas and onions as if nothing else in the world existed. Merean and Larelle gathered their shawls, gray fringe and blue swaying. They looked eager to be elsewhere. They looked as though their feet had been nailed to the floor.

"So this girl does not want to be a novice," said a woman's voice from the stairs. A voice Moiraine had heard only once, two years ago, and would never forget. A number of women were stronger than she, but only one could be as much stronger as this one. Unwillingly, she looked over her shoulder.

Nearly black eyes studied her from beneath a bun of iron-gray hair decorated with golden ornaments, stars and birds, crescent moons and fish. Cadsuane, too, wore her shawl, fringed in green. "In my opinion, girl," she said dryly, "you could profit from ten years in white."

Everyone had believed Cadsuane Melaidhrin dead somewhere in retirement until she reappeared at the start of the Aiel War, and a good many sisters probably wished her truly in her grave. Cadsuane was a legend, a most uncomfortable thing to have alive and staring at you. Half the tales about her came close to impossibility, while the rest were beyond it, even among those that had proof. A long-ago King of Tarabon winkled out of his palace when it was learned he could channel, carried to Tar Valon to be gentled while an army that did not believe chased after to attempt rescue. A King of Arad Doman and a Queen of Saldaea *both* kidnapped, spirited away in secrecy, and when Cadsuane finally released them, a war that had seemed certain simply faded away. It was said she bent Tower law where it suited her, flouted custom, went her own way and often dragged others with her.

"I thank the Aes Sedai for her concern," Moiraine began, then trailed off under that stare. Not a hard stare. Simply implacable. Supposedly even Amyrlins had stepped warily around Cadsuane over the years. It was whispered that she had actually *assaulted* an Amyrlin, once. Impossible, of course; she would have been executed! Moiraine swallowed and tried to start over, only to find she wanted to swallow again.

Descending the stair, Cadsuane told Merean and Larelle, "Bring the girl." Without a second glance, she glided across the common room. Merchants and craftsfolk looked at her, some openly, some from the corner of an eye, and Warders too, but every sister kept her gaze on her table.

Merean's face tightened, and Larelle sighed extravagantly, yet they prodded Moiraine after the bobbing golden ornaments. She had no choice but to go. At least Cadsuane could not be one of the women Tamra had called in; she had not returned to Tar Valon since that visit at the beginning of the war.

Cadsuane led them to one of the inn's private sitting rooms, where a fire blazed on the black stone hearth and silver lamps hung along the red wall panels. A tall pitcher stood near the fire to keep warm, and a lacquered tray on a small carved table held silver cups. Merean and Larelle took two of the brightly cushioned chairs, but when Moiraine put her cloak on a chair and started to sit, Cadsuane pointed to a spot in front of the other sisters. "Stand there, child," she said.

Making an effort not to clutch her skirt in fists, Moiraine stood as directed. Obedience had always been difficult for her. Until she went to the Tower at sixteen, there had been few people she had to obey. Most obeyed her.

Cadsuane circled the three of them slowly, once, twice. Merean and Larelle exchanged wondering frowns, and Larelle opened her mouth, but after one look at Cadsuane, closed it again. They assumed smooth-faced serenity; any watcher would have thought they knew exactly what was going on. Sometimes Cadsuane glanced at them, but the greater part of her attention stayed on Moiraine.

"Most new sisters," the legendary Green said abruptly, "hardly remove their shawls to sleep or bathe, but here you are without shawl or ring, in one of the most dangerous spots you could choose short of the Blight itself. Why?"

Moiraine blinked. A direct question. The woman really did ignore custom when it suited her. She made her voice light. "New sisters also seek a Warder." Why was the woman singling her out in this manner? "I have not bonded mine, yet. I am told Bordermen make fine Warders." The Green sent her a stabbing look that made her wish she had been just a little less light.

Stopping behind Larelle, Cadsuane laid a hand on her shoulder. "What do you know of this child?"

Every girl in Larelle's classes had thought her the perfect sister and been intimidated by that cool consideration. They all had been afraid of her, and wanted to be her. "Moiraine was studious and a quick learner," she said thoughtfully. "She and Siuan Sanche were two of the quickest the Tower has ever seen. But you must know that. Let me see. She was rather too free with her opinions, and her temper, until we settled her down. As much as we did settle her. She and the Sanche girl had a continuing fondness for pranks. But they both passed for Accepted on the first try, and for the shawl. She needs seasoning, of course, yet she may make something of herself."

Cadsuane moved behind Merean, asking the same question, adding, "A fondness for . . . pranks, Larelle said. A troublesome child?"

Merean shook her head with a smile. None of the girls had wanted to be Merean, but everyone knew where to go for a shoulder to cry on or advice when you could not ask your closest friend. Many more girls visited her on their own than had been sent for chastisement. "Not troublesome, really," she said. "High-spirited. None of the tricks Moiraine played were mean, but they were plentiful. Novice and Accepted, she was sent to my study more often than any three other girls. Except for her pillow-friend Siuan. Of course, pillow-friends frequently get into tangles together, but with those two, one was never sent to me without the other. The last time the very night after passing for the shawl." Her smile faded into a frown very much like the one she had worn that night. Not angry, but rather disbelieving of the mischief young women could get up to. And a touch amused by it. "Instead of spending the night in contemplation, they tried to sneak mice into a sister's bed—Elaida a'Roihan—and were caught. I doubt any other women have been raised Aes Sedai while still too tender to sit from their last visit to the Mistress of Novices. Once the Three Oaths tightened on them, they needed cushions a week."

Moiraine kept her face smooth, kept her hands from knotting into fists, but she could do nothing about burning cheeks. That ruefully amused frown, as if she were still Accepted. She needed seasoning, did she? Well, perhaps she did, some, but still. And spreading out all these intimacies!

"I think you know all of me that you need to know," she told Cadsuane stiffly. How close she and Siuan had been was no one's business but theirs. And their punishments, *details* of their punishments. Elaida had been hateful, always pressing, demanding perfection whenever she visited the Tower. "If you are quite satisfied, I must pack my things. I am departing for Chachin."

She swallowed a groan before it could form. She still let her tongue go too free when her temper was up. If Merean or Larelle was part of the search, they must have at least part of the list in her little book. Including Jurine Najima here, the Lady Ines Demain in Chachin, and Avene Sahera, who lived in "a village on the high road between Chachin and Canluum." To strengthen suspicion, all she need do now was say she intended to spend time in Arafel and Shienar next.

Cadsuane smiled, not at all pleasantly. "You'll leave when I say, child. Be silent till you're spoken to. That pitcher should hold spiced wine. Pour for us."

Moiraine quivered. Child! She was no longer a novice. The woman could not order her coming and going. Or her tongue. But she did not protest. She walked to the hearth—stalked, really—and picked up the long-necked silver pitcher.

"You seem very interested in this young woman, Cadsuane," Merean said, turning slightly to watch Moiraine pour. "Is there something about her we should know?"

Larelle's smile held a touch of mockery. Only a touch, with Cadsuane. "Has someone Foretold she'll be Amyrlin one day? I can't say that I see it in her, but then, I don't have the Foretelling."

"I might live another thirty years," Cadsuane said, putting out a hand for the cup Moiraine offered, "or only three. Who can say?"

Moiraine's eyes went wide, and she slopped hot wine over her own wrist. Merean gasped, and Larelle looked as though she had been struck in the forehead with a stone. Any Aes Sedai would spit on the table before referring to another sister's age or her own. Except that Cadsuane was not any Aes Sedai.

"A little more care with the other cups," she said, unperturbed by all the gaping. "Child?" Moiraine returned to the hearth still staring, and Cadsuane went on, "Meilyn is considerably older. When she and I are gone, that leaves Kerene the strongest." Larelle flinched. "Am I disturbing you?" Cadsuane's solicitous tone could not have been more false, and she did not wait for an answer. "Holding our silence about age doesn't keep people from knowing we live longer than they. Phaaw! From Kerene, it's a sharp drop to the next five. Five once this child and the Sanche girl reach their potential. And one of those is as old as I am and in retirement to boot."

"Is there some point to this?" Merean asked, sounding a little sick. Larelle pressed her hands against her middle, her face gray. They barely glanced at the wine Moiraine offered before gesturing it away, and she kept the cup, though she did not think she could swallow a mouthful.

Cadsuane scowled, a fearsome sight. "No one has come to the Tower in a thousand years who could match me. No one to match Meilyn or Kerene in almost six hundred. A thousand years ago, there would have been fifty sisters or more who stood higher than this child. In another hundred years, though, she'll stand in the first rank. Oh, someone stronger may be found in that time, but there won't be fifty, and there may be none. We dwindle."

"I don't understand," Larelle said sharply. She seemed to have gathered herself, and to be angry for her previous weakness. "We are all aware of the problem, but what does Moiraine have to do with it? Do you think she can somehow make more girls come to the Tower, girls with stronger potential?" Her snort said what she thought of that.

"I would regret her being wasted before she knows up from down. The Tower can't afford to lose her out of her own ignorance. Look at her. A pretty little doll of a Cairhienin noble." Cadsuane put a finger under Moiraine's chin, tilting it up. "Before you find a Warder like that, child, a brigand who wants to see what's in your purse will put an arrow through your heart. A footpad who'd faint at the sight of a sister in her sleep will crack your head, and you'll wake at the back of an alley minus your gold and maybe more. I suspect you'll want to take as much care choosing your first man as you do your first Warder."

Moiraine jerked back, spluttered with indignation. First her and Siuan, now this. There were things one talked about, and things one did not!

Cadsuane ignored her outrage. Calmly sipping her wine, she turned back to the others. "Until she does find a Warder to guard her back, it might be best to protect her from her own enthusiasm. You two are going to Chachin, I believe. She'll travel with you, then. I expect you not to let her out of your sight."

Moiraine found her tongue, but her protests did as much good as her indignation had. Merean and Larelle objected, too, just as vociferously. Aes Sedai did not need "looking after," no matter how new. They had interests of their own to look after. They did not make clear what those were—few sisters would have—but they plainly wanted no company. Cadsuane paid no attention to anything she did not want to hear, assumed they would do as she wished, pressed wherever they offered an opening. Soon the pair were twisting on their chairs and reduced to saying that they had only encountered each other the day before and were not sure they would be traveling on together. In any event, both meant to spend two or three days in Canluum, while Moiraine wanted to leave today.

"The child will stay until you leave," Cadsuane said briskly. "Good; that's done, then. I'm sure you two want to see to whatever brought you to Canluum. I won't keep you."

Larelle shifted her shawl irritably at the abrupt dismissal, then stalked out muttering that Moiraine would regret it if she got underfoot or slowed her reaching Chachin. Merean took it better, even saying she would look after Moiraine like a daughter, though her smile hardly looked pleased.

When they were gone, Moiraine stared at Cadsuane incredulously. She had never seen anything like it. Except an avalanche, once. The thing to do now was keep silent until she had a chance to leave without Cadsuane or the others seeing. Much the wisest thing. "I agreed to nothing," she said coolly. Very coolly. "What if I have affairs in Chachin that will not wait? What if I do not choose to wait here two or three days?" Perhaps she did need to learn to school her tongue a little more.

Cadsuane had been looking thoughtfully at the door that had closed behind Merean and Larelle, but she turned a piercing gaze on Moiraine. "You've worn the shawl five months, and you have affairs that cannot wait? Phaaw! You still haven't learned the first real lesson, that the shawl means you are ready to truly begin learning. The second lesson is caution. I know very well how hard that is to find when you're young and have *saidar* at your fingertips and the world at your feet. As you think." Moiraine tried to fit a word in, but she might as well have stood in front of that avalanche. "You will take great risks in your life, if you live long enough. You already take more than you know. Heed carefully what I say. And do as I say. I will check your bed tonight, and if you are not in it, I will find you and make you weep as you did for those mice. You can dry your tears afterward on that shawl you believe makes you invincible. It does not."

Staring as the door closed behind Cadsuane, Moiraine suddenly realized she still held the cup of wine and gulped it dry. The woman was . . . formidable. Custom forbade physical violence against another sister, but Cadsuane had not sidestepped a hair in her threat. She had said it right out, so by the Three Oaths she meant it exactly. Incredible. Was it happpenstance that she had mentioned Meilyn Arganya and Kerene Nagashi? They were two of Tamra's searchers. *Could* Cadsuane be another? Either way, she had very neatly cut Moiraine out of the hunt for the next week or more. If she actually went with Merean and Larelle, at least. But why only a week? If the woman was part of the search. . . . If Cadsuane knew about her and Siuan. . . . If. . . . Standing there fiddling with an empty winecup was getting her nowhere. She snatched up her cloak.

A number of people looked around at her when she came out into the common room, some with sympathy in their eyes. Doubtless they were imagining what it must be like to be the focus of attention for three Aes Sedai, and they could not imagine any good in it. There was no commiseration on any sister's face. Felaana wore a pleased smile; she probably thought the Lady Alys' name as good as written in the novice book. Cadsuane was nowhere in sight, nor the other two.

Picking her way through the tables, Moiraine felt shaken. There were too many questions, and not an answer to be found. She wished Siuan were there; Siuan was very good at puzzles, and nothing shook her.

A young woman looked in at the door from the street, then jerked out of sight, and Moiraine missed a step. Wish for something hard enough, and you could think you saw it. The woman peeked in again, the hood of her cloak fallen atop the bundle on her back, and it really was Siuan, sturdy and handsome, in a plain blue dress that showed signs of hard travel. This time she saw Moiraine, but instead of rushing to greet her, Siuan nodded up the street and vanished again.

Heart climbing into her throat, Moiraine swept her cloak around her and went out. Down the street, Siuan was slipping through the traffic, glancing back at every third step. Moiraine followed quickly, worry growing.

Siuan was supposed to be six hundred miles away in Tar Valon, working for Cetalia Delarme, who ran the Blue Ajah's network of eyes-and-ears. She had let that secret slip while bemoaning her fate. The whole time they were novice and Accepted together Siuan had talked of getting out into the world, seeing the world, but Cetalia had taken her aside the day they received the shawl, and by that evening Siuan was sorting reports from men and women scattered through the nations. She had a mind that saw patterns others missed. Cetalia equaled Merean in the Power, and it would be another three or four years before Siuan gained enough strength to tell Cetalia she was leaving the job. There would be snow at Sunday before Cetalia let her go short of that. And the only other possibility for her being in Canluum. . . . Moiraine groaned, and when a big-eared fellow selling pins from a tray gave her a concerned look, she glared so hard that he started back.

It would be just like Sierin to send Siuan to bring her back, so their worry could feed on each other during the long ride. Sierin was a hard woman, without an ounce of mercy. An Amyrlin was supposed to grant indulgences and relief from penances on the day she was raised; Sierin had ordered two sisters birched and exiled three from the Tower for a year. She might well have told Siuan the penance she intended to impose. Moiraine shivered. Likely, Sierin would manage to combine Labor, Deprivation, Mortification of the Flesh, *and* Mortification of the Spirit.

A hundred paces from the inn, Siuan looked back once more, paused till she was sure that Moiraine saw her, then darted into an alley. Moiraine quickened her stride and followed.

Her friend was pacing beneath the still-unlit oil lamps that lined even this narrow, dusty passage. Nothing frightened Siuan Sanche, a fisherman's daughter from the toughest quarter in Tear, but fear glittered in those sharp blue eyes now. Moiraine opened her mouth to confirm her own fears about Sierin, but the taller woman spoke first.

"Tell me you've found him, Moiraine. Tell me the Najima boy's the one, and we can hand him to the Tower with a hundred sisters watching, and it's done."

A hundred sisters? "No, Siuan." This did not sound like Sierin. "What is the matter?"

Siuan began to weep. Siuan, who had a lion's heart and had never let a tear fall until after they left Merean's study. Throwing her arms around Moiraine, she squeezed hard. She was trembling. "They're all dead," she mumbled. "Aisha and Kerene, Valera and Ludice and Meilyn. They say Aisha and her Warder were killed by bandits in Murandy. Kerene supposedly fell off a ship in the Alguenya during a storm and drowned. And Meilyn . . . Meilyn . . ."

Moiraine hugged her, making soothing sounds. And staring past Siuan's shoulder in consternation. They had learned five of the women Tamra had selected, and all five were dead. "Meilyn was . . . hardly young," she said slowly. She was not sure she could have said it at all if Cadsuane had not spoken so openly. Siuan gave a startled jerk, and she made herself go on. "Neither were any of the others, even Kerene." Close to two hundred was not young even for Aes Sedai. "And accidents do happen. Bandits. Storms." She was having a hard time making herself believe. *All* of them?

Siuan pushed herself away. "You don't understand. Meilyn!" Grimacing, she scrubbed at her eyes. "Fish guts! I'm not making this clear. Get hold of yourself, you bloody fool!" That last was growled to herself. Merean and others had gone to a great deal of trouble to clean up Siuan's language, but she had reverted the moment the shawl was on her shoulders. Guiding Moiraine to an upended cask with no bung, she sat her down. "You won't want to be standing when you hear what I have to say. For that matter, I bloody well don't want to be standing myself."

Dragging a crate with broken slats from further up the alley, she settled on it, fussing with her skirts, peering toward the street, muttering about people looking in as they passed. Her reluctance did little to soothe Moiraine's stomach. It seemed to do little for Siuan's, either. When she started up again, she kept pausing to swallow, like a woman who wanted to sick up.

"Meilyn returned to the Tower almost a month ago. I don't know why. She didn't say where she had been, or where she was going, but she only meant to stay a few nights. I . . . I'd heard about Kerene the morning Meilyn came, and the others before that. So I decided to speak to her. Don't look at me that way! I know how to be cautious!" "Cautious" was a word Moiraine had never thought to apply to Siuan. "Anyway, I sneaked into her rooms and hid under the bed. So the servants wouldn't see me when they turned down her sheets." Siuan grunted sourly. "I fell asleep under there. Sunrise woke me, and her bed hadn't been slept in. So I sneaked out and went down to the second sitting of breakfast. And while I was spooning my porridge, Chesmal Emry came in to . . . She . . . She announced that Meilyn had been found in her bed, that she'd died during the night." She finished in a rush and sagged, staring at Moiraine.

Moiraine was very glad to be sitting. Her knees would not have supported a feather. She had grown up amid *Daes Dae'mar*, the scheming and plotting that dominated Cairhienin life, the shades of meaning in every word, every action. There was too much here for shadings. Murder had been done. "The Red Ajah?" she suggested finally. A Red might kill a sister she thought intended to protect a man who could channel.

Siuan snorted. "Meilyn didn't have a mark on her, and Chesmal would have detected poison, or smothering, or . . . That means the Power, Moiraine. Could even a Red do that?" Her voice was fierce, but she pulled the bundle around from her back, clutching it on her lap. She seemed to be hiding behind it. Still, there was less fear on her face than anger, now. "Think, Moiraine. Tamra supposedly died in her sleep, too. Only we know Meilyn didn't, no matter where she was found. First Tamra, then the others started dying. The only thing that makes sense is that someone noticed her calling sisters in and wanted to know why badly enough that they bloody risked putting the Amyrlin Seat herself to the question. They had to have something to hide to do that, something they'd risk anything to keep hidden. They killed her to hide it, to hide what they'd done, and then they set out to kill the rest. Which means they don't want the boy found, not alive. They don't want the Dragon Reborn at the Last Battle. Any other way to look at it is tossing the slop bucket into the wind and hoping for the best."

Unconsciously, Moiraine peered toward the mouth of the alley. A few people walking by glanced in, but none more than once. No one paused at seeing them seated there. Some things were easier to speak of when you were not too specific. "The Amyrlin" had been put to the question; "she" had been killed. Not Tamra, not a name that brought up the familiar, determined face. "Someone" had murdered her. "They" did not want the Dragon Reborn found. Murder with the Power certainly violated the Three Oaths, even for . . . for those Moiraine did not want to name any more than Siuan did.

Forcing her face to smoothness, forcing her voice to calm, she forced the words out. "The Black Ajah." Siuan flinched, then nodded, glowering.

Any sister grew angry at the suggestion there was a secret Ajah hidden inside the others, dedicated to the Dark One. Most sisters refused to listen. The White Tower had stood for the Light for over three thousand years. But some sisters did not deny the Black straight out. Some believed. Very few would admit it even to another sister, though. Moiraine did not want to admit it to herself.

Siuan plucked at the ties on her bundle, but she went on in a brisk voice. "I don't think they have our names—Tamra never really thought us part of it—else I'd have had an 'accident,' too. Just before I left, I slipped a note with my suspicions under Sierin's door. Only, I didn't know how much to trust her. The Amyrlin Seat! I wrote with my left hand, but I was shaking so hard, no one could recognize my writing if I'd used my right. Burn my liver! Even if we knew who to trust, we have bilge water for proof."

"Enough for me. If they know everything, all the women Tamra chose, there may be none left except us. We will have to move fast if we have a hope of finding the boy first." Moiraine tried for a vigorous tone, too. It was gratifying that Siuan only nodded. She would not give up for all her talk of shaking, and she never considered that Moiraine might. Most gratifying. "Perhaps they know us, and perhaps not. Perhaps they think they can leave two new sisters for last. In any case, we cannot trust anyone but ourselves." Blood drained from her face. "Oh, Light! I just had an encounter at the inn, Siuan."

She tried to recall every word, every nuance, from the moment Merean first spoke. Siuan listened with a distant look, filing and sorting. "Cadsuane could be one of Tamra's chosen," she agreed when Moiraine finished. "Or she could be Black Ajah." She barely hesitated over the words. "Maybe she's just trying to get you out of the way until she can dispose of you without rousing suspicion. The trouble is, any of them could be either." Leaning across her bundle, she touched Moiraine's knee. "Can you bring your horse from the stable without being seen? I have a good mount, but I don't know if she can carry both of us. We should be hours from here before they know we're gone."

Moiraine smiled in spite of herself. She very much doubted the good mount. Her friend's eye for horseflesh was no better than her seat in the saddle, and sometimes Siuan fell off nearly before the animal moved. The ride north must have been agony. And full of fear. "No one knows you are here at all, Siuan," she said. "Best if it stays so. You have your book? Good. If I remain until morning, I will have a day's start on them instead of hours. You go on to Chachin now. Take some of my coin." By the state of Siuan's dress, she had spent the last part of that trip sleeping under bushes. A fisherman's daughter had no estates to provide gold. "Start looking for the Lady Ines, and I will catch you up there."

It was not that easy, of course. Siuan had a stubborn streak as wide as the Erinin. Quite aside from that, as novice and Accepted it had been the fisherman's daughter who led, not the king's niece, something that had startled Moiraine at first, until she realized that it felt natural somehow. Siuan had been born to lead.

"I have enough for my needs," she grumbled, but Moiraine insisted on handing her half the coins in her purse, and when Moiraine reminded her of their pledge during their first months in the Tower, that what one owned belonged to the other as well, she muttered, "We swore we'd find beautiful young princes to bond, too, and marry them besides. Girls say all sort of silly things. You watch after yourself, now. You leave me alone in this, and I'll wring your neck."

Embracing to say goodbye, Moiraine found it hard to let go. An hour ago, her worries had been whether she might be stuck away on a farm, or at worse birched. Now. . . . The Black Ajah. She wanted to empty her stomach. If only she had Siuan's courage. Watching Siuan slip down the alley adjusting that bundle on her back again, Moiraine wished she were Green. Only Greens bonded more than one Warder, and she would have liked at least three or four to guard her back right then.

Walking back up the street, she could not help looking at everyone she passed, man or woman. If the Black Ajah—her stomach twisted every time she thought that name—if they were involved, then ordinary Darkfriends were, too. No one denied that some misguided people believed the Dark One would give them immortality, people who would kill and do every sort of evil to gain that hoped-for reward. And if any sister could be Black Ajah, anyone she met could be a Darkfriend. She hoped Siuan remembered that.

As she approached The Gates of Heaven, a sister appeared in the inn's doorway. Part of a sister, at least; all she could see was an arm with a fringed shawl over it. A tall man who had just come out, his hair in two belled braids, turned back to speak for a moment, but the shawl-draped arm gestured peremptorily, and he strode past Moiraine wearing a scowl. She would not have thought twice of it if not for thinking about the Black Ajah and Darkfriends. The Light knew, Aes Sedai did speak to men, and some did more than speak. She had been thinking of Darkfriends, though. And Black sisters. If only she could have made out the color of that fringe. She hurried the last thirty-odd paces frowning.

Merean and Larelle were seated together by themselves near the door, both still wearing their shawls. Few sisters did that except for ceremony, or for show. Both women were watching Cadsuane go into that private sitting room, followed by a pair of gray-haired men who looked as hard as last year's oak. She still wore her shawl, too, with the white Flame of Tar Valon bright on her back. It could have been any of them. Cadsuane might be looking for another Warder; Greens always seemed to be looking. Moiraine did not know whether Merean and Larelle had Warders. The fellow's scowl might have been for hearing he did not measure up. There were a hundred possible explanations, and she put the man out of her head. The sure dangers were real enough without inventing more.

Before she was three steps into the common room, Master Helvin bustled up in a green-striped apron, a bald man nearly as wide as he was tall, and handed her a new irritation. With three more Aes Sedai stopping at his inn, he need to shuffle the beds, as he put it. The Lady

Alys would not mind sharing hers, certainly, under the circumstances. Mistress Palan was a most pleasant woman.

Haesel Palan was a rug merchant from Murandy with the lilt of Lugard in her voice. Moiraine heard more of it than she wanted from the moment she stepped into the small room that had been hers alone. Her clothes had been moved from the wardrobe to pegs on the wall, her comb and brush displaced from the washstand for Mistress Palan's. The plump woman might have been diffident with "Lady Alys," but not with a wilder who everybody said was off in the morning to become a novice in the White Tower. She lectured Moiraine on the duties of a novice, all of it wrong. She followed Moiraine down to dinner and gathered other traders of her acquaintance at the table, every woman of them eager to share what she knew of the White Tower. Which was nothing at all. They shared it in great detail, though. Moiraine thought to escape by retiring early, but Mistress Palan appeared almost as soon as she had her dress off and talked until she dropped off to sleep.

It was not an easy night. The bed was narrow, the woman's elbows sharp and her feet icy despite thick blankets that trapped the warmth of the small stove under the bed. The rainstorm that had threatened all day broke, wind and thunder rattling the shutters for hours. Moiraine doubted she could have slept in any event. Darkfriends and the Black Ajah danced in her head. She saw Tamra being dragged from her sleep, dragged away to somewhere secret and tortured by women wielding the Power. Sometimes the women wore Merean's face, and Larelle's, and Cadsuane's, and every sister's she had ever seen. Sometimes Tamra's face became her own.

When the door creaked slowly open in the dark hours of morning, Moiraine embraced the Source in a flash. *Saidar* filled her to the point where the sweetness and joy came close to pain. Not as much of the Power as she would be able to handle in another year, much less five, yet a hair more would burn the ability out of her now, or kill her. One was as bad as the other, but she wanted to draw more, and not just because the Power always made you want more.

Cadsuane put her head in. Moiraine had forgotten her promise, her threat. Cadsuane saw the glow, of course, could feel how much she held. "Fool girl" was all the woman said before leaving.

Moiraine counted to one hundred slowly, then swung her feet out from under the covers. Now was as good a time as any. Mistress Palan heaved onto her side and began to snore. Channeling Fire, Moiraine lit one of the lamps and dressed hurriedly. A riding dress, this time. Reluctantly she decided to abandon her saddlebags along with every-thing else she had to leave behind. Anyone who saw her moving about might not think too much of it even this time of the morning, but not if she had saddlebags over her shoulder. All she took was what she could fit into the pockets sewn inside her cloak, little more than some spare stockings and a clean shift. Mistress Palan was still snoring as she closed the door behind her.

The skinny groom on night duty was startled to see her with the sky just beginning to turn gray, but a silver penny had him knuckling his forehead and saddling her bay mare. She regretted leaving her pack-horse behind, but not even a fool noble—she heard the fellow mutter that—would take a pack animal for a morning jaunt. Climbing into Arrow's high-cantled saddle, she gave the man a cool smile instead of the second penny he would have received without the comment, and rode slowly out into damp, empty streets. Just out for a ride, however early. It looked to be a good day. The sky looked rained out, for one thing, and there was little wind.

The lamps were still lit all along the streets and alleys, leaving no more than the palest shadow anywhere, yet the only people to be seen were the Night Watch's patrols and the Lamplighters, heavily armed as they made their rounds to make sure no lamp went out. A wonder that people could live so close to the Blight that a Myrddraal could step out of any dark shadow. No one went out in the night, though. Not in the Borderlands.

Which was why she was surprised to see that she was not the first to reach the western gates. Slowing Arrow, she stayed well back from the three very large men waiting with a packhorse behind their mounts. Their attention was all on the barred gates, with now and again a word shared with the gate guards. They barely glanced at her. The lamps here showed their faces clearly. A grizzled old man and a hard-faced young one wearing braided leather cords tied around their heads. Mal-kieri? She thought that was what that meant. The third was an Ara-fellin with belled braids. The same fellow she had seen leaving The Gates of Heaven.

By the time the bright sliver of sunrise allowed the gates to be swung open, several merchants' trains had lined up to depart. The three men were first through, but Moiraine let a train of a dozen wagons behind eight-horse teams rumble ahead of her before she followed across the bridge and onto the road through the hills. She kept the three in sight, though. They were heading in the same direction so far, after all.

They moved quickly, good riders who barely shifted a rein, but a trot suited her. The more distance she put between herself and Cadsuane, the better. The merchants' wagons fell back out of sight long before they reached the first village near midday, a small cluster of tile-roofed stone houses around a tiny inn on a forested hill slope. Moiraine paused long enough to ask whether anyone knew a woman named Avene Sahera. The answer was no, and she galloped on, not slowing until the three men appeared on the hard-packed road ahead, their horses still in that ground-eating pace. Maybe they knew nothing more than the name of the sister the Arafellin had spoken to, but anything at all she learned about Cadsuane or the other two would be to the good.

She formulated several plans for approaching them, and discarded each. Three men on a deserted forest road could well decide that a young woman alone was a good opportunity, especially if they were what she feared. Handling them presented no problem, if it came to it, but she wanted to avoid that. Woods gave way to scattered farms, and farms faded to more woods. A red-crested eagle soared overhead and became a shape against the descending sun.

As her shadow stretched out behind her, she decided to forget the men and find a place to sleep. With luck she might see more farms soon, and if a little silver did not bring a bed, a hayloft would have to do.

Ahead, the three men stopped, conferring for a moment; then one took the packhorse and turned aside into the forest. The others dug in their heels and galloped on.

Moiraine stared after them. The Arafellin was one of the pair rushing off, but if they were traveling together, maybe he had mentioned meeting an Aes Sedai to his companion. And one man would certainly be less trouble than three, if she was careful. Riding to where rider and packhorse had vanished, she dismounted.

Tracking was a thing most ladies left to their huntsmen, but she had taken an interest in the years when climbing trees and getting dirty had seemed equal fun. Broken twigs and kicked winter-fall leaves left a trail a child could have followed. A hundred paces or so into the forest, she spotted a pond in a hollow through the trees. The fellow had already unsaddled and hobbled his bay—a fine-looking animal— and was setting the packsaddle on the ground. It was the younger of the Malkieri. He looked even larger, this close. Unbuckling his sword belt, he sat down facing the pond, laid sword and belt beside him, and put his hands on his knees. He seemed to be staring off across the water, still glittering through the late-afternoon shadows. He did not move a muscle.

Moiraine considered. Plainly he had been left to make camp. The others would come back. A question or two would not take long, though. And if he was unnerved a little—say at finding a woman suddenly standing right behind him—he might answer before he thought. Tying Arrow's reins to a low branch, she gathered her cloak and skirts and moved forward as silently as possible. A low hummock stood humped up behind him, and she stepped up onto that. Added height could help. He was a very tall man. And it might help if he found her with her belt knife in one hand and his sword in the other. Channeling, she whisked the scabbarded blade from his side. Every little bit of shock she could manage for him—

He moved faster than thought. Her grasp closed on the scabbard, and he uncoiled, whirling, one hand clutching the scabbard between hers, the other seizing the front of her dress. Before she could think to channel, she was flying through the air. She had just time to see the pond coming up at her, just time to shout something, she did not know what, and then she struck the surface flat, driving all the wind out of her, struck with a great splash and sank. The water was *freezing! Saidar* fled in her shock.

Floundering to her feet, she stood up to her waist in the icy water, coughing, wet hair clinging to her face, sodden cloak dragging at her shoulders. Furiously she twisted around to confront her attacker, furiously embraced the Source once more. The test for the shawl required channeling with absolute calm under great stress, and far worse than this had been done to her then. She turned, prepared to knock him down and drub him till he squealed!

He stood shaking his head and frowning at the spot where she had stood, a long stride from where he had sat. When he deigned to notice her, he came to the edge of the pond and bent to stretch out a hand. "Unwise to try separating a man from his sword," he said, and after a glance at the colored slashes on her dress, added, "My Lady." Hardly an apology. His startlingly blue eyes did not quite meet hers. If he was hiding mirth . . . !

Muttering under her breath, she splashed awkwardly to where she could take his outstretched hand in both of hers . . . and heaved with all of her might. Ignoring icy water tickling down your ribs was not easy, and if she was wet, so would he be, and without any need to use the . . .

He straightened, raised his arm, and she came out of the water dangling from his hand. In consternation she stared at him until her feet touched the ground and he backed away.

"I'll start a fire and hang up blankets so you can dry yourself," he murmured, still not meeting her gaze.

He was as good as his word, and by the time the other men appeared, she was standing beside a small fire surrounded by blankets dug from his packsaddles and hung from branches. She had no need of the fire for drying, of course, or the privacy. The proper weave of Water had taken every drop from her hair and clothes while she stayed in them. As well he did not see that, though. And she did appreciate the flame's warmth. Anyway, she had to stay inside the blankets long enough for the man to think she had used the fire as he intended. She very definitely held on to *saidar*.

The other men arrived, full of questions about whether "she" had followed into the woods. They had known? Men watched for bandits in these times, but they had noticed a lone woman and decided she was following them? It seemed suspicious.

"A Cairhienin, Lan? I suppose you've seen a Cairhienin in her skin, but I never have." That certainly caught her ear, and with the Power filling her, so did another sound. Steel whispering on leather. A sword leaving its sheath. Preparing several weaves that would stop the lot of them in their tracks, she made a crack in the blankets to peek out.

To her surprise, the man who had dunked her—Lan?—stood with his back to her blankets. He was the one with sword in hand. The Arafellin, facing him, looked surprised. "You remember the sight of the Thousand Lakes, Ryne," Lan said coldly. "Does a woman need protection from your eyes?"

For a moment, she thought Ryne was going to draw despite the blade already in Lan's hand, but the older man, a much battered, graying fellow though as tall as the others, calmed matters, took the other two a little distance away with talk of some game called "sevens." A strange game it seemed to be. Lan and Ryne sat cross-legged facing one another, their swords sheathed, then without warning drew, each blade flashing toward the other man's throat, stopping just short of flesh. The older man pointed to Ryne, they sheathed swords, and then did it again. For as long as she watched, that was how it went. Perhaps Ryne had not been as overconfident as he seemed.

Waiting inside the blankets, she tried to recall what she had been taught of Malkier. Not a great deal, except as history. Ryne remembered the Thousand Lakes, so he must be Malkieri, too. There had been something about distressed women. Now that she was with them, she might as well stay until she learned what she could.

When she came out from behind the blankets, she was ready. "I claim the right of a woman alone," she told them formally. "I travel to Chachin, and I ask the shelter of your swords." She also pressed a fat silver coin into each man's hand. She was not really sure about this ridiculous "woman alone" business, but silver caught most men's attention. "And two more each, paid in Chachin."

The reactions were not what she expected. Ryne glared at the coin as he turned it over in his fingers. Lan looked at his without expression and tucked it into his coat pocket with a grunt. She had given them some of her last Tar Valon marks, she realized, but Tar Valon coins could be found anywhere, along with those of every other land.

Bukama, the grizzled man, bowed with his left hand on his knee. "Honor to serve, my Lady," he said. "To Chachin, my life before yours." His eyes were also blue, and they, too, would not quite meet hers. She hoped he did not turn out to be a Darkfriend.

Learning anything proved to be difficult. Impossible. First the men were busy setting up camp, tending the horses, making a larger fire. They did not seem eager to face a new spring night without that. Bukama and Lan barely said a word over a dinner of flatbread and dried meat that she tried not to wolf down. Her stomach remembered all too well that she had not eaten that day. Ryne talked and was quite charming, really, with a dimple in his cheek when he smiled, and a sparkle in his blue eyes, but he gave no opening for her to mention The Gates of Heaven or Aes Sedai. When she finally inquired why he was going to Chachin, his face turned sad.

"Every man has to die somewhere," he said softly, and went off to make up his blankets.

Lan took the first watch, sitting cross-legged not far from Ryne, and when Bukama doused the fire and rolled himself up in his blankets near Lan, she wove a ward of Spirit around each man. Flows of Spirit she could hold on to sleeping, and if any of them moved in the night, the ward would wake her without alerting them. It meant waking every time they changed guard, but there was nothing for it. Her own blankets lay well away from the men, and as she was lying down, Bukama murmured something she could not catch. She heard Lan's reply plainly enough.

"I'd sooner trust an Aes Sedai, Bukama. Go to sleep."

All the anger she had tamped down flared up. The man threw her into an icy pond, he did not apologize, he . . . ! She channeled, Air and Water weaving with a touch of Earth. A thick cylinder of water rose from the surface of the pond, stretching up and up in the moonlight, arching over. Crashing down on the fool who was so free with his tongue!

Bukama and Ryne bounded to their feet with oaths, but she continued the torrent for a count of ten before letting it end. Freed water splashed down across the campsite. She expected to see a sodden, half-frozen man ready to learn proper respect. He *was* dripping wet, a few small fish flopping around his feet. He was standing on his feet. With his sword out.

"Shadowspawn?" Ryne said in a disbelieving tone, and atop him, Lan said, "Maybe! Guard the woman, Ryne! Bukama, take west; I'll take east!"

"Not Shadowspawn!" Moiraine snapped, stopping them in their tracks. They stared at her. She wished she could see their expressions better in the moonshadows, but those cloud-shifting shadows aided her, too, cloaking her in mystery. With an effort she gave her voice every bit of cool Aes Sedai serenity she could muster. "It is unwise to show anything except respect to an Aes Sedai, Master Lan."

"Aes Sedai?" Ryne whispered. Despite the dim light, the awe on his face was clear. Or maybe it was fear.

No one else made a sound, except for Bukama's grumbles as he shifted his bed away from the mud. Ryne spent a long time moving his blankets in silence, giving her small bows whenever she glanced his way. Lan made no attempt to dry off. He started to choose a new spot for his watch, then stopped and sat back where he had been, in the mud and water. She might have thought it a gesture of humility, only he glanced at her, very nearly meeting her eyes this time. If that was humility, kings were the most humble men on earth.

She wove her wards around them again, of course. If anything, revealing herself only made it more necessary. She did not go to sleep for quite a while, though. She had a great deal to think about. For one thing, none of the men had asked *why* she was following them. The man had been on his *feet*! When she drifted off, she was thinking of Ryne, strangely. A pity if he was afraid of her, now. He was charming, and she did not mind a man wanting to see her unclothed, only his telling others about it.

Lan knew the ride to Chachin would be one he would rather forget, and it met his expectations. It stormed twice, freezing rain mixed with ice, and that was the least. Bukama was angry that he refused to make proper pledge to the diminutive woman who claimed to be Aes Sedai, but Bukama knew the reasons and did not press. He only grumbled whenever he thought Lan could hear; Aes Sedai or not, a decent man followed certain forms. As if he did not share Lan's reasons. Ryne twitched and peered wide-eyed at her, fetched and trotted and offered up compliments on "skin of snowy silk" and the "deep, dark pools of her eyes" like a courtier on a leash. He seemed unable to decide between besotted and terrified, and he let her see both. That would have been bad enough, but Ryne was right; Lan had seen a Cairhienin in her skin, more than one, and they had all tried to mesh him in a scheme, or two, or three. Over one particularly memorable ten days in the south of Cairhien, he had almost been killed six times and nearly married twice. A Cairhienin *and* an Aes Sedai? There could be no worse combination.

This Alys—she told them to call her Alys, which he doubted as much as the Great Serpent ring she produced, especially after she tucked it back into her belt pouch and said no one must know she was Aes Sedai—this "Alys" had a temper. Normally, he did not mind that, cold or hot, in man or woman. Hers was ice. That first night he had sat in the wet to let her know he would accept what she had done. If they were to travel together, better to end it with honors even, as she must see it. Except that she did not.

They rode hard, never stopping long in a village and sleeping under the stars most nights, since no one had the coin for inns, not for four people with horses. He slept when he could. The second night she remained awake till dawn and made sure he did as well, with sharp flicks of an invisible switch whenever he nodded off. The third night, sand somehow got inside his clothes and boots, a thick coating of it. He had shaken out what he could and ridden covered in grit the next day. The fourth night. . . . He could not understand how she managed to make ants crawl into his smallclothes, or make them all bite at once. It had been her doing for sure. She was standing over him when his eyes shot open, and she seemed surprised that he did not cry out. Clearly, she wanted some response, some reaction, but he could not see what. Surely not the pledge of protection. Bukama's sufficed, and besides, she had given them money. The woman did not know insult when she offered it.

When they had first seen her behind them, outpacing the merchant trains and the shield of their guards, Bukama had offered a reason for a woman alone to follow three men. If six swordsmen could not kill a man in daylight, perhaps one woman could in darkness. Bukama had not mentioned Edeyn, of course. In truth, it plainly could not be that, or he would be dead instead of uncomfortable, yet Alys herself never made any explanation, however much Bukama waited for one. Edeyn might set a woman to watch him, thinking he would be less on his guard. So Lan watched her. But the only suspicious thing he saw, if it could be called that, was that she asked questions whenever they came to a village, always away from him and the others, and she went silent if they came too near. Two days from Canluum, she stopped asking, though. Perhaps she had found an answer in the market village called Ravinda, but if so, she did not seem happy about it. That night she discovered a patch of blisterleaf near their campsite, and to his shame, he almost lost his temper.

If Canluum was a city of hills, Chachin was a city of mountains. The three highest rose almost a mile even with their peaks sheared off short, and all glittered in the sun with colorful glazed tile roofs and tile-covered palaces. Atop the tallest of those the Aesdaishar Palace shone brighter than any other in red and green, the prancing Red Horse flying above its largest dome. Three towered ringwalls surrounded the city, as did a deep drymoat a hundred paces wide spanned by two dozen bridges, each with a fortress hulking at its mouth. The traffic was too great here, and the Blight too far away, for the guards with the Red Horse on their chests to be so diligent as in Canluum, but crossing the Bridge of Sunrise amid tides of wagons and people flowing both ways still took some little while. Once inside, Lan wasted no time drawing rein.

"We are within the walls of Chachin," he told the woman. "The pledge has been kept. Keep your coin," he added coldly when she reached for her purse.

Ryne immediately started going on about giving offense to Aes Sedai and offering her smiling apologies, while Bukama rumbled about men with the manners of pigs. The woman herself gazed at Lan with so little expression, she might even have been what she claimed. A dangerous claim if untrue. And if true . . .

Whirling Cat Dancer, he galloped up the street scattering people afoot and some mounted. Bukama and Ryne caught him up before he was halfway up the mountain to the Aesdaishar. If Edeyn was in Chachin, she would be there. Wisely, Bukama and Ryne held their silence.

The palace filled the flattened mountaintop completely, an immense, shining structure of domes and high balconies covering fifty hides, a small city to itself. The great bronze gates, worked with the Red Horse, stood open beneath a red-tiled arch, and once Lan identified himself— as Lan Mandragoran, not al'Lan—the guards' stiffness turned to smiling bows. Servants in red-and-green came running to take the horses and show each man to rooms befitting his station. Bukama and Ryne each received a small room above one of the barracks. Lan was given three rooms draped in silk tapestries, with a bedchamber that overlooked one of the palace gardens, two square-faced serving women to tend him, and a lanky young fellow to run errands.

A little careful questioning of the servants brought answers. Queen Ethenielle was making a progress through the heartland, but Brys, the Prince Consort, was in residence. As was the Lady Edeyn Arrel. The women smiled when they said that; they had known what he wanted from the first.

He washed himself, but let the women dress him. Just because they were servants was no reason to insult them. He had one white silk shirt that did not show too much wear, and a good black silk coat embroidered along the sleeves with golden bloodroses among their hooked thorns. Bloodroses for loss and remembrance. Then he set the women outside to guard his door and sat to wait. His meetings with Edeyn must be public, with as many people around as possible.

A summons came from her, to her chambers, which he ignored. Courtesy demanded he be given time to rest from his journey, yet it seemed a very long time before the invitation to join Brys came, brought by the *shatayan*. A stately, graying woman with a presence to match any queen, she had charge of all the palace servants, and it was an honor to be conducted by her personally. Outsiders needed a guide to find their way anywhere in the Palace. His sword remained on the lacquered rack by the door. It would do him no good here, and would insult Brys besides, indicating that he thought he needed to protect himself.

He expected a private meeting first, but the *shatayan* took him to a columned hall full of people. Soft-footed servants moved through the crowd offering spiced wine to Kandori lords and ladies in silks embroidered with House sigils, and folk in fine woolens worked with the sigils of the more important guilds. And to others, too. Lan saw men wearing the *hadori* he knew had not worn it these ten years or more. Women with hair still cut at the shoulders and higher wore the small dot of the *ki'sain* painted on their foreheads. They bowed at his appearance, and made deep curtsies, those men and women who had decided to remember Malkier.

Prince Brys was a stocky, rough-hewn man in his middle years who looked more suited to armor than his green silks, though in truth he was accustomed to either. Brys was Ethenielle's Swordbearer, the general of her armies, as well as her consort. He caught Lan's shoulders, refusing to allow him to bow.

"None of that from the man who twice saved my life in the Blight, Lan." Brys laughed. "Besides, your coming seems to have rubbed some of your luck off on Diryk. He fell from a balcony this morning, a good fifty feet, without breaking a bone." He motioned his second son, a handsome dark-eyed boy of eight in a coat like his, to come forward. A large bruise marred the side of the boy's head, and he moved with the stiffness of other bruises, but he made a formal bow spoiled only somewhat by a wide grin. "He should be at his lessons," Brys confided, "but he was so eager to meet you, he'd have forgotten his letters and cut himself on a sword." Frowning, the boy protested that he would never cut himself.

Lan returned the lad's bow with equal formality, then had to put up with a deluge of questions. Yes, he had fought Aiel, in the south and on the Shienaran marches, but they were just men, if dangerous, not ten feet tall; they did veil their faces before killing, but they did not eat their dead. No, the White Tower was not as high as a mountain, though it was taller than anything made by men that Lan had ever seen, even the Stone of Tear. Given a chance, the boy would have drained him dry about the Aiel, and the wonders of the great cities in the south like Tar Valon and Far Madding. Likely, he would not have believed that Chachin was as big as either of those.

"Lord Mandragoran will fill your head to your heart's content later," Brys told the boy. "There is someone else he must meet now. Off with you to Mistress Tuval and your books."

Edeyn was exactly as Lan remembered. Oh, ten years older, with touches of white streaking her temples and a few fine lines at the corners of her eyes, but those large dark eyes gripped him. Her *ki'sain* was still the white of a widow, and her hair still hung in black waves below her waist. She wore a red silk gown in the Domani style, clinging and little short of sheer. She was beautiful, but even she could do nothing here.

For a moment she merely looked at him, cool and considering, when he made his bow. "It would have been . . . easier had you come to me," she murmured, seeming not to care whether Brys heard. And then, shockingly, she knelt gracefully and took his hands in hers. "Beneath the Light," she announced in a strong, clear voice, "I, Edeyn ti Gemallen Arrel, pledge fealty to al'Lan Mandragoran, Lord of the Seven Towers, Lord of the Lakes, the true Blade of Malkier. May he sever the Shadow!" Even Brys looked startled. A moment of silence held while she kissed Lan's fingers; then cheers erupted on every side. Cries of "The Golden Crane!" and even "Kandor rides with Malkier!"

The sound freed him to pull his hands loose, to lift her to her feet. "My Lady," he began in a tight voice.

"What must be, will be," she said, putting a hand over his lips. And then she faded back into the crowd of those who wanted to cluster around him, congratulate him—who would have pledged fealty on the spot had he let them.

Brys rescued him, drawing him off to a long, stone-railed walk above a two-hundred-foot drop to the roofs below. It was known as a place Brys went to be private, and no one followed. Only one door let onto it, no window overlooked, and no sound from the palace intruded. "What will you do?" the older man asked simply as they walked.

"I do not know," Lan replied. She had won only a skirmish, but he felt stunned at the ease of it. A formidable opponent, the woman who wore part of his soul in her hair.

For the rest they spoke quietly of hunting and bandits and whether this past year's flare-up in the Blight might die down soon. Brys regretted withdrawing his army from the war against the Aiel, but there had been no alternative. They talked of the rumors about a man who could channel—every tale had him in a different place; Brys thought it another jak o' the mists and Lan agreed—and of the Aes Sedai who seemed to be everywhere, for what reason no one knew. Ethenielle had written him that two sisters had caught a woman pretending to be Aes Sedai in a village along her progression. The woman could channel, but that did her no good. The two real Aes Sedai flogged her squealing through the village, making her confess her crime to every last man and woman who lived there. Then one of the sisters carried her off to Tar Valon for her true punishment, whatever that might be. Lan found himself hoping that Alys had not lied about being Aes Sedai.

He hoped to avoid Edeyn the rest of the day, too, but when he was guided back to his rooms, she was there, waiting languorously in one of the gilded chairs. The servants were nowhere to be seen.

"You are no longer beautiful, I fear, sweetling," she said when he came in. "I think you may even be ugly when you are older. But I always enjoyed your eyes more than your face. And your hands."

He stopped still gripping the door handle. "My Lady, not two hours gone you swore—" She cut him off.

"And I will obey my king. But a king is not a king, alone with his *carneira*. I brought your *daori*. Bring it to me."

Unwillingly, his eyes followed her gesture to a flat lacquered box on a small table beside the door. Lifting the hinged lid took as much effort as lifting a boulder. Coiled inside lay a long cord woven of hair. He could recall every moment of the morning after their first night, when she took him to the women's quarters of the Royal Palace in Fal Moran and let ladies and servants watch as she cut his hair at his shoulders. She even told them what it signified. The women had all been amused, making jokes as he sat at Edeyn's feet to weave the *daori* for her. Edeyn kept custom, but in her own way. The hair felt soft and supple; she must have had it rubbed with lotions every day.

Crossing the floor slowly, he knelt before her and held out his *daori* stretched between his hands. "In token of what I owe to you, Edeyn, always and forever." If his voice did not hold the fervor of that first morning, surely she understood.

She did not take the cord. Instead, she studied him. "I knew you had not been gone so long as to forget our ways," she said finally. "Come."

Rising, she grasped his wrist and drew him to the windows over-looking the garden ten paces below. Two servants were spreading water from buckets, and a young woman was strolling along a slate path in a blue dress as bright as any of the early flowers that grew beneath the trees.

"My daughter, Iselle." For a moment, pride and affection warmed Edeyn's voice. "Do you remember her? She is seventeen, now. She hasn't chosen her *carneira*, yet"—young men were chosen by their *carneira*; young women chose theirs—"but I think it time she married anyway."

He vaguely recalled a child who always had servants running, the blossom of her mother's heart, but his head had been full of Edeyn, then. "She is as beautiful as her mother, I am sure," he said politely. He twisted the *daori* in his hands. She had too much advantage as long as he held it, all advantage, but she had to take it from him. "Edeyn, we must talk." She ignored that.

"Time you were married, too, sweetling. Since none of your female relatives is alive, it is up to me to arrange."

He gasped at what she seemed to be suggesting. At first he could not believe. "*Iselle?*" he said hoarsely. "*Your* daughter?" She might keep custom in her own way, but this was scandalous. "I'll not be reined into something so shameful, Edeyn. Not by you, or by this." He shook the *daori* at her, but she only looked at it and smiled.

"Of course you won't be reined, sweetling. You are a man, not a boy. Yet you do keep custom," she mused, running a finger along the cord of hair quivering between his hands. "Perhaps we do need to talk."

But it was to the bed that she led him.

Moiraine spent most of the day asking discreet questions at inns in the rougher parts of Chachin, where her silk dress and divided skirts drew stares from patrons and innkeepers alike. One leathery fellow wearing a permanent leer told her that his establishment was not for her and tried to escort her to a better, while a round-faced, squinting woman cackled that the evening trade would have a tender pretty like her for dinner if she did not scurry away quick, and a fatherly old man with pink cheeks and a joyous smile was all too eager for her to drink the spiced wine he prepared out of her sight. There was nothing for it but to grit her teeth and move on. That was the sort of place Siuan had liked to visit when they were allowed a rare trip into Tar Valon as Accepted, cheap and unlikely to be frequented by sisters, but none had a blue-eyed Tairen staying under any name. Cold daylight began to settle toward yet another icy night.

She was walking Arrow through lengthening shadows, eyeing darknesses that moved suspiciously in an alley and thinking that she would have to give up for today, when Siuan came bustling up from behind.

"I thought you might look down here when you came," Siuan said, taking her elbow to hurry her along. "Let's get inside before we freeze." She eyed those shadows in the alley, too, and absently fingered her belt knife as if using the Power could not deal with any ten of them. Well, not without revealing themselves. Perhaps it was best to move quickly. "Not the quarter for you, Moiraine. There are fellows around here would bloody well have you for dinner before you knew you were in the pot. Are you laughing or choking?"

Siuan, it turned out, was at a most respectable inn called The Evening Star, which catered to merchants of middling rank, especially women unwilling to be bothered by noise or rough sorts in the common room. A pair of bull-shouldered fellows made sure there was none of that. Siuan's room was tidy and warm, if not large, and the innkeeper, a lean woman with an air of brooking little nonsense, made no objections to Moiraine joining Siuan. So long as the extra for two was paid.

While Moiraine was hanging her cloak on a peg, Siuan settled cross-legged on the not-very-wide bed. She seemed invigorated since Canluum. A goal always made Siuan bubble with enthusiasm. "I've had a time, Moiraine, I tell you. That fool horse nearly beat me to death getting here. The Creator made people to walk or go by boat, not be bounced around. I suppose the Sahera woman wasn't the one, or you'd be jumping like a spawning redtail. I found Ines Demain almost right off, but not where *I* can reach her. She's a new widow, but she did have a son, for sure. Named him Rahien because she saw the dawn come up over Dragonmount. Talk of the streets. Everybody thinks it a fool reason to name a child."

"Avene Sahera's son was born a week too early and thirty miles from Dragonmount," Moiraine said when Siuan paused for breath. She pushed down a momentary thrill. Seeing dawn over the mountain did not mean the child had been born on it. There was no chair or stool, nor room for one, so she sat on the end of the bed. "If you have found Ines and her son, Siuan, why is she out of reach?" The Lady Ines, it turned it out, was in the Aesdaishar Palace, where Siuan could have gained entry easily as Aes Sedai and otherwise only if the Palace was hiring servants.

The Aesdaishar Palace. "We will take care of that in the morning," Moiraine sighed. It meant risk, yet the Lady Ines had to be questioned. No woman Moiraine had found yet had been able to *see* Dragonmount when her child was born. "Have you seen any sign of . . . of the Black Ajah?" She had to get used to saying that name.

Instead of answering immediately, Siuan frowned at her lap and fingered her skirt. "This is a strange city, Moiraine," she said finally. "Lamps in the streets, and women who fight duels, even if they do deny it, and more gossip than ten men full of ale could spew. Some of it interesting." She leaned forward to put a hand on Moiraine's knee. "Everybody's talking about a young blacksmith who died of a broken back a couple of nights ago. Nobody expected much of him, but this last month or so he turned into quite a speaker. Convinced his guild to take up money for the poor who've come into the city, afraid of the bandits, folks not connected to a guild or House."

"Siuan, what under the Light—"

"Just listen, Moiraine. He collected a lot of silver himself, and it seems he was on his way to the guild house to turn in six or eight bags of it when he was killed. Fool was carrying it all by himself. The point is, there wasn't a bloody coin of it taken, Moiraine. And he didn't have a mark on him, aside from his broken back."

They shared a long look; then Moiraine shook her head. "I cannot see how to tie that to Meilyn or Tamra. A blacksmith? Siuan, we can go mad thinking we see Black sisters everywhere."

"We can die from thinking they aren't there," Siuan replied. "Well. Maybe we can be silverpike in the nets instead of grunters. Just remember silverpike go to the fish-market, too. What do you have in mind about this Lady Ines?"

Moiraine told her. Siuan did not like it, and this time it took most of the night to make her see sense. In truth, Moiraine almost wished Siuan would talk her into trying something else. But Lady Ines had seen dawn over Dragonmount. At least Ethenielle's Aes Sedai advisor was with her in the south.

Morning was a whirlwind of activity, little of it satisfying. Moiraine got what she wanted, but not without having to bite her tongue. And Siuan started up again. Arguments Moiraine had dealt with the night before cropped up anew. Siuan did not like being argued out of what she thought was right. She did not like Moiraine taking all the risks. A bear with a sore tooth would have been better company. Even that fellow Lan!

A near-dawn visit to a banker's counting house produced gold—after the stern-eyed woman used an enlarging glass to study the Cairhienin banker's seal at the bottom of the letter-of-rights Moiraine presented. An enlarging glass! At least the letter itself was only a little blurred from its immersion in that pond. Mistress Noallin did not bother to hide her surprise when the pair of them began distributing purses of gold beneath their cloaks.

"Is Chachin so lawless two women are not safe by daylight?" Moiraine asked her civilly. "I think our business is done. You may have your man show us out." She and Siuan clinked when they moved.

Outside, Siuan muttered that even that blacksmith must have staggered, loaded down like a mule. And who could have broken his back that way? Whatever the reason, it must be the Black Ajah. An imposing woman with ivory combs in her hair heard enough of that to give a start, then hike her skirts to her knees and run, leaving her two gaping servants to scramble after her through the crowd. Siuan flushed but remained defiantly unrepentant.

A slim seamstress with a haughty air informed Moiraine that what she wanted was easily done. At end of the month, perhaps. A great many ladies had ordered new gowns. A king was visiting in the Aesdaishar Palace. The King of Malkier!

"The last King of Malkier died twenty-five years ago, Mistress Dorelmin," Moiraine said, spilling thirty gold crowns on the receiving table. Silene Dorelmin eyed the fat coins greedily, and her eyes positively shone when she was told there would be as much again when the dresses were done. "But I will keep six coins from the second thirty for each day it takes." Suddenly it seemed that the dresses could be finished sooner than a month after all. Much sooner.

"Did you see what that skinny trull was wearing?" Siuan said as they left. "You should have your dresses made like that, ready to fall off. You might as well enjoy men looking at you if you're going to lay your fool head on the chopping block."

Moiraine performed a novice exercise, imaging herself a rosebud in stillness, opening to the sun. As always, it brought calm. She would crack a tooth if she kept grinding them. "There is no other way, Siuan. Do you think the innkeeper will hire out one of her strongarms?" The King of *Malkier?* Light! The woman must have thought her a complete fool!

At midmorning two days after Moiraine arrived in Chachin, a yellow-lacquered carriage driven by a fellow with shoulders like a bull arrived at the Aesdaishar Palace, with two mares tied behind, a fine-necked bay and a lanky gray. The Lady Moiraine Damodred, colored slashes marching from the high neck of her dark blue gown to below her knees, was received with all due honor. The name of House Damodred was known, if not hers, and with King Laman dead, any Damodred might ascend to the Sun Throne. If another House did not seize it. She was given suitable apartments, three rooms looking north across the city toward higher, snowcapped peaks, and assigned servants who rushed about unpacking the lady's brass-bound chests and pouring hot scented water for the lady to wash. No one but the servants so much as glanced at Suki, the Lady Moiraine's maid.

"All right," Siuan muttered when the servants finally left them alone in the sitting room, "I admit I'm invisible in this." Her dark gray dress was fine wool, but entirely plain except for collar and cuffs banded in Damodred colors. "You, though, stand out like a High Lord pulling oar. Light, I nearly swallowed my tongue when you asked if there were any sisters in the Palace. I'm so nervous I'm starting to get light-headed. It feels hard to breathe."

"It is the altitude," Moiraine told her. "You will get used to it. Any visitor would ask about Aes Sedai; you could see, the servants never blinked." She had held her breath, however, until she heard the answer. One sister would have changed everything. "I do not know why I must keep telling you. A royal palace is not an inn; 'You may call me Lady Alys' would satisfy no one, here. That is fact, not opinion. I must be myself." The Three Oaths allowed you to say whatever you believed was true even if you could not prove it, as well as to dodge around truth; only words you knew to be a lie would not come off of your tongue. "Suppose you make use of that invisibility and see what you can learn about the Lady Ines. I would be pleased if we leave as soon as possible."

Tomorrow, that would be, without causing insult and talk. Siuan was right. Every eye in the Palace would be on the outland noblewoman from the House that had started the Aiel War. Any Aes Sedai who came to the Aesdaishar would hear of her immediately, and any Aes Sedai who passed through Chachin might well come. Siuan was right; she was standing on a pedestal like a target, and without a clue as to who might be an archer. Tomorrow, early.

Siuan slipped out, but returned quickly with bad news. The Lady Ines was in seclusion, mourning her husband. "He fell over dead in his breakfast porridge ten days ago," Siuan reported, dropping onto a sitting-room chair and hanging an arm over the back. Lessons in deportment were something else forgotten once the shawl was hers. "A much older man, but it seems she loved him. She's been given ten rooms and a garden on the south side of the palace; her husband was a close friend to Prince Brys." Ines would remain to herself a full month, seeing no one but close family. Her servants only came out when absolutely necessary.

"She will see an Aes Sedai," Moiraine sighed. Not even a woman in mourning would refuse to see a sister.

Siuan bolted to her feet. "Are you mad? The Lady Moiraine Damodred attracts enough attention. Moiraine Damodred Aes Sedai might as well send out riders! I thought the idea was to be gone before anyone outside the Palace knows we were here!"

One of the servingwomen came in just then, to announce that the *shatayan* had arrived to escort Moiraine to Prince Brys, and was startled to find Suki standing over her mistress and stabbing a finger at her.

"Tell the *shatayan* I will come to her," Moiraine said calmly, and as soon as the wide-eyed woman curtsied and backed out, she rose to put herself on a more equal footing, hard enough with Siuan even when one had all the advantage. "What else do you suggest? Remaining almost two weeks till she comes out will be as bad, and you cannot befriend her servants if they are secluded with her."

"They may only come out for errands, Moiraine, but I think I can get myself invited inside."

Moiraine started to say that might take as long as the other, but Siuan took her firmly by the shoulders and turned her around, eyeing her up and down critically. "A lady's maid is supposed to make sure her mistress is properly dressed," she said, and gave Moiraine a push toward the door. "Go. The *shatayan* is waiting for you. And with any luck, a young footman named Cal is waiting for Suki."

The *shatayan* indeed was waiting, a tall handsome woman, wrapped in dignity and frosty at being made to wait. Her hazel eyes could have chilled wine. Any queen who got on the wrong side of a *shatayan* was a fool, so Moiraine made herself pleasant as the woman escorted her through the halls. She thought she made some progress in melting that frost, but it was difficult to concentrate. A young footman? She did not know whether Siuan had ever been with a man, but surely she would not just to reach Ines' servants! Not a *footman*!

Statues and tapestries lined the hallways, most surprising for what she knew of the Borderlands. Marble carvings of women with flowers or children playing, silk weavings of fields of flowers and nobles in gardens and only a few hunting scenes, without a single battle shown anywhere. At intervals along the halls arched windows looked down into many more gardens than she expected, too, and flagged courtyards, sometimes with a splashing marble fountain. In one of those, she saw something that pushed questions about Siuan and a footman to the back of her mind.

It was a simple courtyard, without fountain or columned walk, and men stood in rows along the walls watching two others, stripped to the waist and fighting with wooden practice swords. Ryne and Bukama. It was fighting, if in practice; blows landed on flesh hard enough for her to hear the thuds. All landed by Ryne. She would have to avoid them, and Lan, if he was there too. He had not bothered to hide his doubts, and he might raise questions she did not dare have asked. Was she Moiraine or Alys? Worse, was she Aes Sedai or a wilder pretending? Questions that would be discussed in the streets by the next night, for any sister to hear, and that last was one any sister would investigate. Fortunately, three wandering soldiers would hardly be present anywhere she was.

Prince Brys, a solid, green-eyed man, greeted her intimately in a large room paneled red and gold. Two of the Prince's married sisters were present with their husbands, and one of Ethenielle's with hers, the men in muted silks, the women in bright colors belted high beneath their breasts. Liveried servants offered sweetmeats and nuts. Moiraine thought she might get a sore neck from looking up; the shortest of the women was taller than Siuan, and they all stood very straight. Their necks would have bent a little for a sister, men's and women's alike, but they knew themselves the equals of the Lady Moiraine.

The talk ranged from music and the best musicians among the nobles at court to the rigors of travel, from whether rumors of a man who could channel might be true to why so many Aes Sedai seemed to be about, and Moiraine found it difficult to maintain the expected light wittiness. She cared little for music and less for whoever played the instruments; in Cairhien, musicians were hired and forgotten. Everyone knew that travel was arduous, with no assurance of beds or decent food at the end of the day's twenty or thirty miles, and that was when the weather was good. Obviously some of the sisters were about because of rumors about the man, and others to tighten ties that might have loosened during the Aiel War, to make sure thrones and Houses understood they were still expected to meet their obligations to the Tower, both public and private. If an Aes Sedai had not come to the Aesdaishar yet, one soon would, reason enough for her to make heavy going of idle chat. That and thinking about other reasons for sisters to be wandering. The men put a good face on it, but she thought the women found her particularly dull.

When Brys' children were brought in, Moiraine felt a great relief.

Having his children introduced to her was a sign of acceptance to his household, but more, it signaled the end of the audience. The eldest son, Antol, was in the south with Ethenielle as heir, leaving a lovely green-eyed girl of twelve named Jarene to lead in her sister and four brothers, formally aligned by age, though in truth the two youngest boys were still in skirts and carried by nursemaids. Stifling her impatience to find out what Siuan had learned, Moiraine complimented the children on their behavior, encouraged them at their lessons. They must think her as dull as their elders did. Something a little less flat.

"And how did you earn your bruises, my Lord Diryk?" she asked, hardly listening to the boy's soberly delivered story of a fall. Until . . .

"My father says it was Lan's luck I wasn't killed, my Lady," Diryk said, brightening out of his formality. "Lan is the King of Malkier, and the luckiest man in the world, and the best swordsman. Except for my father, of course."

"The King of Malkier?" Moiraine said, blinking. Diryk nodded vigorously and began explaining in a rush of words about Lan's exploits in the Blight and the Malkieri who had come to the Aesdaishar to follow him, until his father motioned him to silence.

"Lan is a king if he wishes it, my Lady," Brys said. A very odd thing to say, and his doubtful tone made it odder. "He keeps much to his rooms"—Brys sounded troubled about that, too—"but you will meet him before you—My Lady, are you well?"

"Not very," she told him. She had hoped for another meeting with Lan Mandragoran, planned for it, but not here! Her stomach was trying to twist into knots. "I myself may keep to my rooms for a few days, if you will forgive me."

He would, of course, and everyone was full of regret at missing her company and sympathy for the strain traveling must have put on her. Though she did hear one of the women murmur that southlanders must be very delicate.

A pale-haired young woman in green-and-red was waiting to show Moiraine back to her rooms. Elis bobbed a curtsy every time she spoke, which meant she bobbed quite often in the beginning. She had been told of Moiraine's "faintness," and she asked every twenty paces whether Moiraine wished to sit and catch her breath, or have cool damp cloths brought to her rooms, or hot bricks for her feet, or smelling salts, or a dozen more sure cures for "a light head," until

Moiraine curtly told her to be quiet. The fool girl led on in silence, face blank.

Moiraine cared not at a whit whether the woman was offended. All she wanted right then was to find Siuan with good news. With the boy in her arms, born on Dragonmount, and his mother packed to travel would be best of all. Most of all, though, she wanted herself out of the halls before she ran into Lan Mandragoran.

Worrying about him, she rounded a corner behind the serving girl and came face-to-face with Merean, blue-fringed shawl looped over her arms. The *shatayan* herself was guiding Merean, and behind the motherly-looking sister came a train of servants, one woman carrying her red riding gloves, another her fur-trimmed cloak, a third her dark velvet hat. Pairs of men bore wicker pack hampers that could have been carried by one, and others had arms full of flowers. An Aes Sedai received more honor than a mere lady, however high her House.

Merean's eyes narrowed at the sight of Moiraine. "A surprise to see you here," she said slowly. "By your dress, I take it you've given over your disguise? But no. Still no ring, I see."

Moiraine was so startled at the woman's sudden appearance that she hardly heard what Merean said. "Are you alone?" she blurted.

For a moment Merean's eyes became slits. "Larelle decided to go her own way. South, I believe. More, I don't know."

"It was Cadsuane I was thinking of," Moiraine said, blinking in surprise. The more she had thought about Cadsuane, the more she had become convinced the woman must be Black Ajah. What surprised her was Larelle. Larelle had seemed bent on reaching Chachin, and without delay. Of course, plans could change, but suddenly Moiraine realized something that should have been obvious. Black sisters could lie. It was impossible—the Oaths *could* not be broken!—yet it had to be.

Merean moved close to Moiraine, and when Moiraine took a step back, she followed. Moiraine held herself erect, but she still came no higher than the other woman's chin. "Are you so eager to see Cadsuane?" Merean said, looking down at her. Her voice was pleasant, her smooth face comforting, but her eyes were cold iron. Abruptly glancing at the servants, she seemed to realize they were not alone. The iron faded, but it did not disappear. "Cadsuane was right, you know. A young woman who thinks she knows more than she does can land herself in very deep trouble. I suggest you be very still and very quiet until we can talk." Her gesture for the *shatayan* to lead on was peremptory, and the dignified woman leaped to obey. A king or queen might find themselves in a *shatayan*'s bad graces, but never an Aes Sedai.

Moiraine stared after Merean until she vanished around a corner far down the corridor. Everything Merean had just said could have come from one of Tamra's chosen. Black sisters could lie. Had Larelle changed her mind about Chachin? Or was she dead somewhere, like Tamra and the others? Suddenly Moiraine realized she was smoothing her skirts. Stilling her hands was easy, but she could not stop herself trembling faintly.

Elis was staring at her with her mouth open. "You're Aes Sedai, too!" the woman squeaked, then gave a jump, taking Moiraine's wince for a grimace. "I won't say a word to anyone, Aes Sedai," she said breathlessly. "I swear, by the Light and my father's grave!" As if every person behind Merean had not heard everything she had. They would not hold their tongues.

"Take me to Lan Mandragoran's apartments," Moiraine told her. What was true at sunrise could change by noon, and so could what was necessary. She took the Great Serpent ring from her pouch and put it on her right hand. Sometimes, you had to gamble.

After a long walk, mercifully in silence, Elis rapped at a red door and announced to the gray-haired woman who opened it that the Lady Moiraine Damodred Aes Sedai wished to speak with King al'Lan Mandragoran. The woman had added her own touches to what Moiraine told her. King, indeed! Shockingly, the reply came back that Lord Mandragoran had no wish to speak with any Aes Sedai. The gray-haired woman looked scandalized, but closed the door firmly.

Elis stared at Moiraine wide-eyed. "I can show my Lady Aes Sedai to her own rooms now," she said uncertainly, "if—" She squeaked when Moiraine pushed open the door and went in.

The gray-haired servingwoman and another a little younger leaped up from where they had been sitting, apparently darning shirts. A bony young man scrambled awkwardly to his feet beside the fireplace, looking to the women for instruction. They simply stared at Moiraine until she raised a questioning eyebrow. Then the gray-haired woman pointed to one of the two doors leading deeper into the apartments.

The door she pointed to led to a sitting room much like Moiraine's own, but all of the gilded chairs had been moved back against the walls and the flowered carpets rolled up. Shirtless, Lan was practicing the sword in the cleared area. A small golden locket swung at his neck as he moved, his blade a blur. Sweat covered him, and more scars than she expected on a man so young. Not to mention a number of half-healed wounds crossed by dark stitches. He spun gracefully out of the forms to face her, the point of his sword grounding on the floor tiles. He still did not quite meet her gaze, in that strange way he and Bukama had. His hair hung damply, clinging to his face despite the leather cord, but he was not breathing hard.

"You," he growled. "So you are Aes Sedai *and* a Damodred today. I've no time for your games, Cairhienin. I am waiting for someone." Cold blue eyes flickered to the door behind her. Oddly, what appeared to be a cord woven of hair was tied around the inner handle in an elaborate knot. "She will not be pleased to find another woman here."

"Your lady love need have no fear of me," Moiraine told him dryly. "For one thing, you are much too tall, and for another, I prefer men with at least a modicum of charm. And manners. I came for your help. There was a pledge made, and held since the War of the Hundred Years, that Malkier would ride when the White Tower called. I *am* Aes Sedai, and I call you!"

"You know the hills are high, but not how they lie," he muttered as if quoting some Malkieri saying. Stalking across the room away from her, he snatched up his scabbard and sheathed the sword forcefully. "I'll give you your help, if you can answer a question. I've asked Aes Sedai over the years, but they wriggled away from answering like vipers. If you are Aes Sedai, answer it."

"If I know the answer, I will." She would not tell him again that she was what she was, but she embraced *saidar*, and moved one of the gilded chairs out into the middle of the floor. She could not have lifted the thing with her hands, yet it floated easily on flows of Air, and would have had it been twice as heavy. Sitting, she rested her hands on crossed knees where the golden serpent on her finger was plain. The taller person had an advantage when both stood, but someone standing must feel they were being judged by someone sitting, especially an Aes Sedai.

He did not seem to feel anything of the kind. For the first time since she had met him, he met her eyes directly, and his stare was blue ice.

"When Malkier died," he said in tones of quiet steel, "Shienar and Arafel sent men. They could not stop the flood of Trollocs and Myrddraal, yet they came. Men rode from Kandor, and even Saldaea. They came too late, but they came." Blue ice became blue fire. His voice did not change, but his knuckles grew white gripping his sword. "For nine hundred years we rode when the White Tower called, but where was the Tower when Malkier died? If you are Aes Sedai, answer me that!"

Moiraine hesitated. The answer he wanted was Sealed to the Tower, taught to Accepted in history lessons yet forbidden to any except initiates of the Tower. But what was a penance alongside what she faced? "Over a hundred sisters were ordered to Malkier," she said more calmly than she felt. By everything she had been taught, she should *ask* a penance for what she had told him already. "Even Aes Sedai cannot fly, however. They were too late." By the time the first had arrived, the armies of Malkier were already broken by endless hordes of Shadowspawn, the people fleeing or dead. The death of Malkier had been hard and blood-soaked, and fast. "That was before I was born, but I regret it deeply. And I regret that the Tower decided to keep their effort secret." Better that the Tower be thought to have done nothing than to have it known Aes Sedai had tried and failed. Failure was a blow to stature, and mystery an armor the Tower needed. Aes Sedai had reasons of their own for what they did, and for what they did not do, and those reasons were known only to Aes Sedai. "That is as much answer as I can give. More than I should have, more than any other sister ever will, I think. Will it suffice?"

For a time he simply looked at her, fire slowly fading to ice once more. His eyes fell away. "Almost, I can believe," he muttered finally, without saying what he almost believed. He gave a bitter laugh. "What help can I give you?"

Moiraine frowned. She very much wanted time alone with this man, to bring him to heel, but that had to wait. "There is another sister in the Palace. Merean Redhill. I need to know where she goes, what she does, who she meets." He blinked, but did not ask the obvious questions. Perhaps he knew he would get no answers, but his silence was still pleasing.

"I have been keeping to my rooms the past few days," he said, looking at the door again. "I do not know how much watching I can do."

In spite of herself, she sniffed. The man promised help, then looked anxiously for his lady. Perhaps he was not what she had thought. But he was who she had. "Not you," she told him. Her visit here would be known throughout the Aesdaishar soon, if it was not already, and if he was noticed spying on Merean. . . . That could be disaster even if the woman was as innocent as a babe. "I thought you might ask one of the Malkieri I understand have gathered here to follow you. Someone with a sharp eye and a close tongue. This must be done in utter secrecy."

"No one follows me," he said sharply. Glancing at the door once more, he suddenly seemed weary. He did not slump, but he moved to the fireplace and propped his sword beside it with the care of a tired man. Standing with his back to her, he said, "I will ask Bukama and Ryne to watch her, but I cannot promise for them. That is all I can do for you."

She stifled a vexed sound. Whether it was all he could do or all he would, she had no leverage to force him. "Bukama," she said. "Only him." Going by how he had behaved around her, Ryne would be too busy staring at Merean to see or hear anything. That was if he did not confess what he was doing the moment Merean looked at him. "And do not tell him why."

His head whipped around, but after a moment he nodded. And again he did not ask the questions most people would have. Telling him how to get word to her, by notes passed to her maid Suki, she hoped she was not making a grave mistake.

Back in her own rooms, she discovered just how quickly news had spread. In the sitting room, Siuan was offering a tray of sweetmeats to a tall, full-mouthed young woman in pale green silk, little older than a girl, with black hair that fell well below her hips and a small blue dot painted on her forehead about where the stone of Moiraine's kesiera hung. Siuan's face was smooth, but her voice was tight as she made introductions. The Lady Iselle quickly showed why.

"Everyone in the Palace is saying you are Aes Sedai," she said, eyeing Moiraine doubtfully. She did not rise, much less curtsy, or even incline her head. "If that is so, I need your assistance. I wish to go to the White Tower. My mother wants me to marry. I would not mind

Lan as my *carneira* if Mother were not already his, but when I marry, I think it will be one of my Warders. I will be Green Ajah." She frowned faintly at Siuan. "Don't hover, girl. Stand over there until you are needed." Siuan took up a stance by the fireplace, back stiff and arms folded beneath her breasts. No real servant would have stood so—or frowned so—but Iselle no longer noticed her. "Do sit down, Moiraine," she went on with a smile, "and I will tell you what I need of you. If you *are* Aes Sedai, of course."

Moiraine stared. Invited to take a chair in her own sitting room. This silly child was certainly a suitable match for Lan when it came to arrogance. Her *carneira*? That meant "first" in the Old Tongue, and plainly something else here. Not what it seemed to, of course; even these Malkieri could not be that peculiar! Sitting, she said dryly, "Choosing your Ajah should at least wait until I test you to see whether there is any point in sending you to the Tower. A few minutes will determine whether you can learn to channel, and your potential strength if you—" The girl blithely broke in.

"Oh, I was tested years ago. The Aes Sedai said I would be very strong. I told her I was fifteen, but she learned the truth. I don't see why I could not go to the Tower at twelve if I wanted. Mother was furious. She has always said I was to be Queen of Malkier one day, but that means marrying Lan, which I would not want even if mother weren't his *carneira*. When you tell her you are taking me to the Tower, she will have to listen. Everyone knows that Aes Sedai take any woman they want for training, and no one can stop them." That full mouth pursed. "You *are* Aes Sedai, aren't you?"

Moiraine performed the rosebud exercise. "If you want to go to Tar Valon, then go. I certainly do not have time to escort you. You will find sisters there about whom you can have no doubts. Suki, will you show the Lady Iselle out? No doubt she does not wish to delay in setting off before her mother catches her."

The chit was all indignation, of course, but Moiraine wanted only to see the back of her, and Siuan very nearly pushed her out into the corridor.

"That one," Siuan said as she came back dusting her hands, "won't last a month if she can equal Cadsuane." The Tower clung like iron bands to any woman who had the smallest chance of earning the shawl, but those who could not or would not learn did find themselves put out, and channeling was only part of what had to be learned.

"Sierin herself can toss her from the top of the Tower for all I care," Moiraine snapped. "Did you learn anything?"

It seemed that Siuan had learned that the young footman knew how to kiss, a revelation that did not even pinken her cheeks, and aside from that, nothing whatsoever. Surprisingly, learning that Moiraine had approached Lan upset her more than Merean's appearance.

"Skin me and salt me if you don't take idiot risks, Moiraine. A man who claims the throne of a dead country is nine kinds of fool. He could be flapping his tongue about you right this minute to anybody who'll bloody listen! If Merean learns you're having her watched. . . . Burn me!"

"He is many kinds of fool, Siuan, but I do not think he ever 'flaps his tongue.' Besides, 'you cannot win if you will not risk a copper,' as you always tell me your father used to say. We have no choice but to take risks. With Merean here, time may be running out. You must reach the Lady Ines as quickly as you can."

"I'll do what I can," Siuan muttered, and stalked out squaring her shoulders as if for a struggle. But she was smoothing her skirt over her hips, too.

Night had long since fallen and Moiraine was trying to read by lamplight when Siuan returned. Moiraine set her book aside; she had been staring at the same page for the past hour. This time, Siuan did have news, delivered while digging through the dresses and shifts Mistress Dorelmin had made.

For one thing, she had been approached on her way back to Moiraine's rooms by "a gristly old stork" who asked if she was Suki, then told her Merean had spent almost the entire day with Prince Brys before retiring to her apartments for the night. No clue there to anything. More important, Siuan had been able to bring up Rahien in casual conversation with Cal. The footman had not been with the Lady Ines when the boy was born, but he did know the day, one day after the Aiel began their retreat from Tar Valon. Moiraine and Siuan shared a long look over that. One day after Gitara Moroso had made her Foretelling of the Dragon's Rebirth and dropped dead from the shock of it. Dawn over the mountain, and born during the ten days before a sudden thaw melted the snow. Gitara had specifically mentioned the snow.

"Anyway," Siuan went on, beginning to make a bundle of clothes and stockings, "I led Cal to believe I'd been dismissed from your service for spilling wine on your dress, and he's offered me a bed with the Lady Ines' servants. He thinks he might be able to get me a place with his Lady." She snorted with amusement, then caught Moiraine's eyes and snorted again, more roughly. "It isn't *his* bloody bed, Moiraine. And if it was, well, he has a gentle manner and the prettiest brown eyes you've ever seen. One of these days, you're going to find yourself ready to do more than dream about some man, and I hope I'm there to see it!"

"Do not talk nonsense," Moiraine told her. The task in front of them was too important to spare thoughts for men. In the way Siuan meant, at least. Merean had spent all day with Brys? Without going near Lady Ines? One of Tamra's chosen or Black Ajah, that made no sense, and it went beyond credibility to believe Merean was not one or the other. She was missing something, and that worried her. What she did not know could kill her. Worse, it could kill the Dragon Reborn in his cradle.

Lan slipped through the corridors of the Aesdaishar alone, using every bit of the skill he had learned in the Blight, avoiding the eyes of passersby. His own servingwomen took Edeyn's commands ahead of his, now, as though they believed that some part of Malkieri ways. She might have told them it was. He expected that anyone in the Aesdaishar wearing livery would tell Edeyn where to find him. He thought he knew where he was, now. Despite previous visits, he had gotten lost twice, without a guide. He felt a fool for wearing his sword. Steel was no use in this battle.

A flicker of movement made him flatten himself against the wall behind a statue of a woman clad in clouds, her arms full of flowers. Just in time. Two women came out of the crossing corridor ahead, pausing in close conversation. Iselle and the Aes Sedai, Merean. He was as still as the stone he hid behind.

He did not like skulking, but while Edeyn was untying the knot in his *daori* that had kept him penned for two days she had made it clear that she intended to announce his marriage to Iselle soon. Bukama had been right. Edeyn used his *daori* like reins, and he did not believe she would stop just because he married her daughter. The only thing to do when faced by an opponent you could not defeat was run, and he wanted to.

At a sharp motion from Merean, Iselle nodded eagerly and went back the way they had come. For a moment Merean watched her go, face unreadable in Aes Sedai serenity. Then, surprisingly, she followed, gliding in a way that made Iselle look awkward.

Lan did not waste time wondering what Merean was up to, any more than he had in wondering why Moiraine wanted her watched. A man could go mad trying to puzzle out Aes Sedai. Which Moiraine really must be, or Merean would have her howling up and down the corridors. Waiting long enough for the pair to be out of sight again, he moved quietly to the corner and peeked. They were both gone, so he hurried on. Aes Sedai were no concern of his today. He had to talk to Bukama.

Running would end Edeyn's schemes of marriage. If he avoided her long enough, she would find another husband for Iselle. Running would end Edeyn's dream of reclaiming Malkier; her support would fade like mist under a noon sun once people learned he was gone. Running would end many dreams. The man who had carried an infant tied to his back had a right to dreams, though. Duty was a mountain, but it had to be carried.

Ahead lay a long flight of broad, stone-railed stairs. He turned to start down, and suddenly he was falling. He just had time to go limp, and then he was bounding from step to step, tumbling head over heels, landing on the tiled floor at the bottom with a crash that drove the last remaining air from his lungs. Spots shimmered in front of his eyes. He struggled to breathe, to push himself up.

Servants appeared from nowhere, helping him dizzily to his feet, all exclaiming over his luck in not killing himself in such a fall, asking whether he wanted to see one of the Aes Sedai for Healing. Frowning up the stairway, he murmured replies, anything in hope of making them go away. He thought he might be as bruised as he had ever been in his life, but bruises went away, and the last thing he wanted at that moment was a sister. Most men would have fought that fall and been lucky to end with half their bones broken. Something had jerked his ankles up there. Something had hit him between the shoulders. There was only one thing it could have been, however little sense it made. An Aes Sedai had tried to kill him.

"Lord Mandragoran!" A stocky man in the striped coat of a palace guard skidded to a halt and nearly fell over trying to bow while still moving. "We've been looking for you everywhere, my Lord!" he panted. "It's your man, Bukama! Come quickly, my Lord! He may still be alive!"

Cursing, Lan ran behind the guard, shouting for the man to go faster, but he was too late. Too late for the man who had carried an infant. Too late for dreams.

Guards crowding a narrow passage just off one of the practice yards squeezed back to let Lan through. Bukama lay facedown, blood pooled around his mouth, the plain wooden hilt of a dagger rising from the dark stain on the back of his coat. His staring eyes looked surprised. Kneeling, Lan closed those eyes and murmured a prayer for the last embrace of the mother to welcome Bukama home.

"Who found him?" he asked, but he barely heard the jumbled replies about who and where and what. He hoped Bukama was reborn in a world where the Golden Crane flew on the wind, and the Seven Towers stood unbroken, and the Thousand Lakes shone like a necklace beneath the sun. How could he have let anyone get close enough to do this? Bukama could *feel* steel being unsheathed near him. Only one thing was sure. Bukama was dead because Lan had tangled him in an Aes Sedai's schemes.

Rising, Lan began to run. Not away from, though. Toward. And he did not care who saw him.

The muffled crash of the door in the anteroom and outraged shouts from the servingwomen lifted Moiraine from the chair where she had been waiting. For anything but this. Embracing *saidar*, she started from the sitting room, but before she reached the door, it swung open. Lan shook off the liveried women clinging to his arms, shut the door in their faces, and put his back to it, meeting Moiraine's startled gaze. Purpling bruises marred his face, and he moved as if he had been beaten. From outside came silence. Whatever he intended, they would be sure she could handle it.

Absurdly, she found herself fingering her belt knife. With the Power she could wrap him up like a child, however large he was, and yet. . . .

He did not glare. There certainly was no fire in those eyes. She wanted to step back. No fire, but death seared cold. That black coat suited him with its cruel thorns and stark gold blossoms.

"Bukama is dead with a knife in his heart," he said calmly, "and not an hour gone, someone tried to kill me with the One Power. At first I thought it must be Merean, but the last I saw of her, she was trailing after Iselle, and unless she saw me and wanted to lull me, she had no time. Few see me when I do not want to be seen, and I don't think she did. That leaves you."

Moiraine winced, and only in part for the certainty in his tone. She should have known the fool girl would go straight to Merean. "You would be surprised how little escapes a sister," she told him. Especially if the sister was filled with *saidar*. "Perhaps I should not have asked Bukama to watch Merean. She is very dangerous." She *was* Black Ajah; Moiraine was certain of that, now. Sisters might make painful examples of people caught snooping, but they did not kill them. But what to do about her? Certainty was not proof, surely not that would stand up before the Amyrlin Seat. And if Sierin herself was Black. . . . Not a worry she could do anything about now. What was the woman doing wasting any time at all with Iselle? "If you care for the girl, I suggest you find her as quickly as possible and keep her away from Merean."

Lan grunted. "All Aes Sedai are dangerous. Iselle is safe enough for the moment; I saw her on my way here, hurrying somewhere with Brys and Diryk. Why did Bukama die, Aes Sedai? What did I snare him in for you?"

Moiraine flung up a hand for silence, and a tiny part of her was surprised when he obeyed. The rest of her thought furiously. Merean with Iselle. Iselle with Brys and Diryk. Merean had tried to kill Lan. Suddenly she saw a pattern, perfect in every line; it made no sense, but she did not doubt it was real. "Diryk told me you are the luckiest man in the world," she said, leaning toward Lan intently, "and for his sake, I hope he was right. Where would Brys go for absolute privacy? Somewhere he would not be seen or heard." It would have to be a place he felt comfortable, yet isolated.

"There is a walk on the west side of the Palace," Lan said slowly; then his voice quickened. "If there is danger to Brys, I must rouse the guards." He was already turning, hand on the door handle.

"No!" she said. She still held the Power, and she prepared a weave of Air to seize him if necessary. "Prince Brys will not appreciate having his guards burst in if Merean is simply talking to him."

"And if she is not talking?" he demanded.

"We have no proof of anything against her, Lan. Suspicions against the word of an Aes Sedai." His head jerked angrily, and he growled something about Aes Sedai that she deliberately did not hear. "Take me to this walk, Lan. Let Aes Sedai deal with Aes Sedai. And let us hurry." If Merean did any talking, Moiraine did not expect her to talk for long.

Hurry Lan surely did, long legs flashing as he ran. All Moiraine could do was gather her skirts high and run after him, ignoring the stares and murmurs of servants and others in the corridors, thanking the Light that the man did not outpace her. She let the Power fill her as she ran, till sweetness and joy bordered pain, and tried to plan what she would do, what she could do, against a woman considerably stronger than she, a woman who had been Aes Sedai more than a hundred years before her own great-grandmother was born. She wished she were not so afraid. She wished Siuan were with her.

The mad dash led through glittering state chambers, along statuary-lined hallways, and suddenly they were into the open, the sounds of the Palace left behind, on a long stone-railed walk twenty paces wide with a vista across the city roofs far below. A cold wind blew like a storm. Merean was there, surrounded by the glow of *saidar*, and Brys and Diryk, standing by the rail, twisting futilely against bonds and gags of Air. Iselle was frowning at the Prince and his son, and surprisingly, farther down the walk stood a glowering Ryne.

". . . and I could hardly bring Lord Diryk to you without his father," Iselle was saying petulantly. "I *did* make sure no one knows, but why—?"

Weaving a shield of Spirit, Moiraine hurled it at Merean with every shred of the Power in her, hoping against hope to cut the woman off from the Source. The shield struck and splintered. Merean was too strong, drawing too near her capacity.

The Blue sister—the Black sister—did not even blink. "You did well enough killing the spy, Ryne," she said calmly as she wove a gag of Air to stop up Iselle's mouth and bonds that held the girl stiff and wide-eyed. "See if you can make certain of the younger one this time. You did say you are a better swordsman."

Everything seemed to happen at once. Ryne rushed forward, scowling, the bells in braids chiming. Lan barely got his own sword out in time to meet him. And before the first clash of steel on steel, Merean struck at Moiraine with the same weave she herself had used, but stronger. In horror Moiraine realized that Merean might have sufficient strength remaining to shield her even while she was embracing as much of *saidar* as she could. Frantically she struck out with Air and Fire, and Merean grunted as severed flows snapped back into her. In the brief interval, Moiraine tried to slice the flows holding Diryk and the others, but before her weave touched Merean's, Merean sliced hers instead, and this time Merean's attempted shield actually touched her before she could cut it. Moiraine's stomach tried to tie itself in a knot.

"You appear too often, Moiraine," Merean said as though they were simply chatting. She looked as if there were no more to it, serene and motherly, not in the slightest perturbed. "I fear I must ask you how, and why." Moiraine just managed to sever a weave of Fire that would have burned off her clothes and perhaps most of her skin, and Merean smiled, a mother amused at the mischief young women get up to. "Don't worry, child. I'll Heal you to answer my questions."

If Moiraine had had any lingering doubts that Merean was Black Ajah, that weave of Fire would have ended them. In the next moments she had more proof, weavings that made sparks dance on her dress and her hair rise, weavings that left her gasping for air that was no longer there, weavings she could not recognize yet was sure would leave her broken and bleeding if they settled around her, if she failed to cut them. . . .

When she could, she tried again and again to cut the bonds holding Diryk and the others, to shield Merean, even to knock her unconscious. She knew she fought for her life—she would die if the other woman won, now or after Merean's questioning—but she never considered that loophole in the Oaths that held her. She had questions of her own for the woman, and the fate of the world might rest on the answers. Unfortunately, most of what she could do was defend herself, and that always on the brink. Her stomach *was* in a knot, and trying to make another. Holding three people bound, Merean was still a match for her, and maybe more. If only Lan could distract the woman.

A hasty glance showed how unlikely that was. Lan and Ryne danced the forms, their blades like whirlwinds, but if there was a hair between their abilities, it rested with Ryne. Blood fanned down the side of Lan's face.

Grimly, Moiraine bore down, not even sparing the bit of concentration necessary to ignore the cold. Shivering, she struck at Merean, defended herself and struck again, defended and struck. If she could manage to wear the woman down, or . . .

"This is taking too long, don't you think, child?" Merean said. Diryk floated into the air, struggling against the bonds he could not see as he drifted over the railing. Brys' head twisted, following his son, and his mouth worked around his unseen gag.

"No!" Moiraine screamed. Desperately, she flung out flows of Air to drag the boy back to safety. Merean slashed them even as she released her own hold on him. Wailing, Diryk fell, and white light exploded in Moiraine's head.

Groggily she opened her eyes, the boy's fading shriek still echoing in her mind. She was on her back on the stone walk, her head spinning. Until that cleared, she had as much chance of embracing *saidar* as a cat did of singing. Not that it made any difference, now. She could see the shield Merean was holding on her, and even a weaker woman could maintain a shield once in place. She tried to rise, fell back, managed to push up on an elbow.

Only moments had passed. Lan and Ryne still danced their deadly dance to the clash of steel. Brys was rigid for more than his bonds, staring at Merean with such implacable hate it seemed he might break free on the strength of his rage. Iselle was trembling visibly, snuffling and weeping and staring wide-eyed at where the boy had fallen. Where Diryk had fallen. Moiraine made herself think the boy's name, flinched to recall his grinning enthusiasm. Only moments.

"You will hold a moment for me, I think," Merean said, turning from Moiraine. Brys rose from the walk. The stocky man's face never changed, never stopped staring hatred at Merean.

Moiraine struggled to her knees. She could not channel. She had no courage left, no strength. Only determination. Brys floated over the railing. Moiraine tottered to her feet. Determination. That look of pure hate etched on his face, Brys fell, never making a sound. This had to end. Iselle lifted into the air, writhing frantically, throat working in an effort to scream past her gag. It had to end now! Stumbling, Moiraine drove her belt knife into Merean's back, blood spurting over her hands.

They fell to the paving stones together, the glow around Merean vanishing as she died, the shield on Moiraine vanishing. Iselle screamed, swaying where Merean's bonds had let her drop, atop the stone railing. Pushing herself to move, Moiraine scrambled across Merean's corpse, seized one of Iselle's flailing hands in hers just as the girl's slippers slid off into open air.

The jolt pulled Moiraine belly-down across the railing, staring down at the girl held by her blood-slick grip above a drop that seemed to go on forever. It was all Moiraine could do to hold them where they were, teetering. If she tried to pull the girl up, they would both go over. Iselle's face was contorted, her mouth a rictus. Her hand slipped in Moiraine's grasp. Forcing herself to calm, Moiraine reached for the Source and failed. Staring down at those distant rooftops did not help her whirling head. Again she tried, but it was like trying to scoop up water with spread fingers. She would save one of the three, though, if the most useless of them. Fighting dizziness, she strove for *saidar*. And Iselle's hand slid out of her bloody fingers. All Moiraine could do was watch her fall, hand still stretched up as if she believed someone might still save her.

An arm pulled Moiraine away from the railing.

"Never watch a death you don't have to," Lan said, setting her on her feet. His right arm hung at his side, a long slash laying open the blood-soaked sleeve and the flesh beneath, and he had other injuries besides the gash on his scalp that still trickled red down his face. Ryne lay on his back ten paces away, staring at the sky in sightless surprise. "A black day," Lan muttered. "As black as ever I've seen."

"A moment," she told him, her voice unsteady. "I am too dizzy to walk far, yet." Her knees wavered as she walked to Merean's body. There would be no answers. The Black Ajah would remain hidden. Bending, she withdrew her belt knife and cleaned it on the traitor's skirts.

"You are a cool one, Aes Sedai," Lan said flatly.

"As cool as I must be," she told him. Diryk's scream rang in her ears. Iselle's face dwindled below her. "It seems Ryne was wrong as well as a Darkfriend. You were better than he."

Lan shook his head slightly. "He was better. But he thought I was finished, with only one arm. He never understood. You surrender after you're dead."

Moiraine nodded. Surrender after you are dead. Yes.

It took a little while for her head to clear enough that she could embrace the Source again, and she had to put up with Lan's anxiety to let the *shatayan* know that Brys and Diryk were dead before word came that their bodies had been found on the rooftops. Understandably, he seemed less eager to inform the Lady Edeyn of her daughter's death. Moiraine was anxious about time, too, if not for the same reasons. She Healed him as soon as she was able. He gasped in shock as the complex weaves of Spirit, Air, and Water knit up his wounds, flesh writhing together into unscarred wholeness. Like anyone who had been Healed, he was weak afterward, weak enough to catch his breath leaning on the stone rail. He would run nowhere for a while.

Carefully Moiraine floated Merean's body over that rail and down a little, close to the stone of the mountain. Flows of Fire, and flame, enveloped the Black sister, flame so hot there was no smoke, only a shimmering in the air, and the occasional crack of a splitting rock.

"What are you—?" Lan began, then changed it to, "Why?"

Moiraine let herself feel the rising heat, currents of air fit for a furnace. "There is no proof she was Black Ajah, only that she was Aes Sedai." The White Tower needed its armor of secrecy again, more than it had when Malkier died, but she could not tell him that. Not yet. "I cannot lie about what happened here, but I can be silent. Will you be silent, or will you do the Shadow's work?"

"You are a very hard woman," he said finally. That was the only answer he gave, but it was enough.

"I am as hard as I must be," she told him. Diryk's scream. Iselle's face. There was still Ryne's body to dispose of, and the blood. As hard as she must be.

Next dawn found the Aesdaishar in mourning, white banners flying from every prominence, the servants with long white cloths tied to their arms. Rumors in the city already talked of portents foretelling the deaths, comets in the night, fires in the sky. People had a way of folding what they saw into what they knew and what they wanted to believe. The disappearance of a simple soldier, and even of an Aes Sedai, escaped notice alongside grief.

Returning from destroying Merean's belongings—after searching in vain for any clue to other Black sisters—Moiraine stepped aside for Edeyn Arrel, who glided down the corridor in a white gown, her hair cut raggedly short. Whispers said she intended to retire from the world. Moiraine thought she already had. The woman's staring eyes looked haggard and old. In a way, they looked much as her daughter's did, in Moiraine's mind.

When Moiraine entered her apartments, Siuan leaped up from a chair. It seemed weeks since Moiraine had seen her. "You look like you reached into the bait well and found a fangfish," she growled. "Well, it's no surprise. I always hated mourning when I knew the people. Anyway, we can go whenever you're ready. Rahien was born in a farmhouse almost two miles from Dragonmount. Merean hasn't been near him, as of this morning. I don't suppose she'll harm him on suspicion even if she is Black."

Not the one. Somehow, Moiraine had almost expected that. "Merean will not harm anyone, Siuan. Put that mind of yours to a puzzle for me." Settling in a chair, she began with the end, and hurried through despite Siuan's gasps and demands for more detail. It was almost like living it again. Getting to what had led her to that confrontation was a relief. "She wanted Diryk dead most of all, Siuan; she killed him first. And she tried to kill Lan. The only thing those two had in common was luck. Diryk survived a fall that should have killed him, and everyone says Lan is the luckiest man alive or the Blight would have killed him years ago. It makes a pattern, but the pattern looks crazy to me. Maybe your blacksmith is even part of it. And Josef Najima, back in Canluum, for all I know. He was lucky, too. Puzzle it out for me if you can. I think it is important, but I cannot see how."

Siuan strode back and forth across the room, kicking her skirt and rubbing her chin, muttering about "men with luck" and "the blacksmith rose suddenly" and other things Moiraine could not make out. Suddenly she stopped dead and said, "She never went near Rahien, Moiraine. The Black Ajah knows the Dragon was Reborn, but they don't bloody know *when*! Maybe Tamra managed to keep it back, or maybe they were too rough and she died before they could pry it out of her. That has to be it!" Her eagerness turned to horror. "Light! They're killing any man or boy who *might* be able to channel! Oh, burn me, thousands could die, Moiraine. Tens of thousands."

It did make a terrible sense. Men who could channel seldom knew what they were doing, at least in the beginning. At first, they often just seemed to be lucky. Events favored them, and frequently, like the blacksmith, they rose to prominence with unexpected suddenness. Siuan was right. The Black Ajah had begun a slaughter.

"But they do not know to look for a boychild," Moiraine said. As hard as she had to be. "An infant will show no signs." Not until he was sixteen at the earliest. No man on record had begun channeling before that, and some not for ten years or more later. "We have more time than we thought. Not enough to be careless, though. Any sister can be Black. I think Cadsuane is. They know others are looking. If one of Tamra's searchers locates the boy and they find her with him, or if they decide to question one of them instead of killing her as soon as it is convenient . . ." Siuan was staring at her. "We still have the task," Moiraine told her.

"I know," Siuan said slowly. "I just never thought. Well, when there's work to do, you haul nets or gut fish." That lacked her usual force, though. "We can be on our way to Arafel before noon."

"You go back to the Tower," Moiraine said. Together, they could search no faster than one could alone, and if they had to be apart, what better place for Siuan than working for Cetalia Delarme, seeing the reports of all the Blue Ajah eyes-and-ears? The Blue was a small Ajah, but every sister said it had a larger network than any other. While Moiraine hunted for the boy, Siuan could learn what was happening in every land, and knowing what she was looking for, she could spot any sign of the Black Ajah or the Dragon Reborn. Siuan truly could see sense when it was pointed out to her, though it took some effort this time, and when she agreed, she did it with a poor grace.

"Cetalia will use me to caulk drafts for running off without leave," she grumbled. "Burn me! Hung out on a drying rack in the Tower! Moiraine, the politics are enough to make you sweat buckets in midwinter! I hate it!" But she was already pawing through the trunks to see what she could take with her for the ride back to Tar Valon. "I suppose you warned that fellow Lan. Seems to me, he deserves it, much good it'll do him. I heard he rode out an hour ago, heading for the Blight, and if that doesn't kill him—Where are you going?"

"I have unfinished business with the man," Moiraine said over her shoulder. She had made a decision about him the first day she knew him, and she intended to keep it.

In the stable where Arrow was kept, silver marks tossed like pennies got the mare saddled and bridled almost while the coins were still in air, and she scrambled onto the animal's back without a care that her skirts pushed up to bare her legs above the knee. Digging her heels in, she galloped out of the Aesdaishar and north through the city, making people leap aside and once setting Arrow to leap cleanly over an empty wagon with a driver too slow to move out of her way. She left a tumult of shouts and shaken fists behind.

On the road north from the city, she slowed enough to ask wagon drivers heading the other way whether they had seen a Malkieri on a bay stallion, and was more than a little relieved the first time she got a yes. The man could have gone in fifty directions after crossing the moat bridge. And with an hour's lead. . . . She would catch him if she had to follow him into the Blight!

"A Malkieri?" The skinny merchant in a dark blue cloak looked startled. "Well, my guards told me there's one up there." Twisting on his wagon seat, he pointed to a grassy hill a hundred paces off the road. Two horses stood in plain sight at the crest, one a packhorse, and the thin smoke of a fire curled into the breeze.

Lan barely looked up when she dismounted. Kneeling beside the remains of a small fire, he was stirring the ashes with a long twig. Strangely, the smell of burned hair hung in the air. "I had hoped you were done with me," he said.

"Not quite yet," she told him. "Burning your future? It will sorrow a great many, I think, when you die in the Blight."

"Burning my past," he said, rising. "Burning memories. A nation. The Golden Crane will fly no more." He started to kick dirt over the ashes, then hesitated and bent to scoop up damp soil and pour it out of his hands almost formally. "No one will sorrow for me when I die, because those who would are dead already. Besides, all men die."

"Only fools choose to die before they must. I want you to be my Warder, Lan Mandragoran."

He stared at her unblinking, then shook his head. "I should have know it would be that. I have a war to fight, Aes Sedai, and no desire to help you weave White Tower webs. Find another."

"I fight the same war as you, against the Shadow. Merean was Black

Ajah." She told him all of it, from Gitara's Foretelling in the presence of the Amyrlin Seat and two Accepted to what she and Siuan had reasoned out. For another man, she would have left most unsaid, but there were few secrets between Warder and Aes Sedai. For another man, she might have softened it, but she did not believe hidden enemies frightened him, not even when they were Aes Sedai. "You said you burned your past. Let the past have its ashes. This is the same war, Lan. The most important battle yet in that war. And this one, you can win."

For a long time he stood staring north, toward the Blight. She did not know what she would do if he refused. She had told him more than she would have anyone but her Warder.

Suddenly he turned, sword flashing out, and for an instant she thought he meant to attack her. Instead he sank to his knees, the sword lying bare across his hands. "By my mother's name, I will draw as you say 'draw' and sheathe as you say 'sheathe.' By my mother's name, I will come as you say 'come' and go as you say 'go.'" He kissed the blade and looked up at her expectantly. On his knees, he made any king on a throne look meek. She would have to teach him some humility for his own sake. And for a pond's sake.

"There is a little more," she said, laying hands on his head.

The weave of Spirit was one of the most intricate known to Aes Sedai. It wove around him, settled into him, vanished. Suddenly she was aware of him, in the way that Aes Sedai were of their Warders. His emotions were a small knot in the back of her head, all steely hard determination, sharp as his blade's edge. She knew the muted pain of old injuries, tamped down and ignored. She would be able to draw on his strength at need, to find him however far away he was. They were bonded.

He rose smoothly, sheathing his sword, studying her. "Men who weren't there call it the Battle of the Shining Walls," he said abruptly. "Men who were, call it the Blood Snow. No more. They know it was a battle. On the morning of the first day, I led nearly five hundred men. Kandori, Saldaeans, Domani. By evening on the third day, half were dead or wounded. Had I made different choices, some of those dead would be alive. And others would be dead in their places. In war, you say a prayer for your dead and ride on, because there is always another fight over the next horizon. Say a prayer for the dead, Moiraine Sedai, and ride on."

Startled, she came close to gaping. She had forgotten that the bond's flow worked both ways. He knew her emotions, too, and apparently could reason out hers far better than she could his. After a moment, she nodded, though she did not know how many prayers it would take to clear her mind.

Handing her Arrow's reins, he said, "Where do we ride first?"

"Back to Chachin," she admitted. "And then Arafel, and..." So few names remained that were easy to find. "The world, if need be. We win this battle, or the world dies."

Side by side they rode down the hill and turned south. Behind them the sky rumbled and turned black, another late storm rolling down from the Blight.